This book contains scenes of graphic violence, abuse, sexual abuse and rape, torture, child abuse, murder, sexually explicit scenes, mutilation, self mutilation, death, magic use, shifting, depression, pregnancy and childbirth.

If you are sensitive to these subjects, please consider your personal mental health before continuing.

Part 3

A Path
Of
Peaceful
Destruction

Written by Kristy Pearson

For the Darkness.

For that little piece of regret, sadness, grief or loathing that lives inside of all of us. For that little voice that whispers in our minds, constantly nigging at our inner critic. Telling us to quit, to give up, to stop pushing, to just roll over and take it.

Fuck that voice.

Fight back.

Chapter One

Zelena

So much has happened in such a short time. And it really has been a short time, I first met Gunner just shy of six months ago. That is when my life completely flipped upside down. I went from being an abused, quiet and disconnected little girl, to a strong and powerful woman. So far, I have discovered that I'm a Werewolf, the man I thought was my father isn't my father, and I have a soulmate. I found a family and a home. I have made friends, and I have lost friends. I have discovered that I am capable of wielding unimaginable power, gifted to me by my ancestor, the Moon Goddess. I went from being all alone to having multiple strong and everlasting connections. I have fought for what I have come to love, and I have killed to keep it. Now I sit here, in front of the woman who claims to be my mother, destined to soon become a mother myself. With all that has changed already, I know there is still more to come. I can feel it in the air, there is more drama on the way.

The silence was drowning me. Sitting this close was making me feel seriously uncomfortable. After all, I still don't know anything about this she-wolf. Gunner was at my side, his large hand resting on my thigh, but it did nothing to calm my racing heart. I can't avoid it any longer, there's no denying that. But deep down I'm dreading hearing what she has to say. I want to be mad at her. I want to hate her, and I want to keep blaming her for how I grew up. I have a feeling though, that once I hear her story, I will change my tune. I gripped Gunner's hand, digging my nails into his skin. If he felt any pain from my death grip, he didn't show it, he just sat there and let me hold his hand. I nodded to Lunaya, indicating that she could begin. She sat back in her chair and casually crossed her legs.

"Firstly, there is something that you need to understand. Something very important passed down by our ancestors. The power of the Triple Goddess works like a beacon. It draws Weres in, like a magnet. Just our genes are enough for it to happen, even for those who don't bear the mark, they still hold a piece of the Goddess inside them. Our heritage makes us stronger, faster, our senses are more evolved, and we are more disciplined over our wolves" Lunaya began,

"That must be why you had so much control over your wolf. When you first changed in the carpark at the school, and again in the field, the initial instinct to attack wasn't there" Gunner cut in, "That would be normal for a daughter of Selena" Lunaya confirmed as she crossed her arms over her chest,

"I also assume many Weres have already sought you out, yes? Even the ones that you had no prior contact or alliance with?"

"Many diplomats have visited since her arrival, yes" Gunner grunted in a gruff tone.

"That is why we can never settle for too long. Our ancestors have moved about all over the world. If the line stays in one place for too long, trouble usually finds us. Whether it be hunters, power hungry Alphas, or other supernatural's. They always come" Lunaya said sadly.

"Is that why you left me, why you didn't come for me? Some weird way of keeping me safe?" I hissed at her sarcastically. Gunner squeezed my thigh and shifted closer to me.

"I was born into a pack called Shining Star. They were a small and unknown pack, hidden in the wildlife refuge on Kodiak Island of Alaska. After my parents died when I was nine, I was sent to Moon Light in Northern Alaska, to be raised by an Elder that lived there" Lunaya began. I huffed and squeezed Gunner's hand tighter,

"Do we really need the history lesson?" I grumbled. Lunaya smiled and looked down at her lap, shaking her head slightly.

"You are so much like your father" she mused with a chuckle,

"All about the quick action with no interest in the fine print. But yes, you need to hear all of it" she answered firmly as she raised her eyes to mine. I was a little taken aback by the authority in her stare. I didn't snap back like I wanted to, and instead just nodded my head.

"After my parents were killed by the hunters, I was sent to Elder Maxine of Moon Light. She was a close friend to my grandmother and a big part of my mother's life. She knew everything about our history. About Selena and the line of chosen daughters. It was her that trained me, she prepared me for the possibility of bearing the mark of the Goddess. Ever since I was young, I felt like I was destined for something great, something important. Being the cocky teenager that I was, I was sure that I was going to be the next Triple Goddess. Clearly, that was not meant to be" she said smiling at me with so much pride and affection shining in her eyes.

"It was not my destiny to be the next Goddess, but it was my responsibility to birth, raise and protect her". Lunaya paused and looked down at her lap. The scent of her sadness and despair filled the room. She looked back up to me with tears brimming in her eyes.

"I failed the task, and I will never be able to express how sorry I am for that" she choked out. We sat quietly, each of us gazing at each other solemnly. I couldn't talk. If I opened my mouth, I was worried that a sob would burst out.

"The moment that I met your father, I knew that he was made for me. We may not have been True Mates like you two, but I knew there was no one else for me. After I realised that I wasn't the Triple Goddess, I thought he would love me less. Moon Light knew who I was, and what I was possible of becoming. This brought me a lot of unwanted attention from the males, those who wanted to use me for my status. But your father wasn't one of them. He wasn't bothered by it at all. Triple Goddess or not, he only ever wanted me. The moment I told him that we were pregnant, that smile that covered his entire face, I will never forget that look. He was so happy, so excited" Lunaya uncrossed her arms and interlaced her fingers. Her smile enveloped the bottom half of her face, but her eyes held so much grief and longing.

"What was his name?" I asked softly,

"Micha. Micha Alvar" she answered. Her voice held so much love, I could feel it flowing from her. It made me feel happy and appreciative. I came from love. Real and pure love. Regardless of what came after, I was wanted. That has to account for something.

"What was he like?"

"Your father was the strongest pack warrior I had ever met. He was fiercely protective of his pack and his family, and yet he was so kind and generous. He was the kind of Were to help the elder she-wolves move furniture and chop their firewood. And he loved you. He loved you so damn much. I wish you could have known him. You may not know it, but you are so much like him" she said with a widespread smile across her face.

"I wish I knew him too. I wish I knew the both of you" I whispered. Lunaya sat quietly, lost in her own thoughts while I waited impatiently for her to continue. Gunner sat beside me, unmoving, apart from his thumb rubbing circles on my thigh.

"When the hunters attacked, we were completely unaware. They had managed to get to the border patrols and scouts before they alerted us to the incoming danger. The hunters knew exactly what they were looking for, and they knew just where to find it. They ripped their way through Moon Light, slaughtering anyone and everyone in their path. Your father and I had a plan, something we tried and tested many, many times. We were to separate, him going in one direction and me going in the other. There was a small log cabin hidden in the snow at the base of Mount Logan. We had readied the cabin with supplies and necessities, for if there ever came a time to use it. But your father never showed".

"And where was I during all this?" I asked, interrupting her spiel.

"With me. When your father and I separated, I didn't get too far before the hunters had me surrounded. They knew exactly what I looked like, and they knew how to find me" she answered without a pause,

"How?"

"That is a question I have asked myself many times over the years. Each time I arrive at the same conclusion. We must have had a spy in the pack, a traitor, someone selling information to the hunter clan".

"You really think one of your pack members betrayed you?" Gunner interjected,

"There is no other explanation. Besides, it can't be too hard to believe, you yourself had a spy. Artemis was working with the Origin Alpha".

"Working with another pack and working with a hunter is very different" Gunner growled lowly,

"Are you defending him?" Lunaya half asked half scoffed, her voice raising in volume.

"Of course not!" Gunner growled back. Lunaya raised her hand and shook her head, stopping the argument in its tracks.

"We're getting off topic. Artemis is dead now, what he did doesn't matter" she said calmly.

"You were up to the part where the hunters had you surrounded" I reminded her. She nodded and continued her story.

"I hid you in a hollowed-out tree and then fought them off the best I could. I am a very skilled warrior, your dad and Elder Maxine made sure of that. But there were so many of them, and I was quickly overwhelmed. Plus, they had bullets and weapons laced with Aconite. All the fighting didn't matter once the poison flooded my bloodstream. Even with my veins on fire and my wolf riddled with bullets, I couldn't quit. My body gave out on me. My wolf form retreated, and I was left dying slowly in the snow as I watched the lead hunter carry away my baby". Tears flowed freely down her cheeks as she recounted the events that led to my kidnapping. I was right. I knew once I heard her version of the truth, I would feel differently. And I do. I am even more angry with her.

"So, you let them take me" I said firmly, I let her feel all of the anger I was feeling.

"Of course I didn't" she said shocked as she leaned back in her chair and gaped at me wide eyed.

"Zelena, if I could change things, I assure you that I would. I didn't want to leave you, I was meant to raise you, train you and guide you. If I had known, if I thought there was any possibility that you were alive, I would have never stopped looking" she pleaded,

"Yeah, but you can't change things, can you? It's too late for that! So, can we skip the tears and the attempt at reconnecting, and just

move on to you telling me what you know about these attacks?"
I growled snidely.
"What makes you think I know something?" she asked me,
disguising the shock in her voice,
"Because I saw the look on your face as Daniel was describing the
deaths. You looked worried".
"Yes, I am worried, these attacks are happening not two days
away from here. I told you that trouble usually finds the
daughters of Selene. How could I not be afraid for my daughter?"
Lunaya quipped back. My body tensed and my fingers gripped
tightly onto Gunner's hand. I felt my anger swirling in my
stomach. I don't care who she is, I hate that she keeps calling me
that.
"Don't call me that!" I growled lowly,
"Call you what? My daughter? Well, sorry to break it to you
Sweetheart, but you are my daughter. I've spent enough time
away from you and I have allowed you more than two weeks to
absorb the idea. You may not be ready, but I am, I won't hide from
it any longer".
"You are not my mother. I had a mother. She kept me safe when
I was being tortured. She fed me when I was hungry. She is the
one who took care of me. And where were you? Globetrotting
with your replacement Mate. You don't get to call me daughter.
For all I care, you are nothing, no one". I was leaning forward as
I screamed at Lunaya. More tears ran down her face as my hurtful
words washed over her.
"Zelena" Gunner growled and dug his fingertips into my thigh,
"Did you not listen? She fought for you, she nearly died for you. I
know why you can see it as her giving up, but you don't know
how Aconite feels for a Were. Thankfully, you've never been
exposed to it. But the fact that she was able to not just move after
it hit her blood, but also keep fighting, it shows her willpower to
protect you. She thought you were dead, what more was she
meant to do?" Gunner said with a deep gruff voice, not his usual
smooth calming tone.
"You're defending her?" I snapped at him,
"I'm listening to her. You should try it" he snapped back. The fact
that he was snapping at me, that he was defending her instead of
me, just made me angrier. He is meant to be on my side. He is MY
Mate! I stood up from the chair and turned to glare at Gunner.

His face was contorted, and his eyes flickered black as he glared back up at me. Fuck. He was absorbing my anger again, feeling it through our bond as well as drinking it in from my aura. The darkness was eating it up, growing inside him. The black whisps swirled around his iris, covering the bright blue. The contortion on his face was proof enough that he was fighting it. But I keep making it worse, I keep letting my own emotions take control, and it's not helping him. I felt a soft hand grab my wrist and I turned to see Lunaya standing behind me. She gently tried to pull me back from Gunner. I growled at her and snatched my arm away from her grip.

"Zelena, he needs calm, and you are not calm. Gunner, I think you need to remove yourself from the situation" she said slowly and coolly. Gunner stood from the couch, slow and steady with his movements. I held out my hand to stop him and huffed,

"You know what, you two can stay here, seeing as you're such good friends now. Let me save you the trouble and I'll go". With that, I turned on my heels and stormed to the living room's double doors,

"Wait!" Lunaya shouted and I paused with my hand on the doorknobs,

"There is more, I have to tell you the rest. It's important" she pleaded with me. I snarled and let a small growl bubble from behind my clenched teeth,

"I don't care" I growled and pushed open the large doors with more force than was necessary. They slammed against the walls and bounced back again. Gunner called out to me as I stomped out of the front door. My heavy footsteps thudded against the wooden porch deck and stairs. I continued to march through the village, no idea as to where I was going. The pack members scurried out of my way as I walked. I looked over my shoulder and saw Tobias, following behind me. Even with his impending presence, I would guess that the foul look on my face was enough of a reason for them to keep their distance. Veering off through some of the cabins, I decided where I wanted to go. The trip was longer this time because I was walking instead of running. I was almost about to question my sense of direction, thinking I was going the wrong way, when the flurry of colours became visible through the trees.

The flower field was still in full bloom, and just as beautiful as I remember it when Smith brought me here the first time. I flopped down in the tall grass and flowers and laid on my back. I threw my arms out at my sides and twisted my fingers in and around the grass. The blue sky held small puffs of clouds, but not enough to block out the sun. I could still feel all of the anger, frustration, and betrayal churning around inside my body. It was making my chest tight, and I felt like I couldn't breathe. I dug my fingers into the dirt, scrunched my eyes closed tight, sucked in a large breath, threw my chin up and screamed. I screamed with everything I had been holding inside me. I screamed out all of the sadness, the anger, the frustration and the fear that had been living within me. As the deep and anguished sound left my body, I felt all the negative energy go with it. After a moment, I had nothing left. I stopped screaming and took a deep breath. I kept my eyes closed and continued to take slow, deep and soothing breaths.

"Do you feel better now?" a soft feminine voice said with a giggle. I sat up and shielded my eyes from the sun. As I looked up, I found one of the people I wanted to see least of all right now. I huffed and flopped back down on the grass. She chuckled and sat down next to me.

"Your pack lands are beautiful, you should feel very proud" she said as she fiddled with the petals of a purple flower. I didn't respond, just pretended that she wasn't there. I know I'm being childish, first with my unwillingness to talk to or even hear out Lunaya, and second with my reaction to Gunner defending her. I can blame it on pregnancy hormones maybe. I don't even know if she-wolves suffer from raging hormones like humans do.

"Your Alpha must be overjoyed with having an heir" she continued, fishing for something that would get me to respond.

"I never had a child of my own. Though with watching how much Lunaya has suffered, perhaps I'm a little relieved for that" she chuckled awkwardly. I need to put her out of her misery,

"Look, Alyse, if you've come to bat for Lunaya, you can save your breath. I'm not interested in hearing anymore, okay" I said exasperatedly and turned onto my side, with my back now to Alyse.

"To be blunt with you Luna, you've barely heard anything yet. Definitely not enough to form a proper opinion. Why won't you hear her out?" she quipped back. I felt her lay down at my side, not too close, but close enough to make it awkward.

"Why should I? She abandoned me. I was raised by a hunter who hated me. He beat me daily, tortured me, starved me, made sure that every day of my life was a living hell".

"Yes, but you were alive. Lunaya has lived the last seventeen years with half of her heart dead. She lost everything the day you were taken. She lost her home, her pack, her Mate, and her family. She has nightmares every night, reliving the moment over and over and over again. Imagine the kind of toll that would have on a person. Reliving the worst day of your life every night when you fall asleep". Alyse paused for a moment as I absorbed what she had said. I didn't really think of it from her perspective. I've been wrapped up in my own thoughts and feelings, I had wondered why she held so much hatred for hunters. If that's not a good reason, then I don't know what is.

"But she still gave up" I said softly. I rolled onto my back and looked up at the sky.

"Oh child, she didn't give up. After I found her, I thought she was going to die, and she was very close to it. But the All Mother still had use of her, so she brought her back" Alyse said fondly. I stayed quiet and let her continue,

"Even before she was fully healed, she began the search. She looked at each and every body of her fallen packmates. Each face she looked upon, and each time that she didn't find her family, another piece of her heart died. Together we buried and burned what we could. She had to see her entire pack, including her Alpha, buried or cremated. She held the weight of that responsibility over herself. After she realised that you weren't on the pack lands, I followed her to a wooden hut somewhere out in the mountains. It was there that we waited, for weeks we waited. But no one came, and again, I saw more of her die. After that, she began to hunt the hunters"

"She what?" I interrupted as I flew upright. Did I hear that right? Alyse sat up and gazed at me with sad eyes.

"The hunted became the hunter. Lunaya believed that it was her duty, her responsibility, to kill all those who were there that day. I don't think that she would have told you this part of the past, but I think it is important that you know. The things she did in the name of retribution, what she had to become in order to enact her revenge. She was a beast. She was merciless and brutal" Alyse spoke with so much sadness and regret laced through her voice. I could tell this was not a story she liked telling. I could also feel how regretful her past actions make her feel now.

"And you? You stayed with her, you helped her?" I cut in,

"I did. For years she tracked down and killed entire hunter clans, in numbers well into the hundreds. And I stuck by her the whole time. She was unlike anyone I had ever encountered before. Her grief and anger were controlling her, but underneath all that darkness, there was love and loyalty. She may have become a monster to do what needed to be done. But she did it for honourable reasons. She did it for her family, for her pack. She did it for you". Alyse is giving all of the credit to Lunaya, but she is downplaying the fact that she stayed. She didn't just stay with her, she helped her. She must have a lot of love for Lunaya in order to do that.

"She killed for me?" I asked, somewhat confused at how this is considered a good thing,

"Of course she did. Hasn't your Mate, your pack members, your friends, haven't they all killed for you too?"

"That's different, it was during a battle. Lunaya chose to kill those humans".

"It's not that different. They killed to protect you. She killed to protect your memory. In her mind you were dead. We had no other reason to think any differently. Everywhere we went, all the places we searched and hunted, we found no signs that any of you were alive" she said with conviction,

"How is that possible? It's not like I was hidden. I was right here, living, going to school and all that crap. I couldn't have been that hard to find"

"Zelena, did you ever see any of the other hunters? Did the one that raised you ever have anyone come to your house, or did he take you to meet with anyone else?"

I thought about it. Hank was a hunter, so he had to have had some kind of contact with his brother or the other hunters. Right? But as much as I wracked my brain, I can't remember ever meeting another person. Hank had us completely cut off from the rest of the world. The only other time I had human contact was at school. But I was Zelena Baxter. He used his last name as my own. I suppose it's pretty strange that he kept my first name. Wait, that is my name, isn't it? Is that why she couldn't find me, Hank gave me a fake name.

"My name, Zelena, is that even my name?" I'm not sure I could handle any more changes. My whole life I have been Zelena. What if that is a lie too? Alyse smiled at me and reached forward to touch my hand.

"Zelena is the name your mother gave you. She told me once that you wore a small gold bracelet with your name engraved on it. It never came off. When you were taken, you were still wearing the bracelet. I guess the hunter didn't see fit to change your name". Alyse smiled softly and squeezed my hand.

"Or he didn't care enough" I grunted. Alyse let go and sat up straight, pulling her shoulders back.

"Sweet Girl, I am so sorry for how you were raised. The things that you had to go through at the hands of the hunter, your suffering, all of it. But you must know, that was not your mother's fault. She would have done everything in her power to keep you safe. She would have torn that man apart if she knew about it" Alyse said with her voice now taking a firmer tone. I wiped a stray tear from my cheek. It still hurts to think about my past. Even with the returned memories of Selene added to them. But somehow Alyse's apology felt good. As much as I want to disagree, as much as I want to hold onto this blame, I know Lunaya couldn't have done anything to help me. Like they keep telling me, she thought I was dead.

"I know" I whispered quietly. Alyse shifted closer and gently placed her arm over my shoulder. I rested my head on her shoulder and we sat quietly, just watching the flowers dance with the breeze. I've been really tough on Lunaya. On my mother. But I think it has more to do with my own sadness. She was out there, somewhere in the world, all this time. The part that hurts, the part that I'm mad about, it's that I could have been with her. We could have been a family. It's not her fault, but it is easier to be angry and blame her for not being there than it is to accept the truth. I miss her. Even though I never knew she existed. I miss the life we could have had.

After a while, I heard heavy footsteps coming our way. I turned to see Tobias looking down at us.

"Come on Little One, you need to eat now" he said gruffly and extended his hand for me. I hadn't realised how hungry I had become. My mind was preoccupied. But now at the mention of food, my mouth salivated, and my stomach twitched with hunger. I looked at Alyse who smiled back at me,

"Go on. I'll be around if you ever want to talk" she cooed gently. I wrapped my arms around her neck and pulled her into me for a tight hug.

"Thank you" I whispered into her ear. She squeezed me back and ran her hand over my head and down my hair.

"Any time" she answered me before letting go. I grabbed Tobias's hand and he pulled me to my feet. I groaned loudly as my numb legs protested under my slowly increasing weight. I rubbed my hands down my thighs and tried to squeeze them back to life. Tobias wasted no time in wrapping his arms around me and lifting me to his chest. With one massive arm supporting my legs, and the other holding my back. I cradled my belly and let him carry me. I've given up on trying to protest when he or Gunner decides to carry me. It's a lost cause trying to argue with my protective Alpha's, best to just sit back and enjoy it the best I can.

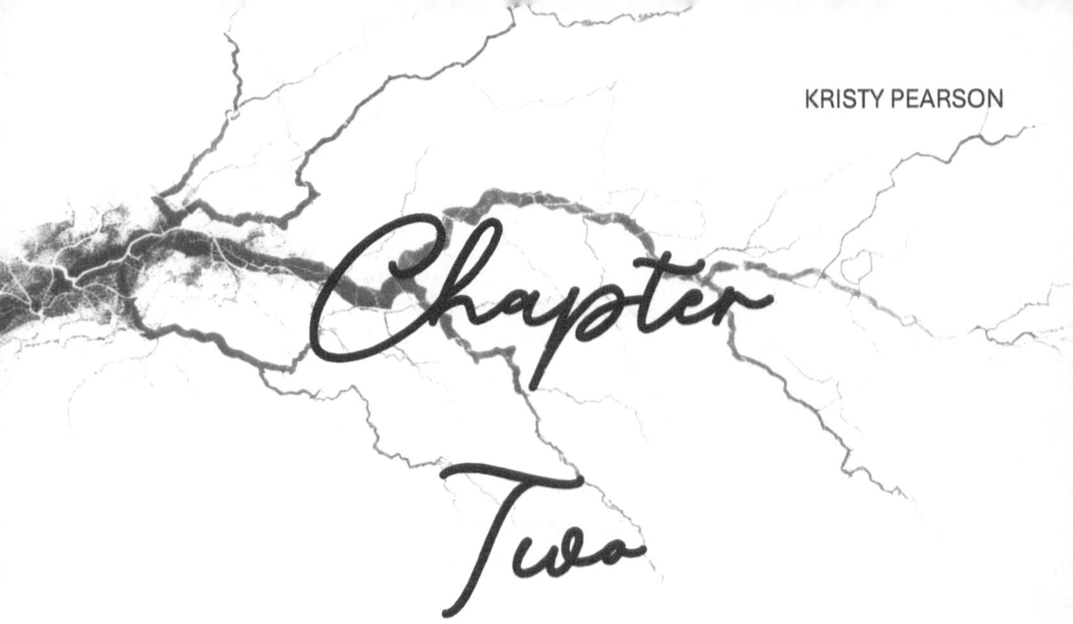

Chapter Two

Zelena

I lay in Gunner's arms as his fingers gently traced circles over my bare back. The house was quiet at this time of night, letting the sounds of the forest slip through the open window. It was peaceful, listening to the insets and other forest animals sing through the night. Just as calm as the gentle caress of Gunner's hand over my skin. The sparks and tingles that he is able to inflict on me are still the most wonderful sensations. A sensation that I hope never goes away.

I turned my head and nuzzled my nose against his firm and perfectly hairless pectoral muscle. I spattered kisses across his chest as I worked my way up to the place where my mark sat. I poked out my tongue and let the tip run along the raised scar. Gunner groaned and tightened his hold on me. I sucked the skin into my mouth and repositioned myself on his lap, one knee on either side of his hips. I pressed my backside down and felt the hard length of his cock press against my core. I cupped his beautiful face in my small hands and kissed him hungrily. I rocked my hips back and forth, sliding my seeping slit along his hardened length. Gunner gripped my hips and pressed his fingertips hard into the soft flesh. He lifted me slightly and positioned himself at my entrance. I slid back down slowly, taking all of him inside of me. As Gunner groaned with pleasure, I sucked his tongue into my mouth and rolled my own around it. I ground my hips into him slowly, letting him fill me completely before rolling back again. It was slow, sensual, full of passion and love. It was just us. Gunner sat up and I wrapped my ankles around his back. His lips and mouth desperately devoured my chest and neck as I rocked in his lap. My fingers twisted and gripped into his soft shaggy hair and pulled. Gunner growled and sucked one of my nipples into his mouth, biting and tugging on it gently. With them being extra sensitive lately, the sensation sent me soaring. My hips increased their pace and Gunner lifted and rocked his hips to meet my movements. It took no time at all for the tightness to come to my stomach. My legs were starting to shake, and I knew I was only seconds away from reaching my bliss. I bucked my hips and my head fell back, I groaned loudly as the orgasm hit me. Gunner moved his hands to the top of my shoulders and thrust into me a few more times before finding his own release. I rested my head on his shoulder and curled my arms around his back. Gunner laid his head on mine and ran his hands up and down my back. And we stayed like that, with him still inside me, just embracing each other.

"I'm so sorry" I croaked, trying not to let my wayward emotions get away from me again. Gunner lifted me off him and sat me between his legs, still facing him. He gripped my face and gently stroked his thumb over my quivering bottom lip.

"Whatever for, my Love?" he said softly,

"I'm sorry for getting angry at you, I'm sorry for making you lose control, and I'm just sorry for being so horrible" I rushed out, followed quickly by a small sob. Gunner slipped his arms around my back and pulled me flush against his chest. He held the back of my head and heaved a heavy breath.

"It's not your fault, Little Wolf. Of course you would be upset about me getting close to another she-wolf, even if she is your mother" he huffed.

"You're not mad at me? I keep making things worse, I keep letting my anger out and I can see how it's affecting you".

"Zee, you're a Were, a very powerful one in fact. It's only natural that you have a hot temper. And it's not fair on you to have to force control over yourself all the time, especially not because of me"

"I don't see it like that. I'm your Mate, I should be helping you"

"It's not me you should be worrying about anymore" he said calmly and pulled back from me. He lowered his hands and placed them over my swollen belly.

"It's him, or her. It's our pup that should be getting all of your attention, not me and my issues" he said while staring at my stomach.

"No, Gunner, you've got my darkness in you. That's not just your issue, it's mine too. And even if you didn't, you would still be at the top of my list of things to worry about. Alongside our pup" I told him earnestly while cupping his cheek.

"That's the problem, isn't it. All the worry I'm putting onto you, it's not good for you, for either of you" Gunner hissed. He was frustrated, with himself mostly, but I would imagine with a lot of other things too. There are only four days left, and I don't know what's going to happen at the end of them. I can't imagine that Selene, the being that raised me, cared for me, and claims to love me, could possibly hurt me so much by taking away my Mate. I don't think that she would really do it. She couldn't. But Selene is not the kind of being to give empty threats. When she says something, she means it. Just the fact that she showed herself to Gunner, is enough to prove that she means business. But still, I just can't imagine that she would do that to me. At least, I hope she won't.

"Zelena" Gunner whispered softly,

"You're using my full name again, this must be bad" I answered back. He paused and took a few deep breaths while letting his hands roam over my body.

"Zee, I have to leave". He said it quietly, but I definitely didn't mishear him. Leave. Leave where?

"What are you talking about?" I asked, examining his face closely. His eyes fell on mine and I gulped. They were so full of sorrow and fear. I don't think I have ever seen him look like that. It just about broke my heart. I reached up with both hands and grabbed his face.

"Gunner, what's going on?" I asked urgently. He grabbed my wrists so that my hands would stay there and nuzzled into my hand.

"I can't stay here, in the house or in the pack. I am putting you in danger. I can't risk hurting you, or our pup, or anyone else for that matter. I don't have a handle on this darkness. I can feel it churning inside me. The closer I get to Thursday the more scared I feel. And the darkness, it's eating away at that fear Zelena. I'm making it stronger, not weaker".

"You're being stupid, don't say stuff like that" I growled and shook my head,

"Maybe if I leave, if I take away the threat to you, Selene won't take my wolf. If you're safe from me, maybe she'll grant me more time to expel the darkness. I can't lose you Zelena, I won't survive it". My heart was pinched, and pain radiated through my chest. He can't be serious. He wants to leave me. I searched his face, looking for a sign that this was all just a cruel joke. I found nothing. Only pain and heartache. Gunner's tears rolled down his cheeks and his bottom lip was pulled between his teeth. He leaned his head forward and pressed his forehead to mine.

"You can't" I managed to get out. Tears welled in my eyes and my head spun.

"I have to" he whispered.

"No, you don't. We'll do this together. You can't leave. You know what your mum said, True Mates can't survive without each other" I sobbed and tried to pull my hands away from his face, but he didn't let go.

"That's only if one dies Zee. I'm not dying, just going away for a little bit. You'll be fine"

"No, I won't. If you leave me, I will die!" I screamed. A burst of energy flew out of me, sending Gunner flying back across the bed. I stumbled to my feet, dragging the bedsheet with me and wrapped it around my naked body. Gunner quickly jumped up and rushed to stand in front of me. He picked me up and held me against his large chest. I struggled and thrashed and kicked my legs while growling and grunting for him to let me go, but it was no use. His grip on me was firm and unbreakable.

"Zee stop" he pleaded,

"Put me down" I growled back,

"Not until you stop and listen"

"I have listened, but what you're saying is stupid"

"It's the only way Zelena". I kicked out and tried to push out of his grip, but his hold wasn't wavering.

"You don't know that! Maybe she'll just punish you more for leaving me, for abandoning your Mate and pup" I growled at him, feigning anger.

"I'm not abandoning you, I'm coming back"

"No, you're not, because you're not fucking going". I flung my head around and it collided with his collarbone. I won't lie, it fucking hurt. But it didn't stop my struggling, it only made me more determined. Whatever anger I felt at his idea to run was all but gone. All that was left was fear. Deep-seated and intense fear. He wouldn't really leave me, would he? He wouldn't leave us. I hadn't realised I was crying, not at first. But I wasn't just screaming at him not to go, I was howling with the pain at the thought of him not being here, not being close to me. The tears ran from my eyes like never ending pools of sadness.

"Zee, stop it, please" he pleaded with me, his own voice was cracked and broken as he begged me. My heart squeezed and wrenched at the sound of his breaking voice. I went limp in his arms and pressed my forehead to his chest. More sobs wracked my body as I continued to weep.

"You can't leave, I won't let you" I sobbed and wriggled my arms around his back and gripped onto him.

"You know that I'll just follow you anyway". Gunner didn't respond, he just held me in his arms. After a while, I became very uncomfortable, and my body was screaming for food. The sobbing had stopped, but my fear of being without Gunner was still the main focal point of my mind.

"Can I put you down now?" Gunner's voice whispered softly,

"Yes" I answered after a deep breath. Gunner placed my feet back on the ground but kept his arms around my shoulders. My stomach grumbled loudly, breaking the silence of our combined sadness.

"Come on Preggers, let's get my pup some food" Gunner teased with a forced cheerfulness. I nodded my head and let him lead me back to the bed. He picked up one of his t-shirts from the ground and motioned for me to lift my arms. I did so and he dragged the very large shirt down my body, it stopped about halfway down my thighs, proving just how big Gunner has gotten since taking on the Alpha role. Gunner pulled on a pair of basketball shorts, then turned and reached his hand out for mine. I grabbed his hand and interlocked our fingers, then I let him lead me from the room. The moment we opened the door, we were greeted by both Tobias and Lunaya. They were standing opposite the door, Tobias with his arms crossed, leaning on the wall, and Lunaya with a worried look on her face.

"Everything okay here?" Tobias asked while glaring at Gunner,

"Yes, we're just going for a midnight snack" I answered him. I moved to stand in front of Gunner and glared up at Tobias, not feeling completely impressed with his hostile tone or expression.

"What are you doing here?" I asked him firmly,

"We heard some yelling, and I could feel your power being used. Is everything alright?" Lunaya asked stepping closer to me. I didn't know she could do that, sense my power. I suppose it makes sense. She must be talking about my little freakout when I threw Gunner off the bed. I guess I was yelling a little too loudly, so of course they would have heard us. However, I don't think the welcoming committee is really needed.

"Yes, everything is okay. Thank you for checking up on us though" I said with a weak smile directed to my mother. Her eyebrows shot up and she straightened her stance. She seemed surprised by my response. Which is warranted, given how awful I have been to her. Tobias looks a little surprised as well, his hard exterior cracked for a second and a small smirk spread across his face. I've missed that side of Tobias. His playful silly side hasn't been seen since the day of the battle, not since he came home from the forest, changed.

"You're sure you're okay? What I felt, your power... It was, it was different" Lunaya said slowly, like she was struggling for the words. In a spontaneous decision, I stepped forward and placed my hand over hers. She froze, watching me closely.

"I'm okay, I just got a little upset is all. But everything is fine now. At least it will be once I stuff my face with a fist full of bacon" I said with a grin. Lunaya's body relaxed and she offered a smile in return.

"Well, okay then. I'll leave you to it" she sighed and went to walk away.

"Wait" I called, and she turned back around,

"I know it's late, but would you like to join us?" I asked her, I felt Gunner step closer to my back and slip his hand around my waist to the side of my belly. She smiled at me as her eyes brewed tears. She walked back over to me and stopped right in front of me. She's so much taller than I am, and I had to crane my neck to look up at her. As I did, the back of my head rested on Gunner's chest.

Lunaya lifted her hand, and she very gently brushed her fingers over my cheek. For the first time, I didn't want to push her away. If anything, I wanted to draw her in.

"I would love that. Really, more than you know. But I think the two of you need a little time for yourselves" she said as he quickly looked up to Gunner before bringing her gaze back to me.

"Are you sure?" I question. I was a little confused as to why she turned me down, I thought she'd jump at the chance. Isn't that what she has wanted this whole time, for us to reconnect? Well, here I am, offering her the opportunity, right now.

"I'm sure, my gorgeous girl. We'll talk more in the morning, or tomorrow, or the next day. We have all the time in the world now, I'm not going anywhere" she said with the most soft and gentle voice, so filled with love and devotion. The kind of tone I haven't heard from her before. It tickled me. And right there, I honestly wanted to jump into her arms and cry.

"Okay" I said slowly, trying to swallow the ball of emotion in my chest. She cupped my cheek and smiled, then patted Gunner on the shoulder. Then she walked back towards her room. Gunner leaned down and whispered softly in my ear.

"I'm proud of you" he said before kissing my cheek. I gripped my hand around the back of his neck and held his lips there for a moment longer.

"Alright love birds, go and have your snack" Tobias snickered as he too walked off towards his room, not giving us a second look. We headed down to the kitchen and Gunner placed me on a stool by the bench. He walked over to the cupboard, and just like the first time I set foot in this kitchen, he pulled on one of Roe's floral aprons. We laughed and joked about his cooking abilities as he got to work on the bacon and a few rare minute steaks. With nothing else on but the shorts and the apron, he looked completely out of place. Still totally delicious and good enough to bite into, but out of place nonetheless. Gunner has grown. Like, a lot. He is bigger, broader, even taller. The Alpha position suits him, and he has taken to it well. But as he is standing in front of the stove with a floral apron on and a pair of tongs in his hands, I can't help but laugh at how silly he looks.

Gunner brought the plates over and sat one down in front of me and one for himself. Since I've been keeping up a regular eating schedule, the desire to 'wolf it down' hasn't been so prominent.

Thankfully. The uncontrollable urges were starting to make me feel like a wild animal. I tucked my arm through Gunner's and leaned my head on his arm. He kissed the top of my head and stabbed his fork into his steak. I picked up a piece of bacon and plopped it in my mouth, and I watched Gunner's perfectly sculpted jaw move with his chewing. There is no one more handsome than Gunner. I may be biased, but I just don't see how anyone else in the world could possibly be this ridiculously good looking. Our baby is one lucky little nugget.

Then it dawned on me again. He wants to leave me. He wants to run away and figure this whole darkness thing out all alone. Who knows how long that could take. Maybe days, maybe weeks, maybe years. Would he really leave and miss the birth of his firstborn? Would he really leave me alone to birth and raise this baby alone? I can see why he may think it is a good idea. He thinks leaving the pack would protect everyone. But what he doesn't seem to see is how much the pack will suffer without their Alpha. Or how much I would suffer. Even more so now that Cole is gone. The pack can't survive without an Alpha and a Beta. I'm still learning about pack law and logic, but surely that is common knowledge. A pack needs a Beta and an Alpha. If he left, would his father then take back up the mantle? What would that make me? Will Roe become Luna again, or will I still be? Oh Goddess, they wouldn't name the Pup Alpha or Luna, would they? No. That's silly, that wouldn't even work. It would have to be Lupus then. Perhaps Gunner is going to name a new Beta. He hasn't said anything to me about it. Could he replace Cole so quickly? Will Smith get the title of Beta and then someone else will become Delta? Maybe even Tobias would take over. He is probably the most powerful Were here, besides me. If the pack accept him as their leader that is. I don't think Gunner has thought all of this through. There are too many blank spaces that need to be filled, and too many unanswered questions.

"Zelena" Gunner's voice broke my train of thought. I shook my head free of the crazy whirlwind of scattered thoughts and looked up at him.

"Yeah?" I asked dumbly,

"What are you thinking about? You stink of anxiety and confusion, and you've barely touched your food" he said with a quirked eyebrow.

"It's nothing, sorry. Baby brain just got me a little carried away for a second" I lied with a fake smile.

"You're lying" he quipped and turned back to his plate. I snuggled into his arm again and ate another piece of bacon.

"It doesn't matter for now" I said after I swallowed the delicious porky goodness.

"For now" Gunner grunted quietly. We finished the rest of our food in silence. Gunner finished first and wrapped his arm around my side so that I could lean back on his chest. With one hand on my stomach, he used the other to spoon feed me the rest of my bacon. It was sweet, romantic even. He'd lift the fort to my lips and kiss my head when I bit off the meat. Then he'd do the same thing again until the plate was clear. By the time we were headed back up to bed, I was pooped. I flopped down on the bed while Gunner kicked off his shorts and turned off the lights.

I turned onto my side so that Gunner could curl up behind me. My small body fit perfectly with his, like we were truly made for one another. With my head resting on Gunner's arm and our fingers interlocked, he used his other hand to rub slow circles on the mound of my stomach. I have been feeling the baby move more and more as the days passed. And right now, its little limbs were pounding against my uterus where Gunner's hand was roaming. We giggled and laughed, marvelling at the strength of the pup's kicks.

"She's a strong one, isn't she?" Gunner laughed,

"He is very strong" I answered him with a cocky tone,

"That's the kick of an Alpha-Son, it's a boy for sure" I added.

"No, that is pure Triple Goddess power. You're feeling the next descendant of the moon making her presence known".

"You really think it's a boy?" he asked as he lifted his chin to rest on my shoulder,

"I don't actually care what it is. So long as it's healthy, happy and safe" I answered him. Gunner's fingers spread out over my stomach as the pup landed another kick to his palm. He was quiet for a moment, just gripping his hand firmly over my belly. He dropped his head back down and sighed,

"Me too" he mumbled. We lay like that for a while longer, peacefully, silently. Revelling in the calmness of the moment. My eyes were closed, and I could feel the sleep creeping up on me.

"I have to do this, Zelena" Gunner said quietly. Though he held more strength and determination in his voice than I held in my entire body. My eyes flew open, and I bit down on my bottom lip to stop it from shaking. It took everything in me not to argue. I want to. Goddess, do I want to. But arguing further would be pointless. The decision has been made, I can hear the finality in his voice. Even if I fought him on it, I don't think there is any chance of changing his mind now. A feeling of dread filled my veins, I felt my skin turn ice cold and the muscles of my arms and legs tensed. I took a long and shakily drawn-out breath and whispered back to him,

"I know". At the very moment the words left my mouth, my heart split in two.

Chapter Three

WG-02

Some time ago.

I've dealt with a lot up until this point. I'm proud to say that through it all, I have not broken. All my life I've known pain. I've grown up on it. Lived it, learnt it, tasted it, endured it. I know pain. Intimately. I have been pushed to the furthest limits imaginable, both in mind and body. And I've still not broken. I am stronger because of how far I have been pushed. I have endured and survived more than anyone else possibly could. I have been moulded into the ultimate weapon, created from pain to cause havoc. I am the shadow in the dark, the monster under the bed. I am the bringer of death. Nothing could ever break me. But this... This is unlike anything else that I have endured before. This is beyond the point of physical pain and mental torture. This is worse. This is a line I was naive enough to believe would never be crossed. This could break me.

His cold clammy hands slid slowly along my exposed thigh. The feel of his callused skin made me want to vomit. His breath was heavy and ragged, and his heartbeat was thumping excitedly in his chest. With my cheek pressed against the frigid metal of the table, and my hands bound tightly behind my back, my options were limited. I'd been trained for situations like this, I knew exactly what to do, but my energy was nearly depleted. My punishment this week was withholding my meals, so it's been six days now since my last scrap of food. I already gave everything I could once I figured out his intentions, but that just made him even more angry. He got off on the struggle. I could feel how much it was getting him off, by the firm lump in his pants that was pressed hard against my backside. Everything about this was making me feel nauseous and weak. From the injuries I already sustained and the disgusting stink of his desire. My body was giving out and I know I can't hold off much longer.

In one last-ditch attempt to get free, I flung my body upright with my head angled back and collided the top of my head with his nose. The satisfying crunch of breaking bones and his pained grunt told me I was successful. I turned my body in a shot to run, but he was too quick and kicked out with his leg, connecting it with my knee. I lost my footing and was stumbling forward, with my hands still bound behind me, I couldn't steady myself and I slammed headfirst into the rough concrete wall. I was out.

The pain in my head was pounding like jackhammers, vibrating all through my body. My ears were ringing with a high-pitched screech that made me wince. The rhythmic thumping against my back alerted me to more pain. My crotch was burning in agony. I tried to open my eyes, but they were heavy and felt sticky. I tried to stand up, but I couldn't move. My hands were still bound, and something heavy was pressed against them. The thumping at my back increased in speed and the pain in my gut intensified. Oh god no. Please no. I cried out in pain, begging for him to stop. Grabbing the hair at the back of my head he pushed my face into the table hard. His grunts and groans filled the room.

Through the cloud of the throbbing pain in my head, I was able to piece together a few things. The stickiness in my eyes was blood. My Blood. And by the feel of it, it was coating my entire face. I was bent over the cold metal table with my hands tied and my bottom half bare. The guard was thrusting himself deep inside me, and it hurt like fucking hell. I tried to thrash under his grip, but he just lifted my head and slammed it back into the table, making my already aching head scream for mercy. His other hand was gripping my bound hands to restrict my fighting movements. The more I tried to fight him, the more he hurt me. So I stopped. I just lay there, begging silently for him to stop. As he pounded his hard dick into my aching nether region, tears pooled in my eyes. What more could I do? He is a 6'2 giant beast, built like a wrestler, and I'm just a small framed sixteen-year-old genetically engineered demon.

After what felt like hours, he finally had enough. He let me go and stepped back. My limp body lay unmoving on the cold metal table. His breathing was heavy and the smell of his sweat and cum filled my nostrils. I didn't move, I couldn't. The pain in my body was too much. I heard him pull his pants back up and then he cut the rope around my wrists. My arms dropped to the table like limp noodles. They were too heavy, and I was too weak to lift them. I listened as he walked to the door, it creaked open slowly before closing again behind him.

"I'll be back for more" his gruff voice called through the slot in the door. I pursed my lips and furrowed my brows together. The pounding pain in my body was replaced by an intense fiery rage. The choice was made then and there. He'll never get the chance.

After a while I built up enough energy to move from the cold metal table, I lifted my torn pants and hobbled to the bed in the corner. The metal springs creaked and squeaked as I lowered my raw body onto the filthy mattress. I lay down on my side and curled my knees to my chest. I pulled the thick dirty blanket up to my shoulders and wrapped my arms around myself tightly. Tears once again began to pool in my eyes, but I blinked them away.

This is life. My life. Break a rule, punishment. Lose a fight, punishment. Talk back, punishment. Punishment. Punishment. Punishment. I existed around being punished. My pale skin is littered with the scars of my mistakes, from cuts to burns to lashings and more. They were always creative with my punishment. But I earned each one. I know that. I was bred for this, it's my only reason to exist. But deep down inside of myself, I feel like there must be more. I feel it, in my soul. If I even have a soul. Do monsters have souls? I hope we do. Anyway, this is my world. Born in a lab and engineered for eradication. I don't even have a proper name. Whiskey-Gulf Zero-Two. That's what I'm called, or Whiskey for short. I'm nothing. No one. A monster, created for pure destruction.

Eventually, my beaten body drifted off to sleep, or a sleep like unconsciousness The same old dream taunted me. Always the same thing. Never different. It's just tedious at this point. I was sat on the cold ground of my room. My knees were curled up to my chest and my small arms wrapped around them. I was hurting, I'd just endured another punishment. And just like always, I looked up at myself. A copy, or a hallucination, or a mirror image of me stood looking down at me. The other me tried to speak to me, but I could never hear what I said. That always bothered me more than I cared to admit. Why couldn't I hear it? For as long as I can remember I had this dream. The other version of myself slowly grew up and changed as I did. But I could never hear it. I would daydream sometimes about what it was that the other me was saying. I don't think I will ever be fully satisfied until I know for sure what 'it', what 'I' am saying.

When I woke again, I expected it was still a few hours before dawn. I was aching all over. My head was pounding, my arms were heavy, and my wrists stung from the rope burn. But above all, one pain stood out among the rest. The place between my legs was burning, any movement brought on an annoying stinging pain. I slowly moved my hand down between my thighs and touched the area. I hissed and whipped my hand back again. It hurt to touch. It was swollen and sensitive, tender and raw. That fucking bastard. A dark red colour on my fingertips caught my attention and I moved my hand in front of my face to inspect. My fingers had fresh blood coating them. I wiped my hand on my dirty blanket and slowly sat up on the bed. My wrists were red and raw, the burns from the rope left dark purple bruising as well. My knuckles were swollen and split from where I tried to fight him off. What a pointless venture that turned out to be.

I struggled to my feet and swallowed the whimper that nearly came out. No crying. Monsters don't cry. One lashing for one tear. Growing up, I learned quickly not to cry. The scars on my back are a testament to my lesson. One tear, one lashing. My scars are years old now. No tears mean no lashings, so I let none fall. I limped to the small sink in the corner of my room and turned on the tap. As per usual, the water was freezing. I cupped my small hands under the stream to catch the water, then gently placed my face into the collected water. I ran my wet fingers over my beaten face, letting the moister wash away the blood. I cupped my hands again and washed more water over my face. I did this until the water that dripped from my face lost its red tinge.

I let my fingers roam the skin of my face, feeling for new wounds. There's no mirror in my room, so this is how I learnt to inspect myself. I started at my hairline, where the throbbing was coming from. My hair was matted together and felt like it was covered in dry blood. I quickly found the reason why, just past my hairline, a large open gash. It was dry, risen and crusted over. My hair had somehow caught most of the blood, and once it dried, it seemed to have plugged the wound and stopped the bleeding. Is it any wonder I knocked myself out, it was gnarly. I moved down to the swollen area around my eye, it was twice the size it should have been, and a deep cut ran across my cheekbone to just below my eye. The skin was tender to the touch and felt warm. Could mean I've fractured my eye socket, or maybe my cheekbone. My fingers moved to my mouth where my bottom lip held a small split. I let my tongue poke out and slid it along the lump on my lip. It wasn't too bad, I've had worse. I let my hands trail down to my neck and again met with sore tender skin.

I flashed back to when he had me pinned against the wall. My feet had been lifted off the ground, as he held me at his eye level. He had both of his hands wrapped around my neck, supporting all my weight. I was coughing and gasping, desperately trying to get another breath. I managed to kick him between his legs, that's why he let me go. I dropped to the floor and rolled to the side away from him. I ran for the door as he stood crumpled over holding his junk. Of course, the big dumb lump remembered to lock it behind him, especially after last time. As I turned around from the door, I was met with a punch to the face. His fist connected with my cheekbone, and I dropped to the floor like a sack of meat. I lay there still, letting him think that he knocked me out. Once I felt his hands grab my shoulder to roll me over, I flung my arm around, smacking my closed fist to the side of his head. He snarled and grunted but didn't let go of my shoulder. I flew the palm of my hand upright, colliding it with the bottom of his chin. The sound of his teeth slamming together made me dry heave. He stepped over me so that I was now lying on the cold ground between his legs. He swung his arm, and the back of his hand slapped against my face. I could feel my lip pop open from the pressure. The force of his backhand made me roll onto my side. He didn't waste the opportunity and quickly kicked his steel capped boot into the soft of my stomach. He kicked the air right out of me, and I lay there wheezing like a broken recorder. Before I got the chance to catch a breath, he reefed me off the cold floor by my hair and dragged me over to my small bed. With an effort that felt too easy, he tossed me onto the bed and started to crawl his way on top of me. My lip was stinging, my stomach was aching, and now with the smell of his sweat and lust so close to my face, I was about to chuck. He had my hands pinned on either side of my face and his face was buried into my neck. His sloppy mouth hungrily devoured the soft skin of my neck, I could feel his teeth biting my flesh. I hooked my foot around his and in one quick swift movement, I rolled us both off the bed. He hit the floor with a thump, and I was now straddling him. Without a moment of hesitation, I began beating down on him with my closed fists. I didn't get to land too many, he was blocking most of them. With the injuries I had already sustained, I was wrecked, what remained of my strength was dwindling fast. He laughed. The fucker started to laugh as I worked my fists into his face and arms. The sound of the door unlocking caught my attention, pulling me from my flashback. I whirled around and waited anxiously to see who would come through the door this time. Spencer's face appeared and he looked over my battered and blood covered body with disgust. Spencer was one of the more uncaring and brutal guards. If anything, he would have been all for my little punishment last night. Actually, if he'd known about it, I'm sure he would have happily joined in.

"Get up Whiskey. Shower time" he spat at me. I pushed myself up from the sink and stood on shaky legs. I carefully walked over to the doorway that he was still standing in and squeezed past him. I knew the way. I've walked this hallway plenty of times. Spencer shoved his hand into the back of my head and pushed, trying to get me to walk faster. All he accomplished though, was sending me sprawling across the floor. The impact of my body hitting the ground again sent a new wave of pain coursing through my body. I wasn't overreacting when I said that everything hurt.

I lay with my cheek on the cold concrete while Spencer snickered behind me. The pain flowing through my body intensified. I could feel my bones twist with anger under my skin. An audible snap filled the hallways and Spencer's laugh halted. Another snap sounded, and another. The first was my rib, the second was my shoulder. I was fighting it as much as I could. If I let the beast free without permission, the punishments that I endure are unlike anything else. They will break my bones, my spirit, my resolve.

They will starve me, chain me up, and leave me to sit constricted for days on end. But worst of all, they have ways to make me feel like I am burning from the inside out. That horrible purple liquid, that's the worst punishment by far.

"Oh, please give me a reason to hurt you" Spencer sneered down at me. He knelt down beside me, right next to my face. He grabbed my chin and turned my head so that I would look at him. "Show me the monster, then I can really have my fun with you. Johnny Boy had his turn last night, now I want mine" he hissed with venom and disdain dripping from his words. He is the worst. I hate it when Spencer is here. Like a lot of the others, he gets satisfaction from my pain and torment. But unlike the others, he was the main cause of it. The breaking and reforming of my bones stopped, but the fiery rage that was flowing through me only sped up. My head started to spin, and I felt a little weightless. I turned onto my back and slowly sat up, propping myself up with my hands. Spencer stood up and took a step back. A moment of fear flicked through his eyes before he masked it back over with his usual hard glare. He took a prepared attack stance and lifted his gun, the barrel pointed right at my head, but I felt no fear. All I felt was anger. I took in a deep breath, in an attempt to calm myself. All of the air filled my lungs and swirled around my body. My chest swelled with the crisp air. Something I had never felt before overwhelmed my body. It was like the air was gripping hold of my blood vessels and contracting my muscles. It felt like it was giving me strength. Spencer let go of his gun and it swung down at his side by the strap over his shoulder. He dropped to his knees and grasped at his throat. I scurried away a little further, unsure of what he was doing. Horrible choking and gasping sounds came from Spencer as his face started to turn a shade of blue. I didn't speak, I didn't move, I just watched. What else was I meant to do? Save him? I don't think so.

Spencer's eyes were glued firmly to mine. Even with his face turning an ungodly colour, and the nightmare inducing gagging sounds he made, he still managed to glare at me with more hatred and disgust than ever before. I don't understand what is happening. One second he is standing over me, hissing threats of violence, and the next he is doing this... whatever 'this' is. After a minute or two, Spencer's glassy eyes rolled to the back of his head, and then he fell to the floor face first. The thump of his body seemed to echo down the hallway. I sat completely still, staring at his unmoving body that was lying right in front of my legs. What am I meant to do now? Do I continue on to the showers myself, or do I go back to my room? As I sat contemplating my options, the decision was made for me. A swarm of guards came around the corner and paused, they took in the sight of their comrade on the ground and then me sitting not a meter away. It was only a brief pause before they burst into action, and quickly surrounded me with their guns pointed down at my shaking body. Of course they would think this was my fault. Everything that goes wrong around me is always my fault. Even if the big idiot choked to death on his own. The guard's angry voices filled my head. They were too loud, and their voices were too muddled together, I couldn't understand what they were screaming at me. I raised my hands in surrender and was met with the butt of a gun slammed into the side of my head.

A few weeks ago.
I walked through the now empty village. The sun was setting in the distance, painting the clouds in the sky in hues of pink and orange. The warmth that the sun offered was slowly drifting away with its light. I prefer the cold, my body is accustomed to the frigid rattling of my frozen bones. The cold is better suited for my icy heart. I walked up the steps of a small hut and pushed open the door. I stood in the doorway and closed my eyes, letting my other senses take control. I could hear a single heartbeat, thumping erratically from inside the small home. I stepped through the doorway and stood in the middle of the living space. The lounge room, dining room and kitchen were all in the same area. A well-worn brown couch sat against the wall, with a small wooden dining table against the other wall. The kitchen was old and held a small, rusted fridge and a wood fire stove. This is definitely one of the poorer packs I've found. At least this place has power though. Once again, I closed my eyes and listened. The heartbeat was coming from the back area. I lifted my nose and sniffed. A male, only a young one, his wolf hasn't been born yet. I followed the scent and the sound of his fear filled heartbeat to a bedroom. I slowly pushed open the door and filled the doorway. This little cat-and-mouse game excites me. I love the chase, the

hunt. Evoking fear in others is my happy drug. I giggled and stepped into the room.

"I know you're in here, why don't you come out and play" I said with a cheery tone. The sound of his heartbeat accelerated, and I turned my head to the source of the sound. A small wooden wardrobe sat beside a single bed with a blue bedspread. I walked over to the wardrobe and knocked twice.

"Vykhodi, vykhodi, gde by ty ni byl" (Come out, come out, wherever you are) I sang and gripped the cupboard door handle. I pulled the door open and flung back the coats hanging inside.

"Gotcha!" I laughed. The boy was curled into a ball, pressing himself into the back of the cupboard. Whisps of blonde hair poked out from the faded blue beanie on his head. It was summer here, but the air was still cold. The brown knitted jumper the boy wore was littered with holes. I grabbed the boy's shoulder and pulled him out of the cupboard and into the room. He cried out and tried to run past me, but I gripped his arm and knelt down in front of him so that we were at eye level.

"Tsk, tsk, tsk" I clicked my tongue as I waved my finger back and forth in his face. The boy was crying and struggling in my hold, but he was not a match for me.

"Gde Troynaya Boginya, malen'kiy mal'chik?" (Where is the Triple Goddess, little boy?)

"Ya ne znayu" (I don't know) he wailed. I huffed and grabbed both of his shoulders. The tips of my nails dug into his skin, and he screamed and struggled even more.

"You wouldn't lie to me, would you?" I asked him sternly. He stared at me blankly with tears streaming down his young face. Judging by the stupid look on his face, the little shit doesn't understand English.

"Ne lgi mne" (Don't lie to me) I growled at him and flashed my teeth.

"Ya ne znayu" (I don't know) the boy cried again and continued to struggle in my grasp. I grow bored of this insolence. I exhaled an exasperated breath and frowned at him. When I ask a simple question, I expect a simple answer. Am I asking too much of this little stray dog? What a waste of my time this turned out to be.

"Nepravil'nyy otvet" (Wrong answer) I sighed and squeezed his shoulders, pressing my sharpened engineered talons into his flesh. The boy screamed and cried out as he tried to break out of my grip. I sucked in a lung full of air, drawing the air from the boy's lungs. He choked and gasped for air, but there was none left for him to breathe. After a minute of gaging and thrashing, the boy's body fell limp to the floor. I stood up and looked down at the dead boy. I wiped the blood from my hands onto my pants and scoffed. Disgusting maggot.

"Onto the next" I said to myself as I stepped over the boy's lifeless body.

Chapter Four

Whiskey

I hate this place. I hate this smell. The stench of wet dog and fear. It's repugnant. When someone dies suddenly, they leave behind the stench of their last thoughts. I've come to find that most of the time those thoughts are ones of fear. I hate the smell of it. It's what comes after, that I like the most, the scent of death. Blood, mixed with pain and a hint of helplessness, all thrown together with the scent of decaying flesh. That is the smell I like. That is what I want to be able to smell all day. If I could, I would infuse the horrendous stench into a perfume and wear it daily. The bringer of death, carrying with her the scent of your doom. Sounds good, doesn't it?

This tedious task is starting to wear on my patience. Proven so by my rush to get through this damned village. I usually love the chase, the thrill of scaring the life out of the mangey mutts, before I literally take their lives from them. But lately, the excitement is dwindling. I'm getting more and more frustrated, angry even. I have never had to work this hard before, and I'm growing bored of it. No one wants to talk. Even in the face of their death, they all remain silent. Tenacious little fuckers these Weres. But in the end, it doesn't matter. I will get what I came for sooner or later. And they will die, all of them, eventually. I'll make sure of it.

I walked through the deserted village and gazed at the small forest space. I can't believe that these creatures live like this. Tiny little huts in the middle of the forest. Some of them looked to be powered by generators, others seemed to have no electricity at all. They live so removed from civilisation, so rough and rogue. I understand why. It's so that their existence remains hidden from the humans. But like this? They couldn't manage something a little more civilized. Either way, this is my nightmare. I did my time in the dark and squaller. Never again. Now, I avoid it the best I can. I would much prefer the few luxurious things this shitty life has to offer. Fancy cars, fancy hotels, the works. I have my very own little stash of items that I've collected over the years. Just little things I have found along the way. A very old Faberge Egg, a gold jewel-encrusted crown stolen from a European Queen who lived a few centuries ago. Multiple pieces of jewellery with big chunks of diamonds, and smaller more delicate diamonds. Plus a few other pieces of jewellery, all made with various coloured precious stones. Apparently, people get really sentimental about their belongings, they pass them along to their kids and all that crap. So pitiful. But it worked out alright for me. Now, I have all of their precious little family heirlooms. I like to consider it payment. Along with all my other little knick-knacks, I have more cash than I could ever spend in this lifetime. I've grown accustomed to the high life, and I will never go back to the scum. I would never choose to live like these creatures do, at least not voluntarily.

I fucked up on this one. In my haste to get what I came for, a few of the mongrels got away. That will probably come back and bite me in the ass at a later date. But I will punish myself for it later. I picked one of the better looking houses, the biggest, cleanest looking one. I pushed open the door and paused in the doorway, letting my eyes shut and focusing on my hearing. I could hear the wind rustling through the trees and the sound of my own heartbeat. Nothing else. Whoever lived here is either gone or lying out in the village somewhere, dead. I headed in and found the kitchen space. This must be the Alpha's residence. It's too nice to belong to anyone else. The kitchen is still a crap heap, but it's big-ish, nicely decorated, and most importantly, it's fully stocked. I helped myself to the cupboards and got to work making a proper meal. Something I've been missing out on the past couple of days. Once I was content with the overfilled plate of bread, cured meat and a bunch of different kinds of chutneys, I went and made myself at home on the decent sized lounge chair. I stuffed the food into my mouth as I looked around at the heavily decorated walls. Were themed memorabilia was placed in every possible place it could fit. Paintings, carvings, tapestries, all of it. It was as if a heavily invested Were fanatic spewed up in here. Disgusting. One item in particular caught my attention, and as I honed my gaze in on it, I was thrown back into my memories.

Eight years ago.
I sat in the decked out electric chair, wearing nothing but my underpants and a crop top. Freezing cold air was blowing through the only window in the concrete room, a small 40cm by 60cm open block with steel bars across it. The icy temperatures from the thick blanket of snow and the ice-covered trees outside had turned the room into a freezer. I was shaking uncontrollably with the nonstop shivers shooting through my young body. My forearms were stinging from the lashes, but I could do nothing to soothe them. My wrists were locked in place by the frigid metal cuffs. The steel bit into my skin each time I tried to move, so I had to stay still. My ankles were also locked in place, along with my waist and head. I couldn't move, even if I wanted to. The shackle around my forehead had screws and padding on it, meaning it kept me from being able to turn away. All I could do was close my eyes and scream. I managed to stop the tears, thankfully. Only a few got loose, but it was enough to earn a punishment. I'm glad I stopped myself from crying more, I wouldn't have been able to take another lashing. The skin of my arms was bright red and bleeding. Any more hits and I think they may hit the bone.
The bright light of the projector screen flickered over my face. The same horrendous pictures would flick through quickly, over and over again, until finally landing on just one, long enough for me to study the depicted scene closely. The same process, going on for hours now. The flickering stopped and a picture of a mangled wolf's body appeared on the screen. Its head was partially severed, and all of its legs were bent in the wrong direction. There were gaping wounds and patches of missing fur scattered over its body. The amount of blood was sickening. Blood was covering every inch of its remaining grey fur, and all of the ground around it. A gentle warmth spread over the chair I was sitting in, momentarily easing the shaking of my tiny bones.

For just a moment I could relax the tension of my jaw, just long enough to take a breath without the sting of the icy air burning down my throat. A new picture appeared. This time it was of a woman with her arms wrapped around the neck of a large brown wolf. She looked happy. A soft smile was on her face, and she had her eyes closed. The wolf was pressing its head into her chest as they stood together. It was a nice picture. Woman and beast, together in love and happiness. A burst of pain shot through me, coming from the collar around my neck. Shoots of electricity flowed through my little body, as I shook and screamed through the torture. Everything hurt, it was like I was on fire. The need to run, or roll, or shake it off was overpowering, but pointless, I was pinned in place. I'm not going anywhere. I screamed out, my small voice filling the room in a high pitched shrill. Eventually, the electricity stopped, and the pictures began flickering again.

I breathed heavily through the pain, forcing the tears to keep away. Just as I was able to catch my breath, the pictures stopped again on another grotesque image of a dead wolf. Only this time, the wolf was hanging upside down from a pole. Its bottom half was that of a wolf, but the top half, the arms and chest, was human. The human head sat on a spike next to the body, only it had large fangs poking out of its open mouth. It was gross, sad, and scary. It made me want to cry again. I closed my eyes tight and tried to shake my head.

"Stop it. Please stop it" I pleaded. Even with my eyes closed I could feel some tears forming behind the lids. A hand collided with the side of my face, forcing my forehead to bang against the steel bar that was holding it down. I opened my eyes again and the tears fell. He laughed. He sounded both happy and really creepy.

"Are those tears?" he chuckled and wiped his finger over the wet streak on my cheek,

"No!" I screamed,

"I'm not crying, I promise, I'm not crying" I begged, but it was too late. The whip came down over my arms in a swift strong movement. The thin leather whip sliced through the skin, and I screamed again. I tried to look down at my left arm without moving my head. A fresh streak of blood trickled from the new slash.

"What's the rule?" he yelled. He was bending down in front of me, his face only inches away from my own.

"One tear, one lash" I yelled back, trying my best to keep my voice sounding strong. Even though all I wanted was to cry.

"Again!" he roared, his hot breath bashed against my face as he screamed,

"One tear, one lash" I screamed back loudly.

"What are you?" he demanded,

"A monster"

"What are you?"

"A monster!"

"And what do monsters not do?"

"Monsters don't cry" I yelled as loud as I could.

"And why don't monsters cry? Tell me beast, what's the rule?"

"One tear, one lash" I repeated again. My voice was becoming hoarse from the screaming and the cold. But I was used to this. It was a daily occurrence. The lash came down again across my arms. I bit into the side of my cheek to hold in the scream. It didn't work. A strangled cry fell from my clenched teeth as the taste of blood filled my mouth. He grabbed my chin and leaned in close. So close that I could smell the fresh tea on his breath.

"Watch the screen" he snapped. He let go of my chin and backed away from me, letting the screen come back into view. The pictures began to change in quick succession, flicking through the gruesome images. It stopped again on another wolf, its belly was cut open and its guts were spilled out on the ground. The chair warmed again, and for a brief second, I wasn't cold. Then it changed to a small group of giant wolves, all standing together with their big teeth facing the camera. The collar whirled to life and the pain shot through me once again. I trembled and shook violently as I screamed in pain. I'm not going to be able to hold out too much longer. The electricity stopped and I took a large gasp of air. I was panting and sweating, but no tears fell. I think dying would be easier than this. I wouldn't even care how painful the death was, as long as it resulted in me not being here any longer. I would take that over this. No question. The pictures started to flick through again, giving me time to calm my quick breathing and racing heart. The screen stopped on a pile of charred remains in the snow. It was still smoking, and fresh blood was all over the ground. From what I could tell, the bodies were both humans and wolves. I bit down on the inside of my cheek again, drawing more blood. Then, I closed my eyes. No more. I don't want to see any more. A fresh crack of the whip and sharp pain across my arms, made me scream out.

"Open your eyes, Whiskey" he demanded. I held them closed tighter and tried to shake my head, but it couldn't move from under the shackle.

"Last chance you little beast, open your fucking eyes and watch the screen" he roared,

"No more, please" I pleaded, but my begging was only met with another whip across my arms. I tried to thrash in my seat. A desperate attempt to free myself, but all that accomplished was more pain in my restricted limbs.

"I warned you" he hissed angrily. I jolted in surprise when a hand came around the top of my neck and squeezed tightly. I gagged and coughed, and my eyes flew open. The second that they were open again, more hands appeared. Multiple people were working on holding open my eyelids as others tried to fit some kind of pointy bracket thing to my face. I screamed from under the pressure on my throat and tried to shake the hands away from my face. Sharp spikes poked into the top and bottom of my eyelids on both eyes, then the hands went away. I tried to blink, but I couldn't.

"What did you do?" I yelled and pulled on my hands. My eyes were starting to sting from being held open for so long.

"Take it off" I yelled. But no one responded. All I could hear was soft laughter. They were laughing at me, they were enjoying doing this to me. Why? What did I ever do to them? Someone stepped forward and tipped some kind of liquid into my eyes. It stopped the stinging, but it didn't help the pain and uncomfortableness.

"I told you Whiskey, but you didn't listen" he teased and tapped his hand on my cheek. I tried to snap my teeth at him, hoping I could move my head just enough to reach a finger. But I couldn't, and he just laughed more.

"Watch the screen" he sneered. I had no choice now anyway. The pictures flicked through quickly before stopping on a picture of two men holding up two severed wolf heads. They looked very proud and happy with themselves. They wore matching black uniforms and each man had big guns slung over their shoulders.

The seat started to heat up again, letting my frozen bare skin warm up for a few seconds. Then the picture changed to the outlined shape of a woman's body. The background was a mix of pink, blue and purple, with stars and a crescent moon. The body of the woman was made up of blinding white light, with a symbol in the middle. A symbol I have become very used to seeing. The picture was beautiful, and for a brief second, I was enjoying looking at it. Then the pain went through me. It was stronger than all the other times. I wanted to scream, but I couldn't even manage that. I couldn't take it. I couldn't do it anymore. Everyone has a limit, and at eleven years old, this was mine. Everything went fuzzy and I was out.

Present Day.
I stood from the couch and walked over to the picture on the wall. I stood in front of it, moving my eyes over the mix of colours. It was like a galaxy of stars, glitter, and beautiful colours. It was the kind of picture that would make someone calm and happy. It was the type of picture someone could marvel at for hours. It was the kind of picture that someone would smile at. But not me. It was the same picture that I have been forced to look at thousands of times throughout my life. I crossed my arms and my fingers moved slowly over my forearm. The fingertips traced over the countless raised scars left behind from my childhood education. I let my eyes glide over the lines of the symbol. Two crescent moons on either side of a full moon. The waxing moon, the full moon and the waning moon. The symbol of the Were deity, the Moon Goddess. This symbol is meant to be a beacon of life and love for Were-kind, their most cherished and worshipped image. What a load of shit. Three stupid shapes that mean nothing. This symbol has caused me nothing but pain. This symbol has controlled my entire life. I am so fucking sick of this stupid fucking symbol!
I grabbed the picture from the wall and threw it through the air. It smashed against the wall on the other side of the room, exploding into a thousand small shards. All of my anger and pain bubbled to the surface. Heat swept through my body making my bones ache. I lifted my chin and screamed. The high-pitched shriek burst from my mouth and filled the room. The windows shattered and a whirlwind of cold air came flying in. The air

whipped around me like cracking ice, slicing through everything in the room just like a hot knife through butter. The shrill scream reached its crescendo, as the fierce tornado of my own making blew out the walls of the lounge room. I gasped in a deep breath and hunched forward, catching myself with my hands on my knees. That fucking symbol. The wind died down, but the cold was more present now. I stood up straight and looked around the room. Wow, I really tore this place to shreds. Broken art, furniture, and stuff that could only be described as scrap was now strewn all over the floor. Two of the walls had been completely blown out, exposing the outside world, and the roof seemed to be hanging lower than before. Fuck. Now I'll have to find somewhere else to sleep tonight. Me and my fucking temper. All because of that stupid useless symbol. I growled and huffed as I stood upright.

I began to trudge through the debris and made my way back outside. I remember seeing another semi decent looking house not far from this one, I suppose that will have to do for now. At least until I find where they keep their records, and then I can get out of this shit hole. I made my way back through the village towards where I spotted the small house. As I walked through the clearing, a far-off howl broke the silence. I stopped in my tracks and searched the surrounding trees with my piercing gaze. The forest was thick, and the setting sun meant it was getting dark. But my senses are phenomenal. I can see better, hear better and smell better than any other human. All thanks to my scientifically engineered genes. Most of the time, these beasts all sound the same. But this howl was different, it was like I could understand what it was saying. I could hear its sadness and its grief. I knew at that moment that it was a member of this pack, and I also knew that I couldn't let it get away.

I set off in a run, towards where the howl came from. Darting between two huts and into the trees. The scent was strong, but it was running away. I pumped my legs harder and pushed forward. My feet crunched over the foliage and the cool air whipped through my chocolate hair as I ran. I could smell the beast up ahead. The foul creature stunk of fear and grief. It made me laugh. Here it is. Here's the kind of chase that I like so much. This is the hunt that I live for. My bones were pulling at me from the inside, twisting and turning as I raced after the runaway. My inner beast was screaming out for the chance to make chase, my body was begging for it. If my education has taught me anything, it's how to suppress that beastly side. And that is just what I need right now. Control. Hunting an animal that is bigger than me, that is meant to be stronger, faster and by all means more powerful than me, and then taking it down in human form. It is the most erotic, fervent, intoxicating feeling you can imagine.

I spotted a flash of dark reddish fur through the trees ahead. From the quick glimpse I got, I could tell it was a big one, probably a male. I pushed harder and caught up to him quickly. The closer I got, the more I could smell. It was definitely a male, and he was a wreck of emotions. I wasn't even breaking a sweat yet. This was easy for me. Fun, but still easy. The wolf was just ahead, one jump and I'd have him. I prepared myself to launch, I saw a rock up ahead that I could push off from, and I measured my steps to get the right footing. Only when we reached the rock, the wolf used it to launch himself through the air. His body went up and then backwards, somersaulting over my head and landing behind me. I skidded to a stop, stirring up dirt and brush all around me. I flung around and was just in time to catch his jaws as he landed on my chest, knocking me to the ground. We slid along the ground, coming to a stop under a tree. I held his snapping teeth back with my hands wedged in the corner of his jaws. I lifted my knee and anchored my foot to his underbelly and pushed. I kept a hold of his head and kicked hard with my foot. The wolf flew up over my head and slammed against the tree trunk above me. I rolled to the side as it came down and landed on the ground on its side with a pathetic whimper. My talons pushed through the ends of my fingers and my sharpened teeth dropped down from my gums. I growled at the beast as it struggled to its feet. The wolf got up and turned to look at me. It was a blow to the gut. All the air left me at once. I stared into its bright blue eyes, and it was like I was looking into my memories.

"No" I breathed out in a breathless huff. Those eyes, the bright ocean blue eyes. They always managed to enchant me, to lead me away from my duty. As I stood unmoving, lost in the past, the wolf tilted its head to the side with confusion, probably unsure as to why I hadn't attacked it yet. I stood up straight and my weak and pitiful body stepped towards the beast, drawn in by those alluring eyes. The wolf took its chance and ran, shooting off through the trees and away from me. I should have taken up the chase again, I should have continued the hunt and brought the beast to its end. But I couldn't. I was planted to the spot where I stood. Glued in place by those goddamn eyes. They took me back to a person who owned eyes just like those ones. A person that I will never forget. That I could never forget. Even if I wanted to.

Chapter Five

Whiskey

I searched the village before it got too dark. It was only a small one. I'd say home to maybe less than sixty. Well, it was home to them, not anymore. I did manage to find the pack library after a bit of ransacking. It was quite small, but the books and scrolls were very old, the oldest one dating back six hundred years. It was a journal kept by an Alpha at the time. He had decent handwriting, though my old Russian was a little rusty, so a lot of the text was a mystery to me. The yellowing pages were filled with pictures, diagrams, and detailed notes. One word stood out among the rest. Boginya. Goddess. I read through the journal a bit more, until I was fully satisfied. This pack have definitely had contact with the Moon Goddess or at least one of her descendants. I slipped the journal into my bag to go through it more thoroughly another time.

Having a heightened sense of smell is usually a great advantage, but when the bodies start to smell, it feels more like a burden. The scent of their decomposing organs hits me quicker than it would a human. Making that part a definite disadvantage. I wasn't going to move them or bury them though. In all the years, I have not once felt the internal pull to take care of the bodies. They're dead, they don't care where their bodies lay, so why would I. If I had to guess, I would estimate that about ten got away. I couldn't know for sure, but I'll stick with ten. And as punishment for letting ten filthy fucking dogs escape, I endured ten lashings. I have never been able to inflict the same severity of punishment upon myself, that my teachers could do to me. But I still manage okay. The extra strength and stamina help. Plus, the accelerated healing means I'm always ready for more, whenever it is needed.

Now I was lying on top of this stranger's really uncomfortable bed, with my hands behind my head, staring up at the ceiling. My back still felt a little tender from my lashings, but the wounds had already closed over. Like I said, the benefits of the healing process. When you have worked and practiced, and experienced as much changing as I have, the wounds start to close again instantaneously. Even with all the windows open, it still stunk of dog. The mattress was like a pile of rocks and the open windows weren't letting enough of the cold in. And of course, there is no air conditioning in this crap hole. Nothing was going right for me today. The blue-eyed wolf didn't come back. Neither did any of the other escapees. Luckily for them. I was in no mood to play nice. I haven't been able to get those damned eyes out of my head. Each time I close my eyes, they take me back again. Back to a place I don't want to be. Back to memories that I don't want to remember. Damn, that fucking wolf and his blue fucking eyes.

Two years ago.
I scaled the side of the building with ease. The darkness of the alley kept me protected. I hung from the windowsill with one arm as I pulled the pocketknife from my belt. I wedged it between the window frames, and they popped open. You would think that these morons would have better security. Cocky bastards. I placed the knife back in my belt and then twisted around so that I could grab the windowsill with that hand too. I was now hanging from the window with my back against the wall, roughly twelve meters above the ground. If anyone came down the alley now, they would be in for a right surprise. I curled my legs up and over and pushed them through the open window. Once I was in, I crouched down and quickly looked around the room. There was an unmade bed and a tallboy. Nothing else. And by the smell of it, the owner hadn't been here for a few hours. I pulled one of the two specially made Sai daggers from its holder on my back and crept over to the door. I pressed my ear up against the wood and listened. Voices are coming from the floor below, but I don't think there is anyone awake up here. I turned the handle and pulled the door

slowly open. A loud creak filled the silence, and I froze. I waited to see if anyone else had heard that, and if they were coming to investigate. After a minute, and no one had come, I decided it was clear. I stood up and got my face nice and close to the hinges of the door, and then spat. A little trick I learned a while back. Doesn't work every time, but now and then it creates enough lubrication to quiet the creaking. I went back to the handle and pulled slowly again. This time, no creak. Bingo.

I stepped out of the door and onto the narrow walkway. There were more doors on either side of this one. Probably more bedrooms. It's a little after three in the morning, so I assume everyone is sleeping, those of them that aren't on night patrol. Opposite me was a waist high wooden railing. I stepped forward and looked over it. I could see parts of the second floor and another set of stairs that I assume lead to the first floor. I'll get to that soon. I have to clear the top floor first. I crept along the wall, keeping far enough back that I couldn't be seen by anyone who happened to look up from the second floor. At the next door, I paused and listened. I could make out some soft snoring, and only one heartbeat. I carefully pushed open the door and stuck my head in. One person was asleep on their side, facing away from the door. I ducked in, went to the side of the bed and looked down at the sleeping being. The man was older looking. No hair on his head but had a full beard. I could see tattoos all over his neck, leading up to the side of his face. I placed the edge of the dagger at his throat and in one swift movement, I sliced open his neck. His eyes flew open and he rolled over onto his back, he then grabbed at the seeping slice on his neck and looked up at me. Blood poured out all around his fingers and down onto the pillow under his head. As he started to gargle on his own blood, I covered his mouth with my hand to silence the sound. I watched the life drain from his face and he eventually stopped gagging. Grabbing his blanket, I wiped the blood from my hand and blade, then I lifted it over his shoulders to cover his dead body. I left the room and closed the door behind me, then proceeded to do the same thing with the six other sleeping people on the top floor.

After the top floor was clear, I made my way back to the first room. I peered over the railing once again, there was still no sign of movement. There were two empty rooms up here, so they must be around and awake somewhere. I slowly made my way down the stairs, stopping before I came around the corner and onto the landing of the second floor. I could hear movement. Someone was walking this way. I pressed my back against the wall and held my dagger in front of me, ready for the kill. The footsteps stopped and the door next to the stairs opened and then closed again. I leaned my ear against the wall and tried to listen. It was muffled, but I could hear some shuffling around for a moment and then silence. I took a breath and peeked out around the corner. The hallway was dark, and I couldn't hear anyone else moving about. I went for the door that the person just went through and pushed it open quickly. It creaked at the last second, alerting the man in the bed that someone was there. He sat up and went to turn on the lamp beside the bed. I launched forward, landing on his lap, with one hand over his mouth and the other holding the blade that I just buried into his chest. He grabbed at my hand and tried to pull it from the hilt of the blade. I withdrew the dagger and stabbed it again a little higher on his body. His muffled scream was louder than I would have liked, the stupid prick may have just woken the rest of the floor. I pulled it out again and stabbed it into the side of his neck. This time he didn't scream. His eyes went wide, and he grabbed his neck. I pulled out the dagger and jumped off his lap and he flopped back down on the bed. Dead.

I turned back to the door, just as another man entered. This one was big. Really big. He filled the whole door frame. He stepped in and I leapt forward. I wrapped my legs around his upper body and gripped hold of his head with my arms, making sure to cover his mouth and nose. He punched at my sides, tried to grab my arms and spun himself around in circles. I would say he resembled a drunk octopus trying to dance. If I was watching from the bed, I probably would have been laughing my ass off. He landed a blow to my ribcage, it hurt, but all it accomplished was making me angry. Things never end well for these dipshits when I get angry. With one hard pull and twist in the right direction, his neck snapped with a satisfying crunch, and the guy dropped to the ground like a sack of shit. I quickly moved to stand next to the open door and waited to see if anyone else heard these two thundering idiots.

When no one came, I dragged the big guy from the doorway and propped him up against the wall. I checked the hallway was clear, then closed the door and moved on to the next room. It must have belonged to the big octopus, the door was wide open, and it smelt like him. I was about to turn away when a glimmer from something on the bedside table caught my eye. I hesitated for just a second, but my curiosity got the better of me. I dashed over to the small table and picked up the item to inspect it. It was a folding knife with a gold dragon melded into the handle. Pretty. I slipped the knife into one of the pockets of my pants and went back to the door. The hall was still quiet, so I assumed no one else had heard the commotion we created. I moved to the next room and found both a woman and a man sleeping in the same bed, naked. They had their arms and legs wrapped around each other and the woman had a peaceful look on her face. If I wasn't so infuriated by the sight, it might have been sweet. The room stunk of alcohol and sex. On the tall boy against the wall was a few empty glass bottles that once held scotch. These fools got plastered and then banged it out. Disgusting.

I went to the male's side of the bed first. I crouched down low so that if the woman woke, she wouldn't be able to see me right away. Then I plunged the Sai blade into the back of the man's skull, at the same time I gripped his forehead so that the force of the thrust wouldn't move him too much. He was dead before he even got the chance to wake up. I slipped quietly around to the woman's side of the bed and looked over her sleeping face. As I watched the blissful and unaware smile on her face, an idea popped into my mind. I smirked down at the two bodies and slipped my blade away, then I went about putting my idea into motion. Silently I moved around the bed, the whole time the woman stayed peacefully asleep, completely unaware of the scare she was about to get. I rolled the dead man's face in his own blood, covering him all over. Then very gently I grabbed the woman's hands and covered them in the blood as well. As I smeared the blood over the sleeping woman's hand, I couldn't contain the evil smirk that spread across my face. She was stupid to let her guard down. She was more stupid to get involved with a man. Love is weakness. She'll learn. I'm making sure of that. Once they were both sufficiently covered in blood, I pulled out the knife I stole from the last room and stabbed a few more holes into the dead man's upper body. Then I gently placed the blood covered knife in the woman's hand and closed her fingers over the handle. I stood back to admire my handiwork and was pretty impressed with myself. It looked like a proper murder scene, and she definitely looked like the murderer. Perfect. She'll eventually wake up and think she killed her lover. Fuck me, I can be pretty funny sometimes. With that, I left the room and went to the next. There were only three other rooms on the second floor and one of them was empty. Once the floor was clear, I went to the stairs and snuck down to the first floor. There was much more movement on this level. I could hear a few voices coming from the end of the hall, and one or two more from a room just a few doors down. I pulled both my Sai blades from their holders at my back and crept forward to the first door. I pressed my ear to it and heard nothing, no talking, no snoring and no heartbeats. I moved to the next and got the same result, empty. The next door is where some of the voices were coming from. I listened for a moment, counting the number of voices. I could only pick up on two, both of them were speaking Italian. I wasn't completely fluent in Italian, I knew the basics, but conversation was hard to follow. As I listened to the voices argue, I was able to pick up on a few important words.

"Missione"

"Macellato"

"Sta arrivando"

"Dobbiamo partire"

I'd only be guessing, but it sounds like they have caught wind of my visit to the last outpost and they're fucking scared. The pussies. The two men continued to argue, but as their conversation got faster, I couldn't follow it any longer. I can't hang around in the hallway forever. I took a deep breath and quickly pushed open the door. Both of the men turned to me at the same time, and the same confused look dawned on both their faces. Time seemed to stand still in that moment. The three of us looked back at each other until a look of recognition grew over the face of the man on the right. As if everything was moving in slow motion, I took a step forward and his skin paled. I took another step, and his eyes went wide. Another step, and he started to retreat. All the while the man on the left was still looking at me confused. Clearly, this one isn't as bright as the other. I jutted out with my arm, stabbing the blade into the man on the left's stomach. Only using half of my available strength, I reefed my arm upwards, slicing the man from stomach to chest. His blood spurted out, splashing all over me, and then the contents of his abdomen began to fall to the floor. I pulled my arm back, removing the dagger from his body, and he dropped to the floor face first. The other man's mouth opened wide as he looked down at his disembowelled friend's body. A small, whispered scream came from his open mouth, but it started to get a little louder. I threw my blade at his head, and it sliced right through his forehead. That shut him up. He fell backwards from the force of my throw and his body hit the ground with a loud thump. I quickly jumped over to his body and withdrew my dagger from his head. As I crouched over his dead body, I watched the door and waited for someone else to enter.

I could hear footsteps approaching quickly. Only light footsteps, so either a female or maybe a child. A body came around the corner and into the doorway, without hesitation I threw the blade across the room. It hit the person in the chest and sent them tumbling backwards into the hallway. Great. Everyone is going to know I'm here now. I jumped up and over the bodies and stopped before I went through the door. Another set of footsteps were running down the hallway towards me, the owner of the footsteps was screaming out something I couldn't translate. I stood back against the wall next to the door and waited. The person stopped at the body in the hallway before checking the room. Rookie mistake. Always check your surroundings. Assess the danger first. Confirm the kill second. It's basic knowledge. And kind of essential. Because why this dumb idiot was checking the dead person in the hallway, I slipped through the door and plunged my other dagger into the side of his head. He didn't even get the chance to see his killer. So stupid. The person I threw the blade at was indeed a woman, a small one too. I threw the dagger so hard, that the blade had gone all the way through her body, impaling her against the wall opposite the door. Impressive kill. If I had a camera, I'd take a photo. I should probably look into that. Getting a camera. Some moments like these deserve to be memorialised.

I pulled the blade from her chest, and she dropped to the floor. I could hear frantic yelling coming from the room at the end of the hall. I was right, they all know I'm here. No point in waiting and listening now. I kicked open the door and threw the blade in my left hand at the first person I saw. Then threw the blade in my right hand at the next. They both hit the floor and I did a quick intake of the room. There were five other people in the small kitchen space. All men. All a whole lot bigger than me. One of them was holding a gun and was slowly lifting it to take aim at me. I threw forward my arm, calling forth the power inside me. A strong gust of wind picked up the man and sent him flying into the wall hard, really hard. Another man was running towards me from the side, I flicked my hand in his direction, and he too got swept up in the air and flew backwards.

As I was distracted by those two men, another managed to wrap his large arms around my upper body, pinning my arms to my sides. I growled lowly and flew my head back, connecting the top of my skull to the bottom of his chin. He grunted but didn't let go, instead, he picked me up, lifting my feet off the ground. I hooked my ankle behind his knee and called the wind back towards me. With the force of the air and my foot locking his leg, the man went falling backwards, with me still in his arms. As we hit the ground, another man had rushed over and was standing over me. I lifted my leg and kicked him in the face. I snapped my head back again, this time connecting it with the man's nose. A crunching sound and a muffled yell, then his arms around me loosening, was enough to know I was successful. I let my nails grow forward and then slammed them deeply into the soft sides of the man's stomach. He screamed and released me completely. I whipped around on his lap and swiped my fully extended talons across his neck, tearing away a large chunk of flesh. As I went to swipe at him again, my arm was grabbed. I looked up to a man with blood all over his face, and more still pouring from his nose. It was the man I kicked in the face. I slashed my nails across his stomach, and he screamed and jumped back, but still didn't let go of my wrist. I stood up and dragged my talons up his abdomen in a quick sharp motion. That made him let me go. He grabbed at his stomach and hunched forward. I jumped up and around, landing a flying roundhouse kick to the side of his head. The man dropped to the ground with a lifeless thump.

I quickly looked up to find where the remaining men were standing. One of the ones that I had sent flying into the wall was starting to come too, and he had started groaning and crawling along the floor. The other was still unmoving, lying face down in his own blood. That just left one more unaccounted for. I whipped around just in time for a bullet to whizz past my head. The anger bubbled deep inside me, and my ribs began to twist with the need to release my beast. I slowly turned my head back to the man holding the gun and growled ferociously. My sharp fangs had descended down and were now on full display. He paled and lifted the gun again. I turned my body so that I was facing him completely, but I didn't move toward him. He fired another shot and then another right after it. I dodged them both easily. I have trained to discipline my reflexes and heighten my senses every day of my life. I have been moulded into the perfect weapon, able to kill and destroy anyone that I come face to face with. And this human thought he could take me out with a mere bullet. So naive and clueless.

His mouth dropped open as he realised that he missed me both times, and then he proceeded to empty his magazine. Firing shot after shot until he had nothing left. My body moved and glided through the air, dodging the bullets effortlessly. As I straightened my posture and glared over at him, he dropped the gun and raised his hands in surrender. A laugh burst forward before I could stop it.

"Mi arrendo" (I give up) he stuttered with his hands in the air,

"Troppo tardi" (Too late) I chuckled and shook my head. I put my hands on my hips and breathed in a slow deep breath. All the air in the room slowly filled my lungs, leaving the man gagging for breath. I kept sucking it in as I watched him fall to his knees. His mouth was gaping open and shut like a fish out of water and his skin went a sickly shade of grey, then he fell forward, face first into the floor. I let the air go free from my lungs and refill the room. I stood and listened, checking for the sounds of heartbeats. Nothing.

As I stepped out of the room, the sound of a woman shrieking from above me filled the silence and echoed through the building. I laughed out loud again and turned for the stairs to the bottom floor. I suppose the woman is awake now and my little plan worked perfectly.

I went down the stairs and paused at the bottom. There's no chance that anyone still alive in this place didn't hear the gunshots and screaming, surely they would have come running if there were. Humans are dumb, for some reason, these ones run towards the sounds of danger, not away from it. But just in case they were trying to hide from me, I focused my hearing and listened. I could make out the faint sounds of heartbeats. Three different rhythms, belonging to three different people, one of which was racing, the other two were slow and weak. I stepped around the corner with my Sai blades ready in front of me. I walked cautiously down the darkened hallway. This part of the building was made of mostly stone and brick. It was cold and stunk of mould and piss. I think I could take an educated guess and say this was their holding cells, or dungeon, or whatever the idiots called it. I crept further along the walkway, pausing at each heavy-duty iron door to listen for signs of life.

Once I got to the end of the hall, there was only one door left, and I still hadn't found the source of the heartbeats. I pressed my ear up against the last door and listened, all three of them were coming from this room. I stood back and looked at the large iron door. There was a sliding locking mechanism, but it was unlocked. I lifted the lever and pushed open the heavy door, standing slightly to the side, just in case. After a beat, I stepped through the door and took in the scene before me. One person, a female, was hanging from the ceiling by thick chains around her wrists. She was naked and covered in dried blood, dirt, and grime. Next to her was a floor to ceiling brick wall, and on the other side of that, was a man hanging from the ceiling with the same kind of chains. He too was butt naked and covered in shit. That was two, where was the owner of the third heartbeat? I did a slow turn around the room, letting my eyes adjust and focus through the darkness. There. Huddled in the far left corner of the grubby cell, a small body was curled up into a ball. I stepped toward the person, only realising once I was closer that it was a child, maybe nine or ten years old. Apart from reeking of fear and shaking uncontrollably, it was definitely in better condition than the two hanging from the chains, which leads me to believe it is not a prisoner here.

"Alzarsi" (Get up) I barked at the kid. It whimpered softly but didn't move. After the past hour in this stinking hunter outpost, my patience level had already reduced down to point zero one. This kid was doing itself no favours.

"Get. Up!" I yelled, the sound echoed around the stone walls of the cell. I heard the chains rattle and looked over the see the male was trying to free himself. Impressive. I could hear how weak his heart was, not to mention the visible state that his body was in, and still he wasn't giving up. That shows strength, a quality I can admire. I growled and stepped forward, grabbing the child by its hair and pulling it upright. Once it was standing up, I could tell for sure that it was a hunter's offspring. It was clean, well fed, and had the stench of privilege all over it.

"Are there more of you?" I asked it firmly. I glared down at its scared little face as tears poured from its eyes. The show of weakness just made me angrier. One tear, one lash. That's what I was taught. Obviously, this little beast didn't get the same lesson. I huffed with frustration and threw the child to the side with all the strength I had. Its head hit the wall with so much force that it basically burst open, splattering blood all over the stones. That was probably a little too rash of me. It didn't tell me if there were more. I think I can safely say that I have gotten all of the ones that are here.

I turned my attention back to the two hanging from the ceiling. The male had gone limp again, probably overexerted himself trying to get free. I went to the female first and inspected her body. She was thin and obviously malnourished. Her skin was clammy and cold and covered in bruises and cuts. I leaned my face close to hers and listened to her breathe. She wheezed in shallow and broken breaths over a barely-there heartbeat. Even with her Were healing, she'd be dead by morning, tomorrow night at the absolute latest. I moved over to the male and looked over his body. He too was covered in bruises, but his cuts were still in the process of healing. I leaned in close to his face and listened. His heart was weak but still held strength. If I left him here, without the hunters to continue his torture, he'd be recovered and able to break free of the chains in a day or two. I couldn't have that. I grabbed his hair and lifted his head, then pressed my blade against his neck. He groaned quietly, opened his eyes and looked directly into my own. Something I had never felt before began to grow inside me. And for the first time in my entire life, I hesitated. I looked into his eyes, and he looked back into mine. The strange feeling intensified and without realising it, I withdrew my blade from his neck. His skin was darkened by the dry blood and dirt, but I could see hints of the smooth caramel colour underneath it all. He stunk of rot and sickness, but hidden behind that, I could pick up hints of cherries. Above all, I was transfixed by the look in his eyes. He looked at me like he knew me, like he had known me all his life. There was something there I had never seen before, something that resembled fondness. He looked at me like he loved me, like I was his everything. I was lost in those bright blue eyes and the feeling of peace that they instilled in me. All I have ever known is death. But in his eyes, I could see life.

Present Day.
I huffed and rolled onto my side, curling my legs up to my chest. After everything I have done, and everything I have endured, how could those eyes still affect me the way they do. That first meeting is still as fresh in my mind as if it were only yesterday. The feeling that those eyes gave me when they looked into the deepest corners of my mind, it still haunts me. It feels like another life ago now. Little did I know back then, what that all meant. Little did I understand what that man, those eyes, what they would come to mean to me. I had no idea of the shit storm I unleashed that day.

Chapter Six

Zelena

When I woke in the morning, the bed was empty. I reached out my hand and felt the space beside me, it was cold. Gunner has been gone for a while. Panic set in immediately. He couldn't have left without saying goodbye, he wouldn't do that, at least I don't believe he would. I pulled on a pair of shorts and one of Gunner's t-shirts and raced downstairs. I checked his office first, nothing. Then I checked the hall and the library, again nothing. I pushed open the kitchen door and found Nat sitting at the bench, playing absentmindedly with her bowl of cereal.

"Have you seen Gunner?" I asked her as I stepped up beside her, but she didn't respond.

"Nat, have you seen Gunner this morning?" I asked again, but still got no response. What the fuck is her problem? What have I done to warrant being ignored. I hit her on the shoulder with the back of my hand and she jumped and squealed, dropping her spoon and spinning around to glare at me,

"What the fuck Lena?" she huffed and gripped at her chest in fright,

"Not me what the fuck, you what the fuck. Why are you ignoring me?" I grunted at her angrily,

"I'm not ignoring you, why on Earth would I ignore the mother of my beautiful little niece or nephew" she cooed and placed both her hands on my belly, then rubbed her cheek on the not so small mound. It was sweet and has become one of her favourite things to do of late. But I was still mad at her for ignoring me, and then denying it to my face.

"I just asked you the same question twice and you ignored me both times" I growled and pushed her head away from my stomach.

"You did not. Did you? Oh Lena, I'm so sorry, I've been off in my own little world this morning. My mind is a mess and I'm completely lost". Nat began to ramble, as Nat usually does. I would usually sit and listen. I do care, and I want to know what's going on with her, but first I need to make sure that Gunner hasn't left already.

"Nat, take a breath for a second will ya. Have you seen Gunner this morning" I interrupted her fast talking. She sat up straight and frowned at me. I've hurt her feelings, shit. I stepped forward and grabbed her hands and placed them back on my stomach. Both Nat and her mother are easily pleased these days, all they need is to feel the pup move.

"I'm sorry, I want to hear all about it, I do. But first I really need to find Gunner. It's important, I swear" I said earnestly. I will come back to this. She seems very upset, and I love her too much to just let her wallow in it alone.

"He's outside somewhere, he was up early this morning" she sighed and turned back around to her bowl of soggy cereal.

"I'll be back soon, I promise" I said softly and kissed her cheek. She nodded and hummed before stirring her spoon through the milk with a spacey look on her face. I took a few steps back but kept watching her for a minute. She rested her head on her hand and slumped forward on the counter. She had deep frown lines in her forehead, which is weird enough on its own. She is always so pristinely dressed and made up. But her hair was clipped up in a messy bun, and not her usual straight and sleek bob. Her skirt hadn't been ironed and she was barefoot. Another very unusual thing for Nat. Whatever is going on with her, it must be huge. I have never seen Nat look so dishevelled. But even in her current state of unravelling, she is still supermodel beautiful.

I kept my eyes on Nat as I backed out of the kitchen, I hated leaving her like this. The door closed and Nat disappeared from my eyesight. I quickly turned on my heels and speed walked for the door. If I could run, I would, but this quickly growing belly is making everyday activities very hard. I've got maybe seven weeks left. But at the rate I am growing, I don't think I can make it that far without bursting open. I made my way onto the porch and scanned the surrounding area. That's when I spotted Gunner, he was sitting on the steps of Smith's cabin, next to Smith. The two were in a deep conversation and Smith's face looked unusually pale. I can only assume that Gunner has just told him that he's leaving. I walked slowly down the steps and continued on my way towards them. Gunner saw me coming and offered a half smile as he kept talking. I walked very slowly, my hands on my stomach and my eyes glued on Gunner's moving lips. I've never been one for lip reading, I wish I was. I could probably hear them if I focused hard enough. But ears dropping on this conversation feels like it would be a severe invasion of privacy.

As I reached the bottom step, Gunner grabbed Smith's head and kissed his cheek hard. He then stood up and raced down the stairs to meet me. He grabbed my face with both hands and bent down to kiss me.

"Good morning, my beautiful Luna" he said softly before dropping down to one knee, to then embrace and kiss my stomach as well,

"Good morning my handsome little Alpha-Son" he snickered and winked up at me. He seemed to be really cheerful. After our argument last night, and our little talk, I expected a more solemn Gunner. Not this. This upbeat and happy Gunner. Not that I am complaining, I love when Gunner is happy, which is a rarity these days. But it seems a little out of place under the current circumstances. Gunner stood back up and kissed the top of my head,

"I've got a bit to do today. Why don't you go and have some breakfast, then maybe chill out and watch a movie. I'll come find you a bit later, okay" he said quickly before kissing my cheek again and dashing off before I could argue. I watched him rush away as I stood dumbfounded and a little lost. He's leaving soon and he thinks I'm just going to sit and watch a movie? I turned around to face Smith and ask him what that was all about. But that thought was gone once I saw him. Smith was slumped forward with his face in his hands. His body was shaking with harsh and ragged breaths, and the smell of despair was all around him. I wobbled up the stairs and sat down next to him, pressing myself right up against his side. I slipped my arm around his, holding onto it tightly, and rested my head on his shoulder. After a beat, Smith leaned over and rested his head on top of mine. We sat like that for a little while. Not talking, just sitting together in silence.

"He told you, huh?" I finally said,

"Yeah" Smith answered softly. I didn't know what to say back. There was nothing to say. Gunner had made up his mind, and if I couldn't change it, I really doubt that Smith could.

"You're okay with him just leaving the pack, for Goddess knows how long?" Smith grumbled as he sat up right again. I sat up too and looked at the side of his face. His nose was red and his under eyes were red and wet.

"Of course I'm not okay with it. I tried to argue, I tried to beg, I tried to reason with him, but he's made his decision. What more am I meant to do?" I answered him with a fake firmness to my voice.

"You're the Triple fucking Goddess, force him to stay" Smith grunted back. I was quiet for a second, thinking about his words. Goddess knows I have thought about using my power on him. I've thought about locking him up, keeping him in place and forcing him to stay. But it would never work. Gunner would lose control and the darkness would take him over, completely defeating the purpose.

"You know why I can't do that" I said slowly after a few seconds. Smith huffed and wiped his face with the back of his hand,

"Yeah, I know" he mumbled.

"He named you the Beta, didn't he?" I asked as I looked back at him. Smith took a sharp breath and looked at me. His soft hazel eyes looked sad and withdrawn.

"He did" Smith confirmed half-heartedly,

"I thought you'd be more excited" I teased and shoved my shoulder into his. But Smith was in no mood to play around. He huffed and leaned forward with his elbows on his knees. His scent changed from despair to anger.

"How could I be excited. The Beta position was never meant for me. I'm a Delta, that was who I was meant to be. Not this. This was Cole's thing. He was born for it, and he was the best fucking Beta I have ever seen, until he wasn't. I could never live up to that" Smith rushed out as he twisted and squeezed his fingers together. He was both angry and sad, I didn't have to be able to smell him to know that. A lot of people have been openly angry about Cole, about his death and about what he did. Well, those of us that knew about what he did anyway. We thought it best to keep the finer details a secret. As far as the pack is concerned, it was Artemis that betrayed us. Only those in the inner circle know the full truth.

"Besides, I don't know if I want to live up to it. I don't know if I want it at all" Smith said softly after a brief pause. I grabbed his shoulder and pulled him back to me so that he was looking at me.

"We haven't talked much since that day. Since Cole..." I paused and swallowed,

"Since Cole died" I forced out.

"We've both been a bit preoccupied" Smith tried to shrug it off,

"That's no excuse. You're my best friend Smith, you were my first friend. I'm sorry I haven't been there for you. I should have tried harder"

"Don't beat yourself up princess, I haven't really made much effort either" he replied and took my hands.

"You found your Mum, Zee. That's kind of huge"

"I did, and it is. And you lost your best friend" I answered while nodding. I knew he was trying to avoid talking about it. About Cole. But I'm no fool and he can't play me anymore. Smith pulled his hands away from mine and snarled,

"Don't call him that" he hissed.

"Why not? He was your best friend. Being dead doesn't change that" I answered, keeping my shocked expression from appearing. Why on earth would he say something like that? I never picked Smith to be a grudge holder.

"But being a traitor does" Smith snarled. I looked over Smith's face before I answered him. His brows were frowning and pushing together in the middle. His lips were pulled into thin tight lines. His whole faced looked pinched tight.

"Do you really think he betrayed the pack? Cole, the best Beta you had ever seen. You really think he betrayed you?" I asked him smoothly.

"It doesn't matter what I think, it's what he did" he answered without hesitation.

"I don't believe that. Cole was angry about his dad, and upset about a lot of things, but I honestly don't think he intended to betray anyone" I said as I shook my head slightly,

"How can you defend him? It was your life he put in danger. If he hadn't taken that damned phone call then that stupid Origin Alpha never would have come here, he never would have taken you, and Cole never would have fucking died" Smith growled, his voice raising in volume with each word. And there it was. Smith wasn't angry at Cole for talking to Galterio. He was mad that Cole was killed. I reached over and took one of Smith's hands and wrapped it in both of mine.

"Smith, he answered the phone when it rang. He didn't reach out to anyone, and he didn't plan on betraying anyone. In a moment of weakness, he let slip that the Triple Goddess had risen. That was all. Just one phone call. There was no sinister plot and no big plan. It was just a simple mistake".

"And look at everything that came from that simple mistake. We went to war and lost more pack members. We hadn't even healed from the last battle we were in. Gunner got infected with that dark shit and Cole went and got himself killed"

"You're angry at Cole for dying?"

"Of course I fucking am! How could he just die? He was meant to grow old in this pack with Gunner and me. He was supposed to find a Mate and adopt a bunch of little pups. He was meant to be here Zelena. He was meant to be the Beta. He was meant to fucking live" Smith blurted out angrily. But that anger quickly turned to sorrow, and tears filled his eyes. Just as quickly, those tears began to flow down his face. I wrapped my arms around Smith and pulled him into me. He heaved and huffed with broken sobs and my own tears started to fall. Smith's arms came around my back and he laid his head on my shoulder. We stayed that way for a long while. The both of us crying and taking comfort in each other. He had been holding it in. This whole time Smith had been denying his sadness. And now it had burst like a broken dam.

"Cole died, it's horrible and tragic. But you couldn't do anything to change it, none of us could. It's okay to be sad about it, and it's okay to be angry. But don't let your grief control your future. Cole would be so pissed at you if he knew that you were flaking on being the Beta. Do it for Cole, and for yourself. You deserve it Smith. And you'll do great" I told him while holding him against me. He didn't respond right away, but his crying had seemed to stop.

"You're right. I'm sorry" he sniffed and sat up. He wiped the tears from his face and smiled weakly,

"You don't need this right now".

"This is exactly what I need. I've missed you" I smiled and wiped away a patch of wetness from his cheek that he missed.

"I've missed you too" he smiled and flicked my nose,

"Do you feel better now, after getting that out?" I asked him with a smile,

"I do actually" he smiled back,

"Do you forgive him?"

"I do. You're bloody smart, you know that"

"Yeah, I know" I chuckled and flicked my hair over my shoulder. Smith took a deep breath and looked out over the pack grounds.

"I think it may have been for the best you know, with how things ended the way they did" he said slowly,

"How do you mean?" I asked confused,

"I mean, even if I understand and I believe what you said, even if it all was just a mistake, Gunner never would have forgiven him. He probably would have banished him"

"He would not!" I squawked. Banishment, seriously. Gunner wouldn't have done that, surely not.

"He would. When it's about you and his pup, he would do anything" Smith said with confidence,

"Even to Cole though?"

"Even to his own mother, Zee"

"But banishment? That's extreme" I said quietly and turned to look away. Some of what he said makes sense. Gunner has still been so angry about Cole. Would he have kicked him out though?

"Yep. And Cole would never have gone to another pack. His soul is with Tri-Moon. He would have ended up becoming Feral, and no one wants that"

"What's Feral?" I asked. I've not heard the term before. How has that not come up in any of my werewolf training?

"That's a conversation for another time, princess" Smith said as he stood up,

"I have some work to do. Your bodyguard is over there, will you be okay?" he asked with his hands on his hips. I looked over his shoulder and sure enough, Tobias was sitting and watching us from the fire pit.

"Yeah I'll be fine, will you be okay?" I asked him with a small chuckle,

"I'm alright. Here" he said and reached his hands forward for me to grab. I took his hands and he pulled me to my feet and helped me down the steps.

"Geeze woman, you're like a walking beachball already" Smith laughed as I stepped off the last step,

"Hey!" I cried and slapped his chest. He laughed and jumped back and swatted my hand away,

"Just kidding, you know you're gorgeous. Pregnancy suits you" he teased and placed his hands on my belly.

"You're mean" I sulked and pushed my bottom lip forward. He laughed and leaned forward to quickly kiss my cheek.

"And you're round" he giggled and turned around to run before I could hit him again.

"Asshole!" I shouted as he headed for the main house,

"She's all yours, mighty warrior" Smith called to Tobias with a laugh as he passed him. Tobias shook his head and stood up, he brushed his hands on his pants and walked over to me.

"I'll hit him. If you want me too, I'll punch him right in that pretty face of his" Tobias said with a hopeful tone. He crossed his arms over his chest and raised one of his eyebrows.

"No, I don't want you to punch him" I laughed,

"Just say the word Little One, and I will happily deliver the blow" he smiled and held out his arm for me to take,

"I'll keep that in mind" I chuckled as I stepped forward and wrapped my arm around Tobias's,

"Your breakfast is ready for you" he said warmly and started walking us back towards the house. At the mention of food my stomach grumbled loudly and I smiled,

"Perfect, because we're starving" I mused. When we reached the kitchen, Nat was gone, but on the counter was a spread worthy of royalty. We sat down and I ate my fill happily. I was too busy feeding my face to worry about conversation with Tobias. Not that he was overly chatty these days. After I had eaten all that I could, I was exhausted. From either the deep emotional breakthrough with Smith, the stress of Gunner's imminent departure, or the fact that I'm growing a werewolf in my womb. Either way, exhaustion has become my second language. I stretched my arms out above my head and yawned.

"You're tired already?" Tobias questioned,

"I'm pooped" I answered mid yawn,

"Come on then, I'll take you upstairs for a nap" he said as he stood up and held his arms out,

"My hero" I teased and turned around on my chair. Tobias picked me up in his usual style and carried me upstairs. He plopped me down gently on the bed and threw the throw blanket over my legs, he then proceeded to surround my body in pillows, like he was building me a nest or something.

"Didn't know you were the maternal type, Tobi" I teased and smiled at him cheekily. He grunted in a half laugh and lightly pinched my calf.

"Shut up and go to sleep" he huffed back and sat down on the chair by the window,

"So grumpy" I yawned and snuggled into the pillow,

"And don't call me Tobi, that's a terrible nickname" he grunted,

"Sorry, oh Mighty Warrior" I giggled, closed my eyes and was out.

~

I rolled onto my back and stretched out my arms and legs, accompanied by a mighty growl and a relaxed groan. I sat upright and turned to Tobias, who was still sitting in the chair by the window. He closed the book he was reading and placed it on the desk, then crossed his arms over his chest and pulled the corner of his mouth up in a half smile.

"How long did I sleep?" I asked him,

"Just over an hour" he answered,

"Has Gunner come back to the house yet?". Tobias didn't answer, he just leaned forward and rested his massive elbows on his knees. He looked at me and shook his head slowly.

"He's putting his affairs in order" Tobias's deep voice rumbled softly around the room,

"You say it like he's dying" I quipped back annoyed. Again, he didn't answer, just stared at me. And that felt like more of an answer than if he were to say it out loud.

"You think he is going to die?" I screeched more urgently,

"I don't know, Little One"

"You know something, I can see it written all over your face. What has she told you?" I demanded of him and shuffled further along the bed.

"I promise you, I know no more than you do" he answered gently,
"Don't lie to me Tobias" I growled and shifted to the edge of the
bed,
"Tell me the truth, I'm a big girl, I can handle it".
"Calm down, stress isn't good for the pup" Tobias grunted and
stood up. He stepped up to the edge of the bed and gently pushed
some of my stray hairs back down. I hit his hand away and
scowled at him. He looked down at me softly and I glared back up
at him, neither one of us blinking or breaking. After a second, he
huffed and dropped onto the bed beside me.
"Like I said, I don't know anything for sure. But I have a feeling"
Tobias started. His voice was soft and quiet, I could tell he was
trying not to rile me up.
"What kind of feeling?" I demanded,
"If his wolf is taken from him, your bond will be too"
"Yes, Gunner and I have already gone over that"
"But what I don't think Gunner has taken into account is the effect
it will have on him, on his body and his soul" Tobias said while
looking at the wall opposite us. I don't understand. Didn't Gunner
say that he could still live without a wolf? What has changed since
then? Well, a lot, I know that now. But this still doesn't make any
sense.
"What do you mean?" I asked Tobias as I shifted to face him.
Tobias turned to face me as well and took a deep breath,
"Everything about Gunner has changed since he met you. Your
True Mate bond made him stronger, then he became an Alpha,
which made him stronger again. He has felt and used your power,
which in itself is another form of strength. And now he has sired
a pup. Everything that has happen over the past few months has
completely altered his physiology. Once all that is stripped away,
what will he have left?"
"If! You said once all that is gone. But he is leaving the pack, so
that Selene won't have to take anything away from him" I rushed
out, interrupting his spiel,
"But if she does?" Tobias snipped back,
"Do you think she will?"
"I think she is angry, and very disappointed in the both of you.
This is punishment for you, just as much as it is for him".
Punishment. Wow. I didn't really think of it like that. She is
punishing me, for taking on the darkness, for using it, and for

enjoying it. Is that all that I have done wrong in her eyes, or could there be more? I wish I could talk to her again. Maybe then I could get a little more clarity on this whole three week deal.

"What do you think the chances are, when Gunner leaves, do you think she will leave him be?" I was afraid of the answer, but I trust Tobias and his counsel, more than almost anyone else.

"Selene is above all things merciful. I think if she sees him sacrificing all that he knows and loves, if she sees just how far he will go and how much he will do, just to prove to her that he is worthy of you. I think she will give him a chance". It wasn't a promise. It wasn't guaranteed. But it was hope. It was enough just to know that Tobias thinks Gunner still stands a chance.

"And do you think he can do it? Gunner, I mean. Do you think he'll be able to get rid of the darkness on his own?" I asked while looking up at Tobias hopefully.

"I know that he is already close. Your birth mother has done very good work with him. But the extra strain that he is under, the animalistic urge to protect and fight when he is around you, it's not helping things". Ugh. That was brutal, like a punch to the guts. I know it's true. But hearing it said out loud that I am hindering Gunner's progress. It hurts a little bit more than a lot.

"Sounds like you agree he should leave" I said sadly,

"I think it's the only chance he has left" Tobias confirmed.

"Damn, I was kind of hoping you'd be on my side on this one" I huffed and turned back around to throw my legs over the side of the bed.

"I'm always on your side little Goddess" he said and shifted to sit back next to me again. I rested my head on his gigantic bicep and sighed.

"Yeah, I know you are. It still hurts though" I conceded. Tobias wrapped his arm around me and pulled me flush against his side. He held the side of my face with his other hand and gently traced his thumb across my cheek, wiping away the stray tear that had started to roll away from my eye.

"I'll be here Zelena. No matter what happens. I'm not just your guardian, I'm your friend. You'll get through it. And when you do, you and Gunner will have a beautiful little pup to make the days shine brighter again".

Chapter Seven

Zelena

Tobias helped to calm my nerves. His words offered a small sliver of hope, but it was enough to lift my spirits. We headed back downstairs to get more food, and then I went in search of Nat. Our little talk is way overdue. After a half attempt at checking her usual loitering spots, the movie room, kitchen, and library, with no luck in any of them, we headed out to the village to see if she was with Smith. It was mid-afternoon but the village was unusually quiet. I walked past the cabins and around the communal areas. A few pack members were out and about keeping themselves busy, but the atmosphere just felt unusually still. Each person I passed offered a warm smile and would either nod, wave or even bow. Yeah, some of them were still bowing, and I'm still so not comfortable with it. We got to the edge of the clearing where most of the visiting packs had been staying when the Alpha ceremony happened. But they were all long gone now, back to their own realities and homes, left to deal with the aftermath of the war. All except for one. Alpha Lace from the Howlers Pack was still here.

I haven't been able to get a clear reason from Gunner as to why he stayed for so long. He did go back to his homeland for a minute, but returned again a day or two later. I've always thought it strange that he was still here. He's an Alpha, after all, he has a pack to run. But here he still is, with seven of his men. Gunner said something about building a stronger alliance, but I don't see why he'd have to live in our pack for weeks on end for that to happen. It's weird.

We approached the large tents that the Howlers were staying in. They had moved to the other side of the clearing, a fair enough distance away from our main village. They had also arranged the five remaining tents to form a circle around a communal area with a fire. I suppose this was to give them a little extra privacy. Which again, I think is weird. If they want privacy, why not go back to their own pack. The closer we got to the tents, the tighter Tobias stuck to my side. Laughing and hollering was echoing from the middle of their little set up, along with the soft thrum of music. Whatever they were doing, they were enjoying themselves.

A crowd of people had made their way over here, and it looked like the beginnings of a party was underway. Two of the Howlers men each had their arms wrapped around a Tri-Moon she-wolf. I knew that one of them had Mated with one of our pack members, Olive, I believe is her name. She will be heading off to live at the Howlers pack with her new Mate. Whenever it is that they eventually leave that is. The other pair looked to be getting very close and comfortable. It was sweet though. He held her to his chest and had his face buried in the crook of her neck, and his arms wrapped tightly around her body. All the while she was laughing wildly while holding a bottle of beer. She looked unapologetically happy. Her bright young face glowed from the smile that was covering it. I don't remember the last time I smiled like that. Not just a regular smile, but a full beam, grown from uncontainable happiness. Honestly, the thought upset me. I am happy here. I love Tri-Moon. I don't know when I stopped smiling like that.

I managed to push my way to the inner edge of the crowd and was both shocked and confused by what I found. Alpha Lace was on his back, shirtless, in the dirt, with a man lying on top of him. He had his arms around the other Weres neck, and his legs wrapped around his body. I recognised the other male immediately. It was Ari. He is one of our top fighters, on the fast track to becoming a commander. And one of Gunner's friends. Alpha Lace had Ari's legs pinned and was squeezing his arms around his neck in a strong chokehold. Ari's face was turning red and was screwed up into a strained grimace. Alpha Lace was laughing and looked like he wasn't struggling in the slightest, even though Ari looked exhausted. I didn't know if I should yell, or scream, or try to pull them apart. But everyone else was cheering, so I froze and just watched. After a few more seconds Ari tapped on Lace's arm, and Lace released his hold. Ari rolled out of his arms onto his hands and knees, coughing and spluttering. Lace jumped up with a mighty roar and threw his hands in the air. He laughed and screamed and revelled in the cheering of the crowd. It wasn't just his arms that were covered in tattoos, his entire torso was covered as well. The intricate pictures and designs rolled over his bulging muscles until they disappeared below the waistline of his pants. All the while Lace was eating up the excitement of the crowd, his eyes seemed to linger in just one direction. I followed his line of sight and saw Nat sitting on a log, staring back at him just as intensely.

I carefully pushed my way through the crowd of people towards Nat. It was actually pretty easy. Tobias moved most of them out of the way for me. As I squeezed closer to Nat, I looked back to Lace and Ari. Alpha Lace helped Ari to his feet and pulled him in for a hug. They were both covered in dirt, dry grass and sweat, but even after the fight they just had, they hugged each other anyway. Nat saw me coming and waved me over to her enthusiastically.

"What's going on?" I asked her as I sat down on the log beside her. She took hold of my hand and rested her head on my shoulder.

"Just testosterone filled men acting like wild animals" Nat said back with a groan,

"Um, what?" I blanked with a scoff,

"They have all been wrestling with each other for about an hour now. So far no one has been able to beat Alpha Lace" Nat said casually, while still looking at the Alpha. Her eyes moved slowly over every inch of his body. The moment his name left her lips, his head snapped around in her direction again. The way he looked at her, it was like he was showing off just for her. Like he was trying to get her attention and impress her. I leaned my head on top of Nat's and slyly sniffed. The sweet scent of arousal was all over her. I sat up straight and stared at the Alpha, then back to the top of Nat's head, and back to the Alpha again. How had I not realised this already? Have I really been that blind? How could I have possibly missed it.

"What's going on with you and the Howlers Alpha?" I asked her sternly. Nat snapped upright and stared at me wide eyed.

"What?" she blurted out quickly,

"You and Alpha Lace, what's going on?" I repeated,

"Nothing! What makes you think there's something going on? Why would you say that?" she snapped and dropped my hand. She looked panicked and flustered, and at the same time terrified.

"I can see it. The way he looks at you, and the way you were looking at him. There's something happening" I said again. A little more gently this time, to try and calm her down,

"Why would you say that to me? I'm with Smith. I love Smith. Nothing is happening with me and Lace" she snapped and jumped up. Before I could even stand up, she was gone. I struggled to my feet and tried to chase after her, but I was too slow and she was fast. Tobias, as per usual, came to my rescue. He swooped me up into his arms and gently jogged us after Nat.

We reached the bottom of the porch steps, just as Nat slammed the front door behind her. Without missing a beat, Tobias followed through the door after her. Nat was stomping up the stairs towards her room as Tobias gently let me down.

"Nat, wait" I called after her, but she ignored my plea. Roe came out of the kitchen, wiping her hands on her apron and looking over the three of us.

"What the name of the Goddess is all the slamming and screaming for?" she demanded,

"I... I think I upset Nat" I answered her sheepishly,

"You think?" she laughed and placed her hands on her hips,

"What happened, Dear?" she asked with her usual soft and welcoming smile.

"I asked her if something was going on between her and the Howlers Alpha. Then she just kind of snapped at me and ran away".

"What made you ask her that?"

"Well, there was a vibe, an energy between them. He was looking at her, but not like a normal look, the kind of way that Lupus looks at you sometimes. And she smelt sweet and kind of like lust or desire. I don't know Roe, maybe I was wrong, I just had a feeling. I didn't mean to make her angry, I just kind of blurted it out like an idiot" I answered her and dropped my head. I really didn't mean to upset her. Maybe I was a little too blunt. I could feel my emotions starting to race. The tears were welling in my eyes and my breathing started to quicken. Roe huffed and stepped closer to me. She gently placed her hands on both sides of my face and lifted them so that I could look at her.

"It's okay Sweet Girl. I have been having the same feeling" Roe said softly and leaned forward to kiss my forehead.

"You have?" I sniffed,

"Yes, Dear. Tobias, there are fresh pastries in the kitchen, why don't you go help yourself. We need to have a little girl time" Roe said over my shoulder to Tobias. I didn't hear him answer but his footsteps started to walk away.

"I was hoping she was going to come to me herself with this, but now is as good a time as any. Come on, Darling, let's go have a chat with that girl of mine" Roe said with her gentle smile and took my arm. She helped me up the stairs and to Nat's room. She didn't knock or call out, she just opened the door and stood to the side to let me in before her.

"Seriously, I do not want to talk to you right now" Nat growled from her spot on the bed. She was lying on her stomach with her face pressed into the pillow.

"Too bad young lady" Roe answered her. Nat growled in frustration and rolled onto her back before sitting up and scowling at the both of us.

"I'm not in the mood" she grunted,

"I don't care. When you slam my doors and yell at your sister, you don't get to choose not to talk to us" Roe quipped back. She strode over and sat down on the bed beside Nat, then she patted the spot next to her for me. I hesitated as I looked between the two of them. I don't want to make things worse than I already have.

"Come on" Roe insisted. I shuffled forward and slowly sat down on the end of the bed. After a few awkward seconds of silence, Roe finally spoke.

"You know, I wasn't born into the Tri-Moon pack" she said with a faraway tone,

"You weren't?" Nat snapped,

"No. Lupus found me at an allied pack when he was on a diplomatic visit" Roe began to explain,

"You're my mum! How did I not know this?" Nat asked, interrupting her. I could tell she was surprised, annoyed even.

That is a weird thing for her to not know. I wonder if Gunner knows.

"Because it's not something we share openly" Roe answered her,

"Why?" I asked,

"Our meeting was somewhat complicated" Roe answered,

"I didn't know that" Nat said sadly,

"It's not something either of us are very proud of"

"What happened?" I asked,

"Well, Lupus had just become the Alpha of Tri-Moon and was out visiting with the Alpha's of the aligned packs. He strolled into my life on a gust of air and everything changed in an instant. The moment we saw each other, something changed in the both of us. We aren't True Mates of course, but it sure felt that way at the time" Roe said as she recited her memories fondly.

"I was still quite young, and I thought my life's plan was already set. Boy was I wrong" Roe chuckled and grabbed Nat's hand and held it in her lap.

"I already had a Mate when I met your father"

"You did?" Nat screeched,

"I did. In fact, I was Mated to the Alpha of the pack I was born in"

"Mum! How could you never tell me this?" Nat yelled and jumped up from the bed.

"First of all, don't you raise your voice at me. Secondly, like I said, it wasn't something I was proud of, and not exactly something you needed to hear until now".

"You cheated on your Mate" Nat scoffed angrily. That was enough to get Roe fired up. She stood from the bed and stood in front of Nat.

"Watch who you're talking to girl, I am still your mother" Roe scolded,

"Sorry Mum" Nat whispered sheepishly. Roe pulled Nat into her arms and held her for a hug.

"No. I did not cheat on my first Mate. But I did break his heart" she said softly. The mother and daughter held each other for a minute before letting go.

"I want to tell you this story, I think it could help you with your current predicament. But no more screaming, understood?" Roe asked while looking over Nat's face. Nat sniffed and nodded, and then they both sat back down on the bed.

"I loved my first Mate. He was handsome, charming, and kind, and he made me feel like the most important person in his world. But I always thought something was missing. That thought only became a reality when I met your father. There was this pull, this animalistic urge to be near him. It was unlike anything I had ever felt before. That was what I was missing with Ambrose" Roe paused and smiled at me, she reached out her arm and motioned for me to move closer. I shuffled along the bed until I was sitting right beside her. She then lifted her arm over my shoulder and held me to her, then pulled Nat's hand onto her lap with her other hand.

"I was so torn up with all my contradicting emotions. Plus, I didn't think that I had a choice. I was Mated to the Alpha, I thought that if I ended our Mateship in favour of an Alpha from an allied pack, I would start a war. But your father was persistent. He would find or create ways for us to be alone together, even if it was just for a few seconds. And with each moment that we spent together, even in the presence of my former Mate, our attraction towards each other grew exponentially. In the end, I realised I no longer had a choice. My heart belonged wholly to Lupus and if I stayed with Ambrose, I would have been miserable, which in turn would have made him miserable. I couldn't do that to him, I loved him too much to make him suffer like that. I went to my mother for help. She was upset of course, but not at the fact that I wanted another, she was upset because she knew I was going to leave my birth pack. In her eyes, there was no choice. Destiny chose my Mate, chose Lupus, and there was no going against destiny. Together, my mother and me, we sat down with Ambrose, and I told him everything. It was hard to hurt him so much, and I did hurt him. He was furious, he even wanted to kill your father. But somewhere along the way, I don't know when or how, he came around. He wished me well and he let me go. It worked out for the best. He met the she-wolf of his dreams and together they made the most wonderful family and ran the pack together. To this day our packs are still allies". Roe sat quietly as both Nat and I digested her story. It was a true Romeo and Juliet fairy tale. I always knew the love they shared was more than anything else I have witnessed. Their history just proves it true. They are truly destined.

"What pack did you come from?" I asked her,

"I was born in a little pack called Lua Chei" she answered me fondly,

"Oh, they were here for the party, weren't they?" I asked her. The name sounded familiar, I think I may have seen the Alpha at the party. I knew of the Alpha-daughter, Analah. She went back to New Zealand, to Luna Eclipse, when the Alpha Hina left.

"Yes, Ambrose was here with one of his sons" she said with a nod,

"I met the Alpha's daughter, she came here with Lunaya"

"She did, yes" Roe smiled.

"Mum?" Nat said softly,

"Yes, Darling?" Roe answered and turned to face her,

"Why now, why are you telling me all this now? I've been with Smith for ages" Nat asked. Roe placed her hand on Nat's cheek and sighed,

"I think you know the answer to that question already, Sweetheart" she cooed softly. Nat stared at her mother for a moment, then she burst out into tears and threw herself into Roe's arms.

"I don't know what to do" Nat sobbed. She pressed her face into her mum's shoulder and squeezed her arms tightly around her back. The fear and sadness coming off her was choking me. Nat cried and cried, muttering about Smith and Lace and how confused she was. All I could do was sit quietly and watch. After a few minutes, Nat had calmed down enough to start making a bit more sense.

"You feel something for Alpha Lace?" Roe asked her gently,

"I don't want to, I love Smith" she blurted out,

"I know honey, but you love the Alpha too, don't you?"

"I think I do. Everything about him is addictive. I crave him, his presence, his scent, his touch. I go to sleep thinking about him, I dream of him, and then I wake up thinking about him again. How could I do this to Smith, he has been so good to me" Nat sobbed and started to cry again.

"Nat, you told me once that Smith wasn't your forever Mate. Maybe you were right, maybe you have found your forever Mate now?" I said softly as I ran my hand over her arm.

"But Smith" Nat choked,

"Smith is a big boy, he'll be okay" I said encouragingly,

"You think so?"

"I do. And it's like your mum said, there's no going against destiny"

"That's easy for you to say. The first Were you ever met was your True Mate. You haven't had to deal with something like this" Nat scoffed,

"Natalia!" Roe yelled angrily,

"No, it's okay" I said and waved off Roe's anger,

"She's right, I got lucky when it comes to Gunner. But I do know a little about making hard choices, and a little more about destiny and following the plan it sets out. Nat, I love you. You are the sister that I never had, and my first ever girlfriend. As much as I hate the thought of you leaving, I hate the thought of you throwing away a bond like the one your mum and dad share more. If Alpha Lace is what you really want, then you should follow your heart. Smith will be okay, he'll understand. You can't give this up just to spare some hurt feelings". Both Nat and Roe watched me as I spoke. Roe nodded along, and more tears fell from Nat's eyes. She wiped her face and turned to look at her mum when I finished. Roe lifted her hands in surrender and smiled,

"Don't look at me, she said it better than I could have" she chuckled and nodded at me,

"You think I should be with Lace?" she asked,

"I really do" I answered confidently,

"Me too" Roe chimed in. Nat dropped her head and played with the hem of her shirt. After a few seconds, she lifted her head and sighed.

"I better go find Smith then" she said sadly,

"I think that's for the best" Roe said encouragingly as she stood up. She kissed my forehead again and gently patted Nat's cheek,

"Now, excuse me, I have a roast in the oven" she cooed and strode out of the bedroom. I shifted over to Nat and placed my hand over hers.

"You really think I should do this? Leave Smith, my home, my family?" she asked as she stared into my eyes anxiously,

"I think you should get to feel the kind of love that makes the ground beneath you shake. I also think that kind of love doesn't exist between you and Smith. But Alpha Lace. He is your Earth-shaking love". Nat twisted her fingers through mine and lifted my hand to her cheek,

"I'm sorry I said those awful things to you. You know that I love you too, right?"

"I know Nat, and it's okay. Now will you go claim your Mate, please? I saw him without his shirt. So… if you don't, then I might have to" I chuckled. Nat growled and quickly slapped a hand over her mouth, her eyes wide in shock.

"I'm so sorry, I don't know where that came from" she balked.

"From your heart" I winked and tugged on her ear. She smiled warmly before pulling me into her arms for a tight hug.

"I love you, Sis" she said softly into my ear,

"I love you too".

Chapter Eight

Whiskey

I was awake before the sun, and had already ransacked through the rest of the huts still standing. I found a few interesting items, some jewellery, a bit of silverware, nothing worth taking with me though. I decided to go back and search the Alpha's house a little more thoroughly. I let my anger distract me last time, and I have suffered the punishment for losing focus. Now to get back on track. The study or office space proved to be worthwhile. I found another journal on a bookshelf in there. This one only dated back three generations, the first entry being date marked as 12th October 1935. He wrote about his desire to have the chosen daughter come back to them. Which confirmed my original theory, this pack have had firsthand contact with the Moon Goddess. I'm getting closer. I took this journal, and the other older one I found yesterday, and went to get comfortable on an armchair that I hadn't destroyed yet. I opened the newer book first. I know all too well that I am going to have a difficult time trying to decipher the old text in the other journal. Best to leave it for last.

After reading the first few pages, my first impression is that this Alpha was a total quack. All he wrote about was the chosen daughter. The time that she lived with them brought them joy and prosperity. Apparently, he believed that her presence gave the pack well wishes and good fortune. Even though she had died three hundred years before he was the Alpha, he still wrote like it was only recent. If he hadn't written the dates, I would have thought that he had been there for it, that he knew her personally. This idiot. Believing in fairy tales like a child. Is it any wonder it was so easy for me to wipe out this pack. I flipped through the rest of the pages more quickly, becoming more and more frustrated and annoyed at how this Alpha glorified the Moon Goddess and her chosen daughters. It's all a crock of shit. All this bullshit about how great and powerful she is. How she is the light in the dark, and how she loves all of her children. Blah blah blah. Yerunda. Spletni i slukhi. And yet nothing about how to find her or her so called chosen daughter. I slammed the book shut and threw it across the room. It hit the wall and dropped to the floor with a thud. I curled my fingers into a tight fist, letting my nails press deep into the palms of my hands. I took a few deep breaths, and along with the grounding feeling of the pain in my hands, I was able to calm down again before losing all control. Damn this temper of mine.

I opened the second book, the older one, and began to slowly read my way through the pages. It was taking a lot longer this time, due to my inability to understand the text. I should have worked harder in the old language, stupid me thought the current dialect would be enough. I only ever did just enough to make them happy. It was lazy of me, and in turn, it has made me weak. Just like they said I would be. They may have been ruthless bastards, but they knew what they were talking about.

Each page took me roughly twenty minutes. It was time well spent. This journal is very different to all of the others I have found and read. Other Alphas spoke of being saved and blessed by the Moon Goddess. This Alpha spoke of doing things differently. He wanted to force change and make things happen, not just sit around and wait for a blessing. I like this Alpha. He knows how to get things done. The more I read, the more I admired him. Even if he was just a filthy dog, he was a beast with a brain. About halfway through the book, his mention of the word 'Boginya' started appearing multiple times in the same sentences. From what I could translate, the chosen daughter had risen into his pack. Finally. I am getting somewhere. He wrote about her being a young she-wolf, only fourteen and still a pup. The birth of her wolf had only come about a week prior to her Goddess stature arising. The news of the young girl travelled far and wide, and celebrations lasted for weeks. The she-wolf was tested and trained daily until her power revealed itself. Vozdukh. Dykhaniye. Air or wind, I believe. How interesting.

The fact that this dog could control the wind, struck a chord with me. If anything, I became more invested in this journal and its proper translations. A talent much like my own. How could that be? The hunters gave me my abilities when they created me. I was a lab rat. They told me as much, repeatedly. How could a daughter of the Moon Goddess share the same gifts? I must be translating it wrong. There is no other way, this isn't just some random coincidence.

Three years ago.

I was puffing hard, gasping for breath as I was hunched over on my hands and knees. My forearms were still tender and raw from my last lesson. I could feel the fresh lashes on my back, they stung like a bitch, but with each new hit, the feeling was melting away to the numbness.

"Opyat' taki!" (Again) he screamed,

"I can't" I gasped. My lungs felt like they were ready to explode. My body has been pushed to its limits, and I'm not sure how much more it can take before it gives up on me completely. The whip came down on my back with a crack. I winched and clenched my teeth, swallowing the scream. A new trickle of blood ran down my side and dripped onto the floor. The sounds of the droplets hitting the cool concrete was unusually calming.

"Again, Whiskey!" Pasha yelled through his deep Russian accent. I huffed and pushed myself up. I slowly stood up straight on shaking and worn out knees. The room was freezing, as per usual. I've attended my lessons in this same frigid ice box for as long as I can remember. Always the same. Don't live up to their expectations, punishment. Argue or refuse an order, punishment. Fail, serious punishment. Only when they approve of my efforts am I rewarded. Which is a very rare occurrence. Nothing is ever enough for them. I remember when I was a child, my reward was warmth. I was so easily pleased back then. Now my rewards vary. Sometimes it's food, sometimes it's small things like books or new training gear. They realised, after a little trial and error, that a night without beatings was more of a reward for them than it was for me. Especially since I am becoming better at the use and control of my power. There were only so many men they could send in to die. And anyone who tried to attack me now, well, they would die, very painfully. I promised John that he would never get the chance to touch me again. Well, that vow went for anyone who tried it. And a few did. Though, none succeeded.

"Last chance!" he screeched over at me. I snarled and curled my lip up with a growl. These fuckers are damn impatient. I straightened my back and gritted my teeth. I held my arms out in front of me, facing my palms towards the two hundred kilo weighted ball. I forced the power through my tired body. The weightlessness and airy feeling tickled across my skin. The room filled with a soft breeze, but steadily increased into a rapid whirlwind. The ball lifted slightly off the floor and spun around in place. If I want this lesson to stop, I'd have to really show them something. And this wasn't going to be enough. Anger and hatred filled my veins, burning me from the inside out. The air twirling around my hands began to mix with thin whisps of black smoke. I tensed my fingers and screamed out loud. I flung my arms to the side, sending the heavy ball flying across the room and slamming into the concrete wall. The weight hit the wall with so much force, it cracked through the bricks and embedded itself into the fixture.

I once again fell to my hands and knees, gasping for air. I was past the point of weakness now. My energy levels were completely depleted. I doubt I will even be able to stand up and walk back to my room. My head spun with dizziness, and I wanted to vomit from the overexertion. A slow clap sounded from the protective barrier. I looked over to see my teacher smiling widely and strolling towards me.

"See" he cheered,

"YA znal, chto ty smozhesh' eto sdelat'" (I knew you could do it). I flopped onto the freezing cold floor and rolled over onto my back. The coolness of the frozen concrete was nice against the fresh wounds to my back. I had almost forgotten about them. I took a deep breath and swallowed my vomit. Fuck, I think I'm going to pass out.

"You just need the, pooshchreniye (encouragement)" he laughed and leaned over my body. The wrinkles around his eyes deepened when he smiled. Which he only did when he was getting his kicks out of punishing me, or on the rare occasion like this when I have impressed him. He always wore the same thing. A stupid grey Ushanka, a black V-neck sweater, and a military vest that has way too many pockets. Like, why does he even need that many pockets? And then also black cargo pants, again with too many pockets. All rounded out by his black heavy leather boots. They all wear black, I'm not totally sure why. But on this arsehole, with his light blue eyes and white-blonde hair poking out from under his dumb hat, it just looks weird. Like a very tall little boy trying to play soldier. I groaned and flipped him off. A risky move, but seeing as he is smiling right now, maybe he will laugh it off. He chuckled and stood up straight, and started walking back to the barrier.

"Opyat' taki!" (Again) he called happily. There was no way I was even getting up off the floor, let alone summoning the power again.

"Net" I spat back at him. I heard the scraping of his boots as he stopped walking.

"Net?" he snapped,

"I can't. Ochen' ustavshiy (Too tired)" I groaned,

"Ty budesh' delat' tak, kak tebe govoryat" (You will do as you are told) he yelled and came to stand back over me. I could feel my body quitting on me. I was about to pass out, any minute now. May as well have a little fun before I do.

"Not today" I crooned and waved my arm out in front of me. The air I was able to summon was just enough to send him flying across the room and into the wall. I heard him hit the bricks with a delectable thump, and I smiled. Then everything went black.

Present Day.

I shook away the memory and continued reading, struggling to translate the text the best that I could. But I couldn't help but feel like it wasn't good enough. I took longer to work my way through the pages, making sure I checked and double checked the words carefully. The Alpha wrote about an incident. A death. I pieced together as much as I could.

Uzhe god minoval, yakozhe Bozhestvenna vozneslasya. Ona prinesla radost' i blagopoluchiye v dom nash. S nadezhdoyu ya vosprinimal, chto yeye prikhoda dast blagodat' nam. No ta nadezhda, kazalos', vpustuyu. Vo nachale ona blazhenna byla. Sila yeye velika, dazhe pred nachalom ucheniya. No s vozrastom i sliyaniyem s siloyu svoyeyu, v ney snev slubochayshiy razsorayetsya. T'ma tam prisutstvuyet, i blasorodnym moim lyudyam ya uzhasayus'.

It had been a year since the Goddess had risen. She brought them joy. But then she became angry. She was dark inside? What does that mean? She was dark inside, like her blood? This is looking more like the ramblings of a madman. My admiration for the Alpha was given too fast. Clearly. He admitted that he was scared of her. Damn my stupid illiterate brain.

Posly vse pribyvayut, prinosya vesti o mire, soyuzakh i bogatstvakh, nedosyasayemykh dlya nashego uma. Legko bylo otverznut' ikh vnachale. Ona byla Boziney. Nichto ne moglo sravnit'sya s yeyo bogatstvom. No nyne. Ona vnushayet mne strakh.

Many delegates, I think is the word. It makes the most sense. They came to trade and bring money. Fuck me, this is fucking ridiculously difficult! He turned them away because the Goddess was rich. Whatever the fuck that is meant to mean. But again, he was scared of her. Weak piece of shit.

Nakonets-to, nebesnyy triumf nash uzron. Pervozdannyy Al'fa yavilsya. Velikuyu zainteresovannost' yavil on v yeyo prikhode i zhelayet k nashemu smirennomu v'yuntsu prisoyedinit'sya. Siye mozhet znachit' slavnyye dela dlya rodnogo nashego usla i dlya sem'i nashey.

Oof. This is hard. His triumph had been seen. Seen by who? The Primordial Alpha. No, that can't be right. The Primitive Alpha. No, that doesn't make sense either. The First or the Original Alpha ? Maybe. Doesn't matter. Moving on. He had shown interest in the Goddess and wanted to join them? Why would someone he called "The Primordial Alpha" want to join this shitty dirt patch of a pack. Whatever.

Bozhestvo nashe yavilo nam opasnosti i ugrozy s nebesnykh prostorov. Pervobytnyy Al'fa ne ustupit. On ne stanet torgovat'sya. Yemu nuzhna Bozhestvo, i ne men'she togo. I yesli ya ne otdam yeyo yemu do kontsa nedeli, on pogubit nas vsekh. Izbran'ye sdelano za menya.

So, the Primordial Alpha sought her out and tried to trade with the Alpha, so that he could claim her, or own her. I'm not sure about that translation. But he wanted her, and this guy wasn't willing to let her go. I guess a threat was made, and the Alpha had no choice? Now things are starting to get interesting. This Alpha offered him an ultimatum. Either give him the she-wolf, or everyone dies. So, I suppose a deal was struck?

Se budet moy posledniy zapisok. Boginya sokrushila nashe stado. Moya radost'. Moya zhizn'. Ver'te, chto yesli ya dash' pervobytnomu Al'fe ubit' yeyo sem'yu, ona smiritsya i uydot tikho. Byt' mne durakom. Videl zlo vnutri neyo, i vybral otvergat' yego. Yeyo vspyshka stoila mne mnogo.

Oh, how dastardly. They killed the girl's parents and siblings, then sold her to the Primordial Alpha. Dogs are such vicious creatures. But, she did not go peacefully. She escaped.

Zhestokoye ubiystvo zheny i yedinstvennogo syna donyne terzayet menya. Ona vysosala vozdukh iz ikh logkikh, i posledniye mgnoveniya ikh byli polny stradaniy i muk. V razgar yego pobega, ona ukrala moy tselyy mir. Day, da otslezhivayet Al'fa yeyo. Day, da vosprimet yeyo siloy. Day, da zastavit yeyo zaplatit'. Molyus' Vsevyshney Materi, da osvobodit nas ot etikh uz. Day, da vossoyedinit menya s moim semeystvom.

The drama just gets better. My word, I hope I'm translating this right. It's just too juicy. So the Goddess escaped, and while doing so, she killed the Luna and the son of the Alpha.

I paused my translation. My enjoyment of the story was gone in an instant. It was the way in which she killed them that stopped me. If I have this right. And I must, I re-read the same sentence twenty times. She suffocated them. She pulled the air from their lungs, leaving them in torment. No! It's one of my favourite skills, a skill I use very often. And this mut was able to do the same thing. The thought enraged me.

I closed the book and wrung my fingers tightly around the cover. I am supposed to be special. I am supposed to be unique. And yet all this time I spent believing that I was one of a kind, another had already mastered my abilities. I am the strong one. I am the trained killer, the silent assassin, the ghost in the night. I am the powerful one. This bitch has nothing on me. A ripping sound pulled me from my rage spiral, I looked down to see the journal now in two shredded pieces in my hands. Fuck. I kneeled down on the ground and laid the two halves together. I opened them both back up to the page that I was last reading, and tried to line them up so that I could see the handwritten words. I really shredded the damned thing. Once I got past the section that had been torn, and down to the bottom end of the page, I could see more clearly. All that I could make out on the last page, was that the she-wolf had escaped custody. The Alpha was distraught over the death of his family. He asked that the Primordial Alpha take her down, and make her pay? It's hard to tell through the crumpled pages.

I got to the end of the page and turned it over, there was nothing. The next page was blank, as were the rest of the pages. I guess she did get him in the end, or the pissant killed himself in his grief. Either way, that means my trail has once again gone cold. I tossed the two torn pieces of the journal away, and the pages were scattered around the floor.

Nothing. Once again, I'm back to the start. Maybe. If I could find a way to figure out who this other pack was, the one with the Primordial Alpha. Maybe if I find them, I won't have to start again on an empty slate. That Alpha wanted her, bad enough to threaten the lives of his own kind. Maybe I will find out more about the Moon Goddess and her chosen daughters in his pack.

What was its name again? New Wolf or something. I rushed over to the scattered pages and rummaged through them, looking for mention of the powerful Alpha's pack. Ah, there it is. Proiskhozhdeniye Volk. Origin Wolf. That's where I need to go next.

But where are they? I have no clue. I haven't heard of that pack before. I mean, I haven't really heard of any of the packs. Not until I'm in the middle of ripping them apart. But if this Alpha is as tough and powerful as the journal claims, then there must be something about him, about his pack somewhere. I just need to find where. I made my way back to the small library. I wasn't expecting to find anything useful. This little shithole was too small and insignificant to have anything worthy of my time. But I had to look regardless. There is always a small possibility of error on my part. However unlikely that may be. My patience had withered down to nothing, and that resulted in no care on my part. I grabbed a book, roughly flicked through the pages, and then threw the book across the room when it revealed to hold nothing of substance. This went on for a while, until the small wooden floor was no longer visible under the spread of ripped and tossed pages. When I moved onto the scrolls, same thing. Rip it open, find nothing, and toss it away.

I was just about to throw another scroll to the side when I spotted something, and so I forced my exasperated eyes to look again. I held the scroll up to the light and inspected it more closely. It was a map of almost the entire Northern Hemisphere. It displayed parts of land from Poland, all over Russia, down to Mongolia and the top of North America, to what we now know as Alaska and Northwest Canada. It was old. I could tell just by looking at the markings and roughly hand drawn borders. In the bottom right-hand corner of the scroll was a scribbled signature next to the date 1689. So, it's very old then. The outlined borders weren't any kind of commonwealth borders and didn't look to follow any set shape or form. Some didn't even connect to anything else, and some were just a rough circle in the middle of nothing. I studied the map, trying to understand what the shapes and borders were for. But it wasn't until I leaned right over and put my face up close and personal with the yellowing paper did I notice some small scribbling in the middle of one of the shapes. Black Wolf. What the fuck is Black Wolf meant to mean? I looked at another outline, and there was another scribble in the centre of that one too. Polnoch. Midnight. Are these names? After noticing the first one, the rest were all blatantly obvious. They are names. Pack names. And the borders are pack lands. Bingo.

The map is super outdated, but unless killed off or taken over by stronger Alphas, these packs usually last for generations. So, it is very possible that most of the pack lands on the map are still in existence. There were multiple outlined sections of land throughout Russia. But I have already cleared a lot of them. Some of them were on the map, but most were not. There are a few more to the East I can search before I make my way to Alaska, and then on to Canada. It was interesting to see the sheer size of land that the packs took ownership of. It piqued my curiosity about how they maintain and protect their land, especially those of the larger regions. I have learnt about their aggressive and possessive ways. They're quick to violence and have little to no care for human life. I was taught about their infighting, and about some of the wars between the packs. Wars that spread to human territories and towns. But I was never shown or taught about the times of peace. If these beasts are capable of peace at all.

Unfortunately, of all the names on the map, Origin Wolf wasn't one of them. This fact frustrated me to no end. The vast expanse this map displayed, and that fucking name wasn't on it. Which leaves me the entire Southern Hemisphere to search. Maybe they're in Australia. The Aboriginal Australians have been proven to be one of the oldest civilisations on Earth. If anyone would be worthy of the title 'Original Wolf', surely, they would have to be from the indigenous Australians. I have not heard of wolves in Australia though. But there are dingos. Perhaps the packs there have evolved to look more like dingos than they do the modern wolf. If my theory is true, that could be why the Alpha of this pack was so scared of the Origin Wolf's Alpha. But this is all just a theory, I need proof before I jet off to the land down under. Alaska and Canada first. If I have no luck around there, then I will travel to Australia. At least then I would be closer to New Zealand. There is a very powerful pack in New Zealand, they hide themselves in the snow-covered mountains somewhere on the South Island. Finding and destroying that pack has been a desire of mine for a long time.

After spending more time carefully, and much more closely examining the rest of the scrolls, I had no further luck. I rolled the map up and placed it in a cylinder document case, after discarding the previous scroll that was already packaged inside it. I went back to my temporary accommodations and packed up my things. I was out of this dump at first light. And that time couldn't come soon enough.

Chapter Nine

Whiskey

Being in the form of my inner monster was one of the absolute worst things for me. To say I hate it would be a serious understatement. It makes me feel wild and untamed, like the feral beasts that I hunt. But when I don't have access to a car, helicopter, or motorbike, it is the next best way to travel across the country. I will have to stop at the next town I come across and steal a car. I was fast in this form, even with my bag and the map case in my mouth. My beast side may be smaller than the natural born dogs I hunt, but I was undoubtedly stronger, and faster. My lifelong training had moulded me into the perfect killing machine, plus with the addition of my power, it meant I was impossible to beat. No matter how big the beast I faced was, I was always better.

I slowly made my way East through Russia. Checking the areas marked on the map for packs. I found and decimated two more. Both were small and irrelevant, and neither housed anything of value to me. It felt like a bit of a waste to take them out. I took care of them quickly, but my time could have been better spent elsewhere. The feelings of anxiousness and impatience to hurry up and move on had been gnawing at me. It was becoming more instant, and getting hard to shake. Something was pulling me to move more quickly, to move towards Alaska. Once I am off this godforsaken continent, everything will be less stressful. I fucking hate this damned country. The things I endured as a child, all for the sake of making me what I am today, the memories of those lessons always hit me harder here. This is, after all, my birthplace. Mother Russia, my creator. I bet the fuckers never thought things would end up the way they have. They always thought that they were superior to me. Well, I showed them, didn't I.

Two and a half years ago.
My body was healing at an exponential rate. With all the times I have been forced to change form over the past year or so, it has made both the time it takes to shift into the beast, and the time it takes to heal my wounds, almost instantaneous. Most of them were afraid of me now. I could smell it all over them. They are weak and pitiful things. Every now and then one of them would grow a little extra courage, and try and intimidate, scare or even beat me. They usually end up dead. Just like John did when he eventually came back to my room again. Killing him was the closest I have ever gotten to feeling true happiness. Looking over his bloodied and mangled body, after I beat him senseless and sucked the air from his lungs, it was a dream come true.
But this monstrous cunt has never shown any fear of me. He has lost any and all toleration of me, and my outbursts of anger. The deep wrinkles around his eyes are now a permanent fixture. As is the scowl on his face. He still wears the same stupid clothes. That fucking vest. I want so bad to rip apart that dumb fucking vest. He has had enough of me, and I have sure as shit had enough of him. Every fucking day, since I killed Spencer, this cunt has been here. Pushing me, testing me, training me. He has been in charge of it all. And I want nothing more than to wring his neck.
"Opyat' taki!" (Again) he yelled. A growl bubbled in the pit of my stomach and made its way up to vibrate in my chest. Control Whiskey, keep control, I told myself over and over again. My body was shaking with anger. I could have blamed it on the cold, but I have long since gotten accustomed to being frozen. I swallowed down the ball of fury for the umpteenth time and snapped my head to the side. The fire flew over my body like a tidal wave, and a second later I was standing on four legs. Pasha stood leaning his back against the wall, with his arms crossed over his chest, glaring at me. He didn't even flinch when I changed. My senses were always better in tune when in this form. I could

smell his hatred and disgust, I could basically taste it on the tip of my tongue. It only fuelled my own hatred towards him.

"I nazad" (And back) he snapped without moving a muscle. I bared my fangs at him and growled my hatred. The sound reverberated around the room, bouncing off the concrete walls. Again, he didn't flinch. It only infuriated me further that I could not scare him like I could all the others. I huffed and rolled my head back. My body shifted back, and I stood up on my human legs. I prefer it much more this way. Fangs are good, but blades and thumbs are better. I stood before him, completely naked from head to toe. My every mark, my every scar, the remanence of not just his teachings, but every man that had come before him, all laid bare for him to gaze upon. And he did. But he wasn't just looking at the scars he had left on my body. No. He was looking at what was under them. He was looking at me.

I sniffed the cool air and his subtle scent of desire crept into my nose. My lips curled back and my teeth sharpened and extended into fangs. This disgusting old bag had the nerve to desire me. The teenager he has been torturing for over a year now. I wanted to puke. I wanted to scream. Most of all I wanted to rip his wrinkly old dick off. I felt the path of his heated gaze burn down my body and back up again. Pasha clicked his tongue and stepped forward, pushing himself off the wall. He shifted his hands into the pockets of his pants and began to slowly walk in a circle around where I stood. For what felt like an hour, I felt him roll his eyes over every inch of my naked flesh. He stood close to my back, so close I could feel the warmth of his body. His finger slid up my arm, over my shoulder and to my neck. He wrapped his hand around my throat and stepped in closer. His body was now pressed up against mine. A growl vibrated through my chest and forced its way through my clenched teeth.

"Takaya trata" (Such a waste) he sneered into my ear.

"You are a beast. Skrytyy (Hidden). Under this vkusnyye (tasty) body". His mouth connected with the soft flesh of my neck, his slimy tongue tasting my skin. Any control I had left was gone at that moment. All I could see was black, and all I wanted was blood. In less than a second, I snapped my arm back and wrapped it around his neck. With a firm tug, I pulled him over my shoulder and sent him flying across the floor in front of me. He slid along the ground and stopped once his body hit the far wall with a hard thud. He grunted but wasn't hurt. He quickly jumped to his feet, but I was faster. I launched myself through the air, landing on him with my legs around his midriff and my hands at his neck. He tumbled backwards until his back hit the wall. I lifted my arm and struck it down across his face. My long and sharply extended talons slashed through the feeble skin of his cheek and nose. The flesh burst open like spring flowers, blooming like bloody petals. It was glorious. Pasha screamed and tried to push me off, but I was stronger. I lifted my other arm and struck it down with the same amount of gusto. He was able to block my strike and instead, my talons ripped through his forearm. He threw me away from him and grabbed his arm to his chest. I landed on my feet and whipped around ready to attack once more. I crouched down and scraped my nails over the frosty concrete floor. My growl filled the room as I eyed down my prey. He was now sitting on the floor, slouched against the wall. Blood poured from the open wounds on his face and seeped through his fingers on his arm. The sight filled me with a joy I had never felt before. Seeing my torturer hurt and in pain, it brought me the kind of happiness that the child I used to be could only dream of. I decided in that moment, I will never let go of this sensation. If I have to kill each and every one of them to prolong this feeling, then I will do it without hesitation.

Just as I was about to charge, I was struck from the side and sent flying across the room. I was so caught up in the sight of Pasha, that I forgot about my surroundings. Four more guards piled in and stood in front of Pasha, blocking him from me. As I stood on the other side of the room, looking over their scared and angry faces, I smiled at them. The idea of now ripping apart all of them, it got me all excited and jittery. One of the guards lifted his gun and aimed it at me. As it fired, I weaved to the side, dodging the track of the bullet. He fired again, and again I dodged. Bullets now rained down on me, and I dodged them all. Just like they trained me to do. As I jumped and spun and twirled out of the way, I got closer and closer to where they stood. The anger on their faces was quickly morphing into terror, as the realisation came to them. They trained me for this, but they never expected me to use it against them. I got to the first guard and sliced his throat with my talons before he could even grasp how close I was to him. I jumped through the air, landing on the shoulders of another. I snapped his neck and let the body fall. I jumped over to the next one before the last guy's body hit the ground. I ducked behind him and dug my talons into his sides, burying my fingers deep into his flesh. I turned him around, just in time for his body to take the shower of bullets from the last guard. I held him in place like a shield as he shook and jolted with each hit. I carried his limp body forward, towards the last guard. As the gun clicked, signalling he was out of ammo, I dropped the body. He was fumbling with his gun, trying to push the new cartridge into place. The scent of his fear, mixed with the blood and gunpowder, it was the most delicious thing I had ever smelled. I laughed out loud as he dropped the cartridge. He then threw the gun to the side and raised his arms in surrender.

Remembering the way in which I killed Spencer, I decided to give it another go. This was a skill they hadn't let me train. They didn't want to sacrifice the men. Well, I now deem this scumbag a worthy sacrifice. I stepped forward and grabbed his shoulders. He stood not too much taller than me, and if I had to guess, he wasn't too much older than me either.

"YA sdayus'" (I give up) he screamed. I smiled at his terrified young face and cupped his cheeks.

"YA znayu" (I know) I said and offered a sweet toothy grin. Though I imagine it looked nothing close to sweet. I leaned in close and sucked in a slow deep breath. My feet felt planted to the ground, but my head felt light and airy. As I breathed in, the guard's face contorted and turned grey. His lips went blue, and he made a wonderful gagged choking sound. I kept sucking in the air as his eyes bulged and started to roll back. My grip on his face was now the only thing that was keeping him upright. After a beat, I felt as though I couldn't take any more air into my lungs, and so I stopped. I held it in for a few seconds and let go of his face. He dropped to the floor like one of the lifeless dummies I had used during my training. I released the air from my lungs, the airiness feeling left as well.

"You stupid bitch" Pasha groaned from behind me on the floor. For a second, I forgot he was still there. His entire face was covered in blood and he was now sitting upright against the wall. He was holding his arm up to his chest, but it did nothing to stop the blood that was now covering his other hand and steadily dripping down his arm and onto his leg. I guess I got him good.

"Tsk, tsk, tsk" I clicked my tongue and came to crouch down in front of him.

"Kontrol' (Control), master. You must keep your control" I said teasingly. Repeating the same phrase that he has said to me a thousand times over. He snarled and spat his blood into my face.

"Fuck you" he hissed. I wiped the blood from my cheek and smiled down at him as I licked the blood from my finger. I don't know what possessed me to do it. It was like some kind of animalistic urge to taste my kill. I smiled at him wickedly as my tongue lapped at his blood. I could still smell his disgust thick in the air. But now, I could taste his fear. Finally. After all this time, he is finally afraid of me. I chuckled and looked back up at him. He reached for the gun at his hip, but his movements were slow and clunky. I leapt forward and straddled his legs. I grabbed his wrist and lifted it above his head, squeezing my talons into the already ripped open flesh of his arm. He threw his head back and hissed in pain.

"Don't do that" I crooned and grabbed the gun with my other hand. I tossed it across the room and shifted closer to him.

"Isn't this what you wanted master? To have me naked and on top of you, pleasuring you?" I said with a low sultry voice. I reached down and squeezed the flaccid lump between his legs.

"Uberi ot menya ruki" (Take your hands off me) he grunted and hit my hand away. I grabbed his other wrist and held it above his head with his other arm.

"Don't do that" I growled and leaned in close to his face.

"You can't win" Pasha jeered with a weak smirk,

"My vsegda naydem tebya" (We will always find you). I hadn't considered running before now. I don't know what I expected to happen after killing Pasha. I didn't think that far ahead. Of course, they would kill me after this. They would be stupid to keep me alive now. So I guess running was my only option. He was right though, I knew that. They will never stop looking for me, no matter how far I ran, or how well I hid. They would never stop trying to bring me back. And that could never happen. So, there is really only one way to make sure that they can't. I tilted my head to the side and pressed my cheek against his torn open and bloody face.

"Not if there is no one left to search" I whispered and ran my tongue over his bloodied cheek. He reared back and glared at me.

"There are too many. Vy ne mozhete ubit' nas vsekh" (You cannot kill us all). I smiled and called forward the magic.

"Watch me" I cooed and smashed my lips to his. He fought against me, but his blood loss had made him weak, and I was still stronger. I sucked the air from his lungs in a sharp hard movement. I was not gentle and slow like I was with the guard. This was painful. I tore apart his lungs with the forcefulness of the action. I could taste his blood as I breathed it in.

He was scared, he was in anguish. I loved every second of it. It was like a drug rolling through me. My body felt a type of pleasure I hadn't known before. Oh, I could bathe in the feeling. Once he was dead, I released my hold on his arms and leaned back to inspect my handy work. His eyes were wide with fear and pain, hidden under the stain of his blood, his normally pale skin was a shade of blueish grey. The man that had caused me so much pain, the man that taught me how to use my power, that man was now dead. I chuckled to myself as I stood from his lap. Well, he can't watch me kill all his friends now, can he?

Pasha was just the beginning. There are more, many more, and all of them will meet the same fate. I'll start here of course. I will kill every worthless meat sack that lives in this frozen wasteland. And once they are dead, I will move on to the rest of the world. I will find every single hunter outpost, every clan, every member, in every corner of the globe. I will search far and wide until I am sure that they are all dead. I vow this to whatever demon I was born from. I promise this to the evil and darkness that lives inside me. And once I am done with the hunters, once they are gone from this earth forever, I will move on to what I was created for. The Werewolves. This is my mission.

Present Day.

It has been nearly three years since I set out on my new path, since I killed every single being in that stinking ice hole. I was merciless. I ripped them to shreds without hesitation or a second thought. Every man, every woman, and every child. They all suffered at the hands of my newfound courage and power. I imagine by the end of it I looked like some kind of demon. A small framed naked girl covered head to toe in blood. What a sight I was. When everyone was dead, I gathered together all the weapons, jewels, money, anything of value really, and filled an armoured car. Once that place was in my rear vision mirror, and I had officially escaped, I did exactly what I said I would do. I hunted those who hunted me. Clan after clan, outpost after outpost. They all fell victim to my rage. I took my vengeance out on them with a barbaric eagerness, to an extent that most would find horrific. Each kill gave me satisfaction. Each time a new compound was cleared I felt elated. Accomplished. Fulfilled. This was what I was created for. Killing. And I loved it.

The first two years were spent in a constant state of travel. Moving from one location to the next. I have been to England, France, Italy, India, Brazil, Mexico, Thailand, South Korea, Turkey, of course Russia, and everywhere else in between. I decimated outposts, villages, and entire towns even. I never stayed in one place for longer than a few hours. The severity of my revenge always differed at each location. Some of them would try to run like cowards. And so those ones I killed quickly, they weren't worthy of my time. Some of them would try to fight back. Those ones I killed painfully, and enjoyed every second of it. And then the ones that turned on each other, that tried to sacrifice their comrades in order to get away. Well, those cowards I killed slowly, taking my time to enjoy their pain and suffering. When I no longer had hunters to hunt, I turned to what was next. The Weres. That was when things took a turn for the worse. But that's not something I want to relive right now.

It took me eight days to reach Lavrentiya. With the stops I had to make along the way, plus finding a new car each time it ran out of gas, it took much longer than I was happy with. The pull to the East was strong, it was sickening even. I felt anxious and nervous, which is not something that is a common sensation for me. I hate it. I don't like not knowing or understanding my own mind. I have no idea what is awaiting me over there, but the ever present need to just get there was growing stronger and stronger the closer I got. Thankfully during this time of year, the water wouldn't be frozen over. Which makes the journey much easier. So now all I need to do is find a boat, then I'll be on my way. One step closer to figuring out this weird feeling, that I just can't seem to shake.

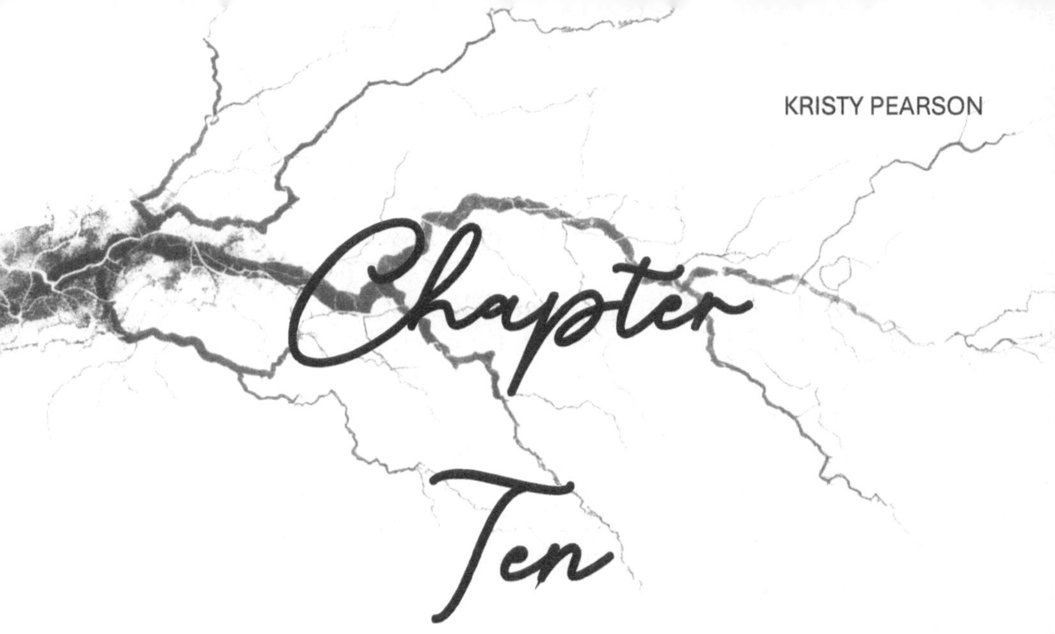

Chapter Ten

Zelena

I felt pretty good after Nat left in search of Smith. She found her true love, and I had figured out what had been making her so down. I was so happy for her, and yet selfishly sad for myself. Nat was the first girl that I ever connected with. She is literally my first girlfriend. But now she will be moving away, hours away. I'll be losing my friend, my sister, and my baby will be losing its aunt. I know I shouldn't feel like this, I should be overjoyed for her. But I can't help it. Through all my own selfish sadness, I keep coming back to poor Smith. He'll be devastated, at first, but I know he'll be okay eventually. It's still going to hurt him though, and with him hurting, I'll be hurting too. Gunner has told me a bit about Smith and his past ways with his many she-wolves, so I can only assume he'll work himself out. Now that I think about it, Smith and I never really talked about his relationship with Nat. That is a lapse on my part. I have really been a shit friend to him. I remember Nat told me once that she didn't think he was her forever, I wonder if he feels the same way. I at least hope he feels the same way.

I eventually waddled back downstairs. Tobias was waiting with a freshly made steak sandwich. He's such a good guardian. I smiled widely as I took the sandwich from the plate and shoved almost half of it into my mouth. The steak was warm and the butter on the bread had melted. I could still taste the blood on the piece of meat. I almost feel guilty. The poor beautiful cows, such sweet, beautiful creatures. Why do they have to taste so damn delicious. It's official, I would never survive as a vegetarian. I took my wonderful sandwich out to the porch swing. I sat down, and unsurprisingly, Tobias sat beside me. He began to swing us gently as I finished off my sandwich. As I was licking the juice that had dripped down my wrist, I noticed Smith walking over to his hut, and Nat standing on his porch waiting. The two sat down on the steps, the same steps where I had my heart to heart with Smith just this morning. I shouldn't be watching. It feels like an invasion of privacy. But I couldn't look away.

Nat placed her hand on Smith's leg and looked at him. Her chest visibly heaved with the large breath she took in. They talked for a little bit, and then Smith's face fell. She was talking animatedly, using her hands a lot, waving them around in front of her. All the while Smith stared straight ahead with a weird sad but neutral look on his face. A little while longer and Nat was crying and trying to pull at Smith's chin so that he would look at her. Smith stood up abruptly and clenched his fists at his side. I could see him shaking with anger from this far away. He was talking at her now, not talking but also not yelling. If he was yelling, I would hear it. I can't stand them being angry with each other, hating each other. How do I fix this? I went to stand up, but Tobias gripped my hand and held me on the swing.

"Don't interfere" he said sternly,

"I have to do something" I snapped back,

"Little One, I understand that you care for each of them, but this is not your place. They have to work it out alone" he said much more softly. Damn him and his wise ways. I looked anxiously back over at Smith and Nat. They were both now standing facing each other and I could only see the sides of their faces. Neither one was talking, and both of them looked upset. They were just standing still, staring at each other. Smith stepped forward and cupped Nat's face with both of his hands, she gripped his shirt and then they stood like that together. Foreheads pressed together, holding onto each other. After a few more minutes, Smith leaned back and pressed his lips to the top of her head. He stroked her hair and then stepped back. She dropped her hands to her sides and watched as he walked away. It was heartbreaking. Nat stood perfectly still, with her heaving chest being her only movement, as Smith's rigid frame walked off. Nat slowly sat back down on the steps and buried her face in her hands.

"Can I go to her now?" I turned and asked Tobias. I don't know why I asked. I haven't really been one to ask permission for anything these days. I just trust his judgment is all. His only answer was a nod of his head. I waddled as fast as I could over to where Nat was sitting. The sounds of her crying grew the closer I got. I leaned my heavy body back and lowered myself onto the step beside her. I wrapped my arm around her shoulder and pushed the hair from her face.

"You okay?" I asked her softly. Her crying changed to harsh sobs as she turned on me in a flash. She threw her arms around my neck and tucked her face in under my hair. I could feel her tears hitting my shoulder as she cried.

"Hey, it's okay. You did what was right. He'll be okay eventually" I said soothingly. Nat sniffed and lifted her head.

"That's the thing, he is okay" she cried.

"But Nat, why is that bad?" I asked surprised,

"It would have been easier if he just hated me. If he was angry and not so damn understanding".

"Aw, honey, those are all good things though. It means you can still be friends".

"I don't know if I can be his friend. I still love him, so much, Lena. What if I'm making a mistake? What if Lace isn't really who I'm meant to be with, and it was really Smith all along? Why couldn't I just have a True Mate like you, then I would know for sure. I could be blowing up the best thing I've ever had for a chance, a chance that may not even be real. Oh Goddess, what am I doing? I have to fix this".

"Nat!" I screamed, pulling her from her downward spiral,

"Take a breath" I said with authority. Nat stopped blabbering and took in a slow deep breath, then huffed it out in one quick puff. She looked at me with sad eyes, full of panic. Her bottom lip was shaking and her eyes were brimming with tears.

"You know you are making the right choice. In your heart, you can feel it. It's okay to still love Smith. But you need to follow your heart, and it's telling you that your future is with Alpha Lace" I told her. She took a shaky breath and nodded her head. I pulled her into my arms for a tight hug. After a minute I pulled back and wiped the tears from her cheek.

"I think there is someone that would really like to hear about your decision" I said with a sweet smile. Nat's face lifted and a smile crept across her lips.

"Will you come with me?" she asked hopefully,

"Of course, as long as you can lift me off these steps. I'm like a whale these past couple of days" I chuckled and rubbed my belly. Nat jumped to her feet and grabbed my belly to press her face into me.

"But you're so smushy and cute. Hello, my sweet little niece, Aunty Nat loves you" she cooed affectionately while rubbing her cheek over my belly. I swatted her away and held my arms out for her to help pull me up.

"You don't know it's a girl" I grunted as Nat pulled me to my feet, "Babe, you're the daughter of Selene, of course your firstborn will be a girl" she said with a chuckle, like it was obvious. I looked down at my swollen stomach, I could only just see the tips of my toes now. I rounded my hand over my bump and hummed.

"I hope you're right" I said quietly. I have felt from the beginning that it was a boy. Maybe because I pictured a mini Gunner running around. I was never able to see a future for myself when I was young. So, I suppose it makes sense that I can't picture my face on a baby version of me now. But having a little girl. My own little mini-me. A built in best friend for life. To have someone I can share a bond with, just like the one Nat and Roe share. That seems too good to be true. I really do want her to be right. A little girl. It would be wonderful. She will be our little princess. She will have Gunner wrapped around her tiny little finger, and be able to command Tobias and Smith to her will with nothing more than a chubby cheeked smile. The future doesn't seem so scary any more. I wish I could pinpoint the exact moment that changed for me.

Nat and I walked slowly over to where the Howlers were camped, Nat babbling about all things baby on the way. As we got closer, Nat went dead silent, which was very a strange thing for Nat. I looked up to see her staring ahead. I heard her heartbeat start to race, and I could smell her anxiety. I followed where she was looking and saw Alpha Lace. He must have spotted us as we approached and started walking over to meet us.

"I'm nervous" Nat whispered,

"Don't be. You'll be fine". I squeezed her hand and pushed her forward a little. She gave me a stiff nod before she walked over to Alpha Lace. I stopped where I was to give them a little extra space. They had only spoken for a minute when he started yelling. "Don't tease me!" he said loudly, barely able to contain his smile. "Are you kidding?" Alpha Lace yelled happily, "You're coming home with me?" he cheered. The sounds of his joyful voice filled the clearing and echoed across the sky. Lace grabbed Nat by her waist and hoisted her into the air, spinning her around above him. Nat laughed and squealed with joy as she held onto his shoulders. The usual stone-cold Alpha Lace with a wide and undeniably happy smile on his face, was truly a sight to behold. Even with his stocky frame and tattooed body, when he looked at Nat, he looked like a puppy with hearts in his eyes. Eventually, Lace lowered her feet back onto the ground. He wrapped his arm around her waist and pulled her into him. He then cupped her face and smashed his lips into hers. Nat's arms went up around his neck as she melted against his body. A tear slid down my cheek as I watched their blossoming love. I was so happy for her. Two arms snaked around my waist and the smell of sunshine filled my nose.

"Looks like she finally got her shit together, ay?" Gunner's smooth velvety voice whispered into my ear before he pressed his lips to my temple.

"You knew?" I asked him a little surprised,

"It was kind of hard to miss" he chuckled,

"What do you mean?"

"I mean why else would he still be here? Plus, the sickly way they constantly gaze at each other. Not to mention the scents. Goddess, I would gladly burn my nose off if it meant I never had to smell my sister's desire again".

"I didn't notice any of that" I said sadly. Gunner knew about their secret passions, but not me. How blind have I been? I have been a worse friend than I thought. I've been neglecting everyone, caught up in my own selfish disaster zone. Gunner's hands moved down to my stomach, just as the pup gave a mighty kick.

"You've been a little busy, my Love" he said softly and nuzzled his nose into my neck. He moved his lips over my neck and the top of my shoulder. Butterflies came to life in my stomach and a gentle heat came to life in my nether region. I love how he can make me feel so hot with nothing more than a kiss. I tilted my head back to give him more access and he gladly to advantage of it, hungrily moving his lips over my skin. The heat in my groin intensified and a low growl bubbled through my parted lips.

"Little Wolf, if you keep that up, I may just have to take you back to bed" Gunner cooed seductively,

"I'm not opposed to that" I moaned back,

"Mm, you're a minx. But I have a better idea" he chuckled and lifted me into his arms. In a heartbeat, we were slowly running away from the clearing towards the forest.

"Where are we going?" I asked as I looked up at his smirking face.

"You'll see" he answered and held me tighter. We only ran for a few minutes, stopping when we came to a stream in the middle of the forest. Gunner wasted no time in setting me down and capturing my lips in his, in a steamy passionate kiss. I leaned into him and gave myself over to the intoxicating taste of his mouth. He made quick work of my shorts, pulling them down my legs and helping me step out of them.

"Have I told you how sexy you look in my shirts?" he mumbled as his mouth roamed up my bare legs. I brushed my fingers through his hair and gripped hold of his dark blonde locks.

"Once or twice" I answered with a breathy voice. Gunner's mouth found the spot between my legs, forcing me to gasp in surprise when he ran his tongue along my lips.

"Take it off, then lay down" he commanded. I didn't hesitate and quickly tossed the shirt aside. Gunner growled with delight when he noticed I had no bra on. He took my hands and helped to lower me to the ground. The brush was soft under my back, and the ground was cool against my heated skin. Gunner shifted his body to move completely between my legs. He pushed open my knees and dived into my waiting slit. I gripped hold of his hair, anchoring his mouth to my pussy, and my sanity to him. Gunner sucked and teased my clit, leaving me a moaning mess, writhing beneath him. My body was vibrating with the pleasure his tongue offered. His fingers slipped inside me, bringing me closer to the edge. I could feel the pressure building and I was ready to ride this wave into oblivion. Gunner moved a finger further back and pressed against my back entrance, then began to rub his finger in a circle. The pressure was incredible, but it wasn't enough.

"More" I moaned and lifted my hips. Gunner attached his lips to my clit and pushed his finger into my tight rear. I tossed my head back and called out in bliss. Everything was moving, his tongue, his lips, his fingers. And I was lost. The building pressure burst through me, rolling down my arms and legs in waves. When the fireworks ceased, I looked down at Gunner, he smiled back at me with a triumphant gleeful look.

"That was..." I huffed and dropped my head back,

"Wow" I chuckled.

"I aim to please" he cooed proudly,

"Oh no, that was so cheesy" I said looking back down at him. Gunner crawled up my body until he was hovering over me.

"Cheddar cheese baby" he smiled happily. With his perfect smile spread across his face, the blue of his eyes sparkling with the sunlight through the trees, the scent of his desire and my own fresh elated feeling, all the troubles of the world just slipped away. It was just us. Me and my Love, relishing in the nature that surrounded us. Wild and free, as we should be.

Gunner laid down beside me and I lifted my head so he could stretch his arm out. I snuggled into his side, curling my leg around his and resting my arm on his chest. I could feel the thumping of his heart under his shirt and his steady breathing. The sounds of the forest animals climbing the trees, scampering across the brush and talking to each other, could be heard for miles. The faint smell of the ocean was in the air, along with an incoming summer storm.

"We should get back" Gunner said sullenly.

"You don't want to… you know?" I asked as I lifted my head. He chuckled and leaned up to look at me. He swiped his thumb over my cheek and smiled.

"I get all the pleasure I need from just gazing at your beautiful face" he cooed. Oh my, he is smooth with his words. I never knew love like this existed. It's hard to believe that I am worthy of it. I leaned forward and pressed my lips to his. Gunner cupped his hand around the back of my neck to anchor me to him. I was overflowing with emotion, the urge to cry was at the tipping point. I wasn't sad though. I wanted to cry from happiness, from love. I was so full of it, it was overflowing from every open part of me. Gunner pulled back and pecked my nose before standing up. He held his hands out to help me up. Once I was standing, he knelt down in front of me and helped slide my shorts back up my legs. He then moved his hands up to my stomach and pressed his forehead and nose to the swollen most part of my belly.

"Hello, my little pup, it's me, your daddy" he spoke lovingly. I curled my fingers through his hair and smiled down at him.

"I want to make you a promise, my precious boy. One day, when you're big and strong, you will lead this pack. I promise that until that day comes, I will help guide you the best that I can. And if it's a little girl in there, you will be Daddy's Goddess-blessed little angel. No man will ever hurt your heart and survive it. I will show you everything I know about life, about love and happiness. I will teach you how to have fun and to enjoy the little things. I will teach you about truth, honesty, loyalty and friendship. I will protect you and lift you up. I promise to love you with my whole heart, until the day I die, and then some. Daddy loves you Little One, and I can't wait to meet you". Gunner smattered kisses over my stomach and then stood up. I, of course, was blubbering like an emotional mess. He smiled at me softly and pressed his lips to my forehead.

"That was really sweet" I sobbed. He chuckled and looked down at me,

"I mean it. I will always protect you, the both of you. No matter what it takes".

"I know you will". I curled my arms around his waist and rested my head on his chest. Gunner held the back of my head and rubbed his hand down my back. I breathed out heavily, trying to slow my racing heart.

"I think I might want a girl now" I said quietly.

"A boy would be good, but I want to see you in a princess crown with nail polish and lipstick" I smiled into his chest. Gunner laughed and let me go. He swept me up into his arms and chuckled down at me.

"You could be so lucky" he mused and started on our way back to the village. Once we got back to the firepit, Gunner put me down again.

"I need to go see Dad, I'll come find you for dinner, okay?" Gunner said as he waved someone over from behind me. I glanced over my shoulder and saw Tobias walking towards us. Unsurprisingly, he was waiting for us. I'm not allowed to be alone any longer. I smiled and turned back to Gunner.

"I want to find Smith, to see if he's okay" I told him,

"Okay, my Love" he said and kissed my forehead before jogging away. I turned to Tobias who was waiting for me a few steps away.

"Smith?" he asked with a knowing look. I shrugged and nodded my head with a smile.

"He's over here" Tobias said and indicated to the front of the house.

"Thanks, Tobi" I smiled, which encouraged a soft growl from Tobias's lips.

Smith and Felix were working on something in the workshop. I've come to learn that Felix is not just an incredible commander, but he has a wicked mind and a hint of genius in him. Felix has become the mastermind of most of our boundary defences and battle preparations. The two were arguing over a piece of machinery as we approached.

"That's not for the spring motion, that's for the compression tank" Felix groaned.

"Well, how the fuck am I supposed to know that? You're the bloody genius here" Smith fired back.

"Do I even want to know?" I asked as I stepped up behind Smith. He turned around with a wide smile, which shocked me. He doesn't look like a man who just had his heart broken.

"Lena" he cooed and came to wrap his arms around my shoulders for a tight hug. Long gone are the days of no touching other males. Gunner learnt real quick that I wouldn't stand for that shit. As Smith lifted my feet off the ground and low growl rumbled from beside me.

"Calm down, Mighty Warrior, I'm not hurting her" Smith chuckled and let me back down, then quickly flashed me before stepping away.

Overprotective much

Stop it, you know it's just his instincts

Felix stepped forward, placed his hand on his chest and bowed low.

"Luna" he said proudly. Smith hit him on the back of the head and laughed loudly.

"Luna" Smith mocked him,

"Easy Felix, if you suck up any more your dick will turn into a vacuum nozzle"

"What does that even mean?" Tobias grunted quietly. Felix turned to Smith and growled lowly,

"Showing honour to my Luna is not a suck up, it's respect. You should learn some" he snapped.

"Hello Felix, it is always nice to see you. I would ask what you're working on, but I don't think I would understand" I said as I glared at Smith. He scoffed and sat down on a metal box, leaned back against the wall and crossed his arms over his chest.

"Well, it's quite simple Luna, we are building a mechanism that can be remotely triggered" Felix said and he stepped back beside the weird machine thing.

"What kind of mechanism is it?" I asked,

"It is a pressurised spring system that will quickly eject large wooden spikes out of the ground. They are to be placed at the end of the driveway" he answered proudly. I was a little shocked, it sounds so brutal. Then again, I have inflicted some pretty brutal things on some very unpleasant people.

"Spikes, wow" I gasped.

"The spikes are designed to flip any unwelcome cars that enter the driveway, not to impale people" Felix said with a reassuring smile. And strangely that information made me feel a hell of a lot better.

"Oh, good" I said with a deep breath.

"I was hoping to speak with Smith, but if you need him, I can come back later"?

"No, no. Please take him. He is more of a hindrance than he is a helper" Felix rushed out,

"Hey" Smith whined and stood up.

"Well, I had better take him off your hands then" I chuckled,

"I'm standing right here" Smith groaned.

"Thank you, Luna" Felix bowed again and winked cheekily at Smith.

"Well, I guess I'm coming with you then" Smith grunted and lightly pinched my elbow. Which of course drew another growl from Tobias.

"See you later, Felix" I smiled and waved,

"Bye for now, Luna" he smiled. I inhaled deeply and smiled back. With Gunner around, it's easy to forget sometimes just how gorgeous Felix is. Boyishly handsome with a dark sexiness thrown in. I can probably blame it on the hormones, but he definitely makes me blush. He'll make a she-wolf very happy one day.

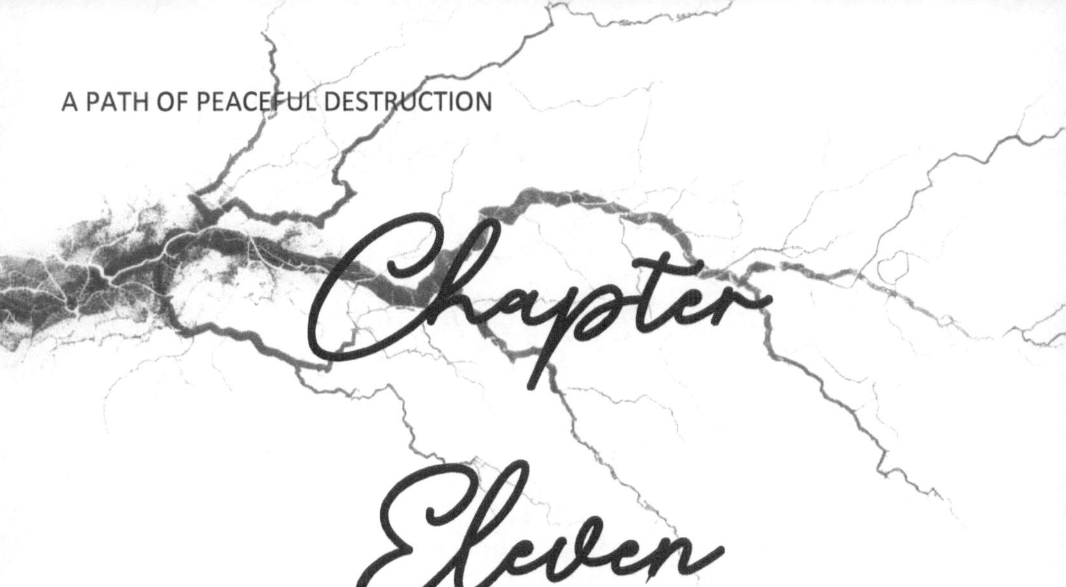

Chapter Eleven

Zelena

Smith and I headed back to the main house, with Tobias close behind. We sat down on the porch swing as Tobias perched himself on the railing opposite us. We sat quietly for a minute or two, with Smith rocking us gently. I studied the side of his face as he looked out over the village. His dark red hair sat in a mess of shaggy curls on top of his head. Some tendrils were long enough to reach his eyes, while others hung down past his neck. Smith's chin was hard and straight, chiselled and defined. His nose was straight and turned up a little at the end. But it only added to his rugged good looks. When Smith smiles, with his broad mouth and perfectly white teeth, it's hard not to smile along with him. He has always had this happy-go-lucky way about him. I kind of envy that part of him.

"Tobias, can we have a few minutes alone please?" I asked and looked up at him,

"No" he grunted back.

"What do you mean no?" I challenged, annoyed.

"I mean I don't trust him" he said firmly.

"What the fuck is that supposed to mean?" Smith growled and shot to his feet. The swing swung back with the force of his movement. I grabbed my belly with one hand and the chain with the other. Tobias stepped forward and looked at me over Smith's shoulder. I put my feet down to stop the swing and carefully stood up. Tobias inched closer to Smith and bared his teeth.

"You're careless" Tobias growled. I stood next to Smith and placed a hand on his shoulder, pulling him back a little.

"Tobias, you're being unreasonable. You know that Smith would never hurt me" I snapped at him,

"Not on purpose. But he is childish and hasty, he doesn't think. That makes him reckless and dangerous" Tobias stated firmly.

"I would die before I let anything hurt her" Smith growled angrily at Tobias. He stepped forward, puffing out his chest and trying to make himself look taller. It was pointless though, Smith is almost half the size of Tobias. I jumped between them and pushed them apart as much as I could. Tobias was growling, Smith was growling back, and I was smack bang in the middle of their display of masculine dominance. Enough of this. Summoning my power, I let it flow through to my hands. With a firm blast, I sent them both sliding backwards.

"Enough!" I yelled.

"Smith, sit down. Tobias, go and cool off" I demanded. Smith growled lowly but complied and sat back down on the swing with a grunt.

"No" Tobias rounded out,

"Smith may be free spirited and a little hasty, but when it counts, he comes through. Every time".

"I. Don't. Trust. Him." Tobias punctuated each word with a rumbling growl.

"I. Don't. Care." I hit back with an angry tone.

"Not that I need to, but I can take care of myself. Now go!". I was pissed. More than pissed, I was infuriated. I get it, he's my guardian, but he also knows that Smith is no threat. I don't understand what he is thinking. Tobias glared at Smith once more before looking down at me. His face was still hard, but he nodded stiffly and walked off towards the fire pit.

"What the fuck is his problem?" Smith grumbled as he took my elbow and I sat back down beside him.

"I have no idea, that is so unlike him" I replied, my eyes following his retreating form. I'll have to have a serious talk with him about boundaries. Maybe try and suss out what is really going on. I know he and Smith like to give each other shit, well more that Smith likes to give him shit. But Tobias never really seemed to mind before. He sure as shit didn't get aggressive over it.

"Whatever. What did you need me for anyways, Princess?" Smith asked. He leaned back on the swing and crossed his arms.

"I just wanted to make sure that you were okay, after Nat, you know?"

"Aww, were you worried about me?" he teased and nudged my shoulder.

"Yes" I answered back with a serious tone. Smith dropped his smile and uncrossed his arms. He was quiet for a minute, so I sat and waited for him to speak.

"It fucking hurt you know. I really do love her. But it wasn't a surprise" he said sullenly.

"What do you mean?"

"Nat had been pulling away for a while. When I think back on it, it started when that fucker first got here. They had a bond from the very beginning, she was just too damn stubborn to let herself feel it". He spoke so evenly and calmly, like he had full control over his emotions. It was surprising, if I was in his place, I would be a wreck.

"You knew she had feelings for him?" I asked him softly,

"I did. I didn't like it, of course. But I have known for a while that it was only a matter of time until she accepted them. I have just been waiting for it" Smith said with a sense of calm finality.

"If you knew all along, why didn't you just end it with her?"

"I didn't want to force her hand. Plus, I still had a little bit of hope"

"Hope?"

"Yeah, that I was wrong".

"Oh, Smith" I said sadly and shifted across the bench until my body was next to his. He lifted his arm and shifted it over my shoulders, so I could let my head rest on his chest.

"Don't worry about me, alright. I'm fine" he said encouragingly.

"I was meant to be the one making you feel better" I said with a chuckle,

"Well mission accomplished, Bestie" he chuckled and squeezed my shoulder.

"I'm sorry about Tobias, he was out of order".

"Nah, don't be, he's just doing his duty. Don't fret on it".

"Well for the record, I don't think that you're reckless, or dangerous. You're my big fluffy puppy dog" I snickered and ruffled his shaggy hair. Smith feigned a growl and nuzzled his mop of hair into my face. When he sat up again, he pulled me close and rested his head on top of mine.

"Thanks, Princess" he said gratefully and pressed his lips to the top of my head.

"You know that I love you, right? You were my first friend. You're my best friend" I told him as I peered up at him. He smiled and shifted his eyes back out to the village.

"I know, I love you too" he smiled and rested his cheek on the top of my head. We sat that way for a while, just listening to the sky rumble. The rain came in fast and hard, quickly soaking the ground. The sky got dark and danced with flashes of lightning. This is going to be one hell of a storm.

"So, what are you going to do now? There aren't that many she-wolves our age around here" I asked as I sat upright and held my belly.

"I'll figure it out, I never had trouble with girls before, so I'm not worried".

"Yes, I heard all about your scandalous ways" I giggled.

"But on a serious note" he said with a deep breath,

"Did you get a load of that Hindi hottie that came with the Luna Eclipse she-wolves?" he crooned. He kicked a leg out, snapped his fingers, and whistled. I huffed and laughed. Of course, he wasn't being serious.

"Venus" I said with a nod of my head. I remember her for sure, she's not the type of girl you see every day. Tall, muscular, hard eyes and feminine features. With her long sleek hair, dark tanned skin and lashes that reach to the sky. Smith was right, she was remarkably beautiful.

"Yeah, Venus. Good Goddess she was something else, wasn't she?" he said with a faraway tone.

"Well, I could arrange for another visit from the Luna Eclipse she-wolves. And put in a request for a specific diplomat" Lunaya said from the bottom of the porch steps.

"Oh, hi" I said with a happy smile,

"What are you doing here?" I asked as I struggled to my feet. Thankfully, Smith pushed from behind to help me the rest of the way up. How could I not be growing the next Alpha-Son, this kid is already twice my size, and it hasn't even left the womb yet.

"Roe invited us for dinner, I hope you don't mind" she said as she and Alyse walked up the steps.

"No, I don't mind". I walked over to them and stopped in front of Lunaya as she let down her umbrella. I was set to give her a hug, then second guess myself, which resulted in me flailing my arms back and forth awkwardly. Alyse chuckled and stepped forward, wrapping her arms around my upper body.

"Hi beautiful, you're positively glowing" she said into my ear,

"Hi Alyse" I smiled. She stepped back and cupped my cheeks, smiling back at me with her whole face. She then let go and stepped back for Lunaya to move forward. I swallowed the hesitation and quickly stepped up to her, wrapping my arms around her waist and leaning my head into her chest. When she didn't immediately hug me back, I went to step away again. Her arms moved to circle around my back and held me to her tightly. The sudden sensation of feeling trapped made me feel stiff, but after a quick second, my body relaxed into her embrace. I found myself sniffing her, breathing in her scent. I listened to her heartbeat thumping and the air expelled from her lungs. It was weird. The feeling of being in her arms. It felt so familiar and safe. Even though I had never held her like this before, it felt like I was home. I could have stayed there for hours. Eventually, Lunaya let me go and stepped back. She wiped freshly fallen tears from her cheeks and sniffled. Alyse moved to her side and sniffled as well.

"Sorry, I don't mean to be all emotional" Lunaya chuckled awkwardly.

"I just… I never thought I would get to hold you in my arms again" she said sadly with a forced half smile. Tears started to well in my eyes as I gazed at her. I can see traces of myself in her features. The shape of her eyes and the curve of her chin. We have some similarities, here and there, but not as many as I imagined. When I was a child, I pictured her often. I thought of what she looked like, the shape of her smile and the sound of her laugh. I wondered what kind of perfume she would wear and the colour of her eyes. I pictured her in a thousand different ways. But now that I'm looking at her beautiful face, my imagination never did her justice.

"I'm sorry that happened to you" I said sadly,

"Oh, Sweetheart, you have nothing to be sorry for" Lunaya said as she stepped forward and took my hands.

"If anything, it's me that should apologise. But I'm afraid there aren't enough hours in the day to express how truly sorry I am. I should have never given up. I should have fought harder for you".

"No. You really don't have to. I'm sorry for what I said to you. It was wrong of me and not at all warranted" I said with a shake of my head.

"You were right to say what you did. Never apologise for feeling the way you feel" she replied and fondly stroked my cheek,

"But I need you to know that I was wrong. I know you tried. You did your best. You fought hard and you gave up so many years of your life. I'm sorry that I made you feel like it wasn't enough. My childhood, the attack on your village and the death of my father, none of that was your fault" I told her earnestly. Lunaya pulled me into her arms once again and held my head to her chest.

"Goddess bless you" she cried.

"I'm so sorry to interrupt" Roe's voice came from the door. Lunaya let me go and we both stepped back from each other, each of us wiping the fresh tears from our face. I turned to smile at Roe, who was looking back at me with love and pride shining in her eyes.

"Dinner is on, ladies" she said and looked at each of us,

"And Smith" she said smiling at him.

"Thank you, we're coming" I said back. I went to walk for the door when Lunaya took my hand again.

"Zelena, when you have some time, there are some things that we really need to talk about" Lunaya said urgently. I was actually a little shocked by the alarm in her voice.

"Okay, sure. Tomorrow?" I said slowly,

"Yes tomorrow, I'll come by after breakfast" she said with a shallow exhale. Alyse took her hand and looked up at her proudly. I don't like this, I think this may be something big. Great. Now I feel nauseous.

"Come on, you need to eat, you look green" Smith laughed and wrapped his arm around my shoulders. We went into the dining room to sit and wait for the others. Lunaya and Alyse sat across from me, leaving the head of the table for Gunner and the two seats to their right for Roe and Lupus. As Smith sat down at my right, the place that Tobias would usually take, Lupus came in. He smiled and greeted me with a kiss on the cheek before greeting Lunaya, Alyse and Smith. A minute later Gunner came in with

Felix hot on his heels. I kissed Gunner before he sat down and then I smiled at Felix. The conversation heated up all around me. I sat back in my chair, closed my eyes and rubbed my belly as I listened to the happy voices. A minute later Tobias entered, I opened my eyes and peered at him. He was glaring at Smith as Smith was talking animatedly with Lunaya and Alyse.

Let it go, please

I pleaded with him through our bond. He visibly clenched his teeth, fighting the growl that was begging to be let out. The room seemed to get quiet as everyone looked from Tobias to Smith. Tobias's body appeared to shudder with rage. He looked at me and nodded once before taking a seat next to Felix. In came Nat, dragging Alpha Lace behind her by the hand. She said hello to Gunner as Lace stood tall and still behind her. I glanced at Smith who was watching them closely. Smith stood up and I grabbed at his wrist in a panic. He patted my hand and smiled at me with a nod, mouthing the words 'It's okay'. He stepped around my chair and walked over to Alpha Lace. Gunner tensed as soon as he saw Smith in front of the Alpha. I held my breath, ready for fists to start flying. The whole room was quiet, all of us watching what Smith was going to do next. Nat placed herself between the two of them, with her hands behind her back, holding onto Lace's shirt. Smith took a deep breath and smiled, then held out his hand for Alpha Lace. Nat's eyes went wide and Lace stepped forward, taking Smith's hand. After a second Lace pulled Smith forward and pressed his forehead to Smith's. Sevasmo. That's a good sign. Smith's mouth moved as he whispered something to Lace. Lace laughed and stood up straight, letting Smith go. He patted Smith on the shoulder and pulled Nat to his side, placing a kiss on her cheek.

"You don't have to worry about that" Lace chuckled. Smith turned and came back to his seat beside me, as Nat and Lace went to sit at the other end of the table. Nat grabbed Lace's face and spread kisses over his cheeks and lips. I turned to Smith and leaned into his ear.

"What did you say to him?" I asked in a whisper,

"I told him that if he hurts her, I will kill him" he answered with a shrug. I blurted out a snorted laugh and quickly covered my mouth with my hand. The image of Smith trying to knock Alpha Lace over, hitting his fists against his chest, like a toddler hitting their parent filled my head. Smith is more than capable of hurting someone, just probably not a Were like Alpha Lace.

"What?" Smith grumbled and frowned at me,

"Nothing. That was a really nice thing you did" I told him proudly. He shrugged again and flicked my nose with his finger, "I'd do it for you too".

"And that's why we love you" I beamed up at him. Once again, the conversation picked up, filling the room with chatter. Not long later, Roe and a few she-wolves brought out the food. I sat and watched, eating quietly as the rest of the table laughed and joked and talked with each other. Gunner, as per usual, would occasionally brush my cheek with his fingers, or lean over and whisper that he loves me, or squeeze my knee, or rub my belly. He never went more than a few minutes without touching me in some way. It was the little things that he did without realising, the small displays of love and affection, that meant the world to me. The feeling of joy and happiness that Gunner and everyone else at this table instil in me still feels so foreign. There are times when I wonder if I deserve this. To be this happy, to have these people at my side. They are my family, my world, and I love them all.

The house shook with thunder from the storm outside, meaning no fire and pack stories tonight. Normally we would just brush it off and tough it out, but this storm was a little too rough. Probably for the best, because I'm beat. I ate my fill, as did everyone else. The laughter and conversation flowed effortlessly around the table. It was only when Gunner shook my arm gently, did I realise I had dozed off. I looked up to see multiple sets of eyes gazing back at me with amusement and pity.

"Come on, my Love, let's get you to bed" he whispered into my ear as he started to pick me up from my chair. I didn't fight him on it, I was too tired. A chorus of 'goodnights' and 'sleep tights' sang out to me as Gunner carried me from the room. We headed upstairs and straight to the ensuite bathroom. Gunner placed me down on the toilet seat and turned on the shower to warm up. He helped me remove my shirt and released my hair from the hair tie. It fell over my face and down my back, I could probably use a haircut. It was getting very long and kept growing much faster than it used to. I suppose that would make sense. Now that it was no longer being used as a handle to drag me around the house, being ripped straight from the roots, it's got an actual chance to grow out. Funny how quickly your body can flourish in a safe and happier environment.

I sat quietly and stared blankly at Gunner's beautiful face as he brushed my hair, and then continued to undress me. Taking care of me like I was a helpless child. Only he didn't see me that way. He looked at me with more love and adoration than anyone else ever had. This was just Gunner, doing his best to take care of me. And I love him for it. It was a tender moment, one that didn't need words.

Once my sandals and shorts were off, he carried us into the shower and slowly sat down on the floor under the stream of hot water. With me in his lap, he lathered his hands in soap and washed my body, then moved onto my hair. I sat with my legs crossed between Gunner's legs. As he massaged the conditioner into my scalp, he started to sing,

"In the dark of the night, not a star in the sky. I can feel your love pull against the tide. And I see you shining bright like a lighthouse. And the winds got the water running wild. But I'll swim to you, swim for my life. And I pray that I'll make it before the night's up. I won't let you go, I feel it in my bones. No matter where I go, you're where my heart belongs. All I know, I'll follow every road, 'til I find my way back home. You're where my heart, you're where my heart, You're where my heart belongs" his smooth voice carried around the tiled corner of the shower cubicle. I hadn't heard Gunner sing before, I wouldn't have guessed he could sing like that. I sighed and leaned back into his chest.

"That was really beautiful. I didn't know you could sing" I said with a yawn,

"That's because I don't sing. Not unless I'm in the shower" he answered with a chuckle. He wrapped his long arms around my waist, resting his hand on my round belly and kept singing softly.

"I belong right here in your open arms. The world can try to tear us apart, but our love will guide us home like a lighthouse. Walk a thousand miles in the pouring rain, and a million years couldn't change the way, the way I feel, I feel about you right now".

Tears welled in my eyes at the hidden meaning behind the words. Gunner is leaving, but I'll bring him home again.

"What song is that?" I asked, swallowing a ball of emotion.

"It's Calum Scott" he answered,
"The song is called Lighthouse". He nuzzled into the crook of my neck and licked a line of water that was dripping down my skin.
"You're my lighthouse, Baby. And I'm coming back home to you" he whispered.
"You better" I whispered back and turned around in his lap. I laid my head on his shoulder and closed my eyes as the water ran over my face. Gunner rubbed his hand slowly over my belly as he cradled me against him.
"I won't let you go, I feel it in my bones. No matter where I go, you're where my heart belongs" Gunner started to sing softly again. With his smooth velvety voice, the warmth of the water and the feel of his heartbeat under my cheek, I was easily lulled into a comfortable sleep. I woke again as Gunner laid me on the bed, wrapped in a towel. I sat up and went to stand to put some clothes on, Gunner pushed gently on my shoulder and kissed the top of my head.
"I'll do it, you rest" he whispered and held one of his t-shirts out in front of me. I smiled and held my arms up so he could slip it over my head. He then pulled a pair of underpants up my legs, I lifted my hips so that he could pull them into place. I grabbed his pillow and curled myself around it, snuggling into it and breathing in his scent. The bed dipped behind me, and Gunner crawled across the mattress. He pulled me back flush against his chest and wrapped his arms around me. I was out in seconds.

~

A shiver ran down my spine, the room felt cold. I pulled the blanket tighter around my shoulders and curled myself into a ball. A while later, maybe minutes, maybe hours, I was in that very first stage of light sleep. I knew I was sleeping, but I also knew I wasn't fully asleep. I felt restless and fitful. I tried shifting back a little, seeking out Gunner's body heat. More time passed and my body started to ache. My chest squeezed and my back pulled taught. I tried turning and rolling around, trying to find a more comfortable position. Nothing helped to alleviate the ache. A while later, I reached out and snatched Gunner's pillow away. If I was too uncomfortable to sleep, then he could be too. I snuggled into it, breathing in his scent. That seemed to do the trick, and I drifted off again.

I opened my eyes, they were still sore and achy from exhaustion. That poor excuse of sleep did nothing to revitalize my depleted energy. I rolled onto my back and took a deep breath. My chest ached. Like tight rope was tied around my heart, restricting its regular beating pattern. I rubbed at my chest and took another deep breath. It's probably indigestion. As I pulled in a lungful of air, the realisation washed over me in an icy cold wave.

His scent wasn't as strong as it should be. The room wasn't as warm as it usually is. The bed felt colder than normal. I didn't need to look at the empty space beside me to know that he was gone. I could feel it. The hollowness, the emptiness, it was hard to ignore. Pain radiated through my body as a deep set and torturous sorrow smothered my heart. I squeezed my eyes tight and gripped the sides of my head. The pain was too much, it was flowing through me like sharp shards of ice, cutting through my veins. I knew it was coming, I knew he was leaving. But I wasn't ready for it. My skin prickled and dizziness flooded my head. I can't hold it. I tossed my head back and cried out into the air. The furniture around the room burst into tiny pieces. The glass of the window shattered, turning to dust. The walls creaked and groaned with the force of my power flying out from within me. The sound from my mouth felt like nothing I had ever heard before. I wasn't even sure that it came from my body. The high-pitched whistling wail sounded otherworldly, ghostly even. The pain and sorrow rolled out of me in uncontainable waves. My head was spinning, and it was like the air was being sucked from my lungs.

A pair of gigantic brown arms slammed around my tiny frame. It was like he had wrapped me in a protective blanket, shielding me from the outside world, warding off the fear and the pain. The sound pouring from my open mouth stopped, and the air filtered back into my lungs. My body was as heavy as my head was light and floaty. I could no longer recognise the room I was in. It was a mess of dust and debris. Dark spots danced across my vision as I inhaled a sharp full breath. I gave myself over to the feeling of emptiness, letting my body go limp in the arms of my guardian. My head dropped back, and I looked up into Tobias' deep brown orbs. He stared down at me with a look of fear and worry that I had never seen on his face before. That look, that terrified look, it was the last thing I saw before it all went black.

Chapter Twelve

Whiskey

It was a small little town, spread out over a vast amount of land. However, the constant traffic and movement made it feel closed in and busy. People were actively moving around the streets, going in and out of buildings. All of them, just going about their day as if it was any other normal day. Little did they know there was danger hiding among them. I tried to blend in as much as I could, I played myself off like a curious tourist. However, I think I stuck out like a sore thumb. I feel awkward around civilians. Their deluded sense of freedom, and their complete obliviousness to the horrors of the world around them, it infuriates me. I don't want to be here any longer than I need to be. The longer I stay, the more risk there is of being noticed. And attention is not something I need. What I do need is a boat.

I made my way towards the water's edge. The buildings became more spread out and isolated the closer to the water I got. That worked to my advantage. Down by the shore, I found a few boats, all of which were anchored far up on the beach. I am strong and could probably drag one down on my own. But there is no telling how much damage the rocks would cause to the boat. Plus, the point is to be inconspicuous. A small woman pulling a boat to the water on her own is far from blending in. No. I need to find a boat already in the water. I strolled along the water's edge, pretending to pick up shells and throw rocks in the water. Thanks to my shorter than average stature, to anyone who may have been watching, I would look like a board kid. But I was searching, scanning the waters both close in, and further out, trying to find an appropriate vessel. Far out on the horizon, I spotted movement. It was a smaller looking fishing trawler, probably privately owned. It would be perfect.

I found a place out of sight to wait. I kept my eye on the boat as it slowly moved across the top of the water. A few hours off sunset, the boat started coming back in. I moved along the shoreline, in line with the boat, until it docked at a small wooden jetty. I watched as they unloaded a few buckets of fish and a smaller whale. I wonder if this is legal. Actually, I don't care. I only want the boat. They can get back to hunting whatever it is they want after I'm gone. After a few more hours, they started to leave. Another hour later and they were all gone, except for just one man. I waited a little longer, but he didn't leave. I'm out of patience and one human is an acceptable disturbance to the plan.

I hid my bag and the document case in a dried out sea log and then kicked off my shoes. As expected, the water was freezing. I waded in until I was waist deep and lowered myself the rest of the way in. I need to be quiet so as to not raise alarm, and I need to be invisible. I swam further out so that I could approach from the rear of the vessel. I purposefully kept my arms and legs under the water, to one, stop from getting cold in the night air, and two, not make any splashing sounds. I swam up to the boat and circled around twice. I had only been in the water for roughly thirty minutes, but the cold was starting to bother me. I know I can last another two to three hours or so, but my fingers won't be very useful if I wait too long. I floated up to the rear of the boat and extended my nails. Using my talons as anchors, I climbed up the side of the boat and quietly plopped on the deck. I crouched down and scanned the area. There was a small hutch door in the middle of the deck, it was open, and a dim light was shining from inside it. Clattering and light banging sounds were echoing from deep inside the hull, indicating that was where the remaining man was located. Keeping light on my feet, I did a quick check of the upper deck and the bridge. There was no one else here, just the man down below. I snuck down the stairs and followed the sounds of clattering and scraping. Whatever he was doing, he was not being gentle. I found him lying on his back with his head inside a cabinet. He was working on some kind of plumbing, whilst swearing like he was making money out of it.

I like this man, he was funny. He talked to himself as he worked on the pipes. Do civilians normally talk to themselves? The only humans I've dealt with were hunters. So not your average everyday person. Which means I don't exactly have anything to compare them to. In all my travels, I've steered clear of people as much as I could. There were rare occasions where I was forced to interact with them. Places like hotels, restaurants, airports. But outside of them serving me in some manner, I never just talked with one casually.

I hid silently for a moment watching the strange man work. He smelt of salt water and frustration. I have never heard someone curse so much. Even the brutes I grew up around didn't curse this much. I found this old man fascinating. It was a pity he had to die. He threw his tool across the floor in frustration, and it came to land just in front of my hiding place. As he got up off the floor, wiping his greased hands on his faded and well-worn overalls, he spotted the tool on the ground. Then he spotted me standing above it.

"Kakogo cherta ty zdes' delayesh'?" (What the hell are you doing here?) he shouted angrily,

"Soydi s moyey lodki" (Get off my boat). He waved his hand at me and stomped over to where I stood. The old man had grey curly hair and a thick bushy grey beard to match. The dark skin around his slanted eyes was thick with wrinkles and looked like worn leather. I could tell he had worked hard for all of his life.

"YA skazal uyti" (I said leave) the man shouted and stood in front of me. He had his chest puffed out and his arms rigid at his sides. Due to how much taller he was, he looked down his nose at me with an angry scowl. I suppose he was trying to intimidate or scare me off. Unfortunately for him, he didn't know who I was. I snapped my hand forward and tightly wrapped my fingers around his neck. Because of how tall he was, I had to lift my arm high over my head in order to lift him off the ground. His eyes went wide with shock, and he grabbed both hands around my wrist, trying to pull my grip free from his neck. His legs were flailing around under him, like he was looking for something to stand on, or trying to find his footing. It was a little amusing.

"Pomoshch'!" (Help!) he screamed at the top of his lungs. I put my finger over my mouth and shook my head,

"Shh" I hissed and smiled wickedly up at him,

"Chto ty?" (What are you?) he choked out, as he tried to pull at my grip again.

"Smert'" (Death) I answered him. He gasped and kicked his legs wildly. I pushed my talons through the tips of my fingers and buried them into the soft flesh of his neck. His warm blood spilled over my fingers and ran down my arm. He opened his mouth wide like he was about to scream, and I tightened my grip. I felt his windpipe crunch under my fingers. His mouth was still wide open, but no sound was coming out. His eyes turned bloodshot, and a trickle of blood ran down his chin. After a few seconds, he stopped kicking and the spark of life left his eyes. I let his body drop to the floor with a heavy thud. I stood over him and listened carefully for signs of a heartbeat. He was dead.

I dragged the fisherman's body back up to the deck and pushed him over the railing. He splashed into the water and bobbed there for a minute before sinking under the surface and out of sight. I went back down to the hull and made sure that the things he was working on looked alright. I know a lot of things, but boats aren't exactly my forte. The pipes were all clean and attached to one another. Nothing looked out of place, at least not to my untrained eye. I suppose I'll just have to see how I go. I headed up to the bridge and turned the engine over. It spluttered but kicked to life without issue. I guess that human was good at fixing boats. I ran back to shore to collect my bag and the map. I dropped them in the bridge and then pulled in the anchor and untied the ropes from the jetty, and away we went.

The instruments were basic and easy to read and understand. I set the course and let the boat do the rest of the work. I was still wet and also hungry, so I decided to check out the cabin. I found some dry clothes in a cupboard, they smelt like fishy sea water, mixed with an old man smell, but they were better than being wet. So, I swallowed my distaste and pulled them on. It was a good decision. The jumper was very big on my slight frame. It came down to just above my knees and the sleeves went far past my hands, but it was cozy, like wearing a giant woollen blanket. I hung up my clothes to dry and went in search of food. I struck gold in the gally. Cupboards filled with tinned fish, packet soup and crackers. Along with a chocolate bar, I also snagged two bottles of booze. A half empty bottle of Praskoveyskiy Whiskey and an unopened bottle of premium Russian Vodka. Russia may have birthed some of the most brutal supernatural hunters I have ever come across, but they also birthed some of the best vodka I have ever tasted.

The trip across the water was slow and incredibly boring. The water was calm, thankfully. But the boat was fucking slow. I was only able to push it up to nine knots before I thought it was going to fall apart. Which meant I was in for a long night. I took a nap, I skimmed through a book I found, I tinkered with the pipes that the old man was working on, and I downed what was left in the whiskey bottle. When I laid back down on the cot I found in the hull, I was pretty well tipsy. The buzz wouldn't last long, but long enough to knock me out for another short sleep. I closed my eyes and drifted off, only to relive the same dream that has taunted me all my life.

~

She was back. Just like always. She stood before my small and beaten body, looking down at me. She looks just like me, or like I did as a child. Her mouth was moving as per usual. She was talking to me, but she didn't make a sound. I strained my hearing trying to hear her words, but there was nothing. I stood up slowly, and as I rose, I grew. I went from being a small broken child to the strong woman I am today. Just like a mirror image, the me in front of me changed as well. She grew as I did. I watched her body change, and get taller and more womanly. I watched her face grow, chubby cheeks morphed into a slim face with big eyes. But when she stopped aging, she looked back at me and smiled. She moved her hands down and placed them over her swollen stomach. She was pregnant. I looked down at my own stomach, and I was pregnant. This had never happened before. How could I be pregnant? That's not possible. I want to wake up now. The other me stepped forward and smiled softly at me. She moved her hand and placed it over mine. Her mouth moved as she spoke, but again, she made no sound. I was becoming more and more frustrated. Why can't I hear her? Other me lifted her hand and placed it on my cheek. The touch was soft, and calming, it felt familiar. I blinked and we were no longer standing in my old frozen cell. We were outside, but it was snowing. There was snow all around us, everything was white. The other me looked to her left and I followed her line of sight. Buried in the snow beside us was a crib. As I peered into the crib, I saw two babies. Fat little babies, holding hands and smiling up at us. This dream has become something else completely. Why am I dreaming about babies? Why am I pregnant? This is fucked up. Other me stepped up to the crib and peered down at the chubby little babies. I felt compelled to follow her, and so I did. I stood at her side, and she took my hand. I felt it. I know that I'm dreaming, but I can feel her hand in mine. I can feel the warmth and the smoothness of her skin. I can actually feel her, for real.

~

I shot up and looked down at my stomach. It was back to normal, flat, with no signs of growing life. Thank fuck for that. I lifted my hand and looked it over. It was like I could still feel my mirrored self holding it. Her fingers pressed into my hand and the warmth left behind, it was all too real. What the actual fuck was that about. I have dreamt about myself for as long as I can remember. But it was always the same, another me talked but I could never hear it. This was something else entirely. My body was shaking, and I felt wired. This dream rattled me, more than anything else ever has. All of the anxiety and frustration I have been feeling over the past few days just increased tenfold. I don't understand what is happening.

There has only ever been one other time that I felt this out of control. I may have a temper, and I am definitely no pillar of self-control. But I always knew what I was doing and why. When I got angry and when I lashed out, I could always pull it back to a single moment, the reason or the cause of my outburst was never unknown. But this. This dream, this unnerving feeling that I have. I can't trace it to any one thing. It is making me question myself. And I swore to never do that again.

Eighteen months ago.

If you asked me two years ago how I thought my life would turn out, this was definitely not it. I didn't think it was possible to stray this far from my training. I was raised a certain way, I was taught to think and do things a certain way. I didn't think it was possible to push that part of me so far to the side. That part of me feels like a whole other life ago now. And it is all because of Saxton. I have no idea why I didn't kill him, or at the very least, leave him hanging from those chains in the dungeon. He was unlike any beast I had come across. I was drawn to him in a way I have never felt with another soul. It's been nearly six months and the feeling hasn't lessened. If anything, it is getting worse. I worry about him. When we run through a new compound, I am more focused on him and if he is okay then I am on me and what I am doing. He has become the most dangerous of distractions. But I can't give him up.

"Tesoro" his smooth and creamy voice called me. I wrinkled my nose and walked over to him,

"Don't call me that" I hissed up at him as I walked past. As much as I enjoy hearing it. As much as my heart flutters each time I hear him call me by my given pet name, I can't let it show.

"Do you prefer I call you Stellina?" he crooned and ran his fingers up my arm. I shivered and stopped walking. My skin was prickling with a thousand needles over the path his finger had traced. My body was alight with a burning desire. I wanted him to call me anything he wanted, as long as he was mine. I wanted his hands on my body, and his lips against mine. I wanted to smell him, taste him, feel him. I wanted him. But it could never happen. I turned to face him and glared the best glare I could muster.

"I want you to call me by my name. Whiskey" I grunted. He smiled and stepped closer to me. One arm came around my lower back and he pulled me into him. The other hand came up to slowly push some stray hair behind my ear. He angled his head down so that his mouth was hovering not far above my own. Even over the stench of gunpowder and smoke, I could still smell him. The scent of dark chocolate and cherries. It's intoxicating.

"You are too beautiful to be called something as horrid as Whiskey. You are a treasure, and so I will call you as such" he said softly in a low and seductive tone. His sweet breath hit my face and I gulped. My heart thundered in my chest and my stomach turned in on itself. My breath caught in my throat, and I was frozen. Saxton has never stopped trying to win me over. Since the day I freed him and took him away from that place, he has tried to win my affection. Little does he know it is a losing battle. I have no love to give. No affection, kindness or attention. I have nothing to give him. Nothing but pain and death. I gazed into his deep ocean filled eyes. He looked back at me with all he had. He looked at me like he was ready to jump on a pyre and burn himself alive, just to make me smile. His thick long lashes blinked and fluttered over his perfect caramel skin. The small mole on the corner of his chin, his wide set mouth with deliciously plumped lips. The way his muscles tensed and twitched when they rubbed against mine. The scent of his arousal wrapped around me, lulling me into a sexual haze of need and desire. The spot between my legs throbbed and I forgot how to breathe. The sound of an explosion from the other side of the building snapped me out of the hypnosis he had me under.

"Let's move" I choked out after a beat and pushed him away from me. The corner of his lip twitched up from a suppressed growl. And he curled his hands into fists. His face was pinched and tight, but he offered a forced smile and nodded his head.

"After you, Tesoro" Saxton said and held his arm forward for me to lead the way. I stepped over the bodies littering the ground and made my way to the large wooden door. I planted my feet, took a deep breath and held out my hands. Summoning the power, and letting it roll through me, it made me lightheaded. But the feeling of absolute power was addictive and thrilling. I loved using it. The door flew open, and half fell off its hinges. It hung on by one screw at the top of the heavy door and swung back and forth from the force of the blow.

I pulled my blades from their holders and walked through the door, with very little care as to what could be on the other side. The courtyard was filled with smoke and rubble. Small fires were still burning around the space in amongst the debris and dead bodies. The homemade bombs we made fulfilled their purpose perfectly. I counted eight bodies in the first quick sweep. I moved further into the courtyard, scanning the area for any other signs of life. The shout was the first thing I heard, followed closely by the explosion. Then I was knocked to the ground. As I fell, my head hit hard against some scattered rubble. Everything went black after that.

As I lay on the ground, trying to regather my mind, I could hear shouting and more gunfire. I tried to lift my head, but each time I moved, my body screamed back in pain. Pain is something I was used to. I was able to shift myself so that I was sitting up, leaning against a large piece of concrete. I grabbed at the spot on my head that hit the ground. My warm blood was seeping down my face

and getting into my eyes. I wiped it away and tried to peer through the blurriness and the pain. I followed the sounds of the shouting and was able to make out a few shapes. People shapes. But their attention wasn't on me. I wiped away the fresh stream of blood and looked to where they were focussing. It was Saxton, or Saxton's wolf. He had his jaws buried into the neck and shoulder of one of the hunters, he was shaking his head furiously as the man screamed in pain. The other men were lining up their guns and aiming at Saxton. A feeling of fear filled my entire being. In a split second, I wanted to scream, cry, vomit and run, all at the same time. But that's not who I am. It only took half a second to form the plan in my mind. The two men were standing directly in front of a wall that had been hit by one of the bombs. The large stone bricks were crumbling and ready to fall. All they needed was a push. That is what I gave them. I waved my hand out towards the wall, letting the wind flow from my fingers. The pain was excruciating, but I had no choice. I couldn't let Saxton die.
It wasn't enough, the bricks weren't moving, I was too weak. I grasped at the wound on my head, for some reason, I thought that would help. I screamed through the pain and summoned the power I needed. Thin wisps of black smoke curled around my fingers, as they have done many times before. But this time they slithered further down my arm and up over my shoulder. My body felt icy cold and filled with more power than I had summoned before. The large stone bricks broke apart and showered over the hunters, burying them beneath the heavy cascade of stones. My pain was gone, the hunters were dead, and Saxton was safe. I pushed myself off the ground and turned to see Saxton's wolf trotting over to me. He nuzzled his head into my chest and neck and sniffed at the blood that was dripping down from my head. He began to lick the blood off my chest and neck and slowly moved his way up to the area of the wound. It was a strange sensation. But I liked it, so I let him. I twisted my fingers through his long shaggy grey fur as he cleaned the blood from my face. As I played with his fur, I felt something sticky and matted into the hair. I lifted my hand and it was now covered in thick blood. Saxton's blood. He was bleeding, pretty badly. I looked closer and saw the large open wound on his shoulder. Saxton was licking at the cut on my head, taking care of me. As I

looked at the open wound on his shoulder, I felt compelled to do the same. I leaned forward and licked my tongue over his wound. I have tasted blood before. In fact, I've lost count of how many different people's blood I have tasted. But this was different. This act felt so intimate. I could always taste the fear in the blood of the ones I killed. But Saxton held no fear towards me, he tasted like what I imagine is love and devotion. Though, I couldn't be sure. I have never felt those feelings from another. Not directed at me anyway. Saxton rested his large wolf head on my shoulder as I moved my tongue over his wound. He whimpered but didn't pull away. The more of him I tasted. The more of him I wanted. Soon his whimpers turned into something more like a low purring. The sound vibrated through me, making me shiver.

Tesoro

Saxton said softly. I reared my head back away from him and looked into his deep blue eyes. Eyes that looked back at me from his wolf form. How did he speak to me when he was still an animal?

"What did you say?" I snapped. He nuzzled into me again and growled lowly. Again, the sound hit me like a wave of heat and need. I clenched my thighs together and bit down on my lower lip.

You are mine now, Tesoro

He spoke again. But the sound didn't come through my ears. It originated in my head. How was that possible? Does Saxton have a power? Or is this another one of mine that has manifested? Could I hear thoughts now? I pushed his huge head away and stared at him.

"Change back" I commanded of him. He growled and huffed but stepped backwards, he turned his head to the side and the crunching and snapping of his bones sounded. Then he stood before me. Naked and human. My eyes rolled over his bare muscular body hungrily. I bit down on my lip and pressed my extended talons into the palms of my hands. Each ripple of skin, every mark, and every scar, I wanted to bite into all of it. My eyes moved lower to the manhood between his legs. I had seen him naked many times before, but I never felt this much need to be naked with him. Like he knew I was staring at it, his dick twitched and slowly rose, coming to life and staring back at me.

Tesoro

His voice sounded in my head again. I looked up at him and he was staring at me intently, waiting for me to do or say something. "How did you do that?" I questioned,

"Do what, Love?" he answered and stepped towards me. I stepped back and held my hands out, indicating for him to stop.

"How did you speak into my head?". He jolted to a stop and tilted his head slightly. He was confused, but of what?

"I flashed you" he answered like it was common knowledge,

"What is that? You have never had this power before now, what has changed?" I demanded. I was trying to mask my desperate desire for him with anger. It wasn't working.

"It is not a power, Tesoro. It is just a flash, it's how we talk to each other".

"No one has ever spoken inside my brain before" I snapped,

"You have not been Mated before, Mi Amore" he said seductively and moved closer to me again. Mated. Did he say Mated? I am human, humans and Weres don't Mate. What is he talking about? "Mated?" I demanded.

"You took my blood, right after I took yours" he chuckled and grabbed hold of my waist,

"That's usually how it works, Tesoro" he cooed and went to press his lips to my neck, but I pushed against his chest so that I could look at him.

"How what works, Saxton? What did you do?" I asked him angrily. This back and forth, sexual teasing and mind games, it was boiling my blood. And not in a good way.

"I didn't do anything" he answered me gruffly. He stepped back and looked down at me with furrowed brows.

"I didn't force you to take my blood, you chose to do that on your own. You know how I feel about you. I've been clear with that. Why are you acting like I made you do this?". He was upset, that was obvious. But I was lost trying to wrap my head around what he was telling me. We're Mated now? That was how they did it, by drinking each other's blood like vampires. First off, gross. And second thing, I'm not a Were, how can I be Mated.

"I can't have a Mate" I said softly. I wasn't saying it to him exactly, just saying it out loud in general. He was shocked by it anyway.

"What are you talking about, Tesoro, any Were can have a Mate" he said and gripped my hips once again. He pulled me into his body and pressed himself against me. The warmth of his skin, his scent of cherries, it was dizzying. And I wanted more. But not yet. "I'm not a Were" I whispered.

Present Day.
I rolled over on the cot and pressed my nails into the palm of my hands. The sting is always grounding. I swallowed the ball of emotion in my throat and dug my nails in deeper. One tear, one lash. What a pointless memory. I was weak and driven by emotion. I pushed all of my training and everything I worked for to the side. And for what? For a filthy beast that played me like a violin, made me think I could believe in magical fairy tales. I was a fool. But never again.

Chapter Thirteen

Whiskey

I headed back to the top deck and peered out into the darkness. The air coming off the water was cold, and I liked it. The icy freshness seeped into my skin, chilling my bones. My skin prickled with goosebumps, and a shiver ran down my back. I love that feeling. It tickles at my dark, frozen heart. I knew I was getting close, I could sense it. Perhaps an hour out now, maybe less. And just in time. Dark storm clouds were rolling across the sky, coming from the direction of the land. Hopefully, I can dock before they hit.

The waves were bashing against the sides of the fishing boat, throwing it all around the place. The metal screamed under the pressure of the water. The land was right there, I could see it through the pouring rain, I just couldn't manoeuvre the stupid boat through the storm to reach the shore. Fuck it. I collected my bag, shoving my clothes and shoes back inside it. I then put the bag, and the document case, into a watertight bag that I found in the cabin. With some extra rope I found, I tied the bag to my chest, securing it tightly around my body. Back on deck, I clumsily climbed onto the railing, gripping hold of the ropes, careful not to fall overboard prematurely. I could see the line of the land on the horizon as the boat dipped up and down over the tremendous waves. I can make it easily. I dived into the water, going deep under the swell. I kicked my legs hard, moving my arms in synchrony, to propel myself through the freezing waters.

Another helpful aspect of being able to manipulate the air, I can hold my breath for a very long time.

I had to come up for air and get my bearings only four times. Each time, I was smashed around by the rough water. If I were any other regular human, I would have drowned in a matter of minutes. The current was strong, trying to drag me back out into the open water. But I am stronger. When I did finally pull my waterlogged body up the beach, I was exhausted. I untied the bag from my chest and flopped my limp body onto the sand. My chest was heaving up and down, and my heart was racing. The rain poured down on me and I opened my mouth, drinking it in. The lightning flashed across the sky, lighting up the dark clouds. I stood up on my tired, shaky legs. The air felt heavy, thick even. At first, I thought it was just the effects of the storm. But that wasn't it. I curled my toes into the sand, burying my feet into the earth. The ground itself felt different. It was almost like it was flowing with a subtle electricity. I couldn't make sense of it.

I knew where I was going next. Thankfully, I set out all my possible paths back on the boat. Which is good, I wouldn't want to risk damage to the map in this storm. The heaviness in the atmosphere surrounded me, filled me, pushed at me. I knew I was headed East. I wanted to cross into Canada from the Northern mountains, then sweep across to find the Inuit Packs in the Northwest Territories, Nunavut and Qikiqtaaluk Region, before skipping over to Greenland. But that doesn't feel like the right plan anymore. Blame it on the storm or my boredom, but I think I should cross into Canada from the Southeast part of Alaska. The mountains there would be prime ground for dogs. I don't know what it is, but North just doesn't feel like the way to go anymore. And I know what happened last time I ignored my instincts. I won't make that mistake again.

Sixteen months ago.

I don't like this. It doesn't feel right. It goes against everything I know. I was made to hunt werewolves, I don't associate with them casually. I certainly don't live with them. Saxton was dead set on going back to his pack land. I don't know why. He's been away from them for what, a month or two short of a year? Why couldn't he just stay gone. He says it was unfair for them to keep thinking that he was dead. Says that he needed to tell his family that he's okay. If the big dumb beast didn't have me so entranced by him, I would have just ditched him. Maybe I still should. I should let him stay here with his family of mutts, and then I can continue on alone. Fuck, I want too. I just can't bring myself to abandon him. I was sitting off to the side on my own, watching the festivities underway around me. Saxton's pack was on the larger side. Roughly two hundred or so. Saxton's family is huge as well, not just his pack members, but his actual family. Siblings, cousins, uncles and aunties. There are so many of them, and they haven't left his side since we got here. We're onto day four of celebrations, and I am at my wits' end. It's good, everything is fine. Saxton is clearly very popular, and his pack are just really happy to see him back again. But if I have to watch one more fucking horny bitch rub up against him, I will kill something.

Saxton's mother made her way over to where I was sitting and plonked herself down next to me. She absolutely stunk of alcohol and was swaying in her seat. She's a pretty she-wolf. Tall like Saxton and with the same bright blue eyes. She was muscular for a female, but Saxton did say that she was a warrior like his father.

"I can't believe my little boy has a Mate" she slurred and draped her arm over my shoulders.

"He may be my eldest, but he is still my baby boy, you know?".

I leaned away from her as she spoke right up in my face. I could feel the saliva hitting my cheek as it flew from her mouth, and I could basically taste the wine on her breath. She pulled me back to her and grabbed my chin. A low growl rumbled through my chest at her harsh fingers touching me.

"You better be good to him. I may be getting up there in years, but I can still kick around a little girl like you. Look at you, you're so tiny" Pia laughed and squeezed my chin. I pulled my face from her grip and curled my lips back, snarling at the drunk woman.

"What kind of a name is Whiskey anyway? Why would your mother call you that? Was she a booze hound?" Pia mumbled and glared at me.

"Ma!" Saxton shouted and grabbed hold of her shoulders. He knelt down in front of her and pushed her hair back behind her ear,

"I told you to behave yourself" he hissed quietly,

"Can't a mother talk to her new daughter-in-law?" she slurred back.

"You're not talking, you're interrogating her, and you're being rude. Remember, I wouldn't be standing here right now if it wasn't for her" he grunted angrily. I filled with pride as Saxton scolded his mother on my behalf. He shot me a quick wink and my heart fluttered. She was lucky he was there, because another disrespectful word from her and she would have ended up a puddle of blood on the floor.

"Puh-lease! This little girl couldn't save a fly if it was drowning in an empty glass" she spat and motioned her chin in my direction, "You need a warrior, someone to fight beside you. Not a weak little flea like this one".

"That's enough!" Saxton hissed and shot to his feet.

"You know I'm..." Pia started, but Saxton cut her off,

"You don't know anything" he screamed at her. He grabbed my hand and pulled me to his side, securing me against him with his large arm around my body.

"Didn't you wonder why I didn't come back right away? Didn't you once ask yourself where I've been for the past year?" Saxton yelled,

"I didn't…" Pia muttered, but Saxton cut her off once again.

"We were doing something noble. We were doing something for the betterment of Were-kind. Me and her. Her and me. Together. And what have you been doing, Mother? Sitting at home drinking yourself to death".

I could feel the anger radiating from Saxton. His grip on my hip was tight, his protruding claws were digging into my skin. His yelling had attracted more attention, as many of the pack members started to move over toward us, getting a better look at the fight unfolding.

"Well then, Son, please tell us what kept you away. Tell us all about your noble mission" Dante, Saxton's father, called from behind us. He was glaring at his son, with his brothers and other warriors standing at his sides. Saxton's siblings also came to stand at the side of their father. All of them stared him down, looking ready for a fight. So quickly they were able to turn on him, on their own blood. It infuriated me. I looked around at the crowd of people, all of them glaring at both Saxton and me. It would appear that Saxton was alone on this ledge. Perhaps there was more to this than I knew. Maybe he isn't quite as popular as I thought.

"You wouldn't believe me anyway. You never have before, why would you now?" he growled at his father.

"Well, you seem so damned sure of yourself. Please, enlighten us" Dante mocked. A growl bubbled from behind my clenched teeth at his disrespect. Saxton's grip around me tightened.

All is well, Tesoro. Keep your calm

"Whiskey is a talented fighter and a strong warrior. I would bet she could put you on your back in a matter of seconds" Saxton said loudly. He spoke to his father, but he made a point of talking loud enough for the entirety of the hall to hear him easily.

"Her? This small child?" Dante laughed. His laughter was echoed by the rest of the people around him. My body heat skyrocketed, and I was ready to launch at him. I wanted nothing more than to watch the laughter die from his face as I sucked the air from his lungs.

"Yes, her" Saxton replied with conviction,

"She had no problem with entire compounds filled with hunters. Taking you down would be a cake walk" he laughed and mocked his father.

"What are you on about?" Dante scoffed.

"I'm happy to explain it all Father, only once she has put you on your ass".

"I would pay to see that" one of the warriors laughed.

"I accept your challenge" I growled lowly. Laughter ensued once again, echoing all around the hall.

"No. I'm not going to fight a weakling like her. I have more dignity than that" Dante chuckled.

"Are you afraid, Father?" Saxton snapped back quickly. A hush fell over the crowd and Dante snarled. Clearly, Saxton had hit a nerve.

"I fear no one and nothing".

"Then you will have no problem defeating me" I said smugly. Dante growled and nodded his head stiffly.

"If you want a beating, I will serve you a beating, Little Girl" he hissed. I smiled up at Saxton and puckered my lips. He leaned down and pressed his lips to mine.

Hurt him all you want, just don't kill him

Why not?

He is still my father, and the Alpha won't take kindly to you killing his warriors

Fine

I rolled my eyes in annoyance, and Saxton chuckled deep from within his chest. We turned to see that the crowd had moved back, creating a large circle in the middle of the hall. Dante removed his shirt and danced around the middle of the space, showing off to the crowd. I am really going to enjoy this. I do wonder what Saxton is trying to prove by having me fight his father. Perhaps it's just some kind of unresolved childhood vendetta thing. Lord knows I have enough of those.

"Last chance to back out, Little Girl" Dante teased.

"No. I'm good" I said with a smile. This seemed to anger Dante more. He stretched out his arms and jumped up and down on the spot, warming his body.

I stood facing him with my hands behind my back, waiting for him to advance first, which I knew he would. He is going into this too cocky, he already thinks he has won. He'll be sloppy, and he will concentrate more on showing off for his comrades than he will on his movements. Plus, he, like everyone else here, has consumed copious amounts of alcohol. I can use that against him. Unsurprisingly, I was right. Dante launched himself forward in a bid to tackle me. I stepped out of his way at the last second, which meant he went sprawling to the ground. Laughter and jeers rang out through the crowd. Dante jumped to his feet and snarled at me. He came at me again, this time swinging for my ribcage. I twirled to the side out of his way, and then back around behind him. I slapped the back of my hand to the back of his head. Dante didn't like that. He kicked out with his leg, aiming for my stomach. I caught his leg easily and threw my elbow down into the side of his knee. Dante screamed out and jumped back away from me. He stood holding his knee while glaring at me. I could see the fear in his eyes now. He is starting to understand that he's underestimated me.

"Fucking get the bitch, Dante" Pia screamed from the side. I looked over at her and growled. I can always take her next, after I've finished with her pathetic husband. I was distracted just long enough for Dante to wrap his arm around my neck. I could smell the pride seeping out of his skin. The silly beast thinks he has me beat now. I lifted one hand to grab the back of his neck and held onto the wrist that was pressing against my throat with my other. With a strong push and pull at the same time, I was able to fling him over my shoulder and slam him onto his back at my feet. The jeers and cheers from the crowd slowly started to die down the more I deterred his attacks. They were all now coming to realise that I am not to be trifled with.

"Stop playing with the girl and put her on her ass already" Pia screeched. Dante rolled away from me and jumped back to his feet. He didn't wait this time and came charging at me once again. His extended claws were out in front of him, and mud brown fur was starting to sprout along his arms. He has no control, is it any wonder this is so easy. Dante swung and I dodged, over and over. I was enjoying the game, toying with him like this. I like watching his anger rise and his frustration grow. It amuses me to no end.

In a split second, I flicked my eyes to Saxton. He was standing tall and proud with his arms crossed over his chest, and a shit-eating grin on his face. He nodded his head once, indicating it was time to end it. Dante was recovering from his last attack, spinning on his heels to come back at me again. As he launched forward, I did too. I used his bent knee to jump up and perch myself on top of his body. I wrapped one leg under his arm, securing my ankle behind his back. And the other came over his shoulder and around his neck. He reached up to dig his claws into my leg, but I caught his hand at the wrist. I squeezed his wrist and twisted it, snapping the bone at an ungodly angle. I squeezed my thighs, tightening the hold on his neck. Dante dropped to his knees from the lack of air. He went for my leg again with his unbroken hand. I went to grab it but just missed, instead my talons ripped through the feeble flesh of his forearm. I put my right leg down to anchor my position and kept my left leg securely around his neck.

He was growing weaker, slowly but surely. Pia was screaming, his other children were screaming, even the other warriors were all screaming. They all seemed to think that he still had a chance to beat me. The fools. My eyes locked onto Saxton. He stood glaring down at his father with a smug look on his face. The way Saxton looked at him, the slight raise of his brow, the small quirk of his lip and the evil glimmer in his eye. It wasn't because he was proud of me for pinning his father, it was because his father was in pain. Then it occurred to me. This whole show of dominance had nothing to do with me proving myself to his pack. It was all about getting back at his family, it was about revenge. For what?

I don't know. But it was clear now. Saxton was using me as a tool in his game of retribution. Just like the hunters did.

Present Day.
I think they are onto me. This pack were very prepared for an attack. Almost like they were expecting it. The mistakes I have made previously, especially by unintentionally letting some of them get away, those errors are coming back to bite me now. It would seem word of my little expeditions has spread further than I would have liked. Unfortunate, but not the worst thing in the world. I had been feeling bored of the mission lately, perhaps now I will have more of a challenge. Maybe if more of them are as prepared, if more of them start to push back and resist their inevitable deaths, maybe the beasts will offer a little bit more excitement to the hunt again. This village seemed empty, rather void of women and children. Which leads me to believe that they had enough time to evacuate. The idea infuriated me. I am better than that. I don't let people escape, I am more efficient and faster than this. I ransacked their houses and other buildings, killing anyone and everyone who got in my way. And surprisingly, there were a lot of them. They all fought back. I am used to people running and hiding, it has been a while since anyone put up a fight. Do these beasts not know who I am? Is the legend of Besomar only known in Russia? Do they not understand that I am evil incarnate. Pure rage and death. Put on this earth to destroy all who stray upon my path.
It was roughly the middle of the day. I had been in Alaska for just 2 days now. I had my talons into the neck of a warrior, about to rip its throat out, when it washed over me. A tidal wave of pure energy. Something that I had never felt before. My skin prickled, and my hair stood on end. My body felt heavy, like it was being dragged into the ground. And yet my head filled with air, like it was about to pop off my neck and float away. I ripped my claws through the warrior's skin, letting his blood spray from the gaping wound. I let his body fall to the ground, and I followed, dropping to my knees and digging my fingers into the dirt. I tried to shake my head free of the obscure feeling clouding it, but it didn't work. The energy rolled through my body, filling me with a pain I had never experienced before. It was unsettling. I flew back up onto my knees, sitting on my feet. I tossed my head back

and screamed up into the air. The strange energy burst from my body like an explosion, knocking down the trees and houses that were in close range. The pain radiated through my veins and out into the air around me. I screamed until I had nothing left. I screamed until I felt empty and void of life. I dropped forward, pressing my face into the dirt. Before I knew what my own body was doing, I cried. For the first time in a decade, I cried. Tears rained from my eyes like they had a never ending supply. My body shook and heaved with the sobs that racked through me. I had lost myself completely, and I had no idea why.

As the tears fell, I lost myself. I lost any sort of feeling. I have never really been one for emotions, I was taught better than that. But the usual rage and anger that I strived on, it was all gone. Only nothing had replaced it. I was left with a giant gaping hole inside my body.

I forced myself off the ground and looked around. Everything that had been standing around me was now gone. The trees, the houses, and even the dead bodies that were on the ground, were all gone. I was left kneeling in a crater of some sort, and it was huge. Meters wide and deep into the ground. The earth around me was barren, just dirt and rocks. The trees off in the distance were now standing at an angle, all leaning away from me. I did this. I created this hole in the ground. A crater caused by my own uncontrollable outburst of power. Interesting. I had never done something like this before. Not to this magnitude anyway. But why? And how? What was the energy that I felt? Why did it cause me so much pain? And why do I feel this black hole of emptiness in the pit of my stomach? Something bigger is happening to me. Something isn't right. I just need to figure out what it is and then put a stop to it. I have to, no matter the cost.

Chapter Fourteen

Zelena

One week.
Emptiness.

Chapter Fifteen

Zelena

Two weeks.
Pain. So. Much. Pain.

Chapter Sixteen

Zelena

Three weeks.
Silence. Darkness.

Chapter Seventeen

Zelena

Four weeks.

Nothingness.

Numb. That's what I was now. Numb. Numb to the pain, numb to the fear, numb to the emptiness. I had nothing left. No emotions, no feelings, just deep dark nothing. The happiness that my memories were meant to evoke, was non-existent. The sadness that I thought his departure would cause me, was nowhere to be found. I had nothing. My lifeless body lay motionless on the bed. I don't know what day it is, nor do I care. I don't know how long it's been since he left, nor do I know where he is. I just know that he isn't here. And without him with me, there was nothing for me here. Hours turned to days and days turned to weeks. But in my mind, it was one long and unbroken patch of darkness. I was conscious of the faces that appeared in the room around me. I could hear the low whispers of pleading and encouragement that accompanied them. But I had nothing to give them in return. No motivation, and no desire to be present. I didn't want to be here without him. I wanted to close my eyes and leave this place. Only to return when he did.

"She can't last like this much longer" a hushed whisper rang out. "We've tried everything we can. She has to choose to fight, she has to want it" another person whispered back.

"The medication isn't working. The forced feeding isn't working any more either. She's slipping away, we're going to lose her, we're going to lose the both of them". I should care. I can hear the pain and frustration in the voices. I can hear the pleading and fear. I should care. I just… I don't.

"She won't let that happen, it's her pup. She may be a little checked out at the moment, but her instincts are still sharp. She won't allow any real harm to come to the baby"

"Look at her! She is already harming the baby" one of the voices shouted.

"Calm down, losing your temper won't help anyone".

"She needs to eat, like actual food. If she loses any more weight the pup won't survive the birth".

The pup. His pup. I had almost forgotten. I shifted my hand over the bed and spread my fingers across the large mound that was my stomach. It's grown. It's grown a lot. I had forgotten there was life growing inside me. His life. I no longer felt the movements and the kicks. I blocked it from my mind, along with everything else. I opened a sliver in my mental wall and allowed myself to feel my body. Everything hurt and I hissed in response. My first instinct was to slam that mental shield back down, to block it all out again. But I hesitated. I spread my out over the bulge of my stomach and concentrated. Now that I opened myself to it once again, the movement was all too present. It must be close now. The pain in my chest and my back was ever present and still excruciating to bear. But the strain and the pressure in my abdomen and the lower half of my body was overwhelming. It couldn't possibly grow any more, there's no room left.

My movements must have caught the attention of whoever was in the room. The bed dipped in front of me and a hand gently ran down my arm.

"Zelena, Sweetheart, are you awake?" Roe's soft voice asked quietly. I should answer, I want to. I just... I can't.

"You need to eat Zelena. You're hurting the pup, and if you don't eat soon, the damage may be too great" the other voice hissed angrily.

"Natalia!" Roe scolded.

"What? I'm not wrong. Enough is enough! She has sulked for long enough, now it's time to suck it up and be a Goddess-damned Luna" Nat snapped back.

"Cut it out. You know perfectly well that it's different for her than it is for us. She's his True Mate. She'd be feeling unimaginable pain with him not here. She isn't just missing him, she's missing a part of herself".

"Well, I'm missing my Mate too. I had to come back here and do her duties instead of getting to know my own fucking pack" Nat whisper shouted. What was she talking about? This is her pack. Oh, that's right, she found her true love. She was meant to leave with him. Why is she here? A low and harsh rumbling growl reverberated around the room. A small flicker of comfort sparked through me, but it was gone as quickly as it came.

"Get out" the deep and looming voice growled.

"Tobias, we are only trying to get her to eat something" Roe said cautiously. I could hear the worry in her tone. I couldn't force myself to care why she was worried. But I could still hear it.

"Leave" Tobias said slowly. His voice had a strange ethereal echo to it. Something about him had changed. More so than he already had. I felt Roe lift off the bed and heard the rushed footsteps leave the room. A moment later, the bed dipped again, and I was pulled into Tobias's side. His arms came around my body and I was pressed into his side with my head on his arm. This is strange. The feel of his skin was different. He smelt different. I pressed my cheek into his skin, trying to understand the strange new sensation I was feeling. Pins and needles rushed over my body where his skin touched mine. I think I have felt this from him before, but this was different, stronger somehow. It doesn't matter. Nothing matters. My body wanted to relax, to be calm and happy. But my heart, or the empty space where my heart should be, wouldn't allow it. I slammed down my walls to the pain and let myself go, letting the vast darkness of sleep take me once again.

~

More days passed. I could again see the faces and hear the voices of the people that I love. But I had nothing to offer them. I wanted to stay in my head, my own quiet world, and away from the place where I knew that Gunner wouldn't be.

Pain shot down my back and I flinched, scrunching up my face and hissing. The warm body that was behind me, pulled me closer. I could smell him before I knew he was there. His scent was far too overpowering. The devotion and protectiveness, it was seeping out of him. Tobias' large hand was under my shirt and his fingers were splayed over my round stomach. The connecting points of our skin tickled, it burned nearly. The sensation was wildly unfamiliar and yet positively addictive. The scent of him, his essence, it filled my empty cup. Just a little a first. But the longer we lay together, the more of him filled my soul. And for the first time, in I don't know how long, I spoke.

"What are you doing?" I asked. My voice was hoarse and quiet. My throat burned and itched from the dryness.

"I am feeding you" he answered. His deep and rumbling voice still held that ethereal echo. It was actually very eery to hear. I cleared my throat and tried again.

"What are you doing?" I choked,

"I am feeding you my energy. Keeping you strong" he answered. I moved to lay my hand over where his rested on my stomach and tried to concentrate. I could feel it now. The gentle vibration coursed through his fingers. The tingle of electricity spreading through my body, and the warmth in my veins. All of it was originating from where his hand was resting on my stomach.

"Why?" I asked,

"It's nearly time" was all he said. Time? Time for what? Time for Gunner to come home maybe? Before I got the chance to ask, the door opened, and a set of heavy footsteps entered. Tobias growled a warning from behind my head. I forced open one of my eyes and looked at the person in the doorway. I squinted through the brightness of the lights. My eyes stung and I had to blink away the heavy feeling.

"Watch yourself, Guardian. Don't forget who I am to that girl" Lunaya growled back. My blurry vision cleared enough for me to see her standing at the edge of the bed. She looked dishevelled and tired, but her eyes held a wildfire deep in the brown of her iris. She shifted her angry gaze from Tobias and down to me. Her face softened the moment our eyes connected.

"Zelena" she huffed.

"Lunaya" I croaked back. Her eyebrows shot up and she stared at me with wide eyes.

"You're talking again?" she said surprised. I didn't answer her. There was nothing to say. She stood there unmoving, and I just lay on my bed watching her. A second later, another searing pain shot down my back. I hissed again and jolted on the bed, colliding my back into Tobias's chest. Lunaya jumped forward and onto the bed in front of me. One of her hands went to my stomach and the other to my forehead. Tobias growled and moved his hand lower on my stomach. Lunaya looked over my shoulder at him and nodded her head. She moved back off the bed and knelt down at the side so that we were now at eye level.

"Zelena, Sweetheart, your contractions have started. We need to move you downstairs to the delivery room" she said softly and slowly, like her words were going to hurt me. I know I should be excited or happy, or even scared. But I felt nothing. Nothing but the huge hole where my heart should be, where Gunner should be.

"Okay" I answered quietly.

The bed shifted and Tobias's body was gone, only for him to reappear in front of me. He gently moved his arms under me and lifted me off the bed. Another pain rushed down my back and I winced. I gripped onto Tobias's shirt and held on until the pain passed again. I rested my head on his shoulder as he carried me down the stairs and into the hall. The room has been cleared of all the furniture and pack memorabilia and replaced with medical supplies. It smelt like a hospital, with that sterile clean scent overwhelming my nose. A large hospital bed sat in the middle of the room with screens and monitors all around it. Trolleys lined with tools, clothes, and other supplies were against the wall, next to what looked like a clear plastic bassinet. When did they do all this? How did they even get all this equipment?

Tobias laid me gently down on the bed and moved to stand at the head. I rolled over and curled my legs up as far as I could. I should be excited. I want to be excited. I want to let myself feel this. But I can't move past what is missing. I can't ignore the missing presence of my Mate. That pain is too much to endure. Another contraction hit and I tensed my body. I've felt worse pain. My entire childhood was built on a foundation of pain. This will be nothing compared to that. Right?

"Roe has called for the doctor, he should be here soon. He did show me how to administer the morphine though. Do you want something for the pain?" Lunaya asked as she walked over to the side of the bed and into my line of sight.

"I don't feel any pain" I answered her numbly.

"Oh, I... um. Okay" she mumbled and shuffled away. I closed my eyes and tried to go back to sleep. But apparently, that wasn't in the cards for me either. So, I did what I have been doing for the past few weeks. I closed myself off to the rest of the world and lay in a comatose state. I blocked out the numbness, the emptiness, I ignored the voices and the faces. And now, I cut myself off from the shooting pains echoing through my body, warning me something was coming.

A little while later Roe came in, a huge smile on her face and an excited hop to her step. She gently caressed the side of my face, sweeping my hair behind my ear.

"Beautiful girl" she cooed and pressed her lips to my forehead.

"The doctor is here, are you willing to talk to him?" she asked me. I huffed and closed my eyes again. I don't want to talk. I don't want to do anything. I just want to go back into the darkness and be left alone. Another contraction rolled through me, causing me to hold my breath and wince as I tried to sit up. They were getting closer together and the intensity was increasing, it was becoming impossible to ignore it.

"Breathe through it, Miss Baxter. You have to work with the contractions, not fight against them" the doctor said as he walked into the room. I gazed blankly at his face, a whisper of familiarity wash across me. I think I remember him. Dr Tenner. The doctor who helped me after I was shot. He was also at the pack grounds after the battle with the Origin Wolf.

"You?" I croaked out.

"Yes, me. It's nice to see you again, Miss Baxter" Dr Tenner said with a smile. He turned to Roe and his smile quickly disappeared and was replaced with a frown.

"Even though I should have seen you a lot more regularly during your pregnancy. Not just when you're in labour" he said firmly while glaring at Roe. She stood up and placed her hands on her hips.

"She-wolves have been delivering their own babies for thousands of years. I don't need a human, let alone a man, to explain childbirth to me" she growled and flashed her canines at him. His face paled and he stumbled back a little. He got too comfortable, too brave. I don't think that will happen again for a while. Roe looked at me and winked. I tried to force a smile back to her, but it didn't work. If anything, I just twisted my mouth upwards in an awkward grimace. She moved away from the bed and sat down on a chair next to Lunaya.

"I apologise" Dr Tenner grunted and came over to the side of the bed. Tobias stepped closer and a low growl vibrated from him. Dr Tenner froze and looked up at my giant guardian. If he was pale before, he was almost translucent now. It looked like he was going to faint.

"It's okay Tobias" I said in a monotone voice. Tobias stayed at my side, but his growling stopped.

"I am just going to feel your stomach, and then we'll do a quick exam to see how far you've dilated" Dr Tenner said while looking at me. I could tell he was trying his darndest not to look at Tobias again. But the bead of sweat on his forehead, the pale clamminess of his skin, not to mention the stench of his anxiety, it all gave him away. He was a nervous wreck. I nodded in agreement and lifted my shirt, well Gunner's shirt. Dr Tenner went to work pushing and poking my stomach. Another contraction hit and he coached me through it as he felt my baby belly. Dr Tenner showed me how to breathe, encouraging me to participate by doing it with me. I tried to follow along, but I had no energy and no motivation. Once the contraction stopped, I slumped back on the bed.

"Very good. You're right where we want you to be. Now if you could please slip out of your underpants, we'll do your exam" he said and quickly moved away. I pulled my underpants down my legs and discarded them on the floor. I would normally be embarrassed or uncomfortable with another man, any man that wasn't Gunner, looking at my nether regions. But I didn't have it in me to care.

"Put your feet together and let your knees drop to the sides, please" Dr Tenner said calmly. He dragged the trolley with the ultrasound machine on it over to the end of the bed. He then placed a blanket over my legs before he sat down on a small stool. After a minute of feeling around, he sat back up and pulled his gloves off.

"You're about five centimetres and progressing quickly" Dr Tenner said as he moved away from between my legs. I attempted to breathe through another contraction, just like he showed me.

"Can't you just put me under and cut it out" I asked blankly. Roe gasped loudly and Lunaya shot to her feet.

"You want a caesarean?" Dr Tenner asked hesitantly,

"I just want it over with" I answered him honestly.

"Zelena, Honey, you don't want that" Lunaya said softly as she stepped towards the bed.

"What would you know?" I asked her. I don't know if she was stunned by the question or by the lack of emotion in my voice, but she was surprised nonetheless.

"I know that you're hurting right now. I know that you probably feel like you have nothing left in this world. I know that there would be this gaping hole in your life that cannot be filled by anything other than your Mate" she answered and stepped up to the bed. A pang of pain radiated through my chest as a small crack appeared in my wall. She was pretty much spot on. But I will not allow myself to feel that pain. I don't want to. When I didn't answer, she went on.

"I lost my Mate too, remember. He may not have been my True Mate, but he was everything to me. When he died, my life collapsed".

"GUNNER IS NOT DEAD!" I screamed. Another contraction hit, this one worse than the others. With the surprise of the contraction and my sudden burst of anger, I lost my hold and a surge of energy exploded out of me. It shook and rattled the instruments and forced Lunaya to her knees. I could feel my wall breaking. The barricade that I had put in place to keep out all of the feelings, all the emotions, all the bad stuff, was starting to crumble. Lunaya struggled back to her feet and gripped the bed railing for support.

"I know he is not dead. He is coming back to you. Don't you want to tell him about how strong you were? Don't you want to share with him the birth of your pup" she said with a strained voice. I took a deep breath in, and with it, I felt another brick come crashing down.

"I don't want to do it without him" I told her.

"You're not doing it without him, Darling. He is still here" she said, pointing to my chest,

"And here" she pointed to my head.

"I understand this isn't how you thought it would go. I know that you wanted him to be here with you, to coach you through it, to hold your hand. But we make do with the hand we've been dealt. Look around you, Sweetheart. In the end, you've been dealt a pretty good hand" Lunaya said as she looked over at the door. Nat was standing just inside the door, with Smith's arm around her shoulder, both of them were looking at me with tears in their eyes. Lupus stood behind them with Alyse under his arm. I looked over to Roe, who was smiling back at me with tears streaming down her face. I looked up to Tobias, with his stone-cold expression. He shot me back a smile. A full ear to ear smile with his white teeth shining from behind his full lips. The kind of smile that I haven't seen on his face in a long time. More of my wall tumbled and the pain in my chest thumped with every heartbeat. I looked back at Lunaya. She smiled sweetly and wiped a tear from my cheek.

"You are stronger than you know" she said quietly as she cupped my face. I stared into her soft brown eyes, and I saw everything that I was afraid of feeling. The rest of my wall shattered into a thousand tiny pieces, and it all came rushing back. The pain in my chest was the feeling of my heart breaking. Of remembering how my life was before Gunner came into it, and the crippling fear of going back to living that way. The unbearable terror of losing him, of him being taken away from me, from us, forever. I can't let my baby grow up without a father, he has to come back to us. Gunner gave me everything. Gunner saved me. The thought of living without him is the scariest notion I have ever encountered. I looked to my mother-in-law, my two best friends, my guardian, and my mother. Then I lost any semblance of control I had left. I began to hyperventilate as the sobs racked my body. Tobias lifted my weeping body and crawled onto the bed behind me, he wrapped himself around me like a protective blanket. Lunaya took my hand and kissed my knuckles. Roe came over to the other side of the bed, took my other hand and held it to her chest.

"I... can't..." I forced out between sobs.

"You can, Sweet Girl" Roe said encouragingly.

"I need him" I cried.

"I know, Baby. He'll be home soon" she said encouragingly. Another contraction came on, the intensity caught me off guard. The pressure, the pain, it's indescribable. I breathed hard, trying to calm myself down. I've been so selfish. I've put my baby at risk, all because I wouldn't face the heartache of Gunner's departure. If something happens to my baby, it will be all my fault. And then I will truly have nothing left to live for. I took a deep breath to steady my heart and turned back to face Roe.

"What if he doesn't come back? What if Selene really did take his wolf? What if losing his wolf made him weak and he couldn't get home again? Maybe that's why he isn't here. He should be here. This is his baby. He should be here. Why isn't he here?" I was crying hard and began to hyperventilate once again. The pain was too much, letting it all back in was overwhelming my senses. The onslaught of contractions wasn't helping either.

"You can't think things like that right now, Honey. Let's bring your little one into the world safe and sound first, and then we can come back to that later" Lunaya spoke.

"I can't. I can't do it alone".

"You're not alone, my beautiful daughter. And you will never be alone again". Lunaya cupped my cheek and wiped some of the tears from my face. So much pain was rolling through me. So much fear as well. And it wasn't just caused by my body preparing itself to push a baby out. My heart was aching. A sharp and constant strain was pulling it in two different directions. One was back to the dark emptiness where I didn't feel or care about anything. And the other was towards my pup. To bear down, be strong and be the mother this baby deserves. I looked around at my loved ones again and rested my head back on Tobias's shoulder. The feel of his body warmth and the tingle of his energy seeping into me. It was just enough to make me see clearly, there was never really a choice.

"You're at eight centimetres, Miss Baxter. But I need you to start working with your contractions and not against them" Mr Tenner interrupted. I looked over to Roe and then back at Lunaya and nodded my head. I can do this. I have to.

"He will be home soon" Tobias whispered into my ear. I turned my neck and looked at him. He had a gentle smile on his face as he nodded his head to the corner of the room. I looked to where he was indicating, but there was nothing there.

Look closer. Feel for it, Little One

He flashed me. Another contraction swept through me, and I did as instructed by Dr Tenner. When it passed, I looked back at Tobias. He again nodded towards the corner and rested his chin on my shoulder. I took a deep breath and tried to concentrate. It was hard to focus on anything other than the pressure in my lower stomach. After a second, I picked up on the tingle in the air, and a gentle and comforting chill brushed over my skin. I focused my eyes, and there she was. Selene. Standing in the corner with her hands held in front of her. Her long white hair swept around her shoulders like it was caught in the breeze, and her long dress did the same. Her pure white eyes were focused on me, and she wore a proud smile on her face. Tears pooled in my eyes as I smiled back at her. She bowed her head a little and blew me a kiss, then disappeared again.

Lunaya spun around next to me and stared at the corner where Selene had been standing. She grabbed at her chest and turned back to me with wide and suspecting eyes.

"Was that...? Was she...?" Lunaya stuttered.

"It was" I confirmed and leaned my body into Tobias's chest. I rested my head on him and revelled in the warm comfort her emanated. Lunaya started to cry and pressed my hand to her cheek.

"Lunaya, Dear, why are you crying?" Roe asked her with an amused chuckle,

"I'm just, I'm very happy is all" she answered and leaned forward to kiss my cheek. Something about Selene's appearance and Tobias's words stuck with me. I think Gunner is coming home. I think Selene came to me to show me that everything will be alright. Her visit was the last push I needed. I gritted my teeth and breathed through my next few rounds of contractions. Roe shooed everyone else from the room, leaving just Dr Tenner, Lunaya, Tobias and herself. The contractions came on quickly and in no time at all, I was ready to push. I don't know what I would have done without my two mothers and Tobias. They gave me so much strength and encouragement, helping me every step of the way.

"You're doing very good, Miss Baxter, you're crowning" Dr Tenner called from between my legs. The pain was intense, it was like a fire was raging in my vagina. The burning sensation was unlike anything else.

"I don't want to do it anymore" I cried and shook my head,

"You're doing great, Baby Girl, just a little more and you'll have your pup in your arms" Roe said encouragingly. I bared down and pushed.

"The head is out Miss Baxter, one more big push for the shoulders okay, just breathe" Dr Tenner called. I scrunched up my eyes, screamed, and pushed. The fire dissipated and soft cries filled the room.

"Congratulations, Miss Baxter. You have a healthy little boy" Dr Tenner said as he stood up. He held a bloody and screaming baby bundled in a blanket in his arms and walked to the side of the bed. Dr Tenner carefully placed the baby in my arms and stepped away. I looked down at my little boy's red face and I cried. He is just perfectly beyond perfect. He has whisps of dark hair like me and a small smushy face. His eyes were closed and he smacked his lips as little cries fell from his perfect little mouth.

"An Alpha-son" Roe cried and gently ran her finger over his tiny little hand.

"Oh Zelena, he is beautiful" Lunaya clucked.

"He really is" I breathed out. Tobias's head was resting on my shoulder, as he too stared at the tiny creature in my arms. The baby gripped onto my little finger tightly and I gazed at him adoringly. I thought I knew what love was before now. But this is something different entirely. There is nothing in the world I wouldn't do for this little boy. A pain ran through my body and the burning sensation started again. I winced and grunted and sat up straight. Tobias tensed behind me, his hands coming to the sides of my still round stomach. That felt like a contraction, why did that feel like a contraction?

"Ah, baby number two is ready I see" Dr Tenner said as he disappeared between my legs again.

"Excuse me?" Roe gasped,

"What do you mean baby number two?" Lunaya snapped,

"Twins, ladies, I mean there's twins" Dr Tenner called. How in the bloody hell did we not know there were two babies in there? Make sense given how huge I was.

"No. She can't be having twins, Weres almost never have twins" Roe argued. There was no point in fighting it, I could sure as shit feel another one was coming out. But I don't understand why she isn't more excited.

"It's not possible" Lunaya breathed quietly.

"It's fucking possible" I screamed and placed the baby into Roe's arms.

"And it's coming now" I yelled and pushed hard. With a few more pushes, Dr Tenner stood up holding another little pink baby in a bundled blanket. He placed it in my arms and wiped his forehead with the back of his hand.

"A sweet little girl, Miss Baxter. Well done" he said and walked off to begin cleaning up his tools and supplies. I looked down at the little pink faced blob of love in my arms. She too had dark whisps of hair and looked exactly like her brother. Her brother... Holy shit. I have two babies. How am I going to handle two babies?

Roe handed me back my boy and I looked down at my two perfect little angels. Tobias's arm snaked around my waist from behind me and he slipped his huge finger into my baby girl's hand. She gurgled and cried and pulled his finger to her mouth.

"They are perfect" he said proudly and kissed my cheek.

"You did good, Mumma" he cooed affectionately. I laughed and leaned back into him.

"Thank you for being here" I told him,

"I wouldn't be anywhere else".

"I'm going to go tell the others. They're waiting very impatiently in the kitchen" Roe smiled and bounced on her feet. She seemed much more excited now. Thank goodness. She gently kissed each baby on the forehead before kissing my cheek too.

"I am so proud of you Zelena. Gunner is going to be over the moon" she cooed happily. Tears welled in my eyes and I smiled.

"Thank you" I said while swallowing a sob. Roe rushed out of the room and I turned to Lunaya. She was staring down at the babies with a blank expression on her face.

"Do you want to hold one, Grandma?" I asked her with a chuckle. Instead of rushing forward to take a baby, or smiling at her new nickname like I thought she would, she took a few steps away from the bed. She shook her head and mumbled to herself.

"Lunaya. Do you want to hold one of your grandchildren?" I asked again a little more firmly.

"No" she snapped. I reared back and raised my eyebrows. I felt Tobias's body tense behind me and the vibration of a suppressed growl rumble in his chest.

"It can't be twins. You can't have twins. This isn't right" she said in a harsh whisper.

"Excuse me?" I asked angrily. I was so happy. Just one moment ago everything was okay again. The pain and the emptiness, it was forgotten. I was here, present and responsive. Just a moment ago, everything felt like it was going to be alright. And she ruined it. How could she react so harshly to her own grandchildren? What on Earth could be so terrible about having twins?

"I'm sorry, I can't be here right now" she mumbled and rushed for the door. She shoved past a smiling Lupus and a crying Nat on her way out.

"What's her problem?" Nat snapped as she stepped into the makeshift delivery room, following Lunay's retreating form with her glare.

"I don't know. I guess she only wanted one grandbaby" I answered with a frown.

Chapter Eighteen

Whiskey

The numb emptiness didn't leave me, it faded somewhat, but I could still feel it. If I wasn't so used to blocking myself off to pain and emotion, I would guess that it would frustrate me. But I actually kind of enjoyed it. The uncaring and unfeeling state of mine was freeing. I lost any guilt I had for what I had done over the past few years, however small that piece of guilt may have been. However, that slight sliver of doubt still lingered in the back of my mind. Always on repeat, eating inside my thoughts, 'Did I do the wrong thing?' With this new hollow feeling, I could no longer see or feel that small slice of doubt. It was fantastic. All that aside, the fact that I still don't know what has brought on or caused this new state of mind, it bugs me. I am determined to find out. And I will, I always do.

I'd made my way to the South of Alaska, to the mountains near the Canadian border. I know that packs like to reside in either thick forests, large open plains, or snowy mountains. I'm not sure why I was drawn to this mountain exactly, but I felt like I needed to go there. And if I've learnt anything in my cataclysmic life, it's to trust my instincts.

Fifteen months ago.

I laid in Saxton's arms with my head on his shoulder, tracing my fingers through the soft curls of hair on his chest. His gentle snores filled the small room. I lifted my leg and splayed it up and over his, rubbing myself against him. I can't believe we're still here. I thought we would have left after the fight with his father. But it seems my winning did exactly what Saxton expected it would do. All of the pack members show me the utmost respect, and in turn, Saxton too. He is thriving on it, soaking in their love and attention. Me, I hate the extra attention. But if he is happy, then so am I. His parents have kept their distance. And lucky too. I have in no way forgotten or forgiven Pia's disrespect. I am still chomping at the bit to give her a good run around.

Saxton has been spending a lot of time with his Alpha. He seems very excited about it. He excitedly tells me every night about how the Alpha thinks he would be a great asset to their warrior ranks, and that his experience with taking down hunter compounds makes him a real contender to be a commander. I love the way his face lights up when he talks about his future as a commander. Even if I still feel like there is more work to do, more hunters to track down, more compounds to demolish, I could never take away that spark from him. Life in this pack with Saxton wouldn't be the worst thing in the world. I love that he is happy.

Sparks tickled along my exposed flesh as I pressed myself against Saxton's side. I lifted my head and smattered kisses over his chest and up to his neck. His arm tightened around my shoulder as a seductive growl vibrated in his throat. He grabbed my leg with his other hand and pulled it so that I was now straddling his waist. I leaned down and sucked and nibbled at his neck. His hands gripped my hips tightly as I gently rocked back and forth along his hardened length. He grabbed my hair and roughly ripped my head away from his neck, he smashed his lips to mine, forcing his tongue into my mouth. I moaned into his mouth and lifted my hips, I reached down and angled his tip to my entrance, then slowly slid down along his member. Before I got to slide all the way down, Saxton hissed and bucked his hips into me, making me bounce on top of him. The harshness of it was delicious, and so I continued the movement, lifting myself along his rod, before slamming back down onto him hard. The slapping of our flesh and the grunts and groans played like an erotic symphony. I pushed his face away from mine, making his back hit the bed. I wrapped my fingers around his throat and increased my speed. Saxton's claws extended and he buried them into the skin at my hips. The added pain was incredible. I moved on top of him, taking control of the pace. Something I know he hates, giving up control. So I do it just to torture him. He tried to move, to flip us over so that he could be on top. I slammed his head back into the pillow and bared my teeth in his face, while squeezing my hands a little tighter around his neck. He hissed and showed me his extended fangs. I tossed my head back and laughed out loud as I slammed myself down onto his length.

Saxton growled loudly and as I was laughing, he flipped me off his lap. Grabbing my hips again, he pulled me back and rammed into me from behind. Moving with deep and hard thrusts, he sent me jolting forward with each push. Saxton grunted with every upshot. The brutal penetration forced a scream from my lips every time. He grabbed the back of my head, tracing his thumb down the length of my neck, before he glided his hand around to my throat, and squeezed it tightly. He lifted my face off the mattress until my back was against his chest. He kept me anchored to him with one hand around my waist and the other at my neck, interrupting the blood flow to my head. As he slammed into me relentlessly, my head became dizzy, and my orgasm loomed closer. I reached up and curled my fingers into Saxton's hair, forcing his mouth to my neck. My other hand rubbed eagerly at my clit, giving myself that extra push.

Saxton's claws ran across my stomach, slicing the skin open. I screamed out and pulled hard at my handful of hair. The pressure was building, and the pain he was inflicting was bringing it along quickly. We have done this dance many times now. He knows how to hurt me in the best ways. Saxton released his grip on my neck with a possessive growl and pushed my body back into the bed, forcing my face into the pillow. He pulled out of me and I growled in frustration. Without warning, he then pushed himself into my ass, in one swift and unforgiving thrust. The moment that he sleuthed himself all the way inside me, I came. I came hard and I wasn't quiet about it. I rolled my hips with each wave of my orgasm, pressing my hips back onto his dick. My moans slowly subsided, and I started to come down from my high, only for Saxton to start thrusting again. My tight hole constricted around him through the last of my orgasm. He pushed at my lower back, making me stick out my ass higher with the deep arch of my back. He grunted and growled as he ploughed into me mercilessly. A minute later and he found his own release, emptying himself into my ass.

We both collapsed onto the mattress, breathing heavily. As I caught my breath again, I started to feel sleepy. I closed my eyes and listened to the sounds of Saxton's harsh breaths. He sat up next to me and ran his fingers over my back, tracing over the multiple scars and markings left behind from my years of education. He moved his fingers higher to the back of my neck, tickling the spot gently and affectionately. Saxton is a neck man. He is always kissing, sucking, tickling and touching the back of my neck and my throat. Not just in moments of passion like this, but any chance he gets. It started the second we Mated.

Saxton sucked his teeth and stood up abruptly, disturbing my almost sleep. I rolled onto my side and looked at him as he pulled on a pair of jeans and a black t-shirt.

"Going somewhere?" I asked him with a smirk.

"Going to see the Alpha" he answered. Again? He was only just there last night, just how much is there to talk about?

"He can wait, I want another go" I teased seductively and reached for his hand. He pulled away and frowned.

"Later. I'm trying to organise our future" he said with a grunt.

"Shouldn't I be a part of that conversation?" I asked. Anger bubbled in my veins at his rejection. I just about had enough of coming second to that damned beast.

"No Tesoro, you can go and clean up and I'll meet you for lunch" he answered blankly. I sat up and growled lowly at his brush off. Saxton whipped his head to me and smiled softly. He knelt on the bed and pulled my face to his, kissing my lips gently.

"I love you, Tesoro. Go have a shower, I'll meet you again in an hour" he said and quickly stood and left the room before I had time to argue. I sneered and moved to the edge of the bed, throwing my legs over the side. I went to the bathroom and looked at myself in the mirror. Pale pink marks were all that was left of his scratches on my stomach, though there were lines of dried blood running down my stomach and the front of my legs. I looked back at the bed and the white sheets were covered in blood. It looked like someone had been murdered. More little marks littered my hips where his claws had been, with more patches of dried blood. Why didn't Saxton have this much blood on him? Surely I left a mark or two on him as well.

I washed off in the shower and then put on some clean clothes. It was still half an hour before I was supposed to meet Saxton for lunch, but I figured I'd go and meet him at the Alpha's office early. I headed down the stairs. Saxton and I were on the second to the top floor, there were four levels, including the underground basement. It was a rather large village, sophisticated in an old-timey, rustic kind of way. It had narrow stone walkways, with large stone buildings, none of which were placed in any kind of pattern. It was like someone just threw a bunch of rocks at the ground and said 'Build your house where it lands'. A large stone wall surrounded the entire village, and on the other side of that were sprawling green fields, littered with rows of grapevines. Saxton's pack, the Red River pack, owned a large vineyard and produced a shit ton of wine. That's how they made their money.

The Alpha's office was pretty much on the other side of the village. It isn't a walk I want to do, especially not at this time of the day when everyone will be out and about. I sucked it up and got to walking anyway. Each pack member I passed smiled and waved, some wanted to stop and talk to me, and some wanted to invite me for food. These people never stop eating. I'm not used to the friendliness and the constant need for conversation. I'm a loner, I like being on my own. It took a lot for me to allow Saxton into my little bubble. I don't know how I am meant to open up to this whole pack-life thing. It's just not for me.

It was another fifteen minutes until I finally got to the Alpha's residence. Unlike everyone else, he didn't need to share his building. It was just him and his wife, and their youngest child. I was always taught to be wary of the Alpha. Not only are they meant to be the strongest among the pack, but they can be sneaky and vicious. Alphas are so greedy. Always taking the best for themselves and leaving the scraps for the rest of their pack. They draw on the energy and strength of their pack members to make themselves stronger. They expect their members to do all the hard work while they sit back and watch, soaking up all the benefits for themselves. The one thing I have never understood is why. Why let one man rule over them? They can survive on their own, right? Why not live as solitary creatures? The whole pack mentality doesn't make sense to me.

I knocked on the front door and the Luna answered a second later.

"Ah, the mysterious Whiskey. Come in Dear" she said with a smile. She opened the door and stepped aside to let me in. She had paint on her clothes and her young one was hanging off her leg, also covered in paint.

"Don't mind us, we were just doing a little arts and crafts" she chuckled and wiped her hands on her shirt.

"I'm looking for Saxton" I told her, trying to cut off the opening for small talk.

"Oh, sure, he is in the office with Antonio. Up the stairs, first door on the left" she said politely. I nodded my head in thanks and headed up the stairs, leaving the Luna and her child in the foyer. As I approached the closed door of the office, I heard Saxton speaking excitedly.

"You know what this could mean for us, for the pack. It's huge. The world will bow at our feet" he said happily.

"There are still tests that need to be done. We need to confirm this, multiple times over. We must be one hundred percent sure of it before we make any moves. Which includes alerting the rest of the pack. You are not to say a word to anyone until I give the go ahead" the Alpha spoke firmly.

"What else is there to confirm, I've given you all of the information you need" Saxton clapped back.

"This is no small feat. We can't go off half-cocked and start a war" The Alpha growled. What war? What are they talking about? If Saxton is so excited about it, why hasn't he told me anything?

"The war has already started. In case you haven't noticed, it's been going on for centuries. At least Whiskey has been doing something about it. We both have. But this, this will help us. This will rally packs from all over the world. We can finally end this, for real this time" Saxton argued. What is he talking about? What have I been doing? Could he mean the hunters and me wiping out their compounds. I am doing that for me, not for them, for the werewolves. I don't care if they benefit or suffer from my actions. I only care about setting out to do what I planned to do. And that is to kill every single one of the monstrous bastards that walk this earth. And then, once they are all dead, I will kill off their families. Their children, their brothers and sisters, cousins, grandparents, uncles, all of them. I will not stop until the earth beneath my feet runs red with blood. I will not stop until the word 'hunter' has been wiped from the history books.

"I know, I know. But this... This is not something we can chance. If we spread the news and it turns out that you're wrong, it will not end well for Red River" Alpha Antonio said softly.

"I'm not wrong" Saxton said strongly. I could hear the confidence in his voice. Which leads me to wonder, what is he so sure of? The Alpha sighed loudly. I heard a chair scrape and footsteps. A moment of silence and then he spoke,

"Tell me again, from the start" Antonio said slowly,

"The start you already know" Saxton groaned,

"Tell me anyway, I need to get my head around this".

"We were caught and taken to a compound in Naples".

"You and Giana?"

"Yes".

"The same compound that she died in?"

"Yes".

"Okay, go on".

"We were beaten and tortured for maybe two weeks, could be more, it was hard to keep the time down there. One night the whole building lit up like a Christmas tree. Shouting, gunfire, the lot. It was clear that they were under attack. After a while, it went completely silent, and then she came through the door. I thought she was going to leave me there for a minute, but she broke the chains and helped me escape".

"Giana was already dead at this point?" the Alpha interrupted,

"Yes" Saxton replied quickly. He lied. Why would he lie? He knew she was still alive, he fought me to save her too. But once I told him that she wouldn't make it, and he either left with me now or I'd leave them both, he gave up and left her hanging there. Why would he lie to the Alpha about that, who was she to him?

"As she was carrying me through the compound, I saw all of the bodies. They were all dead. I must have passed at least twenty of them. When I asked her where her team was, she said it was just her".

"And you didn't see anyone else?"

"No. It really was just her".

"Okay, continue".

"She didn't say a whole lot at first, wouldn't even tell me her name. It took maybe a week to get back to full strength, and it was fucking hard trying to convince her not to leave me during that time. When she found the next compound, she demanded I go, but by that time I was already in too deep. She's cold and withdrawn, but she also has this magnetism about her. I watched her tear that compound to shreds, killing the hunters without mercy. It was an incredible sight. I can't... I can't even describe it" Saxton spoke so proudly when he retold our first few weeks together. I could hear the astonishment and adoration in his voice. It was nice to hear how he really feels about me, unfiltered and honest.

"That was the night I first realised she had a power. I couldn't believe it, I was sure I was hallucinating. But I wasn't, I saw it, it happened. I was determined to learn more about her. I had my suspicions from the get-go, but I had to be sure before I brought her home. The next few months, I worked on gaining her trust and winning her heart".

We agreed that my power would be kept a secret between the two of us. How could Saxton betray me like this? Why would he share that with the Alpha. And now I learn that it was his plan all along to bring me back here, but why? He has told so many lies, but I still don't understand why. What piece of the puzzle am I missing here?

"And you did win her over, after six months?" the Alpha asked,

"Yes, it was six months later that we Mated. Though she didn't know what it meant, she didn't know anything about our ways or traditions".

"That part I can't get my head around. She knows about hunters, and she knows she is a Were, how could she not know more about her own kind?"

"Well, after we did the ritual, she said she isn't a Were" Saxton said slowly, like he was remembering it as he spoke.

"That is the first time you have told me that part" the Alpha said loudly,

"I didn't think of it, and I didn't remember it until just now. I honestly didn't think she meant anything by it, just that she didn't grow up with a pack, so she didn't consider herself a real Were".

"She told you that? Well then, where did she grow up?"

"I don't know".

"Who are her parents?"

"I don't know".

"Why did she start hunting the hunters?"

"I don't know that either".

"Then what the fuck do you know, Saxton? You have given me nothing but more questions and wild possibilities. This girl is a complete mystery, how could we even know for sure about who she is if she won't even tell you, her Mate" the Alpha screamed. I could feel the tension in the room rising, it was seeping through the door. My own anger was growing considerably. The nerve of these beasts. Talking about me behind closed doors, trying to guess and speculate about my past instead of asking me directly. Granted, I wouldn't tell them anyway, but still. I was ready to break down the door and demand answers of my own, but then Saxton began shouting back at the Alpha,

"What more do you need to know, Antonio? She has power over the wind and air. She bears the mark of the Goddess on her skin. Everyone thought the line had ended what? Eighteen, nineteen years ago. She can't be older than twenty. It fits Alpha, you can't deny that all the pieces fit. If she isn't the Triple Goddess, then I'm not a Were".

Triple Goddess. What is that? And what mark is he speaking of, I have literally thousands of marks on my body. My skin is littered with scars, how could he think that just one of them makes me a what? A Goddess? These fucking dogs and their fucking gods and goddesses. I've had enough of this.

I kicked the door with my foot, sending it crashing to the floor across the room. Both Saxton and Alpha Antonio spun to face the door, both of them ready to fight. Only when they saw me, did they relax some. That was a mistake on their part.

"Tesoro, why didn't you tell me you were coming here?" Saxton said softly as he stepped towards me. I curled my lips back and growled a warning to him. He froze in place and lifted his head quizzically. I let the fire burn through my veins, allowing the rage to fuel my power. I summoned the air around me and used it to lift the Alpha off his feet. I threw him across the room to crash high into the wall. He hit the ground with a hard thud, and I quickly picked him up again. This time I held him upright against the wall with his feet dangling above the floor. The wind whipped around the room, sending my hair lashing against my face, and a mess of paper soaring through the air.

"Stop, what are you doing?" Saxton screamed as he rushed over to me. He grabbed my shoulder and tried to pull my attention away from the Alpha. I snapped my hand out and wrapped my fingers around his neck. He didn't fight me, just stared at me with sad eyes. I pulled him close to my face and growled lowly.

"You lied to me" I hissed angrily,

"I'm sorry" he choked out. He lifted his hand and gently stroked my face. The show of affection after his blatant betrayal just enraged me more. I squeezed my grip and growled.

"You promised that it would stay between us".

"I know, let me explain" he said as he tapped the hand that was holding his throat. My mind was in two. I wanted to trust him, to believe him. But all of my instincts were telling me to snap his neck.

"Please, Stellina" Saxton whispered. His eyes held so much emotion, so much longing. I looked over his pleading face, his smooth caramel skin was starting to get red and his mouth was gasping in deep breaths. I know that he loves me, I can see it, even if he did break his promise. I sighed deeply and released my grip. He dropped to his knee and coughed. As I left him to catch his breath, I turned back to the Alpha and snarled. He had been watching me closely the whole time. His body was pressed up against the wall, his arms splayed at his sides, unable to move due to the pressure of the air around him. His eyes were so wide that his thick eyebrows were almost touching his hairline. His normally tanned skin was looking pale and sticky with sweat.

"Don't try anything" I demanded of him. He nodded his head furiously in agreement, and I called back the wind. Antonio dropped to his feet and ran his hands over his body. I'm not sure what he was feeling for, or if he found it, but a second later, he turned back to face me. Saxton stood back at my side and slid his arm around my waist.

"I tried to tell you" he said with a cocky tone, like he had just proven his point. I peeked at him out of the corner of my eye, he had a proud smirk on his lips and his eyes looked down at the Alpha with a glint of malice. Could he have possibly known I was listening on the other side of the door, and that I would have reacted this way? Did he use me again, manipulate my anger to his own advantage? Would he go that far, again?

"Mia Dea" Antonio whispered before dropping to his hands and knees.

"My Goddess" he said softly. He bowed his head and lifted his hands out in front of him, holding his palms forward to face me. What the fuck is the idiot doing now?

"My Goddess" he said softly. He bowed his head and lifted his hands out in front of him, holding his palms forward to face me. What the fuck is the idiot doing now?

Chapter Nineteen

Whiskey

Present day.

I've ignored my training and instincts for too long. I pushed them aside and tried to be a 'normal girl' all for the sake of another. What did that get me? A fuck ton of nothing, that's what. I won't make that mistake again. I know who I am now. I know what I am and what I am capable of. I know now what I am fighting for, and who I am truly fighting against. My intended direction is clearly laid out at my feet, no one could come between me and my path now.

I was making my way up the mountain, trudging through the snow, when a flutter of electric sparks ran down my spine. It made my neck tingle and my body shiver. I looked around at the snow-covered trees and lifted my nose to the air. I sniffed around until I caught a scent. It was sweet and somehow, despite the fridged snow, it made me feel warm. I followed the scent through some trees to a small clearing. Before I broke through the line of trees, I spotted him. A man. At least I think he's a man. He was sitting on a large rock with his legs crossed and his hands resting on his folded knees. Only he wasn't sitting on the rock, he was floating a foot above it, in some kind of meditative state. I swiftly and silently moved through the snow, staying hidden amongst the trees, until I was positioned in front of the strange man. I lowered myself into the ground and watched him closely.

He was rather large. Long legs and long arms, all with defined and bulging muscles. His dark blonde hair was long on the top and short on the sides and sat pushed back off his face. His face was mesmerizing. Strong jawline, brushed with a slight array of hair, a straight nose and thick yet neat eyebrows. His eyes were closed, but I could see them moving behind his eyelids. My eyes moved down his relaxed arms to his fingers. They were moving slowly, flicking and twitching in a rhythmic way. My neck stiffened and I quirked my eyebrow as I zeroed in on his fingertips. Seeping from his fingers were black whisps of smoke. Curling out and around his fingers, before disappearing into the air. It was something I had seen many times before. I lifted my hand out in front of me and summoned my own power. A tiny whirl of wind bounced in the palm of my hand, mixing with it, was tendrils of the black smoke seeping from my skin. I looked back at the strange creature floating above the rock and stared intently at his hands. It's exactly the same. The way it pours from his skin, and twists and twirls around his fingers, the way it floats and dances through the air. It's the same. How could he have this same power? It's not possible. Unless... No. There's no way. He can't use this power, not unless he too is a creation of the hunters.

Fifteen months ago.
Saxton convinced the Alpha to stop bowing at my feet, and we all sat down at a large table. Alpha Antonio sat across from me, and Saxton sat at my side, his hand placed firmly on my leg. It was silent for a moment, uncomfortably so. The increasing tension and awkwardness was relentlessly picking at my anger.
"If you're ready, I'm ready. Explain" I snipped at Saxton. I shifted a little further away from him, still reeling at his betrayal. But he just pulled my chair back to his side.
"If I may start, my Goddess" Antonio interrupted meekly. The strong and frustrated voice I had been listening to was now gone, in its place was a softly spoken and timid squeak. Surely that tiny little show of power didn't scare this beast so much.
"What?" I spat,
"May I see it, may I see your marking?" he asked and quickly dropped his head in a bow. It was almost like he was ashamed to speak to me or to even look at my face.

"What mark? I have thousands of scars, take your pick" I groaned annoyed. Saxton chuckled and pulled me to his side to press his lips to my cheek.

"Not your scars, Tesoro, he means the mark of the Goddess" he said into my cheek. I pushed his face off me and glared at him.

"I don't have a mark of the Goddess, or whatever you want to call it" I snapped angrily. At least I don't think I do. The symbol he is talking about, I know it well. I was tortured while being forced to stare at it for hours on end. That would be the last symbol I wanted to see on my skin, a daily reminder of what I had to endure. I have enough of those already.

"You haven't seen this mark, Amore Mio. It's hidden. Here" Saxton said as he let his fingers gently brush the back of my neck. I reached up and ran my fingers over the spot he touched. I couldn't feel anything there, obviously, I haven't seen it if he says that's where it is. Also, who would take the time to consciously examine the back of their neck, no one. But, why should I believe him? I slapped his hand off me and turned to glare at him.

Every single time that Saxton had affectionately brushed his fingers over my neck, came flooding back into my mind. He does it often, very often. He did it just this morning after we finished fucking. The spot he is talking about is one of his favourite places to touch and kiss. He has always seemed to like rubbing his cheek and face along the back of my neck. I always thought it was just a werewolf thing. But if he has been doing this all this time, it means he has known about this mark for months. How could he not have told me. If it's true, I feel like it would be important information to share. Why would he keep that from me?

"Really?" I asked him softly. I was suddenly feeling much less hostile now, and more extremely confused. I couldn't possibly be starting to believe him. Am I actually considering that he could be right, that maybe he and the Alpha aren't as crazy as I first thought.

"Yes, Tesoro, really" he chuckled and pulled my hand from my neck. He rested his own hand over the place that he claimed the mark was, and squeezed slightly. His scent wafted around me, slipping into my nose, pride, excitement and strong hints of adoration, or perhaps its possessiveness.

"Goddess?" Antonio questioned again, I had forgotten about him for a quick second. I shrugged and stood up, I turned around and lifted my hair, exposing the base of my neck to the Alpha. He gasped loudly and when I turned around, he was once again on his knees.

"What's his deal?" I whispered to Saxton in annoyance as I sat back down.

"This is a big thing for him. In his eyes, you are a God. Apart from the Moon Goddess herself, there is no one else above you. You are the divine power, the ultimate being, the highest ranking Were. And we are Mated, meaning I will stand at the top of the world beside you" Saxton told me proudly. He was reeking of confidence, pride and cockiness. He believed every word he said. There's only one problem, this can't be right. I'm not a Goddess, I'm not even a real Werewolf. But how could I possibly tell them that now, they wouldn't believe me. The both of them have dived so deeply into this fantasy world they have created. I could feel their resolve and the unshed excitement and anticipation that they are still keeping buried, I could basically taste it on the tip of my tongue. And it is making me want to vomit. I don't want to be anyone's God. I don't even want to be here, in this pack, I'm only doing it for Saxton.

"I'm sorry, I don't know what else to tell you, but you're wrong" I said abruptly as I stood from my seat. Saxton jumped to his feet and scowled at me.

"What are you talking about?" he snapped. He has never spoken to me like that before. He had always been tender and loving with his words.

"Excuse me?" I grunted in surprise at his harsh tone. Since when does he speak to me like this. The Alpha slowly stood and watched us bicker warily.

"I'm not wrong. How would you know anyway, you barely know anything about Weres. I know what you are, I know what this means for me" he shouted and stepped closer towards me. He puffed out his chest and stood as tall as he could. He was trying to assert his dominance over me. The fucking idiot. He should know by now that no one is the boss of me.

"For you?" I almost laughed. It's all making sense now. Saxton's eyes went wide, realising what he had just said. The façade he had put on was falling apart, the fake mask he had been wearing was showing its cracks. That scent of his, the one I always assumed was adoration, is not. It's pure possessiveness. I was never a thing he adored. No, I was just something he wanted to possess and control. A toy for his own amusement.

"That's... I didn't... That's not what I meant" he stuttered as more of his cockiness shattered. My anger boiled to a bursting point in a mere moment. I had just discovered the game that I'd been inadvertently playing all this time. My erratically thumping heart shrivelled and froze in that moment of realisation, and I was ready for blood. His blood.

"Oh, it's what you meant alright" I hissed. The venom and fury dripped from my words menacingly. The Alpha backed away from us and lowered himself to the ground. The power, the rage, the violence that I was emanating, it was clearly too much for his weak soul to bear. Saxton let his gaze go soft and his eyes hooded, and a gentle loving look spread over his face. It was a look he had given me a thousand times before, a look I had come to cherish. All this time I had thought that look was filled with his true love and adoration. But now I can see the cracks, now I know there's a game in play, I can see that look for what it truly is. A manipulation. Saxton never truly cared for me, nor did he love me. He saw me only for what I could give him. He saw me as a tool for power and dominance. And I, being the weak and feeble bitch that he turned me into, drank in the fake love and attention like it was Kool-Aid at the cult picnic.

They were right. The hunters. My entire life they told me about werewolves and their vicious and violent tendencies, about their never-ending quest for more power, and unquenchable thirst for dominance. I should have listened more closely. I should have believed them. All this time I have been fighting the wrong enemy. I had been going after the ones that I thought hurt me. They didn't hurt me, not really. They made me strong, they toughened me up and prepared me for the cruelty this world has to offer. The hunters gave me everything I needed to put an end to Were-kind. They were my true protectors. They saw the beasts for what they truly are. Manipulative, greedy, power hungry, selfish animals. The hunters knew that the werewolves needed to be stopped, no matter the cost, whatever the sacrifice. They did what they did to me out of necessity and desperation. They needed me, the monster that they turned me into, because they couldn't do it alone. I've been so stupid, letting myself get tricked by the very beast that I was trained to kill. I know now. I know what I must do.

The anger burned through my body uncontrollably. The black whisps of smoke snapped out of me like a whip, cracking against the walls and furniture. I summoned my power and let the air fill my lungs, then I turned to the Alpha. I opened my mouth and screamed at the top of my lungs. The high-pitched echoed screech stung my ears. The Alpha covered his ears and tucked his head into his arms. Saxton dropped to the ground beside me, also holding his ears. I wailed like a banshee, filling the room with more air, and increasing the pressure around the Alpha. I could see him screaming in pain as he cowered from me. I could see the blood pouring from his ears and nose as he tried to shield himself. After a few seconds, the Alpha's body dropped to the floor. I pulled the air back into my lungs and looked down at his lifeless body. His blood spilled out onto the floor around him as his heart thumped its last beat.

Saxton cried in pain at my feet. A sound that filled my broken heart with joy. I grabbed him by the back of the neck and lifted him to his feet. Blood was dripping from his ears, nose and eyes. He was still holding his ears, like the pressure was still pushing against his brain. He blinked and stared at me in horror. The realisation of what was to come crossed his face and he paled.

"Now you will watch as I destroy your world, just as you did to mine" I sneered with a venomous smile. Saxton immediately tried to fight, to free himself of my grip. He kicked off with his legs and swung out with his extended claws. But he is untrained, his pain made him slow, unlike me. I launched my head forward, cracking my forehead into his nose. The audible crunch and Saxton's cry told me that I had broken it. When he still tried to get free, I lifted my leg and slammed my foot back down into the side of his knee. A loud snap filled the room, along with Saxton's painful scream. I looked down at his leg and smiled. The bottom half of his leg poked out at an awkward angle, and the bone of his shin had broken through the skin. I tightened my grip on the back of his neck so that he wouldn't drop. I leaned in close to his face and smirked,

"Now if you behave, I won't have to break the other one" I said in a cheerful threatening manner. Saxton nodded in understanding and let me lead him from the room. Just as we arrived at the top of the stairs, the Luna appeared at the bottom. Fear filled her face as she looked over Saxton's blood covered body, her eyes hovering on his leg the longest.

"Run!" Saxton screamed, and she didn't hesitate, taking off around the corner and out of sight. I heard two sets of quick footsteps, and then the door slammed closed as she bolted from the house. I growled angrily and threw Saxton's body tumbling down the stairs. He reached the bottom and sprawled out on the wooden floorboards. His broken leg looked even more deformed and more blood covered his face.

"You shouldn't have done that, now I will have to make them suffer" I seethed as I strode casually down the stairs. Saxton rolled onto his back with a groan. He looked up at me with a crooked and bloody nose. Terror filled his eyes as he tried pointlessly to scamper back away from me. A laugh burst from my lips at his pathetic attempt at escaping. I stomped my foot down on his broken leg, feeling the crunch of his bones shattering further. A chilling scream flew freely from his open mouth as he writhed in pain. I grabbed him by the scruff of his shirt and dragged him to the door. He begged and pleaded with me for mercy. Offering me his love, his loyalty, offering everything he has to give. None of which I wanted or cared about. No. I was going to kill every animal in this pack and make him watch as I did it. And then, once I have painted the stones red with the blood of his loved ones, I will kill him too.

Present Day.

I stared gobsmacked at the strange creature. I needed to know more. I need to study him, learn, and find out where he got his power. Once I have the answers I need, then I will act. I watched the man closely, day and night, for over a week. He was a creature of habit, doing the same thing each day. He would wake early with the sun, then he'd change into a large silver wolf. Which only leads me to believe my original theory. He is the same as me, an abomination, a created tool of death. After he hunts through the forest for food, he returns to his rock. Once there, he spends the rest of the day in the same meditative state. The black whisps twirled around his fingers before disappearing into the air. What an unusual man.

The more I watched him, the more curious I became. I noticed that the numbness was slowly fading. Much to my dismay. I was enjoying the blank nothingness. Emotions make you weak, they cloud your judgment. Being cut off from them was liberating. I was starting to find that my surveillance of the mystery man was somewhat comforting. His repetitive nature and the lack of surprises and variations was a nice change. It was good to slow down and just watch, without the need for immediate action. The man was enjoyable to look at as well. He was basically perfect, he would be, if it weren't for the scar on his ear. There was a large burn mark with a chunk of his ear missing from the top. Besides that, he was basically a living Greek God statue. Male beauty incarnate. I want to see him up close, to touch his porcelain skin and see the colour of his eyes. I must be losing my mind. Or I've gone too long without some semblance of decent interaction.

On the ninth day, he surprised me, by doing something out of routine. First, he woke late. He didn't emerge from his small tent until close to noon. Second, he looked ragged. Dark circles surrounded his eyes and his skin looked pale and sickly. He walked with his shoulders slumped forward and a slow thump to his step. He looked terrible. I'm not blind, I know he is insanely attractive, even from a distance. But not now, now he looks like he is dying or something. He skipped his hunt today and headed straight for the rock. I watched silently as he struggled to climb and perch his weak body on the top of the large stone surface. It took him a little longer than usual to get settled comfortably on his crossed legs. And even then, nothing happened. He didn't rise above the rock and the black whisps of smoke didn't pour from his fingers. He struggled. This continued on for hours, well on until after the sun had disappeared. The entire afternoon he struggled and groaned, he tried and failed. He was only making himself weaker.

This would be the optimum time to attack, while he is weak and tired. Too weak to defend himself. I can't risk underestimating this beast. I still don't understand the extent of his capabilities, or how he came to possess this power. The chance to take him out and end the threat is alluring. But I need to know more, I can't let the possibility of important information slip away.

After another hour of the big dumb lump's growling and groaning, he finally gave up and slinked away to his tent. I allowed enough time for him to fall asleep, and then I headed off into the trees in search of a meal of my own. I fought with my own mind, arguing between changing and not changing. I hate it, I always will. But it will be quicker and easier to catch something as the beast. Ruefully, I removed my clothes and hid them in a hollow tree. I let the shiver of heat run down my spine as I twisted my head. The snap sounded and I dropped to the ground on four paws. I stretched my back and shook out my deep black fur. I lifted my nose to the air and sniffed hard. The mountain air was moving through the trees quickly, but I was able to pick up the soft scent of a spruce hen.

Tracking the hens was easy enough, catching them was just as simple. After I had eaten a couple, I wrapped my jaw around two more, with the thought of bringing them back with me to eat later. I headed back to the clearing where the mystery man had made his camp. I slowed down and was careful with my footing as I got closer. I didn't realise what I was doing until it was already done. I placed the two birds at the foot of the tent and went back to the tree where I had hidden my clothes. I don't know what possessed me to leave the man food. I don't care if he dies from hunger, I do care if I don't discover his secret before he dies though. I'll put this down to selfish reasoning, at least for now.

After I dressed, I went back to my hiding spot among the trees. Sleep didn't find me, instead, I lay staring at the hens at the foot of the tent. What was I doing? I can't leave them there, that would be stupid. It was a dumb, rash decision, one I didn't give any thought to. I pushed myself up off the ground and walked quietly over to the tent. I grabbed the birds and slung them over my shoulder. As I was tiptoeing back to my spot, the zip of the tent ripped open. I spun on my heels and came face to face with the mystery beast. Fuck. The moment he saw me, his head tipped to the side and his eyebrows went up. He was surprised to see me, shocked even. I could see the confusion on his face as he was trying to understand what he was seeing. But after a quick second, the strangest look crossed his face, and he gazed at me like he knew me.

"Zee?" he said softly as his eyes looked me up and down.

What the fuck is a Zee?

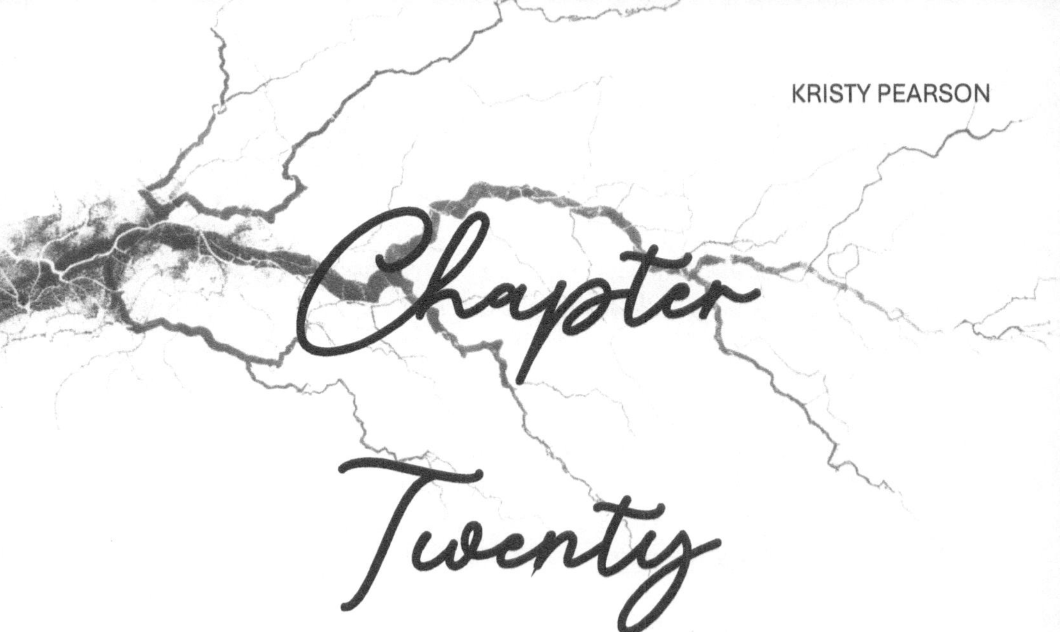

Chapter Twenty

Zelena

All those feelings of darkness and loss, the hurt and pain, the emptiness. They were all gone now. All I had to do was look at the beautiful sleeping faces of my babies, and my heart was full. I haven't named them yet. It doesn't seem right to do it without Gunner. Though I have some ideas that I'm pretty set on already. In the meantime, I have nicknamed them B. for my sweet little boy, and G. for my very loud little girl. They are both so similar, yet I can already pinpoint their very different characteristics. B. is quiet and rarely cries. He eats like a typical Alpha-son, but he loves to be swaddled and held tight. G. is very vocal about her demands. If she wants something or if something isn't right, the whole pack, and I'm sure half the town, will hear about it. I think I may have given birth to a Banshee, not a Were. Unlike her brother, G. likes to flail her arms and kick her legs, being swaddled with restricted movement will bring on the apocalypse. Or so she seems to think.

All that being said, their similarities are endless. Each of them has a pair of bright blue eyes, just like their Daddy. They each have smooth creamy pale skin, free of any imperfections. Their tiny little heads are adorned with dark black hair, like their Mumma. Their tiny little faces have pouty pink lips and a small squishy nose. If it weren't for the small round freckle that G. has on her cheekbone, they would be identical. I couldn't be more in love with them.

I am so full of joy and happiness, it is pouring out of me, quite literally. I find myself crying uncontrollably, even when all I am doing is looking at them. They don't need to do anything in particular, the waterworks will start at random. Roe said that it was just hormones, and she was a mess of emotion for days after both Gunner and Nat were born. I do hope she is right, I don't want to be a sobbing mess forever. Still, with all the love I feel, it still hurts when I remember that he isn't here. He should have been here, he would have loved to see his babies enter the world. It's not fair that he isn't. It feels selfish of me to enjoy this, to enjoy having them while he isn't here. Perhaps it's just the hormones making me angry, but every time one of the twins does something cute or makes a face or a sound, I look to see if Gunner saw it too. But then I remember, he isn't here, he is missing it all, and it gets me mad.

I'm thankful for Tobias, more than I ever have been before. Not only did he help me through the birth, but he has been a constant support since. He sleeps in my room with me now. His soft snores and his body heat help me feel less alone. Especially in the dark of the night when my heart aches the most. All I have to do is curl up into Tobias's side and let our bond do the rest. I don't know what I would do without him. G. has him wrapped around her finger, just like I knew she would. I said from the start that if I had a girl, she would have all the boys whipped. I was spot on. When she cries in the night, it's Tobias who calms her back down. He feeds her, settles her, cuddles with her and puts her back to bed. He is doing everything that Gunner was supposed to do. I am thankful, I really am. But I can't ignore the pain anymore.

I wish I could breastfeed them. During my breakdown, when I stopped eating or talking, or just existing, I lost too much weight. Even after giving birth to twins, I am sickly thin. My body just isn't strong enough to produce the milk. I hate myself for it. I feel like I have not only deprived my children of this important nutritional dietary need, but I have also deprived myself of that special bonding moment. No one ever tells you about all the gross stuff that comes after birth. All the bleeding and the hormones, the fear of spontaneously pooping my pants or pissing myself. I never worried about that before. Not to mention the exhaustion. Maybe it's worse because of how weak I am at the moment, my body is still in recovery mode. Not just from giving birth, but also from my near starvation.

It was dark, possibly early hours of the morning. I had not long ago settled G. back down. After a change, a feed, and a burp, she was out again. Little B. babbled quietly as he stirred awake. I picked him up and held him to my chest. I bounced him gently as I walked quietly around the room. G. was in the bassinet and B. was sound asleep in my arms. Instead of risking it and waking G. again, I laid down on the bed with B. tucked tightly in my arms. I was lying tucked under Tobias's huge arm, with B. in between us. I just started drifting off again when G. screamed herself awake. Tobias rolled carefully onto his side and kissed B. on the forehead, then did the same to me.

"I got her" he whispered softly. I hummed in response and curled myself around B. pressing my lips to his forehead.

"No, I'll do it. You were up with her last night" I mumbled incoherently.

"I don't mind, Mumma. I like her cuddles. Plus, she smells like strawberry ice cream" he chuckled and lifted her from the bassinet. I slowly moved off the bed with B. still in my arms. Tobias had her held up to his face and was smattering kisses over her soft little cheeks, hushing her and whispering how pretty she is.

"She likes you better than she does me" I grunted full of jealousy. I pouted and rolled my lip forward. Tobias chuckled and pulled my head to his chest, he kissed the top of my head and squeezed me gently.

"You're still my favourite Triple Goddess" he teased. I pushed myself out of his hold and huffed,

"I'm the only Triple Goddess" I clapped back.

"And that's why you're my favourite" he chuckled and kissed G. one more time before handing her to me.

"Come on little Alpha, you and me get to have some man time" Tobias said quietly as I shushed him harshly.

"He's still asleep" I whisper yelled, as he took B. from my arms.

"Fine, big boy cuddles then" he teased and laid back down on the bed with B. in the crook of his elbow. I rocked G. in my arms a little and watched as Tobias ran his huge finger over B.'s smushy cheek, whispering to him softly. Watching Tobias with my pups, seeing how good he is with them, seeing how much he loves them both, it only makes me more grateful to have him in my life. I decided to go for a walk, hopefully, the movement will lull G. back to sleep. I did a few laps of the hallway, and although the screaming stopped, she still kicked and punched her little limbs vigorously. I headed downstairs to grab myself a cool drink. The house was silent, everyone lost in peaceful sleep, or at least I hoped they were, and G. hadn't woken everyone.

Once in the kitchen, I was drinking from my glass of crisp cold water, when I saw movement through the window on the porch outside. I looked at the clock on the wall, 4:47 am. Not too early for warriors and hunters to be moving around, but they never come to the house this early. I held G. closer to my chest and tried to peer out the window. My body was swarming with worry and protectiveness. It tickled and buzzed through my veins like electricity. I strained my eyes through the darkness when the figure walked past the window again. I released the breath I was holding and let my worry fade away. I headed for the front door and stepped out onto the porch.

"Lunaya?" I said softly. She stopped her pacing and snapped her head up at me. She looked terrible. Dark circles sat under her eyes, and her hair was an array of messy knots and loose strands. Her body jittered and shook as she stood frozen staring at the bundled blanket in my arms.

"What are you doing awake so early?" I asked as I pulled the door closed behind me and walked over to her, still bouncing G. gently. She didn't move and didn't answer my question, just stared at the back of G's head.

"Lunaya?" I whisper hissed a little louder. She shook her head and looked up at me, forcing a smile onto her fear filled face.

"Couldn't sleep" she said with a shaky voice.

"I haven't seen you since the birth" I said sadly,

"I know" she answered and looked back down to G.

"That was four days ago" I said and bent my knees, trying to move my face down to her line of sight, to capture her attention.

"I should go" she snapped and went to turn around. I reached out and grabbed her arm.

"Stop" I demanded of her. She froze but didn't turn around again. "What is going on? You were so attentive up until now, and so excited about having a grandchild. What's changed?" I questioned her angrily.

"It doesn't matter" she answered and tried to push my hand off her,

"It does matter. You're my mother, everything was going so well between us, and now you can't even look at me. Tell me why!" I said raising my voice. G. gurgled and began her crying once again. I let Lunaya go and shifted G. in my arms, patting her bum and shushing softly into her cheek.

"It's okay Sweet Girl. Mumma didn't mean to yell" I told her gently. I pressed my lips to her cheek and closed my eyes, rubbing the side of my face against hers. When I opened my eyes again, Lunaya was looking at me, tears running down her face in endless streams. I was taken by surprise by her show of emotion. I thought she was mad, angry at me for something. I didn't realise that whatever it was that was bothering her, was hitting her so hard.

"I'm sorry" she sobbed and stepped closer.

"Please, can I hold her?" she asked with her hands out. I hesitated, looking over her distressed face and shaking frame. I don't understand where this extreme reaction is coming from. But I still trust her. At least I think I do. I don't think she would hurt G. or me. I kissed G's forehead and carefully placed her in Lunaya's arms. Lunaya sobbed and pulled G. to her chest, holding her tightly against her body.

"I'm sorry. I'm so sorry" Lunaya cried into the blanket that G. was wrapped in.

"It's okay. You're here now" I said softly, trying to sooth her.

"This isn't right. This can't be right" she cried out, bending her face into the blanket. That got me mad again. Having twins isn't that terrible. She just needs to get over it now. Enough is enough. I was done with trying to soothe her, and I just wanted to let rip with my own disappointment now.

"I get it alright. Roe has filled me in on the rareness of twins. Trust me, I get it. Only one in a million she-wolves have twins. But is it really so difficult to grasp? I'm a werewolf, and I'm the Triple Goddess, and I have a True Mate. Why not just add one more impossibility into the mix. I've already shattered all of the other Were-kind myths and legends" I snapped at her. I took a small step back and tried to keep myself from shouting so as to not bother G. But I failed. I was nearly yelling by the end of my little rant. Lunaya looked up at me with red eyes and tear stained cheeks.

"You don't like that I have twins. You've made that very clear. But you either get over it and get on board, or fuck back off out of my life" I hissed. I stepped forward and all but ripped my child out of her arms. I could feel my body shaking and the anger burning through my bones, making them stretch and twist with the need to change. I haven't been able to change into my wolf since I fell pregnant. But now that the twins were here, I've been feeling the itch to change crawling incessantly under my skin.

"It's not that. I am happy. I love them, both of them. There are just things that you don't understand" she cried desperately, trying to reach for me.

"Then make me understand! Explain it to me!" I yelled. The front door burst open, and Tobias stood there with the small blue blanket in his arm. Roe stormed out from behind Tobias and glared at Lunaya. She stomped over and carefully took G. from my shaking hands.

"What are you doing here? Haven't you upset her enough already" she hissed at Lunaya.

"Please, let me explain. I need to tell you the truth" she pleaded and stepped closer towards me. I held up my hand to stop her, just as the bone snapped out to the side. I winced and scrunched up my face in pain. The change hurts so much more when you are fighting against it.

"You need to let your wolf out first" Lunaya said cautiously and took a few steps back.

"I'm fine" I growled through the stinging feeling of my canines trying to extend from my gums.

"She's right, Little One. Change first, we can talk with your m..." Tobias started but I cut him off mid-sentence with a threatening growl,

"With Lunaya, we can talk with Lunaya at breakfast. You need to go for a run first" he said calmly and handed B. to Roe.

"Fine" I ground out and stomped down the steps to the clearing. Roe spoke quietly with Tobias as I removed my pyjamas. Lunaya just stood awkwardly on the porch, shifting her gaze between Roe and myself. After a minute Tobias nodded and jogged down the porch steps, pulling his shirt off as he went.

"After you" he said and threw his shirt on the pile where my own clothes were already sitting. I stopped resisting the fire and let it run through me freely. The snapping and cracking of my bones sounded as I ground my teeth together. I felt my tail slowly push through and my claws scratch into the dirt. My face and jaw stretched and elongated into my snout, and the fur burst through my skin. The change was done, and I stood panting softly as I looked up at Tobias.

"Such a pretty little puppy" he teased and went to pat my head. I growled and snapped my teeth at his approaching hand.

"Someone woke up on the wrong side of the bed" he feigned hurt and dropped his pants. His change was instant. A fact that enraged me further. I growled lowly and bared my teeth.

You'd be mad too if she was your mother

I am still mad, but I believe there's an explanation

I'm not sure I even care anymore

You can spout that shit all you want, but I know you better than to believe it

Whatever

I huffed and took off into the trees. Unsurprisingly, they were right, Roe and Tobias. A run is just what I needed. I felt like my body had been curled up into a tiny little ball, locked away inside a tiny wooden box, hidden inside a dark cupboard, buried six feet in the dirt. But now I was able to stretch out, unfurl my arms and legs and enjoy the freedom and release.

Tobias's fur and my fur were close in colour. Though, where his fur was black like the forest on a dark night, mine was more like the black sky on a moonless night, so black that it shone with a purple tinge under the light of the stars. I was half the size of Tobias as well. His ginormous wolf looked more like a large mutant bear. I was so small that I could almost blend in with a pack of regular wolves. But Tobias and I still moved through the forest together in perfect synchrony. Where he jumped, I ducked, where he dodged, I weaved. Each of us ran gracefully between the trees and brush. I didn't even know where we were running to, I was just enjoying the feeling. Who would have known that turning into a wild animal and running through a dark forest, would turn out to be an enjoyable experience. Definitely not me, and definitely not a year ago. Now though, I can't imagine not having this freedom, not having my wolf, and not having my special powers. I can't see my life like that anymore.

Tobias and I ran for hours, well after the sunrise, and long past the point where the morning air felt crisp and fresh and had turned warm and steamy. I got the scent of a stream off in the distance and ran toward it. I didn't hesitate and walked straight into the running water. I plopped down and let the stream flow around me, rushing over my tired legs and silky fur. I lapped at it as it flowed past. Tobias dropped his massive hulk like body down on the water's edge, he was panting with his tongue hanging out the side of his mouth. It was amusing to see such a large terrifying creature with a dopy look on its face. Tobias caught my staring and lifted his head, sucking his tongue back into his mouth.

What?

He flashed, with his black wolf eyes glaring at me. I chuckled, if a wolf even can chuckle.

Nothing, you just look adorable

I am not adorable

You are. Just like a fluffy little black cloud

Tobias stood up and took up a stance like he was going to attack. Head low, front paws apart, canines on full display, and his hackles at full attention along his spine.

Still adorable?

He growled through the flash and his wolf growled as well, shaking the ground beneath him. I climbed out of the water and shook out my fur, spraying the water all over him.

Yep. Still adorable

I teased him as I smacked my head into the side of his neck. He huffed annoyed and shoved me back easily with his humongous head. I pretended to trip and fall down, I laid still and whined like I was hurt. Tobias was quickly at my side, sniffing around my neck and shoulder.

I'm sorry Zelena, I didn't mean to hurt you

He flashed in a frantic tone. I quickly whipped over and snapped my jaws around the scruff of his neck, well, as much of it as I could fit in my jaws.

Just kidding

I laughed and tried my best to pull him to the ground, but it was like pulling the side of a building. Tobias growled gleefully and rolled down onto his back, making me fly up off the ground and land on top of him. I pushed my front paws into his fluffy chest and shook my head, growling playfully. For anyone watching us wrestle, with the stark size difference between us, I probably looked like an annoying bear cub pestering its mother. He chuckled and growled back at my attempts to get him to move. He managed to get his hind legs under my belly and flipped me over his head, sending me landing onto my back on the ground above his head. He quickly jumped to his feet and wrapped his giant jaws around my neck.

You need more wolf training

He teased me and easily fought off my ineffective kicks.

You need to stop slobbering on me

Tobias's wolf chuckled and let me go. I jumped to my feet and shook out my fur.

Maybe a little extra training wouldn't hurt, I suppose

Thought you might say that. Are you ready to head back?

Yes. I'm starving, and I miss my babies

Me too

You too, you're starving, or you miss the babies?

Both

You're a big softy, you know that

I'm not soft, or adorable

Sure, sure, you keep telling yourself that

I love making fun of Tobias. No one else would see it, because no one else has the bond that we have. But even now, with all the serious and mysterious changes he went through since that day in the forest with Selene, he is still my closest confidante. Tobias understands me on an entirely different level to everyone else. That's why he is so good for me. The perfect guardian. The best friend.

When we got back to the village, it was bustling with activity. Tobias and I strode through the clearing side by side. I nodded my 'hello' to each pack member that greeted me. Many of them wished me well and told me how excited they were to meet the new baby. We have yet to share with the pack that there are twins. I'm hoping Gunner will be back soon, so then I can share the news with him before I do so with the pack. Which reminded me.

The other day, in the delivery room, you said that Gunner will be home soon

I did

Did you mean it?

Of course

Do you like know, know. Or are you just guessing?

Tobias snapped his large head to the side, and I watched as his body swiftly morphed back into his human form, allowing him to stand up on two feet.

"I know he will come back to you. He is your True Mate, and the father of your pups. No sane Were would ever leave you all behind on purpose" Tobias said as he pulled on his jeans. I concentrated on my human form and felt the pinch of the change. I slowly stood up on my own human feet and took the pyjama bottoms that Tobias was holding out for me. Great, I'll be wearing my pj's in the middle of the village. Didn't consider that when we left before dawn. I slipped my pants on and then the top and walked quickly to the main house.

As soon as I entered the smell of food hit me like a ton of bricks, and my stomach grumbled with enthusiasm. Tobias laughed beside me with a slight shake of his head.

"Anyone would think that you're still pregnant." he scoffed and headed into the kitchen, with me close on his heels. Roe was busy behind the counter with another she-wolf. I recognise her, Amy, she works in the kitchen during special occasions and guest visits. Really any time that cooking requires extra hands. Not sure what special occasion calls for help this morning though.

"Smells good, Roe" I cooed with my nose in the air.

"Thank you, Darling, grab yourself a plate and dig in" she said with a wave.

"Good morning, Amy" I said with a smile. She seemed surprised that I remembered her name, and answered me with a quick low bow.

"Hello Luna" she said from her bowed position.

"What's going on, why the big cook up?" I asked and took a plate and handed it to Tobias, then took one for myself. I began filling my plate with the delicious smelling bacon, pancakes, scrambled eggs, and freshly cut fruit. If there is one thing I love about my wolf being born, it's that I can now eat like a sumo wrestler. Growing up, eating was never something I looked forward to, or held much regard for. Maybe because I didn't remember ever eating a decent meal, not until Selene gave me back my memories. But now, I love eating, especially Roe's cooking.

"I was awake at the ass crack of dawn and couldn't get back to sleep, so I thought why not cook the pack a nice breakfast" Roe mumbled as she continued mixing the pancake batter. I filled with guilt and regret at her words. I didn't mean to wake anyone up this morning. And the last thing I would want is to upset Roe.

"Oh, I'm sorry. I didn't mean to wake you" I said remorsefully. Roe's head snapped up and her gaze softened as she looked at me. "Oh, Darling, I'm not upset at you. If anything, I'm annoyed with that woman" she huffed and threw her head towards the kitchen door. I didn't need to ask, I knew she was talking about Lunaya. Roe has been huffing and grunting about Lunaya since she ran out of the delivery room. The fact that she didn't come back until this morning has probably made her even angrier.

"Well, I'm sorry regardless" I said with a small smile. I looked around the kitchen and the breakfast nook, where Tobias was sitting with his overflowing plate of food, but I didn't see the twins.

"Where are the twins?" I asked nervously, my voice going a little high.

"They should be in the nursery, Smith is with them" she answered over her shoulder as she flipped another pancake.

"Thank you" I called and headed out of the kitchen. I was about to head up the stairs but was stopped before I climbed the first step.

"Zelena?" Lunaya called from the library door. I groaned and turned to look at her.

"Can we talk please?" she asked as she fiddled with her fingers.

"Can it wait, I want to check on the twins" I snipped and put my foot on the first step.

"It can't wait any longer" she said quickly. I froze and looked at her over my shoulder with my brow raised,

"I understand that you're angry with me, and you should be. My behaviour was atrocious. But this has waited long enough and I'm afraid it's become rather urgent" she insisted. The tone in her voice gave me a chill. She sounded scared and anxious. So, I stepped down from the step and followed her into the library. I sat down on an armchair and lifted my plate to sit under my chin.

"Do you want to call for Tobias or Roe, or anyone else?" she asked hesitantly as she sat on the couch opposite me. I shook my head and shoved a spoonful of eggs in my mouth.

"Okay" she breathed heavily and leaned back in the chair, crossing her hands on her lap.

"Where do I start?" she chuckled awkwardly and rubbed her sweaty palms over her legs.

"I've said a few times that there are things about your past, your family, that I've been wanting to talk to you about" she started. I nodded in recognition. There have been a few times she has said we needed to talk, I never knew what about though, but she did always sound urgent when she mentioned it.

"Well, I think the best place to start is when I was pregnant, and I was told about the prophecy for the first time".

I groaned loudly and placed my half eaten plate of food on the coffee table.

"Yes, I've already heard about the prophecy. Galterio told me all about it when he tried to replace Gunner as my Mate" I grunted and folded my arms over my chest.

"Galterio was an overconfident ass, who came from a long line of self-absorbed asshats, and that particular asshat put his faith in the wrong person" Lunaya growled ferociously. Her quick turn to anger had me surprised.

"Let me guess, he told you the prophecy was about you having two Mates?" she hissed with annoyance.

"Yes, he did" I answered her cautiously. This sudden change in temperament had me a little worried.

"Artemis was a fool, he knew nothing of the true prophecy. He spouted bullshit and lies, disguising them as the word of the Goddess. Only a self-important, power hungry, dick like Galterio would believe he had a chance to Mate with a Triple Goddess" Lunaya snapped. My eyes went wide with shock as I gazed at her angry and reddening face. This was personal for her. Like, really personal. My interest piqued and I sat up a little straighter.

"Okay, I hear you. If not two Mates, what was the prophecy about?" I asked her sincerely. Lunaya took a deep breath and interlocked her fingers on her lap. She looked up at me to meet my gaze and then spoke so softly I could only just hear her.

"Spawned by the one who gave us breath. Vanished from life but spared from death. The Ethereal one gives she who is promised. To wield the power of the Triple Goddess. Where the moon is three, two will come. Once the seal is made, destiny is done. With one comes death, pain and destruction. The other comes life, love and devotion. Peril will end and the wolf will thrive. But for peace to reign, only one can survive".

Galterio didn't recite the actual prophecy, he only told me the meaning. Or what he thought was the meaning. I can understand how he may have thought it was about Mates. But hearing it for myself is different. It's not about Mates. Not even close. My stomach dropped and I had a dark feeling in the pit of my stomach. I know what it's about. But I need to hear her say it.

"Tell me" I squeaked. My voice shook with uncertain terror.

"It's about twins" Lunaya said, confirming my fear.

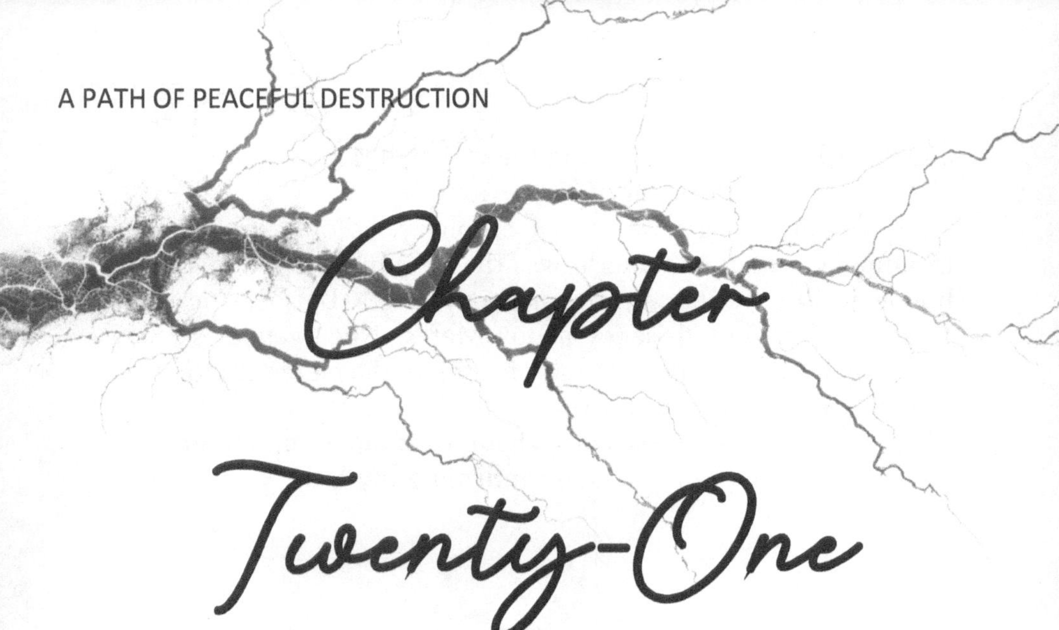

Chapter Twenty-One

Whiskey

What is a Zee? And why is he calling me a Zee? I didn't respond to the strange beast, instead, I backed away slowly and watched as he fully emerged from the tent. I turned my body slightly to the side, bent my knees and lifted my arm over my shoulder. I wrapped my hand tightly around the handle of my blade, ready to pull it from its holster. I was prepared to fight if that's what the beast wants. He was taller up close. He stepped closer toward me, lifted his nose to the air and sniffed. He furrowed his brows and stepped closer again.

"Who are you?" he demanded in a loud and earth-shattering voice. Again, I gave no response, I just curled my lips back and snarled. Come on, Beasty Boy, let's dance.

"What did you do to her?" he demanded again. His voice took on a deep and rumbling roar. A shiver ran up my spine. I'm not sure how or why, but this mutt felt different, his aura, it was more powerful than others I've faced. A quick flicker of curiosity passed through my brain. Who could he be talking about I wonder? I shook the questions from my mind and forced my concentration back to the situation at hand. I pulled the blade slowly out of its holster and pointed it at the large man. His canines extended and he growled. The sound echoed through the trees and shook the ground beneath my feet. Oh yes, this beast will definitely put up one hell of a fight. I smiled at the thought, which seemed to provoke the man further. I glared at him, waiting for him to charge first. They always do. The stupid animals take one look at me, weigh up my size and stature and think it an easy win. Each one of those fools is dead now. This beast will be no different.

I waited, and nothing. He didn't charge, he stood patient, holding his ground. So, he's smart then. Fine. I can adapt. I lunged first, aiming to plunge my blade into the stomach of the man. He was quick for his size, spinning out of my reach at the last second. I didn't wait for him to charge this time and I went for him again. I ran forward, launching myself through the air, I came down on him with my blade aimed at his chest. Just as the blade was about to pierce his skin, I was blocked. Not by his hand or a weapon, the blade was halted by nothing, some kind of invisible shield. What kind of magic is this? I glared at the man, trying to understand what had just happened. He glared back at me with haunting eyes, eyes that were glowing a brilliant silver.

A low and threatening growl burst from his lips, and before I had a moment to react, he grabbed me around the throat and slammed my back into a tree. I rounded my blade on him but once again, I was stopped by that same invisible shield. I growled in frustration and swung my weapon again. This time the blade was ripped from my grip. Though not by his hand. The blade hung in the air not far above my head. I marvelled at it as it turned slowly through the air, held up by nothing. It twisted and turned, and then folded in on itself until it dropped to the ground as a crumpled mess of steel. This fucking bastard, I loved that blade. I lifted my arm for the other blade but he grabbed my wrist and held it at the side of my head. I'll give him one thing, he certainly wasn't weak anymore.

He pressed his body up against mine, pushing himself between my legs and holding me in place with his hips. He ran his nose slowly along the nape of my neck. My body betrayed me and responded with a shiver. I gasped and unknowingly tipped my head to the side, giving the stranger more access to my neck. Fuck. I need to snap out of it. I growled and kicked my leg out, connecting the tip of my foot to his shin. He growled back and lifted me off the ground by my neck and wrist. I kicked my legs out furiously, aiming for anything I could reach. What am I doing, I'm thinking like a trapped animal. I am not capable of being trapped, nor am I a helpless animal. I am powerful, I am death. I glared down at the beast and sucked in a deep breath, taking with it all of the air around him. His eyes went wide and he coughed once. But then he was fine. No. He should be choking, suffocating, dying. Why isn't my power working, why kind of beast is he? I threw my fist forward at his face, but it slammed against the invisible shield. I felt my knuckles crunch and break under the pressure of the blow to the impenetrable wall. The man gazed at me, both anger and curiosity filling his glowing silver eyes.

"Enough" he demanded. He pulled my other blade from its holster and threw it across the ground to the other side of the clearing.

"I don't want to hurt you" he said slowly and cautiously as he lowered me back to my feet. He loosened his grip on my neck, enough for me to breathe unobstructed, but not enough for me to get free. His other hand kept my non broken hand pinned to the tree above my head. Though I could already feel the broken bones shifting and realigning back into place.

"Will you stop trying to kill me?" he asked, his voice was gravelly and rough and held an aura of dominance to it. I looked over his handsome face as he waited for my answer. He is more powerful than I expected. I underestimated him. I won't do that again. But I can't let him go free until I understand how, or where, his power came from. If he is truly like me, a creation of the hunters, that could mean there are more of us. If that's the case, I have to find out how many, and where they are. They could assist me in my mission. I swallowed down the need for blood and buried my desire to cut him into small pieces. I relaxed my furious face and nodded my head slowly.

The glow of his eyes slowly melted away, giving way to the bluest of blue. A tinge of guilt ran through me and a sense of longing filled my shrivelled heart. I stared into his eyes as his face morphed into Saxton's. Smooth caramel skin, long thick lashes, wide plump lips, and that small mole on his chin. His deep blue ocean eyes stared back at me with love and adoration. No! This isn't real. I blinked my eyes and shook my head. My lips curled back and a growl bubbled through my exposed teeth.

"What are you?" he asked me, his head again tilted to the side as he studied my face. He held no malice or fear in his intense gaze, only confusion and curiosity. But wait, he asked 'what' am I, not 'who' am I. Does that mean he can tell I am not a normal human? I didn't answer his question, instead, I tried to get a read on him. I breathed in through my nose, taking in his scent and emotions.

He was confused, but his scent was filled with pain and anguish. He was tormented, like he was grieving. His scent was like warm ocean air, with hints of citrus. I realised I was staring blankly at the man when a chuckle fell from his pink lips.

"I can see you scenting me, little she-wolf, have you figured out if you can trust me yet?" he asked teasingly. He was joking with me, playing even. He doesn't know me, he doesn't know that I am a threat, and yet he is so calm and fearless. Why? He leaned his face closer to mine and sniffed up the side of my neck, all the way to my cheek. His face was so close, I could feel his breath on my cheek. But surprisingly, I wasn't disgusted, I was intrigued.

"It's uncanny" he whispered to himself. He moved his body back and roamed his eyes from my face and down my body, then back up again.

"If I let you go, are you going to attack me again?" he asked gently. I slowly shook my head from side to side, and he removed his fingers from around my neck. He took two large steps away from me, giving me room to breathe and think, which came a lot easier without his intoxicating scent filling my senses.

"Can you speak English?" he asked me as he crossed his arms over his chest, making him look three times bigger. I had a choice to make here. One, kill the beast and forget about all the questions of how, where, and why, coursing through my brain. Or two, speak to him. I can ask him questions, let him ask me questions in return, trick him into trusting me, and then go from there.

"Yes" I answered him, deciding on option two.

"Excellent, that makes things easier" he huffed with a smile. I gasped slightly at the beauty of his smile, he is truly remarkable to look at.

"Do you want to tell me your name?" he questioned. I swiftly shook my head in response.

"Maybe you can tell me why you tried to kill me then?" he asked with a raised eyebrow. I thought about it for a second, then shook my head again. He laughed and walked over to a tree, he lowered himself to the ground and leant back on the trunk.

"Not a big talker, are you?" he said with a hint of amusement. He seemed to be laughing at something, not out loud, but I could see a fond or happy memory flash through his faraway gaze. After a beat, he wiped the smile from his face and looked back up at me, waiting for my answer. I shook my head and very slowly sat down at the base of the tree behind me, not once taking my eyes off the man.

"What are you doing all the way out here?" he asked. His eyes once again travelled the length of my body, making me shiver.

"Hunting" I grunted lowly,

"You're an Omega" he said with a nod. He wasn't asking me, he said it like he already knew. I shrugged my shoulders and pursed my lips. I won't correct him, at least not yet. For now, I will let him think he knows what I am. It's interesting though, how is he still so calm in the face of an unknown threat? Unless he doesn't see me as a threat, like many Weres that came before him.

"So, mystery girl, where have you come from?" he said nonchalantly, like it was no big deal. Though I could see the flicker of interest sparkle in the depths of his blue eyes.

"Why so curious?" I snapped back quickly.

"Woah, just making conversation. It's either chat with you, or have you trying to gut me again" he chuckled with his hands up in surrender. I rested my back against the tree and sat quietly. The man did the same, not saying a word. I scanned the ground for my blade, the one he threw away. I spotted it, on the other side of the clearing. I could make a run for it, but he'd probably either reach it first with his weird power, or he catch me first. So that's not really an option. He can somehow resist my power, so that's out too. I guess if it comes down to it, I'll just have to kill him the old fashion way, with my hands. I turned back to the man and met his intense fiery gaze. I stared back at him, refusing to back down or break first. After a beat, he shook his head and chuckled while pinching the bridge of his nose.

"She's testing me. She has to be" he mumbled to himself. If it weren't for my exceptional hearing, I wouldn't have picked up on it.

"Come again?" I grunted,

"Nothing, it's nothing" he smiled and looked back up at me with a fresh resolve.

"Out with it" I snapped.

"You just look like someone I know, someone I miss very much" he answered very sadly. He does miss her, a lot, I can see it all over him. I think maybe he loves her, whoever she is.

"Is she dead?" I asked without thinking,

"No, she's not dead. She is back at home, waiting for me. Well, I hope she still is" he said without looking at me,
"Waiting for you, why?"
"There's something I have to do before I can see her again".
"And what's that?"
"Well, look who's chatty all of a sudden" he laughed and looked at me with a bright smile. I swallowed the lump in my throat and frowned.
"Would you prefer I go back to trying to gut you?"
"No, not at all. This is nice. I haven't spoken to anyone in a while".
"Me either" I answered softly.
"My name is Gunner" he said after a few minutes of silence. I looked up at him, and he was once again staring at me in a way that made my skin burn. I can't place it, this strange feeling of warmth and comfort that he gives me. No one else, ever, has made me feel like this, not even Saxton. There is a tingle deep in the pit of my stomach, it is screaming at me to trust him. I don't like it. And I sure as shit don't want to listen to it.
"You can call me Whiskey" I said cautiously.
"Whiskey?" he asked. His surprise is warranted. It's a dumb nickname, but it's better than the actual scientific name the hunters gave me. Viski Gol'f Dva (WG-02). Otherwise known as, Wolf-Girl Zero-Two. Pretty fucking dumb, and yet perfectly typical of the hunters to be so uncaring as to not even give their creation a name.
"Whiskey" I confirmed with a nod of my head. He shrugged and stood up, brushing the dirt from his jeans.
"Well, alright then" he said and offered me his hand to help me to my feet, not that I needed it. I looked at his large hand and then up at his waiting blue eyes, then back to his hand.
"I'm not going to hurt you, Whiskey" he said gently and with a half-smile. I very slowly slipped my palm into his hand, and he lifted me to my feet. His skin was unusually warm, and it sent a stream of goosebumps exploding over my arms. I stood with my hand still in his, staring into his bright blue eyes. They flashed with a glimmer of silver, before returning to their natural colour again. That is unusual for a regular Were. I have come to know that their eyes can darken with rage or lust, but they don't glow, and they don't shimmer. He has to be like me, what other explanation is there?

"Do you have a camp nearby?" he asked as he dropped my hand and shifted his eyes around the dark trees. He wouldn't see a camp, as I didn't make one. He doesn't know I've been watching him. I shook my head in response to his question and he chewed on his bottom lip. He sucked on his teeth and sighed.

"If you want, you can bunker down close to me. As long as you promise not to kill me in my sleep" he chuckled dryly. This Were is an idiot. Why would he let a complete stranger share his camp, especially one that just tried to kill him? He must have had one too many hits to the head. I furrowed my brows and stared at him, completely dumbfounded. He must have noticed my blank stare, as he laughed and gently touched my shoulder.

"I don't think you're all that bad. You were just startled or scared. I have a good feeling about you, Whiskey" he said with a reassuring smile. That same tingle in my stomach exploded into a thousand butterflies, all of them begging me to trust him. He is dumb to think I was afraid, I am scared of nothing. But this odd feeling, this overwhelming desire to trust him, to let him in, is only growing stronger.

"Okay" I said slowly and cautiously. I hope I don't regret this.

"You don't have a bag, a tent, a sleeping bag, anything?" he asked looking over my body and again at the surrounding trees, I wonder what he keeps searching for. Then again, it's cold and I'm not wearing my jacket. Maybe he isn't as dumb as I thought.

"Actually, yes. I have a bag" I said and pointed to the shrubs where my things were hidden.

"But didn't you come from that direction?" Gunner asked, pointing to the area of trees where I had hidden my clothes. His voice took on a cautious tone as he eyed me intently, waiting for my response.

"I did. I came across your tent on my way back from a hunt. Must have missed it the first time" I told him, the lie falling effortlessly from my mouth.

"Uh huh" he mumbled and looked back at his own tent. The two hens I left him were still sitting on the ground. Fuck. I'm caught.

"Well, I can come with you to grab your bag" Gunner said and started walking in the direction I pointed. He knows I'm lying, he must. No one is that dumb, even a damned werewolf. But why isn't he calling me out on it?

"No, it's okay, it's not that far away. I'll be right back" I said quickly, stopping him in his tracks. I smiled my best friendly smile and turned to run from the clearing. I ran further than I needed to. Way further. I listened carefully for footsteps, making sure he wasn't following me. When I was sure that he didn't, I circled back and grabbed my bag on the way into the clearing again. He couldn't know that I was staying so close, that I'd been spying on him. It would ruin all my plans. Gunner sat at the open door of his tent, legs crossed and eyes watching me walk toward him.

"That's all you have, where's your tent and camping equipment?" he asked looking at the backpack draped over my shoulder.

"I don't have any of that" I answered bluntly. He furrowed his brows and seemed to be thinking, as he once again looked around at the trees.

"It gets pretty cold here at night" he said and looked at me out of the corner of his eye.

"I didn't know that" I lied. Of course I know it gets cold. I've been sleeping out in it every night. He doesn't need to know how much I actually like the cold, how much I have in common with the cold dark night.

"Hmph" he grunted and ran his hand through his hair.

"Sleep in here" he grumbled lowly and shifted back into his tent until I couldn't see him any longer. He can't be serious. Offering to share a campground is different to sharing a tent. Does he have a death wish. He seemed to notice my hesitation and poked his head back out.

"You don't need to worry about me, I told you I have someone waiting for me. I won't touch you, I swear it" he said with a nod. Funny he was more worried about reassuring me of my safety and less afraid for his own. Such a strange Were. I tossed my bag in through the door and slipped in after it. Gunner had laid out an extra blanket next to him and tossed another out over the span of the tent. He came prepared obviously. He patted the spot beside him and climbed under his own blanket. He rolled onto his side with his back to me. Another dangerous decision. I slowly moved to the area he had set up and sat down, tucking my bag into the far corner.

"Whiskey?" Gunner said without moving,

"Yes" I answered,

"Please don't kill me" he said firmly. I looked at his back and watched his chest rise and fall with his breaths. I could smell his caution and his protectiveness. Though I couldn't pinpoint what he was protecting. Himself perhaps.

"Okay" I said softly and laid down on the makeshift bed beside him. I have no intention of sleeping. He doesn't trust me, as he shouldn't. But I don't trust him either. There is no way I will let my guard down, regardless of what my stomach is telling me. I lay quietly, listening to the slow steady breaths of the recklessly brave Were next to me. Gunner is unlike anyone else I have come across, I'd be lying if I said I wasn't intrigued by him.

Unknowingly, the calming and steady breaths of Gunner slowly lulled me into a peaceful sleep. The same old dream floated through my unconsciousness. The other me was there, her mouth moving with no sound coming out. She wasn't pregnant this time, but she was holding two little babies. She stepped toward me, and I stepped toward her. We did this until we were only inches apart. I looked down at the small little bundles in her arms, two fat little babies smiled back at me. The blue of their eyes was startling. I took some steps back and looked at the other me. Her mouth was still moving as she spoke, but I couldn't hear her. As I looked around at the tall trees and green shrubbery, I felt two strong arms curl around my waist. I looked back at the other me and Gunner was now standing behind her, his arms around her waist and his face in the crook of her neck. I felt hot breath tickle at the top of my shoulder and then soft warm lips skim up along my neck. I tilted my head to the side and moaned into the soft sparks that trailed behind his lips. I looked up and Gunner's face was in the crook of my neck. I looked back at the other me and it was like I was looking in a mirror. I held the two babies in my arms, like her. Gunner's hands were around my waist, his mouth devouring my neck, like her. I was her and she was me. She looked happy and was smiling blissfully as Gunner's mouth ran over the soft skin of her neck. Gunner's face looked up from her neck and his eyes flashed silver as he stared directly at me. She too looked up and stared right at me. And for the first time ever, I heard her speak.

"Come back to me" she sang in a soft and echoed voice. The gentleness wrapped around me like a warm blanket. It made me feel safe, wanted, loved. It made me feel everything that I had been missing my whole life.

I didn't fly up in a panic like I usually do after that dream. Instead, I woke gently from my sleep, my mind filled with calm and peace. I have struggled all my life with not knowing what the mirrored version of me was saying. The unknown has plagued my dreams for as long as I can remember. And now I could hear it. It was like a giant weight had been lifted from my shoulders. But why now? And what was Gunner doing in this dream? That was strange. He was an attractive man for sure. But I still haven't ruled him out as a threat, and I sure as shit don't want him wrapping his arms around me like that. I could be horny but I'm not stupid, and exposing myself to a stranger would be very, very stupid.

I stretched my legs out and realised my movements were restricted. Something hard was pressing against my back and a heavy weight was on my shoulders. My eyes flew open, and it all came rushing back in. Where I was, who I was with, what I was meant to be doing. I stared at the wall of the tent in front of me. Before I moved any more, and alerted him that I was awake, I tried to understand what was holding me down.

Steady and low breaths were what first caught my attention, followed by a gentle snore. Next was the warm breath on the back of my neck. I lowered my eyes and saw a large arm hanging over my shoulder, with his hand wrapped around my wrist. Then a leg, which was thrown lazily over my waist. Gunner had moved himself behind me, right behind me. It was his firm chest that my back was pressed against, his limbs that were pinning me down. But he was snoring, he's still asleep. Is he holding me down on purpose, so that I can't run away, or attack without waking him. That would be smart. Though a strange way of doing it. Tying me up would have been just as effective.

Gunner stirred behind me, shifting himself forward and squeezing his arms around me tighter. I tried to pull myself free, but he only gripped me harder. His body warmth was like a furnace, his skin burning against mine like a gentle flame. As he shifted himself closer, the hardened length between his legs pressed into my backside.

"Zee, five more minutes" he mumbled sleepily and buried his face into my hair. He is getting way too familiar, and why does he keep calling me Zee? I growled a warning, letting the sound rumble loudly through the tent. Gunner's arms and legs disappeared from around me and his body flew back away from me and across the tent. I took the opportunity and rolled away from him. I spun around to face him, crouched and ready with my talons extended. His face had paled, and his eyes were wide. He looked back at me with a half awake and remorseful expression.

"I am so sorry, I forgot myself for a moment there" he grumbled and ran his hand over his face. He rubbed his eyes hard and combed his fingers through his dishevelled hair. When he looked back up at me, he seemed annoyed at my prepared stance.

"I've already told you that I'm not going to hurt you" he groaned and laid back down on his back. Still, I didn't move. I know what men are like, I know what male Weres are like too. Horny lust-filled beasts, insatiable and forceful.

"Tell that to the weapon you've got concealed in your pants" I snorted. Gunner looked down at himself and burst out with a thunderous laugh. He grabbed the corner of the blanket and placed it strategically over his lap, trying and failing to conceal the raised section of his pants. He chuckled lowly and while keeping hold of the blanket, he flopped his other arm over his eyes and sighed deeply.

"I guess some things never change" he mused to himself. I growled again and shifted a little further away from his still form. As I watched him, waiting for him to pounce, I wondered at the meaning behind his little inside joke. What hasn't changed and why does this giant buffoon seem so calm and unbothered by my presence?

Chapter Twenty-Two

Whiskey

"So, where have you come from?" Gunner asked me. He sat across from me at the small firepit. We cooked one of the spruce hens that I caught. It was a fat one too, with lots of meat on it. He was slowly ripping the flesh off the breast, while I gnawed at its leg. After the unexpected cuddle I got from Gunner this morning, I've become more curious about the girl he mentioned, the one waiting for him. I think her name is Zee, or at least that's what he calls her. He has called me Zee twice now, so he must be missing her a lot to be seeing her face in mine.

"Nowhere in particular" I answered. Giving him something, while still giving him nothing. A tactic I have been using all day, every time he has asked me something.

"This isn't exactly a populated area. No towns for miles and the closest pack are hours away. Why would you come all the way out here?" he pushed. He is slowly becoming more brazen and intrusive with his questions. He is curious, that's a given, but his questions are persistent.

"Why did you?" I fired back without hesitation. Gunner chuckled and shook his head.

"Still so defensive" he teased me as he sunk his teeth into the chicken meat.

"Well, I came here for the emptiness, the space and the quiet. Because there is no one else for miles. At least there wasn't meant to be" he mumbled through the chicken in his mouth.

"Now you" he prompted,

"No reason. Or, well, the same reason, I guess" I answered with a careless shrug of my shoulders.

"Did you come from one of the packs close by?"

"No".

"It's very coincidental that you, of all people, just happen to stumble upon the mountain I was camping out on" he said cryptically. He's been doing that a lot today. Saying little things, and making little comments, all of which seem to have a hidden meaning, one that I didn't know about. It's starting to drive me insane. Me of all people. He says it like I'm someone special to him and the universe is playing games with him. Maybe I'll just kill him and be done with it.

"I don't believe in coincidences" I told him while looking him dead in the eye.

"I'm starting not to either" he mumbled and threw a chicken bone into the fire.

"Will you stop with that" I growled annoyed,

"Stop with what?" he chuckled back. The laughing and chuckling are also starting to enrage me. It is almost like he finds my anger and frustration amusing. I wonder how amusing he would find my anger when I am sinking my blade into his chest.

"First of all, stop laughing at me. And then you can stop with the whole cryptic bullshit. You want to say something to me, then out with it" I demanded and threw my chicken bone into the fire. The bone crackled under the heat of the flames, and fresh embers floated away into the night sky.

"I'm sorry, I'm not laughing at you" he said sincerely,

"Liar" I hissed back,

"I'm not lying, I swear it, and I'm not laughing at you. I am, however, laughing at myself, and this whole situation that I have gotten myself into" he said with a shake of his head.

"That, that right there" I yelled and stood up,

"That's the cryptic shit I'm talking about. Just fucking say what you want to say already" I yelled in his face. I could feel the heat fluttering over my skin, the anger inside me starting to bubble. Gunner huffed and ran a hand through his unruly hair.

"Do you know who I am?" he asked me. Not in a cocky sort of way, but in a curious way. Like he expected me to know already. Why? I have no fucking clue.

"No" I scoffed in response,

"You really have no clue? You don't feel anything when you are near me, you didn't feel anything when I touched you? Nothing at all?" he asked as he tipped his head to the side. Something about the way he asked the question surprised me. He was so sincere, so genuine, he really expected a certain answer. I hesitated as I looked at his waiting face.

"No" I blurted out quickly, maybe a little too fast.

"Now you're the one who's lying" he said amused and stood up slowly.

"Tell me. Tell me what you feel" he said as he walked around the fire and stepped in my direction. I stepped back away from him and he halted in his tracks.

"I don't know what you're talking about" I said shakily. I have never before felt nervous, or unsure of myself. Saxton never made me feel weak or less than him. He wouldn't have succeeded even if he tried to. In fact, the one time he did try to push his dominance over me ended quite badly for him. But this Were, Gunner, he has a way of making my skin crawl in the most unexpected of ways. He can get under my skin and make me question everything, just by staring at me with those terrifyingly deep blue eyes.

"You're still lying. Tell me what you feel when you're around me" he commanded. His power and authority rolled over me like boiling water. I have never felt anything like it. It was unnerving.

"You make me feel safe" I answered unknowingly,

"Is that all?" he asked, his voice low and even, almost like he was singing or chanting a spell. I know in my head that I don't want to answer him, I want to keep my secrets for myself. But his voice rang through my ears like a gentle and calming embrace, convincing me to spill my deepest and darkest secrets.

"I feel like I know you, like I can trust you" I answered him,

"You can trust me" he cooed peacefully,

"I know" I said. My voice no longer sounded like my own. It was like I was dreaming. I could see what was going on, I could feel his influence slipping over me. But I didn't want to fight it. I welcomed it. It tickled at my skin and fluttered around my heart. I liked it.

"Go on" he prompted and walked slowly towards me,

"You're what I've been looking for" I said in my faraway voice,

"Just me?" he asked as he stopped in front of me.

"No" I answered,

"What else are you looking for?"

"For me".

"For you? What do you mean?" Gunner said softly and gripped hold of my waist.

"I've been seeing myself in my dreams for as long as I can remember, I want to find out why" I answered. Inside my mind, I was screaming at myself to shut up, to stop talking. But it was like I no longer had control over my mouth. My mind and mouth had become completely separated.

"Interesting, is that all you're looking for?"

"No".

"Tell me, what else is it you're hoping to find?"

"I don't know" I sang,

"You don't know?" he repeated. He looked into my eyes, and I gazed blankly back at his glowing silver orbs.

'I don't know" I repeated.

"Good girl, Whiskey" he said as he pressed my back against a tree.

"I'm going to help you, okay?" he said lowly as he cupped my cheek,

"Okay" I agreed.

"But for me to help you, you need to trust me, okay?" he said softly. The warmth and calmness of his voice melted over me. Any worry I had was gone. The screaming of my inner voice to stop speaking was gone. The concern of him finding out my plan, my mission, vanished. I wanted to tell him everything. I wanted him to know everything there was to know about me, about my mission, my plan, everything.

"Okay" I repeated again.

"You cannot try and kill me again, okay?"

"Okay" I nodded, keeping my eyes locked on his silver gaze,

"Now Whiskey, you're going to forget about this little talk, okay?"

"Okay" I agreed.

"You won't remember telling me about your dream, or anything else we have just talked about. Alright?" he said smoothly. His voice seeped into my ears, twisting itself through my mind. All of my doubts were non-existent. All there was him. His voice. Just Gunner and his words.

"Okay" I agreed. Gunner slowly let me down, sitting me against the tree. He crouched in front of me, still cupping my cheeks. My mind became cloudy, and my eyes felt heavy.

"You won't remember" I heard him whisper. My eyes closed, and all I could see was the two glowing silver balls shrouded in darkness.

~

My eyes flew open, and I sat forward with a start. I huffed in surprise and felt a mighty headache pound through my brain. I gripped the sides of my head and groaned. How the fuck did I get over here, and when the fuck did I fall asleep? It was dark now. It wasn't the last I remembered, the sunset was still an hour off.

"Are you alright?" Gunner's voice called from the other side of the fire pit. I glared at him and dropped my hands. He looked at me over the fire, his eyes full of concern. He slowly stood up and walked around the fire.

"What happened?" I grunted,

"You fell asleep" Gunner answered while looking down at me.

"Whiskey, you look a little pale" he said as he crouched down in front of me. A wave of DeJa'Vu swept over me, and the feeling that I had seen him like that before, stuck to the front of my brain.

"I have a headache" I grunted and shot to my feet, I took a few steps back away from him.

"You should get some proper sleep" he said slowly, his voice dripping with concern.

"Yeah" I mumbled and waddled over to the tent. Gunner followed closely behind me, crawling into the small space after me. I laid down and wrapped my arm over my head.

"Are you alright?" Gunner asked,

"I'll be fine" I snapped back.

"You can trust me" he said softly, and gently placed his hand on my shoulder. Goosebumps broke out across my skin and a shiver ran down my spine. That same feeling of DeJa'Vu hit me like a truck and I couldn't shake it. But I also couldn't shake the feeling that he was right. I could trust him. If I allowed myself to trust anyone, the person it would be is him. I let his words swirl around my head, drinking in the sincerity and truth of his comment.

"I know" I said back to him quietly. I shut my eyes and listened as he breathed out a relieved sigh and lay down. Neither one of us fell asleep. I could tell by his breathing, and because he stank of anxiety. I don't know what he was anxious about though. We lay silently for hours, side by side, neither one of us speaking. It was strangely comfortable.

"Whiskey?" Gunner's voice whispered, breaking the silence.

"Yes?" I whispered back. He took a deep breath and shuffled on the spot,

"I want to take you back with me. Back home, to my pack" he said quietly. I rolled over onto my side to face him. He was lying on his stomach, cuddling his pillow under his chin.

"Why?" I asked with a frown. He laid his cheek on the pillow and looked over at me. It was pitch black, yet I could see the blue of his eyes swirling through the darkness.

"I don't know where you've come from, or where you're going, but I know that I was meant to find you" he said surely. I rolled back over onto my back and crossed my hands over my stomach. It's what I wanted and what I've been trying to accomplish. To get him to trust me enough to lead me to his people. I'm surprised it happened so quickly, I thought it would have taken days. I suppose the quicker he takes me to them, the quicker I can kill them all and move along. But what does he mean, he was meant to find me. He didn't find me, I found him, not that he knows that of course.

"Why do you think that?" I asked him.

"I want to explain it. But I don't know how to yet. Heck, I'm still not convinced that this is all real" he chuckled.

"What's not real?" I asked and rolled to face him again. He looked at me and huffed out a heavy breath.

"I promise, I will explain it. Just not yet" he answered and rolled onto his side to face me.

"Why not yet?" I pushed,

"It won't make any sense, and I'd probably sound like a crazy person" he chuckled softly.

"I already think you're a crazy person" I snorted.

"I'll take that as a compliment" he teased and flicked his finger at my nose. My instincts kicked in and I grabbed his wrist before he could pull it away again. I soft growl bubbled in my chest as a warning. I was actually surprised by his playfulness. People, or werewolves, they don't often surprise me. Very slowly he moved his hand forward towards my face and ran his fingers over the curve of my cheek. The action was tender and gentle, almost affectionate. My heart thundered in my chest and my stomach turned in on itself. I liked the feel of his touch. But I hate that he thinks he can touch me on a whim. I let his fingers roam, for far longer than I should have, before I came back to my senses. I growled and pushed his hand away roughly. He was silent for a moment, a moment that seemed to span forever. The noise of the forest outside dulled to nothingness, the rapid beating of my heart slowly disappeared, and soon all that was left was the sounds of our soft breathing. Gunner huffed out a sharp breath and turned onto his back.

"You're just going to have to trust me" he whispered, and then rolled onto his side, facing away from me. Goosebumps ran over my skin, and I felt like I was forgetting something. It gnawed at the back of my mind. What could I possibly have forgotten? I don't forget things. Ever. But I can't shake it, that feeling in the pit of your stomach that tells you, you've left the oven on. Whatever. I dropped the subject and rolled back over. I do trust him. That alone makes me feel uneasy. I've known this Were for all of a day. I've watched him for a lot longer than that. But I still know nothing about him. Maybe I'm losing my mind. Maybe my life has a shelf life, and I'm slowly crawling towards my used by date.

I woke the next morning without Gunner's arms wrapped around me. I was both happy and sad about this. Gross. Could I have actually liked being in his arms, not a chance. I told myself, never again. His scent in the tent was faint, meaning he'd been up for a while. When I emerged from the tent, I found him on the rock. Not hovering like the many other times before, just sitting with his legs crossed. Many options crossed my mind at that moment. Snap his neck while he is distracted. Sneak up behind him to see if he is using the black smoke magic. Call out good morning, like I know nothing. Even run my hands over the firm ridges of his shoulder muscles, feeling them flex and tighten beneath my fingers. Gunner chose for me though.

"Good morning" he called over his shoulder. I walked over to his rock and looked at his large frame, bent and folded in that position.

"Morning," I grunted back. He opened his eyes and smiled brightly. His skin looked like it was glowing in the early morning sunlight, and his eyes sparkled with flecks of blue diamonds.

"What are you doing?" I asked as I nodded at his crossed legs.

"Meditating" he nodded back and unfurled his long legs.

"Does it help?" I asked and crossed my arms over my chest.

"It did" he answered and smiled brightly. He looked happy. A little too happy. What have I missed here?

"Did?" I asked with a tilt of my head. He laughed and jumped off the rock.

"You're funny, has anyone ever told you that before?" he teased and poked my shoulder.

"No" I barked back.

"Well, I think so. Anyways, what I said last night, about taking you back to my pack. Have you thought any more about it?" he chirped and sat down on a log by the fire pit.

"I have" I nodded.

"Annnnnnnd?" he drawled out, looking up at me through his thick lashes.

"I'll come. But I am making no promises, especially when you refuse to explain why I should go" I conceded and dropped my arms to my sides.

"I'll take it" Gunner shouted happily and shot to his feet. He went about the small clearing, gathering things into a pile. I watched with confusion as he moved busily around the campsite.

"What are you doing?" I asked him from my place by the fire.

"Packing" he called back and disappeared into the tent.

"Why?" I yelled back to him,

"So that we can go, of course" he chuckled. I stood up and walked over to the door of the tent. Gunner was shuffling about, folding blankets and shoving clothes into a duffle bag.

"You want to leave now?" I asked surprised,

"Absolutely" he responded without looking up at me.

"But I thought you couldn't go home yet? You said there was something you had to do first" I said while crouching down to see him better. He stopped his packing and smiled at me with a full set of white teeth.

"And now I've done it, so it's time for me, for us, to go home" he said cheerfully. I don't get this guy. He literally makes no sense whatsoever. He couldn't go back to the woman he missed because he had to do something. Now he claims he has done it, so he wants to go. But I've been here the whole time, apart from meditating and hunting, he hasn't done anything. So, what's the deal? What have I missed during the past couple of days, what is the big thing he needed to do?

"Uh, okay" I said slowly.

I went and sat back down at the fire and watched in complete silence as Gunner ran around the clearing, packing and cleaning up the few things that he had. It was roughly an hour, an hour and a half later that he was done. There wasn't a lot to pack, as he didn't have a lot of stuff. More than I do, but nowhere near as much as a human would take camping. But it was still a large hiking backpack and a smaller duffle bag. I imagine it would have been annoying carrying them all the way up here on his own. He finally came over to where I sat and looked down at me, bags in hand and a smile on his face.

"Ready?" he asked with a grin. He was excited. It was written all over his face, but also, he stank of it. Excitement, anticipation, longing. He was just a giant ball of joy and happiness. It makes me sick to my stomach.

"Yep" I said with a pop of the P. I stood up and threw my bag over my shoulder.

"I'm not helping you carry those" I said gruffly and nodded my head at his bags. Gunner laughed and shook his head.

"Don't sweat it, Little Wolf, I can manage just fine" he chuckled and dropped the bags at his feet. Little Wolf, what's that shit? Is that supposed to be an endearing nickname or something? I was about to argue when Gunner tilted his head to the side with a mighty crack. I watched in awe as his clothes tore off and his large frame grew and reformed into the shape of a giant wolf. His thick silver fur shone under the sunlight, it made the blue of his eyes sparkle with a frightening depth to them. I looked over his huge beast, easily the biggest wolf I have ever seen. I can't believe I hadn't realised it until now. I'm such an idiot.

"You're an Alpha" I said dumbly. So many questions were answered at that moment, and yet so many new ones formed in their place. I understand now why he has such an aura of power to him. To be as huge as he is, he must be very strong. Thank goodness I didn't try to kill him. If he had changed form before I got to the finishing blow, he most definitely would have defeated me.

Gunner's wolf snorted and shook his head, trying to regain my attention. He whined softly and nodded his huge head up and down while scratching at the dirt. I know what he wants. I was pretty certain of that. But there's no chance. I he wants me to change too, he's going to be sorely disappointed. It's not going to happen. I hate travelling in beast form. I hate doing anything in beast form.

"No" I said firmly. He growled lowly and smacked his head into the side of my leg.

"No!" I growled back and kicked him away. Gunner's wolf snorted and huffed. He snapped his head back and slowly the silver fur receded into his human skin. Gunner stood back upright on two human legs, naked and in full view. I tried to avert my eyes, but it was like I lost any and all function over my body. My hungry gaze traced over every bump and every dip that his muscles created. His smooth creamy skin was basically hairless, with broad shoulders and thick defined biceps. The soft pink battle scars that marred his chest and arm only added to his painstaking beauty. My eyes followed the natural path that his muscles created, past the well-defined V formation, and down to the monster hanging between his thick thighs. Every inch of tantalising skin was stretched tightly over his firm muscles. Leading me to wonder what that huge member would look like with the skin stretched tight over the pulsating thickness. My mouth went dry and my eyes just sort of dazed over. My skin prickled and a hot wave flew through me. I have never felt such an instant and intense desire. All I knew was that I wanted to taste him. Every part of him.

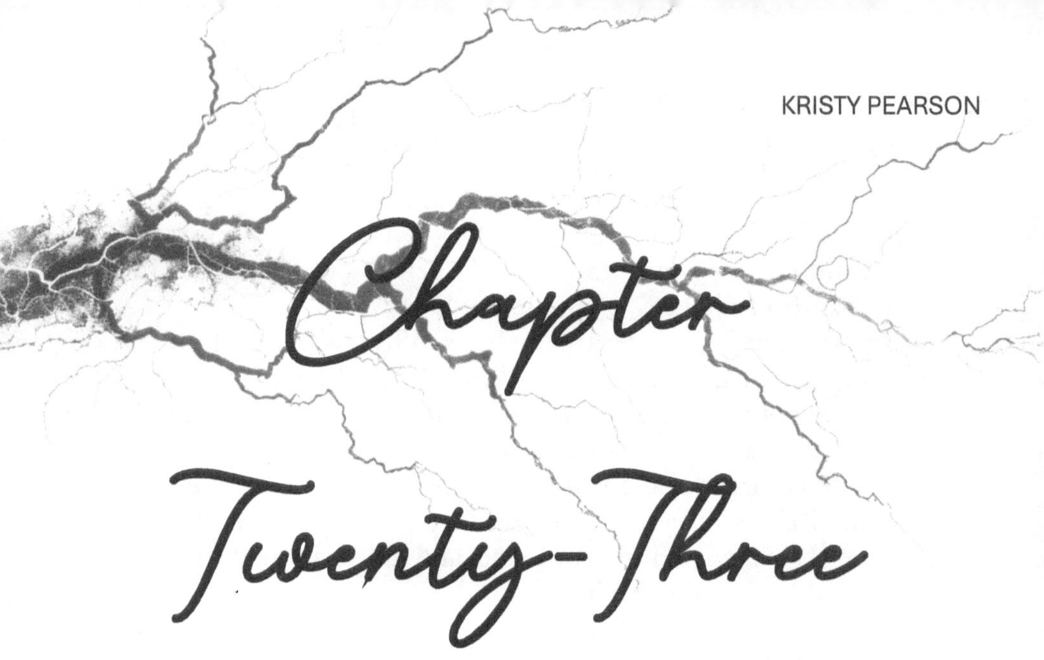

Chapter Twenty-Three

Zelena

I know fear. I lived my whole life in fear. I have worn it, bathed in it, ate it, and abide by it. It has shaken me to my very core, and attached itself to every inch of me. But the kind of fear that was currently swarming through my stomach, was something I had never experienced before. Before now, fear was all about me. What if he kills me, what if he disfigures me, what if I never escape him? Then after I found Gunner, it became, what if he doesn't love me, what if he tires of me, what if I lose him? And now, I no longer matter. Everything is for them. What could this prophecy mean for them, will it hurt them, how can I protect them from this? A million and one possible terrible things ran through my mind in quick succession. Disaster after disaster. And my two sweet and beautiful children right in the centre of it all. I looked up at Lunaya. She was sitting on the edge of her seat, watching all of the emotions flicker across my face. I took a deep breath, my lungs burned with the force of it. I swallowed down the sob that wanted to fly free and the scream that was turning in my stomach. "Are you sure?" I asked her. My voice sounded small and broken. For a moment I sounded like my old self. I could feel my skin prickle and the heaviness start to settle over me. The power was starting to swarm through my veins, looking for its opening.

"Yes, love. I'm very sure" she answered. A small whimper fell from my lips before I was able to stop it. I gripped the sides of my head and tried to steady myself before I lost complete control.

Lunaya moved and sat on the coffee table in front of me. She reached to place her hand over the top of mine. But I quickly pulled away.

"Why did you wait until now to tell me? You've had weeks to do it and multiple chances" I shouted at her.

"Why wait until they are already here! Why wait until the danger is real! I could have done something, I could have stopped it, I could have protected them. Why! Why would you wait?" I screamed. Tears were flowing from my eyes, my chest heaved with broken breaths as the panic started to settle over me.

"Zelena, Zelena, breathe, Sweetheart. Calm down, it's okay, just breathe" Lunaya tried to soothe me, and failed. I stood to my feet and paced back and forth in front of her.

"It's not alright, don't tell me to calm down. They are my children, this is about their lives. It says one of them has to die. How can I be calm when destiny calls for the death of my baby" I screamed, waving my hands around my head as I did so. The door to the library burst open and Tobias stood with a murderous look on his face. He stepped through the door, looking over the both of us.

"What is going on, I can feel you're in distress" he grumbled and then glared at Lunaya. I paused for a moment and stared back at him. Would he know about this? Would Selene know about this? Did this begin with her, did she create the prophecy? If she is involved, that would mean Tobias could be too. I don't know what to do. If there is something I can do to break this prophecy I will do it, no matter the cost. If the cost is my life however, I know that he will do everything he can to stop me. I don't know if I can trust him with this. I don't know if I can trust anyone with this.

"It's nothing, I'm sorry. We were just arguing" I said slowly and glared at Lunaya. I tried to indicate that I wanted her to keep her mouth shut. She looked back at me with surprise in her eyes. Her gaze flicked quickly between Tobias and me before she huffed and dropped her shoulders.

"I was trying to apologise for my behaviour" Lunaya said softly without looking at Tobias.

"And I clearly didn't take it well" I added, still glaring at the top of Lunaya's head.

"You're okay, Little One?" Tobias asked me. He was hesitant, I don't think he was convinced. But I can't tell him about this, not yet, not until I know that both he and Selene have no involvement.

"I'm fine. I'll try and keep it together, I promise" I said as calmly as possible. Tobias looked over the both of us closely, and then backed out of the room, closing the doors behind him. We listened as his feet walked away from the door, then waited for a moment longer.

"You lied to him?" Lunaya said softly, unsurely.

"I did" I nodded.

"Why? He is your guardian" she said with some more bite.

"I don't know if I can trust him yet" I answered. I knew I had to tell her the truth. If she is the only other person that knows about this, then she is the only other person able to help me right now. I need her on my side.

"Zelena, he is your guardian, sworn to protect you, to help you, to guide you. Why would you think that you can't trust him?" she whispered loudly.

"Because I need to put an end to this prophecy, and I will give my life to do it if I need to. I can't trust him because if he knew that, he would try and stop me" I told her bluntly,

"And you think I won't?" she gasped.

"I think you will help me save my babies. I think you owe me that much" I grunted angrily.

"I won't let you kill yourself to do it" she hissed.

"You will help me do whatever it takes to end this prophecy. You should have told me the truth. You shouldn't have waited this long. You owe me!" I yelled. She was quiet for a moment. Just staring at me as I huffed and puffed through my anger.

"Oh, Sweetheart" she said sadly and dropped her face into her hands,

"You can't stop a prophecy" she mumbled through her fingers,

"How would you know?" I barked,

"Because I already tried" Lunaya answered and looked up at me with a new kind of sadness in her eyes. She looked utterly defeated. It was an expression I had never seen her wear before. It honestly terrified me.

"What?" I snorted in disbelief and shock,

"Sit back down, Zelena, there is more we need to discuss" she stated firmly. I did as she asked and slowly placed myself back into my chair. Lunaya looked overly pale, which is unusual for her, seeing as she usually has a nice sun kissed complexion.

"Don't try and talk me out of it" I said harshly. Lunaya chuckled awkwardly and shook her head.

"I wish you knew your father. I wish I could explain just how much alike you both are. He was stubborn and determined too, just like you. Almost to the point you could call him pig headed".

"Are you calling me pig headed?" I scoffed,

"No, Darling, but you can't deny that you have a strong will and an unwillingness to bend".

"So, you are calling me pig headed?" I laughed. I don't know why I'm laughing. This is definitely not a time to laugh or joke. But the whole thing is just so unbelievable, that if I don't laugh now, I may scream. And things tend to blow up when I scream.

"Not in those words exactly" Lunaya teased. I huffed and rolled my eyes with a smirk.

"You know, I first heard about the prophecy when I was pregnant. But, when your father learned of it for the first time, phew, he went into overdrive. He was always protective, but he kicked that up tenfold" she said fondly. I could see the memories flashing through her eyes. I felt envious that she had memories of him to look back on. I wish I had something, anything to help me think of him.

"Did you love him?" I asked her softly.

"More than I can ever express. I really thought that I would die without him. I wanted to die. When I couldn't find him again, after the attack, I felt my heart break. I wouldn't wish that pain on anyone" she said firmly. I nodded my head in understanding. I feel the same about Gunner.

"I wish I could meet him. Just to see him, you know. So I knew what his voice sounds like, what he smells like, what he looks like. All of it".

"Well, to me, his scent was like wet leaves and freshly cut grass. He reminded me of nature, of the forest. He could sing too, oh, he was a beautiful singer, and he often sang to my belly" she said with a sad smile. I can see how much it still hurts her, even after all this time. A stab of heartache shot through my chest. I want to make it all better, I want to make her feel better, but I know that could never happen.

"As for what he looks like, I lost everything when the hunters destroyed my pack. Everything except this". Lunaya pulled a gold chain from around her neck and flicked open the small locket that hung from it. She handed it to me, and I took a deep breath. I slowly turned it around and studied the picture inside. Lunaya stood smiling brightly, her hands over the top of her large swollen belly. The tall man standing beside her was also smiling. I gazed at his face and saw myself. His golden eyes, were just like mine. His deep black hair, was just like mine. His light pale skin, was just like mine. We have the same nose, and the same shaped lips, even our smiles are similar. It bugged me that I couldn't see myself in Lunaya, but I get it now, it was because I look exactly like my father.

"He looks just like me, or I look just like him" I gasped.

"You sure do" she smiled adoringly at me.

"I can't believe it" I chuckled and a small sob broke free.

"Are you okay?" Lunaya asked softly,

"Yeah, I'm just... I'm happy, I think. I feel so much more connected to him now" I smiled and wiped the tears from my cheeks.

"I'm glad" she smiled back.

"And you're pregnant. I'm technically in the photo too. It's a family picture" I chuckled and pointed at her large belly in the photo. When Lunaya didn't respond, I looked up from the picture to see her looking down with furrowed brows.

"What is it?" I asked,

"Yes, you are in the picture. So is your sister" she said as she looked up to meet my gaze. What? I furrowed my brows and shook my head.

"I'm sorry. What?" I blurted blankly.

"The reason that I know you can't break a prophecy, the reason your dad became so protective, it's because we've already tried to. And we failed" she answered.

"I'm not following".

"Zelena, baby, you had a sister. A twin sister" she said with more firmness. I could hear the words just fine. I couldn't quite grip onto them though. They just weren't computing. This can't be true. I have a sister, a twin sister. What does that all mean? Is the prophecy not about my babies, is it actually about me?

"That's not funny" I sneered.

"I'm not telling any jokes" Lunaya snipped back.

"You had twins too?"

"I did".

"I have a sister?" I said slowly. My mind began to wonder, and I could see her, clear as day. I could see the future we could have had together. Growing up side by side, playing together, learning together. She would have been my best friend, and I hers. I could picture her face too, it is just like mine. We would have played pranks on the other pack members, switching places and laughing hysterically when we got found out. We would have made so many wonderful memories together as we experienced the world. Together, as sisters.

"No, Darling, you 'had' a sister" Lunaya said, cutting off my daydream.

"Huh?" I blanked.

"She's dead, Zelena, she died during the attack on Moon Light" Lunaya said sadly. Only I wasn't sad at her words. No, I was angry.

"How can you be so sure? You thought that I died too" I snapped at her. With the rise of my voice came a dull creaking sound from the bookshelves. Lunaya was quiet, staring at me wide eyed and a little afraid.

"How do you know for sure!" I screamed and jumped to my feet, but she still didn't answer.

"Did you see her body? Did you see her die? Tell me!" I yelled. My legs grew heavy, and I could feel the weightlessness fill my head. The books on the shelves started to shake, and the coffee table bobbled slightly off the ground. My emotions were all over the place and my control over my power was weaning. I steadied my feet and closed my eyes, then took a few deep breaths and pulled the power back in. The heaviness evaporated and the airy feeling left. I looked down at Lunaya and she had fresh tears falling from her eyes. I felt bad for yelling at her. It was her daughter too, not just my sister. I imagine it hurts her a lot more than it does me. But this is kind of an atomic bomb drop of information.

"I'm sorry" I said sincerely and sat back down in my chair.

"Lunaya, did you see her die?" I asked with a gentler tone. She shook her head and wiped the tears from her eyes.

"So, it is possible then. She could still be alive" I said with a nod of my head. My heart was beating so fast it was almost like a hummingbird. I could hear the blood pumping around my ears. My excitement was palpable. She could still be alive. The story that Lunaya told me, that first day I spoke to her, like really spoke to her, she said something that I didn't understand at the time.

"When you first told me about my father, about the attack on Moon Light, you said that you and he split up" I said slowly. The story was making more sense now, the pieces of the puzzle were fitting together.

"I did tell you that" Lunaya confirmed cautiously. I think she also knows where this is going.

"That part never made sense to me. I didn't question it before, maybe I should have, but I think I get it now" I said and turned to look at her more closely.

"You split up, to split us up. Me and my sister. Right?" I asked and lowered myself onto the couch opposite where she was sitting.

"Yes" she nodded in confirmation,

"Why would you do that? Why wouldn't you stay together, wouldn't it have been safer that way?"

"It was clear from the start of the attack that the hunters were looking for us specifically, but we didn't know for sure if they knew there were two of you. We couldn't risk them finding out and getting their hands on the both of you" she confessed.

"But you said that you never found Dad's body, and you never saw my sister die. So maybe they got away" I said hopefully. She was quiet for a moment then a soft weeping came from her.

"You called him Dad" Lunaya sobbed.

"Well, he is my Dad"

"I know, I just, I haven't heard you say that before".

"Don't change the topic. They could both be alive, right?"

"No honey, I don't think so"

"Why not"

"Because he never came to the meeting place".

"Maybe he was hurt and couldn't get there"

"Your father would have never quit. He could have lost both his legs and he would still drag his body there"

"You quit" I whispered and stood back up.

"Zelena" Lunaya called.

"Sorry, that wasn't fair, we've already talked about that. I thought I was over it, I guess I'm not" I said as I started pacing again.

"It's okay to be upset".

"I'm not upset, but I'm not ready to give up yet".

"Sweetheart, I searched. I scoured the world looking for traces of your father and you girls. I found nothing. After years of endless searching, countless compounds, and zero signs, only then did I give up hope".

"Yeah, well, I have only just been told I have a sister. I understand you did your time looking, but now I have to try for myself".

"And what of the prophecy? I thought you were going to try and stop that first?"

"Shit, right. First, I'll end the prophecy, and then I'll find my sister. Wait" I said and turned back to face her,

"What's her name?" I asked. Lunaya's face softened and a sad smile spread across her lips.

"Aurora. Her name was Aurora" she said softly.

"Aurora" I said quietly, letting the name roll through my mouth. My sister, Aurora. Zelena and Aurora. Twins. A and Z. The beginning and the end. I like it.

"It's pretty" I said quietly, looking over at Lunaya, as I sat down again.

"I picked her name, it means 'The Dawn'. Your father chose yours, 'The Moon'. The two of you were our lights in the dark. The Moon and The Dawn" she said while reminiscing. I could see her mind had gone back there, reliving the memories once again.

"Fitting" I said with a huff,

"We thought so" Lunaya nodded.

"So, which one of us is meant to bring life and which one is death?" I asked sourly.

"Zelena" Lunaya scolded.

"Oh right, sorry. It's my babies that will bring life and death. Silly me" I said sarcastically.

"That's enough!" she snapped and stood up. She glared down at me angrily, the angriest I had ever seen her before. I can see why some of the other pack members find her intimidating. I leaned back into the chair and looked up at her warily.

"I didn't create the prophecy. Your father and I did everything we could to end it. I thought it ended when I thought you all died. I understand that you're angry, I was angry too. But don't throw that bullshit at me, I won't stand for it" she growled harshly. Holy shit. Did I just get scolded by my mother like a petulant child? I sank further back into the chair and nodded my head meekly.

"I'm sorry" I squeaked out. She breathed out a few deep breaths and sat back down again.

"I'm sorry I yelled at you, that wasn't my intention. But please understand this is a big deal for me too. I know I haven't handled the news of your twins very well, and I absolutely should have told you about Aurora and the true meaning of the prophecy right away. But I'm... I'm scared Zelena".

I watched her face as she sat quietly. This whole time she has been here, and I've been watching her. Then also after I let her get close, and started getting to know her. The whole time I have never felt much of a parental connection to her. I always felt like there was this wall between us, keeping us apart. But now, I see her. I really see her. I can see her maternal instincts shining strongly, the need to protect and shelter. And also, in her eyes and the sharp corners of her tensed mouth, I can see the kind of fear that only a parent could understand. I can feel her maternal love, I can see her motherly desire to keep me safe. How could I have been so blind to it this whole time?

I slowly stood up and walked over to where she sat. She looked up at me curiously and wiped a tear from her cheek. I lifted her hand from her lap and carefully sat myself down on her legs. Her body was tense and unsure. As I curled myself into her lap, pressing my face into her chest, her body relaxed and she wrapped her arms around me.

"I'm scared too, Mum" I whispered. She whimpered and squeezed me tightly, rocking me back and forth.

"I love you, my baby girl. I always have" she sobbed into my hair. Her happiness, her sorrow, her relief and her grief, it all swarmed around me. I could feel every bit of it. I could feel the sadness she had lived with all these years. I could feel her happiness at finding me alive. I could feel her grief at losing her children and her Mate. And her relief that I was finally accepting her as my mother. I could feel all of her emotions like they were my own. I understand her now.

"I love you too, Mum" I said as my own tears fell from my eyes. She held me tightly in her arms, as if I were still the small baby that she held so many years ago. I like being in her arms, I like feeling her love. I like having her here with me. I don't know how long we sat like that. It could have been minutes, it could have been hours. Either way, it was long overdue.

"You will help me save them, won't you? The both of them?" I asked her after a while. She brushed her fingers through my hair and sighed.

"It was never a question. I will do everything I possibly can to help you protect them. We won't let anything happen to either of them, Zelena. I promise you" she said firmly.

"Where do we start?" I asked, sitting up from her chest. Lunaya stroked her fingers across my cheek and smiled softly.

"We start with me telling you everything I know about this prophecy" she said with a nod. She tapped my knees and I stood up.

"And that includes telling your family" she said standing up and taking my hands.

"No, we can't. Not yet" I argued.

"My Darling, the more eyes we have searching books, and the more minds we have trying to solve this, the better it will be for the twins. I know you're scared. But they are your family, your pack, you have to know that they too will do anything to help the babies" she said with certainty.

"I know, it's just..."

"It's nothing" Lunaya cut me off,

"You have to tell them. There's no other option, if you don't, I will. They are your family. They will help you, they will help us" she argued. She's right, I know she's right. It's a hard pill to swallow though. I wish Gunner were here, he'd know what to do.

Zelena

I stood at the head of the table, holding baby B. in my arms. Tobias sat to my right, with little G. happily asleep in the crook of his elbow. Next to Tobias was Lunaya, Alyse, and then Felix. On my left was Smith, taking on his new Beta role. Next to him was Lupus, Roe and Nat. I debated calling Daniel, Gunner named him Delta before he left. I would have thought that he'd give Felix the title, seeing as how experienced and trusted he is. But Felix is the head commander now. He can't be the head commander and pack Delta. I like Daniel well enough, he seems capable and smart, I just don't know him too well yet. This is about my pups, and I won't tell just anyone about this, regardless of their rank. Only the ones I deeply trust. Felix fits into that box, Daniel doesn't, at least not yet.

"What's going on, Sweet Girl? You look all frazzled" Roe asked softly.

"I have to tell you all something, something important" I said with a shaky voice.

"You can't be pregnant again already" Smith piped up jokingly.

"Not unless you and Tobias have something to share with the group" Smith chuckled. Tobias growled threateningly, and the deep rumble shook the table. Lupus smacked Smith across the back of the head and hissed,

"That's not fucking funny" Lupus scolded.

"What? Shit on me for trying to lighten the mood, feels like someone's kitten just died" he snipped back.

"Smith, give it a rest" Nat groaned annoyed.

"Lena, I was meant to leave for Howlers an hour ago, do I need to be here for this?" Nat asked.

"If I have to be here, then you have to be here" Smith fired back.

I couldn't help but pick up on the hints of frustration in their voices. I have never asked everyone together like this before. What makes them think this is all just a big joke? Smith and Nat began to bicker, while Roe tried to get between them. Felix shook his head and rubbed his temples and Tobias went back to cooing at baby G. The whole careless attitude of the room was starting to get on my nerves. I carefully handed B. to Lupus, who took him gladly. I looked around at all the important people in my life, bar one. The only ones looking at all interested were Lunaya and Alyse. I took a deep breath and slammed my fists hard into the table. The edge of the wood cracked and splintered as it snapped off, landing at my feet.

"I am trying to tell you something!" I screamed.

"Zelena!" Lunaya and Roe both growled at the same time. I snapped my eyes angrily to my mother. I was heaving with rage and annoyance, my blood was pumping boiling hot, and I could feel my canines pressing at my gums.

"This is important" I growled back at Roe,

"And this table was crafted by Gunner's great grandfather" Roe snapped angrily. My canines extended through my gums and my bones groaned inside my body. I could feel the sparks of electricity dance through my veins, and the airy feeling fill my head. A hand grabbed my wrist and squeezed.

"Calm" Tobias hissed lowly. The place where his skin touched mine was instantly cool, I could feel that same thrum of vibrations and the gentle feeling spread through me. My canines retracted and I cooled down. I looked down at him and smiled in appreciation.

"Thank you" I mouthed silently. He nodded his head once, let go of my hand and picked up G's chubby little fingers once again.

"I'm sorry. I'm a little worked up" I said with a grunt.

"We hadn't noticed" Lupus teased while looking down and smiling at a babbling B.

"Go on Zelena" Lunaya prompted. I looked at her and she nodded encouragingly. I could see the pride and the love glitter behind her gaze. How have I gone this long without her in my life? How have I gotten by, survived, made it through everything I endured without seeing that look before now? I don't ever want to lose that. And I don't want my children growing up not knowing how that look of pride fills their chests. I smiled weakly back at her and nodded my head.

"I suppose I'll start with something that most of you may already know" I began with a heavy breath and the room listened silently. "Alpha Galterio from Origin Wolf was told about a prophecy, this is why he took me. He and Artemis thought that the prophecy was about a Triple Goddess with two Mates".

"Yes, we know about that. He tried to mark you, but it didn't take" Roe agreed with a nod.

"What was the prophecy?" Felix interjected. I looked over at him and he bowed his head,

"If you don't mind, Luna, I have not heard it" he added quickly.

"Mum?" I said turning to Lunaya,

"Mum?" Roe interrupted with surprise. She was still a long way from forgiving Lunaya and understanding her reaction to the twins. Hopefully, she will understand it all in a few minutes. I nodded at Roe and offered a gentle smile. She pursed her lips and glared at Lunaya, but shrugged and leaned back into her chair.

"Go on" I said to Lunaya,

"Spawned by the one who gave us breath. Vanished from life but spared from death. The Ethereal one gives she who is promised. To wield the power of the Triple Goddess. Where the moon is three, two will come. Once the seal is made, destiny is done. With one comes death, pain and destruction. The other comes life, love and devotion. Peril will end and the wolf will thrive. But for peace to reign, only one can survive" she recited loudly for everyone to hear.

It was still weird hearing it for myself. I looked around the room at everyone's faces, all of them trying to make sense of it. My attention snapped to Tobias, I needed to know if he'd heard it already, if he knew about it. He looked pensive, but not surprised. I don't know what to make of his reaction.

"Where the moon is three, does that mean Tri-Moon?" Felix asked. I lifted my eyes to him and blanked. I had never thought about that before. I looked at Lunaya and she started back at me. "Does it?" I asked her,

"I... I don't know. It could be. I have never been able to decipher that part. But it makes sense that it is speaking of a place" she answered with a half nod.

"There is no other pack that references the three phases of the moon. There is of course Crescent Wolf and Waning Wolf, but they only name one part of the cycle. Tri-Moon names all three. It would make a lot of sense" Roe said to Lunaya and myself.

"I agree" Lunaya replied with a nod.

"The start is obvious, the one who gave us breath, that means Selene" Roe said with certainty,

"As well as the next, vanished from life, because she doesn't show herself to anyone anymore" Roe said with a nod. I assume she means anyone, besides me, but I decided not to voice that out loud.

"And the next part is clear as well, she who is promised, that means the Triple Goddess" Nat said to her mother, they were both now talking to each other while the rest of us watched and listened.

"Zelena, yes. Now, two will come, I assume that means the twins" Roe said pensively as she ran her fingers absentmindedly up and down her forearm,

"But the seal part, what does that mean?" Nat asked while deep in thought.

"The Book of the Goddess, the one that explains Selene and her lineage, it states that the mark of the Goddess can be placed on the wrist or the back of the neck. That could be the seal it is referring to"

"Which means that her destiny is set. As in, she will only become the Triple Goddess after her mark appears? Well, that's already happened" Nat scoffed,

"Yes, but what does that have to do with the twins? Neither of them have any markings, we've checked, many times. If Zelena is the Triple Goddess, why or how does that affect her twins beyond continuing the line. That part doesn't make sense. G. can't be the next chosen daughter, it's too soon after Zelena. I'm just not sure, something isn't adding up here" Roe said confused.

"I may be able to offer insight into that part" Lunaya said softly. She stood up and looked to me for approval. I nodded my head, telling her to go on.

"Zelena is also a twin" she said without hesitation. The room was silent, all eyes now searing into Lunaya's skin.

"And you're only telling us this now?" Roe snapped. She wasn't holding back any punches, that's for sure.

"I was always going to tell her, I just didn't know how to" she snipped back,

"You already know?" Nat said looking up at me. I nodded my head and sighed,

"She just told me this morning" I confessed.

"Is this why you flipped out in the delivery room? Why you ran off all flustered and upset" Nat spat at Lunaya,

"It is" Lunaya nodded.

"And you didn't think that would have been a good moment to bring this all up" Roe sneered angrily while waving her arms around.

"I was a little taken aback in the moment. I had to process it all. The prophecy was meant to be dead, I thought it died with my pack and my family. I never considered that Zelena was alive, or that she too would have twins. This is all a little unprecedented" Lunaya said quickly, she was starting to get flustered or anxious, I could hear it in her voice.

"You should have said something sooner, before the twins were born" Roe growled angrily.

"I know that! But what's done is done" Lunaya growled back. G. started to stir and began with some soft wailing. All eyes turned to Tobias as he tried to calm her back down again.

"Now look what you've done" Roe hissed at Lunaya,

"You're the one yelling" Lunaya hissed back.

"Stop it, the both of you" I said in a hushed yell.

"You're as bad as each other. Yes, Roe, you're right, Lunaya should have said something about me having a twin a long time ago. But she has apologised and is trying to make it right. And she's right as well. What's done is done. All we can do now is figure out how this affects the twins and what sort of danger they are in. If my sister is truly dead, then perhaps the prophecy is too. But if she is, by some miracle, still alive, then we have to find her" I said sternly. I let every ounce of Luna dominance seep into my words, and apparently, it had an effect. No one argued or disagreed, in fact, they all sat quietly with their heads down. I know now that this is a show of obedience.

"A sister?" Nat asked softly, finally breaking the uncomfortable silence of the room. I whipped my head to her and sighed when I caught the sadness in her eyes. I walked around the table and past Roe and Lupus. I pulled out the chair next to Nat and took her hands in mine.

"You are my sister. Also my best friend and one of my most favourite people. I may have another sister out there, or I might not. But Nat, you and me will always be sisters" I told her earnestly. She sniffed and smiled and pulled me into her for a firm hug.

"I love you, Sis" she whispered. I chuckled softly and squeezed her tight.

"I love you back" I said and pulled myself from her vice like grip. She may be a little pissed at me right now, but Nat is Nat. I will love her always, no matter what.

"So what do we do now, Luna?" Felix asked from across the table. I stood back up and looked around at the faces waiting for my answer. The truth was, I have no idea. I don't know what to do or where to start looking. This world is still reasonably new to me. To say I lack confidence is an understatement, but what I lack there, I make up for in determination.

"The libraries" I said with as much certainty as I could force.

"We need to search the library. But not just ours, we will have to branch out to our closest allies too. We need to find any mention of prophecies, fortunes, visions, or anything similar that could help us"

"Luna Eclipse has a Seer" Alyse said softly.

"Of course, Papi" Lunaya squawked and smacked herself on the forehead,

"I completely forgot about her" she said annoyed.

"A Seer, you're sure?" Roe asked, her interest was definitely piqued.

"Yes. She is the one that told me I needed to come to Nova Scotia, she is the one that told me one of you was still alive".

"Wait, a Seer, what is that?" I asked urgently.

"A Seer is someone that can see someone's past and their future, just by touching them" Nat said with a surprising amount of astonishment in her voice.

"They are rare, like seriously rare. Packs kill each other over getting a Seer" she said with wide eyes.

"No surprise Luna Eclipse was able to keep one a secret though" Lupus added nonchalantly while still gazing down at B.

"And this Seer, she told you that I was here?" I asked, walking back over to where Lunaya was standing,

"She said you were waiting for me and that I could find you in Canada" she confirmed.

"It was pure luck we found you as soon as we did" she added. I felt my heart rate pick up and my excitement started to grow.

"And what else did she tell you? Did she mention Aurora, did she say anything about the prophecy or if my sister was alive as well?" I demanded.

"No, Sweetheart, I would have told you already" Lunaya said gently,

"Would you though? You haven't exactly been forthright with information" I yelled. The thin hold I had on my emotions was ripping apart. Why won't she tell me stuff? What is she trying to hide, doesn't she trust me. She claims to care for me, she says she's sorry for not telling me about Aurora, but she keeps withholding information. My hands were shaking at my sides and waves of heaviness were smashing against my body.

"Zelena" Lunaya sighed exhaustedly. I growled lowly. Struggling to get a grip back on my temper and power. I closed my eyes and took a slow deep breath. After a beat, I looked back at her and let my face relax again.

"I know, we've already talked about that. It's going to take a minute for me to get over it. Sorry" I said sullenly.

"It's alright. I promise you that there is nothing more that I'm keeping from you. At least nothing important enough for me to remember at this very moment" she chuckled. I could see she was trying to ease the tension. Though I can appreciate her trying to make things better, I don't appreciate the poor timing.

"So, the Seer told you nothing about your other daughter?" Felix asked,

"No. She was vague with any kind of detail and withheld more than she gave" Lunaya said speaking to Felix.

"Imagine that" I whispered sarcastically, only to be shot a firm glare from Roe. I huffed and sat down. She's meant to be on my side here.

"We will get in contact with Alpha Hina at Luna Eclipse, maybe we can convince Papi to tell us more about what she saw" Alyse said to the room.

"I'll head home and talk with Lace about it, and go through the library there" Nat announced,

"I will call my brother" Tobias said without looking up,

"Blue Moon has an extensive library and he will be happy to help" Tobias offered. I was a little surprised. I was still undecided as to where he was with this whole thing, whether he knew about it, or he didn't. But he is offering to help, so that has to mean he doesn't know anything. At least I hope it does. That glimmer of hope and the reignition of my trust in him, it took a small bit of weight off my shoulders.

"I recommend you keep as much of this on the down low as possible" Lupus interjected. All eyes turned to him, waiting for an explanation.

"Zelena already faces a lot of danger just by being the Triple Goddess, that fact has been proven enough already. If the rest of the world discovered that the Triple Goddess is not only a twin herself, but has also given birth to twins..." Lupus started,

"There will be chaos" Felix added.

"Weres from all over the world will come for her" Smith said cautiously.

The room fell into silence, each of us contemplating the possibilities. Lupus is right, this news will send shockwaves through the gossip channels. Twin births are rare in Weres, this has been said to me enough times over the past week. A twin giving birth to twins, now that would be considered a miracle. Not to mention the addition of the Triple Goddess thing. I'd be a circus act. My pups would be bombarded by strangers from all over the world. We can't let that happen. They have to be protected.

"So how are we going to handle this then?" Alyse asked, breaking the tense silence.

"I have to tell Lace, I won't keep secrets from him" Nat said quickly and firmly,

"No one expects you to keep secrets from your Mate, My Dear" Roe answered her.

"But please keep it to only those who are close to you both, make sure they can be trusted" I said to everyone.

"I trust Lace and his Beta" Nat snipped,

"And everyone here trusted Artemis, look how that turned out" I snapped back. She lowered her head and went silent. I huffed and pinched the bridge of my nose. Artemis betraying Tri-Moon hasn't really been talked about a whole lot. I know that everyone is still angry about it. But mostly there is a lot of shame and embarrassment. A lot of the pack, especially Lupus, Roe and other senior pack members, all feel an air of guilt over it.

"Sorry, I shouldn't have said that" I grunted.

"No. You're right" Lupus chimed in,

"We were all fooled by Artemis. Each of us needs to be very careful with this information, share it wisely and with as much discretion as possible" he said with a heavy warning.

"Of course"

"Okay"

"I will"

The room chorused their understanding and agreement. Finally, it looked like we were getting somewhere.

"And what of the pack?" Smith asked.

"What do you mean?" I replied.

"I mean the twins still haven't been introduced to the pack yet. They know that you've given birth, and they are getting impatient to meet the pup, or in this case pups. Are you going to tell them that you had twins?"

"No" Roe and I said at the same time. Roe raised her hand to me, indicating she had something to say before I explained my reason. I nodded for her to go ahead.

"I've thought about this over the past few days. The twins need to remain a secret, at least for now. But we do need to introduce the pack to at least one of them, otherwise they will start to get suspicious. And suspicion leads to questions".

"You want to keep just one baby hidden?" I asked. I was honestly a little hurt by the idea. The thought of hiding one of my babies like a dirty secret made me angry.

"Yes, and no" Roe continued,

"They look so much alike, I think we can use that to our advantage".

"How?" Nat asked.

"We only take one pup out of the house at any one time. We don't let anyone else hold the pups, this will make sure that no one gets close enough to pinpoint the difference in their scents. Then after we have found more information on the prophecy, then and only then do we admit the truth".

Everyone was quiet, probably doing what I was doing and weighing up our options. It's a good idea. We could probably pull it off without too much trouble, at least for a month or two. Though hopefully, we won't need to for that long.

"And do we tell them they have an Alpha-son or an Alpha-daughter?" I asked.

"Son" Lupus, Felix and Smith spoke together. Nat huffed and rolled her eyes.

"Typical" she sneered.

"No! Not for any of that macho sexist crap you're assuming" Smith argued while waving his hand at Nat,

"Think about it. Zelena is the Triple Goddess, and the gene is passed from mother to daughter. So, if word spreads that she has given birth to a daughter, that could put G. at risk".

Of course, that was one of the many threats I had already thought of. Hunters could come for G. just like they did for me and Aurora. Not just hunters though, but rival packs, other supernaturals, really anyone that considered her a threat or wanted to claim the bloodline of Selena. Smith has a point. An Alpha-son would be cherished more by the pack, and yet probably of less interest to the rest of Were-kind.

"It makes sense" I said offering Smith a half grin.

"Well, I'll be damned" Lupus chuckled,

"I was thinking the same thing" he said proudly and nodded to Smith.

"So, it's settled then. We announce the birth of an Alpha-son" Roe said with finality. When no one said anything further, she slapped her hands on the table,

"I'll make the arrangements" she nodded and stood up.

"I'll head home first thing in the morning" Nat said, also standing up.

"You won't stay for the announcement?" I asked, stopping her before she left. Nat took my hand and sighed,

"I want to, I do, but I have to get back to Howlers. I've already been gone for too long. And the sooner that I'm home, the sooner I can start scouring the library" she said squeezing my hand and offering a small smile. I nodded in understanding and let her go. Just as Nat went to push the door open, loud knocking sounded from the other side of it. She pulled open the door and stepped to the side for Daniel to enter. All eyes now turned to his flushed and worried face. As he looked around the room at everyone in attendance, his worry faded, and confusion took its place.

"Did I miss a meeting?" he asked, turning his attention to me. I swallowed, trying to think of something quickly so as to not hurt his feelings.

"No, no. Just family stuff. What can I do for you, Daniel?" I answered him with a shrug. He hesitated for a moment, the worry once again appeared on his face.

"Daniel, is something wrong?" I asked. I was getting a little concerned that he was going to puke. He was pale and flushed at the same time, if that's even possible. He took a deep breath and turned to face me completely,

"The Alpha has just pulled into the driveway" he said with caution. His words were riddled with fear and anxiety. My knees almost gave out from under me and my stomach hit the floor. He couldn't mean Gunner, why would Daniel be scared that Gunner was home?

"The Alpha?" Lupus asked, he handed B. to Roe and slowly stood up.

"Gunner" Daniel confirmed with a nod.

Chapter Twenty-Five

Aurora

"Why won't you change?" Gunner huffed annoyed. I wanted to answer, I needed to answer. But there was an invisible rope, tying my gaze to his creamy skin and the thick rod between his legs. I swear I could taste him already. Musky, yet sweet. I can see myself running my tongue over those deep crevasses that are his abs.

"Whiskey, we need to get down the mountain, it will be quicker to do that in wolf form" he said with a touch of frustration in his tone. Yet I still couldn't look away. I was positively spellbound.

"Fuckin' hell. Whiskey!" he snapped and clicked his fingers to garner my attention. I managed to drag my eyes away from his body and met his impatient stare.

"What?" I asked blankly. I must sound like a blundering idiot. What is wrong with me. He smirked, a cocky kind of smirk that told me he knew exactly what I was looking at.

"When you're done, we need to change form so that we can get down the mountain" he said with a hint of amusement.

"No" I snapped. I crossed my arms and ground my teeth together.

"What do you mean, no? You said you wanted to come back with me, what's changed?" he asked raising his voice.

"I said I would come back with you. I didn't agree to go galivanting over the mountain as a wild beast" I growled. Just the thought of changing made me angry. Gunner seemed shocked, he dropped his arms and stepped back a little.

"Why would you say something so hateful?" he asked in a hiss.
"Not hateful, just honest. We are perfectly capable of getting down the mountain on two feet, two human feet" I said with a harsh whip to the word human.
"You called your wolf a beast, that is hateful" Gunner argued.
"They are beasts" I snipped back at him. This conversation was going to lead us nowhere but to him asking about my obvious hatred toward the wolf form. That conversation will not be productive or helpful to my plan.
"Look, I'll tell you about it one day, okay?" I sighed and uncrossed my arms,
"But for today, can we just put a pin in it and walk? Please" I asked with a false tone of promise. I put on my most innocent expression and used my sad and pleading little girl eyes. Gunner pulled his bottom lip between his teeth and looked over my face.
"Ah fuck" he whisper hissed and turned to the bags at his feet. He ruffled through one and pulled out some clothes. After putting them on, much to my disappointment, he turned back around to glare at me.
"I don't like this. It will take us twice as long, so you had better keep up a good pace" he grunted and tossed the large backpack over his shoulder. I nodded my head and offered a small smile.
"It's you that will have to keep up" I snickered and readjusted the bag on my shoulder. I pushed past him and headed into the trees. I heard Gunner mumble and groan, but I couldn't make out the words.
I was right, it was Gunner who struggled to keep pace. He is clearly too dependent on his wolf form. Although he is muscular and fit, his human endurance is nowhere near my level. After a couple of hours, Gunner got winded. He was huffing and looked to be struggling with the large bag on his back. Me, however, I'm used to this. My body knows how to handle the distance and agility needed for such treks, I have been doing it for years.
"Do you need to rest?" I asked as I paused and turned back to Gunner. Sweat was beaded on his forehead and his chest was expanding with his deep quick breaths.
"No resting" Gunner grunted back.
"Here then, we'll swap backpacks for a little while" I said as I held my small bag out for him to take. He glared at the bag in my hands and then back up at me.

"Thought you said you weren't going to help" he snipped, "Thought you said you wanted to keep a good pace" I hit back. Gunner growled lowly and let the bag drop from his shoulders. I walked back over to him and picked it up from his feet. As I stood slowly, I realised how close we were. I looked up at his deep blue eyes, eyes that were looking back down at me from only inches away. His sweat smelt like the rain on a hot summer day. It took all of my willpower not to lick him from his chest to his chin. Gunner took a deep breath and stepped back away from me. I was ready to step up to him again, recapturing the closeness we just lost, but I caught the look on his face before he turned away. His brows were furrowed, and deep lines marred his forehead. His lips were pulled into thin tight lines, and he was mumbling to himself. He seems conflicted. Maybe he wants to be close to me, just like I do to him. Maybe I'm not alone in this odd attraction.

I put the large bag on my back and started off again. I can see why Gunner was struggling, the bag is fully packed. It's not heavy, at least not for me, but I can see myself growing tired of carrying it very quickly. This is why I travel light. Material crap just weighs you down, there is nothing you need to survive that you can't find in nature. We switched out the bags a few times on the rest of the hike. I didn't think that Gunner would go through my things, but it made me uneasy all the same. I stuck close each time he had my bag on his back, watching him carefully. Even still, I had to play this game, to be the nice and helpful girl. There is still a lot of information that I want to dig out of him. Letting him believe that I am on his side is the best way to do that. I offered to stop a couple of times, I offered to make some food and take his bag for longer, but Gunner refused. Almost every offer, he refused. I don't know, maybe he was embarrassed or something. Maybe it was his cocky Alpha mentality thing.

The rest of the trip down the mountain was mostly silent. Gunner was still mad at having to do the trip on two legs instead of four. Probably because he got tired quickly in his human form. But that's his own fault. Not my problem if he is weak. I was very surprised when Gunner led us to a vehicle though. He seemed like the type to do the whole trip in wolf form, being all accepting of the wolf and all that shit. We are clearly very different in that aspect, even if we are both creations of the hunters. Though, I am second guessing my first assumptions about him. He seems too normal, or well balanced. If he is like me, wouldn't he have a few more issues? Wouldn't he think the same of his wolf side as I do of mine? If he was tortured and beaten his whole life, wouldn't he have a few more scars to show for it? Plus, how could the hunters create an Alpha wolf, that doesn't seem possible. This isn't adding up. I don't like it when I can't make sense of things. I don't like not knowing. But what I do understand, what I know for sure, is that Weres don't usually have magical powers. So, if he is a regular born Werewolf, how or where did he acquire magical abilities?

"You have a car?" I asked dumbfounded. After Gunner had pulled the protective covering off the large car. He rolled the sheeting up and chuckled,

"Of course" he said as he started ruffling through his bag.

"Oh" I blanked.

"Were you expecting a private jet?" he teased, as he dug through his bag, assumably for the keys.

"I don't know what I was expecting, not this though" I scoffed as I looked over the fancy black SUV. The paint was dent and scratch free, the glossiness shone under the setting sun. I do enjoy nice things, and I have stolen one or two nice cars. But this was very nice. I've not come across many packs that can afford stuff like this. Just where does he come from, I wonder. Gunner pulled out a big black key and hit the button, the car beeped in response and flashed its lights.

"Well, I couldn't very well run the whole way, that would have taken weeks" Gunner said as he opened the trunk and tossed the bags inside.

"Weeks?" I asked,

"Yep" he nodded back and went around to the driver's side door. I hesitated at the passenger door. I'm honestly starting to second guess this whole idea. He hasn't told me where we are going or what he expects to happen once we get there. This whole time, I've been assuming that I am the one playing him, that I'm in control. But what if he is playing me. This could all be a trap. The passenger door swung open and Gunner sat back upright in the driver's seat,

"You coming, or what?" he asked with a smile. I carefully climbed into the seat and shut the door. I looked at Gunner as he started up the engine and backed out of the shrubs and trees that the car had been half hidden amongst.

"Where exactly are we going?" I asked him. He turned to look at me quickly before looking back at the darkening road.

"My pack" he answered like it was obvious,

"I'm aware of that, but where is your pack?" I asked with a little more hardness to my voice. Gunner paused before answering. He looked at me a couple of times out of the corner of his eye as he drove, while I sat quietly watching him, waiting for his answer.

"Are you having second thoughts?" he asked cautiously,

"Not exactly. But driving in a car, with a man I've just met, in the middle of the night, to a destination that I don't know, you can see why that is a little concerning" I told him.

"It's not the middle of the night, it's just off eight o'clock" he said back. He was trying to avoid telling me, but why? What is he hiding?

"Where are we going?" I asked again,

"Why does the destination matter? You said you wanted to come with me" he quipped back.

"Why is it such a big secret? If you're trying to earn my trust, this isn't the way to do it" I snapped angrily. This doesn't feel right. Why is he trying to hide their location? I have a bad feeling about this.

"With all due respect, it was you who tried to kill me at first sight, not the other way around. If anyone should have trust issues here, it's me" he snorted. He's avoiding the question. I'm not stupid, I know how manipulation works, and he is trying pretty damn hard to steer this conversation somewhere else. This must be a trap. What other explanation is there? I was right all along, he is a creation of the hunters and he's been sent out to find me and bring me back. That's what he's doing, he is taking me back to the hunters. Well fuck that, I'm not going back.

"Fuck this" I spat and pulled my door handle. The door swung open and I reefed my seatbelt off.

"Stop!" Gunner shouted. He leaned over my lap, grabbing my legs to stop me from jumping out of the moving car. With one hand still on the wheel, and a lot of his upper body on my legs, he pulled the door closed again with a hard thud. Gunner sat up a little more, then he gently took the seatbelt from my hand and buckled it back into place.

"Please don't do that" he said pleadingly while keeping his hand on the buckle.

"Tell me where you're taking me" I shouted. I had one hand on the doorhandle ready to swing it open, and the other hovering over his hand on my seatbelt.

"To my pack" he said gently. All this time he was still driving, a fact that concerned me. Even if we did crash, I probably wouldn't die, and I would heal quickly. But when there's a scuffle in a car, don't people usually pull over, why wouldn't he want to stop?

"Where is your pack?" I demanded and tried to pull his hand away from the buckle. He refused to let me get to the belt, and instead grabbed my hand and held it tightly on my lap.

"I can't tell you that" he said softly,

"Then I'm not going!" I screamed and tried to pull my hand free. The car screeched to a halt, sending my body jolting forward hard and my head whipping back. Before I had a chance to stop my head from spinning, the seat's backrest dropped down flat, and Gunner's body was hovering over the top of me. His hands were pinning me down on either side of my head, and one of his knees sat between my legs. The position felt very close, intimate even. Once again, my body betrayed me and my heart began to flutter. My breathing increased and my skin ran hot. I arched my back, trying to press myself against him, but he was too high above me.

"Calm down, I'm not going to hurt you" he said gently. I took a long deep breath, trying to rid myself of the pulsating desire in my stomach.

"There you go" Gunner cooed. The big idiot mistook my excitement for fear.

"Get off me" I growled lowly,

"In a minute" he said back softly,

"No, now!" I screamed and thrashed my arms and legs. One of my knees hit Gunner between his legs. He grunted and buckled over, leaning his head on my shoulder. He groaned in pain and moved one of his hands from beside my head, leaving the space open. I took the opportunity and opened the car door, I shoved Gunner off me, sending him toppling onto the ground. I jumped from the car and started to run back the way we came. I won't go back to them. I can't go back there. I ran down the road for a bit, then dodged off into the trees. I was moving fast, constantly changing my direction and backtracking, making it harder for him to follow me. If those bastards want me back, they'll have to kill me first.

I stopped running and pressed my back against a tree trunk. I held my breath and listened to the sounds through the forest. The thumping of my heart was the only thing I could hear. Not even the forest animals were risking being caught tonight. I pushed off the tree and started to run again, only to be hit in the back and pushed to the ground. I rolled over and came face to face with a large set of razor sharp teeth. I pulled my knees up to my chest and planted my feet on its stomach. I pushed hard with my legs, sending the beast flying through the air and slamming into a tree. As I jumped to my feet and glared at the large wolf, I had to pause. This one was smaller, and a darker shade of grey. It's not Gunner. Gunner's beast is huge, and his fur is a silky silver. Who the fuck is this? The wolf charged at me, I lifted my hand for my blade and hissed with anger. My bag is still in the car, the blade that Gunner didn't destroy is in the bag. Fuck. The grey wolf jumped, launching itself through the air, headed right for me. Just at the last second, it was struck in the side and sent rolling through the trees away from me. A whirlwind of growls, grunts and yelps sounded through the forest as the animals fought.

I should have run, I shouldn't have hesitated. But stupid me, I waited, I watched. Gunner's wolf was clearly the dominant creature and could have killed the other wolf ten times over by now. But he didn't lay any lethal blows. He was simply trying to subdue the other beast. Gunner had the other wolf pinned with his large paw on his throat. The smaller wolf was huffing and whining, it had smears of blood seeping through its fur.

"Kill it!" I shouted. Gunner whipped his head to me and flashed his teeth. The wolf struggled and yelped under Gunner's hold.

"Gunner, kill it!" I screamed. But no, the big dumb lump didn't kill it. Instead, Gunner took his paw off the wolf and took a few steps back. His silver fur slowly receded back into his skin, and he stood on two human feet with his hands out in front of him in surrender.

"What are you doing?" I yelled angrily. He was surrendering. What the fuck, he had it, he won, why would he let it go?

"I apologise, friend, we did not mean to trespass on your land. My companion became lost" Gunner said to the other beast. The wolf struggled to its feet and tilted its head back, then howled into the sky. Great, now every fucking wolf in a five kilometre radius will be coming for us. The small beast stepped back, and then it too stood up on two human legs.

"State your business" the man demanded. He was on the older side, maybe early fifties. Though he was still in good shape, he had lived a rough life. His skin was painted with battle scars. The older man was grasping at his side, fresh blood was slowly seeping through his fingers.

"As I said, my companion became lost after we argued, I was just protecting her" Gunner said firmly.

"Can I help you? You're still bleeding" Gunner asked as he stepped closer to the older man. The man scoffed and looked down at his wound.

"It's fine, I just don't heal like I used to" he forced a chuckle,

"My father has said something similar a few times" Gunner joked. What in the bloody hell was going on here. What, are they friends now? As I stood watching the two naked men converse about the disadvantages of growing old, soft growls steadily began to surround us. A large brown wolf crept through the trees, headed right for me. Its long sharp teeth were bared, and it had its head down and ready to attack as it stalked towards me. I curled my lips back and growled at the beast.

"Fuck off" I hissed at it. I will have no issue killing this mongrel, and all of its little friends. A few more wolves appeared and slowly started to shift into humans. The growls of their comrades still echoed through the dark of the trees, letting us know that there were many more of them here. The one that had been growling at me was a bitch, a woman. She was not too much taller than me, with long chocolate brown hair and a medium built figure. She stepped up to me and tried to grab my arm. I hissed and flung my hand out, slicing my talons through her forearm. The girl screamed and grabbed her arm.

"Don't touch me" I growled. Just as I finished the last word, I was jumped on by three other naked men. One of the men grabbed an arm, and another grabbed my other arm. The third man wrapped one of his arms around my waist and one around my throat. I growled and fought but was unable to move.

"Let her go!" Gunner roared. His voice was so loud that it shook the branches above our heads. I could feel the influence of his voice, it was like a heavy weight inside my head.

"Alpha" a deep firm voice called through the trees. All eyes turned to the source of the voice, as a middle aged man walked forward. He had silver tainting the sides of his deep black hair, and dark pink scars all over his exposed chest and arms. He's an Alpha, I can tell just by looking at him. I looked around at the other members of his pack, all of them were covered in scars. Some more than others, but each person held a great many marks. It would have taken years of constant fighting to gather so many scars. Either that, or they are all just terrible fighters.

"Tell your men to let her go" Gunner demanded. He stood up tall with his chest forward and head high, as he stepped toward the other Alpha.

"Not yet" he smirked and looked over at me. I struggled against the six hands holding me and growled back at the Alpha.

"She's feisty, I like her" he laughed. Gunner growled and stepped in the face of the Alpha,

"She's claimed" Gunner growled.

"I'm not trying to claim your Mate, Alpha" he laughed and stepped back. I snapped my eyes to Gunner, to see what he would say. But he said nothing, he didn't correct the Alpha.

"We will be on our way then" Gunner grunted and turned to me. The moment I saw his eyes, I knew we were in trouble. Even with his Alpha strength and his special power, Gunner still had fear in his eyes. Who are these mutts to make Gunner scared?

"Now hold your horses, I can't just let anyone go traipsing through my territory" The other Alpha said,

"We have a vehicle on the road" Gunner told him,

"Oh I know, we found your vehicle. And yet here you are, in my forest, attacking my pack members".

"I told this one that we got lost after an argument, we didn't mean to come onto your land" Gunner growled and pointed at the older man who found me.

"Yes, I know that too" the Alpha smirked. I really want to smack that smirk right off his stupid face.

"Then what's the problem?" Gunner grunted,

"The problem, young Alpha, is that you have both now drawn blood from my pack members. Blood must pay with blood" he answered with a glimmer of amusement in his dark eyes.

I know that look. The look of evil and excitement. He was about to do something bad, and he was going to enjoy it. I know that look because I wear it myself regularly. Gunner turned to look at me just as the Alpha raised his hand. At his signal, the man with his arm around my throat tightened his grip. Upon instinct, I gasped and choked on the air that got stuck. Gunner's face went feral with anger as he turned back on the Alpha. Gunner threw his arm forward, he didn't even touch the other Alpha, but still, he went flying backwards through the trees. One of the other men ran for Gunner, but Gunner waved his arm up into the air, and the man went flying up with it.

I got so caught up in watching Gunner in all his magnificent glory, that I forgot to fight off the three men holding me. I tilted my head back and sucked in a slow, long, deep breath. The coughing was first, then they dropped their grips on me, then the choking sounds of suffocation. I glared down at the three men, watching their faces turn blue as I sucked the air from their lungs. "Whiskey" Gunner called. I turned to look at him and he shook his head before looking down at the three gasping men on the ground. He wants me to spare them, is he fucking crazy.

"Don't" he mouthed and held his hands out, doing the slow down movement. He was indicating for me to stop. I scrunched up my face with annoyance and let the breath go. The three men gasped deeply and clumsily scampered away from my feet. Gunner was at my side in an instant. His arm was around my shoulders, holding me to him protectively. All of the other men and women that surrounded us had started closing in. This was going to be a fight. Good. I could use a decent scrap, maybe let off some steam.

"Well now!" the Alpha called as he sauntered back over to us,

"You are as impressive as I've heard you were" he chuckled and waved his hand. All of his men backed down and walked slowly back, giving us more space.

"What does that mean?" I whispered to Gunner,

"Shh" he hissed back.

"The Alpha Gunner. The Alpha of Alphas, they call you".

Alpha of Alphas, I've never heard that term before. I looked up to Gunner's chin, he was glaring at the other Alpha with his fingers digging into my arm.

"I don't believe I've had the pleasure" Gunner said through his clenched teeth. The Alpha laughed and shook his head.

"No, Mighty Alpha, royalty like you would never foul yourselves with the lowly likes of us. Not until you need something done that you won't dirty your own polished hands with" he sneered angrily. Gunner's body tensed and I couldn't help but press myself against the firmness of his muscles.

"I know who you are" Gunner said in a firm and commanding voice. The other Alpha didn't respond, just snickered.

"You're Alpha Doyle. Alpha to the Meļņasirds, the mercenary pack" Gunner said in a low voice. He was speaking with authority and firmness, though I could hear the underlying caution in his words. He was afraid. Whoever this Doyle and his pack of mercenaries are, they have Gunner worried.

Chapter Twenty-Six

Aurora

I tightened my grip on Gunner's side, digging my fingernails into his flesh. Gunner stared at Doyle, and Doyle stared back at Gunner. I looked around us, we were still surrounded. At a quick glance, I counted nine, ten including the Alpha. Should be easy to take them. I've taken down more than this on my own before. But Gunner doesn't seem like the type to get scared at just anyone. He called these ones mercenaries. I've never heard of Werewolf mercenaries. I wonder if the hunters knew about them. Probably not, or else they would have extinguished them by now. Human mercenaries earn their reputation, similar to that of a hunter clan. I can only assume that wolf mercenaries work the same way. And by the look of Gunner, this pack have built themselves one hell of a reputation.

"So, Mighty Alpha, you have heard of me? I guess my reputation speaks as loud as yours does. Or should I say, as loud as your Mate's" Doyle sneered and turned his glare to me. Why does he think I'm Gunner's Mate, what would have given him that impression.

"We've all heard the stories about you, Tiny Goddess" Doyle teased.

What stories? How does he even know who I am. I have always been careful to keep my identity a secret. There is no way he could know who I am. Also, did he just call me 'Tiny Goddess'? Eww. But wait, he thinks I'm Gunner's Mate. We both know that I'm not, so he's referring to someone else. It must be the Zee person he has mentioned. Gunner refuses to talk about her, so I don't know what she could have done that was special enough to have stories told about her. With all the mystery, and now the new interest from this Alpha, I am well past the point of curious. Once we kill these morons and get out of this forest, Gunner and I are going to need to have a real conversation. But for now, he thinks I am Gunner's Mate, so I guess I can play along.

"Then you should know not to fuck with me" I sneered at Doyle. He glared back at me with his top lip curled back into a snarl. I was ready for his attack, my feet were light and ready to move. My talons were pressing against the tips of my fingers, my gums tingled with the need for my fangs to extend. Gunner's body vibrated with a deep growl, he too was ready for the fight. A roar of laughter burst from Doyle's mouth. He threw his head back and laughed into the sky.

"Didn't I say it, she is feisty. No she-wolf kills that many hunters without a bucket load of fire in her belly" Doyle cackled wildly. Hunters, Gunner's Mate killed a lot of hunters? So she's some kind of super warrior then. I'm starting to respect and hate this mystery woman. Gunner squeezed my shoulder, another growl bubbled out of his mouth.

"Yes, Tiny Goddess. I know all too well not to fuck with you" Doyle teased,

"Then what is this show for? Why try and keep us here, why lay hands on her, and why spout your 'blood pays with blood' nonsense?" Gunner growled. Doyle's amused expression dropped, and his laughter was gone. He glared at Gunner and stepped forward.

"Blood pays with blood, is our way. Do not disrespect our traditions. I don't care who you are, disrespect me and you will regret it" Doyle warned venomously.

"I meant no disrespect, Alpha Doyle, but you threatened my Mate" Gunner grunted back. I nearly choked on my own tongue. Did he just call me his Mate? I heard that, right? I looked up to his face as he stared blankly at Doyle. Not a flinch, blink, delayed breath, nothing. His position was firm and strong, either he is a brilliant poker player, or he means it. No, no. Saxton explained how Mating works, and neither of us has drunk the other's blood. He's just playing along, he must be.

"I made no threat, not to her. I was just curious" he snickered.

"Curious about what exactly?" I snapped.

"About you, of course" he fired back,

"What about me?" I asked. If I can't get Gunner to talk, maybe I can manipulate Doyle into telling me about this Zee woman.

"Stop" Gunner hissed out of the corner of his mouth and pinched my arm.

"I just wanted to know if you really are the badass that the stories claim you are, or if it was just that, a story".

"And your conclusion?" I asked without hesitation. Doyle laughed again and smiled wickedly at me.

"You are a fearless little thing, aren't you" he chuckled.

"That wasn't an answer" I snipped. Doyle stopped his chuckling and stared at me.

"Careful she-wolf. Or else I will be forced to test the full extent of your abilities" Doyle growled his warning. Gunner and I both growled back. He is threatening me. Mutts that threaten me don't usually fare too well.

"Try me" I snarled and flashed my teeth. I went to step toward him, fully prepared and itching to watch the life drain out of his cocky face and dark eyes. But Gunner's grip on my arm pulled me back, smacking my back against his chest. He wrapped his arms around my body, holding me in front of him. As much as there were other things to worry about, the fact that his naked and muscular body was pressed completely up against me, didn't go unnoticed.

"Oh, I have no doubt that you would put up one hell of a fight" Doyle scoffed,

"But we have a more pressing matter to attend to" he said with a sly smile. I don't like this dog. He seems off.

"Are you afraid?" I teased with a chuckle. I don't know what possessed me to bait him. I guess I'm just used to playing with these dumb animals. He didn't seem to appreciate it though. Doyle roared. He didn't just let his canines extend, but his whole face began morphing into a wolf. His nose extended forward as his teeth grew, and his eyebrows increased in size and spread across to his ears, which had grown into furry points.

"I fear nothing" he growled in a deep and rumbling animalistic voice. I had no reaction. I just stared at his disfigured face. Gunner growled and pulled me back away from Doyle. The rest of the people around us were all silently watching. I smirked at the furious Alpha, again probably not the best idea. But I found the whole situation hilarious. This idiot thinks he could actually beat me. Maybe he could beat the girl that he thinks I am, Zee. But the mongrel has zero chance against me, the real me, the incarnation of death. His face slowly returned to its normal state, then he glowered at me.

"Remember this, Tiny Goddess. Remember that I let you walk out of here unscathed. The next time we cross paths, you may not be so lucky" Doyle rumbled.

"Ditto" I snapped back. Doyle curled his lips back over his teeth and snarled. He lifted his hand and snapped his fingers, then they were all gone. I watched as they retreated into the trees, leaving Gunner and me alone, his naked body still holding me to him. I could feel his heart thundering in his chest, his heated skin was warm against mine. I leaned back into him, pushing out my backside like a horny cat. Gunner hissed and pushed me away. I whirled around and frowned at him.

"What the fuck is wrong with you?" he snapped harshly. I didn't answer, just stared at him wide eyed. What's ruffled his feathers?

"Excuse me?" I asked annoyed,

"Do you have any fucking clue who they were?" he yelled stepping toward me and pointing in the direction that Doyle had run off in.

"No. Should I?" I asked dumbly. Gunner seemed to have dropped his anger and stood up straight. He tipped his head to the side and quirked his eyebrow.

"Wait, really?" he asked with a gentler tone.

"Really. I don't know who that was, why would I?" I replied annoyed.

"Oh" Gunner said stunned.

"Who was he?" I asked innocently.

"That's the Alpha you call when your pack is having trouble"

"What kind of trouble?"

"Supernatural trouble, hunter trouble, sometimes even human trouble".

"And they what, they kill them?"

"Well, Yeah. They're called the mercenaries, but I suppose they are more like the Were equivalent of the CIA secret assassins. Only they're not owned or operated by any government or organisation. We don't exactly talk about them, everyone knows about them, but they are a taboo subject" Gunner explained.

He told me more than I was expecting him to. It didn't make sense though, the hunters would have known about an organisation like that. They have a multitude of spies, and many ways of getting sensitive information from places you wouldn't expect. This feels like something they would have known about. Especially if these mercenaries were killing clans of hunters and innocent humans. That's what the hunters are for, protecting the humans, by eradicating the supernaturals.

"Why's that, why the hush hush?" I pushed him for more answers.

"Well, because we don't kill humans. At least we're not meant to. The Meḷnasirds do. If there's money in it for them, they'll kill anything".

"What do you mean you don't kill humans?" I asked with a jeer. I've been told hundreds of stories about the savage wolves that tore their way through towns, slaughtering innocent women and children. I've been shown pictures and videos of the aftermath. I know that Weres kill humans ruthlessly. It's been drummed into me for as long as I can remember. Werewolves are born killers, uncontrollable animals that thirst for blood.

"Huh?" Gunner huffed surprised by my question,

"I've seen plenty of humans killed by wolves" I shot back at him. Was he trying to play innocent or something, what was with the fake shock on his face. Gunner stepped forward and grabbed my shoulders. He crouched down so that we were at eye level.

"What are you talking about?" he asked urgently, I scoffed annoyed and tried to shake out of his hold. He pulled me back roughly to look at him and repeated the question,

"Tell me, what are you talking about?" he ordered. I wanted to sneer at his fake concern, but decided to play along, if only for a moment.

"I'm talking about the thousands of humans that werewolves have slaughtered over the years. Don't act like it's some big surprise" I answered him angrily. Gunner pursed his lips and stared into my eyes, like he was searching for something. When he didn't speak again, I pulled at his hand to release me,

"Will you let me go now" I grunted.

"Whiskey, have you actually seen a Were kill a human?" he asked, no, he demanded He shook my shoulders for good measure. I scoffed up at him. I don't understand what is happening here. Why was he pretending like this, what did he get out of it, of acting innocent? There's no one else here, just me. No one to show off for and play the doting and caring animal. Why act this way when we both clearly know the truth? When I couldn't come up with a witty comeback, I snorted.

"What?" I said with a huff.

"Where? When? Who was it? This is serious, tell me Whiskey" he said gruffly. The pressure of his fingers on my arms was becoming annoying.

"Stop it, Gunner, you're freaking me out" I said and tried to push his hand off my shoulder.

"Listen to me. This is important, have you yourself seen a Were kill a human unjustly" he snapped firmly.

"Unjustly?" I scoffed. Like killing innocent families can ever be justified.

"Where did you see it?" he growled,

"The fuck are you talking about?" I blanked,

"Tell me, Whiskey. Have you seen it?" he shouted and shook me,

"NO!" I screamed back. Gunner let me go and stood up straight. He glared at me and put his hands on his hips.

"Why did you say that, that Weres have slaughtered humans, if you didn't see it, why did you say it?" Gunner asked slowly. I could hear the seriousness in his voice, I could feel the anger radiating from him.

"I don't know what you want me to say" I answered him.

I couldn't tell him about the pictures, the stories, the bodies, not without explaining how and why I saw them. I can't tell him about the time I was dragged through a burnt-out town, forced to stare at the bodies that littered the streets. I can't tell him that I know it was werewolves that killed all those people, without explaining that I knew it because the hunters caught three of them. I can't explain how those wolves were tortured and beaten, begging and pleading for their lives. Right up until the point that they confessed and were then decapitated. I definitely can't tell him that this was a one time only thing. Those hunters took me to many small little human towns and villages. That was the one thing I could never get past, the fact that the werewolves only ever killed off small, isolated villages. Towns that were far away from big cities and other humans. They always went for the most vulnerable and defenceless. It's the one thing that I could never forgive. Seeing those bodies shot to hell, half burnt and even hanging from trees and light poles. Men, women and children alike. Such brutal and ruthless murders. The hunters always showed me the bodies of the wolves responsible afterwards. They made me look upon their misshapen bodies, riddled with bullet holes, patches of fur singed off and completely lifeless. They always made sure I knew it was the wolves responsible, and they made sure it filled me with hate and loathing.

If that information came out, it would ruin everything. Gunner can't know. No one can know.

"I want you to tell me what would possess you to lie" Gunner demanded.

"It's not a lie. Humans are murdered by werewolves all the time" I snipped. Reliving those memories in my head reignited my anger and hatred. Wolves are monsters. My mission to continue the hunter's work is one hundred percent justified. They all deserve to die.

"You have never seen it happen though?" he clipped back.

"So what? You don't see children born in the street, but you know it happens all the time. Same thing applies".

Gunner grabbed my wrist and pulled me back to him. He looked down at me angrily and with concern. Like I just told the world about a secret that he didn't know I knew. Shit. Can he read my mind or something, could see those memories flashing through my mind?

"What did you just say?" he grunted,

"I said, just because you don't see babies born all around you, doesn't mean that thousands of babies aren't born every day. Just because I haven't seen a werewolf kill a human, doesn't mean it doesn't happen" I grunted and reefed my arms from his hold. He looked at me surprised and in disbelief. I thought I had him there. He was silent as he watched me glare at him. Why would he lie about it though? Does he think I'm stupid or something. I know what he is and what his kind does.

"We're done here. Get back to the car" he snapped and stormed off through the trees.

"I'm not going with you" I sneered angrily. Gunner stopped walking and turned back on me.

"What?" he snapped.

"I'm not going anywhere with you, not until you tell me where we're going" I said firmly. I crossed my arms and stuck out my hip, like a real petulant child.

"I'm not doing this with you, not here, not now. Not after the shit you just pulled. Get in the car, Whiskey".

"No!" I retorted.

Gunner's face contorted into one of pure frustration. I would have laughed if I didn't feel a little sorry for him. He lifted his head back and curled his hands into fists.

"Goddess help me!" he yelled at the top of his lungs. I snorted in amusement. Gunner is ridiculously sexy, and I want nothing more than to ride him like a bucking bronco. But holy fuck, he can be really stupid. Calling out to the Goddess like she gives a damn about him. Acting like werewolves aren't murderous beasts. Thinking he can persuade and manipulate me into telling him all my secrets. He's in for a rude awakening when I start killing off his precious pack members.

"Fucking, fucked up, shitting fuck" Gunner growled and stomped back and forth in front of me. I just watched him slowly descend into madness, as I tried desperately not to laugh at his little meltdown.

"I didn't want to fucking do it this way" he mumbled to himself. It was like he forgot I was even there, or that I could see and hear him.

"Why can't you let anything be even just a small bit easy" he growled into the sky.

"Are you talking to me"? I asked him after swallowing down my chuckle.

"No!" he snapped and glared at me.

"Right. Well, I'm just going to leave you to your freak out then" I smirked and turned to walk away. I took three steps and then froze. Only it wasn't me that froze, my body just stopped moving. My legs became so heavy, that I couldn't lift them. Even my arms became too heavy to lift.

"What the fuck?" I huffed and tried to move my feet, but it was like they were pinned in place.

"I can't move" I squeaked. I could feel my panic rising. It was just like all those times I was tied to the chair in the frozen room. My wrists, arms, legs and ankles, my chest, neck and forehead, were all strapped down so that all I could move was my eyes. This felt like that.

"Gunner, I can't move" I called back to him desperately.

"I know" his voice answered. He sounded sad and defeated. I felt my feet lift off the ground, but I still couldn't move. My body slowly turned around in mid air, until I was facing Gunner. He had one hand out toward me and a sullen expression on his face. He was doing this, like when he sent Doyle flying through the air, he's doing the same thing to me now.

"What are you doing?" I growled and tried to thrash free. I put every ounce of strength into my movements, but nothing worked.

"I'm sorry" he said softly.

"Let me go" I screamed.

"I can't, you have to come with me" he said as he pulled his arm into his body. I floated above the ground, closer to him, until my face was only inches from his. He lifted his hand to my face and I closed my eyes. I don't know what I was expecting, I didn't think he was going to hit me or anything. But I definitely wasn't expecting the soft and gentle caress on my cheek. My eyes flew open, and I looked right into Gunner's piercing gaze.

"You can trust me" he whispered. My head felt dizzy and my eyes wanted to droop closed.

"Everything is alright" he said in a soft gentle voice. I tried to struggle again but I still couldn't move. I fought as hard as I could. Pulling and demanding that my limbs move. But when that failed, all that I could do was scream. And I did. I scrunched my eyes closed tight and screamed out in frustration.

"Look at me, Whiskey" Gunner's smooth voice called to me. I wanted to ignore him, to yell at him and demand he let me go. But I didn't. I opened my eyes and looked into his glowing silver orbs. A wave of calm washed over me.

"You're safe" his voice echoed through my ears. I stopped trying to fight, to get free, and just gave over to the warm comfortable feeling. Gunner's eyes shone brightly, deep behind the glow of silver, a bright blue swirled within. I felt like butter melting in a hot pan. I couldn't feel my body anymore, I couldn't feel the anger and the pain and the fear. All I could feel was Gunner and his calmness.

"We are going back to the car now" he said in a soft and even tone. His voice felt like soft silk cascading through my ears.

"Okay" I responded.

"You will sleep and be happy. When you wake up, we will be home" he told me. My eyes felt heavy and I wanted to close them. A heavy tiredness swarmed through me.

"Okay" I said sleepily.

"You won't remember this. You will only remember getting in the car and falling asleep" Gunner's echoed voice rang through my head.

"Won't remember" I repeated. My mind was foggy, I couldn't remember why I was angry. Gunner's beautiful silver eyes were gently lulling me into unconsciousness.

"You won't remember" his voice called through my tired mind. My eyes dropped closed, sleep was pulling me under. I can't remember why I was scared.

"You're okay" the smooth gentle voice caressed my ears.

"Go to sleep" he sang. The rest of my thoughts drifted away. I was left floating in nothing. It was warm, safe and comfortable. Nothing else mattered here.

~

"Whiskey" a soft and gentle voice called to me. I was happy here, in the empty nothingness, I didn't want to leave yet.

"Whiskey, it's time to wake up" the voice sang. It was pulling me from the dark, enticing me back to consciousness.

"Hey, are you okay? Are you awake?" I felt a firm touch on my shoulder and a small shake. My head was pounding, my ears were ringing. I groaned and grasped my head. Where did this headache come from.

"What the fuck" I mumbled. The intense pressure in my skull was making me want to puke.

"Where here, Whiskey, we're at my pack" Gunner called to me, shaking me gently.

"Will you stop shaking me, you're gonna make me chuck" I grunted at him and hunched over, putting my head in my lap. How can we be here already? He said it was going to take a long time to get here, wherever here is. I don't remember any of the drive.

"Did I sleep the whole way?" I asked surprised. I couldn't have. I haven't slept for more than four consecutive hours since I was a child. Maybe that's why my head feels like it's going to explode. Maybe I just slept too long.

"You sure did. You snore pretty good too" Gunner chuckled awkwardly. I turned my head and glared up at him with a huff.
"I don't snore" I quipped.
"I beg to differ" Gunner smiled cheekily. We gazed at each other for a moment. His face turned with an unknown emotion. I couldn't place it. I don't know if it was some kind of fear or concern, it could have even been similar to sadness. He's been going on and on about going home, and now that he was finally home, he didn't seem happy about it. I wonder what is going on inside that beautiful head of his. He pulled his eyes from mine and lifted his head. The moment he looked out the windscreen, the strange emotion left him. His eyes grew five times the size and his mouth hung open with the deep breath he inhaled. I could hear his heart thundering, like a freight train on a rickety track. The cab of the car filled with the stench of his excitement and desire. It was overpowering and sickening.
"Zelena" he whispered with a heavy breath.

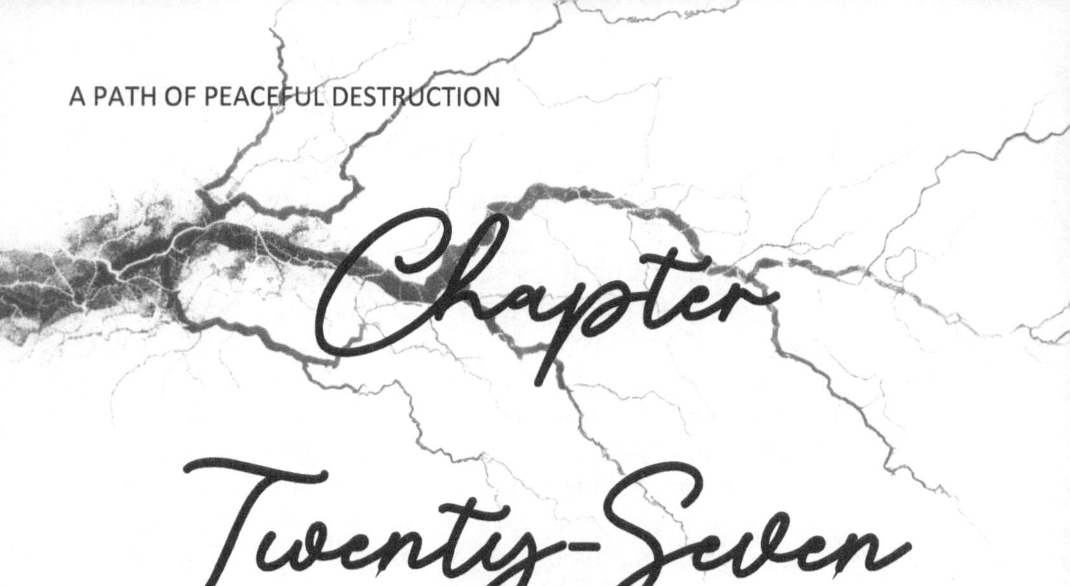

Chapter Twenty-Seven

Zelena

As soon as the name left Daniel's mouth, I flew from the room at lightning speed. My feet barely touched the ground as I ran through the house. A stampede of footsteps thundered closely after me. I ran out the front door and all the way around the building to the driveway, not stopping or pausing for anything. I saw the SUV parked in the middle of the drive, bugs were splattered across the front grill and up along the wheel arch and fenders. He must have been driving through the night. I strained my eyes to peer through the darkly tinted glass. My heart tightened and I gasped. There he is. His hair had grown, and he had a short beard now, but it was definitely Gunner. Tears fell from my eyes as I looked over his figure in the car. He was looking down at the passenger seat, but slowly lifted his head. His eyes connected with mine, and a whimper burst from my lips. He's here, he's really here. He came back to me.

He didn't move from his seat, not at first, he just sat there staring at me through the windscreen. I smiled and half laughed, half sobbed. I lifted my arm to wave to him, like the awkward idiot I am. In a blink, the car door was flung open, and his large frame was running full speed towards me. I reached my arms out for him and tried to run, but I was so overcome with emotions, that my legs gave out from under me before I could even take the first step. Gunner's strong arms wrapped around me as I dropped. He caught me easily and pulled me into his body. I clawed my way up his body to wrap my arms around his neck and my legs around his waist. Once I had him in my arms, I squeezed tight, just to be sure he was real. He is so warm and firm, and just large. I've missed having him in my arms.

"Zelena" Gunner whispered as he nuzzled his face into the crook of my neck. I could feel him breathing me in, becoming familiar with my scent again. I lifted my head to look at him, his bright blue eyes looked back down at me.

"I missed you" I sobbed with a smile. Gunner wiped his fingers over the tears on my cheek and smiled back at me,

"I missed you more" he said sweetly. I was lost in his gaze, making up for lost time. I couldn't see a hint of black anywhere in the startling blue. I ran my hands over his chest, his face, his biceps, everywhere I could reach. He hasn't lost an inch of muscle. He feels strong and sturdy under my touch. This is good, right? It means he's okay, if he lost his wolf he'd be small and weak. He doesn't look or feel that way.

Without warning, Gunner grabbed me from under my arms and lifted me into the air, holding me high above his head. He spun us around quickly, making my long loose hair flutter around my face. I laughed out loud with joy and excitement. Gunner, my Gunner, was finally home. Back in my arms where he belongs.

Sparks of electricity danced across my skin, just like they had always done when Gunner touched me. Overwhelming happiness flooded my brain as I looked down at his beautiful face. Gunner's face was split in two with the largest smile I had ever seen on him. The depths of his eyes sparkled with all the love that I remember they held. He pulled me into him once again, and I wrapped my legs around his waist. He grabbed my face and smashed his lips to mine. I curled my arms around his neck, determined to never let him go again. My face was wet with tears, and they dripped onto our lips as I kissed him feverishly. His hands moved up and down my back, as I rolled my tongue with his. I moaned happily into his mouth as the sparks sent shivers down my spine. Gunner paused and pulled his face away from mine. I pouted and he chuckled, and then he looked down at my now flat stomach. He held my back with one hand and placed the other on my belly.

"The pup?" he asked urgently. I smiled and cupped his face. I pressed my lips to his and held them there for a moment. Then did it again and again, moving my lips all over his face, smothering him in kisses. I leaned my forehead against his and sighed with happiness.

"The pup's fine" I told him in a whisper. He exhaled with a long breath of relief. He moved his hand to cup my cheek and wiped the tears away.

"Thank the Goddess" he huffed. I chuckled to myself and he pulled his head away to look at me with a raised eyebrow.

"More than you know" I smiled mischievously. Oh boy, he is in for a big surprise. He went to ask me something, but I held my finger over his lips, to cut him off. He sucked my finger into his mouth and nipped at it with a playful growl. Oh Goddess, have I missed him. I giggled and flicked his nose before quickly pulling my hand away.

"Do you want to come and see?" I asked and looked into his brilliant blue eyes. My word, I have missed those eyes. I don't want to go another day without gazing into these beautiful eyes.

"Heck Yeah" he exclaimed. He pulled me into him for a tight hug, and I pressed my face into the crook of his neck. I took a deep breath, inhaling his delicious scent. Warm sunshine, forest leaves and love. Everything I remember him smelling like. But there was something else too, something I couldn't place, but it felt very familiar.

"Gunner, my baby boy" Roe cooed loudly with a soft sob, as she came running over. I stayed in Gunner's hold as he greeted his parents, I wasn't ready to let him go just yet. And I don't think either of them would mind.

"Hi Mum" Gunner said back cheerfully. One of his hands disappeared from my back, and I felt Roe squeeze herself in next to me for a hug of her own.

"You've missed so much" she told him, as she rubbed her small hand in a circle on my back.

"I don't doubt it" he scoffed with an amused chuckle,

"Son" Lupus rumbled. He grabbed Gunner by the back of his neck and pulled his head forward to press their foreheads together, I lifted my head slightly and watched as they embraced each other. I have been selfish in my own grief at his absence. I didn't give enough thought to everyone else that would have been missing him as much as I was.

"Hey Dad" Gunner said back with a wide smile, once they separated,

"We're happy you're home, my boy" Lupus smiled and tapped Gunner's cheek lightly. Something I've seen him do often.

"Me too. Hi everyone. Sis, Smith, Lunaya" he said to everyone that had been in the hall with me just a few minutes ago. Everyone except Tobias, he must still be inside with the twins.

"Come inside and meet your pup" I said excitedly and jumped out of his hold. I smiled brightly up at him and then winked at Roe. I took Gunner's hand and went to pull him towards the house. He resisted and pulled me back, I flung around and looked up at him with a frown. I thought he would be running for the house to see his pup. Is he not excited?

"First, I have to tell you something" he said cautiously. My stomach dropped and I felt sick.

"What? What happened, did you lose your wolf, did something happen, what is it?" I demanded urgently. He smiled softly and ran his thumb over my quivering bottom lip.

"Nothing like that, my Love. My wolf is fine, the darkness is gone" he said with a smile. The tears started again and I threw myself into his arms.

"You did it" I cheered through my happy sobs.

"I did" he said back.

"I knew you would" Roe murmured sweetly,

"I didn't have a single doubt" Lupus bellowed proudly. I could hear the others behind me muttering happily amongst themselves.

"Come on then, I have something I need to show you" I told him eagerly and tried to pull him by the hand again,

"Wait, I haven't told you my news yet" he said and pulled me back.

"Can it wait, this is important" I said with a frown,

"She's not wrong" Lupus chuckled,

"So is this" Gunner said firmly. I was getting frustrated, what could possibly be more important than meeting his pups for the first time?

"What?" I grunted annoyed. He looked over his shoulder to the car, just as I heard one of the doors open. Who else was in the car with him, I didn't see anyone else. A loud gasp came from behind me. I turned around to see Lunaya on her knees and Alyse beside her. Lunaya had her hands over her mouth, holding in her sobs. Alyse knelt next to her with one arm over her shoulder and her hand over her mouth too. Smith stood with his mouth hanging open wide, next to Felix with a contemplative frown. Nat was pale and unmoving with wide eyes. What did I miss?

"Holy Mother" Roe exclaimed shocked. I whipped my head to her, and she was looking over at the SUV.

I stepped around Gunner to see what everyone was gawking at. I didn't understand what I was looking at, not at first. It took a minute for the realisation to hit me. And when it did, it was like a building had fallen on top of me. Holy shit. She stood just in front of the car, staring at me with the same kind of expression I imagined I was wearing. Her eyes were wide and her thick brows were lifted high on her forehead. Her mouth hung open and her pale skin looked basically translucent. Without paying attention to what I was doing, I walked forward. She too walked towards me. We both stopped not two steps away from each other. She was me. I was her. Her face was my face, her eyes were my eyes, her hair was my hair. She was me, in every way. I roamed my eyes down her body, taking note of the many dark pink scars that marred her skin. She has lived a brutal upbringing, just like I did. Goddess only knows what they did to her too. I wanted to say something, I wanted to cry, I wanted to smile. But I didn't do any of those things. I just stared at her, and she at me.

"Is this real?" she said softly. Her voice was different to mine, more gravelly and low,

"What are you?" she asked, her voice sounding more angry, panicked maybe. A warm hand snaked around my waist, sending delicious sparks shooting up my side.

"Whiskey, this is Zee, my Mate" Gunner's voice spoke smoothly. Whiskey, why did he call her Whiskey? This is her, isn't it? My sister, Aurora. My twin? Why would Gunner call her Whiskey? She flicked her golden-brown eyes up to Gunner, and a flash of something passed over them. I'm not sure what that was, confusion, sadness maybe. If anything, she looked hurt, but at what? Her gaze moved back down to me and it hardened. Her brows furrowed and she pressed her lips together hard.

"Is this some kind of fucking joke?" she snapped angrily, moving her eyes back to Gunner.

"I told you that you'd think I was crazy" he teased her. He seemed comfortable with her, and she with him. Just how long have they been together. I felt my cheeks grow hot and my stomach turn as jealousy flared through me. I don't like that he was with someone else doing Goddess knows what, especially when that someone is my mirror image. But also, they have already built some kind of relationship between them. Gunner got to meet my sister before I did. Both ideas hurt me. Gunner squeezed my hip, pulling me closer against his side, and flashed me.

Are you okay?

Yes

I can still tell when you're lying

I'm just overwhelmed

"I want to leave now" Aurora snapped and looked around the driveway.

"What?" I blurted,

"Why?" Gunner asked just as quickly.

"Whatever this weird ass game is that you're playing, I don't want any part of it" she growled while looking frantically all around her. I slipped from Gunner's arm and stepped towards her. I need to calm her down and convince her to stay. We have so much that we need to talk about. I want to know where she's been, what she's been through. I want to ask her about the prophecy and if she knew about me. I have to ask her about her life, if she has a Mate, a best friend. I need to know everything about her. I have so many questions. She can't leave yet.

I placed my hand on hers, and fire burned through my skin. My head fell back, and I screamed out in pain. It was like my skin was being peeled away from my bones. My blood was boiling, cooking me from the inside out. I have never felt such agony. I lowered my chin and looked at Aurora. She looked back at me with bright red glowing eyes, the sight was terrifying. Her face was screwed up, like she too was in pain, but she was letting it in, she wasn't fighting it. The burning sensation turned to shoots of electricity. Pins and needles stabbed against my skin, my hair stood up and a dark feeling filled my chest. Next thing I know, I'm being flown backwards through the air. I hit the ground hard, the back of my head slammed against the stone pavement, and I was out.

~

I opened my eyes and sat up slowly. I looked around me but wasn't sure where I was. The last thing I remember was grabbing Aurora's hand, then the extreme pain, like I was on fire. But that pain is gone now, I feel fine actually. What's going on. It's dark, and it's freezing. I breathed in through my nose, sniffing hard.

Blood, mould and rot. I think I'm in the dark room, the one I visited during one of my Drakos visions. I looked around for signs of the girl, the one that spoke to me, but it was too dark to see. I took another deep inhale, but I couldn't pick up on her scent. I don't know if the odour is too strong, or perhaps she just isn't here. There are no windows or any other source of light, I can barely make out anything. A few odd shapes, but nothing clear enough to make sense of. I stood up and walked to the wall and used it to guide me around the room. The smell was rancid, like something had died, or was dying. My bare toes were frozen and hurting from the cold. I wrapped my arms around my body to keep warm. That was when I heard it. A soft murmur in the other corner of the frigid room. I walked over to where the sound came from and looked down at the floor. I forced my eyes to focus, drawing on my wolf for help. There, I could see it, a thin dirty mattress on the floor. Laying on top of it is me, only it isn't me. I know now that this has to be Aurora. She's young, maybe nine or ten years old. Her clothes are torn and stained brown, and her ribs are protruding through them, as are her hips, and spine. I looked over her sleeping face, she's been freshly beaten. There was a deep cut on her lip, and another on her chin, and her left eye looked swollen and raw. I don't need to ask what has happened to her. If it is anything like the way it was with the man that I grew up with, I know too well what she has endured. This must be another Drakos vision. Only it feels different somehow.

"Aurora" I whispered softly. I don't even know if she can hear me, but it was worth a shot. She rolled onto her stomach and curled into a ball. Her back was littered with fresh wounds. Lashings. The same kind of markings once lived on my back. I knelt down beside her ratty bed and reached for her. A soft and gentle hand wrapped around my wrist, stopping me from comforting her. I looked at the person that the hand belonged to, and was surprised to see Selene.

"Mother?" I whispered,

"Hello, daughter of mine" she said back. Her gentle ethereal voice echoed around the room. Even in the darkness, her skin glowed. The silk of her white dress fluttered in the non-existent breeze, and her pure white hair hung in a straight curtain down her back. "Is this the Ethereal Plane?" I asked her and looked back down at Aurora's broken body.

"No" she answered.

"A dream then?" I questioned,

"Not a dream, child, a memory" she sang quietly.

"Who's memory?" I asked, looking up at her beautiful face.

"Mine" she answered sadly. She's showing me her memories, but why. But if she was here, with Aurora, that means she was visiting her too. Just like she did with me when I was this age. If I'm right, why didn't she say anything, why didn't she tell me about her?

"I don't understand" I admitted with furrowed brows.

"Why are you showing me this now, why didn't you tell me about her sooner?".

"This was the last time I was able to visit her" Selene whispered. Even through the musical bells that were her voice, I could hear the sadness.

"Able? Why would you not be able? You're the Goddess of the Moon" I asked perplexed.

"She stopped allowing me in. It was on this day that she closed me off indefinitely".

"I'm sorry, I just don't understand. She shut you off, how does that happen?"

"You are a creation of me, my blood is your blood, as is hers. I have a great many powers, but even I have limitations. For me to visit with you, with anyone, you must be open to it. If you deny me, I cannot come" she explained. I didn't expect such openness from her. I didn't think she would give me the answers, any answers, so easily. Everything is always so cryptic with Selene, why be straight with me now?

"She denied you?" I asked a little shocked. Why would she do that? I remember my time with Selene growing up, I wouldn't have survived without her visits. How could Aurora deny her?

"She did" Selene confirmed,

"But why?"

"Because I could not free her, and she would not accept that".

Oh. My poor sister. I can't pretend to know exactly what she suffered. Our upbringings could have been the same in many ways, but vastly different in others. I remember crying constantly for Selene to take me with her. I remember wishing she'd come back sooner, and just begging her to stay. But I could never imagine living without her. Even though I didn't remember her at the time, each time my memory came back, every time I saw her face again, I never wanted to let her go.

"Why didn't you tell me about her?" I asked,

"You were not ready to hear it" she answered and gracefully stood up. I watched Aurora for another moment. She whimpered and tucked her head into her chest but didn't wake.

"Isn't that up to me to decide?" I said sternly as I stood up and faced my surrogate mother.

"No, child" she answered with a kind smile.

"Is it because of the prophecy? That's why you didn't tell me about her?".

I stood waiting for an answer, but she didn't respond. I opened my mouth to push her for answers when the door opened. A tall, brooding, angry looking man walked in and went straight to the mattress on the floor. We watched silently as he kicked her in the lower back. Aurora cried out in pain and spun around, she scampered back until her small body was pressed into the corner of the two concrete walls.

"Get up, Bitch" he snorted down at her angrily. When she didn't move fast enough, he grabbed her by her skinny little arms and dragged her to her feet. When I saw how rough he was with her, it infuriated me. My blood was boiling and I was ready to kill him. I stepped toward him, not even sure what I was going to do, if anything. But Selene's long thin fingers wrapped around my wrist. I turned to glare at her, and she shook her head and held up her hand, telling me to wait.

The brutish man dragged Aurora from the room and Selene and I followed closely behind. As we walked down the empty hall, the subzero temperature was evident. And yet they had her dressed in flimsy rags. I took my best guess as to where we were. It looked like some kind of military bunker or something. Floor to ceiling, and everything in between, was all made of concrete. Pipes and wires ran along the roof, with air vents and fluorescent lights spread out along the way. I think perhaps we are underground. The sound of marching feet echoed through the many hallways, that splintered off in all directions.

"Can anyone see us?" I whispered to Selene.

"No child, we are not really here. This is just a memory, one I walk through regularly" she answered. She didn't whisper or try to talk quietly, so I guess they couldn't hear us either.

We walked for a little further until the man knocked on a large steel door. After a second the door buzzed open and the man threw Aurora through it. He strode in behind her, holding himself tall and proud, like he was a tough guy or something for beating on a child. Once in the new room, I saw that it was separated by thick metal bars. On the other side of the bars was a chair, all decked out with restraints, wires and electrical looking stuff. A matching chair sat on this side too, one that the man got to work strapping Aurora into.

"What's going on?" I asked Selene as I looked between Aurora and the other chair.

"Wait" she told me. Wait for what? What is all this? After a minute, a door on the other side of the bars opened and another man walked in, dragging someone behind him. It was a man, tall but thin, his long scruffy black hair covering his face. His clothes were in tatters and his pale skin was black and blue with bruises. The guard dropped him into the chair and began with all the straps at his legs, hands and chest. Once he finished with those, he moved behind the chair and lifted the man's head so that he could clip the strap across his forehead. The guard moved the man's hair away from his eyes and I could see his face.

I gasped and covered my hand over my mouth. He looked over at Aurora, fear and sorrow filled his lifeless golden eyes. He looked different than the smiling proud man I gazed at in the photo Lunaya had given me, but there was no denying it. It's my father, our father. It was Micha.

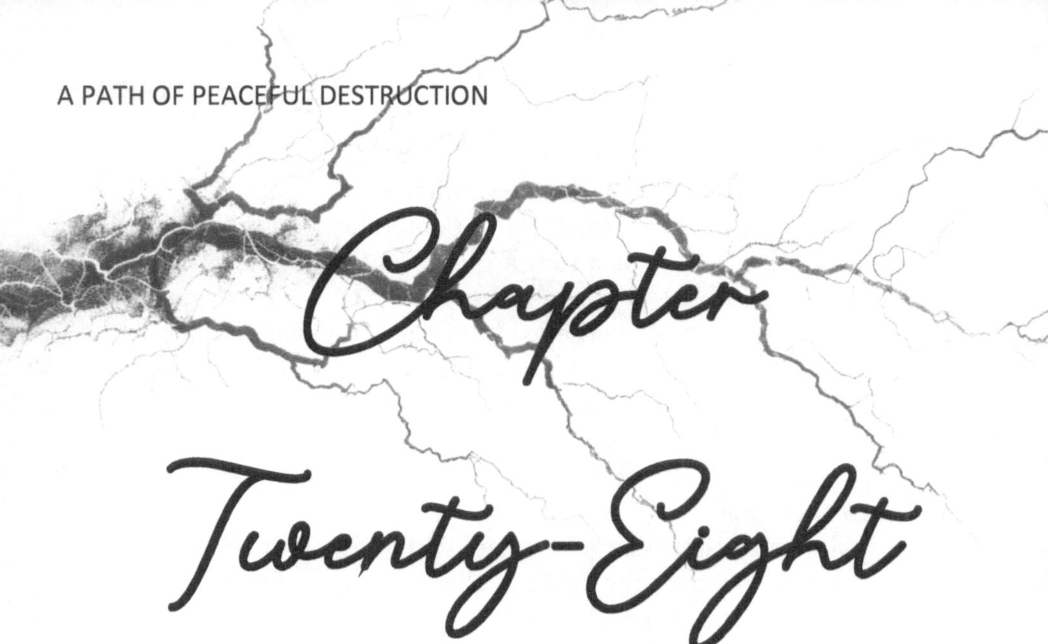

Chapter Twenty-Eight

Zelena

"Dad" I sobbed and stepped forward. Selene's hands laid softly on my shoulders and she gently pulled me back.

"We have to help him" I cried and looked back at her.

"The past is set, sweet daughter. You cannot change what has already been done" she told me as she brushed her fingers over my cheek.

"Then why are we here?" I asked shakily.

"Because, in order to understand, first you must see" she answered cryptically. I turned back around and watched what was unfolding. The soldier that brought in Aurora snapped something around her neck, then the other guard did the same to Micha. I recognised what they were immediately. Shock collars. The exact same ones that Hank used on me the night Gunner rescued me. That answered one of my many questions. If they're using the same gear that Hank used, and he was a hunter, that means these guys are hunters too. Dad and Aurora were captured by the hunters, not killed by them. A clicking sound echoed through the room, followed by a voice through a speaker box.

"Who is the Goddess?" the heavily accented voice asked.

"I don't know" Micha answered. There was a long silence and then a high pitched beep. The guard behind Aurora pressed a button on the back of her chair, and she screamed out in pain. The sound reverberated through my ears. I know that scream, I have made the same sound enough times throughout my life. Her little body shook, what small amount it could from under the straps of the chair. Tears welled in my eyes. I don't want to see this.

"Stop! Stop! Stop!" Micha yelled quickly. He tried to thrash in the chair, but he couldn't move, not with all the bindings holding him down.

"I don't know which one" he yelled. The beep sounded through the speaker and the guard pressed the button, turning off the shock collar. Micha's terrified eyes bore into Aurora's panting face. The guard stepped around the chair and looked over her face. He stepped back and shook his head. He was doing that for someone else, they're watching this. I scanned my eyes around the room quickly. There. A small camera in the corner of the roof was pointed directly at Aurora. I looked up behind me, there was another pointing at Micha. This is an interrogation, not just torture.

"How does she get the magic?" the voice called out.

"She can't. She's too young" Micha huffed. Silence ensued and then the beeping. Both guards hit the buttons on each of the chairs. Micha's face pulled into a grimace, while Aurora wailed through the pain. After a few seconds, the beep sounded again and they turned them off. Micha opened his eyes and immediately searched Aurora's face. It was comforting in a way, to know that even after all these years, and after everything they have been subjected to, he still cares for and loves her.

"Go for option two" the voice called through the speaker. Option two, what is option two? The guard with Aurora grabbed a whip and stood at her side.

"Which one is the Goddess?" the voice in the speaker asked.

"Please, I don't know" Micha answered desperately. The whip came down on Aurora's forearms, splitting her delicate skin. The sound of the snap, mixed with Aurora's squeal of pain, filled the room.

"How does she get the magic?" the voice echoed.

"She can't yet, she may never" Micha answered without hesitation. The whip came down again, just centimetres away from the last lash. Her skin burst open from the force of the hit, blood dripped slowly out of the wounds.

"Stop! Please! I have told you everything I can" Micha pleaded. Everything was silent. All I could hear was the heavy panting of Aurora and my thundering heartbeat.

"You have told us nothing" the angry voice yelled. The man with the whip struck it down on Aurora's legs, just above her knees. The skin split and blood began to run down her legs. I turned on Selene, full of anger at her doing nothing to stop them.

"Stop this!" I demanded of her,

"I cannot" she answered.

"Why not, why won't you help them?"

"I could not interfere".

"That's bullshit, you helped me. Why won't you help her?" I screamed.

"I did for her, as I did for you"

"Then why are you letting this happen?"

"This is not happening now, this is the past" Selene said nonchalantly. She kept her tone even and her voice smooth and silky. As if what was happening didn't bother her in the slightest. How could she stand by and watch this, why wouldn't she help. I don't understand. If she truly does love me, or loves us, why wouldn't she help us?

"When will she get the magic?" the voice rang through the speakers, recapturing my attention. I spun back around to watch my father as he gave his answer. I know that he knows the truth, Lunaya told me as much. He knows that she won't gain the power until she loses her virginity. But he would never tell them that, surely. The monsters would probably rape her, a ten year old child, with no hesitation or remorse.

"I don't know" he yelled. Though he looked weak and sickly, his voice sounded strong as it bounced around the concrete cells. The room was silent, then came the high pitched beep. The guard pressed the button on the chair, and the electricity came to life, coursing through Aurora's small body. Micha yelled and screamed and thrashed around as much as he could. He begged and pleaded for them to stop, but they didn't. She sat there screaming. She screamed until she couldn't scream any longer. A mighty roar came from Micha as he snapped one of his arms free from the bindings. His skin was slowly growing tuffs of greyish-black fur. The guard behind him grabbed at his arm, but Micha was able to grab him first. He flung the guard away and then snapped his other arm free. My heart was racing, my blood was pumping with excitement. This is why I'm here. This is what

Selene wanted to show me. Micha got free, he escaped. Is that what I'm watching?

"Get him back in the chair" the voice screamed manically through the speaker. Aurora's guard turned off her chair and ran for the bars. He fumbled with a wad of keys on his belt while anxiously watching Micha. I hadn't noticed before, there was a locked gate within the bars. I didn't know whether to watch Micha who was continuing to break the remainder of his bindings, or the guard who was hopelessly trying to get different keys into the locks.

"Daddy" Aurora cried. Both the guard and Micha snapped their eyes to her. Micha roared again and broke through his last strap easily. He dropped to his hands and knees and let his body morph. He looked like he was struggling, probably because of all the injuries and how skinny he looked.

"Get him back in the chair" the speaker box voice screeched again. Without realising it, I had both hands over my mouth, holding in my own screams of encouragement. Micha's wolf marched over to the man on the floor, who had now started coming back too. The man reached for the gun on his belt, but Micha snapped his teeth over his arms and ripped it away from his body. The guard screamed and grabbed at the place his arm had been. Without missing a beat, Micha chomped down on his neck, cutting him off mid-scream.

"Ona budet nakazana saa tvoyu derzost" (She will be punished for your insolence) the guard spat. I don't know what he said, nor could I place the language. Russian maybe. Whatever it was he said, it made Micha angry. He growled and charged at the gate, just as the guard had turned the key. I was caught up in the speed at which the escape was happening, I didn't notice when the guard grabbed a gun from his holster. He fired it at my father, but there was no loud pop or bang, it didn't sound like any other gun I'd heard. Micha didn't stop or pause, he just kept charging. The guard fired once more before the gate was thrown open and Micha was on top of him. His jaws went straight over his face. I heard the muffled cry of pain before Micha quite literally ripped his face off.

"Daddy" Aurora cried again. Micha rushed over to her, and using his teeth, he grabbed onto the straps at her ankles and knees, tearing them away from her. He was starting to wobble on his feet a bit, when I noticed the dart sticking out of his shoulder, and another in his chest. They must be tranquilisers. He managed to get one of her arms free when he finally fell.

"Dad!" Aurora cried out as she looked down at him helplessly,

"I can't get the other one" she sobbed and pulled roughly at her arm. The fur receded back into his skin, leaving him panting and naked on the frozen concrete floor.

"I'm coming angel" he huffed out. Tears were pouring from my eyes. I followed behind him as he drunkenly picked himself up off the floor, and tried to pull the other cuff free. But he was too weak, he could barely stand up.

"The aconite, baby, I can't do it" he puffed exhaustedly,

"Please Daddy, get me out" Aurora cried and pulled at her arm some more. Micha bent down and placed one of his hands on her face, with his other hand he supported his weight on the arm of the chair.

"I'm not going anywhere, Baby, I'm right here" he said softly. He sounded exhausted, and he looked terrible. I don't know how they are going to do this. I spun around to stare at Selene, she looked back at me with a blank expression, only her brilliant white eyes looked sad. I realised I didn't need to ask what I wanted to ask, the answer was on her face already. They're not getting out.

"I need you to help me, Sweetheart, can you do that?" Micha asked Aurora. She paused for a moment before nodding her response.

"We will pull together okay, you need to pull as hard as you can. Can you do that for me, Angel?" he said while looking at her young face. Stupidly, in that moment, I felt envious of my sister. She got to meet our father. She got to know him. He calls her Angel. She got a real father, and I got Hank.

"Three, two, one" Micha counted down, and together they pulled at the steel bar that was holding down Aurora's wrist. The metal creaked and groaned, but didn't break. He was struggling, that much was clear, but he didn't give up. While they were both still pulling at the bar, the door that Aurora came through burst open. A stream of hunters poured in, all of them wearing heavy armour, and each holding a gun pointed directly at Micha and Aurora. The twelve men formed a semi circle around the chair, blocking the door and the cage gate.

"Na zemle" (On the ground) one of the hunters screamed.

"Get down" another shouted in English. Micha turned to face the men, flashing his teeth and growling ferociously. There is no way he could take them all, not in his current state. Given the stories that Lunaya has told me, I have no doubt that back in his day, before we were born, it would have been a cakewalk for him. But not now, not like this. I could see him trying to focus, to bring forth the change, but the spurts of fur over his body disappeared just as fast as they grew. He was too weak to change form.

I watched helplessly as the men all pounced on him at the same time. I cried out for them to let him go, but of course, they couldn't hear me. Selene stepped up behind me and placed her hand on my shoulder. After a minute the men began to stand, dragging a blood covered Micha to his feet as well. Four of the men held him steady, one with a large knife at his throat, while all the others stood with their guns aimed and ready to fire. All the while, Aurora continued to beg for the men to stop. A man in military uniform walked into the room, more so sauntered. He stood with his shoulders back and head high. His uniform was pristine and covered in stripes and medals made of gold.

"You have made a fatal mistake, beast" the heavily accented man spoke. It was the same voice from the speaker box. This is the man in charge. Micha didn't respond, just growled. Another man marched in through the door, wearing black combat pants and a long sleeve shirt, with a black vest on over the top. My stomach dropped and my mouth lost all moisture. I know him. He once called himself my Uncle Trevor. Though he was younger and had fewer wrinkles. He still wore the same devilish smirk.

"I ought to remove her fingers" the uniformed man said threateningly. Micha growled and fought against the firm hold on him.

"You won't touch her" he snarled back angrily.

"You are right" the man said smugly, then stepped to the side.

"I won't" he said vaguely. Trevor walked forward and stood in front of my father. My heart was racing as my panic exploded. My whole body was shaking in anticipation. I was on the cusp of full blown screaming for them to get away. The tears in my eyes rolled down my cheeks at their own will.

"You on the other hand" Trevor said with a shit eating tone,

"Serve no further purpose" he chortled. Trevor grabbed my father by his hair and pulled him to the front of the chair, where Aurora was shaking and quivering with fear. Trevor held Micha by the scruff of his hair, holding his face in front of Aurora.

"Let this serve as a warning to you, mutt" Trevor sneered at my sister,

"You will never leave this place. You belong to us. If you are disobedient, you will be punished. If you misbehave, you will be punished. If you ever try anything like this again, you will be punished" Trevor yelled down at the small Aurora.

"Do I make myself clear?" he snapped. Aurora jumped and nodded her head quickly,

"I don't think she understands" Trevor chuckled over his shoulder, to the men behind him. A small smattering of chuckles sounded from the men in response.

"Perhaps this will teach you" he snorted. Trevor lifted his hand to my father's neck, and with zero hesitation, sliced a knife through his throat. My father's blood spurted out of the gaping wound, covering Aurora from head to toe. I screamed a sound that I didn't know I was capable of. My chest throbbed with a stabbing pain. Selene's arms wrapped around me, as I dropped to the ground onto my knees. Why would she make me watch this, what could I possibly learn from watching my father die? Selene's hand brushed through my long hair as I sobbed uncontrollably. She whispered gentle shooshing sounds as she held onto me.

Aurora did nothing. She sat quietly in the chair, her eyes glued to our father as the life left his face. She did not cry, she did not scream or beg. She simply did nothing. After a minute, Trevor let Micha's body drop to the ground and lay in the pool of blood covering the floor. Trevor stepped forward and put both hands on the arms of the chair. He leaned forward, forcing Aurora to lean back. Then silence, all he did was stare at her. All that could be heard was my own weeping and harsh breathing.

"No tears for your dear father?" he finally asked in a teasing manner. She didn't answer and she didn't look away. She glared right back at him, unmoving and not backing down. For a child, her resolve was impressive. After another minute Trevor pushed off from the chair and stood upright.

"She will be a good little bitch. Give her a few days in the cell to make sure" he said as he turned around to face the uniformed man. He nodded with an evil smile.

"Idti" (Go) he shouted to the other men. In a matter of seconds, Aurora was freed from the chair and marched back to the dark room. Selene had to convince me to follow her. I couldn't leave my father. I couldn't look away from his lifeless golden eyes. I wanted so badly for him to still be alive. I hoped with everything I had that he had gotten free. Those hapless dreams were pointless. The only sweet thing I could focus on was that Trevor got his just deserts. Gunner killed that monster. Though I now wish I had been able to do it myself.

Once back in the dark room, Aurora sat silently on the dirty mattress. She still didn't sob or cry, or shed a single tear. She was like a statue, completely unmoving besides the rise and fall of her chest.

"What's going on?" I asked Selene meekly,

"Listen" she whispered and moved to kneel down in front of Aurora.

"Daughter of mine" her voice rang like an echo through the room,

"Go away" Aurora hissed back. Holy shit, she can hear her.

"My child, I am so very sorry" Selene cooed gently.

"Get out!" Aurora snapped harshly. She looked up and glared at Selene. I saw her then, truly saw her. The fear and sadness that I had seen in her gaze, the hope she held when she thought she was going to escape with our father, all emotion was gone. All but one. Anger. She held Selene in her line of sight, with so much hatred filling her childish eyes. Her face was still covered in our father's blood, her hateful eyes narrowed to slits, and her small teeth hissed through her thin lips. In that moment she was terrifying. In that moment, she was a vision of pure evil.

"Please talk to me, Little Light" Selene begged.

"I don't want to talk to you, I don't want to see you, I want nothing to do with you" Aurora snarled angrily. When Selene didn't answer, she continued,

"He died because of you. They wanted us because of you. You're all they ever talk about. You said you wouldn't save me, so why won't you just leave me alone!" she screamed at the top of her lungs.

"Daughter, I explained that to you" Selene answered softly.

"Don't call me that! You are not my mother, I have no mother! I hate you! You hear me, I hate you!".

Aurora was panting, her body was shaking, and her eyes were wide and full of rage and malice. As she was screaming, the room felt like it got colder. An uncomfortable shiver ran up my spine. There was no light in here, but the room felt darker all of a sudden. The space filled with foreboding shadows. Selene sat back on her legs and placed her hands on her lap. They both looked at each other, neither one speaking. I didn't know what to do, or why I was brought here. I understand this is a memory and I'm watching something that has already happened, but I still feel helpless.

"Aurora..." Selene started, but she was cut short,

"My name. Is Whiskey. Aurora died with her dad. I never want to see you again" she hissed venomously. For being just a child, there was so much coldness and so much hostility in her. It was surprising, and it hurt even me.

"As you wish" Selene said sadly. She reached her hand forward and placed her palm on Aurora's cheek. Aurora's eyes rolled back, and after a moment, she slowly laid down on the mattress.

"What did you do?" I asked urgently as I looked down at Aurora. Selene stood up effortlessly, like she was gliding, and looked at me over her shoulder.

"I took her memories" she answered like it was no big deal. I held down the scoff I wanted to let loose. I know firsthand what a big deal it really is.

"She hates you" I said sadly,

"She does" Selene agreed.

"But why you?"

"She needed someone to blame, for all the monstrous atrocities that she endured during the first ten years of her life"

"And she blames you?"

"Yes".

"Why you?"

"Her hatred became her lifeline. She needed someone, something, the hate. It was all I could give her" Selene answered in a monotone voice, though it still sounded like little church bells.

The room was freezing, and my body was still shaking from the shock of what I witnessed. Could she not have explained this situation without making me watch my father die. How could that have been helpful? I would have understood without watching it happen for myself.

"Why did you make me watch that?" I asked softly. I was on the tipping point between crying in hysterics and just shutting myself down.

"To understand, you needed to see" she repeated the same line from before,

"I didn't need to see that, why would you think watching my father have his throat cut open would be in any way helpful to me" I said with a half sob and half yell.

"There was more to see than just that".

"It's hard to think of anything other than that right now" I scoffed.

"Go back to your Mate, your sister, and your loved ones. You will see, when you are ready to see" she said softly and turned to face me completely.

"Wait" I started, but I was too late. Selene waved her hand, and my body was falling, flying backwards through the air. I awoke with a jolt and flew upright on the couch. Gunner's face was the first thing I saw, his worried eyes and furrowed brows looking down at me from where he was perched at my side. The next thing was Tobias, he too was looking down at me, though his expression was more guarded. He held both his hands on my ankles, once I saw them there, I could feel the soft vibration and the warmness. He was doing the energy thing again. I turned back to Gunner, met his worried gaze, and the dam broke. I tossed my arms around his neck, buried my face into his warmth, and howled with grief.

"It's okay, you're okay" Gunner cooed softly. He slowly rubbed his hands up and down my back, while Tobias kept hold of my ankles.

"He died. I watched him die" I cried out harshly,

"Who died, my Love, what happened?" Gunner asked calmly.

"My dad, Trevor killed him, and she made me watch it" I wailed.

"It's alright, it was just a dream" he offered, trying to calm me down. I didn't have the emotional balance to explain right now. It wasn't a dream it was real, he suffered, they both did.

After a while of intense sobbing, I very slowly started to calm down. As my heart rate steadied, I could feel the pain in my body. My head was throbbing terribly, and I felt exhausted, like I ran a marathon.

"What happened?" I asked through heavy breaths, as I peeled my face from Gunner's shirt.

"You hit your head" Gunner answered,

"I figured. But what happened with Aurora and me?" I said plainly,
"Well, you grabbed Whiskey's hand, then the both of you just like convulsed" He answered confused.
"What do you mean?"
"You both lifted off the ground a few inches. Then, you were kind of shaking, while she was stiff as a rock. There was this weird swirling light sort of thing surrounding you. Then boom, you flew apart like you touched a livewire or something. Then when you landed on the driveway, you smacked your head. But whiskey landed on the car, so the windscreen broke her fall a bit more".
"Stop calling her that" I groaned and touched the back of my head,
"Huh?" Gunner blanked. I touched a lump on my scalp and hissed. I really did hit it hard.
"Her name is Aurora" I told him,
"Well according to her, her name's Whiskey" he shot back with a shrug.
"Where is she?" I asked as I pulled my legs away from Tobias.
"She's here, Sweetheart" Lunaya's voice came from behind Gunner. He stood up and moved to the side so that I could see Aurora lying on the other couch, still unconscious.
"Is she alright?" I asked as I sat up. My head spun and my body screamed in argument.
"She's fine, just unconscious" Lunaya answered.
"I saw Mother" I blurted out. The room went silent and I felt all their eyes on me again. I looked up to see everyone looking down at me.
"You saw Selene?" Roe asked.
"She walked me through her memories" I told them honestly. A few gasps sounded and Lunaya moved to kneel in front of my legs.
"What did she show you?" she asked excitedly. Her face was so happy and bright, how could I shatter that. I looked up to Roe, who was also waiting eagerly for my answer.
"I'm sorry, Mum" I said sadly as I turned back to Lunaya,
"What for, Darling, what happened?"
"She showed me a memory of Aurora when she was ten" I started slowly, trying to delay the inevitable.
"And?" Lunaya pushed,

"And Dad was there too" I admitted. Lunaya's eyes went wide and her face paled. A quiet choked sob bubbled through her quivering lips.

"Micha's alive?" she whispered hopefully.

"I'm sorry, Mum, but no" I answered.

"But you said he was in the memory, that means he survived the attack on Moon Light"

"He did. He and Aurora were captured and tortured by the hunters for ten years. The memory she showed me… it was…" I paused and looked at her eyes. They were so hopeful and excited.

"Was what?" she urged. I looked up at Gunner as a tear rolled down my cheek.

I can't tell her

I flashed him. He understood what I meant, I saw the recognition flash over his face as I said it. Gunner has always been able to read me like a book, it's a trait I love about him.

You can, Little Wolf, you must

He flashed me back. He placed his hand on my shoulder and squeezed gently. I reached up for his hand, letting the calmness of the sparks fill me. I took a deep shaky breath and looked at the woman who gave birth to me, who had only just come back into my life, and who might hate me after I told her this.

"The memory she showed me, was of Dad's death" I confessed. Lunaya froze, staring at me blankly while she digested the information. She then fell back onto the floor, landing on her butt. She covered her face with her hands and cried. Alyse was quick to her side, wrapping her arms around her to soothe her.

"I'm sorry Mum, I'm so sorry" I said again.

"Why would she show you something like that?" Roe asked, sounding both shocked and disgusted.

"I don't know. She said I would know when I was ready" I told her.

A deep gasp came from the other couch as Aurora flew up from her lying position. Her eyes snapped around quickly as she took stock of where she was. She narrowed her eyes and appeared to search the room until her gaze found mine. A brief second of sadness or grief crossed through her gaze before her golden eyes hardened into something dark, something angry, something resembling animosity.

Chapter Twenty-Nine

Aurora

One second, he was sitting there beside me, looking at me, smiling at me. And the next, he was gone. I watched him run from the car and embrace the small woman in the driveway. They held each other for what felt like forever. She had her back to me so I couldn't see her face, but I could see Gunner's. His eyes sparkled as he stared at her, his mouth flashed a full toothy grin. He never looked that way around me, he never looked at me like the way he did her. I feared then that these feelings I had, these desires, it may have been one sided. The more I watched, the more I burned. He picked her up and spun her around through the air. Her long hair covered her face, but I can only assume she looked as sickly happy as Gunner did. There was so much joy and happiness. I admit I felt envious. As she wrapped her legs around him, they just about consumed each other's faces. I felt myself growl before I knew it was coming. I hate her. I don't know her, but I know I don't like her. This must be Zee, his elusive Mate. I'm excited to kill her, and I know I'll enjoy it.

I turned away from their nauseating display and looked over the other people who had gathered to greet him. One man, a large bearded man, is quite possibly Gunner's doppelganger. The rest were all a random bunch of nobodies. A tall blonde woman who somewhat resembled Gunner, a strongly built red haired male and a few others. My eyes landed on a taller woman with dark brown hair. She stood holding hands with a shorter woman. The tall one felt familiar somehow, like I had seen her before, but I couldn't place where. Gunner was talking to the girl in his arms when a small dark haired lady ran over to them. She affectionately touched Gunner's face while she held her arm around the girl's back. They're close, it would seem. The bearded man strolled over with a smile and pressed his head against Gunner's. That's weird. So, this must be his family. If he has a family, he most definitely isn't a creation of the hunters like me. Petri Dish babies don't have families. I think that's the final piece of proof I need. But it only makes for more questions, where or how did he get powers like the ones he has?

The four of them talked for a little while, before the woman I assume is Zee, jumped from his arms and tried to drag him away. I suppose I had better get out of the car and make myself known. Even though Gunner has probably already forgotten that I'm still here. As much as I didn't want any part of this happy family reunion, I couldn't hide in the car forever. I pushed open the door and slid out. I slowly marched to the front of the car and waited for Gunner to remember I was there. As I was watching him talk, the tall dark-haired woman spotted me. Our eyes met and for a quick second, I thought she fainted. She gasped for breath and dropped to her knees. I didn't even use my power to steal her air, so what's the deal. After her reaction, I felt all of the other's eyes turn to me. Each and every one of them stared at me like I was some kind of three-headed alien swamp beast. I know I have scars, and I don't give two shits about them, but do they really make me so hideous?

The girl I assume is Zee, pushed past Gunner and now stood clearly in my view, with no hair in her face and no one blocking her from my vision. My muscles stiffened and my jaw clenched. This isn't real. I blinked a couple of times to make sure and then pressed my nails into the palms of my hands, the pain always grounds me, it helps me know I'm not dreaming. If I'm not asleep, then this is some kind of trick. Why does she look like me? The girl took a step toward me, and I did the same. We stopped right in front of each other. With her so close I could see her perfectly. I'm still not convinced that I'm not dreaming. All her features, her eyes, the shape of her nose, the line of her lips, even the shape of her jaw, it's all identical to me. Minus a scar or two, she is my spitting image. Her eyes moved over my body, and mine did the same to hers. Her muscles weren't as defined as mine. She's slender but not sickly thin. Her breasts appear to be larger than mine, and her skin is blemish free. I have to be dreaming, there's no other explanation.

"Is this real?" I asked myself out loud. I can feel the pain in my hands, I can smell the forest, I can hear the birds. This isn't a dream. But if she is my identical copy, then she has to be like me, right?

"What are you?" I snapped. Gunner sauntered up behind her and curled his arm around her waist. Is he trying to rub in how happy they are, is he trying to make me jealous?

"Whiskey, this is Zee, my Mate" Gunner said like it was no big deal. I know I wasn't in this alone for the past couple of days. He felt the attraction too, or at least he acted like he did. Was it only because I looked like her, his Mate, the girl he was missing. Was that what he was doing, placating some kind of longing desire to see his Mate again. He didn't actually desire me, he didn't want me at all, when he was looking at me, he was seeing her. That fucking bastard. I glared at the bitch, it took a lot of self-control not to rip her face off right then and there.

"Is this some kind of fucking joke?" I snarled. I can't believe I let him play me like that. He made me look like a fool.

"I told you that you'd think I was crazy" Gunner said with a slight chuckle. Is he teasing me right now? Seriously. I could feel the rage steadily increasing inside me. Gunner pulled his Mate tighter into his side, really rubbing it in now. I could feel my blood boiling, and an airy feeling filled my head, I was about to burst into a murderous rage.

"I want to leave now" I snapped. I looked around me, trying to find the best and quickest way to run. If I don't leave now, I will kill the lot of them. It will be a sloppy and unplanned attack, leaving me open to avoidable mistakes. Both Gunner and his perfect little Mate began to argue, but it was pointless.

"Whatever this weird ass game is that you're playing, I don't want any part of it" I growled angrily. I hate them, both of them, all of them actually. The other people on the driveway were starting to close in. I don't like being caged, my temper doesn't handle it. I searched the surroundings for an escape route. Trees lined the driveway, leading into a thick forest, they could provide good cover. There was a path that led around to the other side of the large house. I imagine that's where the rest of the pack is, so that way was not an option. I was about to make a break for it back down the driveway when a hand grabbed mine.

My body was engulfed in invisible flames. The pain was incredible. I closed my eyes and let it surround me. I've come to love pain. It makes me feel strong and unbreakable. The mighty Zee, however, she was screaming into the air. Weak little bitch. She lowered her head to look back at me, I was caught off-guard by her glowing yellow eyes. They glowed just like Gunner's did, only his were silver. That's not a coincidence. Bursts of electricity replaced the burning sensation. It shook me with a powerful feeling, like I was a battery on charge. I loved it. I smirked at the pained expression on Gunner's Mate's face. I was then sent flying back away from her, soaring through the air uncontrollably. I landed back first into the windscreen of the car. I felt my body push through the glass as shards of it tore at my skin. Before I was able to get up, I felt like I was falling. Darkness clouded my eyes, then enveloped me completely.

~

When I opened my eyes, a soft glow came from the light above my head. I have no idea where I am. The concrete I was laying on was cold, but not the kind of cold that I'm used to. I sat up and looked around. There are shelves or work benches of some kind. A large dirty mattress in a corner and boxes stacked on top of each other lining the walls. I think this is someone's basement, but how the heck did I get here. Did those fucking bastards lock me in here? Are they trying to hold me like I'm a prisoner? That is a mistake I will make them pay for. I stood up and turned to look at the rest of the space. As I turned slowly, I spotted something. Curled up on the floor at my feet was a body. A female child's body.

"Hello" I said surprised. When the child didn't answer me, I tried again,

"Hey" I said louder. Still no answer. Is she dead or something, was she their prisoner too? The sound of a door opening echoed from the top of the stairs behind me. I turned to see a man come stomping down the steps. I bent my knees and readied myself to attack. I growled a warning, but he paid no mind. How dare this vermin ignore me. As he reached the bottom of the stairs and was just in front of me, I swiped out with my talons. Only my fingers didn't slice through his flesh like I intended, instead, they evaporated right through him, like I was a ghost of some sort. The man continued on his way, walking right through my body. A shiver ran up my spine and I gasped. I lifted my hands to my face and went completely blank. I could see through my hands, they were transparent, with a weird blue glow. What the heck is going on? I spun around quickly to look where the man had gone. He was now standing over the child, holding her off the ground by her hair. Again, I blanked. The child was me. But I don't remember any of this, I have never been here before. How is this possible?

"You stupid fucking cunt" he spat in my face. I stood and watched wide eyed as the ten year old me cried out and tried to pry his hand from my hair. But it was apparently pointless. I was small and weak, and he was large. A little on the fat side but still somewhat well built. He had dark curly hair and tanned-ish skin. Who is he?

"Daddy, stop" the little me yelled. Daddy? I don't have a father, or a mother, why would I call him that. Also, he looks nothing like me. There's no way this is my father. And if he is, how could I not remember him?

"My name is Hank" the man screamed and punched little me in the stomach. I coughed and gasped for breath, as the man called Hank, dropped me like a sack of shit onto the floor. I stepped closer and growled at the man. How could I not remember this, I can remember each and every lesson like it was yesterday. Why have I forgotten this one? The man locked some metal cuffs on the child me's ankles, then pulled her over to do the same to her wrists. I looked over my child self a little closer. Bruises and scars were scattered over her body. Some fresh, some old, but there are a great many. Her hair was long, longer than I remember my hair ever being at that age. I looked around the basement, taking it all in. It dawned on me. This isn't me. This is Gunner's Mate, Zee. Even as a child, we were identical. Of course, I don't remember this, because it didn't happen to me, it happened to her.

The man, Hank, stood up and walked over to a metal loop linked to the floor, just a few steps away from Zee. He pulled on the chain connected to her wrist, dragging her arm until it was fully outstretched. He then walked to the other side and did the same thing to the other chain. Her arms were stretched so far out, that I thought they might rip right off.

"Much better" Hank chortled. He sauntered back over to the young girl, in a way that felt so very familiar. His cocky strut and the proud way he held himself, it all felt familiar. As he stood behind her, I got to see his face more clearly. A strange feeling of rage and sadness washed through me. I don't know why or where it came from, but the sense of familiarity was strong. I knew this face, but I don't know how.

"I'm sorry" she sobbed. Tears rolled freely down her cheeks. I watched closely, waiting to see if he would punish her for crying. One tear, one lash. That was my way of life as a child. Hank scoffed and walked over to a table that was sitting against the wall. He scuffled about for a moment, before returning with a thick brown leather belt. He snapped the belt on his hand and Zee cried harder.

"I'm sorry, Dad, please, I'm sorry!" she screamed through her sobs. He didn't seem the least bit impressed with her screaming, and cracked the belt down over her forearm. She winced and bit down hard on her lip. The belt came down again and a muffled cry left her lips.

"So now you want to stop screaming" the man she called her father sneered at her. Why would her father treat her like this? I've seen Weres die protecting their babies, yet this one is beating on his. I know the beasts to be ruthless and savage to other creatures, especially humans, but not usually to their own offspring. Maybe I just hadn't witnessed it. Perhaps they are all vicious animals after all, so I suppose it's no surprise that one could do something like this to their child.

"I'll be quicker, I will" Zee said shakily.

"Too fucking late, you useless piece of trash" he screamed next to her ear. She flinched away from his voice, but couldn't move far, the chains pulling at her arms had no give.

"It won't happen again, I promise" she pleaded. Such a weak thing to do, to beg and plead for mercy. It disgusts me. Even if she is just a child, she should have a little dignity.

"I had to wait an extra fucking hour for you to get home" he shouted. I'm lost as to what is happening here.

"The teacher made me stay back, I told her I didn't want to. I'm sorry Daddy" she cried. Her teacher, she said. Like at a school, or the kind of teachers that I had, I wonder.

"I don't want to hear your bullshit excuses. You come home, you cook, and then you fuck off out of my sight. You understand?"

"I do, I understand" she told him urgently. He stood up straight, still standing behind her, out of her view. The way he looked down at her, the hatred and disgust in his eyes, it was the same way the hunters used to look at me. Interesting. He bent down again so that his mouth was next to her ear.

"I don't think you do" he whispered with a terrific smirk. He stood back up quickly and whipped the belt down on her forearm. The skin turned a bright pink and she gasped in pain. He did it again and again, on both of her arms. The pink marks soon turned red, as welts formed across her skin. But he didn't let up. I am a lover of pain, and I enjoy inflicting it onto deserving monsters. But this, watching this, it was almost hard to stomach. Even though I don't like the bitch, even though I want to rip the pretty face from her head, she is still just a child here. I don't know a lot about civilian human behaviours and regulations, but this punishment, just for coming home late from school, seems awfully excessive.

After more of the grown man striking the child with the belt, her skin resembled that of a zebra. Dark pink and purple streaks lined her arms. It's amazing that not a single whipping had split her skin wide open. Through the whole experience, the girl barely made a sound. A few gasps, and a couple of whimpers, but that was all. Toward the end, she had obviously become defeated. She hung her head and didn't make a peep. The man, Hank, looked exhausted. He was huffing and sweating, all from just swinging his arms. He dropped the belt at his feet and stepped over the chain to stand in front of Zee. He grabbed her by the hair and lifted her head. Now I know why she didn't make a sound, she was unconscious.

"If it were up to me, you'd be dead" Hank hissed at her pale and unresponsive face. He let her head drop, then he turned to march back up the stairs. The door slammed closed behind him, after he left her there, chained on her knees, unable to move. 'If it were up to me'. I wonder what he meant by that. He is the father, who else would have a say in it? Her mother, maybe? But could a mother, in good conscience, let this sort of thing happen to her daughter?

There is no way she wouldn't know about it. Unless she is drugged up or just as cruel and uncaring as her supposed father. What an interesting turn of events.

I looked around me, unsure of what to do now or where to go. Am I dead, is that why I am all ghost like and watching this shit? How do I go back, can I go back? This is so far beyond the norm. I sat down and crossed my legs. Gunner said meditating helped him, maybe it can help me. Now how did he do this exactly? I pictured Gunner sitting on the rock, back when I was still spying on him. Oh, of course, I moved my hands to my knees and straightened my back. Now what? I closed my eyes and took a deep breath. Nothing is happening. I shuffled my butt and tried again, taking a long deep breath. Still nothing. I groaned and dropped my shoulders. Fuck this. The sound of soft sobbing caught my attention. My eyes flew open, and I looked across at the now awake Zee. Tears streamed down her cheeks as she shifted uncomfortably on her knees. A strange warmth filled the basement and a feeling of electricity tingled around me. Zee looked up, and it was like she was staring directly at me. I turned around to look behind me, but there was nothing there. I turned back to her, and she was still staring desperately at me. She began to cry harder and pulled at her arms.

"Mother" she sobbed and struggled against the restraints. Who is she talking to? I looked around the basement, but there was no one else here.

"Let me out, please, help me" she pleaded. This girl has lost her mind. She is looking right at me, crying and begging. Is she talking to me, can she see me? I pointed to my chest and raised my brows.

"Are you talking to me?" I asked her.

"Mother, please" she cried.

"I'm not your mother" I scoffed in disbelief.

"No, you can't, please, take me with you! Don't leave me here!" she all but screamed. I looked around again, just to make sure there was no one else here. There isn't. Who in the fucking shit is this crazy bitch talking to? Zee thrashed and pulled wildly at her arms, so much so that the cuffs bit into her skin. Blood dripped down from her wrists, but she didn't let up. She cried and fought, begging her invisible mother to save her. Maybe her mother is a ghost too. Maybe only she can see her. Pfft. Now I'm acting crazy too.

"I'll be good, I promise, you won't even know I'm there" Zee pleaded. She had moved on from her desperate thrashing and was now back to begging.

"Why can't you?" she cried. It was like she was having a full blown conversation with someone.

"Please, I don't want to stay here" Zee sobbed. She dropped her head and cried. Her chest heaved with the harsh breaths and her stink of sadness and desperation filled the small basement. There was another scent down here, one that wasn't here before. It's hard to describe, but it smells like spring flowers, and what I imagine the clouds smell like. It's pleasant, if you're into that sort of thing.

Zee's head started to rise, but the way she lifted her head chin first, it was almost like someone else was pulling her chin up. Her crying stopped and she took a few gasping breaths. She stared intently at the one spot, not looking away from it. I followed her line of site, but there was nothing there. She sniffed and nodded her head.

"You promise?" she asked softly.

"Do I promise what?" I blurted out. I've realised now that she isn't talking to me, nor can she see me. I don't know what compelled me to answer, it just came out.

"Okay" she breathed out heavily. Her eyes went blank and her body slowly relaxed. It was kind of like she blacked out or something, but her eyes were still wide open. The warm feeling evaporated, along with the unexplained scent. I think maybe I am dead, there's no other explanation. Zee let her head fall back down and she continued with her quiet sobbing. The room was cold and silent, with only the quiet crying of Zee echoing off the walls. What the fucking hell is going on here. I stood up abruptly and immediately felt dizzy. My head spun and it felt like I was falling backwards. I closed my eyes and grabbed my head, waiting for the feeling to pass. I groaned with the sickening feeling and hunched forward. Then in a flash, it was gone. I paused waiting for it to come back again, but it didn't. Weird. I opened my eyes and looked down at the beaten child. Only she was now gone, and in her place was the grown up Zee. Just like the one I saw before in the driveway. Though this one was skinnier and covered in blood, she was no longer the child I was watching moments ago. What the fuck is going on.

Chapter Thirty

Aurora

What. The. Fuck. What just happened? How did she age so quickly? I don't know what is going on, but I do know that I don't like it. I want out. I looked around the basement, it was still the same, with a few extra piles of crap, but otherwise unchanged. I walked forward and looked down at Zee more closely. This can't be right. The Zee I saw before, in the driveway, she was different. I saw her, she had not a single mark or blemish on her porcelain skin. This one, however, is covered in dark bruises, open wounds and aging scars. There is no possible way this is the same girl. No one can heal scar tissue. Something strange is going on here.

As I gazed down at her unconscious body, I noticed it, an item that I was very familiar with. A piece of equipment that I could never forget about. It was a shock collar. The same kind of one that the hunters used to use on me during my training. How did her father get one though? I know all about this device. Pasha used to tell me all about it as he used it on me. A device of his own creation, he would tell me. Intended to weaken the beast side and cause insurmountable pain. He was always so proud as he spoke about it. If the subject does somehow become able to initiate a change during the process, the electricity would burn the fur right off. I know firsthand, though, through my years and years of experience. The burning it does to fur happens to human flesh too. And it is something else entirely, worse in some cases. I have a few scars caused by this fucking thing.

The door opened, and the same man as before, Hank, marched down. He was older, fatter, and even more gross looking now. Time has not been kind to him. As he went to stomp past me, I quickly stepped out of his way to avoid that disapparating feeling. He leaned over Zee's body and smacked her across the face a couple of times.

"Wake up now little slut, it's time for some fun" he sneered down at her. Fun he says, does he rape her as well as beat her? He pulled the remote for the collar out of his back pocket and waved it in front of her face. Oh, so not that kind of fun, he's talking about the torturous kind of fun. Hank held down the button, and her body started convulsing. She made sickening gagging sounds as she thrashed around on the floor. But above all, the sound of the buzzing electricity was as clear as day in my ears. I know that sound all too well.

Hank roared with laughter as he watched his handiwork. What is the lesson here, I wonder. When this was used on me, it was for either being disobedient or for training. As brutal as Pasha was, he was not one to use the collar without reason. What has she done this time? I hadn't realised before, but she was basically naked, wearing only an overly large and worn-down t-shirt. Is that why she is being punished, because she is dressed indecently? "Oh my God. You should see how stupid you look" Hank cackled joyfully. He bent over with his hand on his hip, like he was trying to catch his breath. He hadn't even stopped laughing when he began the next shock. Zee writhed in pain, and her father laughed uncontrollably. I wondered as to the purpose of this lesson. If the big dumb idiot would stop laughing for just a moment, and try to explain what she has done wrong, then she could learn from it. As the electricity stopped, Hank crouched down and laughed through some deep breaths. This is where he is going to explain the lesson. Zee slowly lifted a hand and tried to pry at the collar. Her movements were slow and unsteady, her arm shook, and her fingers were clumsy as she grabbed at the strap. Hank snarled and quickly stood back up. He marched over to her and without hesitation, he slammed his foot down onto her stomach.

"No you fucking don't" he swore down at her as she rolled to her side and vomited all the contents of her stomach. A slightly exaggerated hit, and probably not necessary. Surely a slap or a whip would have sufficed. Broken ribs are a tough one to take, and I have no doubt in my mind that he just broke one or two of hers. However, I still don't understand the lesson. He hasn't said a thing about why she is being punished. I always knew what I was being punished for. They reiterated it to me with every blow. But this all seems pointless. If he isn't doing this to teach her, is this just plain old pointless abuse?

"Please. Stop" Zee coughed as more blood dripped from her mouth. Her dad leaned over her and laughed.

"Now why would I do that, we're having so much fun" he teased her. I felt anger swirl in my stomach. Even if I don't like the girl, this is excessive. Lessons like this should have a purpose, or at least a reason. Worse things were done to me. Though by the look of her scars, she has taken her fair share of beatings. But I can't shake the feeling of anger. Anger towards her father. I've never been one to care for anyone or anything. Maybe it's because she looks like me. Maybe I can see myself and my own punishments in her pained face. Fuck. If this bitch is making me weak, I will end her before I let her infect me with useless feelings.

Her body shook again with the volts of electricity coursing through her. In no time at all, she was unconscious again. Hank laughed and wheezed as he looked down at her. He placed the remote on the bench and then went back over to her body. I moved to stand directly behind him, so that I could see what he was doing. He then proceeded to roam his hands over her body. At first, I thought he was just being a disgusting pig, getting a feel in while she was out, but that wasn't the case. He rolled her from side to side, and looked over her arms, legs, stomach and chest. The man even examined between her thighs. He was looking for something, but what? Instinctually, I lifted my hand and grabbed the back of my neck. The mark that Saxton told me about, the mark of the Goddess, does this man think she has one too? He pushed her onto her belly and lifted her hair from her neck. He rubbed his fingers roughly over the spot at the base of her neck. But there was nothing there.

"Fuck" he hissed and stood up again. His hands and arms were now covered in Zee's blood, from his thorough work over of her beaten body. He groaned and wiped the blood from his hand onto his shirt. He stood over her, scratching his head while looking down at her unmoving body. He seems disappointed somehow. I walked around in front of him to look at his face. He was biting his lip and fidgeting, his eyes moved all about the room, bouncing from Zee to the wall and back again. He is worried about something.

The door at the top of the stairs flew off its hinges and toppled down the stairs, followed quickly by a large silver wolf. It looked just like Gunner's beast, only smaller. The next few moments seemed to fly by in quick succession. Two more wolves joined the silver wolf, and they all turned on Hank. And Gunner tried to tell me that wolves don't kill humans, look here, these wolves are about to kill Zee's father. The silver wolf stalked, growled and barked at Hank. The brown one barked at the silver wolf while the smaller dark red mutt whined softly. I thought they were all about to start fighting each other. But no, the silver wolf tackled Hank to the ground and snapped at his face. I could see its claws burying into his chest. Hank begged and cried out for help. Pathetic, he was all high and mighty when it was just him and Zee. I was expecting to watch the silver wolf rip Hank's head off, but he didn't. He jumped off the man and ran to Zee's side. The crunching of bones filled the room, and the silver wolf disappeared, leaving a naked Gunner in its place. So, that was Gunner. But when I was with his beast on the mountain, it was almost double the size. Why is he so small here? Even the human Gunner looked smaller than the one I knew.

As Gunner fawned over Zee, checking her wounds and covering her exposed body, that warm feeling from before returned, along with the same sweet scent. I looked around, but I still couldn't see the source of it. The room seemed to grow brighter, but either they didn't notice or couldn't see it. Gunner and the two other wolves paid no mind to the additional light, or the odd scent.

Gunner picked Zee up from the ground and held her in his arms. He carried her so tenderly, with so much care and attention. I felt jealous of how sweet and gentle he was with her. I could see the pain on his face as he looked down at her. I could also see the love and devotion in his eyes. He would set the world on fire for this girl. The realisation hit me hard. He will never look at me the same way that he does her. As much as I hope and wish for it, I can see it now, his heart belongs solely to her.

I instantly filled with anger and hatred, every morsel of my body flooded with it. What does she have that I don't have? We look exactly alike. He should see me, he should look at me, love me, treat me like he does her. Why can't he? The dizzy feeling came back to me, and I once again felt like I was falling. I closed my eyes and grabbed my head, then waited for the feeling to pass again. Once it did, I opened my eyes and looked around. I wasn't in the basement anymore, and Zee wasn't here. I was now standing outside in the snow. Around me were rustic hut type buildings. The area was empty, but I could hear screaming and frantic yelling in the distance. What in the actual fuck is going on. I must be dead. How else could this be happening? To go from one place to the next without explanation, it has to be death. Behind me, I heard rushed voices and rustling. I turned around to see the tall dark–haired woman from the driveway run out of one of the huts. She was younger, more spritely looking, and was also holding a small toddler. Behind her was a tall, muscular, dark-haired man, also holding a baby. My stomach tightened and my heart thumped wildly in my chest. I know that man.

I've seen his face in my dreams, thousands of times before. But they were just dreams, this is, whatever this is. Why would he be here? Does that mean he is real? I don't even know if this ghost walk thing is real, so perhaps I am just dreaming. He looks like I remember. Black hair, pale skin, golden eyes. In my dreams, he would smile at me and tell me he loved me. In my dreams, I called him Daddy. But they were just that, dreams. I don't have a father. He was just a well concocted figment of my childlike imagination. He only existed to ease my suffering when I was young and weak. I never actually saw this man for real. Because he isn't real. This isn't real. I dreamed him up to give myself something to cling to when life with the hunters felt too hard.

The man and woman embraced each other, pressing their heads together. He ran his fingers over her face and through her hair. She grabbed his face and kissed him passionately.

"Come back to me" she whispered breathlessly. The baby in her arms cooed and stirred a little. The man grabbed her by the back of the neck and pulled her lips back to his. He kissed her feverishly, not relenting or giving in to the quick movements of her lips. It was starting to feel awkward watching them. The screams got louder, and I could now hear gunfire in the air as well.

"Always" he breathed out. He pulled back and kissed the top of her head.

"I'll meet you at the cabin" he said assuredly. Even his voice sounds the same as it did in my dreams. Strong and reassuring, calming almost.

"Three days" she nodded and shifted the baby in her arms. He crouched down and brushed his fingers over the babe's chubby little cheek. I watched him with the babe, and a memory came back to me. In the dream I had on the boat from Russia, I dreamt of two babies. Those babies were, or are, these babies. They look exactly the same. Pale skin, dark hair, chubby cheeks, maybe a year and a half old. They're the same babies. That explains it all, this is just a very vivid dream. First, I dreamt of this man that I called Daddy, then the babies. All the abuse and torture, all the lessons I've had to endure, they are finally messing with my mind. "My beautiful Zelena" he whispered into the child's fat cheek. What a strange name. Zelena. It's not one that you would hear very often. Then again, I suppose neither is Whiskey. The man then kissed the child's cheek, and forehead, and fingers. He was so sweet with her, I can see that he really loves her. Once he finished smothering the child in kisses, he then lifted the baby in his arms so that the woman could reach her face. She then did the same as the man had just done. Kissing the baby all over its face and hands. The baby giggled and grabbed hold of the woman's hair. She smiled as tears rolled down her cheeks.

"Take care of her" she said sadly as she stood up straight,

"You know I will" he said back and wiped the tears from her cheek. The baby had its fat little fingers wrapped around her finger.

"I love you, my sweet Aurora" she cooed and bent to kiss the baby's hand once more. An explosion sounded in the distance, and both adults whipped their heads in that direction.

"We have to go" the man said urgently.

"Three days" the woman said to him.

"Three days" he nodded in confirmation. He kissed her once more and swiped his thumb over her lips.

"Go" he demanded and pushed her gently. She looked at him and then down at the baby. A tear ran down her cheek, and then she turned and ran, with the second baby still in her arms.

"Okay, Little Angel, let's go" he said to the baby. He carefully placed her into a bag like thing, and then put her on the ground. While still kneeling, he cracked his head to the side and changed into a wolf almost instantly. I swallowed hard, my tongue felt rough and dry. My heart was thundering as my thoughts raced. Why would I dream of a werewolf being my father? Though in my dreams I never saw him as a wolf, only a man, it still doesn't make sense. I hate these beasts, I would never wish for one to be my family. I need to stop. This isn't real. I have no father, no mother, no family. I was created in a lab. These hapless thoughts are doing me more harm than good.

Using his jaws, the man picked up the bag with the baby in it, and then ran in the opposite direction that the woman with the other baby had gone. I made the snap decision to follow him. I was here, seeing all of this for some reason, I figured I might as well find out what that reason is. I ran behind him as he darted through the forest, skilfully dodging branches and fallen tree trunks. The gunfire was ringing through my ears, the smell of fire, blood and gunpowder was thick in the air. I wonder what was going on. The man slowed down and I quickly realised why. Up ahead, through the trees, I could see a small battalion gathered and moving together in unison. They were all firing on something, but we were still too far away for me to see what. The man stalked forward, keeping behind the trees. The closer we got, the more I recognised. The men firing the guns, they were all dressed similarly. They all carried the same kind of weapons and moved in the same tactical way. They were hunters. That fact was indisputable. What were they doing here? This is a werewolf village, obviously, because why else would this man be living here. From everything I've learnt, hunters don't attack villages, not unless the pack living there has attacked humans first. So, what kind of vicious monster have I been dreaming about? If they have earned the retaliation of hunters, they must be bad. A low growl and a soft whine got my thoughts back on the current events. The man, or the wolf, was watching what the hunters were doing.

I couldn't believe what I was seeing. This isn't right. This is not what I know, what I was taught and shown. This is all wrong. All across the ground were bodies, a sight I've become accustomed to in my mission these past few years. But what I couldn't understand was the lineup. Men, women, children, all bound, blindfolded, and grouped together. The hunters would walk them, line by line, off to the side and force them to their knees.

There, the other hunters would fire on them. It was a kill squad. This is nothing like what I've been taught. They said they are savage beasts. Out to kill until their last dying breath. They said that they fight, and hunt, and kill mercilessly. But none of these people were fighting back. It's not the killing that bothers me, I've done my fair share of that. It's not even the fact that it's children they are killing, I've killed plenty of kids. It's that this doesn't match the stories, the lessons, the mission reports. Brave heroes, risking their lives for the greater good, facing ruthless and unforgiving monsters. Fighting unstoppable and dangerous creatures for the betterment of humankind. These people don't look so dangerous.

Now that I really think of it. In all my travels, all the villages I have destroyed, and the werewolves I have killed. Most of the beasts chose to run first. When the running option was deemed pointless, and surrender was not going to happen, only then did they try to fight. Granted, the fighting was also pointless, no one could defeat me. It would seem that fighting was never their first action, but a last resort. I have killed without mercy or prejudice. Not a care or second thought as to who or what it was that I was killing, only if they were in the way of completing my mission. Have I been blinded by my own rage, so focused on my mission and what I need to do, have I not seen things clearly? Could I have been tricked or misled? It has happened once before, with Saxton and his ambition. But that was a moment of weakness. Before then, I had been strong and unbreakable, never shaken. No. This is all just part of the ghostly thing that is happening. It's messing with my mind.

The baby cried out, and the wolf quickly ran on. I watched a little longer to see if they heard the cry. Two of them did. They pointed and shouted out that there was someone there and gave chase. I caught up to him quickly, just as more of the hunters sprouted through the trees in front of us. Shots began to fly all around us, a few went through me like Hank did back in the basement. But if the man from my dreams was shot, he didn't look like it. He charged through some of them, sending them flying through the air. He manoeuvred around tree trunks, up onto tree branches and over groups of shooting hunters, all the while keeping the baby from being hit. It was quite impressive to witness. I have never faced off against a beast like him, if I had, I may have been somewhat worried.

He was in the clear, running full pelt through the trees and away from the gunfire, the baby still calm and happy in his jaws. Now what, I wonder, am I meant to just keep following him? I was about to stop running alongside the wolf when a shot rang out. The man's beast whimpered and stumbled as it ran, forcing it to fall and roll through the snow. The bag that the baby was in flew from his mouth and slid along the ground, making the child scream. Another shot sounded and the animal whined and tried to stumble forward, towards the baby. He managed to get to his feet and began running towards where the bag had landed, when another shot sounded. It grunted and fell to the side, but dragged itself forward, until it had placed its body completely over the baby, like he was shielding it. I walked over next to the panting wolf and roamed my eyes over its body. A patch of purple liquid was oozing out of a wound on its ribs, and another wound closer to its hip. There were three shots, but I could only see two visible wounds. Aconite. The poison is deadly to werewolves. And one of the favourite tools to use by hunters. With a highly concentrated dose, it can cause death within an hour. With these few wounds, the beast will just be in excruciating pain for the next few hours. If he had been shot a few more times though, death would be coming for him. Such a shame, he was so close to escaping too.

The sound of crunching snow under heavy boots echoed through the trees, and hunters slowly began to emerge from the trees. They encircled the beast, trapping it in. Two figures stepped forward and I recognised the both of them immediately. One was an officer, I don't know his name, but I heard them call him the General. He was a regular at my lessons. He never participated, but he came to watch all the time. The General would stand there and shout orders and yell at the men, he was one of the higher ups in the organisation. The other man was a younger and stronger looking Hank, Zee's father from the basement. What would he be doing out here with hunters? As the two men stood side by side, it became abundantly clear. They were brothers, maybe twins. They looked just like one another, the General was maybe a little shorter than Hank, but their faces were the same. Hank laughed wickedly and kicked the dog in the stomach. He grunted and whimpered, but remained where he was, on top of the child.

"Where's the baby?" the General asked firmly, but the wolf didn't answer. He probably couldn't even see straight. With three rounds of aconite coursing through his blood, I imagine reality is feeling a lot like hell right now. Hank stepped forward and went to kick the beast again, but the animal was too fast and clamped its jaws around Hank's ankle. Hank screamed and fell back, all while his ankle remained locked between the wolf's sharp teeth. The General stepped forward and pulled his gun from his hip. He aimed it at the leg of the beast and fired. The wolf let go of Hank's foot and howled in pain. The other hunters quickly dragged Hank away. The wolf was panting hard and whining in pain. I watched as its fur receded back into his skin and his body reshaped into the man he was before. He kept his body curled around the bundled bag that was holding the baby, but it was now clearly visible, without all the added fur shielding it.

"There it is" the General smiled,

"Take it" he commanded, and all of the hunters converged on the man's naked form. I didn't expect any kind of resistance from him, especially after being shot with the aconite, but I was wrong. The man growled and clawed, and fought fiercer than I thought possible. He sent a few of the hunters flying into trees and even landed a few good punches. But after a minute, they had him on his knees with his hands in handcuffs behind his back. One of the hunters picked up the bag and handed it to the General. He grabbed the baby and laughed.

"You thought you could hide from us. You thought we didn't know where you were. Silly dog. We know everything" the General chortled and handed the baby off to another hunter.

"Let me kill it, Trevor! I want that mutt dead" Hank screamed from behind the General.

"Quiet!" he demanded, and Hank's screams quickly died down. The general bent down in front of the man and grabbed him by the hair, lifting his head so that he would see him.

"No" he said to himself,

"I think this mutt could be useful".

The General stood up and waved his arms about, giving his men silent orders. They must have understood his hand movements, because they pulled the naked man to his feet and began dragging him away. He fought and screamed for the baby, but it was pointless. The hunters marched off with the baby in the opposite direction.

"You're letting it live?" Hank screamed as he came back to his brother's side.

"For now" the General answered,

"It mutilated me, I want it dead" Hank demanded.

"Come now, Brother, we have what we came for, now the real fun can begin" the General smiled and tapped his brother on the shoulder.

"Why do we need to keep them alive? If we just kill them now, the whole line will be gone".

"I've told you why, and I won't have this conversation again. Do your duty, Little Brother" the General hissed angrily. Hank groaned but nodded his head reluctantly.

"Good, now that is settled, I have a special mission for you" the General smirked at his brother,

"What mission? This is the first I've heard of it" Hank snapped.

"We still don't know how to trigger the magic" he told him,

"And, what does that have to do with me?" Hank quipped.

"We are going to try two different tactics"

"Trevor" Hank ground out.

"I will take this one back to the main facility"

"Don't say it" Hank warned, but his brother ignored his plea.

"You will take the other one, Zelena, its name was"

"No".

"You'll raise it like a normal child"

"Not a fucking chance!"

"You'll live in a normal town, with regular civilians and report back any changes with the child".

"No! Not going to happen. You can't do this to me" Hank argued.

"This is an honour. You will have the chance to turn the tide on this war. For too long have those beasts been able to roam free throughout this world, killing humans at will. They have held the power long enough. If one of these kids is the answer, then it's our duty to do all that we can, to use them to the full extent of their abilities" the General scolded.

"And if you're wrong? If neither one of them have the magic?" Hank screamed his question,

"Then you can kill it. But only once we know for sure that it's useless" the General confirmed with a smirk.

"And what will you do with this one?" Hank asked with a general toss of his head.

"This one will have a slightly different upbringing. If the normal childhood doesn't work on yours, then maybe the brainwashing will work on mine".

Both the General and Hank chuckled sinisterly as they walked off after the other hunters. From what I understood, each brother took a baby to raise them separately. One like normal and the other with brainwashing, whatever the fuck that is supposed to mean. But what magic are they talking about? The only magic that the hunters ever mentioned to me, was the dark witch magic that the Moon Goddess used. She has some kind of black magic. She used it to create the werewolves so that they could kill off the humans. At least that's the legend. Why would they think these babies could have magic. Wait, if they do, maybe that's where they got my power from. Maybe they used the babies to help create me. What am I thinking, this is a dream. It's not real. I looked after the brothers, but my head spun and the dizziness took over. I was falling backwards before it all went black again. I kept falling, unable to move or stand or do anything. It was just black nothingness.

Flashes of cloudy pictures started to flood my vision, followed by echoing voices and laughter and cries. The sounds all melded together, I could barely make them out. And the pictures moved so fast, I couldn't see them properly. I spotted Gunner in one of the pictures, with his arms around his Mate.

"I love you, Zelena" he called to her. His voice, and the name he called her echoed all through my ears. Zelena, I thought her name was Zee. Zelena was the name of one of the babies. The pictures shifted, and now the man from my dreams was there. He kissed me on the head and smiled,

"Stay strong, my beautiful Aurora" he whispered sweetly. Why would he call me Aurora, the other baby's name. That's not my name, my name is Whiskey. It doesn't make sense. The pictures faded out, and another took its place. It was Zee and I, standing in front of each other. She grabbed me and pulled me into her body for a hug. A gentle glowing light shined all around us. She looked happy and excited. I was smiling, and I don't smile. This is some kind of black magic, just like the hunters were talking about. That's what's going on here, Zee is a witch, just like the

Moon Goddess. That's why we look alike, she's using magic on me. Well, that will have to stop.

The pictures faded away, the voices fading with them, leaving me in the darkness with the never ending feeling of falling. I landed on something soft and flew upright. I gasped as I sat up and looked around the room. Most of the people that were on the driveway, were now crowded in the room here with me. I searched out Gunner first, he was looking back at me with gentle eyes. Next to him was her, Zee, or Zelena, whatever her name is. The witch.

Chapter Thirty-One

Zelena

Lunaya and Alyse fussed over Aurora, who only seemed to grow angrier and angrier from the added attention. She threw their hands away from her, which stopped their insistent "Are you okay?" and "Are you hurt?" cooing and questioning.

"Get off me" she growled and shot to her feet. She shot up from the couch and slowly backed away from everyone else in the room.

"Aurora, Sweetheart, it's okay" Lunaya said softly and stepped toward her with her hands out. Aurora growled and flashed her teeth.

"My name is Whiskey" she snarled through her clenched teeth. Gunner stepped forward, in line with Lunaya.

"Whiskey, you're safe here. You can trust me" he told her. Her eyes sort of glazed over, and her body visibly became less tense. How did he do that? He was just talking to her, he didn't use magic, I would have felt it. I've never seen that before. Gunner stepped forward again and held his hand out for her to take. She hesitated, staring intently at him, then reached out and took his hand. It's good, I suppose, that she has someone to trust. After what Selene made me watch, seeing the torture that she had to endure, I can only imagine how that has affected her state of mind. My poor sister. I have no doubt that things didn't improve for her after Dad was killed. If anything, it probably got worse without that support. Especially if she blocked out Selene. I'll say it a thousand times, I never would have survived without her. So how did Aurora? We'll need to talk it out. I want to know what happened to her and how she survived. If she is willing to talk to me, that is. With the angry looks she keeps throwing at me, I don't think she is in much of a chatting mood.

Gunner walked Aurora back to the couch and sat her down. I thought he was going to sit down beside her, but he didn't. He came to the couch I was on and sat down at my side. He placed his hand on my knee and I wrapped my arm through his. I leaned my head on his shoulder and took a deep breath, inhaling his scent. It made me feel almost instantly calm. After a few more deep breaths, I lifted my gaze to Aurora, but she was now glaring up at Tobias. Lunaya sat beside her on the couch, trying to get her attention, but Aurora paid her no mind and instead kept her gaze firmly on my guardian. The air crackled with tension. I could feel Tobias inching closer to me from behind the couch. His overpowering aura of protectiveness was flooding the room, it was suffocating.

"Aurora, I mean, Whiskey, are you alright? Did you hit your head? Are you hurt?" Lunaya fussed from beside her. She went to swipe some of Aurora's loose hair from the side of her cheek, but Aurora caught her hand before she was able to touch her.

"Woman, if you touch me again, you will lose your hand" Aurora growled threateningly and threw her hand away. I swallowed the growl that threatened to slip through my clenched teeth. We're overwhelming her, that's all it is. She is just confused, I tried to tell myself. She won't hurt anyone, not on purpose.

"Mum, ease off" I said pointedly to Lunaya. She stood up with tears brimming in her eyes and walked behind the couch to where Alyse was standing. Alyse smiled softly and took her hand. This probably isn't how she thought meeting her other daughter would go. I gave her a tough enough time when I found out who she was, she was most likely hoping it would be a lot easier with Aurora.

We all sat silently, looking back and forth between each other. No one quite knew what to say. As I examined my lost sister, a thousand questions bounced around my mind. What does this mean for the prophecy? Now that she is alive, is it about me and her and not the twins? I prayed as much. I don't want them anywhere near this prophecy. But also, which one of us is the bringer of death, pain and destruction? Since Gunner brought me to the pack, so many Weres have died. For me, because of me, in my name. So much death surrounds me. First, with the hunter's attack, and then the war with Origin Wolf. The idea that I am the one bringing death and destruction, it's firm and ever present in my mind. It makes sense to me. Even if I hope it is not true, it feels like it could be.

A gentle growl caught my attention. I snapped my eyes back up to Aurora, who was now glaring at me with her top lip curled back. I squeezed Gunner's arm and offered her a soft smile. She is probably freaking out.

"Aurora, can I..." I began, but she quickly cut me off,

"Whiskey!" she snapped,

"My fucking name is Whiskey. Yebanyye debily (Fucking morons)" she shouted and shot to her feet once again. Gunner was quick to stand in front of her, blocking me from seeing her face. Tobias's growl filled the small room, while a few murmurs came from Roe and Lunaya.

"Enough, Whiskey! It was just a mistake. You're okay, you're safe" Gunner cooed gently. Her eyes did that same glazed over thing and she slowly sat back down. I'm going to have to ask him about that. Gunner moved to sit back down beside me, but Tobias didn't move back, he stayed at my side, watching Aurora closely.

"I'm sorry, Whiskey it is" I told her with a smile. She blinked rapidly and scoffed, leaning back into the chair with her arms crossed.

"Why don't I get Whiskey some fresh clothes and a hot meal?" Roe piped up and stepped forward. Whiskey moved so fast, uncrossing her legs and shifting to turn towards Roe. It was like she was expecting her to attack or something. I suppose if she was raised by hunters, she would have had to be prepared for them to attack her all the time. Just like I was with Hank.

"Isn't there something you two need to do?" Roe asked Gunner with her eyebrow raised. Gunner grabbed my hand and pulled me to my feet.

"Actually, there is" he answered excitedly. He dropped my hand and crouched down in front of Aurora.

"Whiskey, this is my mum, Roe. And my father, Lupus. I promise you, they will take care of you. You are safe here, you can trust me" Gunner said assuredly. Aurora shot her eyes to both Roe and Lupus, before looking back at Gunner and nodding her head.

"That's Lunaya and Alyse" he went on, pointing behind her to where they were standing. She turned to glance at them and quickly turned back.

"They will also take good care of you. If you need anything at all while I'm gone, any of them will help you. Okay?" he asked, and again she nodded.

"That big guy behind me is Tobias. He's a grumpy old fart, but he is no danger to you, I promise" Gunner said with a chuckle, which earned him a low growl from Tobias. Gunner turned and winked at Tobias from over his shoulder before he stood up again and took my hand.

"You'll be alright, we won't be long" he said once more. He gently squeezed her shoulder, and she just stared at him, not saying a word, like she was in some kind of trance. He nodded to her and then again to his mum, then pulled me out of the room. The doors closed behind us, and he scooped me up into his arms, making me squeal from both excitement and surprise. Halfway up the stairs, he stopped and pressed my back against the wall. He bent his head down and smashed his lips to mine enthusiastically. I met his lips just as excitedly and slipped my tongue into his mouth. I moaned at the taste of him. I have missed him, I've missed this. I wrapped my legs around his waist and brushed my fingers through his hair. Our lips moved together in perfect synchrony, like no time had passed. Sparks danced across my skin where he touched me. His hands squeezed and grabbed and pinched me all over, while his hips kept me in place, pressing me into the wall. I want nothing more than to take him to our room and lick him from head to toe.

"Fuck, I've missed you" he breathed heavily.

"I missed you too" I responded and captured his lips once again. My body was on fire, burning with the desire to feel him. His touch, his kiss, the heat of his naked skin on mine. I was starving for him and was prepared to feast right there on the stairwell. The sound of someone clearing their throat with an awkward chuckle forced us to peel our mouths away. Nat stood at the top of the stairs with her hand on her hip.

"If you're about done" she said teasingly.

"I could go for a few more hours, I have some lost time to make up for" Gunner teased and nipped at my lips. I chuckled and flicked his nose with the tip of my tongue, earning me a lust filled growl from Gunner.

"Gross" Nat scoffed,

"And here I was thinking you'd want to meet your..." Nat started, but Gunner quickly cut her off,

"We're coming" he said with a wide smile. His skin smelled strongly of desire and excitement. I didn't want to let him go yet, but the vibration of pure joy coursing through him was strong. It made me excited too. The thought that he was as eager to meet them as I was to introduce him made my smile widen. Even if I still haven't told him that there are two babies. He is going to flip. At least I hope he will.

"Come on then, I've got stuff to do, you know" she jeered playfully and walked back to the nursery. I laughed and pushed his chest back so that I could crawl out of his arms. Then we marched quickly up the stairs and to the door of the nursery. I jumped in front of him before he could go through it, and stopped him with a hand on his chest. He looked down at me with a quirked brow.

"What's wrong?" he asked,

"Try not to freak out" I said slowly. His eyes went wide, and he quickly pushed past me.

"Why would I freak out?" he asked as he stumbled through the door with me close behind him. Nat turned around and smiled up at her brother. I went over to her side and watched Gunner's reaction with anticipation. He froze on the spot, his eyes glued to the blue blanket in Nat's arms.

"Bout time" Nat said with a cheerful tone.

"Meet your son, Daddy" I said to him with a smile. Gunner looked up at me and smiled as a tear rolled down his cheek.

"A son?" he repeated softly. I nodded my head and he shuffled over to us. Carefully, he pulled the corner of the blanket away from B's face and ran his finger over his cheek.

"He's perfect" Gunner whispered. He then crouched down so that his face was in the blanket and inhaled deeply. I looked up questioningly at Nat. She chuckled and nodded her head.

"He is scenting him, it's an Alpha thing" she told me.

"Oh" I drawled out. When Gunner lifted his head again, I wiped the tears from his face.

"Wanna hold him?" I asked and he nodded enthusiastically. Very slowly and with more care than he needed to, Gunner took B. from Nat. Instantly, he began to sway gently from side to side as he stared down at his son. Nat squeezed my elbow and blew me a kiss before leaving the room to give us some privacy. As Gunner was distracted by B. I looked into G's bassinet, she was still fast asleep.

"We have a son" Gunner said proudly. He looked up, just as I turned around to smile back at him,

"We sure do" I confirmed.

"What's his name?" Gunner asked, gazing down at little B.

"I haven't named him yet, I thought his father should have a say in something as important as that".

"You waited for me?" he asked, sounding very surprised.

"Of course I did" I answered, emphasising the words 'of course'.

"Thank you" he said with a fresh tear,

"What have you been calling him then?"

"We call him B." I said with a shrug, like it was obvious.

"B." Gunner said to himself and continued looking down at his son.

"I told you it was a boy" he teased, sending me a quick wink before going back to staring at the sleeping baby in his arms.

"Wellllll..." I drawled with a high pitch tone. I turned and carefully picked up G. She stirred in my arms and cried out, but didn't wake. As I turned around with her in my arms, Gunner's eyes just about burst out of his skull.

"Whose baby is that?" he almost shouted.

"Shh..." I laughed and walked over to his side.

"She's yours, of course. This is G." I giggled.

"Mine?" he blurted out, shocked.

"Yes, yours" I chuckled,

"There's two of them?"

"Yes, twins"

"You had twins?"

"No, my Love, we had twins".

"Holy shit. She's a girl?"

"Yes, a little boy and a little girl".

"Twins" he said again, like he was still trying to wrap his head around it.

"Yes, Gunner. Twins" I confirmed again.

"Let me hold her" he said as he shifted B. in his arms. He moved B. to his left arm and held out his right arm for G. Once I placed her in his arms, I stepped back to watch him with them. More tears rolled down his cheeks as he looked back and forth between the two of them. He ducked his head into G's blanket and sniffed her like he did with B. I quickly grabbed my mobile phone and took some pictures. It's already filled with hundreds of pictures of them, but I just can't stop.

"When were they born?" Gunner asked, looking up at me.

"Five days ago" I answered. His joyfulness seemed to drop, and his brows pinched together in the middle.

"What is it?" I asked, stepping back over to him.

"I missed it, and by only five days" he said sadly.

"It's okay, Gunner" I said reassuringly as I cupped his cheek.

"No, I should have been here for it. I missed the birth of my children. I made you go through that alone. I'm so sorry, Zee" he rambled off quickly. G. started to cry with the change in Gunner's emotions.

"Shit" he hissed quietly and gently tried to rock her.

"Here" I offered and lifted her out of his arm.

"She's fussy and doesn't like to have her arms restricted. Plus, she cries at literally everything, you didn't do anything wrong" I told him. I took G. to the change table and unwrapped her swaddle. As soon as her arms and legs were free, she flailed them about like an octopus. Gunner laughed and stroked the top of her head.

"I see what you mean" he said adoringly as he put his finger in the palm of her hand. She grabbed onto it tightly, and Gunner started to make a soft purring type sound. As I changed her diaper, I looked up at him with an amused smile.

"Are you purring, like a cat?" I teased. He stopped the sound and cleared his throat.

"I thought you were a big scary werewolf, not a sweet little house kitten" I teased him and leaned my shoulder into his chest.

"I'm not a kitten" he grumbled,

"And I can't help it. It's just something male Weres do to calm their offspring" he said with a shrug.

"I didn't know that" I answered.

"Well, now you do" he smiled and kissed my temple. Once G. was changed, I picked her back up and gave her back to Gunner. Then I took B. to change him too. I leaned down and smattered kisses all over his cheeks.

"Wake up, little boy" I whispered. He whined a little and stirred awake. He blinked open those big blue eyes and looked right at me. I kissed and nibbled on his cheek as I let his arms free. Before

I could move my face away, he gripped onto some of my loose hair. I laughed and pried his fingers away before giving him my finger. I looked over my shoulder at Gunner, who was cooing and babbling to little G. Just like I expected, she has him wrapped around her finger already.

"Come on, my handsome prince, let's get you changed" I told B. as I got to work on his pants. Roe and Nat went crazy in town, buying up all the baby stuff. I swear they cleaned multiple shops out. The twins have more clothes than they will be able to wear before growing out of them. And more toys than they know what to do with. But I wasn't going to stomp all over their joy. They loved the twins as much as I do. Maybe soon, Nat will bring them home a cousin to play with. I smiled at the thought as I picked up B. and turned around to Gunner.

"What's got you all smiley? Has that handsome little devil stolen your love away from me?" Gunner sang as he took B's hand.

"Are you jealous of your own son?" I laughed, teasing him,

"Absolutely, the kid's a stunner. He'll be a right lady killer when he grows up" Gunner chuckled and kissed B's chubby little hand.

"He already is" I cooed down at him, smooching more kisses to his cheeks.

"This one will have to be homeschooled. No boys are allowed near you, are they, Angel?" Gunner cooed. The name he gave her brought tears to my eyes. I pictured the memory Selene showed me, my father calling Aurora his angel.

"Hey, hey, hey. What's all this about?" Gunner rushed out and wiped at the tears rolling down my cheeks. I felt the wetness and used my sleeve to wipe them away, I hadn't realised I was crying so hard. Gunner turned and buckled G. into the bounce chair, and then took B. from my arms and put him in the second bounce chair.

"What's going on?" Gunner asked full of concern, as he took my face between his large warm hands. I nuzzled my face into his palm, revelling in the smell of his warm skin.

"You called her Angel" I said with a soft sob,

"Should I not call her that?" Gunner asked confused.

"No, it's just that... Selene, the memory she showed me. My dad used to call Aurora, Angel" I cried and grabbed hold of Gunner, wrapping my arms around his waist and pressing my face into his chest.

"Oh, Little Wolf. I'm sorry, I didn't know" Gunner said sadly as he rubbed his hands up and down my back.

"You're twins too, right, you and Whiskey?" he asked. I didn't say anything, just nodded my head.

"You just keep surprising me. Impossibility after impossibility" he said astonished, and squeezed me into him tighter.

"Why would she have shown you that though? What a horrible thing to do to someone you love" Gunner said, his tone turning angry. I pulled back and stared up at him worriedly.

"Don't get angry, the darkness" I mumbled quickly. He smiled and grabbed my face,

"The darkness is gone, my Love. It's not coming back, I'm here to stay" he said and pressed his lips to mine. I melted into him, moving my arms to wrap around his neck. My body swarmed with emotions, it was hard to pinpoint each individual one. I was so happy that he was home, yet terrified of who he brought with him and what that could mean for us. I was filled with love for my children and excited that he was here to meet them, yet so worried about what the prophecy meant for their future. I was angry at my sister and the bond she had formed with my Mate, yet so sad for her and the way she grew up. I felt a great amount of loss after seeing my father killed, yet I was excited that my lost sister had found her way to me. I didn't know where to look, or what to feel. It was all so much to handle, it was overwhelming.

I hadn't realised how hard I was sobbing until Gunner moved to lay us down on the carpet in front of the twin's chairs. He wrapped me tightly in his arms, folding his legs around mine as well. My chest to his chest, our arms and legs tangled together, until you could no longer tell where he ended and I began. I listened to the thumping of his heart and breathed in the muskiness of his scent. For those few moments, as we lay in each other's arms, we were one.

Gunner got my sobbing to settle, as the babies happily sat in their chairs. After a while, I was able to breathe without my chest rattling. Gunner's hands never stop roaming over my back and arms and into my hair. The sparks from his skin on mine were even more calming.

"I'm sorry" I whispered.

"You don't have to be" he whispered back and planted a kiss on the top of my head.

"Do you want to talk about it?" he asked gently.
"Not yet, I don't think I can" I answered with a deep breath.
"Whenever you're ready, I'm here".
"I know. And I love you for that" I told him, as I buried my face into his chest,
"I love you more" he whispered.

Zelena

A little while later, it was time to feed the twins. Gunner sat on the floor with B. on his lap, holding a bottle up to his mouth, while I sat right in front of him, doing the same with G. We laughed at the little snorting sounds they both made as they drank hungrily from the bottles. I was filling Gunner in on Nat and Alpha Lace, and how she was helping with the pack while I was still pregnant. And that she was itching to get back to Howlers, and to him. I teased that she could be having her own pup soon, which Gunner refused to hear. He said it was gross and that he didn't want to talk about his little sister's sex life. It only made me laugh at how silly he was being about it. Weres have sex, a lot of sex, even his sister. I was laughing and teasing him when B. made a grotesque snorted rumbling sound when the nipple of the bottle fell out of his mouth. I laughed along with Gunner as he manoeuvred it back inside B's wide open mouth.

"You never wanted to breastfeed?" Gunner asked, catching me by surprise. I blanked, opening and closing my mouth like a fish, trying to think of an answer. I have been trying to avoid telling him about the part where I had shut down for Goddess knows how long. I don't want to hurt or upset him. If he knew how sick I got, how close I was to hurting the twins, he'd be devastated. It wasn't his fault, not in the slightest. He had to go, to get rid of the darkness. But since finding him, I haven't been without him for more than a couple of hours. Not including that whole kidnap scenario. We can just forget about that horrible ordeal. We knew I was going to not be one hundred percent okay with him being gone, but not even I expected to get as bad as I did. I don't think anyone could have anticipated it. Even so, I know that Gunner will still blame himself for it.

"Of course I wanted to breastfeed" I answered quickly. Gunner was quietly watching me, waiting for the rest of my answer. I could feel the panic rising in my belly.

"But you can see how much that little Buddha eats, I couldn't make enough milk to feed just him, let alone the both of them at the same time" I blurted out with an awkward chuckle. I watched Gunner, waiting to see if he bought it. I mean, it's not a lie. I couldn't produce the milk to feed them, I just didn't go into why I couldn't do it.

"Makes sense, this boy can eat" Gunner chuckled and patted his round little belly. I huffed out a strained breath and forced a chuckle, agreeing with him.

"Are you alright?" Gunner asked, looking back up at me,

"I'm good, why?" I shot back.

"You just seem nervous or worried. With all the hormones still sweeping through you, it's hard to get a read on your feelings" he said with a shrug.

"Are you trying to read me?" I asked with a fake look of suspicion on my face. He laughed and shrugged.

"I'm always trying to read you, my Love" he smiled warmly at me. My heart fluttered and I filled with a warm happiness, before it disappeared just as quickly. The unanswered questions were starting to scream inside my brain.

"I'm okay, just tired I think" I told him with a half smile,

"You can go and have a sleep, I'll look after them" he said happily. I scratched the back of my neck and hummed.

"Well, actually, I was hoping we could talk a little more" I said. I've been waiting to ask him about Aurora, I just wanted him to have some baby time first.

"About Whiskey?" he asked, like he already knew.

"Aurora, her name is Aurora" I said annoyed.

"I understand that is what your parents named her, and when she is ready to be called that, I'm all for it. But you heard her. She wants to be called Whiskey, it's the only name she's known for Goddess knows how long" Gunner said defensively. It bothered me a little at how protective he was being over her. What has brought on these defensive feelings?

"You seem to really care about her" I quipped before realising I said it.

"That's because I do" he answered without hesitation. I pressed my lips together to force myself not to say anything else. A low growl bubbled in my chest, working its way up, until it slipped from my mouth. Gunner snapped his eyes up away from B. and looked at me in question.

"What was that for?" he asked surprised,

"Nothing" I grunted back.

"Are you jealous?" he asked, quirking his brow. I didn't answer, just glared down at the bottle in my hands. G's little arms flailed around while she drank enthusiastically from the bottle.

"Zelena?" Gunner called, trying to regain my attention.

"Is that what's been bothering you, you're jealous of your sister?" Gunner asked. He sounded like he was accusing me of some terrible thing. The way he asked, the way his tone rose, he made it sound like I was being ridiculous. I think I'm entitled to be worried. He was prancing around the countryside with a woman that looked exactly like me. All the while I was at home birthing his children. I get that my body isn't as tight and firm as it was before. My boobs hang a little lower now and the skin on my belly is still kind of flabby. I know that don't I look as good as I did, but that's no reason for him to cheat on me, is it? If that's what he even did. Maybe he just thinks I'm too gross now. Aurora has muscles in places I didn't know girls could have muscles. Her lean figure is muscular and healthy, with no flabby skin or saggy boobs in sight. I can see why he'd want her over me.

"Zee, calm down, I can smell your jealousy and sadness. What's brought this on?" Gunner asked urgently. He leaned forward and placed his hand on my knee. A lone tear rolled down my cheek and I quickly wiped it away before pushing his hand off me.

"Zee, talk to me, please" he pleaded.

"Do you love her?" I asked softly, so softly that he probably couldn't even hear me,

"Excuse me?" he snorted. I looked up at him and sighed. He stared back at me with astonishment.

"Do you love her?" I asked again.

"I... I... I don't know how to answer that" Gunner stumbled over his words. His dismissal sent me tumbling off my happy little cloud. It was like a knife through my heart. He didn't deny it, he didn't even try to deny it. What am I meant to think?

"That was answer enough" I said sadly and stood up. I shifted G. in my arms, which meant the bottle came out of her mouth. She didn't hesitate and screamed her little heart out for the four seconds it took me to put it back in her mouth.

"Hold up" Gunner grunted and stood up too,

"Where are you going?" he asked as he stepped in front of the door.

"Away" I answered and tried to push past him.

"Hold the fuck up, what just happened?" he snapped.

"I won't leave, not without my kids, if that's what you were thinking" I said angrily.

"Leave? Why are you leaving, where are you going?" Gunner asked, his voice rising as he became more agitated.

"You can have your house back. Though I may have accidentally destroyed your room, I won't stay in here and be in your way" I told him, ignoring his questions. My heart felt like a dried up piece of beef. The pain was excruciating. But I wasn't about to beg him to be with me, not if he didn't want to be. I went to open the door when he slammed it closed again.

"What the fuck is going on?" he yelled. The sound frightened B. and he started wailing. The sound of his crying made G. start crying too. I stepped back away from Gunner, rocking G. in my arms and trying to get her to take the bottle again. The door handle rattled as someone on the outside was trying to push it open, only Gunner's hand was still holding it. Gunner was breathing heavily, the stench of his anger and confusion filled the room. He stepped away from the door and Roe rushed in, with a worried look on her face.

"What's going on?" she asked urgently, looking down at both the babies in each of our arms.

"I have no fucking idea" Gunner spat.

"Don't you use that kind of language in front of my grand-pups" she scolded and grabbed the crying B. from his arms. She turned to me and her angry eyes softened, I handed her G. and then she left us alone in the nursery. We stood in front of each other silently. Gunner breathing harshly, trying to calm down, and me quietly falling apart and trying not to cry. I don't want to face this rejection by myself. I want Tobias. He would have usually sensed my distress by now and come running. Where is he?

"What's going on Zee, why are you saying all this crap about leaving and giving me my house back?" Gunner demanded, stepping closer to me. I stepped back, so that my back was against the wall. Gunner took another step forward so that he was only inches away from me. I could feel the warmth of his skin, I could smell that usual scent of warm sunshine, mixed with his sadness, confusion and anger. He reached out and took my hand, the sparks that I love so much shot across my skin. I'll miss this.

"Talk to me, please" Gunner said softly. I took a deep breath and looked up into his pained eyes. The crystal blue orbs shone with questions.

"You love her" I said sadly, emphasizing the word 'her'.

"I love you" he said back quickly, putting more emphasis on the 'you'.

"But you love her too. I won't stand in your way. Not if it's her that you want" I told him, using all the strength and resolve I could muster to make myself sound sure.

"Oh, Zelena" Gunner said softly.

"That's what this is all about?" he said as he grabbed my chin to lift my face.

"I could never love anyone the way I love you" he said earnestly.

"But when I asked you..." I started to argue, but Gunner cut me off,

"I love you, only you. You are my True Mate, my only Mate. You're all I could ever want and need. You are everything to me"

"But you..." I started. Gunner placed his finger over my mouth and shook his head.

"Let me finish. You asked me if I love her, the short answer is yes" Gunner said with certainty. The moment the words left his mouth my heart ached. I wanted to cry, and fight, and argue. But I did none of those things, I just stood silently and let him speak.

"The long answer, I love her because she is a piece of you. She is your other half in a way that I could never be. She is your blood, your family, and that makes her my family. I love her like I do my own sister. I will protect her the way I do my own family. There are no romantic feelings there. I admit, I might have flirted a little to gain her trust. That was wrong of me, I shouldn't have done that. But nothing more happened. No wait, that's not true. We shared a tent and when I was asleep, I cuddled her, but I didn't mean to. She just smells a little like you, and I didn't know what I was doing, because you know, I was sleeping. But that's all. Basically. When I first saw her, I thought she was you, and I may have gotten a little too close when I was trying to figure out what or who she was. She is just so much like you, you know. You look identical. I could have sworn she was you. But once I got close enough to smell her, I knew it wasn't you. But I always knew you were connected, you know. I feel very protective over her. But no more than any other member of my family. Okay, that's all. I think".

By the time Gunner finished his ramble, he was panting. He spoke so fast and shot through a lot of information in quick succession. He reminded me so much of Nat in that moment, it was hard not to smile. I felt lighter, more at ease, knowing that he didn't want her like that. I was silly and self-conscious for thinking he did. But then he said the stuff about smelling her and cuddling her, I'd be lying if I said that didn't bother me.

"You don't want to be with her?" I asked. I needed to hear him say it.

"No. I want you Zelena, only you" he confirmed.

"You don't feel anything for her?" I asked again.

"I wouldn't say that exactly. I feel some kind of connection, like we are drawn to each other. Nothing like I am with you, you are like the air I need to breathe, I would die instantly without you. But Whiskey is... I don't know how to explain what she is, but there's something there. She is like destiny, I was meant to find her. It can't just be a coincidence that she ended up on the mountain I was on. It can't all just be an accident that Selene let me go to rid myself of the darkness, only for me to find your long lost twin" Gunner said sternly, like he had already decided this was all a big conspiracy theory.

"You've given this a lot of thought, haven't you?"

Gunner scoffed and threw his arms up in the air, then began to walk around the room as he started a new ramble.

"Of course I have. The identical twin sister of my True Mate just happened to walk into my camp. A camp on a mountain, in the middle of nowhere, with nothing and no one nearby. That's not an accident. The fact that I was able to dispel the last of the darkness the day after she found me, that's not an accident either. She wanted me to bring her back to you. Selene had all of this planned, she knew exactly what she was doing. This whole thing is all part of her master plan, she has had this in the works for months, if not years or decades. It's like we are all playing out a script that she has already written".

"Like a prophecy" I said blankly.

"Uh, Yeah, I suppose. Like a prophecy. Those are already written, sometimes hundreds of years before they happen". As crazy as Gunner sounds, what if he's not. What if this is all just part of the prophecy, making its way together. Everything is coming to fruition, all the pieces of the puzzle are fitting together. I have to tell him about the prophecy.

"Gunner, there's something you need to know" I said as I stepped toward him.

"What? You didn't actually have triplets, did you?" he chuckled and wrapped his arms around my waist, pulling my chest flush against his.

"No" I snorted.

"First, are we okay?" he asked and nuzzled his face into the top of my head.

"We're okay. I'm sorry I freaked out on you" I said and pressed my face to his chest.

"Don't apologise. I can see how it looks, and it didn't look good. I'm sorry I put you through that".

"You didn't mean to, I'm just extra sensitive at the moment".

"Just please know, I will never betray you like that. I could never do that to you. You're my whole world Zee. The twins have made that world a little bigger, but you will always be at the centre of it" he said honestly. I felt the love and devotion fly out of him, washing over me like warm waves. I wanted to cry again, only this time from happiness, not heartbreak.

"I know" I said softly and nuzzled my nose into him, breathing in his scent. We stood together silently, just holding each other. I've missed his warmth, his smell, the feel of his hands, the sound of his heartbeat. I've missed him. I'm not ready to share him with everyone else. I nuzzled my face into him some more, letting my hands roam up and down his back, over his biceps and down his chest. He feels so good. His chest vibrated and his heart rate picked up. He moved his hands down my back and to my backside, with a cheek in each hand he squeezed. I pressed my body into him, feeling the hardened length in his jeans. A lust filled growl burst out of him as I rubbed myself against him. Using his hands on my ass, he picked me up and I wrapped my legs around his waist. He wasted no time in attacking my neck with his mouth, sucking, biting and kissing, all over my neck and collarbones. I ground my hips against him, trying to get as much friction as I could. Gunner moved his mouth up my neck and slammed his lips against mine. We fought each other for dominance, each of us wanting to taste every part of the other. Gunner slid his hand between my legs and cupped my pussy. I whined into his mouth, the need for him becoming too much.

"Wait, not here" I breathed heavily. Without taking his lips away from my neck, Gunner marched us for the door and kicked it open. He went straight to the next closest door, which just so happened to be the bathroom. He placed my ass on the basin and got back to roaming his hands all over my body. I heard the tearing of material and felt a gush of cold air, as my shirt fell in tatters to the floor. Gunner stepped out from between my knees and quickly ripped my pants from my legs, then quickly moved back to where he was. I grabbed the collar of his t-shirt and ripped it down the middle, then Gunner threw what remained of it on the floor. I undid his pants, and he did a little dance to kick his legs free of them. With the both of us now naked, all of my skin rubbed against all of his, it drove me wild. I grabbed Gunner's rock hard cock tightly and stroked it. His fingers went to my already slick slit and he slipped them over my folds. He wasted no time and moved a hand under my ass cheek, he lifted me slightly and I angled the tip of his cock to my entrance. He slammed into me mercilessly and I cried out in euphoria. The pressure of being filled so completely, the sensations of his heated skin on mine, it was perfect.

He slid out slowly and slammed back into me again, and again, and again. Each time he drew a scream of pure bliss from my lips. He ducked his head to my chest and sucked my nipple into his mouth. He teased it between his teeth, making me whine. I could feel my nails sliding across his back as I pawed at him, I was desperate to get him closer to me. The tips of my fingers tingled with the need for my claws to slip out. My canines had already pushed through, and my gums ached with the need to be buried in his flesh.

I screamed out, the pressure building in my belly and my skin alight with sparks. Each thrust was a push closer to the edge. I was ready to throw myself over and give in completely to the tidal waves of pleasure that I knew were coming. My body tingled all over, it was all consuming. Gunner's teeth grazed along my skin, until he landed on my breast, right next to my armpit. I felt the sharpness of his teeth break the skin, before his fangs were pushed all the way through. Rushes of electric sparks flowed through me. I tossed my head back and cried out as the first explosion of my orgasm opened up. I snapped my head back again, finding the place where his neck met his shoulder. My own canines pressed into his skin, and as the blood hit my tongue, I was lost to it. I chomped down hard into his neck, and I felt his hips jerk as he began emptying himself inside me. I rode through the waves of my orgasm, which felt never ending, all the while keeping my fangs in Gunner's neck. He did the same, bucking his hips into me while his teeth were in me.

After Goddess knows how long, I felt depleted. All of my energy had evaporated with the last of my orgasm. I slipped my teeth from Gunner's neck and licked it over with my tongue, cleaning up the blood. Gunner's teeth pulled out of my side, and I felt his warm tongue trail over the fresh mark. I shivered and a gentle throb beat between my legs. He ran his mouth back over my chest, nibbling on my nipple as he went. His lips moved back up over my neck and to the corner of my mouth.

"Let's do that about eighty more times today, and I might be satisfied" he mumbled with a grin. I turned my head and dove my tongue into his mouth, which he accepted willingly. The throb intensified, and I was ready to go again. Gunner growled and I felt his dick twitch inside me. I moaned into his mouth and rounded my hips forward. Gunner's arm slipped under my knee and lifted my leg higher, opening myself to him wider. He pushed his hips forward and he was hard again already. I grabbed his neck and pulled his face to mine, meshing our lips together. I continued to round my hips on him, grinding myself along his shaft. Gunner groaned and thrust his hips forward. With my leg up he hit me deep and I moaned loudly. He did it again, harder, and I moaned louder. We kept on doing this dance for a little longer, until

Gunner surprised me. He picked me up off the basin, tucking his other arm under my other knee. I grabbed hold of his neck so I wouldn't fall backwards. Then he went to town, fucking me into oblivion. The sound of clapping flesh filled the bathroom, echoing off the walls. I was unable to move with my legs trapped in his hold. If I let go of his neck, I would drop. He pounded into me like never before, using me as his own personal fuck toy. And I loved it.

"I missed you" Gunner grunted,

"I missed you so fucking much" he puffed out, not letting up for a moment on his savage pounding. I was incapable of words. I moaned and wailed and called out with the extreme pleasure he was giving me. My stomach was contracting with the need to burst. My arms were shaking as I dug my nails into the back of Gunner's neck. He growled and thrust harder, bouncing me off of him. I was holding on, trying not to cum until he did. I love the feeling of coming on his twitching dick. I was at my limit, about ready to burst when he grunted and bucked his hips. I felt him empty himself inside of me and I let loose, screaming into my orgasm. I could feel both of our juices coating my thighs with his last few pumps. Gunner grunted and pulled me back into him, wrapping his arms around my body. Our chests were flush against each other, our skin coated in sweat as the both of us were panting hard.

Gunner walked us to the shower and turned the taps on, before carrying me under the stream of hot water. I was already burning hot, our vigorous love making had me searing. Yet the hot water still felt refreshing against my flushed skin.

"Do you want me to put you down?" Gunner asked as he peppered kisses across my chin,

"I'm not sure if I can stand yet" I huffed. Gunner chuckled and shifted my weight in his arms,

"I got you" he whispered and kissed the corner of my mouth. He slowly lowered my feet to the cool shower tiles, keeping one arm wrapped firmly around my waist, holding most of my weight. The other was hooked under my arm, with his finger drawing circles on my back. Although I was standing, I laid myself against him, letting him hold me up.

"That was amazing" I sighed, feeling completely sated.

"You're amazing" Gunner shot back and pinched my ass. I chuckled and pushed myself off his chest. My knees felt weak and my legs shook like jelly underneath my weight. Gunner chuckled and grabbed my arm,

"You alright?" he asked with a somewhat cocky tone.

"No, you screwed the feeling right out of my legs" I scoffed playfully and slapped his chest. He lifted his head back and laughed, the sound echoing around the bathroom.

"And that was just the pre-show, I'm nowhere near done with you yet" he teased and ducked his head into my neck. His lips moved over the sensitive skin, leading to his very first mark on the top of my shoulder. I turned my head to the side, giving him more room, and sucked in a breath. Gunner sucked the marked skin into his mouth, and my legs buckled. Luckily, he was still holding me, or I would have hit the deck. He laughed and lifted me back into his arms, so that my legs could go around his waist. His mouth nibbled and sucked at the scared flesh, sending shoots of electricity through my limbs, and shivers of excitement through my body. I'll say it a thousand times over, I will never tire of the effect he has on my body.

A harsh bang on the door had Gunner's head snap in the direction and a low growl left his clenched jaw. His hold on me tightened and he pulled me closer into his body.

"What?" he snapped,

"Gunner" I scolded in a whisper.

"You have visitors" Smith's voice called out. Gunner grunted and went back to attacking my neck and shoulder.

Tell them to come back later

Gunner flashed both Smith and I at the same time. He moved a hand to my breast and teased the perked nipple between his thumb and forefinger. I stifled my moan, knowing Smith was just on the other side of the door.

You'll want to come downstairs

Smith's voice called through the flash. He sounded both excited and urgent. I wonder who it could be. My curiosity was pushing back the insatiable need to have Gunner take me again. Though he didn't seem to care. He ducked his head down and sucked my nipple into his mouth. I groaned and grabbed his head, using his hair as leverage. I ripped his head away from my skin and Gunner pouted.

"We'll be down in five" I called out to Smith and Gunner groaned loudly, smacking the back of his head against the wall. I laughed and pulled his face back down to mine, pressing my lips against his.

"You're so mean to me" he whined and stuck his bottom lip out. I laughed and bit down on it, I pulled it out before letting it go with a pop.

"See, when you do things like that, it only makes me want to bury my teeth into you again" Gunner growled and nuzzled into my neck,

"Among other things" he said coyly and pushed his hips forward so that his hardened length could rub against my thigh. How in the heck is he hard again? This man is a machine. Not that I'm complaining. I plan on taking full advantage of this superpower of his over the next few days. Who am I kidding, I'll be taking advantage of this ability for the rest of our lives.

"Come on. You're still the Alpha, and I'm still the Luna" I scolded him and lifted my hips away from him.

"Which means we can make them wait" he smirked and lowered his hold, meaning my body slid down his, until he was rubbing against me once again. I laughed and kissed him once on his pouting lips.

"We can pick this up again after we see who's here" I told him and climbed out of his arms. Gunner growled and put his head under the water stream. My legs had still not regained full feeling, but if I let him carry me again, we'd never leave this bathroom. I stepped out and wrapped a towel around myself.

"Out" I called, and Gunner swore under his breath, though I still heard it. I tossed him a towel and headed out the bathroom door, with Gunner following behind me. When I turned left down the hallway instead of right, towards Gunner's old room, he stopped.

"Where are you going? Our room's right there" he said and pointed to the newly installed door.

"Oh, uh, I haven't been sleeping in there" I said meekly, Gunner stepped up in front of me and slid a hand under my towel, running his fingers across my hip.

"And why not?" he asked, his voice was low and sultry, it made my skin tingle.

"There was a little accident" I admitted. Gunner's hand stopped caressing my hip and he squeezed it. I looked up to meet his wary gaze.

"What happened?" he demanded. I bit my lip and swallowed.

"I'll um... Can I explain later?" I asked and gave him my sweetest smile. He hummed and pursed his lips but agreed.

"I'm not dropping this" he said as I skipped off to the spare room, "I know" I called back. We both quickly dried off and put some clothes on, much to Gunner's disappointment. It was very hard to turn him down, and my resolve was slipping the more he tried to seduce me. We settled on a midnight wolf run through the forest and then some wild outdoor sex. I'm actually looking forward to it.

We came downstairs and followed the voices to the kitchen. I pushed open the door and stepped through. Roe was busy over the stove, Lunaya and Alyse were standing by the counter, all of them talking animatedly with our guests.

"Hello" I blanked. What are they doing here? Why have they come back?

"What are you doing here?" I blurted out before my mind could stop me.

"My apologies, you're welcome here, always. But why are you back?" I said with a more dignified tone.

"I've brought a message for the Triple Goddess" Elaine, the Beta wolf of the Luna Eclipse pack, said in a low and serious voice as she stepped toward me and away from her entourage. A shiver ran down my spine and a tightness filled my stomach. I have a bad feeling about this.

Chapter Thirty-Three

Whiskey

Once Gunner left the room with his Mate, the warm feeling of calmness left with him. I don't know how he does it, and it's starting to bug me. One moment I'd be filled with rage and ready to kill, the next, he says some words and it's as if I melt like butter. Deep down, buried under a mountain of self-hate, distrust and vengefulness, I think I may trust him. There is still something there. Even though I now see that he could never want me like he does the witch, there is still a connection between us. I just need to find out what it is. Preferably before I kill off the rest of his pack, so I know whether or not he needs to die along with them. I don't want to be here, especially without Gunner, not with these animals. I want the calmness back. The calmness that I only feel from him. The dark-haired woman from my ghost dream thingy, Lunaya, Gunner called her, she was getting on my nerves. She thinks I can't hear her, but I can. Whispering and crying to the small woman at her side. She kept saying that she wanted to hold me. Whatever the fuck that is supposed to mean. I'm not picking up on any anger or hostility from her, so I don't think she means to hold me captive. She had better not mean to embrace me. I let the bitch touch me twice now, that is all she gets. I gave her the warning, and I always stick to my word.

"Well then" Gunner's mother called happily with a clap of her hands,

"I bet you're hungry" she smiled down at me. I can see traces of Gunner in her smile and the twinkle of her eye. But it's his father that he most resembles. The large man moved to stand next to his Mate, giving me the opportunity to look him over more closely. There was a large scar that ran from his lip, across his face and disappeared into his hairline. It made him look dangerous. The smile he wore didn't hide his powerful aura, I could see right through the friendly persona he was putting forward. This man would kill anything and everything for the woman at his side. I guess Gunner got that part of himself from his father. Though I wonder if he, too, has powers like Gunner, if any of them do.

"Whiskey, Dear?" his mother called gently, recapturing my attention. I looked over to her and blanked, I've already forgotten her name. I've never cared for names before. The only time I stuck around anywhere long enough for names to matter, was at Saxton's pack. Even then, it took me days to remember some of their names. I will have to work harder at it here, especially if I am to win over their trust.

I stood up slowly and flicked my eyes to the large man still standing behind the couch. His skin was dark chocolate and it glowed under the soft light filtering through the curtains. His dark endless eyes bore into mine. His face was tense, and he didn't emit any emotion or feelings that I could get a read on. His thick brows were pulled together in the middle, and although his lips were pressed into a line, I could tell they were plump. The longer I stared at him, the more uneasy he made me feel, and that is not a feat easily accomplished. Nothing scares me, nothing bothers me, but this mountain of a man was different. When I look at Gunner, I feel warm and safe. When I look at this gigantic beast, I feel confused, like there is a secret that I'm not a part of.

I hadn't realised it in the moment, but I walked toward him, stopping just inches away from him. I craned my neck, looking up at his hard, expressionless face. He didn't move away, or back down, he stayed put, staring back at me unblinking. I could hear Gunner's mother calling my name, but her voice was lost in the moment. His smooth skin was blemish free, and his bald head glistened under the light. Now that I was closer, I could see the true colour of his eyes. Not black like they appear from a distance, but a rich brown. His unblinking stare matched my own, but I could get nothing from his gaze. The eyes were always the giveaway. In people's eyes, you could see their hidden fear, or sadness, or even love. But his eyes were just deep pools of nothing. Not even a hint of emotion. What is he? He is more than a regular werewolf, I can feel that much, but he is somehow blocking his aura and his emotions. No one has ever been able to do that around me before. I have a knack for reading people, but reading him seems impossible.

A soft growl, almost like a purr slipped out of my mouth, unintentionally. I have never made a sound like that before. My arm moved before my mind, and I reached up and touched the man's face. Tingles exploded over my skin, like a live wire had been connected to my fingers. I gasped and snapped my hand back, but he caught it before I could withdraw. He squeezed his excessively large hand around my wrist, and a rumble sounded in his chest. I pulled my hand from his and stumbled back away from him, crashing into Gunner's father. He held my shoulders to steady my feet. I heard his muffled voice speak, but I couldn't make out the words. I shook my head and rubbed my temple, trying to regain my lost senses. Did the big man do something to me, did he dull them, or block them somehow?

"Don't ignore me, Tobias" Gunner's father growled. I looked back up at him, Tobias, the colossal mystery man. His face had hardened, and his blank eyes now looked almost angry. He rumbled again, this time sounding much more ferocious.

"Tobias" Gunner's mother snapped at him. Lunaya and the smaller woman stepped between us and growled back at him. I was confused as to what was happening, the blurry feeling of my dulled senses hadn't fully cleared. Was he threatening me? No, it doesn't feel like I'm in danger, it feels like his anger is directed more to the people around me. Tobias spared me one last look, and I finally saw it, the flicker of emotion in his eyes that I had been searching for. Concern. As to what, I don't know, but he was worried about something. Tobias then turned and stormed off, not saying a word to anyone. The door slammed behind him and the room fell silent, slowly filling with tension.

"Are you okay, dear?" Gunner's mother cooed softly as she stood in front of my face. She reached forward to touch my face, but quickly stopped herself. She's observant, I'll give her that. She must have remembered that I told Lunaya not to touch me, clever lady. I narrowed my eyes and nodded my head. She smiled and stepped back a bit further away from me again.

"Come, let's get you some food" she smiled and held her hand out to the door. Lupus went first, pushing open the door and holding it while the rest of us walked through. It was the first time I had seen the inside of their home. It was grand, much like the Alpha's house at Red River, Saxton's pack in Italy. But this felt much more homely, and a hell of a lot less showy. That was one of the things I hated about Alpha Antonio, he was all about status and showing off his riches. He cared more about the material things that he thought made him powerful, and less about his actual power, or lack thereof.

I stopped and looked up, above us hung a grand crystal chandelier. It was nice, if you like that sort of thing. I wonder if it's worth anything. I breathed in through my nose and salivated. Roasted meat, fresh pastries, plus something sweet, and traces of Gunner's scent filled the air. Pictures lined the walls all over the foyer area. But not ugly paintings like at Alpha Antonio's residence, these were all photographs. My eyes zeroed in on a picture of Gunner wearing a dark grey suit, and Zee in a dark green dress. They were facing each other, holding an oversized silver cup with two big handles. Only the side of Gunner's face was visible, but he was beaming with happiness. It made my stomach hurt. Gunner's mother caught me staring and moved to lift the frame off the wall and hand it to me. I looked more closely at the picture, taking in the whole scene. White lanterns were lit behind them, making it look like they were both glowing. Gunner looked unbearably handsome in the suit as it clung to his defined muscles perfectly. His face was cleanly shaved and overflowing with love for the woman he was looking at. As much as I didn't want to, my eyes moved to her. She was smiling broadly up at him, the light illuminating her golden eyes. She looked smaller in the picture than she does in real life. Her chest was flatter, her stomach thinner, and her arms leaner. The green dress she wore hung off every curve of her body, accentuating what little shape her body did have. She looks beautiful. And I hate her for it.

"It was their ascension ceremony" Gunner's mother said proudly and ran her fingers over the glass of the frame.

"She's beautiful, isn't she?" she cooed softly and took the picture back to the wall. She turned around again and smiled widely,

"Just as you are" she said cheerfully. She went to grab my hand but pulled back at the last second.

"Sorry" she mumbled and forced a smile, then walked off to a door on the left. She held it open and waved me through. Her Mate and the two other women were already in there, sitting on tall stools at a very large bench. Unsurprisingly, the kitchen was as decadent as the rest of the house. Gunner's mother was quick on her feet, shuffling through the kitchen and whipping out plates and bowls of food. After a few silent moments, she ushered me over to a booth table in the corner and placed multiple plates of food in front of me. She watched me with anticipation as I stared at the mountains of food. How do I know this isn't a trick? She could be trying to slip me drugs, or even poison. I frowned at the food, thinking up a way to get out of this. There was a tugging sensation in the back of my mind, telling me it was okay, screaming out for me to trust her.

"Help yourself, Dear" the woman smiled down at me. She stood waiting, as she wiped her hands on a floral apron. Wait, when did she even put that on, she wasn't wearing that a second ago. After another moment, she went back to busying herself in the kitchen. I watched her for a moment, whilst she flittered around cleaning up the benches. Her Mate and the two other women each had a plate in front of them, filled with the same food I had. But they weren't hesitating, they were eating away happily. I suppose this would be an odd way to kill someone. Killing me while I was unconscious would have been more practical. This whole situation is making my head spin. I looked down at the food, my mouth salivated and my nose breathed in the smells on its own. It does look really good, and I am fucking starving. I don't even know when I ate last. Though it's not uncommon for me to forget to eat. I picked up a piece of tenderised steak and sniffed at it. Barbeque sauce, garlic, a hint of chilli and a lot of smoke. I can't pick out any unusual scents on the meat, maybe it is ok after all.

"You don't like barbequed steak, girl?" Lupus' voice bellowed through the kitchen. I looked up to see he and the three women all watching me.

"You'll never taste better cooking than Roe's" he said with a proud smile over at his Mate. Roe, got it, her name is Roe. I frowned at him and then back down at the meat. What the heck. I placed the corner of the steak into my mouth and tore off a decent sized chunk. The flavours exploded on my tongue as the meat's juices coated the inside of my mouth. I chewed fast, too fast to enjoy the flavours. I put more in my mouth and chewed, once again not slowly enough to savour it. Before I realised it, I was shoving the whole thing in my mouth greedily while reaching for other bits of food. I went full animal, smashing the food against my face and hoping I got enough inside my mouth. Soft chuckling pulled me back and I turned to the four adults. Each of them was watching me wide eyed, while Lupus and the small woman, whose name I have forgotten, were laughing quietly.

"Stop it" Roe hissed and slapped her Mate on the back of the head. I watched with anticipation, to see how he would retaliate for her hitting him. But he did nothing, just chuckled more openly. Since when do werewolves not fight back when attacked?

"Told you she cooks good, ay?" Lupus smiled before putting more food in his own mouth. He wasn't wrong, it was some of the best food that I have ever eaten. But I couldn't move past the fact that he ignored the hit his Mate landed on his head. Why wouldn't he retaliate? I watched them for a moment, Roe leaned over the counter and kissed Lupus, he then hand fed her some of the food from his plate. She took it out of his fingers with her teeth and winked at him. It was like she never hit him at all. How odd. Lunaya and the small woman were still watching me. Lunaya's eyes searched my face for something. When she didn't turn away, I growled.

"What?" I snarled at the woman. She furrowed her brows and slowly stood off the stool.

"Nae" the small woman called quietly and tried to pull her back down onto the stool. She shrugged her off and walked towards me. She stopped a few steps away and stared at me. She was trying to hide it, but I could see the internal battle going on behind her eyes, she was desperate to say something.

"Do you know who I am?" she asked sternly. What a stupid fucking question, why would I know that, also, why would I care? Despite seeing her with the man from my dreams in that weird ass unconscious sleep thingy, I have never seen her before. Perhaps this was an intimidation thing. Alphas often asked me if I knew who they were before I killed them. Like, somehow knowing their identity would stop me from ending their pathetic lives. They always seemed shocked or even hurt that I would tell them no, or that it didn't matter. It seems like status means a lot to these beasts. I looked over Lunaya's face and I realised, she was dead serious, she isn't being cocky or boasting, she is asking a genuine question.

"Lunaya, not now" Roe hissed before shooting me a forced smile.

"No, now. I waited last time and look how that turned out" she grunted back at Gunner's mother. What did she wait for last time and what do they want her to wait for now?

"Nae, please, give her a minute" the small lady pleaded as she came to stand by her side.

"We don't have the time, you know that. You all know that" she shouted behind her to where Roe and Lupus were still sitting. I am completely lost as to what is going on here. These beasts are fucking weird.

"Well? Aurora, Whiskey. Whatever the fuck you're calling yourself" she snarled at me. I wiped my arm over my face and hissed, standing up to face the tall woman. I have said a hundred times now, my name is not Aurora and I am sick to fucking death of hearing it.

"You fucking mutts must be daft as all hell" I snarled, throwing my eyes back to the very concerned looking small woman behind Lunaya,

"For the last time, my name is Whiskey" I shouted and slammed my fist down onto the table. Roe ran around from behind the counter and stood in front of Lunaya.

"She knows that, Darling, she is just being rude" Roe scolded while glaring at Lunaya over her shoulder.

"Lunaya, I understand your urgency, but she is not ready, clearly" Roe said quietly while facing away from me. It was a bold move for her to turn her back to me. I don't know the bitch well enough to garner if it was a show of trust, or just disrespect. I will need to find out. Or perhaps she was trying to speak to Lunaya so that I wouldn't hear her. Maybe she isn't aware I still can hear her, my senses are strong and powerful, more so than any regular wolf. I know that she is talking about me, but why? What is it that they think I'm not ready for?

"If you have something to say" I said loudly, interrupting their whispered conversation. Roe turned around with a smile plastered on her face.

"No, Sweet Girl, nothing that can't wait another day or two" she said sweetly. She is lying, I can smell it on her. On instinct, I growled. I had no intention of attacking right now, not unless they did first, I still have to plan it out. But the growl prompted the protectiveness of Lupus. Like a thundering giant, he placed himself between me and the two women and growled down at me threateningly. Somehow, he managed to make himself look three times larger than he did before. I have only seen this man when he was smiling or joking. This side of him, however, is impressive. The extended fangs, the angry eyes, the tense muscles, the aura of power he was exuding. There is no argument, he is dangerous. I've still taken down bigger animals though.

"You are a guest in my home, you will show respect to my Mate while you are under this roof" he bellowed, the sound echoed around the kitchen, bouncing off the walls. Roe placed her hand on his chest, and it was like he deflated. All the anger and tension left the room and he looked down at her gently.

"If you'll all excuse me, I'm going to check on the t... I'm going upstairs" Roe said before kissing Lupus on the cheek and leaving the room. Lupus glared back at me before he sat back down on his stool.

"Well, out with it then" I blurted annoyed. I glared at Lunaya who still looked angry, but now also sorrowful. She pulled her hand from the small woman's grip, who reluctantly let go after a slight fight. She stepped closer to me and huffed out a harsh breath.

"Do you remember your parents?" she asked me gently. What on earth does that have to do with anything? If I had parents, what would it matter to her if I remembered them or not.

"Your mother or your father, what do you know about them?" she asked again.

"None of your fucking business" I snapped harshly. My mind went immediately to the man from my dreams, the same man that I saw with the babies and Lunaya during my ghost walk thing. That wasn't real though, none of it was real. He isn't real, I don't have parents.

"So, you do remember something" she said with a slight excitement to her voice as she studied my pensive face. I lifted my eyes back to hers and shook the thoughts of the man from my mind.

"I don't have parents" I growled through clenched teeth. She looked at me, not saying anything back. Her intrusion into my private life was infuriating, and I was panting hard, trying to control my anger. I could feel the power coursing through me, looking for a weak point to slip through. I would love nothing more than to drain the air from this woman, along with her life. But not yet, I can't start my attack until I have a better understanding of my surroundings and the pack numbers.

"You do have parents, everyone has parents" Lunaya's soft voice finally said. This damn woman is dancing on my last nerve. She dares to talk to me like she knows me. She knows nothing. I have no mother, no father. I was created in a lab. Made to bring death to the savage beasts that roam the Earth. I am death incarnate.

"No" I growled lowly. I pressed my talons into the palms of my hands, letting the pain bring me back down before I exploded completely.

"No, what? Whiskey, what do you remember about them?" the small woman asked from behind Lunaya.

"Drop it" I grunted. My resolve was weakening, the power was getting stronger inside me, pushing at the constraints.

"You're safe here, you can talk to us" Lunaya said softly and stepped towards me again. That was the breaking point. I felt the power slip through and whirl around me. The wind slapped at my skin as it blew through the kitchen. It knocked the plates from the tables and rattled the pans hanging from the overhead hanger.

"What is this?" I heard Lupus's mighty voice call through the bellowing of the wind.

"It's her" Lunaya yelled back without hesitation. How could she have known it was me causing the whirlwind? She didn't even need to think about it, it was like she already knew. But how?

I managed to rein it back in. Taking a deep breath, I was able to pull the air back into my body. The wind disappeared and the kitchen was once again deadly silent. I glared up at the three waiting and astonished gazes. Lupus was now standing between the small woman and Lunaya, his arms out, trying to keep them behind him. Lunaya was looking at me with wide and gleeful eyes. That sort of display would scare most people, so why not her? If anything, she looked thrilled. The kitchen was a mess. I have caused worse damage in my rampages, this was actually very minor. Lunaya and the small woman, I must find out her name, both of their hair was in shambles.

"You have a gift" Lunaya said excitedly as she pushed past Lupus's arm.

"What?" I snapped at her. How is she still smiling and happy, I just about blew her through the wall, yet she's still smiling at me.

"I mean, of course you have a gift, just like your sister, you're incredible" she fawned proudly. Did she just say sister? I don't have a sister, what is she on about now.

"She is a Goddess too?" Lupus asked urgently from over Lunaya's shoulder. I almost burst out laughing right then and there. Did he seriously just ask if I was a Goddess, are all Canadian Weres this crazy?

"Excuse me?" I chortled, trying to hold back my laughter. This whole situation is laughable. How did I get to this point? There's a girl who looks just like me, a woman I saw in my dreams who seems to think she knows me. Then there are all these other random people that I have never met, all of which are looking at me and watching me expectedly, like they know what I'm going to do next. This whole thing is just bizarre. Not to mention all the weird shit that keep spurting out, that is a whole other nation of weird.

"Don't you see it? Your power, you finding your way here, it's all already been ordained. This was all part of a larger plan. Her plan" Lunaya says quickly.

"Who's plan?" I asked. Not that I really care, but I am slightly curious.

"Selene, of course. The Moon Goddess has it all planned out" Lunaya answered instantly. My anger spiked at hearing the name, the name I had to hear over and over again as I was being tortured. The name of the mystic being responsible for my creation. The original witch herself. The fucking Moon Goddess. I curled my lip back and snarled.

"You're fucking nuts, you know that right? I'm not part of this weird ass fantasy you have cooked up in that coo-coo mind of yours" I spat,

"Oh, you very much are, that's why you're here, with me, with Zelena" she said, looking at me with a gentle smile, a maternal like smile, it was unnerving.

The small woman came to Lunaya's side and took her hand. Lupus too stepped closer. The three of them all looking at me, waiting for me to speak, or to come to some sort of bright realisation. But, I'm not here for them. Well, in a way I am. I'm here to kill them. But I came here for Gunner, to find out how he got his power. I don't give two flying shits about Lunaya, Zee or any other the rest of them. Why would I? Lunaya stepped closer again and smiled invitingly, she reached her hand out for me to take. I think she may have lost her mind, especially if she thinks I'm going to hold her damn hand. I scoffed at her hand and snarled up at her as she spoke.
"You see, My Darling, I am your birth mother".

Chapter Thirty-Four

Whiskey

What the fuck did she just say? My mother, seriously? This lady has lost her damn mind. I was lost for words, completely. Which is odd for me, I always have some sort of smart remark to make. But not this time. I was just stunned into silence by her stupidity. She actually thinks that I'm her child. She believes that I'm a real werewolf. I must have played my part better than I thought. She stood in front of me, watching for my reaction, waiting for me to say something. But I had nothing to say. She isn't my mother, I have no mother. We stood silently for what felt like an hour, though it was only a few seconds. Both Lunaya and Lupus, plus the small woman, were all watching me closely, waiting for me to speak. But I didn't. No. Words had been lost to me, but something was working its way out of me. Slowly forcing its way up my body, ready to burst free. Once it reached the back of my chest, I couldn't hold it in anymore. I tossed my head back and roared with laughter. It spilled out of my mouth effortlessly, making me wheeze for air. I hunched over, leaning on my knees, to try and catch a breath, but the laughter wouldn't stop.

"Aurora?" Lunaya said concerned. At the sound of that name, my laughter cut off and was replaced by a growl.

"My name is Whiskey" I snarled at her low and threatening. She glared back at me and looked to stumble over herself for words. She sucked her teeth and huffed heavily, then shook her head.

"No" she waved her hand back and forth.

"Enough of this" she growled over at me with a frown,
"Your name is Aurora, named for the new dawn. You are the twin sister of Zelena. You are the second born daughter of Micha and Lunaya Alvar. You come from the line of Selena, the chosen daughters, descendants of the All Mother herself. You hold the power of the Moon Goddess, and you bear her mark. You are mine to love, ours to cherish, and the world's to adore. You are Aurora".

I glared at her as she spoke, my anger bubbling inside me. All of that crap she babbled means nothing to me. I don't care who she thinks I am, no matter how much I look like that witch, regardless of all the stories she could spin, that is not me. This is not my life, that's not my story. This isn't where my path leads, I'm not destined for happy endings. I don't believe her, I won't believe her. I am the death incarnate, the bringer of pain, created to end all the werewolves. That is who I am. I am Whiskey. I am not, nor will I ever be Aurora.

When I didn't respond again, Lunaya huffed annoyed and stepped toward me with one giant step.

"All Mother, please help me" she whispered before she connected the palm of her hand to my forehead. I felt like I was falling, or more so, being pulled backwards. Everything around me blurred and a pain rang out in my head. In fact, the pain shot all through me, from the tip of my toes to the end of my fingers. I would usually enjoy the pain, finding it grounding and real. This kind of pain was different. It was like my body was being forced through icy water and burning flames at the same time. I was being pulled to a place that I didn't want to be. I don't know for sure how I knew that, call it intuition. But deep in my stomach, I knew that wherever I was going was not where I wanted to go.

When I opened my eyes, I was back in my room at the facility, back in Russia. Panic filled my stomach as I whirled around on the spot. No, no, no. I can't be here, I swore never to return to this place. How am I here? How did she do that? The heavy door opened with a groan and a thud, capturing my attention. In walked one of the hunters. I remember seeing him in my dream. He was one of the men that captured my father. Or, the man I imagined to be my father. How could he be here? I looked over his face and recognised him as the hunter who carried the child away after my father was captured. I moved my eyes to his arms, and he was once again holding that same baby. This can't be right. I watched as he put the baby on the dirty mattress lying on the floor, the same dirty mattress that I slept on all my life. He then walked away, leaving the crying child alone in the room. I turned on it, glaring at the blubbering baby. What is this thing doing in my old room.

Pain coursed through my body, forcing me to hunch over and grip my stomach. The crying stopped abruptly, and gentle whimpering took its place. I looked up to see what made the sudden change. The baby was sitting upright on the mattress, its hand outstretched, like it was holding something. But there was nothing there. The pain got worse, and I grunted involuntarily. I rubbed my hand over my face and eyes, hoping the pain would go away, but it didn't. I looked back up at the baby, but it wasn't alone anymore. A pale white light, like an apparition or something, was sitting next to her. I rubbed my eyes again, straining to make sense of the weird figure. What the fuck is that. More pain rolled through me, this time forcing me to drop to my knees. My head was ringing with a thousand tiny jackhammers pounding at the inside of my skull. My arms and legs were cramping, the muscles spasming painfully. My stomach was in motion, rolling around inside me, making me want to hurl. I don't know what's going on, but I want it to stop. This forceful pain is unlike anything I have ever experienced. I will take whippings, lashings and starvation over this. I would prefer to be forced to change into my beast and back again, feel the breaking of my bones a hundred thousand times over again, instead of this. I would take the cold room with that horror torture chair over this. Anything is better than this agony.

A strangled scream burst from my lips and echoed around the frigid walls. I curled myself into my knees, pressing my forehead to the frozen concrete ground. I closed my eyes tightly and gripped the side of my head. Please stop. Please stop. Please stop! And just like that, it did. The pain was gone. I stayed perfectly still in my little ball, my head in my hands, crunched over on my knees, with my forehead on the ground. I was afraid that if I moved, the pain would return.

"See, you're okay, Sweet Girl" a voice rang out. Such a soft and angelic voice. It made my skin break out in goosebumps. Yet, I feel like I know that voice, like I've heard it before. The baby cooed happily in response to the voice. Who else was in here, I wondered. Someone else must have come in while I was screaming in pain. I slowly sat up and looked at where the baby was. The pale light was gone, and now a beautiful woman in a white dress was there, holding the baby in her arms. Her long, straight, snow white hair hung long past her shoulders. Her skin glistened and looked like it was sparkling. She rocked the child in her arms, whispering gentle words to calm her down. The dress the woman wore was nothing more than a slip of thin material. Any normal person would be freezing, yet this woman didn't even shiver. Who is she?

"Mother is here, my beautiful Aurora" she sang to the baby. Mother? But I thought Lunaya was meant to be her mother. The woman looked up and met my curious gaze. I looked behind me to check that she wasn't looking at someone else, but there was no one else in here. As I turned back to her, she winked and looked back down at the child. A gust of wind picked up in the windowless room, wind that wasn't coming from me. I looked around but couldn't see the source. When I looked back to where the woman and the baby had been sitting, I frowned. The baby had grown. She was now at least two or three years older. I watched carefully as the child kept growing in the woman's arms. It was like watching a movie in fast forward. The more she grew, the more I recognised myself in the child. How could this be possible? It's not. It can't be right.

The young girl was now around nine or ten, and she was my spitting image. From her ratty hair to her pale skin, all the way down to the scars and markings on her flesh. She was me. I was her. But that's not right. I wasn't born, I was created. I wasn't stolen or kidnapped, I was bred in a lab by mad scientists. How could this be? All my life, they told me what I was created for, why they made me, and what my purpose for being alive was. Am I supposed to believe that they lied?

"Hello, daughter of mine" that same voice chimed, only it wasn't from the woman holding the child, it came from beside me. I snapped my eyes over my shoulder and jumped back. The woman was now standing next to me, but she was still sitting on the mattress as well. I flipped my head from the woman on the mattress to the woman standing in front of me, and back and forth again. She chuckled, the sound sounding more like gentle bells than a laugh.

"I am her, and she is me. Just as she is you, and you are her" she said rhythmically while waving to the young girl. So, she confirmed it then. The girl is me, well, a younger me, but me all the same.

"How are you standing there and sitting down at the same time?" I demanded of the woman. I have never seen anyone so perfectly beautiful. Her skin was like glimmering porcelain, and her pure white eyes were both haunting and peaceful at the same time.

"I am here now, she is but a memory of myself" she answered with a wave of her hand.

"And the child?" I asked.

"The child is my memory of you, many moons ago" she sang out effortlessly.

"How is this possible?" I demanded, not for a moment letting up on my defensive stance.

"I am capable of a great many things. As were you" she answered without hesitation. Something was scratching at the back of my mind, trying to get out, trying to make me remember, but I just couldn't reach it.

"What do you mean by were?" I asked. I didn't miss her very specific choice of wording, she may have thought she slipped it by me, but I don't miss much.

"Time and choice have a hand in all things. The choices we make and the choices of others, they all have a part to play in the final outcome".

Riddles and hidden meanings. I already hate this woman. People who speak like that infuriate me. She is no exception. I have a feeling, and an inkling as to who she may be, though I need to be sure before I act. I growled lowly and snarled. Then her first words came back to me again. I stood up a little straighter and frowned,

"You called me Daughter" I said quickly.

"I did" she said back.

"Why?"

"You are a product of your mother, who in turn is a product of me"

"That doesn't make any sense" I snapped.

"Your blood comes from my blood, your life force is my life force. You were nourished at my breast, born in my image, chosen by my hand" she blabbered on. More riddles and cryptic talk, of fucking course.

"What are you hiding?" I snapped at her.

"Hiding?" she asked. Her brow raised ever so slightly, yet it made not a single crease or line in her perfect porcelain skin.

"You think you can fool me with your bullshit talk. You think I don't see through your stupid riddles. Do you even know who I am?" I growled angrily. The woman paused for a moment, then smiled. If I thought she was beautiful before, it was nothing compared to how she looks when she smiles. And I wanted to rip that smile right off her beautiful face. Then, her smile turned, and her magnificent face held hints of sadness.

"Yes, I know who you are. Do you know who I am?".

I stared at her as she waited for me to answer her question. I could taste the answer on the tip of my tongue, but I didn't know what it was. I couldn't see the answer, or hear it, but I know that I know it, somehow. The itching in the back of my mind got worse. I wanted to bang the side of my head to make it stop, but it was persistent. I pressed my fingers to my temple and scrunched up my face. Why won't this stop.

"Let me help you" the woman said softly as she stepped towards me. I growled and held up my extended claws. She reached for my face, and I told myself to stop her. But my arms wouldn't move. Nothing would move, not my arms, legs, fingers, nothing. In that one split second, I was screaming inside my head to not let her touch me. But it was like my body and my head were separate entities, no longer working together, but against each other.

Her soft hand cupped my cheek, the coolness of her skin on mine made me shiver. It was like electric sparks rolled through my veins, reigniting a dying flame inside my body. A sensation I couldn't recognise swarmed my every thought and feeling. My head spun and it was like everything around me started to blur back into focus. I looked up at the woman, and I knew exactly who she is. I've looked upon her face a hundred times before. Selene. The Moon Goddess herself. I could see every time that she sat with me in this same exact frozen concrete room. I could still feel her warmth from every time she hugged me, held me, and soothed me. I could once again hear her calming words and whispers of encouragement. I could remember her and the stories she told me. She was here, with me, in this room. I remember it all now.

But I don't just remember her, I remember my father, the man from my dream. But I know now, it wasn't a dream, it was a memory. He was real, I remember him. I remember his strong and powerful frame and watching it wither away to skin and bones as the years passed. I remember his face and the love he held in his eyes when he looked at me. I remember the feel of his skin on those rare occasions we could be close enough to touch. I remember the sound of his voice when he told me not to give up. I can still hear his voice, I can hear the love and sorrow mixed into his words. I remember all the stories he told me about the incredible woman who gave birth to me, and about the special bond I shared with my identical twin sister. I remember all of it. How he spoke so sadly about missing them both, how he hoped he would see them again someday, and of course, that he wished I could meet them for myself. I've known all along about Zelena. How could I not? Our father spoke of her constantly. But how could I have forgotten about her, about him, about my mother. Why is it only now that I remember again?

With all these memories flooding back into my mind, like they never truly left, there is one thing that I see clearer than anything else. And that's the day it all changed, the day my father was taken from me. I can still see the fear on his face, it's as clear as day. I can feel his warm blood on my skin as it spurted over me when his throat was cut. I remember the dread and the sorrow, the helplessness I felt. I remember the pain in my chest as his lifeless body dropped to the cold floor. And I remember her. I remember how she did nothing to stop it, how she just let it happen. I remember how she let him die and then left me to suffer alone in this hellish place.

I lifted my gaze to meet hers, and anger filled me to the brim. She is the Moon Goddess. The creature I was trained to hate, to hunt, to kill. She is the reason for all of this. All the things that I had to endure, everything that I was forced to go through, the torture, the abuse, all of it. It was all because of her. She had the ability to save me, to take me away from this place, but she refused. I remember begging and pleading with her to help me. But it was the same answer every time. 'I cannot intervene'. What kind of bullshit is that.

"You!" I growled out and stepped back away from her touch. Her face remained the same but she sighed.

"You remember" she said with a nod.

"Oh, I remember. But why did I forget in the first place?" I demanded angrily.

"It was the only way" she answered after a second.

"Only way for what?" I grunted. My voice took on a low gravelly sound, the anger burning through my body was working its way into my words.

"For you to survive" she quipped with hesitation. I scoffed and began to pace the floor. I need to do something, to move around, busy myself before I tear her beautiful face apart.

"There was another way, you could have taken me away from this hellhole" I shouted as I paced the floor.

"You know I could not"

"That's bullshit!" I screamed and turned to face her.

"Aurora, as I told you before, as I told the both of you many times over, I could not interfere with the decisions of others".

I turned away from her quickly, thinking over the words she used. The both of us. Could she mean... Zee, or Zelena, whatever her name is. I saw it in my dream thingy, the abuse that she endured at the hands of the man she thought was her father. Which leads me to think, that if perhaps Selene was watching over her too, Zelena also pleaded for rescue. The only answer I need to know now is if she helped her whilst abandoning me.

"And yet, she got free?" I said venomously as I turned slowly back around to face her again. Selene looked back at me, not responding to my comment. The silence alone feels an awful lot like an answer. Anger was coursing through me, heating my blood and sending my heart thumping in my chest. After what felt like a long while, Selene sighed.

"In the end, she did. As did you" she said slowly.

"That's different" I snapped harshly.

"You and Zelena are two branches of the same tree. You have grown in different directions, each forging your own path and each suffering through different trials. But in the end, you are still, inarguably, made from the same material. Your differences are what make you, you. Even if you have come from the same roots. You cannot compare your trials to hers. You cannot compare her life to yours. Do you understand?".

Each word from her mouth only made me hate her more. My arms were shaking from the rage. My canines tingled, and my claws pressed against my fingertips. I fucking hate her. She can spin all the stories and tell all the lies she wants to, but the bottom line doesn't change. She left me to rot in that frozen hell. All the while, her precious Zee was living the good life. The life I should have had. She got a shiny new family, she got her own pack, she got friends and people that love her, and she got Gunner. What did I get? Scars, lies and betrayal. I should be the one with the pretty family. I should be the one with Gunner. I deserve it. Not her. She stole the life that was meant for me. And I am going to take it back.

"I'm going to kill you".

The whispered words slipped through my clenched teeth before I could stop them. But it felt better than good to say it out loud, so why not roll with it. I lifted my head slowly and glared at Selene with all the coldness in my heart.

"Maybe not today, maybe not tomorrow. But I swear to you, one day, I will kill you" I proclaimed as I stared her down. She looked back at me with no emotion on her perfect face. The room we were in moments ago was gone. We were no longer in the icebox that was my childhood confines. We were now in a white field, lined with white trees and white flowers. Selene was further away from me now too. She was halfway across the open field, a fair distance, but I could still see her clearly. I could probably even still reach her if I ran for it, with the added help from my power. She stood stoically with her hands clasped in front of her. Her hair and dress blew around her in the non-existent breeze. She stared back at me silently, with her face still void of any emotion.

"I swear it, with everything I am, your death will come by my hands" I hissed venomously. My entire body was trembling, rage coursing through my every atom, shaking me to the very core. Selene sighed heavily and unclasped her hands.

"I never wanted this for you" she said sternly and waved her long thin arm out in front of her. It was like I was hit with a wall of water. The air was forced from my lungs, and I could feel my body flying rapidly backwards. I hit the ground and got my breath back with one large gasp. I scrambled quickly to my feet and crashed into something behind me. A table, where did a table come from? My legs felt like jelly, I was panting hard and feeling disoriented.

I was able to catch myself on the edge of the table before I fell down again. That fucking bitch with her mystical bullshit. Now I will kill her slowly and painfully. To hell with waiting, I'm going to do it right fucking now. I glared up at Selene, but she was gone. Instead, Lunaya, Lupus, and the small woman were all looking down at me with worried expressions.

"Are you alright, Darling?" Lunaya blurted out and rushed to help me steady my feet. Lunaya, my mother. If you can even call her that. She's just the bitch that shat me out. I have no mother. I have lived without one my entire life, why change that now.

"Get away from me" I growled and slashed at her arm with my claws. She yelped in surprise and jumped back away from me. Lupus was quick to drag her behind his large protective frame, where the small woman fussed over the fresh wounds on her forearm.

"Easy" Lupus growled down at me. Lunaya pushed the woman's hands away and shoved past Lupus again,

"What did you see?" she asked me urgently. I curled my lip back and snarled. She knew. She knew all along who I was, what I was to her. By the anxious look on her face, she probably knew I would see Selene when she touched my forehead. That was her plan all along, wasn't it. She wanted to force me to remember her, remember Selene, Zelena, my father, all of them. Did she think that would change things? Did she expect me to weep and jump into her arms, happy to be reunited once again? If so, she was naive. She was straight up stupid. This new knowledge changes nothing.

"Aurora, what did you see?" Lunaya asked more sternly.

"I saw enough" I snorted angrily and pushed myself up off the ground.

"So, you know then? You know who I am?" she asked stepping toward me. I hissed, flashing my sharp teeth and stepped back. Lupus gripped her arm, forcing her to stop coming any closer. Her blood was dripping down her forearm from the slashes I gave her and creating a small puddle on the floor.

"Aurora?" she whispered gently. I hate that fucking name. That's not who I am. Maybe it was, once, when I was still in diapers and blind to the real world. But not anymore. They all made sure of that.

"Don't call me that" I growled,

"What's wrong, My Darling?" Lunaya asked sadly.

"I'm not your Darling"

"Don't you know, didn't she show you?"

"She showed me everything, I remember everything. I know who you are"

"I'm your mother"

"I have no mother, you are no one"

"Aurora, why..."

"You are nothing!" I shouted cutting her off.

"Aurora, please..." Lunaya tried to plead with me.

"DON'T CALL ME THAT!" I screamed at the top of my lungs. The sound of my voice reverberated through the kitchen. With it came the full force of my power. The wind swept Lunaya from her feet and over the benchtop behind her. The small woman skidded along the floor, knocking over a few bar stools as she went. Lupus ducked down low, and after digging his claws into the timber floor, he managed to only get dragged back a few feet. With the three of them down, I took my chance and ran from the kitchen. A large, heavy looking wooden door was to the right. Fingers crossed it's the way out. I pulled it open and ran out onto the porch. Once outside, it took me just a split second to make my next move. The area below looked to be the main village. It was busy with people, all of whom were completely unaware of my presence. I snapped my head around quickly, finding the closest section of bushland. I then jumped over the porch railing and continued to run to the left of the house, avoiding the heart of the village. The trees were closest in that direction, and the area seemed semi empty. I didn't hear any sounds of chase, and I didn't wait to look back to confirm it. I just ran.

After a few minutes of continuous running, I spotted a very large tree with thick, long branches that spanned high into the sky. I didn't slow down as I approached the wide trunk of the tree. Instead, using my power, I launched myself up into the air, landing halfway up the tree trunk. I dug my claws into the bark and climbed up to the first branch thick enough to shield me. I swung my leg over it and pressed my stomach and cheek to the rough bark of the tree. I was breathing heavily, huffing harshly through my nose. It wasn't because I was exhausted from the running, no, it was from my undying anger. I hate them. All of them. Lunaya, my so-called mother. Zelena, the doppelgänger bitch that stole my life. Gunner, the idiot who fell for her witchcraft. And especially Selene, the whore that started it all. As far as I'm concerned, Aurora is dead. She died along with her father ten years ago, back in Russia. I am who I have always been. I am Whiskey. I am the merchant of death. I will destroy these mutts, and every other mutt alive. The werewolf scum will be eradicated by my hand, every last one of them. I will be the ghost in the night that torments their every thought. I will find solace in being their worst nightmare. Before I take my final breath, I will rain down pain and destruction onto their perfectly happy little lives. They will know fear like never before. They will know agony, they will know torture. Those monsters will feel the kind of pain that they never knew was possible. And they will never see me coming.

Chapter Thirty-Five

Zelena

I stared at Elaine's face, trying to get my brain to digest the words. A message. What message, and from whom? My mind swam with possibilities. Could it be bout Aurora, or the prophecy? Could they know about the birth of the twins? Have they been attacked, or are they in trouble? Is there another danger on its way to ruin this brief and happy reunion? My eyes flicked to the Indian beauty sitting beside her, Venus, who stared back with a blank expression. I was quick to realise that I wasn't going to get anything out of her. I moved my gaze over to my mother. She looked worried, maybe even a little shaken. There's definitely something going on here. I could just make out a red line on her forehead, just below her hairline. From a distance, it looks like a partially healed wound. I dropped Gunner's hand and marched over to her, grabbing her face and pulling her head down so I could see it more clearly. I could still smell the blood on her, and the freshness of the mark told me this was recent, like very recent. Lunaya carefully patted my wrist and pulled it from her cheek.

"I'm fine, Hon" she said earnestly.

"What happened?" I demanded. When she didn't answer immediately, I looked over her shoulder to Alyse, who quickly dropped her head to avoid my piercing glare. I then looked over to where Lupus was sitting at the breakfast nook, he had a feral glower etched on his face. Panic was starting to rise in my stomach, making me feel uneasy. There was a thick tension suffocating the kitchen space, I could basically feel the silence crawling over my skin. They're keeping something from me, something big. Luna Eclipse wouldn't have come all this way for nothing. Plus, my mother is hurt, Lupus is angry, and no one is speaking. My skin was getting hot and my fingers were tingling. I could feel my power simmering at the surface. They all still see me as the weak and broken girl that I was when I came here. I'm not her anymore. I haven't been her for a while now. Why can't they see that? Why do they still not think I can handle stuff?

"What happened?" I asked again. There was much more power behind my voice that time. It almost sounded like it echoed. I could feel the words burst from my body, not just out of my mouth. I was honestly surprised with myself, I didn't even know I could make my voice sound like that. Gunner's arm snaked around my waist, startling me a little. He pulled me back flush against his body and buried his nose into the crook of my neck. The feel of his skin and the dance of sparks it immediately evoked instantly calmed me down again.

"Shoosh" his smooth voice called as his breath fanned over my skin. I closed my eyes and lay my head back against him, revelling in the calmness he gave me. My word, I have missed him. I cooled down, and all the worries just slipped away, like they were never there. When I opened my eyes again, they were all looking at me curiously. Roe, Lupus, Lunaya, Alyse, Elaine, Venus and even Smith, all with weird expressions on their faces.

"What?" I blurted out, suddenly feeling very self-conscious. Maybe I have something in my teeth, maybe Gunner and I still reek of sex.

"You, uh, you just went full..." Smith stumbled,

"Nothing, Sweet Girl, come have some food" Roe called, cutting off Smith and placing a plate on the bench. I looked at Smith for an answer, but he shook his head and shrugged. So, I shrugged back and walked over to the bench. Before I sat down, I noticed a new rug was placed in the centre of the kitchen.

"Nice rug" I said casually as I sat down. Roe growled lowly and shot an angry look at Lupus.

"Someone scratched the hardwood" she grunted. I turned to look at Lupus over my shoulder and caught him mid eyeroll. Gunner chuckled, lowering himself onto the stool next to me to take the plate his mother handed him. Like a choreographed routine,

Elaine, Venus, Alyse and Lunaya all turned to look at me at the exact same time. That same feeling of self-consciousness thrummed at my insides. What the heck is going on with everyone today? They are all acting extra weird.

"Alright, what's going on?" I said as I slammed my fork back down. I looked at each of their worried faces, waiting for them to answer, when I realised a face was missing.

"Wait, where's uh, where's Whiskey?" I asked. I hate calling her that, it sounds so vulgar. Granted, I only just found out that she existed, and that her name is Aurora. But I also feel as if I bonded with the name Aurora the moment I heard it. It's kind of like all the possible futures I imagined are connected to the girl with that name, not the girl named Whiskey.

"Well, something happened" Alyse started to say softly. I looked up again at the fading mark on my mother's forehead.

"What happened? Did she do that to you?" I asked urgently as I pointed to the soft pink line on Lunaya's caramel skin.

"Not intentionally" she fired back just as quickly and frowned at Alyse. I stood to my feet quickly, knocking over the stool with the back of my legs.

"She hurt you?" I shouted. After everything I saw from her past, all the things Selene showed me, and all the things that she didn't show me, I wasn't exactly surprised that she lashed out. Goddess knows I have my own issues, thanks to Hank, case and point, my role in his brutal death. I closed my eyes and shivered as the picture of his mangled body appeared back in my mind. It's the one thing that I regret. Not killing him per se, just the way in which I did it. I think that was my first step into letting the darkness into my heart.

"She was just upset and frightened. Remember how the first time I touched you, you passed out and saw Selene, and you remembered everything again?" Lunaya asked me quickly,

"Yeah, of course" I muttered back, confused as to the point of this topic.

"Well, I think I did the same thing to her" she said with a confident nod.

"But I watched you touch her before, when we were in the living room. Why didn't it work then?" I asked.

"I don't know, Darling. But this time, when she woke up again... well, when she came out of it, she was a little angry".

"She was more than angry" Lupus grumbled from his seat.

"She was upset, I think it was perfectly justified" Lunaya snapped at him.

"She sent you flying across the fucking room" Lupus growled back. I was a little caught off guard by his tone. He almost sounded protective, but when did Lupus become protective over Lunaya? I honestly thought that he didn't like her. Or maybe that was just Roe's influence. Anyway, irrelevant, Whiskey did what?

"I'm sorry, she did what now?" I blurted, my surprise evident in my voice.

"There's, um, Sweetheart, there's something we haven't told you yet" Roe said as she pulled her apron off. She quickly came to stand in front of me and took my hands.

"This is bad, huh?" I said softly. I could tell it was. It was written on each of their faces.

"It's not great, Zee" Smith mumbled. He had moved closer to where I was standing. They all did. It was like they had encircled me, but why. Are they assuming I'm going to lash out or something. Or is this all back to the whole 'they don't think I can handle it' thing.

"When Aurora got here" Lunaya started,

"Whiskey" I said, interrupting her,

"She wants to be called Whiskey" I reminded them all.

"Whiskey then" Lunaya grunted, obviously very displeased with using that name.

"Anyway, when she got here and you two collapsed"

"They did more than collapse" Smith snorted.

"Can I finish, please?" Lunaya snapped. Smith held up his hands in surrender and shrugged. I couldn't help the smirk that made its way onto my face. It's just like Smith to make a joke of a serious situation.

"Zelena, Honey, Whiskey has a marking" Roe blurted out quickly. Lunaya huffed at her and turned back to me. Sure, she has markings. I saw heaps of scars on her arms. So what?

"And?" I asked confused.

"She has the same mark as you" Lunaya clarified. She reached up and touched the back of my neck, right on the spot where the symbol of the Goddess sits. I stepped back slightly, just enough for Lunaya to drop her hand. Instinctively, I reached for my mark. As always, I couldn't physically feel it, but in a way, I could. No.

She couldn't mean Whiskey has the same symbol. That's not possible, is it? They all said there can only be one Triple Goddess at a time, and the next one comes decades after the last one dies. How could there be two of us?

"That's not possible, you said so yourself" I spat out quickly.

"There's a lot of impossibilities happening around here lately" Venus quipped sarcastically. Smith snorted and quickly covered his mouth and whispered a 'sorry'.

If she has a mark like me, that means she is a Triple Goddess too. Lupus said she sent Mum flying across the room. There is no way Whiskey could have done that, not without some kind of help. Say, perhaps, magical help.

"She has powers, doesn't she? That's how she hurt you?" I asked, looking up at my mum. She nodded her head and cupped my cheek.

"She does" she confirmed with a nod.

"It appears to be some kind of Aerokinesis" Roe jumped in.

"That's the air one, right?" I asked, looking at her. She nodded and stepped back into Lupus's arms.

"She may have tried to use one of her powers on me" Gunner said cautiously. I turned my gaze on him, and he felt the full force of my anger. She tried to hurt him, and he didn't tell me.

"When, how, and why are you only saying this now?" I growled lowly. I want to love my sister, but she hurt what's mine, and I can't forgive that.

"Relax, she wasn't able to, I used the shield" he said calmly as he stroked my cheek.

"You were able to access her power while you were away? How far did you go?" Lunaya asked quickly.

"Of course I could, she is still my Mate, no matter how far apart we may be, the bond doesn't break because of a little distance" he scoffed back.

"How far?" Lupus repeated Lunaya's question.

"In the mountains, near Kluane National Park, right next to the border" Gunner answered with an annoyed tone.

"Wow" Venus huffed quietly.

"Back to the part where my sister tried to hurt you" I grunted. He isn't getting out of this that easily.

"It was when we first met, she didn't know if I was a threat or not and attacked me on instinct" he started to explain.

"I had her pinned by the throat to stop her from spilling my guts with her fancy knives, and I'm not sure what happened next. All of a sudden, her eyes turned red, and then I couldn't breathe. It only took a second to realise her eyes glowed because she was using a power, like how Zelena's glow yellow"

"And yours glow silver" I interjected,

"Exactly. Well, once that hit, I lifted the shield, and it blocked the power. She seemed very surprised by that, and by me using the other powers. I don't think she knows what she is" Gunner continued as he looked down at the ground.

"Well, she sure as shit knows now" Lupus grunted and went to sit back down at the breakfast nook.

"Wait, so you're saying she is a Triple Goddess, like me. That's what is going on here, right? I'm not reading this all wrong?" I asked shaking my head and waving my arms.

"That's what we're saying" Lunaya said gently.

"It's the prophecy, Zee, remember?" Smith asked slowly. His voice was soft and gentle, like he was trying not to scare me. The prophecy, he said. It speaks of twins. But I thought it meant my twins.

"Where the moon is three, two will come" he said again, just as gently. I replayed that damn thing in my head a thousand times already, trying to figure out every possibility. I have gone over everything I possibly could. This, however, never crossed my mind. They said it wasn't possible. But now, I don't know. Maybe this is it, it's not about two babies, but two sisters. It's about two Goddesses.

"Two Triple Goddesses" I said out loud.

"We think so, yes" Roe answered. We all sat in silence for a moment. I was thanking the heavens that my babies were safe, they have no part in this prophecy. But there is still one blaring alarm in my mind. For peace to reign, only one can survive. But which one? Me? Or Whiskey?

"Only one can survive" I whispered softly. They heard me, I know they did, they're supernatural creatures for crying out loud. But only silence followed. I may be late to this new discovery, but clearly, each of them has already gone through the paces. They know what comes next.

Elaine cleared her throat, bringing our thoughts and attention back to the room.

"If I may, Goddess, the message" she said to me.

"Right, sorry" I answered shakily with a nod of my head.

"The hour is now. The transfer must be complete before the rise of the next full moon" she said sternly. I stared back at her blankly. I don't know what that means. She waited for me to speak, but I don't know what I'm meant to say, that makes no sense to me. I looked down at my feet and pondered the meaning. The transfer? Transfer of what exactly?

"That's it?" Gunner asked from over my shoulder.

"That is the message" she confirmed with a swift nod.

"What transfer?" Roe asked,

"What does that mean?" Gunner questioned.

"Goddess?" Elaine called for my attention. I lifted my gaze back to hers, still with no idea what the message meant.

"It is time" she whispered.

"Time for what?" I asked softly,

"Time for you to fulfil the prophecy"

"I don't know how to do that"

"But you do, my Goddess".

I swallowed hard and looked up at Gunner. He looked back at me, his eyes full of fear, with worry lines etched into his forehead. I can't deal with this right now. I don't know what to make of it. And I'm definitely not ready to accept where my mind is taking me. The horrible thoughts and ideas, the solutions, the dark things that my imagination is throwing at me. I don't want any part in it.

"Where is your guardian?" Elaine asked loudly. I looked up and quickly tossed my eyes around the kitchen. Usually, his presence is hard to miss, but I honestly hadn't noticed that he wasn't here.

"I, uh, I don't know" I mumbled.

"He is with Felix and a few others" Lupus rumbled,

"Why, and doing what?" I asked in return.

"They're out looking for your sister" Lupus answered. Shit, I got side-tracked. They were going to tell me where she was before we got into the whole two Triple Goddesses thing. Lupus grabbed Smith by the shoulder, and the two of them went and sat down at the table.

"And why are they looking for her, where did she go?" I asked sternly.

"Well, if we knew that, we wouldn't need to send Felix to find her" Smith quipped back with a sarcastic tone.

"Right" I grunted dumbly. I was a little surprised that Tobias went. I got the feeling he didn't like her. Maybe I read that wrong too. I'm getting everything wrong of late, apparently.

"And Tobias went too?" I asked Lupus from around Elaine's shoulder. He looked up and nodded back his response before going back to whispering with Smith.

"Huh" I huffed.

"What is it, Darling?" Roe asked, stepping closer,

"Nothing, I guess I was wrong" I shrugged.

"Wrong about what?" she questioned.

"I just got the sense that he didn't like her is all, he was acting funny when we woke up in the lounge room" I told her, remembering the way he glared at Whiskey. Roe looked over at Lupus and he nodded back at her. They were flashing, but about what. What's with all the secrets?

"What is it?" I asked, grabbing Roe's hand.

"Nothing, it can wait" she smiled weakly back at me.

"No, tell me now" I demanded.

"I'm sick to death of all the damn secrets. I'm not a scared little kid anymore, I can handle it" I said angrily, ending the sentence half yelling.

"We know you can, Sweet Girl" Roe cooed back,

"Then stop hiding important information from me and spill" I called. I took a deep breath and stared at Roe. I love her like she were my own mother. She has done so much for me, welcomed me without hesitation, and made me feel at home from the moment I arrived. She's a special kind of woman, Roe, one of a kind for sure. She nodded her head and sighed deeply.

"There was a uh... a moment, between Tobias and Whiskey" Roe answered sheepishly,

"What kind of moment?" I questioned. I felt overcome with jealousy. Tobias is mine. Granted, he's not my Mate, but he is my guardian, my friend. We have a special bond, and it hurts to think I could be replaced.

"At first, she looked to be spellbound by him. She gravitated towards him. They were staring at each other, growling and such" Lunaya chimed in.

"Growling? Like she threatened him?" I interrupted. I couldn't disguise the anger in my voice. Gunner's body pressed into my back and his hands gripped my hips hard. I don't have the mental capacity to stroke his male ego at the moment.

"Not aggressively. Honestly, my first thought was that they were True Mates" Roe chuckled as she stepped beside Lunaya. These two seem to have bonded. Which is good, they are both my mother now. But for a minute there, I was afraid Roe would never forgive Lunaya. I'm glad they are getting along, even if it does mean they can gang up against me.

"You said at first" I pushed, eyeing the two women.

"Yes, well, she may have been captivated by him, but he didn't seem so happy about her" Lunaya snipped.

"Not the reaction you'd expect from True Mates" Roe said, looking up at Lunaya. Lunaya rolled her eyes and crossed her arms over her chest.

"Why are you upset about that?" I asked, narrowing my eyes at my mother.

"It's nothing, just silly hopefulness" she waved me off and turned to walk away and sit at the breakfast nook with Smith and Lupus.

"Right" I said slowly as I watched her go. There's more going on there, I'll ask her about it later.

"Back to Tobias" I demanded, turning back to Roe.

"Why is he looking for her?" I questioned,

"Because she ran off" Roe answered sadly.

"Ran where?"

"Once she used her ability on us, and got us off our feet, Lupus, your mum and I were distracted. Only for a second, but just long enough for her to make a break for the door" Alyse answered softly.

"You were there too?" I asked her.

"Yes, just the four of us" Alyse confirmed,

"And she just left?"

"She was quite distraught after coming out of it. Whatever Selene showed her, it mustn't have been good".

"Yeah, that sounds about right. From what I saw at least, if she just got all those horrible memories back in one hit, I imagine she's going through a lot" I sighed sadly.

I know how she feels, more than anyone else could. When I remembered Selene again, I'd be lying if I said I wasn't angry. I'm not angry anymore, I understand why she did what she did. But in those first few moments, not so much. After seeing Whiskey yelling at Selene in the memory, I can imagine she holds a hell of a lot more anger than I do. But I still did some terrible things. What I did to Hank for example. Not to mention Galterio. But also Cole, Spartan, the pack members, our allies, all of these Weres died because of me. I have brought so much death to these people that I'm supposed to love and protect. What if I'm not the good guy in this story? What if I'm the villain and I just don't know it yet?

"They'll find her, Zelena, don't worry" my mother said soothingly. I looked up at her and felt my face relax. I must have been frowning, lost in my worried thoughts. However, it wasn't just that Whiskey ran away that I was worried about. I knew she'd come back, she has to, it's destined. What's playing on my mind is what happens after she comes back. The same line repeated in my head as I looked at my mother's face. For peace to reign, only one can survive. One of us is destined to die. One of her daughters. Either me, or Whiskey. But which one?

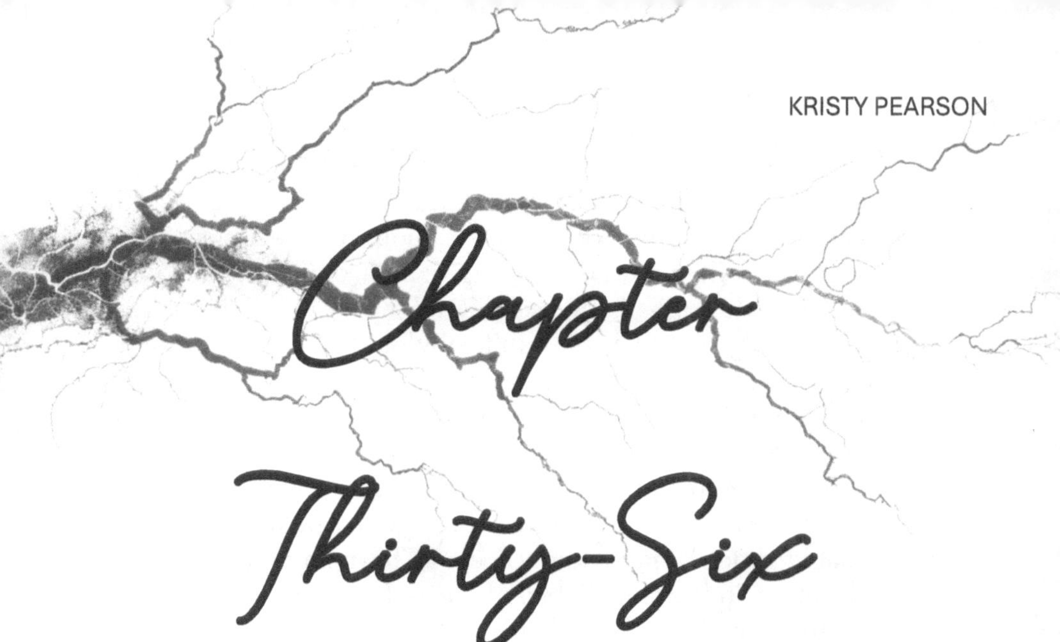

Chapter Thirty-Six

Zelena

Lunaya looked down at me with a warm and gentle smile. She is a good woman, I can see that now. I regret being so hard on her back when she told me the truth about who she really was. I was awful to her then. Even though that feels like a whole other lifetime ago now. I'm actually very lucky to have her. She's so strong and brave, and unbelievably resilient. But there is so much more to her, so much that she hides from everyone else around. She has a softness to her, there's a motherly glow in her eyes when she looks at me. Roe has the same kind of spark in her gaze too. I know I can trust her. In my heart, I know I can share with her anything and everything, including my deepest fears and insecurities. And she will take them on her shoulders like they were her own. That's just what we do. Because she's a mother. She's my mother. So, all of the daunting feelings filling my chest. The fears I have for the fast-approaching end to this prophecy. I know that I can share them all with her without the possibility of her judging me, or seeing me as weak. I know this because she would be carrying many of the same fears. She lost her family, her children. Then, by some miracle, she got them back again. Only for fate to turn around and take one, if not both, of her daughters away from her again. This Merry-Go-Round we call life sure can be a bitch.

I sighed heavily and opened my mouth to speak, to tell her that I was scared, to let her in on all the worries that were still plaguing me. But before I got the chance, a shiver ran up my spine, and loud voices echoed in my head. I closed my eyes, dropped my chin and grabbed at the sides of my face. Though covering my ears was futile, the voices weren't coming from around us, they were being flashed through. I hit the side of my head, thinking that would lower the volume. It didn't, obviously. A flash of anger rolled through me, and I quickly looked up at Gunner. He was shaking his head with his fingers to his temple, an angered look plastered across his face.

"Slow down, one at a time!" he shouted out loud for everyone in the room to hear, but the sound still resonated through the flash at the same time. I didn't know I could hear anyone else other than Gunner, Smith and Tobias. Unless I was in wolf form, of course. How was I hearing all this? I tried to focus on one voice at a time, which was hard, there were a lot of them.

"East border has been crossed"

"They're coming in from the south"

"They're not attacking"

"Intruders at the West"

"They've pushed through"

"All borders have been breached" one voice yelled through above the rest. It was Felix's voice, I was sure of that. But I thought he was out looking for Whiskey. More importantly, who has breached the borders?

"Gunner?" I asked worriedly. He looked back at me quickly before his voice rumbled through the flash.

"Perimeter breach! We are under attack, all fighters to the village!" he bellowed. There was so much dominance and power in his voice. I've heard him give an order before, and I've seen the way it can make a Were bend and obey. It's never had that kind of effect on me though, thankfully. Regardless, this was so much stronger than I'd heard from him before, it felt heavier almost. Smith and Lupus jumped to their feet and bounded out the door after Gunner. Elaine and Venus also jumped to their feet and looked at me in question. I paused before running after Gunner.

"Someone's crossed the borders" I told them quickly as I turned on my heels and ran out of the kitchen. I could hear their footsteps running after me, but it was quickly drowned out by the commotion coming from outside. Once on the porch, I could see our pack fighters coming in from all directions, surrounding the house and filtering through the village. Vicious growls, howls and shouting filled the cool night air. Gunner's large silver wolf stood at the bottom of the steps. A gust of air flew past me, as my mother's black and white wolf stood at Gunner's side. A sharp snap sounded behind me, followed by low growling. Both Elaine and Venus were now in wolf form too, standing on either side of Roe and Alyse. I went to turn back to the village, but quickly stopped. I did a double-take, looking over Alyse again. Her claws were out, and her fangs were fully extended. What surprised me though was that the shape of her face had changed slightly. It was almost like she had stopped mid change. Her nose and jaw had protruded forward, giving her the slightest appearance of a muzzle. Her brow had grown, and her eyebrows were bushy and wild. I've seen Were's in human form with their fangs out, but not with a partially morphed face. It was honestly a little frightening. Howls rang out through the trees, recapturing my attention. The sound felt unfamiliar somehow. I knew the howl didn't come from someone in Tri-Moon, I could feel it in my belly. But I also knew that it wasn't a battle cry. It was like I could understand it, like someone was speaking actual words. This is new, I can speak wolf now apparently. The howl sounded again, alerting us to their approach and informing us that they meant no harm. Soon, there were rows of wolves lining the front of the house and along the middle of the village. They aren't going into the woods to meet the intruders? Why are they letting them get this close to the house? There must already be fighters in the forest, Gunner knows what he's doing. But if they do manage to get this close to the village... I whipped around to Roe and Venus with wide frightened eyes,

"The twins" I whispered. My voice broke slightly with the fear warping into my words. We don't know who these Weres are, or what their intentions are. Do they really mean no harm, or is it just a ploy to get close enough to hurt us. Are they here for me, or for my babies, who knows. I can't take the risk of waiting to find out. The twins are the most important thing, and I will kill anyone who threatens their lives.

Roe nodded back to me in understanding and dashed back into the house. I turned my gaze on Venus, who paused. She looked over at Elaine's wolf, then out to the gathering fighters, before back to me. She was hesitating or unwilling to leave the possible fight.

"Please, I need you to protect my babies" I half pleaded half demanded of her. She growled lowly but was swiftly cut off by a bark from Elaine. With that, she nodded and rushed back into the house. Another howl called out, this time sounding much closer than the last one. I walked to the edge of the porch steps and looked out to the tree line. With the help of my Were eyes, I could make out the trunks of the trees lining the forest through the darkness. They'll be here any second. I took a deep breath and let the power roll over my skin, wrapping around my veins and filling my body. The tingling sparked at my fingertips, and the strength it gave me made me feel tall and powerful.

A figure emerged at the tree line, flanked by maybe a dozen wolves. It may have been dark, but I could still tell that I didn't recognise them. They stopped right at the fringe, where the trees end and the clearing begins. They made a point of coming far enough out of the forest to show us their numbers. I'm unsure if that was an intimidation tactic or a way to show they aren't hiding. Either way, I'm not counting anything out, not until we know their true motives. I stared at the tall man standing among the wolves. He was unusually tall, dark haired, and well built. For just a moment, the pit of my stomach dropped, as the similarities between him and Galterio crossed my mind. But no, that's not possible. Galterio is dead, I killed him. This isn't him. This man was taller and broader, his arms looked longer, and there was something feral about him. Galterio was horrid and delusional, no doubt, but he still carried a poshness with him, something that gave off upper class vibes. Not this man. Everything from the way he stood, to the way his arms hung bent at the sides of his body. This man screamed wild and dangerous.

It was only a few seconds until the small mystery group were surrounded by our pack fighters. Another second and they were being herded into the clearing. They didn't resist or even try to push back against the fighters. I don't like this, something feels off. This doesn't feel the same as the other visiting Weres, the ones that came searching out the Triple Goddess, or to bring offers of alliances. This feels like a trick. The annoyance of the unknown was eating away at the insides of my stomach. By the time the fighters got them to the centre of the village, right next to the fire pit, they were outnumbered three to one. I counted thirteen of them. Definitely more than a regular delegation or visiting group would bring.

My body was shaking in anger, with fear and uncertainty weaved in too. I shifted my eyes down to where Gunner's wolf was standing. His posture was rigid, and the wolves around him appeared to be cowering away from him somewhat. I could basically see the anger rolling through his shoulders. The fur on his back was sticking up and his ears were pulled right back. His low and ferocious growl rumbled around the entire village. I whipped my eyes back to the man standing with the other Weres and gasped. His long arms were spattered with thick hair. His hands were half morphed into claw like talons. His long legs were bent backwards at the knees, and sticking out of holes in his jeans were tufts of dark hair. He was barefoot, but his feet were half deformed. They were half human, half wolf, with sharp claws digging into the dirt. I trailed my eyes back up his thick and fur spattered body to his face. His ears were pointed at the top with more fur like hair covering them. His brow line was large and bushy and furrowed over dark and venomous eyes. His nose and mouth were protruding forward into a half snout. Just like Alyse, though this man's muzzle was more prominent. His fangs hung out the sides of his mouth with slobber dripping from the sharpest point. He was only half a wolf. How is this possible? Is this even normal?

"What is he?" I whispered to myself.

"A half-breed" Alyse answered. I looked at her quickly, I wasn't expecting an answer.

"Like me" she clarified.

"Almost" she added viciously as she flicked her eyes over my shoulder and back to the half-man. I stared at her blankly for a moment, considering the answer she just gave me. I didn't even know a half-breed was a thing. Does that mean one of his parents and Alyse's parents was human? Weird, I wonder if they're common.

Gunner's deep growl rumbled through the village. I turned back around to see that he had stepped forward and the half-man was smiling wickedly back at him. Gunner barked an order and the pack fighters closed in around them tighter, preparing for attack. They all seem so alert and cautious, which is good, they should be cautious. But why is there so much fear in the air? The smell of it is hard to ignore. As I looked around at our fighters and Gunner, I noticed the way they watched the half-man closely, like they were expecting him to do something. The half-man smirked at Gunner, and it hit me. It's so obvious now, I don't know how I could not have seen it before. Gunner and this man know each other, somehow.

The man held out his hands in surrender and chuckled. I watched as the hair slowly disappeared into his skin. His human frame got shorter and smaller as his limbs shrank. I watched in amazement as his face reverted back to that of a normal human. He was a little older, but fit and still somewhat scary looking. He lifted his gaze to me briefly and winked, an act I thought was very forward and familiar for someone I had never seen before. It didn't go unnoticed by Gunner, who stepped forward again and growled. The man turned his attention back to Gunner and relaxed his arms. He smiled widely, placed his hand on his chest and bowed ever so slightly.

"Alpha of Alphas" he spoke teasingly. The look on his face was not one of consideration, but more of mockery. He was baiting Gunner, pretending to show respect while actually mocking him. My whole body heated in anger, and the need to protect what's mine consumed me. And Alpha of Alphas, is he trying to be funny. Without even thinking about it, my body's instincts took over and a rumbling growl burst from my lips. The man's eyes quickly snapped to mine and he smirked.

"Still as feisty as ever, Tiny Goddess" he cooed cheekily. Still? If I didn't know any better, I'd say he is talking like he knows me. But I've never seen this person before.

"Excuse me?" I snapped angrily and stepped down onto the first step.

Enough Zelena, stay where you are

Gunner's angry voice filled my head. I looked down at his wolf. He was standing with his body facing the man, but his eyes were glancing back at me over his shoulder. The man laughed out with a forced laugh. It didn't sound even slightly genuine. He must be deranged or something. What other explanation would he have for coming onto pack land unannounced, then mocking the Alpha, winking at the Luna and then teasing and flirting? He is straight up bonkers.

"Are you fucking insane or what?" I scoffed in disbelief. His laughter cut off instantly, and he pierced me with a furious glare. "Remember what I told you last time, Tiny Goddess, remember what I said about the next time we cross paths" he growled lowly. I stared back at him blankly. What in the world is he talking about, we've never met before. I opened my mouth to question the statement, but was cut off by the sound of the deck creaking behind me. I turned my head to see Tobias's oversized black wolf stalking up behind me. His eyes were fixed on the man below, his hackles were standing tall, and his fur shook with the growl rumbling through his body. He stopped at my right side, with his shoulder and head hanging over my shoulder. He was standing so close that his fur tickled at the back of my neck. The man stood tall and glared up at Tobias. He tried to keep his face hard and emotionless, but I saw the concern flash through his eyes.

"Well, aren't you terrifying?" he laughed awkwardly. To which Tobias answered with a growl loud enough to vibrate the floorboards.

"Oh, so tough standing behind the Triple Goddess, aren't you?" he teased with a smirk. Tobias jumped down the steps in one leap, pushing me into the side railing as he went. I got back to my feet and rushed after him. The man had returned to his half-man, half-wolf form and was snarling at Tobias. Tobias had his teeth bared and was ready to attack. I stood at his side and readied myself, calling forward the magic until I could feel it just below the surface.

"ENOUGH!" Gunner bellowed and moved to stand between us all. My eyes fell on the scar on his shoulder, the remnants of the bullet wound from facing off against the hunters. It's the only mark to mar his otherwise perfect skin.

"State your business Doyle, before I throw you off my fucking land" he demanded of the man, who I now know as Doyle. Doyle dragged his ferocious gaze from Tobias and looked at Gunner. He flicked his eyes back to Tobias's wolf and then down to me. I can't not look at his deformed face. It's so unusual, I wonder how he does that, is it a half-breed thing? And is that why Alyse can do it too? He kept staring at me while his features returned to human shape. His lip curled up into a smirk as he gazed at me.

"Best stop frowning at me, Tiny Goddess. You might start to hurt my feelings. We wouldn't want anyone to think that you're not happy to see me again" he said in an overly sweet tone.

"Last warning, Doyle" Gunner growled and moved to block me from his sight. I am so confused right now. I don't know him, Doyle, I've never met him before, why would he keep suggesting otherwise. Oh, unless... He doesn't mean me. He met Whiskey, and now he thinks I'm Whiskey.

"Just getting reacquainted, young Alpha" Doyle shot back at Gunner with a frown. I saw Gunner's body visibly swell, his shoulders pulled back and his chest expanded. The muscles under his bare skin rippled with anger.

"State your business" Gunner demanded again. His voice held that same strength as before. I felt it wash over me like a cool breeze. The wolves standing around Doyle appeared to lower themselves, to the point that most of them had their bellies on the ground. Even some of our own pack fighters lowered themselves. Everyone felt the power of Gunner's voice, they all responded to the command within it. Even Doyle. His knees buckled and he dropped to one knee. He was fighting against it, the strain was visible on his face, but Gunner proved to be more powerful.

"I have information about some attacks on the smaller packs around Russia" Doyle blurted out quickly. He took a deep breath and huffed angrily. It's been so long since Daniel brought the news back about those attacks. Honestly, so much has happened since then that I forgot all about it.

"What information?" Gunner demanded again, not for a second dropping the aura of his influence. Doyle was trying to get up off the ground, but it looked like his legs were too heavy to lift himself. It was actually quite amusing to watch. I fought the grin wanting to spread across my face.

"We found a survivor" Doyle begrudgingly answered in a strained voice. The grin I was fighting against vanished immediately.

"A survivor?" I rushed out and jumped forward. I gripped Gunner's arm and stared down at Doyle, suddenly desperate for more information. Daniel told us that the packs had been fully wiped out, and no one was left alive. Could they really have a survivor? Tobias was right behind me, not giving an inch of space for anyone to get between us. Doyle looked up at me with a frown and nodded.

"Release me" he grunted turning to Gunner. Gunner, however, didn't relent. His swollen muscles twitched and his chest heaved with heavy breaths. I tapped his bicep and stroked my fingers gently across his forearm.

"Let him go, it's alright" I said softly. Gunner growled lowly, leaning over Doyle's kneeling stance. I felt Gunner's influence scratch against my skin as he pushed his power over Doyle harder. The wolves around him whimpered and pressed themselves into the dirt. Our own fighters lowered their bodies with bowed heads. Doyle struggled visibly against the power. His legs shook, and his knuckles turned white as he balled them tightly. He grunted and dropped down onto both his hands and knees, his head was bowed as he fought against the urge to lie flat on the ground. Then Doyle huffed deeply and collapsed into the dirt. The air around us felt ten times lighter. All of the wolves stopped whimpering and slowly started to rise up again. Gunner took a few steps backwards, wrapping his arm around my waist, and he dragged me further back with him. Doyle growled lowly and pushed himself up off the ground. He brushed the front of his shirt while glaring at Gunner with his lips curled back to expose his teeth.

"Playing dirty, Alpha" Doyle grumbled angrily.

"I'm not playing at all" Gunner fired back without missing a beat.

"The survivor" I interjected before these two went at each other again. Doyle turned his dark eyes in my direction but didn't respond. I felt the heat of his piercing gaze as it ran down my body and up again. When his eyes found mine again, I saw a hint of confusion hidden in them. I tilted my head to the side, waiting for his response. When he didn't answer, I asked again.

"You said you found a survivor. What happened to them?" I pushed him. He paused for a minute before answering,

"Who are you?" he asked in a half whisper, almost like he wasn't sure of the question.

"What?" I blanked. He was so sure that I was Whiskey, basically cocky about his assuredness. What changed?

"You're not the same she-wolf I..." he began, speaking slowly and softly, but he was quickly silenced by a rumbling growl from Gunner.

"Stop deflecting, where is the survivor?" he demanded as he stood in front of me. His voice echoed through the village, but then it hung in the air like a dark cloud instead of dissipating, pressing down on all of us. Gunner is different, I could feel it from the moment he returned. But it's so clear now, and I can't be the only one who can see and feel it. His power, the Alpha aura, everything about him and his energy feels so much bigger, stronger, and more potent now.

I leaned to the side to see around Gunner's body, just as Doyle growled and waved his hand above his head. He looked over his shoulder to the tree line, just as three human figures appeared between the trees. The three people walked slowly towards us through the clearing. Only once they were closer did I realise the man in the middle had his hands tied behind his back. He can't be the survivor, if he was, why was he tied up? Doyle grabbed the man by the shoulder and threw him at Gunner's feet.

"Your survivor" he spat angrily as he pushed him down. With his hands tied behind his back, the man rolled across the ground, landing roughly on his face and chest.

"What the fuck!" I growled and rushed forward to help the man back up. Gunner grabbed at my shoulder and Tobias growled for me to stop, but I ignored them both.

"Are you alright?" I asked gently as I took hold of his shoulders to help him off the ground. He stumbled to his knees and looked up at me with gratitude, but the moment his eyes found mine, that look was gone.

"Besomar" he screamed as he fell back and tried desperately to crawl away from me. I held my hands out in front of me and froze. The man scrambled across the dirt screaming and muttering in Russian. Doyle moved to stand behind the man, making it harder for him to scamper away any further. Gunner pulled me up and away from the terrified man and growled down at him. Tobias, Elaine, Lunaya, all of our fighters growled and moved in closer, ready to attack.

"Stop, stop" I screamed at them all and waved them back away. I whipped around to the man on the ground. He was staring up at me with so much fear on his face. His blond hair had a tinge of red through it. His pale skin was dirty and covered in bloody grazes and fresh bruises. He was thin, strong looking, but still quite slim. Above all, he had the most haunting blue eyes. Gunner's eyes are like pools of crystal blue water, this Weres eyes, however, were so clear and so blue I imagine I could see my reflection clearly in his iris. I was caught in place, struck by the brilliance of his eyes. I blinked a few times to regain my senses. The man was still muttering, saying the word' Besomar' over and over again.

"What's he saying?" I asked Doyle. He smirked and shrugged.

"Don't know, I don't speak Russian" he answered smartly. I looked up at Gunner in question. I don't know any Russian, and he has never said if he could speak it, so what do we do now.

"Mum understands Russian" he said softly. He turned his head to where his father's wolf stood and nodded, I assume to flash her to come outside. I quickly flashed Gunner before it was too late.

She's watching the twins, someone needs to protect them while he's here I flashed and nodded in Doyle's direction. Gunner turned back to Doyle and snarled as he answered my flash.

It's okay, I'll send Smith up

Alright

A second later Smith's wolf took off and into the house. A minute later Roe came marching out to where we were all congregated. She came to my side and squeezed my elbow. I offered her a small smile, to which she nodded back. We didn't need words to understand each other. She was telling me that the babies were okay with Smith and Venus, and I was thanking her for staying with them. She may very well be the perfect housewife and Luna. Whereas I resemble that of a newborn horse learning to run. Either way, I find that we are still quite similar, or at the very least compatible. I think that has had a huge impact on how quickly I was able to trust and confide in her.

The man hadn't stopped mumbling and scurrying across the ground. He was now pressed into Doyle's legs, who was clearly not happy with the close contact, as he kept kicking his legs out to force the man off again. Roe stepped forward slightly and looked down at him with a saddened expression.

"Who is this?" she asked while looking over his cowering body.

"We don't know yet" I answered her.

"Doyle claims to have found him" Gunner interjected.

"Doyle?" Roe questioned looking up at her son.

"The Alpha of the Melṇasirds" he replied with a nod of his head in Doyle's direction. Doyle stood watching the interaction, eyeing Roe hungrily from head to toe. I felt Roe's fear hit me as soon as she heard the name. She knows Doyle and his pack then, why else would she be so scared? I suppose it makes sense why everyone else was scared too. Whoever these Melnasirds are, they must be dangerous. I looked around at the other fighters. They all seemed very wary and overly cautious, none of them had eased out of their attack stance. They were all watching closely and waiting. Who is this guy and why is everyone so damn afraid of him.

"Oh" Roe stumbled out.

"Welcome, Alpha Doyle" she spoke somewhat slowly.

"Well, thank you, gorgeous" he answered with a wink, which of course earned a growl from Lupus's wolf.

"It's definitely my pleasure to meet you, Miss, we don't often come across a beauty such as yours" Doyle cooed seductively. He leaned forward and held out his hand, like he wanted to shake her hand or something. Gunner growled a warning and Doyle quickly stood up straight and pulled his hand back again.

"What's your name?" he asked her in a slightly firmer tone.

"I'm Romea, Alpha Gunner's mother" she answered with a hard voice. I could still smell her fear, but she was doing a good job of masking it.

"Is that so?" Doyle chuckled and looked up to Gunner, who nodded once.

"Such a shame" he chuckled and kicked the man off his leg once again. The man whimpered and kicked his legs to scamper away from me again. What the fuck did I do?

"Privet, tebe ne nuzhno boyat'sya" (Hello, you don't need to be afraid) Roe said gently as she knelt on the ground in front of the mumbling man. He snapped his head to Roe when she spoke, seeming somewhat surprised to hear her speak to him in his language.

"Besomar, eto Besomar" he stuttered out while quickly flicking his eyes up to me.

"Eta devushka?" (This girl?) Roe pointed up at me without turning away from the man. He nodded his head furiously.

"What is Besomar? Why does he keep saying that?" Gunner grumbled annoyed.

"Besomar is from a Russian folk tale, it's like a demon" Roe said over her shoulder to Gunner. A demon, is he saying he thinks I'm a demon? I knelt down beside Roe and smiled sweetly at the man.

"Derzhis' podal'she ubiytsa!" (Stay away murderer) he screamed and kicked out with his leg. He caught my knee with his foot, which made me lose my balance and fall on my backside. Gunner growled and launched forward, but Doyle was faster and reefed the man away. He held his whole body off the ground and in the air in front of his face. Doyle's face had morphed back into the half wolf again, and he roared ferociously at the terrified man.

"Stop, stop it" Roe yelled and tried to pry Doyle's hand from around the man's neck,

"He's just scared and confused, stop!" she yelled angrily. Doyle seemed amused by her anger, but that amusement faded when Lupus changed back into his human form and stormed through the small crowd. He pulled Roe away from Doyle and growled, to which Doyle dropped the man and growled back. This, of course got everyone else fired up too. Doyle's wolves were growling and barking, while our pack fighters were doing the same. All of them were moving in closer, constricting what little space we had left between us.

"Enough!" I screamed and jumped to my feet. I easily captured all of their attention. Just like how Gunner's had done, my voice held an aura of power and heaviness, making it impossible for any of them to ignore it. I stepped between them all and held my hands out. Summoning my power, I let the heaviness fill my body and then pushed them all apart. Doyle seemed surprised at the invisible force field that was forcing him back through the dirt. My pack already knew what was happening and began moving back on their own.

"Roe, will you please take this man away and speak with him privately. Find out who he is, where he came from and what he knows about the attacks" I demanded with a hard and echoed voice. It came out as an order, not a request. I didn't even know I could do that. It was like I used an Alpha command, but I'm not an Alpha. Roe nodded and immediately got the man to follow her towards a cabin at the back of the village. Lupus and two other pack fighters followed after them, along with two of Doyle's men.

"Alpha Doyle, we appreciate you bringing this man to us. However, if you continue to show aggression, you will be swiftly dealt with" I warned him. He growled lowly and tried to step forward, but I hadn't dropped the wall holding them back. His threatening action made me fill with anger, though it wasn't just mine, I could feel both Gunner's and Tobias's anger roll through me also. I twisted my hand and curled my power around his body. His whole body jerked and straightened as I squeezed my fingers, in turn increasing the pressure around his body. He struggled against the force, and panic quickly filled his eyes. His packmates looked on in confusion and fear as he seemingly struggled against nothing. Doyle growled and fought to free himself, but he obviously didn't know how pointless that was. I heard Gunner chuckle as he stepped up behind me, his hand resting softly on my lower back.

"You're not the scariest wolf around here, Alpha Doyle, you'd do good to remember that" Gunner said mischievously. He leaned down and pressed his lips to my cheek.

"Let him go, Sweetheart" he whispered before standing up again. I stayed put, glaring at Doyle the entire time.

"Don't test me again" I warned. Doyle frowned and tried to restrain the snarl from slipping past his lips.

"I apologise, my Goddess" he grunted out painfully. I squeezed tightly once more before dropping my hold. His whole body fell forward as he heaved in a lungful of air.

"And I thought the other you was the nasty one" he huffed and rubbed at his chest.

"The other me?" I questioned harshly.

"Yeah, the one from the forest with this guy" he nodded at Gunner.

"I'm not stupid, you're not the same she-wolf" he grunted.

"Whiskey?" I asked Gunner. He responded with one nod. I turned back to Doyle and growled. Not because I was mad, but because I was surprisingly consumed by jealousy.

"I suggest you try not to test that theory while you are on our pack lands, Alpha. I've been known to lose my temper on people who threaten the ones I love" I snarled down at the Alpha on his knees.

"So I've heard" Doyle replied teasingly. He looked up at me with a smirk, but once our eyes met, he dropped the cocky look on his face. I guess I was showing more resting bitch face than I thought I was. His face blanked and his skin appeared to pale.

"Of course, my Goddess, it won't happen again" he pledged with a bow of his head. If I'm being honest, I expected much more of a fight from Alpha Doyle, he doesn't seem like the type to back down to anyone willingly.

"Head inside, Love, I'll get Mum to meet us in my office when she's done" Gunner said as he pushed a loose tendril of hair behind my ear. I looked over at the group of uninvited Weres before nodding in agreement. I would usually argue about being kept out of this sort of important proceedings. But I wanted to check on the twins anyway. He leaned down and pressed his lips to mine, subtly flicking his tongue against my bottom lip before standing up straight again.

"I'll let you know when we're on the way" he said quickly. He turned to the assembly behind us, snapped his fingers in the air and waved a hand at the group of intruders. The pack fighters converged on the visiting Weres, rounding them into a small circle and ushering them towards the edge of the village. I'll leave Gunner to it, he doesn't need my help. As I whirled around quickly, Tobias was still standing right behind me, making me smack my face into his big furry chest. I gripped hold of the long fur to steady my balance. The aura emanating from him was undeniable. I twirled my fingers through the soft thick fur as I looked over his furious gaze.

"What's up?" I asked him,

I don't like this, they shouldn't be here

"I can tell, but why though?"

It's not right what he does, what his pack does

"You know him then? Doyle and his pack?"

Everyone knows them

"Well, I don't"

You will

"That's awfully cryptic of you, Mighty Guardian" I teased and pulled on his fur. He huffed and nudged me with his giant head.

Come

Tobias ordered and pushed me towards the house with his nose. I know better than to argue with Tobias, especially when he's in a mood, and there is definitely something eating at him.

Chapter Thirty-Seven

Zelena

Once back at the house, I bounded up the stairs to the nursery. This whole situation has me feeling all kinds of paranoid. I know Smith would flash if something was wrong, but that doesn't settle my overactive imagination. I rushed to push open the door and stepped into the darkness of the baby's room. I paused in the doorway and listened for their gentle little snores filling the silence. I flicked on the lamp by the door and both Venus and Smith stared at me with wide surprised and fearful eyes. They were sitting side by side on the floor, both of them leaning against the wall. They each pulled a weird look of desperation and silently waved their hands in front of them, motioning for me to turn the light off again. But it was too late. Little G. stirred awake and her soft cries filled the room. I chuckled at the exhausted look on both Smith and Venus's faces as they slumped back against the wall in unison.

"We just got her back to sleep" Smith grumbled as he pushed himself off the floor. He held his hand out for Venus, who hesitated for a moment before taking it and letting him pull her up.

"She's a screamer huh?" Venus scoffed down at the little pink bundle.

"You have no idea" I huffed with joy as I scooped her up out of the bassinet. I held her up to my face and smiled widely,

"Hello, my little princess. Have you been torturing poor Uncle Smith?" I cooed at her with my lips puckered. Her small cries softened, and her bottom lip popped right out. She is just too sweet, how did I ever make something so perfectly beautiful.

"Aww, my baby girl" I laughed and pulled her to my chest. I rocked her in my arms as she gripped my finger. Venus was standing at my side smiling down at G. while Smith was standing over B.'s bassinet, checking that we hadn't woken him. Which would be unlikely, that boy would sleep through a hurricane. I felt the atmosphere of the room change as soon as Tobias stepped through the door. Venus took a small step back away from where she was looking down at G. in my arms. To anyone else, it would have been nothing, but I know she did it intentionally. Tobias scares and intimidates a lot of people these days. He has done ever since the battle with Origin Wolf. Not me of course, but still, he makes a lot of people very uncomfortable.

"Shall we leave you to it then?" Smith asked subtlety.

"I got it from here, thanks, Smith. And you too, Venus. Really, thank you" I said with a smile up at the two of them. Smith nodded and walked up behind Venus, then gently ushered her out of the room. The door closed with a thud and Tobias marched over to me.

"What did they do to my baby girl?" he grumbled and gently plucked G. from my arms. Her mood changed right away, she went from making soft whines and grumbles, to happy coos and snorts. Favouritism, that's what it is. I snorted in annoyance and slid my finger back into her chubby hand.

"Sure, perk up for him but not for me. I see how it is" I pretended to scold her as I shook her little hand.

"Don't be jealous, she can't help it. After all, I am ridiculously good looking, so of course she adores me more" Tobias teased as he pulled faces at G. It's still weird to see this mammoth of a man turn to mush around a little baby. I don't think anyone else has gotten the chance to see this side of Tobias. The gentle, sweet, caring and loveable side. It's reserved for just me and the babies, but I ain't mad at it though. I feel protective over my bond with Tobias, almost possessive even. I can't even think about him with a Mate of his own. Not because I have romantic feelings for him, but because I wouldn't want to share his attention with anyone else. I can honestly say that the only person I'd ever be completely okay sharing him with is G. or B. I smiled up at my giant guardian and was awed.

"She's got you whipped" I chuckled and turned to plonk down on the rocking chair.

"Yeah, she does" he answered without looking away from her. I watched in silence as Tobias slowly paced around the room, bouncing G. in his arms, gently convincing her to fall back to sleep. After a short while, she was out like a light again. Tobias carefully laid her back in the bassinet and came over to where I stayed seated in the rocking chair. He slumped his large body on the floor next to the chair and lay down on the carpet. He crossed his ankles and interlocked his fingers together, resting his hands on his chest. The room was deathly silent, except for the sound of the baby's snores and Tobias's deep breathing. He didn't speak, he just closed his eyes and lay perfectly still. I rocked slowly back and forth on the chair while watching Tobias's closed eyes. I could see them moving rapidly behind his eyelids. If he had fallen asleep, he was having one hell of a dream. If he is still awake, his thoughts must be going a thousand miles a minute. I remember the cheeky way he looked at me that first time we met. His eyes held so much hopefulness and excitement. Over time that look has changed into one of deep love and respect. Before the twins, he was the other half of my world. Then when Gunner left, he was my everything, my true pillar of strength. I can still feel his love and devotion, which has never faltered. But he has been becoming distant these past few weeks. Not physically, of course, he is always just behind me. But emotionally, he's withdrawn. He's holding something back, or at least keeping something from me.

"What's going on?" I asked in a whisper. I waited silently for an answer, and it took a minute for him to respond.

"Nothing" he said with a deep huff.

"You're lying to me" I whispered back. When he didn't respond, I slid down off the rocking chair and crawled across the floor. I laid down beside him and turned onto my side, perching my head up on my hand. I looked over his face as we lay together in silence. I trailed my eyes over his smooth chocolate skin, along the curve of his nose and to his plump lips. I watched his chest rise and fall with each breath. And still, he didn't say anything. I sighed and shifted closer, lifting his hands I moved my body under them to lay myself half over his chest with his arms around my back. I rested my ear on the centre of his chest and listened to the sound of his thumping heart. It was peaceful, melodic even. To the point, I thought it might lull me to sleep.

My mind went back to the prophecy, to what it could mean for me and my mysterious sister. One of us is going to die, that's a given. But how do we know which one is the right one, which one will bring destruction, and which one will bring prosperity? Selfishly, I don't want to be the one to die. I have so much to live for now. I finally have a family of my own, and I want to be with them. Plus, I'm a mother now, my children need me. I can't be the one, I have too much holding me to this world. But what does that say about Whiskey, am I saying that she doesn't deserve to live? Of course, she does. She deserves the chance to make a family of her own, as I did. She should be allowed to find happiness and peace, if she hasn't already. How could I live, knowing that it was only granted by her death. How could I allow my sister to die in my stead. But also, how could I leave my children, my Love, and my new family. I could never just abandon them. Neither outcome is acceptable, and I need to find a loophole. However impossible it may be.

I opened my eyes and became aware of the tingles dancing across my body. Wave after wave of gentle electricity brushing through my veins. I lifted my head and looked down to where Tobias's hands were resting on my lower back. I could feel the energy slipping from his skin, I could see the pulsating waves dancing over us.

"What are you doing?" I asked him quietly.

"I can feel you stressing" he answered just as softly,

"I'm making you feel better" he whispered. I laid back down, resting my chin on my hands and stared at his closed eyes. Tobias gently rubbed his hands up and down my back. I sighed and laid my arms out, making me lay flat on his chest.

"That feels nice" I groaned, my voice sounded like a purr,

"It feels like pins and needles, but in a good way" I whispered. I let my body go limp in his arms and simply enjoyed the weird feeling. Although this is one of the new super cool guardian bond perks, it's still amazing. I was starting to feel sleepy, but also wired at the same time. My body was full of energy and ready to roll, my brain however was past the point of exhaustion. I pushed myself up off Tobias's chest and sat on the floor beside him. I stretched my arms up and stifled the groan that wanted to scream out of my mouth.

"How do you do that?" I asked as I rolled my neck.

"Do what?" he asked back.

"Make me feel so alive and wired, even when I'm ready to slip away and sleep for the next few days?". Tobias sat up and crossed his large legs in front of him.

"It's what I was chosen for" he said blankly.

"What? You were chosen to keep my energy levels up?" I scoffed with a sarcastic laugh. I quickly covered my mouth and kneeled up to look over the top of the two bassinets. Both B. and G. were still fast asleep, thankfully. I sat back down and turned back to Tobias with a silly grin. He was staring at me with such a stern and serious look on his face, it made my smile melt away instantly.

"What?" I asked worriedly.

"You're stronger than you give yourself credit for" he said in a hushed whisper.

"Uh... Thanks?" I replied awkwardly, feeling a little caught off guard by the sudden shift in the seriousness of the conversation.

"I mean it, Zelena. You have more strength than you know, and you are powerful beyond belief. You're going to change this world for the better before you're done with it".

"I appreciate all the hype, but why are you talking like this?"

"Like what?"

"Like you're saying goodbye". Tobias dropped his head and looked at his hands on his knees. My stomach dropped and fear filled my belly.

"Are you?" I asked with a shaky voice.

"Am I what?" he replied, lifting his head to stare at me again.

"Are you leaving?".

I stared into his deep dark eyes, waiting for an answer that didn't come. The longer he sat quietly, the more fear built up inside me, until I was at the point that quivers were rolling down my arms and legs.

"Tobias?" I asked with a squeak. He leaned forward and wrapped his hand around mine.

"You and I will never be apart, not truly" he said gently. A tear ran down my cheek and he lifted his hand to wipe it away with his thumb.

"You're just, you're my rock, you know. I don't know what I'd do without you" I sniffled as more tears started to fall. I don't even know why I'm crying. I was feeling so energetic one second ago, now I'm overflowing with emotions. I think I need to have a rest. Tobias smiled and held his arms open. I chuckled softly and crawled into his lap, just like a child would with their parent. He wrapped his giant arms around my small frame, cocooning me against him. I sniffed and pressed my face into his chest. I love the way he smells. It relaxes me like nothing else. Gunner's scent gets my heart racing, Tobias's scent keeps me cool. They play off each other perfectly.

"Why are you crying?" Tobias chuckled quietly.

"I don't know" I blubbered out. He laughed and squeezed me tighter.

"Poor little puppy, so full of emotions" he teased and nuzzled his nose into the top of my head.

"Shut up" I whined and pushed out of his arms.

"Let's change the subject" I offered and wiped my nose with the back of my hand.

"Alrighty, go on then" he smiled teasingly.

"Tell me who the Meļņasirds are and why everyone was so scared of them" I said without hesitating. The smile left his face and deep frown lines took its place. His lips curled back, and a low growl sounded in his throat.

"They're dirty, rotten, money hungry scoundrels. They will do anything for a bit of cash, and they have no honour" he snarled in a harsh whisper. Well, that's some rough commentary from a usually quiet Were, consider my interests peaked.

"Wow, okay. Like what?" I asked gently.

"They kill mercilessly. And they have no issues with killing humans" he snapped back. His voice was still quiet, but I could still hear the anger and venom beneath it.

"I don't understand, I've killed humans too" I said slowly,

"No, you killed hunters, they don't count. Doyle and his pack of mutts will kill innocent humans if there's enough money in it for them".

"They get paid to kill people, like some kind of werewolf assassins?" I asked shocked.

"Yes" Tobias growled.

"Who pays them though?"

"Anyone from an Alpha of a competing pack to high-ranking government officials. There have been whispers that they have cleared small human villages or fishing towns to make way for industrial shit. They have even killed off an entire family, all so that their land could be bought for cheap by some big corporation. There's no limit to what that mongrel, Doye, would do" he snarled out the last part.

I had to pause to consider what Tobias was telling me. This is totally new to everything else I have heard about so far. I know that packs fight with each other. Whether it be over territory, money, pack members, or whatever. I understand that things can get heated, considering our possessive and compulsive instincts. But I never would have thought that an Alpha would go as far as hiring assassins. Not just Alpha's but people in the government, human people. That either means that there are regular humans that know about our existence, or there are Weres in the government, or both. Why were Doyle and his pack in Russia though? That was the only place where the packs were being attacked, that we know of anyway. Could it have been targeted, is it political based intentions. Were human homes involved in the attacks, or just Weres. This is a lot.

"That's intense" I huffed and rubbed my temple. I don't know what else to say.

"Why do you think they were in Russia? Do you really think they were just investigating the attacks?" I asked him quietly.

"I don't know. But I do know that Doyle doesn't do anything for free. Someone paid him to look into those attacks. If that's what he was truly doing" he answered. I could basically hear the clogs turning inside his head. He is thinking a lot about this.

"But why would Doyle bring the survivor here? We didn't pay him" I exclaimed.

"I'm still working on that part. It doesn't make sense yet" he said slowly, his voice slowly fading off with the last word.

It's scary, I get it now. I'm not scared of Doyle, that fool doesn't scare me. I am afraid of who is paying his bills though. Could Tobias be right, could he have come here because someone told him to. If so, then we could all be in danger. We need to find out why he was really in Russia, and who sent him here. That must be our top priority. We need to know what kind of danger he presents, to the babies, to the pack, to Gunner, to all of us.

"You're panicking" Tobias whispered.

"Of course, I'm fucking panicking. They could be here to hurt my children" I growled lowly. Tobias took my hand and held it to his cheek.

"No one will ever hurt those children, I swear it" he said convincingly. I took a deep breath and let it out slowly. It's hard not to believe him. I know he will kill for my babies, he would die for them too, as I would. I felt the wave of calm wash over me, along with the sparks of energy tickling across my skin. I could see the aura around my fingers where the back of my hand sat against his face. I turned my hand around and cupped his cheek. He held his other hand over mine, covering it completely.

"I do love you, you know that right?" I said softly.

"I know, Little One, I love you as well" he replied. His voice was still low and quiet, though it held an aspect of sadness.

"What would I do without you?" I smiled.

"You will do what you always do. You'll survive" he answered without missing a beat. He tapped my hand and smiled over at me.

"Come on, you need to try and get some sleep" he cooed quietly. Tobias uncurled his legs and went to stand up, but before he was fully upright, it looked like he tripped and went stumbling forward. I caught his shoulders, but he is a giant and I am tiny. It was like a gerbil trying to stop a walrus, absolutely futile. Tobias's body kept falling forward, forcing me back onto my butt and then onto my back, making my head thump on the carpet. Tobias was half lying, half kneeling over the top of me. He was holding his upper body off me with one hand and grabbing at his temple with the other.

"Holy shit, are you alright?" I questioned urgently. I can't believe we didn't just wake the babies with the sound of my head hitting the floor. When Tobias didn't answer, I stared up at his face. His eyes were closed, and his face held a pained expression. I tapped his chest and quickly grabbed at his cheeks, trying to make him look at me.

"Tobias? Tobias, what's going on? Are you okay?" I repeated his name over and over with no answer. I dragged my body out from under him and then tried to pull him up by the arm.

"Tobias, what the fuck?" I whisper yelled. When he still didn't answer I started to panic.

Smith! Smith help. Tobias needs help!

I yelled through the flash. Smith's thunderous footsteps came up the steps just seconds later. He barged through the door and stood in the doorway for a second. He looked between me holding Tobias's arm and Tobias still kneeling on the ground, before he quickly rushed over to Tobias's side. Smith pulled him up much easier than I could have. He moved to stand in front of Tobias, still seeming to hold up most of his body weight. Tobias swayed on his feet, still holding his head with his eyes pressed closed tightly.

"Hey, Buddy. Tobias? Are you with us mate?" Smith coaxed but got no response. G. grumbled and groaned as she stirred.

"In the hall, quickly" I whispered harshly and began shoving Tobias and Smith towards the door. It looked like Smith was managing with Tobias alright as they shuffled out into the hallway. I looked back at G. to make sure she was still asleep, then carefully pulled the door closed. Smith had Tobias leaning on the wall beside the door while he was holding him up by the chest.

"Tobias, what's going on buddy, speak to me" Smith called out as he snapped his fingers in front of his face.

"What happened?" Smith asked over his shoulder at me,

"I don't know, it looked like he tripped over but then he was like this" I answered, waving my hands at Tobias. Smith turned back to Tobias and gently tapped his cheek. He then tried to lift his eyelid, but that didn't work either.

"What were you guys doing?" Smith questioned while getting up close and personal to Tobias's face.

"We were just talking. I don't know what's going on" I said urgently. My voice broke at the end, and I felt the tears welling in my eyes.

"Come on Tobias. You can't be a very good Guardian if you're freaking out your charge" Smith teased and shook his shoulders. Tobias's eyes flew open and a low growl bubbled from the back of his throat. He pushed Smith back and stood up straight.

"Whoa, I was just kidding" Smith forced a chuckle. He stepped back to my side and pulled me back another step with his arm over my stomach. Tobias moved his eyes to me, and his angry face softened.

"Sorry, I'm okay" he mumbled and stepped toward me. Smith pulled us back another step so that we were both now up against the other wall.

"You sure?" Smith asked cautiously as he moved subtly to place himself more in front of me. Tobias flicked his eyes to Smith and nodded his head once.

"What the fuck Tobias, you scared the shit out of me" I scolded as I wiped the fresh tears from my cheeks,

"I'm sorry Little Goddess, I didn't mean to" he said gently and held his hand out for me. I looked up at Smith and he slowly put his arm down, allowing me to go past. I took Tobias's hand and he pulled me into his chest for a hug.

"What was that?" I asked as I swallowed a small sob. He patted down my hair and hummed.

"I just stood up too fast" he blatantly lied. I could hear and feel it. He must know that I could tell he was lying, he's not that stupid. I stepped out of his arms and glared up at him. He didn't say anything or admit that he lied, he just stared back at me.

"Tobias" I said harshly,

"It's nothing Zee, I promise" he said earnestly. I pulled my bottom lip between my teeth and hummed unconvinced.

"Smith will get you to bed, I need to go... get a drink" Tobias said slowly while flicking his eyes up to Smith.

"I can get myself to bed, I'm not three years old" I snapped.

"I know that" he went to argue.

"Do you though, because you seem to be under the impression that I'm a child that needs coddling" I scolded angrily, interrupting his almost excuse.

"Zee, it's not that" he went to argue again.

"Forget about it, just go get your drink" I said sarcastically while doing air quotes with the word drink. I wasn't in the mood to pretend that I'm not pissed. Tobias sighed and rubbed his hand down his face. I watched, steaming mad, as he looked up at Smith. If it was at all possible under his dark skin, he looked pale. As mad as I am, I wasn't blind to the concern I felt circling around my stomach.

"She's fine" Smith said confidently, any sign of amusement and joking was gone from his tone. Tobias spared me one last glance before he headed off down the stairs. I almost asked him to wait, I wanted to check if he was okay. I may be angry, but that doesn't make me not care about his wellbeing. I went to step forward, to follow after him, but Smith took my hand, stopping me before I could. After he was gone and I heard the front door open and close behind him, I turned to Smith.

"What do you know?" I asked accusingly.

"No more than you" he answered back instantly. I could tell he wasn't lying. I honestly don't think that Smith has ever lied to me, that's one of the reasons I trust him so explicitly.

"There's something up with him" I said more so to myself than Smith. I dropped my hand and rubbed my hands down the outside of my thighs.

"He's acting weird, that's for sure. Well, weirder than usual anyway" Smith answered a little sarcastically. I turned to look in the direction Tobias just walked. I stared at the stairs and scratched the back of my neck. I need to find out what's going on. He lied to me, right to my face, and it wasn't even a good lie. Why would he hide something from me, after everything that has happened. It hurts. Tobias is supposed to be my rock, my anchor, my calm in the storm. Why would he need to lie about anything. Fuck it. I'm going to get to the bottom of this, I won't stop until I figure it out. Tobias can lie and pretend all he wants, but I can see right through him.

Chapter Thirty-Eight

Whiskey

Night fell quickly, and once the sun was gone from the sky the air turned. It was getting cold, winter was fast approaching. With any luck, these beasts won't live long enough to see the first snow hit the ground. In the few hours I've been out here, no one has come. I don't even know if I'm still on pack land. I caught sight of some patrol wolves through the trees, but they were upwind from my tree and didn't catch my scent. These guys either have some serious security concerns, or they were looking for something. Maybe they were looking for me. I mean, I did lash out and expose my power, a dumb move on my part. But why would they care if I left, they've clearly never cared about me before, so why start now.

I'm such a fool. All the lies and all the bullshit. Everything I thought I knew. It was all a lie. And I fell for it, hook line and sinker. I'm so dumb. I'm not fucking special, I'm just like every other mangy mutt out there. The annoyance crawled over my skin, making me itch with need. I know what I need, and I know nothing else will make this feeling go away. It's the only thing that makes it better. But like a stupid, overly trusting, lust filled moron, I left my bag in Gunner's car. I can't risk going back there yet, it's too soon. I'll have to come up with something else. I turned myself around on the branch and looked up into the tree. I spotted what I needed and climbed up a few branches to reach it. I snapped the fresh branch sprout from the trunk and climbed back down to my hiding spot. I peeled the top layer of bark off the stem until I was left with a long thin and flexible piece of wood. I shook off my thin jacket and pulled my shirt over my head. After I unclipped my bra, my naked back was exposed to the evening air. I held one end of the branch and lifted my arm up to my shoulder, laying the other end of the branch against my back. I flicked my wrist as hard as I could, the branch flew out and quickly whipped back against my bare skin. The sting was nice, but it wasn't enough. I flicked my wrist again, and another whip slapped against my back. And another, and another, and another. My back was throbbing as I took a deep breath, but the itch didn't go away. This isn't working. I held my forearm out on my lap and snapped the branch across the softest part of the skin. That felt better, but I still need more. I whipped the branch across my skin countless more times. Hitting harder and harder each time. The skin on my forearm had split open and blood was seeping down my arm and onto my jeans. The pain coursed through my veins, my breathing slowed and the thumping of my heart in my chest was all I could hear. The itch dissipated and a cold relaxed feeling swept over me. Keeping my legs wrapped around the branch I was sitting on, I laid back and rested my head down. The sting of the open cuts throbbed through me, I could already feel the skin stitching itself back together again. The sting, the pain, it reminded me I was still here, I was still alive, I could still feel. I took a deep breath and my body relaxed into the branch. That's better. I can always find calmness in the throbbing feeling of the aching pain. It's my happy place.

I was stirred awake by the sound of a twig snapping. It was close, very close. I carefully rolled onto my belly and scanned my eyes through the trees. My eyesight was perfect, even in the dark. That was something I always attributed to how the hunters made me, but that isn't the case anymore is it. No, it's just how I am. Perhaps how all normal Werewolves are. Normal. That's not something I ever considered myself before. It makes me sick to my stomach to think of myself that way now. I'll make sure that I'm no ordinary dog, I'll be the worst fucking beast they ever encountered.

Back on the ground, not one hundred metres from me, was the largest wolf I have ever seen. It had long scruffy fur as black as the night. Its tail was almost as long as its body. The monster stood taller than any human and was as built as a small brick house. It was beyond huge. I've killed plenty of big scary looking beasts, but this one was on a whole other calibre. I watched in silence as it sniffed at the ground, pushing the brush around with its snout. Was this one of Gunner's? Surely it couldn't be. Any wolf of that size would be an Alpha of its own pack. Size and strength are all that matter to these big dumb creatures. And this beast was definitely top of both those categories. It lifted its head and sniffed into the air. I pressed my body into the tree branch, trying to make myself become part of the tree. I can't take on this giant bare knuckled, I need weapons, I need my blades. If it catches me, I'm toast. The wolf turned its head and seemed to be looking right at me. Something felt different with this wolf, familiar even. I got a sense of danger wash through me, followed quickly by an odd calmness. I watched on as it stood perfectly still, staring in my direction.

The wolf snapped his head to the left and shifted its feet. Something else has captured its attention now. It lowered its body and tapped its front paws as its ears pulled back. I could hear the rumble of its growl from all the way over here. It was mad. I pity whoever crosses this dog. Without warning, it dashed forward and was gone through the trees before I could comprehend what happened. One thing I did understand though, it was fucking fast for its size. A few seconds later the sounds of heavy footsteps against the earth filtered through the forest. That must be what the big wolf heard. I lifted my head and strained my eyes to catch a glimpse of where the noise was coming from, but I got nothing. After a minute, the sounds of snapping twigs and rustling through the brush, along with the stomping of feet on the ground got louder. There are others out here in the forest. I listened closely and tried to count the footsteps. There's a few of them, ten or so, maybe more. But I can't pinpoint if they are the heavy strides of wolf's feet, or the smaller thumps of human feet. Perhaps a mixture of both, maybe that's why it sounds different. My eyes trailed across the earth, looking out into the darkness for any kind of movement. But I still couldn't see them. I pushed myself up and stood on the branch, still holding onto the trunk for support. I can still hear them, and I can tell they're getting closer, I should be able to see them now too. As I looked out through the forest, I noticed the trees were all reasonably close to each other. Most of the lower branches were thick and spread out quite far, connecting most of the trees to the ones around them. I could easily hop from branch to branch and not have to climb back down to the ground at all. I looked around for the next closest branch. I picked one a little higher up than the one I was on, but it looked strong and sturdy. I walked along the branch slowly, eyeing off the next one over. I readied myself and pushed off with my legs. I tried my hardest to land gently on the next tree's branch, so as to not break or crack it. The leaves on the branch rustled, shaking a few loose with the impact. The branch shook and bounced slightly with the disturbance to its otherwise peaceful state, but thankfully remained intact. I smiled to myself, feeling rather proud of the idea. I didn't even hesitate before scampering across the branch and jumping out onto the next one, and the one after that.

I kept going, stopping every third or fourth leap to pause and listen for the sounds of the visitors. Their footsteps slowed and eventually came to a stop. I could now see them, not too far ahead of me. It was a large group, I counted twenty-two, six of which are human. I continued my approach, moving much slower and with far more caution. I made sure not to make a sound as I tiptoed across the branch through the treetops. The wolves were standing in a tight circle, growling and huffing at each other. As I made my way to the tree a few feet to their right, I was able to see the scene more clearly. One of the humans was tied to the back of one of the wolves. From a distance, I thought he was injured and just catching a ride. Now that I was on top of them and could see them all clearly, it was obvious that he was a captive. Ropes were tied to his ankles, with the length of it going under the wolf's belly and connecting to his other ankle. More ropes were around his hands, with them then looped around the wolf's neck. Whoever this man is, they did not want him to escape. Which of course increased my interest in his identity. There must be a reason they haven't just killed him, he is important somehow.

The other beings that I thought were human, were anything but. The biggest of them all was abnormally tall and muscular. His arms hung low and crooked, his knees bent in the wrong direction, and he was hairy like a wild boar. It wasn't until he turned his head, and I could see his features in the moonlight, did

I understand why he looked that way. I covered my mouth with my hand before an audible gasp left my lips. A half-breed. Impossible. I quickly looked at the other humans, and I felt my stomach tighten with anger and something that could have been mistaken as fear. They were all half-breeds. This can't be.

I know all about these abominations, for a time I thought I was one. The hunters did multiple experiments with human and Were DNA. They were trying to extract the strength and speed of the werewolf and give it to the humans. They did everything from having a human woman carry a child made from Were semen, and a Were woman carry a child made with human seed. Not to mention all the disastrous Petri dish babies. Luckily, they never succeeded in their mission. The creatures they bred were worse than any wolf I'd seen. Some of the babies were born half wolf, half human. Some with animalistic features. Some died before birth, some died years later. It was the ones that made it to puberty that were the most rotten. When those children changed form, it was like they were transformed. Once scared and timid kids, changed to become ravenous and uncontrollable monsters. One boy managed to kill his way through half a battalion before they took him out. The creatures were smaller in size, but larger in ferocity. It was like they had no human senses left, no soul, no sense of pain. They were crazed and unstoppable beasts. None of them survived the first change, they had to be terminated almost immediately. That is, all but one. A girl, just shy of fifteen. When she changed, she looked similar to this man. She didn't take the body of a wolf, but her face hands and legs were deformed. She didn't attack or become aggressive. She just cowered in the corner like she always did. I never saw her again after that first change. She was taken away for further experimentation. I never expected to see a half-breed in the wild, let alone five of them.

The way the other wolves and half-breeds stood around him, the way they looked up to him while cowering away from him at the same time, it appeared like they were afraid of him. Either that or he was their leader. But that's ridiculous, why would they allow a weak monstrosity to lead them. I watched in silence as they stood around having a silent conversation. After a few more minutes the large half-breed spoke out loud to the others.

"Stay out of sight" he ordered them. His voice was low and rough, deep and demanding. It made the hair on the back of my neck stand up. The heated desire to kill this beast rose in my belly. My claws pressed at the tips of my fingers. I could just kick myself for leaving my blades behind. The death of this abomination could go one of two ways. One, he will be as weak and pathetic as I imagine him to be and will die in seconds. And the less likely option two, he will surprise me and put up one hell of a fight. I am hoping to be surprised, I need a good fight.

After a few more seconds, the tall half-breed and fourteen of the wolves took off through the trees, taking the human prisoner with them. The remaining four half-breeds and two wolves slowly ran off in another direction. I was torn on who to follow. I could take out the half-breeds and two wolves easily. Then loop back around for the other larger group. But I want to know why they are here, who their captive is and what the go with this giant half-breed is. I snarled and jumped down from my tree, chasing after the larger group. I kept my distance and made sure to stay in the shadows and out of sight. After a while the group split into four and all ran off in different directions. What the fuck are they doing, is this some kind of random attack strategy. I kept on the main half-breed, as much as it infuriated me. Their splitting up only makes it easier for me to pick them off. But I need to know what is going on.

These idiots made no attempt to be quiet or sneaky or to hide their approach from the patrolling wolves in any way. Bold strategy, albeit stupid, but still bold. Why would they not care about being spotted. When a howl rang out through the early night air, the hair rose on my arms. It was a warning. Whoever these beasts are, they aren't meant to be here, and now Gunner's pack know they're here. Another howl sounded from the other direction, then the half-breed stopped running. He lifted his head and howled loudly in return. A shiver ran over my skin, and something pulled at the back of my head. I don't know how or why, but I knew in that moment that the half-breed has no intention of attacking. I'd be lying if I said I wasn't slightly disappointed. They kept going in the direction of the pack house, the half-breed stopped once more to howl into the night air. I kept my senses sharp and alert, I knew Gunner's warrior puppies would be out here tracking these wolves, and I couldn't risk them finding me instead.

I heard the warriors through the trees, chasing after us. Well, chasing them. Their growls and barks of angered warnings filtered through the forest. I caught sight of a small group off to the right. They had their noses to the ground, following the scent of the intruders. If I stay high up, in the trees like before, they may not pick up my scent. I climbed the first tree I reached and planted myself on a branch, and hid there until the small group of warriors were out of sight. By doing so, I lost sight of the half-breed and his pack as well.

I scanned the forest, looking for more patrols. They were all over the place, in every direction. Perhaps that was why the half-breed and his pack split up, to make it harder for them to be caught. Maybe he isn't as dumb as I first thought. I tried to move silently, but it was getting harder to do so without being spotted. With the ducking and weaving, and the climbing and scampering I did to avoid the hunting warriors, I had completely lost my sense of direction. All these trees look the same to me. When another howl rang through the trees, I knew exactly where I needed to go. I climbed back up into the trees and began bouncing from tree to tree as quickly and quietly as I could. The noises from the intruders and the warriors chasing them grew louder, making it easier to disguise my own noises. The closer I got to the village, the more sparse the trees became, which made my own approach more difficult.

Four wolves quickly ran past the tree I was in, following not far behind them were six others. The first four were with the half-breed, the six chasing them must be from Gunner's pack. I jumped down and followed after them, still keeping far enough behind so that I wouldn't be easily noticed. I heard rustling through the forest off to the left, and soon after came another group that was with the half-breed. They are regrouping, why though. More of Gunner's warriors appeared through the trees in front of me. I ducked to the right just in time to avoid them. I kept going towards the village. It's obvious that's where the half-breed and his pack were trying to get to, so I'll just catch up to them there. I kept running until I could see the lights of the village through the trees. I slowed down and kept low as I got closer to the edge of the tree line. I can hear the commotion echoing around the area, the barking and the growling all coming from Gunner's house. I kept my body behind a large tree trunk and peered around it into the clearing. Gunner's warriors had the half-breed and his pack surrounded and were ushering them to the middle of the clearing. I haven't picked a good vantage point to watch the chaos unfold. My view is obstructed by the little houses lining the centre of the village. They stopped and held the half-breed a safe distance from the house. Gunner's large silver wolf stood in front of the group. I was too far away to hear anything, unfortunately. I could only just see the half-breed and three of his wolves, the rest of them were blocked from my line of sight by a cabin. The half-breed stepped forward and held his arms up. His arms and chest started to shrink as he bowed for Gunner. When he stood up straight again, the fiery rage that exploded inside me was phenomenal. It's the man from the forest. The half-breed is the Alpha of the secret assassin pack, Alpha Doyle.

I could feel the itch of need crawl over my skin. I want to feel that abomination's warm blood run down my arms after I impale him with my claws. I want to see the life drain out of him. All this time, that cocky asshole was a half-breed. Gunner's voice bellowed through the clearing, pulling my thoughts away from killing Doyle and back to the current moment. Gunner had changed back to his human form and was standing between the assassin and a giant black wolf. It's the same wolf I saw in the forest earlier. So, he is one of Gunner's lackeys. The wolf stepped back slightly, and there she was. The little witch, the bane of my existence. Zelena. If I could shoot lasers from my eyes, I'd carve my name into her skin, and then she'd be dead right here right now. Doyle dropped to his knee in front of Gunner and the giant wolf moved to stand protectively over Zelena's shoulder. Of course, she has her own guard dog. Stupid fucking princess. Everyone fucking loves her, don't they. Everyone wants to kiss her toes and wipe her ass for her, don't they. The fucking cunt.

After Doyle stood back up, he waved his hand over his head and looked back to the tree line. He was calling someone. I stuck my head further out and looked along the line of the clearing. Three humans emerged, one of which was the prisoner. Is that what this was all about, they want to trade back a hostage. Seems like a lot of effort. When Doyle threw the prisoner at Gunner's feet, Zelena rushed forward to help him. The goody-two-shoes that she is. I shook my head and huffed. I'm so sick to fucking death of this little bitch. When screaming ensued and rung around the forest,

I shot my eyes back up again. The first thing I realised, this man did not like Zelena. Same dude, same. The second thing, he was speaking perfect Russian. Third thing, he called her Besomar. Fuck, this could be bad for me.

Gunner's mother came running from the house to where everyone had gathered. They talked for a little before she turned her attention to the prisoner. I think it's pretty safe to discredit my original theory, I don't believe this is a hostage situation. There was a quick panicked shuffle and my view was blocked by the crowd. When they parted again, the half-breed, Doyle, had the prisoner up in the air and was roaring in his face. Zelena was on her ass on the ground and Gunner's mother was trying to pull the man free. He couldn't possibly be defending her too. Does this bitch have all the men around her whipped into submission. Doyle promised to kill me, but he wants to defend her of all people. This is ridiculous. Zelena jumped to her feet and yelled at the crowd, which made them all go silent. Just proving my point, she has her dark witchy magic twisted around each and every one of them. I don't know what she told them, but Gunner's mother quickly ushered the prisoner away, followed closely by her Mate and two of Doyle's wolves. I flicked my eyes between Zelena and the others, and Gunner's mother and the prisoner. I know enough of what I need to know from Zelena, but I still have information to gather from the prisoner. I snuck forward and dashed to hide behind a cabin. I spared one last look to where Zelena and Gunner were arguing with Doyle, then followed silently after the prisoner.

They took him around the side of the house and into a shed like structure. I ran over to the outside wall and pressed my ear to the cool metal to listen. Roe was fussing over the prisoner while ordering her Mate and the others to bring her water, clean clothing, and blankets. I snuck a little further forward to where there was a small window high off the ground. I'm not going to be able to reach it by myself, I need something to stand on. I ran back to where I saw a car tyre leaning against the shed. Being as silent and as fast as I could, I rolled it to the window and jumped up on top of it. I held my hands out to my sides and used my power to steady myself. For any other person, I imagine standing upright on a tyre that wants to roll you off would be difficult. But I'm not just any other person. With the added height I could just see through the small rectangular window. The prisoner was sitting on a chair with a blanket wrapped around his body. Gunner's mother was sitting on another chair right in front of him, seemingly comforting him. When she stood up to take a glass from her Mate, I could see the prisoner uninterrupted. He was thin, filthy and looked exhausted. His hair was shaggy, and his skin was covered in cuts and bruises. Despite all that, his tired eyes shone with a glistening blue. I have seen blue eyes like that before, just three times. Saxton's eyes. Deep dark blue pools of lies and trickery. Gunner's eyes. Bright blue and endless, filled with care and devotion. And the wolf that escaped me back in Russia. His sparkling blue eyes glistened with sadness and fear. This man's eyes hold that same look. It can't be a coincidence that this man speaks Russian, that Doyle brought him here, and that he called Zelena Besomar. This is him, that same wolf, it has to be. The only Werewolf that has managed to escape my murderous rampages. I knew letting him go would come back to bite me in the ass.

Chapter Thirty-Nine

Whiskey

I watched on as Gunner's mother continued to converse with the man. My mind was running a million miles a minute. If he tells them that it was me that killed his pack, everything will be fucked. It will mess up all my plans of waiting and watching. I need to observe this place, and the idiots that live here, for a longer period. I need to know more before I attack. I've already seen a small part of their defences when Doyle entered their land. I have no doubt that there would be more than just a couple of warriors hidden around the place. I need the time to work out what they are. I can't go in blind this time. Especially seeing as Gunner has powers of his own. They're too strong and I can't risk failing. That's a weird concept to swallow. Failure. It's not something I am used to. I don't fail, I never have, and I don't ever plan to. Which is why I have to plan out this attack and prepare for it properly. If this stupid beast spills his guts before then, I may not have that opportunity. There's an interesting thought. Spill his guts. I could just kill him before he gets the chance to tell them everything. And if I can do it without being seen, then my plan may still be viable. How could I do it though?

I let my power go and silently jumped down off the tyre. I took a quick second to listen to what was going on around me before I made my next move. The hushed conversation inside the shed continued. There was more happening back around the other side of the house, probably Doyle still stirring trouble with Gunner. I should check on them before I kill this flea. I looked up at the small window I was just peering through and listened. Gunner's mother was still trying to coax information out of the prisoner, though he wasn't being overly forthcoming. Just babbling nonsense about the Besomar. So, I think I still have a bit of time before he opens up completely. Just enough to check back in on the others.

I slinked backwards into the shadows and all the way to the tree line. I kept my ears open and my eyes wide. Gunner will have his dogs on full alert, and I can't risk them noticing my return just yet. I slowly and carefully made my way back around the edge of the clearing. Gunner, Zelena and Doyle were no longer in the middle of the village. Everything seemed kind of calm. The people were just sitting in small groups, talking, cutting firewood, or sitting on their little cabin porches. It doesn't look like they have just been invaded by a half-blood killer. Speaking of, where is Doyle? Surely they wouldn't have taken him inside the house, Gunner's not that stupid. They'd be keeping him away from everyone else, somewhere a little safer. I scanned the village and spotted two possible options. One was a large, tall building, possibly a barn. The other was a smaller cabin, similar to the ones the villagers were living in.

I went with the smaller one. I figured the smaller the space they hold him in, the smaller the area they have to guard. The bad part is, it was on the other side of the village, across the clearing. I could hear the patrols in the forest behind me, not close, but still searching and on the move. I can't go all the way around and risk getting trapped or caught. Going right through the middle is suicide. I could maybe stick to the very edge of the tree line and make my way around. But there are too many gaps, the trees are too sparse, and the light from the village is too bright. I have one other option, but it's risky. I've only done it a few times before, and not always successfully. Sucking the air out of my enemy's lungs isn't the only power I have. I can also manipulate the air in other ways. Sometimes, to cast a large, fast wave. Big enough to knock someone off their feet. Or just small enough to push closed an open door. Mostly I use it to give myself an extra boost to jump higher, or to slow and soften a landing. On two or three occasions, I did manage to pull off something that could be misconstrued as flying.

The first time was a total fluke, and not in the slightest bit graceful. I tried to slow a landing after jumping down from a building, but instead, I shot myself back up into the air. I smacked into the side of the building before landing on a fire escape. I'll admit that one hurt, though it was more surprising than anything. Another time, after getting a good run up, I jumped across a wide ravine. I used the air push to help me jump the far distance, but I misjudged the distance and landed way too far away from the bank. That time, I rolled through the dirt before crashing hard into a tree. This kind of use of my power hasn't worked out well for me, so now I mostly just use little bursts of wind to keep myself balanced or something similar. Things go wrong every now and then, but I think I've got enough of a handle on it. The past few months have really tested my abilities and my control. I'm better now than I ever was, so if I really want to, I could probably shoot myself over the top of the village. Maybe.

After quickly looking around again, I've come to the conclusion that I don't have another option. It's either this or get caught. I moved a little to my left until I found a spot where I could shoot through without too many branches or other obstacles. I can't believe I'm about to do this. I planted my feet and twiddled my fingers. I bounced a little on the balls of my feet, trying to hype myself up a bit. I pulled the power forward and felt it twirl around my fingers and legs. My feet lifted off the ground, only slightly, and probably in the most graceful way I have ever done before. I could feel the air wrapped around my legs like tight jeans. I pushed forward and willed the air to lift me higher into the trees. I kept going up, the slowest and most controlled I have ever been before. The darkness took over the ground below me, and the moonlight shone across the sky. I was floating in the air, high above the tops of the trees. Not so high that I could be seen if someone looked up, but high enough that I couldn't see the ground unless I used my wolf eyes. I looked across the clearing and spotted the roof of the barn building thing, the small cabin was not too far to the right of that. While trying my best to keep total concentration over the power, I quickly scoped what was going on below in the clearing. Much of the same, no one really paid too much attention to anything else outside of what they were doing themselves.

This is my chance. While it's clear and no one is watching. If I go as quickly as possible, then I doubt anyone will see me. The only problem there is now, is if I can control the distance, or the landing, or anything after this point. I must be losing my damn mind. I angled my arms behind me and felt the air slither further up my legs to my abdomen and chest. It was holding me, supporting me, but it also felt like it was a part of me. Being embraced by the coolness of the power was like hugging my arms tightly around myself. I always believed that the power was something forced onto me by my torturers. Perhaps that's why I always struggled to control it. I thought it was something to be controlled, as I once was. But it's not. This power is part of who I am. It's something that I was given, not something that was just thrown into my hands. I understand now. The power is me, as I am the power. It's not something I control, it's something I harness.

I took a deep breath and allowed the power to sweep over me completely. I told myself to push forward, and I did. The air tightened around my body, and I was suddenly shooting through the sky over the top of the clearing. I was like a bullet in the wind, too quick for anyone to track. Before I even knew it, I was on the other side of the clearing. I flew my arms out in front of me to stop myself. I came to a sudden halt, and I felt the organs inside my body jolt forward, as if I were in a car that just hit the brakes too hard. A soft grunt left my lips, and I grabbed my stomach. As soon as I lowered my arm, I started falling. I crashed through the tops of the trees, catching branch after branch as I went. I was falling faster and faster and desperately trying to regain control over my movements. I could see the ground getting closer as I hit another branch. The sound of the wood snapping echoed through the forest. Just before my face hit the ground, I put my hands out in front of me. My body stilled just inches off the ground. The air whipped around my body, scattering the leaves and blowing my hair across my face. Just in time.

I kept myself there for a moment, just floating above the cool forest floor. Sounds of stampeding paws filtered through the air, followed closely by rough panting and low growls. Gunner's mutts must have heard my ungraceful descent through the trees. I pushed myself back up and then went a little higher, until I reached one of the branches that I just smashed into moments ago. Once my feet were touching the bark, I let the power go and let the branch take all of my weight. I don't know what it is about this part of the forest, but the trees here are ginormous. I lay my body flat on the branch and peered over the edge. Another moment later, I saw four wolves run past. One of them paused, putting its nose in the air. Its dark grey fur lifted, and its ears went flat as it sniffed around. It may be able to smell my scent, but I didn't touch the ground, so it's also unlikely. I pressed my body into the branch and lifted my arm. I pulled forth a subtle breeze, one that could be considered a natural occurrence. Hopefully, that will sweep away any trace of my scent on the ground. The wolf lowered its head and growled, then took off through the trees after the other wolves. Stupid mutt. I wonder if it is truly me they are searching for, or do they know that more of Doyle's men are out here too.

I waited another minute before jumping down from the branch. I landed with a soft thud and quickly looked around the forest. I could just see the lights from the village through the trees. I'd landed further away than I would have liked, but not too far, thankfully. With one last quick look around, I darted off towards the village. I was quick and light on my feet, didn't make a sound and didn't stay in one spot long enough to be spotted. This is like second nature to me. Moving without being seen, without being heard. I am still the merchant of death, the ghost in the night, just like I was every time before.

In no time at all, I was in view of the small cabin. The patrolling dogs were still out in the depths of the forest, and they probably didn't expect me to get this close to the village again. Their mistake. It's one of the top rules that was beaten into me, never assume. I approached the cabin from the back, keeping myself in the shadow of the building. I lifted my nose and breathed in as I got closer. The lack of wolf stench is becoming apparent. They aren't here. I reached the building and pressed myself flat up against the wall. Another quick perimeter check, good, no one has seen me. I pressed my ear to the wall just to double check, there was no noise coming from inside. I peered through the small window, and I was right, it's empty. Shit.

The barn is further away and in a slightly more open space. It's doable, of course, just riskier. I slinked back into the tree line and snaked my way towards the building. The closer I got to the barn, the more I realised that this was where they had to be. I can smell the filthy wet dog scent, and I can hear the low conversations. I peered out from around a tree and took in my surroundings. The barn was lit up brightly, meaning that if I could see everything illuminated around it, then they could too. I'll be easily spotted. From where I am, I can see four. I have no doubt that there'd be more on the other side of the barn. The cabin didn't have guards. Fuck I'm stupid, of course they'd have Doyle guarded. He's in there.

I watched silently from the tree line for a little while longer. I know he's in there, it's the only place that makes any sense. However, my suspicions were confirmed when I spotted Gunner stomping out of the barn. I was far enough away not to be scented or seen, but not far enough to be unable to see the rotten look on his face. I watched the side of his face as he marched away. Even fuming mad he is still enticing to look at. He should belong to me. Mine to admire, to ravish, to love. Why did the witch get the good life? Why was she more deserving than me? The anger filled my stomach and slowly spread to my chest, slowly boiling me from the inside out. Fucking Selene and her damn favouritism. Zelena is nothing but a weak bug needing to be crushed under the weight of my boot. I am the more powerful one, I am the one that everyone should love and fear. Not her. Me!

The rage spilled out of me, scorching my skin and fuelling my desire for revenge. First the blue-eyed wolf, and then the bitch Zelena. Planning be dammed. I'll kill her and sneak away into the night. Then, when all those pathetic beasts are lost to their grief over the death of Her Highness, I'll come back and finish the rest of them. I slinked back into the forest with my new resolve and made my way further into the shrub. I found a large tree and climbed to the top. I stood on a thick branch and pulled the magic forward. It was like my fury had given me complete control over the power. My skin tingled with icy cold goosebumps. I looked down at my arms, the smooth black smoke I had been seeing over the past few years was now smothering my entire arm. The soft whisps were replaced by sharp and crackling clouds. I could feel the cool sting of it seeping into my veins. I could feel the energy of it shoot through my blood. It was powering me, filling me up with more energy and power than I had ever felt before. This is what true power feels like. Nothing like that gentle breeze crap the supposed All Mother gave me. This is the real me.

Using my newfound dark power, I lifted my body off the branch and hovered above the tree. I could still feel the wind wrapping around my body protectively like before. Only now it was thick, cold, ruthless, more like my blackened soul. Without hesitation, I shot myself through the air to the other side of the clearing. Only this time, I didn't slow down or freeze. I controlled the air around me perfectly. I flew down through the branches of the trees. If anyone saw me, I have no doubt that I would have looked just like Superman. I reached the ground and straightened my body, standing upright and releasing the power. I like this new control I have. It makes me feel invincible, unstoppable, all mighty even. That being said, I still don't want to get caught. I slipped behind some trees and looked around. I was still far enough away from the searching party not to be noticed. Though I couldn't tell if they were expanding their search further away from the village, or if they were giving it up completely. I'm hoping for the former. The further away the warriors are from the house, the better chance I have of escaping after I end their stupid cunt of a Luna. As I slipped back through the trees, getting closer to the shed where they were questioning the prisoner, hushed whispers caught my attention. I should bypass them, give whoever it is a wide berth and keep on going. But something in my chest was pulling me towards the voices. I veered in the direction without even intending to. But as I got closer, something inside me, a feeling of some sort, started to ache. I lifted my nose to the air and breathed in. The scent was too faint to pick up. I closed my eyes and called a gentle breeze through the trees. The wind swept through the people I was spying on and made its way over to my nose. I knew the scent immediately, I couldn't forget it. It belonged to Tobias, the gigantic man I encountered in the living room. His smooth chocolate skin and deep, dark eyes popped into my head. My chest tightened, and my stomach rolled. I don't know what this is, unease, desire, nerves. He was handsome, undoubtedly. And judging by the size of him, I know he could inflict a delicious amount of pain on my body as he fucked me raw. But I don't want that. I shook the image away and cursed myself for feeling any kind of desire towards that beast. I don't like the unknown, and that is what he is. He will die along with the rest of those animals.

I crept forward, being sure to stay downwind and not make a sound. I got close enough to see the huge man through the trees, but I wouldn't dare to approach any further. He was standing under some kind of garden cabana. It was painted white with vines sprouting purple flowers growing around the structure's poles. Tobias was leaning on the railing, facing away from an overly large woman standing beside him. Where the fuck were they hiding this monster of a woman? There is no way I would have missed her wandering around the village before now. A plane flying overhead wouldn't miss this mammoth of a woman. She was sporting tribal tattoos on her chin and both of her exposed arms. I think I am in pretty good shape, I'm strong and fit and have good stamina. But this woman, she was in a class of her own. Her biceps were bigger than Gunner's, and her angry scowl was enough to make me raise an eyebrow. It will be interesting if I come across her in a one-on-one battle.

I slid behind a tree, keeping the rest of my body out of view and focussed on my hearing.

"Guardian, it is time. Why have you not completed your mission?" the angry woman hissed at him.

"What would you know about my mission?" Tobias snapped back at her without turning around.

"Granted, I don't know all the details, but the Seer has told me enough" she replied. Tobias huffed and growled lowly.

"You don't understand" he grumbled.

"Explain it to me. I am to help you however I must, that was my instruction" she said. Her voice was still firm and rough, but the pleading was evident, even from a distance.

"I didn't know, she didn't tell me" Tobias said through clenched teeth.

"Didn't know what?"

"When she gave me the choice, she didn't tell me the whole truth" he growled and beat his fist on the railing of the cabana.

"You need to explain it to me, Guardian" The big woman said in an annoyed tone.

"She didn't tell me about the other one. I didn't know there were two. She didn't say I'd feel like this for her as well" he growled and rubbed one of his giant hands over his bald head.

"What are you babbling about?" the woman snapped. Tobias whipped around and growled ferociously at her.

"I love Zelena, I will die for her. She is mine to protect" he yelled.

"And…" the woman grunted with frustration, seemingly unfazed by his outburst.

"I feel the same way for the other. She didn't tell me I was to guard them both" he yelled with a wave of his arm. A few moments of silence passed between them before the woman spoke with a much gentler tone.

"You are Aurora's guardian as well" she said slowly. My guardian, what the fuck is that supposed to mean. I don't need a bodyguard.

"It appears so" he answered with a huff.

"Does this change things for you?" the woman asked.

"How could it not? I can't ignore my instincts, and they want me to protect her too" he answered.

"Is this what she instructed of you?"

"No".

They stood staring at each other for what seemed like forever. The woman finally turned away and sat on a bench under the cabana roof.

"I will help you, I swear it. But to do that, you need to give me more" the angry woman breathed out heavily. Tobias slowly slid his large body down the pole until he was sitting on the ground. I hissed at him disappearing from my view, but I could still see him enough through the gaps of the wood panelling.

"She said I must choose, I can only help one of them" he grunted reluctantly.

"And how do you do that?" the woman fired back without missing a beat.

"I don't know yet. She said when the moment was right, the answer would present itself".

"She always was the aloof type" the woman grunted as she leaned back on the bench.

I may have an idea as to what they are talking about. Tobias is in love with Zelena, but he seems to have protective feelings for me. Fuck knows why. This appears to be bothering him. Probably because only an idiot grows feelings for someone after looking at them one time for all of two minutes. Also, someone has given him a mission, again fuck knows what that mission is. But for some reason, I believe either Zelena or I am standing in the way of him completing his mission. And to top it off, he thinks he needs to be my guard dog. Whatever the fuck that is meant to mean. And whatever it is he's meant to be guarding me from is a whole other unanswered question. I could be reading this all wrong. Maybe, maybe not. But I seriously don't give a fuck about the big man's dilemma. I have wasted enough time listening to him dribble on about his nonsensical drama. I have mutts to kill.

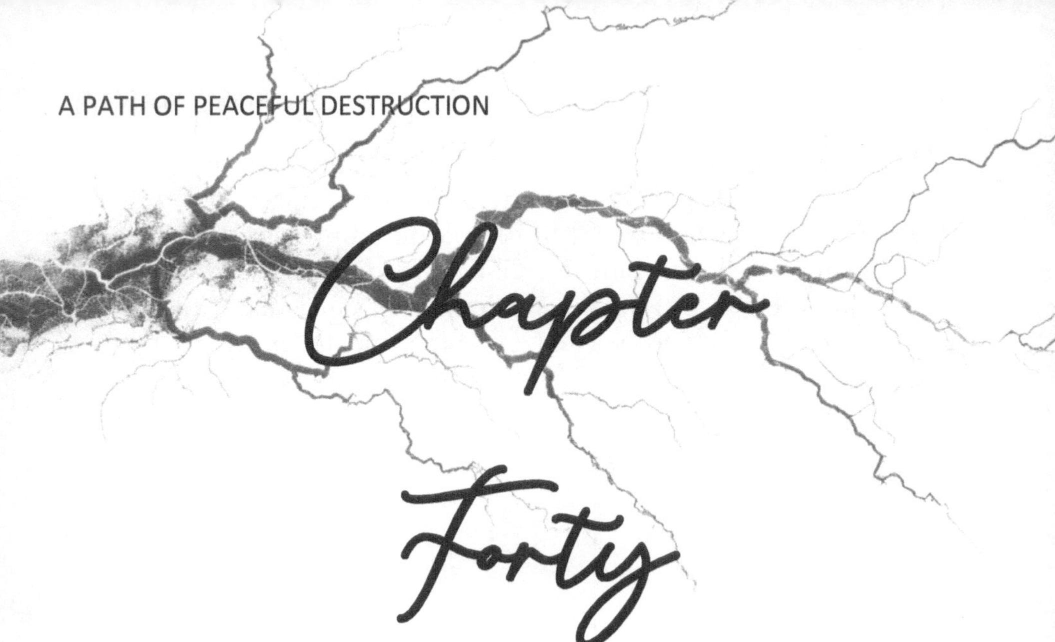

Chapter Forty

Zelena

I lay on top of the bed, unable to sleep. The soft and steady breathing of the twins was enough to keep me calm, but not enough to soothe my racing mind. Too many questions and so much uncertainty. What happened to Tobias, why was he lying to me? Where did Whiskey go, and when will she be back? Who or what is behind Alpha Doyle's visit? Why does everyone seem so afraid that he is a half-breed but not that Alyse is? Is it possible that nobody knows Alyse is a half-breed? No, that can't be right. I saw her, which means others did too. Does Whiskey remember everything now, is that why she left? When will Gunner be finished with Doyle? What is up with Tobias? Now I'm just going in circles. I need to get up and do something, I can't keep torturing myself like this.

I pushed myself up and climbed out of the bed. I grabbed the baby monitor and went to the door. I swung it open slowly and looked over at the twins as I stepped out into the hallway, being careful not to wake them. As I turned around, I smacked face first into Gunner's chest.

"Shit" I whispered yelled.

"Why does everyone need to stand so damned close to me. I'm going to break my fucking nose one of these days" I cursed quietly as I rubbed my nose.

"Babe, I'm sorry, I didn't mean to" Gunner rushed out apologetically. He leaned down so that we were at eye level and watched me rub my nose with a worried expression.

"It's fine" I grunted. He studied me for a moment before standing up straight again. He held onto my shoulders and leaned back slightly.

"What's going on, you're a mess of emotions right now" he said accusingly. I frowned and pushed his hands away.

"Am I not allowed to feel now?" I snapped, perhaps a little too harshly. Gunner seemed surprised at my outburst, as he watched me with wide eyes.

"Of course you are. I just want to make sure you're okay" he said softly. Fuck, I hurt his feelings.

"Sorry" I grumbled half-heartedly.

"I just don't know what's going on right now" I said looking up at him. He stepped forward and placed his hands on my hips. He pushed himself into me and kissed the top of my head.

"I'm sorry too" he said with a deep breath.

"It's hard to breathe sometimes with all this going on. It's like there is never a break in the drama" Gunner said with an exasperated tone.

"We'll get through it" I said as I pushed him back a little so that I could see his face. He smiled down at me softly.

"Together?" he said while staring into my eyes.

"Together" I agreed. Gunner leaned down and pressed his lips gently to mine. Before he got the chance to move away, I wrapped my arms around his neck and held him in place. He got the idea and leaned himself into my body. I pressed against the wall with Gunner's heated body flush up against mine. I moaned softly as I rolled my tongue with his, deepening the kiss. All the worries and the unanswered questions disappeared, if only for a few moments. Gunner grabbed the back of my thighs and lifted me off the floor. I wrapped my legs around his waist and arched my back. Gunner growled lowly as he pushed his tongue into my mouth. His hands grabbed my butt firmly, while my fingers twisted into his hair. We were locked together in this heated kiss, nothing else mattered in that moment. But I know we can't escape reality for too long. I moved my head away and sighed as Gunner peppered kisses down my neck.

"Why'd you come up here?" I asked. Though I could be tempted to keep ignoring it for a little while longer. Gunner grunted and kissed my neck back up to my chin.

"Just a little longer" he mumbled into my sensitive skin. It seems that he too wants to escape the drama for a little while. I chuckled as he hit a ticklish spot under my ear lobe. Gunner growled playfully and sucked my lobe into his mouth, teasing it with his teeth.

"Gunner" I giggled and pulled my head away from his delicious lips. He sighed dramatically and leaned his head against my forehead.

"Let's run away. You, me, and the twins. We can leave all the mess behind and live on the land, wild and free" he said with a grin.

"Make our own little tribe?" I teased joining in.

"Oh, my Love, you doubt my abilities. We'd make our own little town" he said as he licked my bottom lip and growled.

"Yeah right" I laughed.

"And will you be birthing all these town residents?" I asked pointedly. The joyful look disappeared from his face and a sad one took its place.

"I'm sorry I missed it" he said solemnly.

"Missed what?"

"The birth of our pups"

"Oh, Gunner, it wasn't your fault"

"But it is. I'll never be able to get that moment back".

I moved my hands to cup his cheeks and kissed him softly. I had completely forgotten about my own sadness at Gunner missing the birth of the twins. The moment he returned home it all became a nonissue. I never really stopped long enough to think if he was doing okay with it. So much has happened since he got home, I haven't even been able to ask him about it. I've neglected him, again. I sighed and pulled away from his tender kiss to lean my forehead on his.

"There'll be more opportunities, I have no doubt" I smiled sweetly and pecked his lips just once more.

"I love you, so damn much" Gunner chuffed as he slowly let me down.

"I love you more" I quipped back.

"Impossible" he said with a smile and pulled me into his body for a tight hug. I enjoy being in his arms, smelling his scent, and hearing his heartbeat. I could stay here forever. But reality will soon come back to grab us from our little love bubble.

"What happened with Doyle, did he tell you why he came here?" I asked, which immediately soured the mood. Gunner stepped out of the hug and frowned.

"Yes, but also no. Doesn't matter, I don't believe him for a second" he grumbled angrily.

"Is your mum finished with the survivor?" I asked quickly, moving on to my next bunch of curiosities. Gunner's eyes hardened and he squeezed my hip.

"Yes, that's why I came to get you" he said firmly.

"Oh, it's not good, is it?"

"I don't think so".

"Well, my sexy Alpha, let's go find out then" I said as I took his hand.

"After you, my beautiful Luna" he chipped back. As I stepped in front of him to walk down the hallway, a loud slap echoed through the space.

"Ouch!" I screeched as I grabbed my backside and turned on Gunner with a frown.

"To be continued" he said with a wink.

"You're insatiable" I mumbled to myself as I rubbed my butt cheek and stomped down the stairs. I veered left to go straight for the living room, expecting that was where Roe would be.

"This way" Gunner said, taking my hand and leading me to the hall. Why would we be going to the hall? That's used for serious stuff, official type stuff. I thought we were just talking to Roe about what she learned from the survivor. The moment we walked through the door, I felt the tension wash over me. The head of the table was left clear for Gunner, the seat at his left for me. Smith was already waiting in the seat at the right of Gunner, with Lupus next to him. Smith must be stepping up more for his Beta role. I know he had been having a hard time taking it on. He had been letting Lupus take on a lot of the Beta duties, maybe because he knew what it entailed. Smith was never trained as a Beta. That was destined for Cole. I was happy to see Felix in the room, I've always liked Felix. Daniel was here too, the new Delta. Along with Lunaya, Alyse, Elaine, and one of our commanders. No Tobias though, which is unusual.

Gunner pulled out my chair and I slowly sat down while staring at all the waiting faces. Gunner sat down and immediately pulled my hand onto his lap.

"You asked for this gathering, why are we here?" Gunner's voice called, dripping with authority and roughness. Roe stood up and Lupus gently patted her hip in a show of support.

"I've gotten the Russian Were to tell me some info about the attack on his pack" she said softly. Her eyes flicked over to mine briefly before she dropped them again. I didn't miss the glimmer of fear she was hiding in there though.

"And, what did he tell you?" Gunner asked, this time his voice sounding much more gentle.

"He said a monster came, the Besomar, and it killed everyone" Roe said, still not lifting her eyes.

"Besomar?" I asked,

"That's what he called me when Doyle brought him in".

"Yes" Roe nodded.

"What is a Besomar?" Felix asked from across the table.

"It's like a demon" Roe choked a little on the word 'demon'.

"He thinks a demon attacked his home?" Gunner scoffed.

"Besomar is an evil spirit. It is said that the person or animal that Besomar possesses, is no longer themself, but a vessel of pure evil. Besomar is the strongest and can cause the most chaos, out of all other evil spirits combined" Roe said in all seriousness. Daniel snorted and quickly covered his mouth with his hand. Roe, Lupus and Gunner all glared at him at the same time.

"I'm sorry" he coughed as he swallowed his laugh.

"We're telling ghost stories now? You can't be serious" he exclaimed sarcastically. His tone and face were smothered in animosity and disbelief.

"I know I'm still new to all this, but weren't True Mates considered to be a myth as well?" I asked while eyeing Daniel. His expression changed and he frowned slightly.

"That's different" he grumbled and turned away.

"So this Were, what's his name?" I asked, turning back to Roe.

"Konstantin" Roe replied quickly.

"Ok, so Konstantin thinks I have been possessed by this evil spirit, Besomar. Is that right?" I asked. I wonder what kind of vibes I give off for this guy to think I'm a demon in disguise. Maybe I need to work on my resting bitch face. It took me a moment to realise that Roe didn't reply. I looked up at her in question, but she was looking at Lupus, the two of them were flashing.

"What's going on?" Gunner asked firmly. Lupus grunted angrily and sat back in his chair, crossing his arms over his broad chest. Roe cleared her throat and looked at her son.

"I don't think he was talking about Zelena" she said after a minute. The room was silent, all of them lost to their own thoughts. It was me that Konstantin was looking at when he said it, me he was screaming at, and me he was trying to get away from. Of course, he was calling me Besomar. I looked at Gunner, he was rubbing the back of his neck, something he does when he is unsure or concerned. I looked at my mother, she was chewing on her bottom lip while squeezing Alyse's hand on the table.

"If not Zelena, who?" Felix asked, finally breaking the silence.

"You think he saw Aurora there, don't you?" Lunaya asked before Roe could answer. She hesitated for a moment, then nodded her head.

"Wait, how could he think Whiskey is possessed, he's not even seen her. She ran off before Doyle and his men got here" I shot out confused. Gunner squeezed my hand, pulling my attention to him. His face was contorted with his brows furrowed and his lips pulled into a straight line.

"Zee" he said softly. The tone of his voice and the heaviness behind it hit something in me. I understood then.

"You think Whiskey attacked his pack?" I yelled and shot to my feet.

"It makes sense" Smith said quietly.

"There has to be another reason" Lunaya said while shaking her head.

"He called Zelena, Besomar. He was absolutely terrified of her. Who do we know that looks exactly like Zelena?" Lupus interjected angrily. It seems like he has already made his mind up about this.

"It wasn't her" I said vehemently.

"But how could you know for sure?" Felix asked gently. Gunner pulled at my hand, dragging me back down onto my seat.

"Zee, I know you don't want to hear this, but just try" he said softly. I could feel the tears burning at the rims of my eyes.

"You said that Selene showed you things, things about Whiskey and how angry she was" he said while wiping a tear from my cheek.

"That doesn't mean she's a killer" I shot back foolishly.

"But you also saw some of the things that the hunters were doing to her. They were torturing her, why would they do that for no reason?"

"Because they're evil" I pleaded.

"Or because they were brainwashing her" Lupus scoffed.

"You're not even trying to give her a chance!" I yelled at him. The large round table shook as the power of my voice rolled across it. Lupus wasn't fazed though. He grunted and rolled his eyes with annoyance.

"She was emanating all kinds of bad vibes, right from the moment you two touched each other. You may not have seen it, but I did. She attacked her own mother for fucks sake" he growled with a wave of his arm.

"Sweetheart" Roe said sternly, warning her husband to rein in his anger. I whirled on my mother, who had been strangely quiet during this revelation.

"Are you going to say anything?" I snapped at her. She was quiet for a moment, like she was ignoring me. But her face lifted and she looked at me through red rimmed eyes.

"The reports say that all the Weres had been suffocated. We already know that Aurora has the power of Aerokinesis" she said emotionlessly.

"So? What's that got to do with anything?" I growled. The heaviness in my chest was crushing me from the inside out. I knew where this was leading, and I was afraid of the legitimacy behind it.

"Areokinesis, the power of air, like what we need to breathe?" Lupus mumbled with a huff.

"The prophecy talks of two, one that brings love, the other that brings death" Lunaya spoke in a monotone voice.

"We still don't know which one of us is which" I blurted out in a last attempt to reason with them. Though deep down I knew it was futile. The truth was becoming more and more clear. It can't be ignored any longer.

"I think it's a pretty safe bet" Smith said with a slight scoff.

I slumped back in my chair and released the hold I had on my tears. They poured down my cheeks as I sat and silently wept. I know what this means for me. It's been plaguing my mind persistently. One of us will die soon.

Gunner gently rubbed my thigh in some kind of show of comfort or solidarity. But then he stood up and began to address the room, making plans to find and capture Whiskey. I couldn't sit there and listen to him make plans to trap my sister. No matter what she has done, she is still my sister. They are talking about her like she is a wild dangerous animal. After a few minutes of listening to them speak about how powerful and dangerous she was, and the steps they needed to take to reduce the possibility of casualties, I couldn't take anymore.

I pushed my chair back so hard that it toppled over as I stood up. I narrowed my eyes at Gunner before stomping out and slamming the door behind me. I stood on the other side of the door for a moment. My breath was coming out in short harsh bursts as my anger rolled through me. I need answers, and there is only one person that can give me those. I stormed through the house and out on the patio. My anger hadn't dissipated in the slightest. If anything, it increased tenfold. I could feel my bones starting to twist and crack with the need to change. Maybe changing will help relieve the anger a little. I kicked off my shoes and ran down the steps. The change was coming too fast, and I screwed my face up with the pain of my bones rearranging. I tossed my head back with a grunt as my spine twisted and my face elongated. I threw myself forward onto the ground and landed on two midnight black paws. I panted hard and the pain slowly disappeared. I shook out my fur, shaking off the last of the ache in my bones.

"Goddess?" a female voice called to my right, but I ran off before I looked to see who it was. I headed to the edge of the clearing and through the trees, going in the direction of one of my favourite places. When I reached the flower field, a very slight feeling of calmness tickled through me. Even in the dark of the night the field was beautiful. I walked into the middle of the field and flopped down, rolling my wolf body into the soft grass. I stilled after a minute and laid on my back looking up at the moon. I took a few slow and deep breaths, trying to calm the rest of my anger and fears. I closed my eyes and thought of Selene and the Ethereal Plain.

"Mother" I called out in my head.

"I need you".

The feeling of falling pulled me upright. I opened my eyes, and I was now standing on my human feet, in front of me was the ever beautiful Selene.

"Hello, daughter of mine" she sang happily.

"Mother" I smiled half heartedly.

"You heard me" I said with a huff.

"I am always listening" she said as she turned and wondered, more like glided, through the field of white flowers.

"What can I do for you, my girl?" her melodic voice called. There was a lot I wanted to ask her, a lot that I was desperate to understand. But one question stood above the rest.

"I need to know if you knew" I replied, stepping toward her. She didn't answer right away, but I know she heard me, I know that she knows what I'm talking about. Could she have been behind this prophecy the entire time? Did she create us, Whiskey and I, only for us to die? Is this all her doing?

"Yes" she said quietly as she turned back to face me.

"How long?" I asked solemnly. Pain raked through my chest at her confession.

"Longer than you can imagine" she sighed.

"So you've known that one of us was going to die. You've known since before we were even born?" I snapped angrily.

"All living things die" she replied unfazed by my anger. How could she do this to me, to us? Is it all fake, is her love just a ruse? Just a way to fill the lines of a story written hundreds of years ago. Did she write this story? Is all of this her fault?

"Did you do this to us, the prophecy, was it all just part of your big celestial plan?" I growled out. Selena chuckled as she sauntered over to me. She ran her long slender fingers over my cheek but kept walking, gliding through the tall flowers.

"I am powerful, My Darling. But I do not control destiny, nor do I choose how it comes to pass" she sang out. A heavy weight lifted off my shoulders at her words. That means she didn't force this wretched prophecy onto us.

"Can we stop it?" I asked the second most burning question on my mind.

"No" she replied in a monotone voice. A tear slid down my cheek and I dropped my head to the ground. That wasn't the answer I wanted to hear.

"Am I the bad one? Am I the one that brings death?" I asked sadly. I didn't look at my mother as I asked, I was afraid she would see how much I didn't want to know this answer as well. So many people have died around me, people I care about. Maybe they wouldn't have if I never met Gunner. I wiped the fresh tears from my cheeks and looked up. Selene was now standing in front of me, watching me with interest.

"Do you think you are?" she asked me.

"Cole died. His dad, my dad, all of those pack warriors. Heck, even Galterio. They all died because of me". My voice broke as I uttered the last three words. More tears shed and a sob wracked my body.

"If you never gave me Gunner, if I just died in the basement when I was a child, maybe none of this would have happened" I cried. I lowered my head and twisted my fingers together as I sobbed. Not a second later, a cool hand touched my chin and lifted my face. Selene looked at me with sadness in her gaze.

"All living things die, my daughter. Gunner was made for you, as you were for him. Death can make one feel helpless, but death is inevitable either way".

"Are you telling me that I am going to die?" I blubbered out.

"One day" she said with a small smile, though it didn't reach her eyes. Something she said though itched at my brain creating a new question I hadn't yet thought of. Selene let go of my chin and was about to continue her gliding.

"Wait" I said as I turned to her.

"You made Gunner for me. Did you make a True Mate for Whiskey too?" I asked with a tilt of my head. Selene stopped her wondering and turned to face me completely. She watched me with a blank expression as I waited for her response. If we were both destined to be the Triple Goddess, she wouldn't create a True Mate for me and not Whiskey, right? Not unless she knew for sure that it was Whiskey that was going to die. Unless... no. Sickness twisted through my stomach and my chest tightened. I placed my hand over my heart, trying to lessen the pain my thoughts were inflicting on me.

"Was Gunner made for her too?" I choked out painfully. The idea of having to share Gunner was one I could not swallow. There was no way I could ever survive that. He is my everything. Was he made to be her everything too? Selene didn't answer. Instead, she slowly lowered her body into the grass. She looked over her shoulder at me, and without saying a word, I knew I needed to sit beside her. I sat at her side, with my body facing hers, and waited for the answer to my question. I swallowed hard, trying to call forth enough courage to ask it again.

"Gunner is yours, and yours alone" Selene's voice sang out. I sighed audibly and my shoulders slumped with relief. I was about to ask another question, but Selene continued.

"Aurora also had a True Mate" she said while looking off into the distance. That means there's hope. If Selene had planned for us both to have a True Mate, then maybe she planned for both of us to live. Somehow. I smiled, with the newfound hope filling my chest with warmth.

"Is he close by, like Gunner was to me?" I asked. The silence that followed cut my hope in two.

"Aurora killed her True Mate" Selene said sadly as she dropped her head. My chest twisted in pain. Just thinking about Gunner being hurt is enough to make me physically sick. How could Whiskey have survived after being the one to hurt her Mate?

"How?" I managed to choke out.

"Aurora was lost to us many moons ago. Her fated one was nothing more than a casualty of her anger" Selene answered.

"How is she still alive though? I thought you are supposed to die if your True Mate dies" I said gripping my chest.

"There was no connection made. She never saw him, nor did he see her".

"How is that possible?" I blanked.

"Aurora's anger has taken many lives, more than even she knows. So many of my children, gone" Selene whispered. Her voice was laced with so much sorrow. Her sadness seeped into me, bringing forth more tears. I didn't know what to say, I didn't know how to comfort her. So I didn't, I just stared at her blankly.

"Aurora never got the chance to find her anchor, her love. Her anger moves through her so swiftly, pushing her, leading her. She wasn't capable of looking upon each one of her victims. And even then, she may not have seen him". The confirmation swirled through my brain. All those Weres. Their lives, she took them all. "She really is the killer, the one attacking all those packs" I whispered dejectedly. It wasn't a question. I just needed to hear myself say it out loud. Silence ensued between us as I tried to wrap my head around the revelation.

"Does that mean that she is the bad one, the death bringer, it's not me?".

Selene didn't answer, she just picked a flower and played with its petals. I turned away from her and looked out over the pure white landscape. Whiskey is the killer. All those packs, all those Weres. The children, the innocent. How could she do that to them? Why would she do that to them? Is that why she came to Tri-Moon, is she going to kill my pack members, my family? I can't let that happen.

"She won't stop, will she?" I said out loud, more to myself than to Selene. Whiskey has suffered so much, more than anyone else. Probably more than even me. I understand how a lifetime of hate filled abuse can warp your mind. Growing up with Hank, he did everything in his power to make me weak and miserable. And I was, every day I wanted to die. At least I found Gunner at the end of that shitstorm. I know now why Hank never just let me die. He wasn't allowed to. But Whiskey, her life was much different. She was tortured on the daily, like clockwork. Trained and brainwashed to hate her own kind. I can only imagine what other awful things those monsters did to her. Or what they made her do or see. I mean she saw our father die, and Selene showed me what that did to her. She holds so much hate and resentment in her heart. There is no happily ever after at the end of this for her. How can there be? Whiskey never got the chance to find her peace. She destroyed her lifeboat before it could save her. I can't let her destroy mine too.

"What am I supposed to do now?" I asked looking at the side of my mother's face.

"You do as you have always done" she answered cryptically.

"What is that exactly?" I huffed. She turned to face me and cupped my cheek. Her gentle fingers felt cool against my skin. Her loving gaze penetrated through my chaotic thoughts. The sound of her steady and rhythmic breathing lulled me into a sense of calmness that I didn't know I was capable of.

"The right thing" she whispered. As her breath fanned across my face, my body fell back into the grass. I stirred and shot up onto four paws. I looked around at the now dark field and regained my bearings. I was back home again, in the flower field. I stretched my limbs and shook my bottom half and tail. I wasn't worried anymore. I was still sad and still a little scared. But my understanding had become clear now. Whiskey is an unstable force of rage and destruction. She isn't going to stop killing the Weres, not even now that she has regained her memories. If anything, I think it will only drive her further into herself and her pain. I can see how this world will look if she is the Triple Goddess that survives the prophecy. The wolf will thrive, I have no doubt about that. But peace under Whiskey will be all darkness. Oppression, pain, and death. All conceived under a corrupt monarchy. Human and Were alike, they will all kneel to the pressure, stuck under the heel of her foot. She needs to be stopped. It's the right thing to do.

Chapter Forty-One

Zelena

Back at the house, I found Roe in the kitchen. It's as if she doesn't like the other rooms of the house, besides maybe the library. She could have gone back to bed, no one would have thought any less of her for it. But no, even in the middle of the night, Roe will always find a way to busy herself with cooking. It's her love language after all. Feeding her loved ones, it's how she shows her affection.

"Hi" I said as I sat on a stool at the bench,

"Zelena, Sweetheart, are you doing okay?" she asked while putting down the knife she was using to slice a giant watermelon. I pulled a slice off the cutting board and took a quick bite before smiling.

"I'll be alright" I answered her honestly. She narrowed her eyes and put her hand on her apron covered hip. She didn't even need to say anything, she just looked at me with that motherly stare.

"Really Roe, I know what needs to be done. I understand it now" I told her with a nod. She stood up straight, dropping her hand and looking at me with concern.

"What do you mean?" she asked shakily. I put the rind of the watermelon back on the cutting board and stood up.

"Where's Mum?" I asked, ignoring her last question,

"She went for a walk. She's struggling with the news" Roe said while still studying me intently.

"And Gunner?" I quickly added,

"Still in the hall".

"Thanks, Roe" I quipped and headed for the door.

"Zelena, wait" she called, but I was already through the door. I have a feeling I know what she wanted to say. 'We can find a way around it' and 'We can get through to her' or 'Everything will be okay'. And it will be okay, I'm going to make sure everyone will be okay. I have one chance.

I pushed open the door of the hall and let it close with a thud behind me. Gunner and all the other men were still gathered around the table. Gunner stood at the head, while the others were all seated, giving him their undivided attention. The conversation stopped when I came in and all eyes were on me as I walked over to Gunner's side. I pulled his shoulder down so that I could reach the side of his face, and gently pressed my lips to his cheek.

"Where are you up to?" I asked as I slowly looked over the map on the table.

"Zee?" he questioned with a raised brow, not seeming to understand my question.

"Your plan to capture her, what have you got so far?" I repeated. Gunner sighed and turned to face me a little more and placed his hand on my hip.

"Zee, you don't need to be here for this" he said gently.

"Of course I need to be here" I scoffed and pushed his hand away.

"Zelena, we're talking about capturing your twin sister" Smith said, pulling my attention from Gunner's concerned face.

"I'm aware of that" I responded in a 'duh' kind of tone.

"Babe, we can handle it. Go back to bed" Gunner said while taking my hand in a firm but gentle grip. He began to pull me toward him as if to lead me out of the room, and that's when my anger boiled over. I whipped my hand from his and slammed my fist on the tabletop. A wave of energy flew out from the contact point, hitting everyone sitting around the table.

"It's my prophecy, my sister, and my problem" I yelled as I glared out at all of the shocked faces.

"If any of you have an issue with that, there's the door" I snarled angrily while pointing at the door behind me. There was no response for a moment, apart from my harsh breathing, the room was silent. I turned to glare down Gunner. He would be the only one who would dare argue with me on this, and I have no idea which way he will go.

"If you wish, love" Gunner broke the ice and kissed my lips. The sparks danced across my face and calmed me back down again instantly.

"Can one of you please tell me where you're at?" I asked politely with a hint of authority in my voice. I slowly sat down in my chair to Gunner's left and crossed my right knee over my other.

"The warriors haven't found any trace of her yet. I gave the order for them to start looking closer to the pack border" Smith spoke from his seat.

"That far, really?" I questioned.

"Well, we don't have a lot to go on. It looks like she left the area" he shrugged.

"She didn't leave" I said back casually.

"How do you know that?" Gunner asked looking down at me.

"Because she won't leave until she's finished what she came to do" I answered like it was obvious. Clearly, as seen on the questioning faces around the table, they didn't seem to think it was so obvious.

"And that is what exactly?" Felix interjected. I took a deep breath and calmed myself, then turned to look at him.

"To kill all the Weres in Tri-Moon" I told them all.

"Before she moves on to the next closest pack" I continued. I turned to Gunner and explained further.

"That would be Blue Moon, Tobias's old pack. No?".

He didn't answer for a moment, just enough time for the tension in the room to thicken to near suffocating levels.

"You know this how?" Smith growled lowly.

"Because it's what she's been doing in Russia. And who knows where else, she's probably been killing Weres all over the place. She has been making her way through the packs, looking for me".

"Zee, we don't know for sure that it's her" Gunner said while rubbing his fingers over my hand. I rolled my eyes and pinched the bridge of my nose. I know he just wants to protect me and not get me upset, but denying the truth isn't going to do anyone any good.

"Gunner, you know it as well as I do. You spent time with her on the way here, you got to know her before anyone else. Tell me truthfully, do you actually believe that it's not her?" I snapped and looked up at him. He hesitated, his eyes flicked all over the place and he opened and closed his mouth a couple of times. He was trying to convince himself it wasn't true. As much as I hate it, he grew to care for her in the short time they spent together.

"Zee..." he finally drawled out. The big loveable fool. I cursed and stood up again and looked at everyone at the table. Smith, Lupus, Felix, Daniel, the commander who I still can't remember.

"Let's be serious. She was raised in a facility run by Hunters. She was tortured and brainwashed her whole life. She hates us. She hates what she is. She especially hates Selene. She's been killing off the Weres as she was programmed to do. You all know that I'm right, why else would you be in here planning to capture her. You're putting the pieces together, I can see it. The prophecy. The darkness. The mysterious angry twin that shows up out of nowhere. Of course it's her. And I'm not the only one that knows it, you all do too".

When nobody answered I slowly sat back down and crossed my hands over my lap. Gunner's brows were drawn together as he frowned at the table. Smith was looking away from me, also deeply in thought. Lupus looked like the only one that didn't need to think about it. He was nodding along, determined anger painting his face. This was his pack for a long time, it makes sense that he would be so ready to protect it.

"How do you know all that, about her upbringing?" Felix asked.

"I saw it. Selene has shown me a lot" I answered bluntly. I kept it vague. I don't want to betray her confidence and I'm not sure how much of what she shows me is meant just for me. I looked at each of the important men in this pack and in my life, gauging their responses to my revelation, when I realised one was missing. I wonder where Tobias is, it's not like him to miss something like this. I reached out to him through our bond.

Tobias?

I flashed. But nothing came back, just emptiness.

Tobias, is everything okay?

I tried again. But still no response. If something had gone wrong, we would have been alerted. Tobias is a large Were, not easily hidden or unnoticed. But he fainted, just a couple of hours ago. Maybe there is something really wrong, maybe he is unconscious someone out in the forest.

Tobias!

I yelled through the flash, but still got nothing back. I don't like this, something is up. I came back to the room while they were talking about the search parties spreading out towards the borders.

"Where's Tobias?" I asked Gunner a little urgently.

"He was with Elaine and Venus last I heard" he answered casually. I bit my lip and looked over at Smith. He was talking with Felix, but his eyes were on me.

"Did you see him? Was he alright?" I asked Gunner in a whisper. That piqued his interest, and he crouched down next to my chair. "What's going on?" he whispered while twirling his fingers around mine.

"He isn't answering my flash, and earlier he… um. He… I don't know, he fainted or something" I mumbled out while eyeing Smith. Maybe he knows something. Fuck. I should have checked in on him, I knew he wasn't okay, and I still let him walk away. Gunner cupped my cheek and brought my gaze back to his.

"He'll be fine, he's the strongest Were I know" he said soothingly. "Yeah, but…"

"But nothing, he's probably just asleep, like you should be. It is three in the morning after all" he smiled a rubbed his thumb over the corner of my mouth. I swallowed my argument and nodded. Gunner leaned over and pressed his lips to mine before standing up completely. He returned to the head of the table and continued on with the conversation.

I sat back a listened intently as they discussed their options. The main topic of the discussion was about how they can trap Whiskey without her turning her powers on them. They came up with a few different versions of surprise attacks, from power suppressing plants, to normal human drugs. I kept my mouth shut while I listened. I knew that none of them would work. The only option was me. Everyone is constantly on me about how I am yet to realise my full potential. How I am more powerful than I know. That I am strong and undeniable, basically a superhero. Whiskey is my other half. My twin, my equal. Selene created us this way. If I am as powerful as everyone claims, then she is too. No one will be able to stand against her. Not even Gunner. He can access a lot of my power and my strength, but I could always feel the blockage. I am the Triple Goddess, the power is mine. He can't access all of it, not like I can. I stood up and cleared my throat, gaining everyone's attention.

"Can I have a moment?" I asked, stepping up to the edge of the table.

"Of course, my Love, you are the Luna, you can always have a voice here" Gunner said as he pulled me to his side. His arm came around my hip and I wrapped mine around his back. I fisted his shirt in my fist at his stomach and swallowed hard.

"I appreciate what you're doing here." I began with a shaky voice, "I know how hard you are all working. I know the lengths that each and every one of you will go to in order to protect this pack and its inhabitants. You're good men, good people, Gunner and I are lucky to call you our friends".

"What's going on, Zee?" Smith interrupted. I glanced over at him and sighed slightly. This is going to go down like a bag of dicks.

"I understand that you all have more experience with this sort of thing, but I have a plan of my own" I said strongly.

"Are you going to share this plan of yours?" Smith asked with a smirk. I tightened my hand around Gunner's shirt and nodded.

"Firstly, you need to move the women, children, and the elderly back to the safe houses. I know they have had to come and go multiple times now. With the hunters and all that. But if all goes to plan, this should be the last time they will have to leave their homes".

"Agreed" Felix added.

"Second, bring the warriors back to the village. They won't find her out in the forest, not if she doesn't want them to".

"She isn't the only one they are looking for" Daniel spoke up. Confused, I looked up at Gunner with an unspoken question.

"Doyle" he answered with a growl,

"We think he may have more men hidden close by. When I encountered him the last time, he had many more Weres with him than just the ones he allowed us to see" Gunner continued. I had completely forgotten about the scary half-breed.

"Where is Doyle?" I asked,

"We have him secured and under strict guard in the barn" Felix answered.

"Good" I nodded.

"What's next, Zee?" Smith asked, drawing my attention away from the memory of Alpha Doyle's half formed face.

"Right, well, you've all come up with some good ideas already" I started,

"But…?" Smith drawled out,

"But, none of them will work" I said bluntly.

"You can't just simply capture her, she's too smart for that. Like I said, the hunters brainwashed her, and tortured her, and Goddess knows what else they did to her. We know they were looking for us back then, we know they knew about the Triple Goddess's powers. It would make sense for them to use her for her power too".

"What are you getting at, exactly?" Gunner asked,

"I'm trying to say that you can't underestimate her. She has already shown that she's powerful"

"Not like you" Gunner interrupted.

"You don't know that" I clipped back. I reluctantly let go of Gunner and stepped out of his hold.

"Whiskey and I were made as equals. However powerful I may be, she is just a much so. The difference is the hunters would have been training her to use her power. I am self taught. She's going to have more control, she'll be more deadly".

"Where are you going with this, Zee?" Gunner asked with a harshness to his voice. However, I think he has already figured out where I'm going with this. I swallowed hard and drew on whatever courage I could muster.

"The only one that will be able to stop her, is me" I said to the group.

"No" Gunner growled protectively. I knew this was how he was going to react.

"The prophecy says that one of us has to die" I said softly.

"And that will not be you" Smith snapped angrily.

"I don't want it to be either, but that doesn't mean I want her to die. However messed up she may be, whatever evil she has done in this world, she is still my sister".

"Prophecies don't work like that, you can't save her. What is foretold will come about, no matter what you do" Felix added, crossing his arms over his muscular chest.

"I know what the prophecy means, I know what has to happen" I snapped at him annoyed. I closed my eyes and took a deep breath. As I opened them, I looked over at Felix with a softer gaze.

"I'm sorry, I didn't mean to snap. This is hard for me, I'm sure you all understand that, but it doesn't change the facts".

"What are the facts then, Zelena?" Lupus grumbled.

"Whiskey and I are equally matched, power wise at least. She is too strong for any of you, not even Gunner can match her. I have an idea, but I don't know if it'll work" I spat out as fast as I could. Just thinking about it was starting to give me anxiety. I don't even know if it will work, but I have to at least try. Whiskey deserves as much.

"There's something I haven't told you" Gunner piped up. I turned to look at him and frowned. I don't think I can handle any more bad news at this point in time.

"What?" I blanched.

"To get her to come with me, back to the pack, I did something to her" he said hesitantly.

"What did you do?" Smith asked with a snap in his tone. Gunner faced him and growled, swiftly shutting down any possibility of a challenge. Smith stepped back and dropped his head, conceding to Gunner.

"I used some kind of compulsion on her" Gunner admitted. I had to shake my head a little to make sure I heard him right.

"Compulsion? Like an Alpha command?" Felix asked before I did. Gunner shook his head and rested his hands on the table.

"No, I don't think so. It didn't feel like it at least" he said while looking at his hands. I looked down at my feet to think if anything like that had happened to me. I can't picture any time that I managed to compel someone to do something against their will.

"What then?" Lupus huffed gruffly.

"I'm not sure. I think it was Goddess magic. But maybe it was mixed with Alpha power, giving it an extra kick".

"Is that possible?" Smith questioned.

"I said I don't know. I was desperate for her to cooperate and to just trust me enough to come back here. I used my Alpha command, but I pushed with Zelena's magic at the same time. I think I somehow altered her brainwaves while I spoke" he continued.

"Look I don't know the science or the magic of it. But she was out of it, almost like she was hypnotized. I didn't even know what was happening the first time I did it" Gunner answered.

"The first time?" I snapped,

"Meaning you've hypnotized her more than once?" I asked angrily. Something about this doesn't sit right with me. He took away her choice, her free will. After everything that I saw the hunters doing to her, this just seems extra cruel. Accidental or not.

"I didn't mean to, Love. Not at first. But I couldn't see any other way to get her back here without killing me, or trying to escape again" Gunner said gently while reaching his hand out for me to take. I was reaching up for it until he said the last part, and then I swiftly pulled it back.

"She tried to escape. So you forced her to come here, I thought she agreed to it?" I asked angrily. I know what she has done, I know she has killed so many people. But I can't ignore the protective instincts I feel. She is still my family after all.

"She agreed, albeit hesitantly. But she agreed. She was just scared and uncertain, especially after learning I was an Alpha, and everything that went down with Doyle. I didn't force her, I just helped her" Gunner said convincingly. I took a slow deep breath and closed my eyes for a second. I know Gunner would never do something to hurt a woman. He would have felt the urgent need to bring her home, to fulfil the prophecy. Even if he didn't know it at the time. I can't fault him for that. I opened my eyes and took his hand.

"I don't like how it went down, but I know you had to do what you had to do" I told him as I lifted his hand to my cheek. I pressed my cheek to the back of his hand and held it there. He gently turned it over and cupped my cheek, rubbing his thumb across the corner of my mouth.

"Can you show me?" I asked staring into his eyes.

"Hypnotize someone?" he balked with wide eyes and I nodded. Smith stood up and smiled.

"I volunteer as tribute" he announced with three fingers saluting in the air. I don't get it, but Gunner laughed, so I suppose he does.

"Okay" Gunner chuckled as Smith came to stand in front of us. Gunner placed his hand on Smith's shoulder and leaned in close to his face.

"Your right hand is itchy, isn't it?" Gunner said in a low smooth voice.

"Yes Master" Smith replied in a robot voice. I huffed with annoyance and Gunner smacked him across the back of the head. Smith laughed and apologised as he rubbed the spot Gunner smacked.

Gunner moved his hand to Smith's neck and leaned forward again.

"Smith?" Gunner called and Smith stopped giggling and stared back at him.

"Is your right hand itchy?" Gunner called, his voice like ripples over a still pond. So gentle and captivating, I found myself leaning closer. Smith's face blanked and he nodded.

"It is" he answered in an emotionless voice, which was a little disturbing coming from the usually happy-go-lucky Smith.

"You can scratch your hand now, Smith" Gunner's voice carried softly through the room. Smith immediately lifted his hands and began to scratch at the back of his right hand.

"It's still itchy, isn't Smith?" Gunner voiced,

"Yes" Smith answered.

"Try smacking your hand against your head" Gunner suggested gently, and Smith obeyed. He slapped his hand against his cheek, then his forehead, then the side of his head. Gunner took his hand and pushed away a smirk playing on his lips.

"That's better, isn't it Smith?" he crooned like he would with a child.

"Yes" Smith answered.

"It's not itchy any more is it Smith?"

"No"

"Good. You can sit down now" Gunner whispered smoothly. Smith marched back to his seat and slumped down. We all watched, amazed, shocked, and in my case, terrified. After a beat, Smith blinked a few times and grasped his head.

"Ouch. Did it work?" he hissed while rubbing at his temples,

"Because my fucking head is pounding" he whined and pressed his forehead to the table.

"Incredible" Lupus gushed and smacked his palm on the table.

"That's..." I began,

"Unnerving" Felix finished for me. I snapped my fingers and pointed at him while staring at Gunner.

"Exactly" I said loudly.

"How's your head?" Gunner asked turning to Smith. He groaned and lifted his head from the table.

"Like I have the worst hangover of my life" he whined and plopped his head back down.

"Is that normal?" I asked looping my arm around Gunner's bicep.

"I don't know, this whole thing is out of the norm. But Whiskey had headaches when she came to again as well" he answered. I hummed and tightened my hold on Gunner. This is amazing, but also scary. We have no idea what he is doing inside their brains. And if it causes pain, I don't think he should be doing it.

"I know" Gunner whispered so only I could hear him. The others were talking to Smith, to see if he remembered anything.

It could be dangerous

I flashed, keeping my gaze on Smith.

I agree.

We shouldn't do this again, not until we know what kind of damage we could be doing

I know, Sweetheart. I won't use it

Thank you

Gunner leaned down and pressed his lips to my temple, then held them there for a few seconds.

"Okay" he said loudly, recapturing the room's attention.

"What was your plan, my Love?" Gunner said softly. I looked up to meet his adoring gaze. I will never tire of the way he looks at me. The love that he can hold in a single gaze is breathtaking. I lifted his hand and pressed my lips to the palm of his hand then rested my head on his chest for a brief moment. After a few seconds, I stepped out of Gunner's arms again and faced the waiting men.

"The village needs to be cleared of all pack members. She is stronger and more powerful than I think you have anticipated" I began.

"She has been killing off packs across the country, yet she has somehow managed to come out unscathed each time. That's very unusual. We can't risk our people's lives, so we have to get them out of here" I continued.

"That has been agreed to by all of us already" Felix added.

"Good. Next, the fighters need to surround the village, but stay out of sight. If she tries to run, we need to be able to stop her"

"Yes, good idea" Lupus nodded along.

"Then, I will face her" I said sternly.

"Not alone" Gunner growled lowly. I huffed and took his hand.

"Not completely alone, no. I will need you there. You're going to put the force field up around us, keeping everything on the outside safe from whatever happens on the inside"

"And what is it you think is going to happen inside the force field?" Smith snapped. He looked and seemed a little upset. His mouth was set in a mad frown, but his eyes were scared. It could be the headache, or he could just be genuinely afraid.

"Like I said before, I don't know if it will work" I answered hesitantly. I am seriously starting to doubt myself. I don't even know if I can do what I'm thinking of doing, or if it is even possible.

"Do you want to share with the group anyway?" Smith said again, his annoyance clear in his voice.

"I'm going to take her wolf" I answered with a firm nod.

"You're going to do what now?" Lupus blanched, seemingly shocked.

"Selene gave me the idea. When she threatened to take Gunner's wolf. Tobias explained what he thought that would do to him" I answered.

"And what did Tobias think was going to happen?" Gunner asked.

"He said that because you were an Alpha, losing your wolf would make you weak and eventually kill you".

"If you're going to kill her, why would you want to do it so brutally like that? Taking her wolf, taking away that side of her soul, it's barbaric" Lupus scoffed somewhat disgusted by the idea.

"First off, I don't want to kill her. Aurora isn't an Alpha, so it shouldn't have the same effects" I snipped back.

"She avoids her wolf, she hasn't bonded with it. I don't think she even likes that part of herself" Gunner said thoughtfully.

"See, if that's the case, then maybe she'll be okay. If her wolf dies, so will the heightened feelings and instincts. If she has no wolf, if she is just a human, maybe she can stay alive" I said hopefully. Everyone was quiet for a moment, thinking it over, going through the possibilities. Felix was the first to speak,

"It's not a terrible plan" he said slowly while running his hand through his hair.

"The prophecy speaks of Goddesses and wolves. Not humans. If she has no wolf, she can't be a Triple Goddess. So it would be void, right?" Felix talked through his thought process. I was grateful that he had come to the same conclusion that I did.

"But how will you do it?" Smith jumped in.

"I'm not entirely sure. I hope that when the time comes, Mother will help me".

"You are basing your entire plan on The Moon Goddess picking sides? Not just sides, but picking between her children?" Lupus asked incredulously.

"Lupus is right, what if something goes wrong? What if she doesn't help you, what if you can't do it? What if Whiskey hurts you before you can do anything? I'm not sold on this plan, Zee, there are too many variables" Smith said while shaking his head. I sat down slowly and watched as Gunner, Felix, Smith, and Lupus argued through the countless possibilities and unforeseeable problems with my plan. It doesn't really matter what they think though. There is no other way. Either I try to take away her wolf side or I'm forced to kill her. That, or she kills me first. Either they help me, or they don't, this is how it's going to be. I trust the All-Mother, I truly believe that she will help me. I sat quietly and listened. Goosebumps ran over my body, and I shivered. The air turned and something felt different. A blast of nausea hit me and I heaved. I think I'm getting too tired to pay attention. Pain bloomed in my chest, silently taking my breath. I sat forward and rubbed the centre of my chest. I really need to rest. I stood up abruptly and waved my arms, capturing everyone's attention.

"Guys, guys, guys. Stop. We can stay here for days going through all the things that could go wrong. But we don't have that kind of time, and we don't have any other options" I said exasperatedly while still rubbing at the spot on my chest.

"Incorrect" Smith argued.

"One of us could kill her instead" he said with his finger up in the air.

"You know that's not how the prophecy goes" I scoffed.

"It doesn't say specifically who has to kill who, only that one can survive" he continued.

"Smith, please" I started but was cut off by Gunner.

"Smith, enough. I know you're worried about Zelena, we all are. But there has to be..." Gunner was interrupted by the hall door flying open and Roe standing in the frame, her face pale and her eyes wide.

"She's here, in the village. She killed Konstantin and his guards" Roe rushed out. Lupus was at her side in a split second, wrapping his arms around his Mate. My skin ran cold and the pain in my chest got worse. I folded over and grunted, grasping at my chest.

"Zee, what's wrong?" Gunner asked urgently as he grabbed my shoulders.

"Something's wrong. It feels like my chest is being torn open from the inside" I grunted on a harsh breath.

"It's Tobias" Roe gasped.

"He was... He's... He's" Roe stuttered as she began to cry while shaking in Lupus' arms.

"He's what, Roe?" I shouted from my hunched position.

"He's been hurt" she forced out fearfully. My blood froze and the pain exploded, engulfing me completely. My stomach dropped from the all consuming fear I felt. Oh Goddess, no. Please, don't take Tobias.

Chapter Forty-Two

Whiskey

I gave Tobias and the angry woman a large birth and made my way back to the shed where they had been keeping the prisoner. The searching warriors were moving further away from the village, just as I had hoped they would. This should be a quick and relatively easy task. Not even Gunner and his little bitch Mate will get in the way of my mission. I climbed onto the same tyre, under the same window, and peered through the dirty glass once more. Gunner's mother and father had left now, but the prisoner wasn't left alone. One of the dirty wolves from Doyle's pack was now joined by three people, probably members of Gunner's pack. Though, just by looking at the fowl glare and the dishevelled appearance of one of the humans, and the fact that he hung rather close to the wolf, I think it's a safe assumption to guess he is one of Doyle's. Taking down four measly animals is child's play. I'm determined not to let that blue eyed bastard get away from me for a second time. Hopefully, I've gotten to him before he's spilled the beans to Gunner's mother.

I jumped down from the tyre and looked around. I couldn't see anyone, but I could hear them. The searching wolves, far out into the forest. The soft murmuring from the voices inside. The regular sound of nature. I couldn't pick up anything out of the ordinary, but that didn't mean I could be less cautious, it just meant there was no imminent threat. Sticking to the side of the shed, I slid around the outside until I was right beside the open door. I focussed my hearing and listened to the voices from inside. Two of the men from Gunner's pack were complaining about having to watch this guy instead of being on the half-breed detail. They just don't know how lucky they are. They get to die first, quickly and quietly. Many of their friends will die much more painfully, I can say that for sure.

An evil smile spread across my face as I thought about my blade slicing through their flesh. I didn't wait another second before I stepped through the large shed doors, the evil smirk still gracing my face. One of Gunner's guards was the first to see me. He was surprised at first. I assume he mistook me for the witch, Zelena. But it only took a second for the recognition to register, then fear sparked in his gaze. Good, he is smart enough to fear me. He pulled a bat shaped tool from his belt and raised it in the air.

"Stay where you are" he said cautiously, alerting the others of my presence. The wolf snarled and growled and stalked in my direction. The other guard matched the first one's stance, eyeing me warily. The prisoner's eyes bulged from inside his head as he dropped from his chair. The blanket that was around his shoulders fell to the dirt covered floor as he scurried back on his butt.

"Besomar" he whispered, his voice laced with fear and the knowing that his end was imminent.

"Put your hands up" the first guard yelled. I turned my gaze from the pathetic prisoner and sneered excitedly at the guard. His back seemed to straighten as his Adam's apple bobbed. I lifted my hands into the air and tilted my head ever so slightly to the side. My talons extended from the tips of my fingers as I flexed my hands, the sharp nails clicking together as I did. The other man, the one from Doyle's pack, was shaking and grunting. His fear and rage were forcing the change on him. A chuckle burst from my lips at my witnessing his weakness. It was all he needed for the beast to take over from the human. He and the other raggedy wolf charged at me, their growls vibrating through the shed's rickety wooden walls.

"NO!" one of Gunner's guards yelled, but it was too late. I turned to the side to dodge the first wolf and bent my spine back to duck under the second one. The first wolf recovered quickly and came for my thigh. I kicked my leg up and jumped over its head, dragging my talons along its neck as I went. I landed on top of it, with my claws still embedded in the soft flesh at the side of its neck. It was still alive and struggling beneath my hold. The other wolf whirled on me and growled loudly as it took in my position on top of its friend. I smirked at the beast as it took a step forward. I grasped the inside of the beast's neck and reefed my arm back, taking a chunk of its flesh with me. Its death was instant, an unfortunate outcome.

"Stand down" one of Gunner's guards yelled from off to the side. Though I don't think he was ordering it from me, I believe he was telling the other wolf. Interesting, why would they not want to attack me after I killed one of their allies? Thankfully the mutt didn't listen and charged in a furious rage. Stupid, he wasn't paying attention. During my takedown of the first dog, I picked up a short steel pole from the floor next to the bench that we landed beside. The wolf ran straight for me, a wrangled battle howl pouring from between its exposed teeth. I stood my ground as it closed the distance between us. As it launched itself through the air to tackle me, I pulled the pole out from behind my back. The dog saw it, right before the dumb thing impaled itself through the chest, I saw the flicker of realisation pass over its eyes. I like watching that knowing look take hold of a person or a beast. The last flicker of their life, a lifetime of memories passing through in just mere milliseconds. Then, death.

I crashed back into the dirt as the wolf landed on top of me, the pole jammed right through its heart. I lay listening as it expelled the last breath of air from its lungs before I pushed it off me. Its warm blood drenched my shirt, heating my usually cold skin. I slowly stood and turned to face the two remaining guards. They were still guarding the cowering blue-eyed wolf on the floor, blocking my access to him. I smirked and stepped toward them. The guard in front raised his weapon and growled.

"Stay back" he snarled with his teeth bared. The second guard moved himself to better protect the prisoner. A futile endeavour, but it's sweet that he tried. I stepped forward again and the guard rumbled his warning.

"We don't want to hurt you" he said as fiercely as he could, though it did nothing to scare or deter me. I want to play with this little dog a little. I took a step back and raised my hands in front of me. "I don't want to hurt you either" I said in my most innocent voice.

"That's good. How about we get the Alpha out here and you two can chat? Does that sound good?" the guard said with a much softer tone. I stepped back again and nodded my head slowly.

"Yes, please" I added with a weak smile. He was falling for it hook line and sinker. The dipshit behind him though was still glaring at me with furious eyes. The guard pointed to the corner of the shed and nodded his head.

"You have a sit down just there, I'll go fetch the Alpha, okay?" he said warily.

"Yes, okay" I whispered and dropped my eyes to the floor in an act of meekness. My small stature had always worked in favour of making me look unthreatening. Men usually fell for the trick. In my experience, a male could never see a female and consider her a threat. Especially if that female was smaller than him. Too bad for them and their closed-minded way of thinking. I am far more dangerous than any man, no matter his size.

I had walked back far enough now, and thankfully without them noticing my retreating. As soon as the first guard turned his head away to speak with the one behind him, I took my chance. I pulled the pole from the chest of the dead dog on the ground and launched it through the air like a spear. It was a perfect throw, hitting like a bullseye, slicing right through his lower abdomen. The guard gurgled and dropped to his knees. Not a kill shot I don't think, unfortunately. The blue eyed prisoner screamed and began to blubber as the other guard changed into his beast on the fly. The mutt, now covered in scruffy brown fur, flew toward me with his teeth bared. His paws hit the ground hard and in just two steps he was mere meters in front of me. He jumped with his claws out, aiming for my jugular. Just as he was about to connect, I bent my body back so that he flew right over the top of me. I gripped hold of his sides and flipped us both as we soared above the ground, making us land so that I was on top of him. I straddled his fluffy chest as we skidded along the dirt. Without waiting for the dumb dog to regain his balance, I let my own claws protrude through my fingers and sliced them mercilessly through the soft tissue of the wolf's neck. It yelped with a strangled cry and continued to struggle for a moment. I held my position on top of the creature, keeping its back planted on the ground and its front paws between my knees. I watched intently as the life drained from its eyes while its blood spilled onto the dirt around us.

I slowly stood and turned to the half dead guard and the whimpering prisoner. How embarrassing. These are Gunner's best? These are the ones he entrusted to guard and protect these lands. Taking out his pitiful pack looks like it is going to be easier than I thought. I wiped the blood from my hands on my pant legs as I approached the guard. He was gripping the pipe sticking out of his stomach with a grimace on his pained face. A smear of blood coated his chin and lips, slowly dribbling from his mouth. Well, I guess it was a kill shot after all. I smiled down at the man as I watched him grunt and groan while he attempted to pull the metal rod from his body. He looked up to meet my gaze and his eyes hardened. I expected to see fear, pain, or even sadness. I didn't see any of that. No, this mutt was angry, his defiance shone brightly in his dying eyes.

"You'll never beat them" he snarled with a splutter of blood. His confrontation surprised me, I almost blanched, but kept my face still. I let my smile spread wider and crouched down to his level.

"You think so?" I asked teasingly.

"I know it" he growled with a cough as more blood dripped from his sneering lips. I'd be lying if I didn't admit that his lack of fear fascinated me. Beasts are always scared in their last moments of life. Why is this one so different? I tilted my head to the side and reached my hand forward, swiping my thumb across the blood on his chin. He tried to pull his head away from my fingers but failed miserably.

"So confident" I chided then licked his blood from my finger. He growled and sat up as much as he could, which wasn't all that much.

"She's more than you could ever be" he smirked through his blood coated lips and then dropped back onto the ground with a grunt. He didn't say her name, but I could take a good guess as to who he was talking about. Fucking Zelena. It doesn't take much to make me angry, it never has. But I have always been able to maintain a firm grip on my anger. Showing any kind of emotion, even considering letting my anger explode, would have resulted in punishment. Learning to control myself happened very quickly in life. Hearing this dog's words, his dying jesting, his attempt at angering me, it worked a treat. My skin turned icy cold with the fury that rolled through me. This pathetic mutt thinks that she is better than me. ME! He is crazy, he must have lost too much blood, and it's made him delusional. There is no one equal to me. No one even comes close. I am the best killer this world has ever seen. I am an unstoppable force. I am the god-damn merchant of death. I will rip that fucking bitch to pieces, along with every other fucking dog in this pack. And every pack, all over the world. I WILL END THE WEREWOLF SPECIES!

I didn't look back at the guard as I stood up again. I curled my hand around the pipe and watched as whisps of black smoke twirled around my fingers. Pulling the pipe from his chest, I smirked while examining the smoke closer. The dying dog yelped and groaned out a long breath. His head dropped back with a lifeless thud. I twirled the pole in my hands and smiled, then lifted the blood to my nose. I took in a deep sniff, letting the scent of the metallic blood fuel my internal fire. I felt the delicious goosebumps roll over my skin as the itch settled beneath it. Excitement mixed with my thirst for blood, and I knew the hunt was on. Fuck my planning, fucking the research. The time is now.

An array of tools hung from hooks on the wall to my right. I scanned the items slowly, a few rakes, a pickaxe, a couple of crowbars, and some axes. My eyes landed on a hatchet, the blade glinting from the dim light on the roof. It's no Sai blade, but it'll still get the job done. I took the axe from the hook and tossed it up in front of me. The handle spun in a full three-sixty before landing in my hand again. I sucked my teeth and nodded my head with a newfound sense of determination. Clutching the bloodied pole in one hand and the hatchet in the other, I rolled my shoulders back and sauntered out of the shed.

The village itself was dark and quiet. With the dawn not far away, everyone was still fast asleep. That makes it easier to pick them off, though far less fun. I prefer them to run, I enjoy the chase, the hunt. Thankfully, I don't feel the need to hide and be sneaky anymore. I want them to know I'm coming for them. I want her to know I'm coming for her. She'll know that I will be the one to end her. Standing outside the shed, out in the open, in clear view of anyone who thought to look my way, I lifted my head and took a deep breath. I let the air fill my lungs, I let it seep into my bloodstream. I could feel the energy it gave me, the extra power boost shot through my body. Air is my thing. It's my strength, my bond. I am air. And when I wish it, I can take it away. Such a beautiful gift, to deprive anyone of the one thing they need to survive. Their one true life source. That power in my hands was intoxicating.

I turned my gaze back to the village. The pickings in the clearing were slim, with everyone still in their little houses. The barn. I could take care of Doyle and his pack of abominations. At least it would get them off the playing field for when the real fight starts. That's it then. I nodded my head with conviction and strutted off around the house towards the clearing. As I came around the side of the building, before I reached the last corner, a figure appeared in front of me. I didn't wait to examine who the person was or to give them the time to call for help. I swung my arm out, slicing the tip of the hatchet across the person's chest. He screamed and stepped back, but quickly tripped over his own feet. His ass hit the ground as his hands went to the gaping wound on his chest. He opened his mouth to scream again, and I swiftly embedded the hatchet in the top of his head, cutting off any alarm he was about to raise. His eyes did a weird cross-eyed thing that drew a giggle from my lips. I grabbed his shoulder and pulled the axe from his skull. Wiping the blood off using his shirt, I then let him drop into the dirt like the bag of shit that he was. Hiding in the shadows was over now. I am going to march right through the heart of the village and take out anyone who gets in my way. I tossed the hatchet once again and marched in the direction of the barn.

I only got a few yards when the next person spotted me. It was a woman with a small child in her arms. At first, she smiled and lifted her arm to wave. I suppose that is when she saw the feral look on my face, and perhaps the bloodied pipe and hatchet in my hands. Her smile dropped immediately, and she clutched the child to her chest tighter.

"Goddess?" she called fearfully. The chuckle burst from my lips before I could contain it. She turned to run, and I wasted no time in throwing the hatchet into her back as she retreated. Her pained scream broke through the cold silent air as she dropped to the ground. The child wailed loudly as they both hit the dirt. I jogged forward and reefed the small axe from her back. The child squirmed and screamed from under its mother's arm that had it pinned down. I grinned and lifted the axe above my head, ready to bring it down severing the child's head. As I swung the hatchet down, I was slammed in the stomach and sent flying backward. I landed hard on my lower back, but quickly rolled and recovered into a fighting position. A large tan-coloured wolf stood over the body of the woman, seemingly protecting the still living child. I gripped the hatchet tighter and stood up. The wolf was large, not an Alpha, but still one of the bigger wolves I have fought. Though, something was different about this beast. It looked normal, almost like it was an actual wolf, not just a Were. That's if wolves grew to that size. But they don't, that's impossible. I smirked and subtly shifted my grip on the pole.

"Ready to die?" I sneered at the wolf. It growled and lifted its head to the sky, a loud howl filled the air. Fucking coward, it's calling for backup. I threw my arm forward, letting fly the pole I was holding. It swiftly cut the air and hit the hip of the dog. Its howl died in an instant and it jumped back, dislodging the pole from its leg. I didn't wait for the wolf to ready itself, and instead, I charged toward it with the hatchet primed and ready to slice it open. I swung out for its throat as I reached it, but it was faster than I gave it credit for. The wolf jumped back while lifting the top half of its body at the same time, meaning the hatchet only just connected with its chest. Enough to cut through the skin, but not deep enough to debilitate it. As I was running full pelt, I couldn't stop before colliding with the stinky beast, so I dropped my shoulder and rammed myself into its upper chest as we collided. It was enough to flip the beast off balance, the force made it fall backwards and land on its side. I spun on my toes and jumped forward, landing on top of the dog. With the hatchet coming in a downward motion, I caught the look of realisation in the mutt's eyes. It knew it didn't have the time to stop me, it knew it was going to die today. It shifted its body right at the last second, meaning the blade of the axe was embedded into its shoulder and not its head which I was aiming for.

The wolf let out another howl, only this time it was from pain. I tried to pull the axe from its shoulder, but it must have lodged into the bone and was stuck. It squirmed underneath me, growling and whimpering, and I continued to yank at the handle of the hatchet to no avail. I stood up and wedged my foot into the dog's neck to give myself better leverage. As I pulled the hatchet free, blood spurted from the gaping wound, splattering across my face and upper body. The dog howled again before its head lolled to the side. It lay unmoving but still panting hard. I guess I nicked an artery or something. I went to step off the beast but was halted when two massive arms came around my body, trapping my arms at my sides. Calmness swept over me as gentle sparks danced across my skin. I breathed in deeply, taking in the scent of Tobias, the gargantuan brown man. I growled lowly and pushed on his arms, to get him to let me go.

"Calm now, Little Warrior" he whispered into the crook of my neck.

"Let. Me. Go!" I snarled out each word clearly and harshly. His arms didn't budge, if anything he tightened them. I felt the firm ridges of his chest and abdomen muscles press at my shoulders. His heavy breaths blew into my hair, making the stray strands dance. His scent was calming but infuriating at the same time. How can a stranger have such strong effects on my body? I know that he feels some sort of way about me. But that feeling is not mutual.

I slammed my head back, hoping to connect with his nose, but the bastard was too big. The back of my head hit his chest, while just the top of my head nicked his chin. It did nothing to put him off, and if anything, only served to annoy him.

"Enough, Aurora" Tobias hissed.

Hearing that stupid fucking name fuelled the fire in my chest. I felt my skin run cold as my heart rate increased. I looked down at my chest to see the whisps of black smoke starting to spiral out from under my shirt. The power dripping through my blood was delicious. The icy coldness prickling across my skin was everything I knew that I remembered and enjoyed. I've not always liked the cold. When I was a child, it was either like it or let it kill me. I chose to embrace it. Now it empowers me. The cool black smoke was the epitome of my cold blood and blackened heart. Is there any wonder it came to me, this power. It chose me because it is me. We are one and the same.

The smoke spread across my skin, down my arms, around my fingers, and up my neck. Tobias gasped from behind me when the smoke curled around his biceps. His body tensed and a low growl rumbled through his chest.

"Stop this" he demanded. I smirked as I caught the tone in his voice. He was a little worried. Good. He should be. I closed my eyes and leaned my head back against his chest, concentrating, as I felt the power flowing through my body. I focused on the coldness of it, the lightness and the gentle way it skimmed across my skin. I pulled it into me, letting it fill every corner and crevasse. The magic bubbled inside me, pushing and pulling to be let go. And so I did. I let it go. I opened my eyes and let the power fly out of me on a scream. A wave of pressure burst forth, shaking the cabins and violently rustling the trees. It was enough to knock Tobias off his feet. I took advantage of his unsteadiness and wriggled free of his grip. I turned on my heel and watched him slide along the dirt before coming to a stop. He frowned over at me and raised his hands in surrender. I'm a little disappointed, I thought a man of his size would have a little more fight in him.

"Please Aurora, it doesn't have to be this way" Tobias said with a tinge of sadness in his voice. I didn't reply, I just dropped my shoulders and tilted my head to the side.

"Please, put it down and come back inside" he said softly and extended his hand out to me.

"I can't do that" I growled back quietly.

"You can, this can end. Right here, right now" he said with the utmost sincerity. I almost believed him. Almost. A group of men and women ran towards us from both sides, all of them ready to leap into the fight without question. Tobias waved them down and they paused. I snarled and whipped my head back and forth to take in both groups. Nine in total. Easy enough to take out. I lifted my hand to the group on the left and pushed it out. A gust of wind flew forward, knocking the five of them off their feet and sending them soaring through the air and a good twenty meters away.

"Aurora, stop!" Tobias shouted. His loud voice echoed through the village.

"Leave me alone!" I screamed back at him.

"Please. We don't want to hurt you" he pleaded. I sneered at him and fixed my grip on the handle of the hatchet.

"No" I hissed venomously,

"But I want to hurt you" I yelled as I let the hatchet fly from my hand. My plan worked. I distracted him with my words, just long enough for him to not see the axe coming. It lodged into his chest, just off the centre. His feet staggered and he dropped to one knee. Both of his hands wrapped around the blade of the axe as he looked up at me. His face was a blank mask, but his eyes were dripping with sadness. I flashed my fangs and growled. Weirdly enough, Tobias sent me a half smile before dropping back and collapsing into the dirt.

Chapter Forty-Three

Zelena

I swallowed the pain in my chest and stood up slowly on shaking legs. Gunner grabbed my arm, half to help me stand, and I assume, half to stop me from bolting right for the door. Smith and Felix followed my movements, both of them also rising slowly. Smith's growl rumbled lowly through the room, quickly followed by Felix, then Lupus. The symphony of growls rolled around the room, all blending into one angry song. I hadn't realised it at first, but my own growl joined the angry tune. All of us rumbled out how worried, angry, and ready to fight we were. I pulled my arm from Gunner's hold and stepped toward the door. My claws extended and my bones ached through my anger and the desire the change. I pulled the Goddess's power into my body. It tingled across my skin, fed my soul, and filled me with energy.

"Let's get to it then" I snarled. My anger was palpable. Family be damned, if my own sister has hurt Tobias, MY Tobias, I will finish her where she stands. I will reign the pain she has caused back down upon her. However, if I was being honest with myself, it's all just a front. I'm angry, yes. I'm ready to fight and die for my pack and my family. But I'm also terrified. What if Tobias is hurt badly, what if he dies? What if I can't take Aurora's wolf, what if she kills more of my people? What if I fail? Everyone was counting on me now. I can't fail. I won't. For them. I have to do this, for my pack and my family.

I stomped through the doors, brushing past Roe as I went. I was almost at the front door when I was spun around by my shoulders. One of Gunner's arms came to the back of my neck, the other to my waist, pulling my body flush against his. His lips were on mine before I could argue for him to let me go. He kissed me with more passion than I was ready for. I could feel all his love, his devotion, his hopes and dreams. All of him was felt in that single kiss. When he pulled back, he rested his forehead against mine and breathed deeply.

"Come back to me. You hear me? Don't you dare leave me" he whispered desperately. Tears sprang to my eyes as the realisation once again slammed down on me. I'm risking everything for this prophecy. My love, my family, my life. I could lose them all. I swallowed my sob and pulled on every single bit of courage I could find. I grabbed both sides of Gunner's face and ran my thumb across his bottom lip. This man, Gunner, he is more than I ever could have wished for. I looked deep into his crystal blue eyes and pulled him down to kiss him once more.

"I'm not going anywhere" I said as convincingly as I could. He kissed my forehead and stepped out of my arms. He turned to the others, who I hadn't realised were watching and waiting for us.

"We're going with Zelena's plan, do as she instructed. Smith, clear the village as much as you can. Felix, round up the commanders and fighters and place them in the woods where we discussed. Dad, I need you with me, keep everyone and anyone away from me and Zelena. We have to stay focused and uninterrupted. Mum, get to Doyle, make sure he stays in the barn, we can't trust him not to turn on us" Gunner commanded. There was no hesitation, no question. Everyone nodded once and went about their duties. Gunner burst through the door first, with me and everyone else hot on his heels. I could hear commotion towards the far right corner of the village. Orders being yelled, a baby wailing, screams of pain. It was getting louder and louder by the second, all of it echoed across the early morning sky. Whatever was happening was happening fast. The others dashed off on their own missions, leaving Gunner, Lupus, and me standing on the porch. Hearing the screams of pain made my head pound. Feeling the deaths of my pack members snap away from my Luna bond was what was making me nauseous, not being overtired. I should have felt it sooner. Gunner should have felt it. How did we fucking me this?

I growled with frustration and ran forward, headed for the source of the chaos. Gunner came to my side and took my hand as we ran stride for stride. I looked up at him as we raced towards the fight, just as he looked down at me. In the back of his eyes, the soft glimmer of silver was starting to sparkle through. I have no doubt my eyes were shining a golden yellow too. Mother was with us, I could feel her in the air.

We reached the back of the barn, which appeared to be the outskirts of the fight, and I just about fell over my own feet. The scene was frightening, to say the least. It all but fuelled the already heated rage bubbling through my veins. Bodies were scattered around the clearing. Bodies of my fallen pack mates. Some were still alive and screaming in pain, and others were freshly dead and already paling. I raised my hand to cover my mouth. I don't know if I was trying to stop myself from screaming, crying or vomiting. I scanned the scattered bodies and froze when I found my mother. I dashed towards her and fell to my knees at her side.

"Mum? Cleo?" I blanched while moving my eyes between them. Fresh tears were pouring from my mother's eyes, and Cleo's breath was coming out in harsh pants. Alyse was kneeling at Cleo's other side, holding a t-shirt over her neck and upper chest. Mum was clutching Cleo's hand to her chest while gently brushing her fingers through the shaved side of Cleo's head. Blood was covering both their hands and Cleo's face and neck. I looked back at the shirt in Alyse's hands and realised it wasn't red, it was soaked in blood.

"What happened?" I demanded.

"The other one" Cleo panted with a pain filled face.

"Try not to talk" Alyse snipped while repositioning herself. She moved to place more of her body weight over the injury on Cleo's chest. Blood was seeping from beneath the cloth and dripping between Alyse's fingers.

"Aurora" Mum sniffed and swallowed hard. She didn't take her eyes off Cleo as she spoke.

"Cleo was defending a mother and her baby. Aurora got her in the neck with an axe" she said with a melancholy tone. I felt Gunner move in behind me as his hand came to rest on my shoulder. My eyes were wide, and I could hear my pulse thrumming in my ears.

"Aurora did this?" I whispered. Neither of them responded, they didn't need to.

"Zee, we need to go" Gunner said gently as he pulled back on my shoulder. I pushed his hand away and leaned down over Cleo. I pressed my forehead to hers and held it there. Cleo lifted her arm and grabbed the back of my neck. As her grip wavered and her arm started to fall, I grabbed her hand and held it in place.

"Thank you for bringing my mother back to me" I whispered. Cleo grunted and exhaled a sharp breath.

"For the Goddess" she wheezed. Her arm went limp and fell from her grip on my neck. I sat back and stared down at her unmoving body. Her chest had stopped rising and falling as her eyes glazed over. Lunaya sobbed softly, and Alyse tried to shake Cleo back to life.

"Cleo!" she shouted and rubbed at her chest. I moved back as Alyse hit the centre of Cleo's chest with her fist. I stood slowly and backed up into Gunner's waiting arms. I watched as Alyse desperately tried to revive Cleo. I turned my head to Gunner's chest and listened carefully. There was too much blood, as much Alyse tries, it won't do any good. Cleo's heart had stopped. There's no coming back from this one.

"I'm sorry, my Love, but we don't have the time" Gunner whispered gently. He brushed the hair from my tear-streaked face and lifted my chin to look at him.

"If we don't act now, there will be many more deaths to mourn" he said solemnly. I nodded my head and took one last look at my crying mother. Gunner took my hand, and I turned to follow behind him. Lupus was marching at his side, the two of them whispering harshly. I couldn't focus on what they were saying, I was too taken aback by the bodies we passed. My eyes caught on a woman lying face down on the ground with a gaping wound in her back. Another with his neck broken at an ungodly angle. Three or four wolf bodies followed quickly after. How could one person do so much damage? A rush of magic tickled across my skin, and the air around us felt thinner and lighter. Gunner stopped walking and turned to look at me.

"Do you feel it?" he asked. I nodded and lifted my head higher.

"She's literally sucking the air out of the village" I answered.

"How are you supposed to fight against that?" Lupus grunted angrily.

"I have powers too" I said as I lifted my hands and erected a shield around the three of us. The air immediately felt normal again, further proven by the sigh and deep breath Lupus took.

"Let's go" I commanded. The three of us set off on a jog toward where the magic was coming from. We rounded the barn and a growl burst from my lips. Whiskey stood with her back to the barn doors and a circle of bodies around her. She held a small axe in her hand that was red with blood. Her entire body was drenched in blood, so much so that there was barely any clear skin visible. Our warriors were fighting back hard, but their efforts were pointless. Between her brutal and fearless fighting skills and her ability to seemingly pull the air out of people's lungs, she was winning. Each warrior that attacked ended up dead with a swing of her axe or a swish of her hand. Dread weighed down my stomach, and an icy shiver ran up my spine. I don't know if I can beat her.

"Get everyone back, and stay out of sight" I growled over my shoulder at Lupus. He nodded once and changed form, right in front of me. His dark grey, and very large, wolf looked even more terrifying than the human form of Lupus did. I've seen his wolf form before, from a distance anyway. But seeing his wolf up close and personal, with the scar running across his face, his long sharp teeth on full display, plus the furious glint in his eyes. If I didn't know who it was in there, I would be wetting myself with fear.

Lupus dashed off back the way we came. I assume to get around the other side of Whiskey. Gunner once again took my hand and squeezed it tight. Together we cautiously walked forward. A group of seven fighters in their wolf forms spotted us and quickly ran over to flank us on both sides.

"Get out of here, all of you" Gunner commanded. The wolves stopped and looked at him puzzled. A large orange wolf shook his head a growled fiercely. I guess that is a no. Gunner waved them off and growled.

"I order you" he demanded, his voice echoing through the air.

"All of you, get your squad and clear the area". He used his Alpha command. They couldn't refuse him now, even if they wanted to. Unfortunately though, we gained Whiskey's attention. She flung her right arm out, catching a small brown wolf mid jump. Avoiding its chomping teeth, she threw the wolf effortlessly, sending it soaring back to crash into one of the cabins. I followed the wolf with my eyes and winced as it hit the structure and crashed through the wall. When it didn't come back out again, I turned and snarled at Whiskey. She was looking back at me with what I can only describe as a look of twisted insanity. Her smile was wide, her eyes glowed a dark red and her body seemed to be vibrating. But the most disturbing part was the whisps of black smoke that spiralled around her arms and legs. She's given herself over to it, the darkness. I know the enticing feel of it, it's not something I could ever forget. The power, the addictive taste of it, the sense of excitement it instils in you. The darkness was what took Gunner from me, it was what encouraged me to kill Galterio, and it was what made me feel crazy. If Whiskey had let it take her over, Goddess help us all.

I squeezed Gunner's hand once more before pulling my hand from his.

Now or never.

I flashed him as I stepped forward.

I've got you, I'm right here.

Gunner answered as he lifted the shield. Just around the both of us at first. But I could feel it expanding. I felt the power bristle through the air. Gunner's mixed with Whiskey's, with a bit of mine. All of it was Goddess magic, but the differences were astronomical. Whiskey's was cold and dangerous. Gunner's warm and illuminating. Mine was grounding and homely.

Lupus must have been fulfilling his task, as the clearing seemed to clear out almost instantly. I unfurled my fingers from my tightly clenched fist and flexed them. My eyes were fixed on Whiskey, as hers were on me. I spotted a wolf out of my peripherals as it charged for Whiskey. I suppose it thought I was distracting her enough. It was wrong. Whiskey didn't even look away from my gaze as she swiped her arm out, slicing the axe across the chest of the fighter. It yelped and began to tumble back. Whiskey twirled with dizzying speed and swung the axe once more, embedding it in the neck of the wolf.

A scream burst from within me, shooting out a wave of energy that crashed over Whiskey and shook the barn behind her. The wolf was dead, its head half decapitated. Seeing one of my pack members slain before my very eyes is entirely different from seeing the already dead pack-mates on the way here. It hurt differently, just as intensely, but very differently. Fury burned through me, lighting the spark of magic in my soul.

"Whiskey!" I shouted. Regaining her attention. She turned slowly to face me. Her wicked smile was still in place and her eyes held more evil than I thought possible. She laughed. Just a giggle at first, but it quickly turned to a full belly laugh. I think she may actually be crazy. Whatever those hunters did to her all those years, whatever pain and torment they subjected her to. It broke her. They broke her.

"You!" she huffed out between breaths.

"You're the best they have. You're the one that's going to stop me?" she cackled as she looked around the space, as if expecting more fighters to come.

"Stop this, now!" I demanded.

"Or what?" she blanched. All humour was gone, and she was glaring at me through furrowed brows and a tightly pressed scowl.

"What are you going to do, dear sister? You think you can stop me, you think you can beat me? Do you want to give it a go?" she snarled through clenched teeth. I quickly looked at the space around us. Multiple people had already died by her hand, but I couldn't see any more of our fighters.

They're gone, they're all safe. It's just us now, Zee.

Gunner's voice filled my head with the assurance that I needed. This is my shot, now or never right. I lifted my arms at my sides, pulling the power into my command. I manipulated the gravy around Whiskey and gripped hold of her. With her arms pinned to her sides and her legs completely encircled, I held her in place and lifted her off the ground. She struggled against the pressure, only for a moment, but just as quickly stopped again. I stepped closer to her, with Gunner right behind me. His forcefield was around all three of us, expanding out a fair distance over the space around us too. Whiskey watched us both closely as we neared her.

"I underestimated you" she hissed. A tight smile graced her reddening face. She wanted me to think she had given up, she made it look like she wasn't fighting it. She's trying to trick me into releasing her. I guess she doesn't know that I can feel it, the pressure she is putting on the hold I have. I can feel her pushing at the tethers. Just like with Galterio before he broke free of me. I can feel my hold on her weighing. It was just one moment. One quick flash of fear, a second of me doubting myself. Remembering how Galterio broke through my power, and what he did to me afterwards. It was just a flash of memory, but it was enough to interrupt my concentration. Whiskey took full advantage of my slip up and used her power to sweep me off my feet.

I flew off to the side with so much speed. The force at which I hit Gunner's shield made my brain wobble inside my skull. My hold dropped and Whiskey landed back on the ground on her feet. Keeping the shield in place, Gunner growled and stepped toward Whiskey with his claws ready. I quickly stood up and raced to stop him, but I was sent flying back into the shield once again. When I went to get back up again, a sharp pain shot through my chest, and I yelped out in pain. I looked down to the source of the irritation and froze. Shit. A long black jagged piece of ice was protruding from my chest.

I stared at the protruding icicle and gaped. It's made from the darkness. I produced the same type of weapon once. I killed with the same type of weapon. The sting of ice in my veins intensified and the cold emptiness of the darkness filled my chest. I gasped and snapped my head to Whiskey, who was about to launch another shard in my direction. Before the fresh shard of black ice left her hand, Gunner swung his arm out in her direction. The shield around us dropped and Gunner retrained all of his attention on Whiskey. As the shield fell away from behind me, I laid back onto the dirt.

Each breath was like a punch to the gut. I could hear the air wheezing in my lungs. My skin grew cold and I could feel the darkness taking over my body once more. I can't let her win. I can't give myself over to it, not again. There's no coming back a second time. I know that for certain.

I breathed in a deep lungful of air, as deep as the pain would allow. I held my breath and gritted my teeth to ready myself for the pain that was coming. I wrapped my fingers around the jagged piece of darkness lodged in my chest and yanked it out. An anguished scream cried out of me before I bit my lip to cut off the last of it. I pressed my hands down over the wound and forced myself to sit back up again. I lifted my hand to look at the damage done. Blood was covering my hands and quickly drenched my shirt. Fuck me. This isn't good.

The skin around the open wound was crawling with whisps of black smoke. The blood seeping from the wound looked more black than it did red. It was still infecting me, the ice shard, or the darkness. Whatever it is, I can basically feel it oozing into my body and soul. I tried to stand again and grunted with the excruciating pain.

"Little One" a voice called from the other side of one of the cabins. I whipped my head in the direction the voice came from and squinted. The morning sun was starting to brighten up the sky, which helped me spot a pair of legs lying on the ground around the corner. It was the gigantic pair of bare feet that made it click. Tobias. What is he still doing over there? Roe said he was hurt, why wasn't he taken to get help? I whipped my gaze back to Gunner who was dealing magical blow for blow with Whiskey. He appeared to be handling himself fine, for the moment at least. But it wouldn't last. He is strong and determined, but he isn't the one to end this prophecy. That burden is mine.

I tried to get up, but the strain only made me cough up blood. Fucking shit! I looked over to where Tobias's legs were poking out from the side of the cabin, and then over to where Gunner just blocked an ice shard flying for his face. To hell with it. I wiped the blood from my chin, then scrambled across the dirt on my hands and knees. The short distance felt like climbing a mountain. My chest felt like it was tearing apart. The icy feeling of the darkness was like cold needles jabbing into my skin, intensifying the pain tenfold. I wheezed and coughed out more blood as I dropped onto my side at Tobias's feet.

"Fuck" I hissed and put pressure back on my seeping wound. I swallowed the agonized sob in my throat. It went down like a lump of hot coal. I winced and glared up at Tobias, ready to tear him a new one for getting himself hurt. I'm so damn mad at him right now. For still being out here when wounded. For being his same old typical overprotective guardian beast, and staying at my side, circumstances be damned. But as our eyes met, my heart split in two.

"Tobias?" I cried and dragged myself up his body to his side. He was sitting up against the side of the cabin. His usually dark skin was terribly grey and dripping with sweat. There was a hole in his chest, long and very deep, that sat just to the left of his heart. Although blood was covering his chest, arms, and hands, the wound itself was no longer bleeding. The stench of death was all over him. His arm came around my side to my hip and he basically pulled me half on top of him.

"What happened, why is no one helping you?" I cried and went to touch his chest but quickly pulled my hands back before I did. Tobis slipped one of his hands under my shirt and let it rest on the skin of my lower back. His other hand he lifted and placed it over the gaping hole in my chest. The moment his skin touched mine I could feel the singe of his energy flowing around me.

"Aurora" Tobias croaked out.

"I thought I could talk her down, I was wrong" he chuffed out a forced laugh, which only made him cough.

"You need help, we need to get the doctor" I cried. I didn't know where to put my hands so I just kind of waved them around in front of me in a panic. Tobias took my hand and held it at the centre of his chest. I half choked, half sobbed. I don't know how to help him. I don't know what to do.

"Calm, Zelena. Be calm" he shooshed me and squeezed my hand.

"You're telling me to calm down, right now? You have a hole in your chest, I have a hole in my chest. We both have fucking holes in our fucking chests" I screamed out the sentence as I bounced on Tobias's lap. It was then that I stilled. It didn't hurt to move anymore. I looked down and my chest and my eyes bulged. The black whisps of smoke were gone, but the hole was also three times smaller. I felt it then. The zing. The gentle sparks where Tobias's skin was touching mine. He was doing that thing he did when I was pregnant. Feeding me his energy or some shit. I pulled my hands away from him and growled.

"What are you doing?" I yelled and glared at him. Tobias smiled weakly and reached out to take my hand again. I pulled it away from him and went to slide off his lap.

"Stop, don't do that. You need your energy, you need it to heal yourself" I scolded him. Tobias chuckled and grabbed both my hands, pulling them to rest in the middle of his chest.

"There's no healing this one" he said softly. Fresh tears fell as I glared down at him. I shook my head wildly and looked around us. I need a cloth or a bandage, something I can use to wrap up his wound. I'm not giving up, he can still heal. Tobias moved one of his giant hands to cup my face and pulled my gaze back to his.

"It's okay, Little Goddess" he whispered and pulled me closer to him.

"It's not okay, you're not okay, Tobias" I sobbed. My body was shaking rapidly, my heart was hammering, and my breaths were fast and sharp.

"Breathe, Zelena" Tobias said soothingly. He pulled my head forward and pressed our foreheads together. The energy swirled around us. It tickled my skin, eased my pain and filled me with calmness.

"Stop it, Tobias" I sobbed and tried to pull away again. His hand came around the back of my neck and held me in place.

"Everything is going to be okay, Zee".

"It's not. You're dying" I heaved. Tobias shook his head slightly and made a tsking sound.

"I'm fulfilling my destiny" he answered and squeezed the back of my neck. I moved my hands to his shoulders to steady myself.

"Let me do this. Let me complete my mission" he pleaded. His voice was becoming softer and weaker. The scent of death was growing stronger. But his energy never stopped flowing between us.

"What are you talking about?" I asked harshly,

"What mission?"

"This is always the way it was going to be". Tobias grunted and his face scrunched up.

"I made my choice" he wheezed.

"What do you mean?" I demanded.

"Selene. She gave me the choice. You or her" his voice broke on the word her and I swallowed another sob.

"She said I could stay with you. Be your guardian. Till we're old and grey" he said slowly through broken breaths,

"Or give my life to you. Give you my strength and my power. And ensure you live".

"What kind of crap is that?" I blubbered.

"It's okay. I chose you. You were always mine to save" he said with a weak smile.

"Please don't. You have to stay with me. I can't be without you" I pleaded as fresh sobs wracked my body.

"I will always be with you. You just need to feel for it" Tobias answered in his typical wise old owl ways.

"I need you" I begged and shook at his shoulder.

"You're my family" I wept through my river of tears.

"I'm here" Tobias strained and moved his hand to the centre of my chest, over the now healed wound. His energy fizzed and a soft blue glow lit up the space around us.

"This has been my greatest honour" his voice muttered weakly.

"Tobias, please" I whimpered and cupped his face. He pulled me forward and whispered stiffly,

"I love you, Little One". Tobias pressed his lips to my forehead and exhaled a laboured breath.

"Be the light" he croaked weakly. The blue glow evolved into a bright sparkle. Tobias's hand fell from the back of my neck and his head lolled to the side. I leaned back a look over his sickly face. The blue light was coming from him. It was his energy, his life spark.

The bright twinkling glow was pouring out of Tobias's skin and evaporating into mine. It twirled through the air, twisting and weaving in beautiful patterns. Like stars in the night sky dancing with the light of the moon, the blue light spun its magical web, illuminating the space around me. I watched as the whisps of his magic entered my skin. I felt it as it filled my soul with life and love.

When there was nothing left in him, his body just sat there, unmoving and empty. I stared blankly at the shell of my guardian. The tears didn't stop as I wept silently. How could he be gone? He was everything, my rock, my best friend. He was the big brother I didn't know I needed. How can I possibly get through this life without him at my side. I cupped my hands over my face and howled through the pain. My shoulders slumped and I curled in on myself. My broken heart beat in agonizing thumps. The emptiness he left inside me was beyond comprehension.

A tingle brushed against my cheek, like fingers caressing my skin. I turned to look at who it was, but no one was there. The blue glow was still spiralling around me, now shining brightly at my back. I felt the prickle of magic across my skin and a burst of energy ignited deep inside my soul. I convulsed with the force of the power, and my back arched, forcing me to sit straighter. I can still feel him. Tobias. He was still with me, he was showing me the way forward. His light moved and twirled through the air as it reshaped itself. I stood slowly and watched over my shoulder as the light spun and transformed into its final shape. I gasped loudly as I gazed at the wonder of it. This was Tobias's mission. He was to give me one final gift in order to defeat the prophecy. And now, with his glittering light a part of me, with our souls forever blended together as one, I can do it.

Chapter Forty-Four

Whiskey

Tobias hit the deck like a wet sack of shit. A pulling sensation tugged at my heart, like the shrivelled piece of brown beef thumping in my chest would suddenly come to life and feel something for the big dumb oaf. Yeah right. Once he was down, the fighters that he waved away all charged at me in unison. Some shifted into their beasts, others tempted fate on their human legs. It didn't really matter either way. They were all going to die by my hand, one way or the other.

I cut each of them down easily, and all the others who tried their luck with me. It appears these animals are just as dumb as all the other stupid dogs that I've fought. Never learning where they lay on the food chain. Never realising that they're doomed from the moment they decide to fight against me. They're all the same. Single minded, foolish animals. The fight had us slowly moving through the village, leaving a breadcrumb trail of bodies along the way. They just kept coming, one after the other. I was surprised that they didn't attack in one single wave. That's what all the other packs have done. It made killing them all in one fell swoop so much easier. This tactic, though, the constant drip, drip, drip of fighters, is becoming annoying. It's not that I'm tired. I don't get tired. But I want to find Zelena. These fucking mongrels are slowing me down.

I swung my arm up and let the blade of the axe tear open the stomach of the dog that just jumped for me. It yelped and dropped to my feet. I looked down at it as it tried to drag its body away, leaving a trail of blood and guts behind it. I lifted the axe to my face and inspected the blade. It's no Sao blade, that's for sure. But I'm really starting to like this little treat of a weapon. I may have to look into hatchets in the future. A shiver ran up my spine, and the air pressure changed, it felt heavy. Weird. That wasn't done by me. I've been purposefully keeping the air thin. Taking their oxygen makes the big dumb animals slower, weaker, and more sloppy with their movements. I looked around at the few wolves that were left. Not many of them now, and their numbers are shrinking by the minute. As I scanned the semi-circle I had made myself, I caught sight of a figure standing at the edge of the barn. Excitement bubbled in my stomach at her furious expression. The thumping of feet on the dirt made me aware of another incoming attack. I turned quickly, just in time to catch the small wolf by the neck before it landed on top of me. I flashed my teeth and jerked my fingers and wrist. Once I felt the crunching of its neck under my grip, I tossed the wolf back across the clearing. I turned back on Zelena, who was watching where I threw the dog. The pathetic look of concern on her face proved to me how weak she was. She was scared, scared for that stupid mutt, scared for herself. Her fear surrounded her. Ending her life will bring me so much pleasure. The thought alone brought a smile to my face.

I could feel the excitement inside me building. The unquenchable thirst for her blood. The insatiable hunger, the uncontrollable rage. All for her. The Witch. My bitch 'sister'. The air around me grew thick as the power grew. I could feel the coldness slithering along my skin. It only worked to increase my hunger.

Out of the corner of my eye, I spotted movement. A slow and fat little dog was trying to sneak up on me. Tsk, tsk, tsk. So stupid. I glowered at Zelena, mentally begging her to charge at me, to begin this fight that I am so desperately excited for. The fear in her eyes was overflowing. She pulled her hand from Gunner's and stepped toward me. I followed along and made the same move. Gunner's body flinched, drawing my eye to his. He seemed to be flexing or tensing, or something. The air around me fell still. The sounds of the forest, the cries of pain, and the scent of fear all but vanished. I zeroed in my gaze on Gunner, this was his doing, his magic. I shifted my burning gaze to Zelena and licked my lips. Come on, little bitch, let's do this. Her eyes shifted to my right, the same direction that the fat dog was approaching from. The thumping of paws on dirt came next. They never learn. As the sound grew louder, I swung my arm out, letting the blade of the axe slice across the dog's body. It yelped in pain, letting me know I got it good. Without wasting another moment, I spun on the ball of my foot, swinging out with the axe once again. As my body turned, the axe lodged into the neck of the falling wolf. The power of the blow just about cut the dog's head clean off, an image that brought another satisfied smile to my face.

A scream filled the air, and the ground shook beneath my feet. I was hit by what felt like a wave of water. I turned away and covered my head with my arm. The pressure of it was intense, unlike anything I could describe. When Zelena's angry voice filled the air, filled with so much pain and anger, I turned slowly to gaze upon her once again. As my eyes met hers, and I caught those pitiful tears brimming along her golden glare, I couldn't help but laugh. She is nothing. Crying over a meaningless nobody of a dog and showing her pain so openly, for all to see plain as day. She is weak. Why was everyone so afraid of her? All those years I spent learning and training. All the punishments that I endured, just to prepare me for what? This? Her? It all just seems like a waste now. Zelena could cut off one of my legs and stab out one of my eyes, and I would still destroy her without fail. It would be as easy as scratching my own arse.

Before I knew it, I was laughing. I was laughing harder than I ever had before. Just thinking about my wasted life, about how simple it will be to kill her, the famed Triple Goddess. It was such a disappointment.

"You!" I huffed out between laughs. Her! She is meant to be the pinnacle of my mission. Killing her is meant to be the great finale of my life.

"You're the best they have. You're the one that's going to stop me?" I wheezed as I looked around me. Surely this has to be some cosmic joke. There has to be more to it than this. It's too easy.

"Stop this, now" the bitch screamed. She may be a quick and easy kill, but it won't make it any less enjoyable for me.

"Or what?" I snarled. What could this pathetic tick possibly do to me?

"What are you going to do, dear sister? You think you can stop me, you think you can beat me? Do you want to give it a go?" I teased her, seeing if she was dumb enough to take the bait. She was hesitating. But she wants to, I can see it on her face. Her eyes darted around the clearing before coming back to mine. Her expression changed then. She's made up her mind, it seems, she's going for it.

Her arms lifted, outstretched toward me, and it was like she had an invisible hold on my body. My arms and legs were pinned and unable to move. I lifted off the ground as I pushed and pulled at my limbs. This is just what Gunner did to me, the invisible force field. So, they share the same power. How fascinating. I wasn't able to free myself from Gunner's magic, so if they truly were the same, wasting my energy now would be pointless. I eyed the happy couple as they approached me. I wonder if Gunner was gifted his own powers, like Zelena and I, or does he tap into hers somehow? Curious. Gunner was right at her back, staying close. But he was not focused on us, he seemed to be off in his own little world.

"I underestimated you" I whispered. Fuck, I didn't mean to say that out loud. I forced a smile and pushed again at the pressure keeping me captive. My legs moved, my arms too. Only slightly, but I can move them, so maybe the all-powerful princess isn't all she's cracked up to be. A flash of fear passed through Zelena's eyes, and I knew I had her then. I pulled all my power forward and threw my arms free with a great gust of wind. The force of my power sent both Zelena and Gunner flying off in different directions. Zelena's hold on me fell, and I dropped back to the ground, landing effortlessly on my feet. Gunner was quick to recover, turning on me with his teeth and claws ready. I prepared myself to charge for him when Zelena's movements caught my eye. A shiver of icy coldness slipped over me, and I was suddenly filled with power and energy once again. The black smoke curled around my body, leaving that trail of frost that I love to feel. I felt the jagged edges and frosty texture of the new weapon in my hand. I don't know how I summoned it, but it sure feels right.

I swung my arm towards Zelena, letting fly the spear of black ice. It got her in the upper right side of her chest, sending her flying back to the ground. A proud smile filled my face as another weapon materialised in my grip. I was about to hit her again when I was sent flying back through the air. I dropped the shard of ice and used my own power to cushion the landing. Gunner was poised and ready to attack. Zelena was still lying on the ground. I knew she was going to be easy to get rid of, just one hit and she was down.

I pulled on that dark feeling inside me, tugging on the string of power that was in me now. Another icy shard appeared in my hand, and I hurled it toward Gunner. He dodged to the side, missing the spear, and then charged toward me. I didn't even need to think about it now, the weapons just came to my hands as I thought of them. I leaned on my back foot and steadied my feet, then I hurled dagger after dagger at Gunner. One hit his shoulder, but it didn't slow his charge. Just three steps from reaching me, he dropped his shoulder and poised to shoulder barge right into me. I summoned the air and pushed myself off the ground and over his head. I landed and swirled to watch Gunner slide along the dirt, trying to stop himself before hitting the side of a cabin. As he turned to face me, his teeth bared, and his face screwed up with anger, I saw where two daggers had hit. One on his shoulder and the other on his forearm. The area had black blood seeping from the wounds and black spider veins slowly spreading under his skin. Isn't this a nice surprise? It would seem that the black magic works like a poison.

Gunner came for me again, only slower this time. His heavy feet stomped as he marched my way. He raised his arms with his hands clenched into fists and stopped just in front of me. He growled and flashed teeth, then raised his head to me in a nod. Hand to hand it is then. I matched his stance and smirked, ready and set for him to throw the first blow.

"It doesn't have to be this way" Gunner hissed through his clenched teeth.

"So everyone keeps telling me" I answered with a giggle.

"Please, Whiskey, don't do this" he pleaded dejectedly. His face dropped, losing the anger and fierceness. His big, beautiful blue eyes begged me, pleaded with me to surrender. For just a second, my fists unclenched, just slightly, but enough for the hesitation to sweep through me. I swallowed hard, my mouth suddenly felt awfully dry. My heartbeat thumped hard, so hard I could hear it. Could he be right? Could Gunner still be my reason to quit my mission? Could he be my salvation? As I watched him, reading him, waiting for a sign of some sort, I caught the movement of his eyes. He looked at something behind me, and his face instantly hardened again. I snapped my gaze quickly over my shoulder to find what he saw. There she was, fucking Zelena. My view of her was blocked by the wall of a cabin, but I could still see that she was bent over something on the ground. Of course. I will never be able to compete against her for his attention. The way he looks at her, the way he gravitates toward her. She is his everything. I am now, and always will be, nothing to Gunner.

I squared my shoulders and re-clenched my fists. The snarl on my face was for me, for my own disgust. How could I be so naïve, so stupid, even to entertain the idea? My lips curled back, and a rumbling growl bubbled up from my chest.

"Let's do this" I snapped as I leapt forward, colliding my fist with the corner of Gunner's chin. He stumbled back from the blow but quickly recovered. We traded punches as the both of us moved about the clearing. I imagine it would have looked like a well choreographed dance. I must admit, Gunner was well trained. He's big and a little clumsy, and he could not match my speed, but he has power behind his hits. He is not at my level of combat, but he still managed to land a few good hits.

Gunner was leading in for an uppercut, I ducked in the last second and drove an ice dagger into his abdomen. He grunted and stumbled back, quickly pulling the shard from his body before it evaporated into smoke. I pushed off the ground and flew through the air, coming to land with my fist on his eye socket. I recovered with a jab to his ribs and another hit to his nose. He grunted, and then, he was down. Gunner tried to stand again, but he was weak and disoriented. Now is my chance.

I walked over and stood above Gunner's failing body as he knelt before me. I was ready to land the final blow while he glared up at me. He was panting hard with his hand grasping at the fresh wound in his side. Blood was dripping down his chin and his eye was already looking red and angry. He held so much hatred in that glare. It poked at my cold heart, trying to make me feel something. But all I felt was contempt. I hate him. I really do. Just as much as I hate Zelena. This was personal now. Maybe it always was, and I just didn't know it until now. It had always just been about the mission, and I don't know when that changed. Gone were the thoughts of desire and envy, the idea of wanting him. I want nothing from this beast, nothing but his death. I lifted my arms, holding the newly created sword shaped icicle in both hands. A sneer fell across my face as I snarled down at the so-called mighty Alpha. There is no other on my level. I am more than any other beast could ever hope to be. I am above all of these creatures. There is a reason that I am undefeated. There's a reason that no one has ever been able to come face to face with me a walk away. It's because I am the ultimate killing machine, I am the apex predator. Once I have finished here, with this pathetic dog, I won't stop until the entire Were species has been wiped from this earth. The sky slowly lit up all around us, pulling me from my delicious dreams of grandeur. A bright blue light came from around a cabin, half blinding me as it did. I shielded my eyes with my arm and hissed as the light approached. As it got closer, I could start to pick up on the makings of a shape. A long, winding tail whipping around behind it, a strong and outstretched neck, with razor sharp teeth inside a large, open mouth. And above that, two glowing crystal blue eyes. Two large and intimidating wings spread out across the sky, lighting it up in a bright blue glow. It was a fucking dragon.

The glowing light dimmed, just enough for me to find a small human frame within the dragon's glow. It was Zelena. The dragon was with Zelena. How could this be possible?

"Whiskey" a voice called out. I took a step back and looked up at the beast. Dragons aren't real, I told myself. Plus, this dragon was odd. It wasn't a physical being. Its face, its wings, its body, it was all made out of light. I could see the electrical currents tethering all the pieces together, almost like it was made of pure energy.

"Whiskey" the voice called again. It came from both Zelena and the dragon, almost like they spoke at the same time, in the same voice. I stumbled back a few more steps, but Zelena and the dragon just kept coming.

"You're reign of death is over" the dragon called. This is unexpected. But I've never quit before, and I sure as shit won't be starting today. I steadied my feet and squared my shoulders. I summoned another ice sword, now holding one in each hand.

"We'll see about that" I snarled and pressed forward. I took three large steps and pushed off, jumping high enough to slit the dragon's throat. I pulled on my power for that extra boost of speed. I poised my weapons to slide right through the dragon's neck as I flew past it. But as I soared through the air, right past the body of the beast, the blades went right through the energy currents. It was like I was cutting smoke. Not a single mark or wound was made. I landed with a skid and turned as I slid along the dirt. Zelena and the dragon turned to face me, now standing between Gunner and me. Though Gunner hadn't moved. I don't know if it was because of his injuries or that he was too taken aback by the giant fucking dragon surrounding his Mate.

I couldn't wait, I reformed the swords of ice into one long spear and charged again, this time aiming for Zelena. Before the tip of the spear was able to pierce her heart, I was stopped. The spear in my grip evaporated, and my body was lifted off the ground. The dragon's wings flapped as they lifted us into the air, not stopping until we were high above the trees. I tried to break free from Zelena's hold, just like I did last time. But I couldn't move, not even a wiggle of my finger. I shifted my gaze from the ground to Zelena and then my body. The hold on me wasn't invisible this time. No, this time, my body was being held firmly in the grip of a giant dragon's talon. I snarled at Zelena, who was floating just in front of me in the centre of the dragon's glow. As I took her in, I saw the differences in her. Her eyes were now glowing a bright yellow with swirls of blue. She looked strong and powerful. Her arm was outstretched towards me, looking like she was holding something in her hand. I took in the shape of the dragon holding me, from its claws to its wings, its body to its head. This can't be possible. The dragon wasn't just guarding Zelena, the dragon was Zelena. The blue glow of its body was all around her, twisting and turning its current of energy through the sky. The waves of light were weaving through her body. The energy of the dragon wasn't just surrounding her, it was emanating from her. She was the dragon. She was the heart of the beast.

"I'm sorry this was the life you had to live" Zelena's voice called to me. I turned my gaze from the swirling blue glow of the dragon and glared at the bitch. I hate pity, and I certainly don't want anyone to pity me.

"Fuck you" I hissed. The glow of the dragon flashed brighter.

"I'm sorry this happened to you. I'm sorry this happened to the both of us. I never asked for this" Zelena pleaded. Her voice was filled with pain and sadness. It makes me sick. I struggled in the hold of the dragon's hand, Zelena's hand, but I could not get free. "I didn't want it to be this way" she said sorrowfully. So fucking weak. Trying to explain her way out of it. What does she expect, for me to feel sorry for her. She wants me to tell her it's all okay, that she can kill me, I don't mind. Just pitiful.

"I don't want..." Zelena started again, but I quickly cut her off.

"Enough with the sob story. If you're going to kill me, just fucking do it. Stop being a coward and do it already" I snarled. She glared at me, and the dragon's hold tightened, its glow growing brighter again.

"I don't want to kill you" she hissed through clenched teeth.

"I want to save you".

I almost laughed. If this fucking dragon wasn't squeezing the air out of me, I would have. Save me? Oh please. She is more deranged than I am. I don't need saving. I am exactly where I want to be. I am exactly who I want to be. This mission is mine. I chose it. She wants to save me? To hell with that. I curled back my lips, let my fangs extend and I growled at Zelena and her desperately depressing glare. I have no intention of being saved. I am here for one reason and one reason only, to kill. And I have every intention of making her my next victim.

I called my power forward, letting the icy blackness fill me from the inside out. My veins swirled with back magic, and my chest thumped hard with the exhilaration. Turned my power on Zelena, letting fly a shower of tiny icicle blades. The dragon's wing came down between us, blocking Zelena. The black ice turned to smoke as it hit the energy of the giant wing. The grip of the dragon loosened enough for me to free myself. Using my power, I flew out from between the long claws and into the open air in front of Zelena. I spun around to face the witch and her dragon, my hair whipped around my face with the force of the wind this high into the sky. I sneered and clenched my fists at the sight of Zelena. She floated in the air, like some kind of graceful Goddess. The form of the dragon that surrounded her was just as majestic. The whole thing was infuriating.

Rage was alight in my veins. I hate her. I hate her more than I have ever hated anything else in this world. My magic poured out of me, engulfing me in the coldness of the dark power. I looked down at my body, which was now covered head to toe in the black smoke. It covered me like a second skin. Like battle armour. I smiled and looked back up at Zelena. Let's finish this.

I flew forward at breakneck speed, colliding with her half a second later. I gripped a hand to her throat and used my other to deliver jab after jab to her ribcage. We tumbled through the sky, with me punching with all my strength, and her managing to block a couple of my blows. My power was keeping me up in the air by icy shards of wind that were stabbing against my skin, offering wonderous pins of pain. Whatever power this bitch had was allowing her to stay up here with me, seemingly unphased by the thinness of the oxygen.

Zelena put a hand on my forehead and shoved hard. Her surprising amount of strength managed to unlock my hand from around her throat. We both went careening back through the air. I pulled the wind to my back and steadied my roll. As I straightened myself, I found that Zelena was already upright. She floated there, watching me, the glow of the dragon all around her, just waiting for my next attack. I screamed and pushed my hand forward, sending a torrent of black ice throwing stars right for her. As if in slow motion, she sighed and waved a hand. My weapons immediately dropped to the earth below us. I screamed in frustration and sent another barrage of ice blades towards her. Zelena raised both her hands, and they all froze in their spot, hanging in mid air. As she lowered her hands, the blades all fell away. What the fuck is this? She may be able to dodge my magic, but she can't dodge my fists, that I know for certain.

I flew for her again, tackling her around the waist. We rolled and tumbled through the sky as I punched and punched at her face and body. Zelena grunted and huffed with each blow that I landed, but she didn't scream. That alone was enough to set my anger over the edge. I pulled the power to my hands and formed Sai blades out of black ice. I stabbed at Zelena's stomach and smirked as I felt the blade slice deep into her abdomen. She screamed in pain, which only made my smirk grow to a full smile. I pulled the blade out and stabbed again, drawing another scream from the witch. I couldn't help myself, I twisted the blade and laughed manically. I reefed my blade back, and as I went to stab again, I was blocked. The blade evaporated in my hand, and the blue light that surrounded Zelena brightened.

My body was suddenly engulfed in an air-constricting hold, and I was pulled away from Zelena. I watched in disgust as the electric swirls of light smothered Zelena. They washed over her blood covered torso and seeped into the wounds I had inflicted. I sneered and growled as I watched her stab wounds stitch back together. The glow of the dragon healed all of her injuries, until it was as if they were never there at all. I managed to free one of my hands, and I slammed my ice dagger into the claw of the dragon that was gripping my body. Nothing happened. There was no blood, no hole, not even a scratch.

I screamed with frustration and called forward a barrage of sharp, jagged, ice-encrusted blades. I pushed them out in all directions. Some toward the body of the dragon, some toward Zelena. But it was the same as before. They hit against the swirling energy of the dragon, and against the wing used to protect Zelena, and they all just evaporated. The exertion to pull weapon after weapon, while keeping myself flying through the air, was draining. My limbs were feeling heavy, and I couldn't get a full breath with the tight grip on my chest. I took as deep a breath as I could and screamed out with another wave of ice knives. The attempt was pitiful. They made no mark and didn't appear to weaken Zelena or the dragon in the slightest. My energy was spent, and I began to feel dizzy.

"I will kill you" I spat.

"You can turn yourself into a million dragons, I'll never stop" I seethed with gasping breaths. The wing pulled back, and Zelena's face came into view again. She didn't look sad or scared anymore, she just looked settled. She sighed and let her dragon wings expand behind her.

"I know" she whispered with a slight nod of her head. Zelena pushed her other arm forward with her palm facing me. A wave of energy hit me, like a truck hitting a mountain at top speed. My entire body jolted with the force, down to the tiniest atom. The air was stolen from my lungs, and my vision went black. I felt like a giant hand was inside my body, pulling it apart piece by piece. The pain was incredible. I could feel every part of myself being torn to shreds. I tried to scream, but no sound came. I tried to fight, but my body was no longer under my control. This must be what death feels like. I can't imagine it being anything else. There was a pressure inside my chest, like something was pulling it open. It built and built, tearing and ripping at my essence. It was almost too much. I was ready to give in to it. After all that I have endured and all the pain that has been inflicted on my body over my lifetime, I still kept fighting. I was never worn down to the point of giving up. But this, I can't bare this, I want this to stop.

I need this to be over. The pressure in my chest, the pain that was radiating through my body, it burst like a radioactive bubble. A stillness came over me, and the pain was gone. I could still feel the remnants of it though. Under my skin, in my fingers and toes, in the slow beat of my heart. The echoes of it rolled through me. What was that?

My body touched down, and I was lying on something hard. Gravity came back to me and the floatiness of the air was gone. I moved my hands over my body, making sure everything was still attached. As far as I could tell, it was. But something isn't right. Something is missing, it feels wrong. A feeling of warm calmness swished through my veins. I want to cry. Why the heck do I want to cry? I opened my eyes and looked up at the clear blue sky. It's beautiful, the softness of the baby blue colours and the gentle whisps of white clouds. I've never taken the time to appreciate the natural beauty of the sky. I pulled myself up to sit, and a shudder ran through me. I feel weak. I'm tired and my body aches. I looked down at my fingers and flexed them out in front of me. I pulled on that string of darkness that was tied to my heart, trying to summon the power, but I couldn't find it. The string was gone, the whole icy feeling of the black magic was gone. I pushed forward on my claws, forcing them to protrude through my fingertips, but they didn't. I couldn't reach that part of me. I swallowed the unease that balled in my throat and rolled my neck. I tugged at that part of myself that I hated so much and tried to shift. I flopped my head from side to side, but the change wouldn't come. I can't feel that side of me at all. The animalistic urge, the need for blood, the untameable anger, it's all gone.

"What's happening to me?" I asked myself as I squeezed my arms around my body. I feel so... so empty.

"I took your wolf" a voice came from behind me. I whirled around and stood up at the same time. Zelena stood a few steps away from me, with Gunner close at her side, his hand holding her hip protectively.

"You what?" I blanched. She took my wolf, how is that possible?

"I took your wolf. You're not a Were anymore" Zelena answered immediately.

"How do you feel, Whiskey?" Gunner asked, his voice was hard and angry. I ran my hands over my body, feeling the bumps of my scars and the strong muscles undeath my skin. I still feel the same, physically, at least. But inside, it doesn't feel right. I've never been one for emotions, not unless that emotion is anger, of course. But my chest was tight with the need to cry. My mind was swimming with thoughts and feelings. Feelings I have never felt before, feelings I never thought I would feel, ever. I want a hug. I want to lie down and cry. I want my dad. A wetness hit my cheek, and I looked up at the sky. There aren't enough clouds for it to be raining. I wiped at the wetness on my cheek. Am I crying?

"Whiskey?" Zelena called gently. I shot my gaze to hers, and more tears poured down. I don't cry. One tear, one lash. That's the rule. I can't cry. My breaths became shaky, and my legs felt wobbly underneath me.

"What did you do?" I screamed. Gunner grabbed Zelena's arm and pulled her back a few steps. The movement of their feet drew my gaze, and I saw something on the ground between us. I dived for it, grabbing the small hunting knife before quickly standing again. I held it tight and spread my feet, readying myself. But something is wrong, something is missing. I don't want to fight them. I don't want to fight anyone. The desire I felt to kill Zelena was gone. The need to kill anyone is gone. I wiped my eyes, trying to clear away the moisture so I could see properly.

"Whiskey, stop. You don't have to fight anymore" Zelena pleaded with me. Gunner was holding her arm, but her body was leaning forward like she wanted to come to me. I wanted that too. My body craved her touch. This isn't right, this isn't me.

"What did you do?" I asked through my jagged breaths and incessant tears.

"I took away the part of you that craved violence. I took away the animal inside you". Zelena paused, waiting to see if I would speak. When I didn't, she went on.

"You're human now. You can live a human life" Her voice was soft and sweet.

"You don't need to fight anymore" she whispered. I could feel the love and hope in her words. It lit something in me. After everything I have done, she still wants me. The tears came harder, my chest squeezed and I could barely catch a breath. I don't understand. I don't deserve kindness. I especially don't deserve her kindness. The knife in my hands shook as my hand dropped ever so slightly.

"Whiskey?" Zelena called. I looked over at her, meeting her golden eyes with my own. My sister. My twin. The person I just tried to kill. And she was right there, looking back at me with a soft smile. That smile said more than any words ever could. She loves me, for just me. Not for some kind of power I could give her. Not for status or personal greed. Not because she wants anything from me. But because she is my sister. Pain radiated through my body. I've never had that before. That kind of unconditional love. At least not since I was ten years old and my father was killed. I'd forgotten what this felt like. It hurts. It hurts so fucking much.

"I can't" I choked out through my sobs.

"You can. You just need to put the knife down. I'll help you, we both will" she sang softly, as she gestured to Gunner over her shoulder. My eyes flicked to him, and I saw it plainly in his hardened gaze. Zelena may love me, but no one else ever could. I have hurt so many people. I've done so many terrible things. The way that Gunner was looking at me. The anger and mistrust simmering in the back of his beautiful blue eyes. He said all I needed to hear without saying a word. There is no redemption for me. Not as a Were, a hunter, a merchant of death, a descendant of a Goddess, and not even as a human. There is no coming back from what I've done. I turned my gaze back to Zelena and forced my trembling lips into a soft smile. She stood up straighter and smiled brighter, the hope in her eyes was more than I could have ever asked for. She deserves so much more than me.

"I'm sorry" I whispered.

Zelena's face fell as her eyes tracked the knife in my hands. She followed my hand as I pulled the steel of the blade to my throat. I pressed it into my flesh and cut it cleanly across my carotid artery. Zelena's screams filled the air as I dropped the knife and fell onto my knees. She was at my side, pulling my head onto her lap as I dropped back. Warmth ran down my neck and chest as blood filled my mouth. I looked up at my sister and grabbed her hand from around my throat. I squeezed her fingers, trying to get her attention. She was screaming and crying, looking all around us. I reached up and grabbed her face, pulling her eyes to mine. Tears were pouring from her golden eyes. Eyes that looked just like mine. I tried to smile, but more blood just poured out of my open mouth. I smiled through the gagging and choking and caressed her cheek softly. I wished I had a life with her. I wish we could have known each other. Staring into her face, a face that looked just like mine, and knowing that my death was beating down on me, I could see it now. In her golden eyes, I could see it, playing out like a movie, the life I could have had with her. Zelena and me, growing up together. Playing with dolls as young girls, learning to swim and ride bikes. Our first change and meeting our wolves. Fighting with our parents and making up again. Discovering boys and finding love. Building our own families and sharing our lives together. She would have been my greatest ally and my biggest annoyance. She would have been my best friend and my favourite person. She would have been my everything. She should have been my sister.

Epilogue

Zelena

Grief is difficult. It's a hard feeling to navigate. With the addition of my bouts of guilt and regret, I wasn't sure I was ever going to find my way through it. If I'm honest, I'm still working my way through it. Every new day is different from the last. It's strange, really. One day, I will be fine, filled with happiness and joy, enjoying my family and my life. The next, something as simple as hearing the term 'Little One' will set me off on hours of crying and wishing for things to be different. Grief is weird. It's true when people say that you never actually get over the pain, you just learn to live with it. Not being alone with my pain is a huge help. Gunner and I are both working through our grief. Everyone is. Losing Cole, Tobias, and Aurora. Plus, Cleo and all the other fighters who sacrificed their lives. Those losses hit us all really hard.

Even with all that loss, we've gained a lot as well. Thanks to Aurora, the hunters are basically extinct. A special team of Were-hunters has been created to track down and stop the remaining hunter clans. All headed by my newly revealed cousin, the head of the Melnasirds. Doyle is definitely not who we thought he was. Who the world thought he was. As a descendant of Callisto, one of the daughters of Lycaon, he is as related to me as Galterio was. So, in a way, not at all, but in another way, my cousin. He and the other Melnasirds have shed a whole new light on the dangers of gossip. Oh, how the truth can be twisted and turned into a pretty fairytale. Or, in his case, a nightmare. All these years, Doyle had been fighting to find and protect half-breeds. After he found out that the hunters had been breeding half-breeds, trying to create their own team of super soldiers, he began searching for them.

And for years, that's what he'd been doing. Finding half-breeds, protecting them from hunters, other Weres, and everyone else that wanted to hurt or use them. He had been creating his own pack of half-breeds and anyone else that believed as he did. That they aren't all monsters like the stories have told. Alyse and Doyle are living proof. I'm glad he found us, and I'm happy he told us the truth of his history. Who would have thought that he would become a truly valued ally, and a strange and unexpected addition to our family? The fact that Doyle and the other Melnasirds are deadly assassins and have been demolishing the hunters from the inside out, well, that's just icing on the cake.

The prophecy really did come to fruition, not in the way I hoped, but in the best way possible way it could have. I may have lost Aurora in the end, a fact that still haunts me most days, but she left on her own terms. I can forgive her for that. Peace is in full effect in the Were world. One of our first acts as High Alpha and Triple Goddess was to install a Were council. They will help us keep the peace between the pacts. Laws have been voted in, and disciplinary justices have been put in place. Warring between packs is quickly becoming a thing of the past. With the threat of a dragon's wrath, the laws have been easily upheld. The whole dragon thing is still really weird for me. Gunner, Roe, Mum, and I have discussed it in great length, many, many, many times. The dragon has always been a part of me, and the initial connection came through my Drakos Mati gift. When Tobias gave up his life, giving his essence over to me, he unlocked the full potential of Selene's dragon. Well, my dragon now, I suppose. I've only summoned it twice more since that day. I mean, a dragon, whoa-wee. It's kind of a huge deal, one that I haven't fully come to terms with yet, and I probably never will.

Life has been moving along so quickly. Nat has started her own family now, she and Lace welcomed a baby boy just a few months ago. I couldn't be prouder of the woman she is becoming. She is a powerhouse Luna, a prized ally, and a respected voice to she-wolves everywhere. And now also a bomb-ass mother.

Tri-Moon is still healing. There is a lot of pain to unpack and loss to work through. It's been a huge few years for the once 'secret' pack. They are now the head of Were-kind, home to the leaders of an entire species, and the ground zero of the Moon Goddess' prophecy. Tri-Moon is a celebrity in its own right. I rocked myself on the porch swing as I recounted all my favourite memories. Some bad, some good, but all of them are mine.

"That's enough roughhousing, you two, it's time to pack it up" I yelled over to the twins. At three years old, they can now run circles around me. It's true when they created the saying 'it takes a village'. Without my village, Gunner and I would be swamped. The pack took the news of the twins well. Some were understandably cautious and concerned. After everything we have been through together as a pack, it makes sense that they would be wary. Others were overjoyed by the idea of two descendants. One to take over the throne of Alpha, and one to carry the line of the Goddess. Though to me, they are more than a future Alpha and a future Goddess, they are my heart and soul. I laughed and rocked back on the porch swing. Watching my little girl, wearing a pink dress with pigtails, dominate my little boy, who happens to be nearly twice her size. It sure is a sight to behold. I chuckled and rubbed my hand over my swollen belly. I hummed a lullaby as my hand circled my stomach. My childhood lullaby. Well, Selene's lullaby, as it has come to be called. It's become a staple in the household. Now that I remember it anyway. The twins love it, and even Gunner, Roe and Nat sing it. I love that I have something special and personal to pass on to my loved ones.

This next month is going to drag out. I sat up a little straighter as I noticed Gunner closing in behind the twins. They hadn't noticed him yet and were still preoccupied rolling around in the grass, growling and grabbing at each other. Gunner got a few feet away and dove for them. He grabbed one toddler in each arm and rolled so that he landed on his back with them on top of him. Squeals of joy and laughter filled the air as the twins wrestled with their father. I love watching him with them. He is the best father, constantly showering them with love and affection. I couldn't have asked for a better man to be my Mate.

I swung back on the porch and decided to let them have a few more minutes of playtime before their bath. A sharp kick slammed into my rib cage, and I grunted with the force of it.

"Ease up in there, peanut. Mummy isn't a punching bag" I chuckled and ran my hands over the round of my pregnant stomach. The happy squeals got louder as Gunner approached with the twins on his shoulders. I stood up and shuffled over to the stairs.

"Where are my babies?" I cooed and held out my arms.

"Mumma" little Collette squealed as she launched herself into my arms. I caught her under her armpits and spun her around before pulling her into my chest. I kissed her nose and then gave her an Eskimo kiss. She giggled and grabbed my face, then planted a slobbery kiss on my nose.

"Love you, Mumma" she babbled with a chubby cheeked smile.

"And I love you, my little princess" I cooed back. Collette kicked her feet so I could let her down, and I did. I watched her run through the open door while screaming out for Gran. Her wild and unsettled nature as a baby has transformed into an untamed and sassy toddler. She is strong and confident, just like the man we named her after. Cole would have been tightly wound around her little finger, jumping to her every need and demand. Just as Tobias was, just as everyone now is.

"Mumma?" Toby called softly. I sniffed and looked up at him with a bright smile. Gunner pulled him down from his shoulder and held him out in front of me. Toby has gotten a little too big for me to hold now, especially with the added weight of the giant child currently in my womb.

"You sad?" Toby sighed with a pout and wiped a stray tear from my cheek. I beamed at him and pinched his cheek.

"Not sad, Baby. I'm happy" I told him and leaned forward to kiss his nose. He giggled and pushed my face away, but held onto my cheeks.

"Happy?" he asked with a tilt of his head.

"Happy" I nodded and pouted my lips. He rubbed his little fingers over my cheeks and stared at me. Toby sees himself as my little protector. He is always so worried about my happiness. He growls at anyone who raises their voice with me. He pushes people to get them out of my way. Recently, he has taken to hitting anyone who touches me, besides our family members, of course. His protective instincts are rivalled only by that of his namesake. Tobias would be proud of the little force of nature that Toby is becoming.

"Ok" Toby chirped and jumped out of Gunner's arms. He ran off into the house, also screaming for his Gran. I watched him go and sighed. They're growing up too damn fast. Gunner's arms came around my stomach, and he leaned his chin on my shoulder.

"You okay?" he asked softly.

"I'm good" I answered and reached up to tap his cheek. He turned his face and kissed the palm of my hand.

"You were crying again" he said, like I hadn't already known that.

"Well, pregnant ladies cry, Mighty Alpha" I quipped and turned to face him with a smirk. He didn't answer me right away, just gazed down at me.

"You sure you're alright?" he asked more gently. He cupped my cheek, and I leaned into his touch.

"I'm fine. Thinking of Cole and Tobias just makes me sad sometimes". Gunner smiled sadly and ran his thumb over the corner of my mouth.

"Me too" he said softly before leaning in to press a soft kiss to my waiting lips.

"I love you" I said, looking up into his beautiful blue eyes.

"I love you more" he smiled back.

"It's not a competition" I grumbled and pinched his pec. He laughed and rubbed at the spot.

"It's not. There's just more of you to love" he cooed and dropped to his knees in front of me. I laughed and twirled my fingers through his shaggy hair. Gunner rubbed his face into my swollen belly and began to purr. I've become accustomed to Gunner doing this. I think it's his way of connecting with the baby. He is so caring and attentive, jumping to my every whim. I think he still feels a lot of guilt over missing out on most of my pregnancy and the birth of the twins. His protective Alpha still comes out here and there, thankfully nowhere near as bad as the first time round. That probably has a lot to do with the fact that we knew about this one right away. He was able to control himself better because he knew what he was dealing with. But with both Gunner and Toby working the protective Alpha role, I don't need to worry about a thing, not even a simple splinter. They are doing all of the worrying for me.

Gunner's purr tickled across my belly and hit right between my thighs. I'm honestly really enjoying it. The way he purrs, the vibration, the way it rumbles in the back of his throat. It licks me in the most delicious way. If I had thought Gunner was irresistible before, it would have been nothing compared to now. Having him close while pregnant was like having a constant boner pill. My last pregnancy was rocked by the trauma of missing my Mate, making me numb to everything. This time around, I am feeling all of my erratic hormones. Especially the never-ending randy horniness.

A seductive growl bubbled from my half open mouth. My heart was beating hard in my chest, and my lady bits were throbbing and seeping with need. Gunner's head moved from my belly to the spot between my thighs. He breathed in deeply and growled with excitement.

"That is the best scent on this earth" he sighed and pressed his nose back between my legs. I chuckled and pushed my pelvis forward.

"I could live between these legs and bathe in your delicious juices" he mumbled with his nose pressed against my clit. I never knew how erotic and exciting dirty talk could be. But the more time I have with Gunner, the more his filthy mouth excites me.

"MUMMA!" Collette's voice screamed from inside the house. Gunner growled and fell back onto his backside. I laughed at his forlorn face and tapped the top of his head.

"Sorry, tiger. Save it for later" I teased and went to walk past him. Gunner growled and launched forward. I squealed and quickly skipped away from his snapping teeth.

"MUMMA!" Collette called again.

"Come help Mummy. Daddy is trying to bite me" I screamed and dashed away from Gunner as fast as I could waddle. Staying on his hands and knees, he chased me down the hallway, still snapping at my ankles. Toby came out of the library and charged down the hall. An angry look plastered on his face and eyes trained on Gunner, he leapt through the air, tackling his father as he landed. Gunner laughed wildly and rolled onto his back with Toby on his chest, throwing his tiny fists into his father's chest.

"No biting" Toby yelled while smacking his little fists into Gunner's muscular chest. I turned at the sound of singing and saw Collette skipping down the hall, swinging her dress as she danced towards us. She stopped at my side and looked up at me while shaking her head.

"Boys" she scoffed. I laughed and twirled a strand of her hair around my finger.

"What are we to do with them?" I asked while shaking my head with feigned disappointment.

"I got it, Mumma" she said with a smile. A second later, she dived through the air like a WWE wrestler, landing on top of both her brother and her father. I tossed my head back and laughed madly. I clutched my heavy stomach and hunched forward with the force of my uncontrollable laughter. My three great loves wrestled on the floor, growling, laughing, and yelling. The ruckus they were making pulled everyone in the house out into the hallway. Roe and Lupus stood behind me with their arms wrapped around each other. Lunaya and Alyse came from the loungeroom and laughed at the scene on the floor in front of them. A moment later and Smith appeared from the kitchen with a plate of food in his hand. His Mate was right behind him.

"Backup! I need backup" Gunner yelled while holding a squirming Toby in the air above him.

"I'm coming, brother" Smith mumbled with a mouthful of chicken. He handed the plate to his Mate and kissed her cheek. I'm beyond happy that Smith found someone who fits with him so perfectly. I had my doubts for a little while there. But typical Smith, with his charm and charismatic ways, he somehow managed to thaw her frozen heart.

Smith plucked Toby from Gunner's hands and flew him around the room like an aeroplane. Toby kicked his legs and pulled at Smith's fingers.

"Uncle Smith" Toby screeched. He was flailing his arms and legs like a wild rabbit that's just been caught. Gunner had Collette tucked in his arms and was leaning over her, smothering her with kisses. She was giggling and screaming for him to let her go. Another kick landed on my pelvis. I guess this little one was having a little bit of FOMO. I rubbed my belly and tried to catch my breath after the fit of laughter. I looked slowly around the room, stopping to take in the smiling faces of each and every one of my loved ones. I took a deep breath and let the overwhelming feelings of happiness, fulfilment, and love fill me to the brim. If this is what the prophecy meant by how the wolf will thrive, then this is looking like a pretty great life.

The End